THE SOUL SUMMONER SERIES
BOOKS 1 -3

ELICIA HYDER

ISBN: 978-1-945775-07-9
Inkwell & Quill, LLC

For More Information:
www.eliciahyder.com

This collection is dedicated to my husband Chris.
None of this would have happened without you.
I love you, Mr. Spouse

There's a FREE Book from Elicia Hyder waiting for you at
www.thesoulsummoner.com/detective

THE DETECTIVE
A Nathan McNamara Story

THE SOUL SUMMONER

ELICIA HYDER

BOOK ONE OF
THE SOUL SUMMONER SERIES

The Soul Summoner is for my kids…
in hopes that it pays for college.

1.

HER HAZEL EYES were judging me again. *God, I wish I could read minds instead.*

Adrianne spun her fork into her spaghetti, letting the tines scrape against the china. I cringed from the sound. She pointed her forkful of noodles at my face. "I think you're a witch."

I laughed to cover my nerves. "You've said that before." Under the white tablecloth, I crossed my fingers and prayed we would breeze through this conversation one more time.

A small, teasing smile played at the corner of her painted lips. "I really think you are."

I shook my head. "I'm not a witch."

She shrugged. "You might be a witch."

I picked up my white wine. "I wish I had a dollar for every time I've heard that. I could pay off my student loans." With one deep gulp, I finished off the glass.

She swallowed the bite in her mouth and leaned toward me. "Come on. I might die if I don't get to see him tonight! Do you really want that kind of guilt on your hands?"

I rolled my eyes. "You're so dramatic."

She placed her fork beside her plate and reached over to squeeze my hand. "Please try."

My shoulders caved. "OK." I shoved my chair back a few inches and crossed my legs on top of my seat. I closed my eyes, shook my long brown hair off my shoulders, and blew out a deep slow breath as I made circular O's with my fingertips. Slowly, my hands floated down till they rested on my knees. I began to moan. "Ohhhhhmmmm…"

Adrianne threw her napkin at me, drawing the attention of the surrounding guests at Alejandro's Italian Bistro. "Be serious!"

I dropped my feet to the floor and laughed as I scooted closer to the table. "*You* be serious," I said. "You know that's not how it works."

She laughed. "You don't even know how it works!" She flattened her palms on the tablecloth. "Here, I'll make it easy. Repeat after me. Billy Stewart, Billy Stewart, Billy Stewart," she chanted.

I groaned and closed my eyes. "Billy Stewart, Billy Stewart, Billy Stewart."

She broke out in giggles and covered her mouth. "You're such a freak!"

I raised an eyebrow. "You call me that a lot."

"You know I'm only joking. Sort of."

Adrianne Marx had been my best friend since the fifth grade, but sometimes I still had trouble deciphering when she was joking and when she was being serious.

I picked up my fork again and pointed it at her. "It's not gonna happen, so don't get too excited."

She let out a deep breath. "I'm not."

I smirked. "Whatever."

Our waiter, who had been the topic of our conversation before Adrianne began gushing about her new crush on Billy Stewart, appeared at our table.

"Can I get you ladies anything else?" His Southern drawl was so smooth I had nicknamed him Elvis over dinner. He was a little older than the two of us, maybe twenty-three, and he had a sweet, genuine smile. His hair was almost black, and his eyes were the color of sparkling sapphires. I had drunk enough water that night to float the Titanic just so I could watch him refill my glass.

I looked at his name tag. "Luke, do I look like a witch?"

His mouth fell open. "Uh, I don't think so?" His response was more of a question than an answer.

Across the table, Adrianne was twisting strands of her auburn ponytail around her finger. I nodded toward Luke. "See, he doesn't think I'm a witch."

Luke lowered his voice and leaned one hand on our table. "You're too pretty to be a witch," he added, with a wink.

I smiled with satisfaction.

Adrianne laughed and pushed her plate away from her. "Don't be fooled, Luke. She has powers you can't even dream of."

He looked down at me and smiled. "Oh really?" He leaned down and lowered his voice. "How about you let me take care of this for you"—he dangled our bill in front of my face—"and later, when I get off, I can hear all about your powers?"

Heat rose in my cheeks as I took the check from his hand, and when I pulled a pen from his waistband apron, his breath caught in his chest. I flashed my best sultry smile up at him and scribbled my name and phone number on the back of the bill. I stood up, letting my hand linger in his as I gave him the check. "I'm in town on a break from college for the weekend, so let me know when you get off."

He smiled and backed away from the table. "I will"—he looked down at the paper—"Sloan."

I took a deep breath to calm the butterflies in my stomach as Adrianne followed me toward the front door. She nudged me with her elbow. "You should win some kind of award for being able to pick up guys," she said as we passed through the small rush of dinner customers coming in.

I shrugged my shoulders and glanced back at her with a mischievous grin. "Maybe it's part of my gift."

"Witch," she muttered.

The icy chill of winter nipped at my face as I pushed the glass door open. When we walked out onto the sidewalk, I stopped so suddenly that Adrianne tripped over my legs and tumbled to the concrete.

Billy Stewart was waiting at a red light in front of the restaurant.

* * *

Adrianne might never have even noticed Billy's official game warden truck at the stoplight had my mouth not been hanging open when she struggled to her feet. She was cursing me under her breath as her eyes followed the direction of my dumbfounded gaze across the dark parking lot. When her eyes landed on the green and gold truck, she fell back a step.

Her fingers, still coated in gravel dust, dug into my arm. "Is that…?"

I turned my horrified eyes to meet hers when traffic started moving again.

Frantically, she waved her finger in the direction of the traffic light. "That was Billy Stewart!" She was so excited that her voice cracked.

"Yeah, it was." Mortification settled over me, and I pressed my eyes closed, hoping to wake from a bad dream. When I focused on Adrianne again, I realized she had taken a pretty nasty fall. Her blue jeans were torn and her right knee was bloody. "Oh geez, I'm so sorry."

She looked at me, her eyes wild with a clear mix of anxiety and amusement. She glanced down at the gash on her knee. "Can you heal me too?" Her question had a touch of maniacal laughter.

I shoved her shoulder. "Shut up." I tugged her toward the restaurant's entrance. "Let's go to the bathroom and get you cleaned up."

Once we were behind the closed door of the ladies room, Adrianne's curious eyes turned toward me again. She hiked her leg up on the counter beside the sink. "What the hell just happened out there?"

I ran some cold water over a paper towel and handed it to her. "I need a drink." I splashed my face with cold water and, for a moment, considered drowning myself in the sink.

She pointed at me as she dabbed the oozing blood off her kneecap. "You and me both, sister. You've got some major explaining to do."

Alejandro's had a small bar near the front door where I had never seen anyone actually sit. When we pulled out two empty bar stools, the slightly balding bartender looked at us like we might be lost. His eyebrows rose in question as he mindlessly polished water spots off of a wine glass.

"I think I'm going to need a Jack and Coke," Adrianne announced.

I held up two fingers. "Make that two."

"IDs?" he asked.

Getting carded was one of the best things about being twenty-one. Any other time, I would have whipped out my finally-legal-identification with a smile plastered on my face. But in that moment, fear of what the next conversation might bring loomed over me like a black storm cloud that was ready to drop a funnel.

I had already learned the hard way not to talk about these things.

People are scared of what they can't comprehend, and the last thing

I wanted was for Adrianne to be afraid of me. Despite my unnatural propensity toward popularity, Adrianne was one of the only real friends I had.

I knew the jabs she made about me being a witch were all in jest, but there was a part of her that had been genuinely curious about me since we were kids. Adrianne, above anyone else, had the most cause to be suspicious of the odd 'coincidences' that were happening more and more frequently around me.

Summoning Billy Stewart had been a complete accident. God knows I had tried my whole life to summon all sorts of people—my birth mother and Johnny Depp to name a couple—without any success at all. Sitting next to Adrianne at the bar, I knew from the look in her eyes that seeing Billy at that stoplight solidified to her what I already knew to be true: I was different. Very different.

Swiveling her chair around to face me, she pointed to the dining table we had just vacated. "OK, I was kidding about Billy at dinner. That was some serious David Copperfield shit you just pulled out there, Sloan. Totally creepy."

I groaned and dropped my face into my hands. "I know."

An arm came to rest behind my back, and Luke appeared between our seats with a tantalizing grin that would normally make me swoon. "Did you miss me that much?" he asked.

Adrianne pointed a well-manicured fingernail at him. "Not now, Elvis," she said without taking her eyes off me.

Stunned, Luke took a few steps back.

I offered him an apologetic wink. "We need a minute."

He nodded awkwardly, stuffed his hands into his pockets, and left us alone.

When he was gone, I turned back to Adrianne. "I don't suppose you could be convinced this was all a really big coincidence?"

"Sloan, when we ran into my Gran after you said you needed to pick up some canned green beans from her, that was a coincidence. When we were talking about going to Matt Sheridan's keg party and we ran into him at the beer store, that was a coincidence. When you said you hoped Shannon Green would get syphilis and we saw her walking out of the Health Department, maybe even that was a coincidence." We both laughed.

She tapped her nails against the bar top. "Billy Stewart is supposed to be working on the backside of a mountain right now, Sloan. He shouldn't be anywhere near the city. I was joking and trying to get you to make him magically appear...and then *you did*. That's not a coincidence."

I groaned.

She lowered her voice and leaned into me. "What are you not telling me? Did you make that happen or not?"

It was too late to try and recover with a lie. I had no other choice but to tell her the truth. My legs were shaking under the table and a trickle of sweat ran down my spine. "I'm not a hundred percent certain, but yes. I think so."

She sucked in a deep breath and blew it out slowly. Her eyes were wide and looking everywhere but into mine. "I'm going to be honest. You're kinda freaking me out a little bit right now."

I nodded and pinched the bridge of my nose. "I know. I wish I had a grand explanation, but I've never had anyone explain it to me either."

I felt her hand squeeze mine. "I love you, so let me have it. Tell me everything."

My stomach felt like an elevator free-falling through the shaft. "You're going to think I'm crazy."

"Sloan, I think we bypassed crazy about twenty minutes ago," she said with a genuine chuckle.

The bartender placed our drinks in front of us, and I wrapped my fingers around the short tumbler. Adrianne drained half of her whiskey in one swallow.

I took a deep breath. I let my thoughts roll around for a moment in my head, and I tried to choose my words carefully so I didn't sound as nuts as I felt. Finally, I looked at her and lowered my voice. "You know when you're out and you see someone you really feel like you know, but you can't remember how or who they are?"

She nodded. "Sure."

I paused for a moment. "I feel that way around *everyone*. Like I already know them."

Her face contorted with confusion. She tried to laugh it off without success. "Well, I've always said you've never met a stranger."

I looked at her seriously. "I haven't *ever* met a stranger, Adrianne."

She cleared her throat. "I really don't understand what you're talking about."

Sadly, I didn't understand what I was talking about either.

"I see people I've never met and feel like I've known them forever. I can even just see a picture of someone and know if they are alive or dead and what kind of person they are. I don't know their names or anything specific, but I have a weird sense about them before ever talking to them. It's like I recognize their soul."

She let my words sink in for a moment. "Like the time you told me not to go out with the exchange student in the eleventh grade, and then he date-raped that cheerleader?"

"Yes. I knew he had a lot of evil in him," I said.

"And you get these 'vibes' from everyone?" she asked.

I nodded. "Absolutely everyone."

"So that's why you're so good with people...why you can talk to anyone and everyone at any time?"

I nodded again. "It's easy to befriend people when it feels like you've known them for years, and I seem to be somewhat of a people-magnet."

She interrupted me. "But what does that have to do with Billy Stewart showing up here tonight?"

"There's more."

She sat back, exasperated. "Of course there is."

"I think it's somehow related. People are naturally drawn to me, and somehow I can manipulate that."

Her eyes widened. "You can control people?" Her voice was almost a whisper.

"I don't think I would call it *controlling* people..." My voice trailed off as I sorted through my thoughts. "I know things about people, and sometimes when I talk about someone, it's like I can summon them to me."

She laughed, but it was clear she didn't think it was funny. "Come on, Sloan. Really?"

"Just think about it." I looked at her over the rim of my tumbler and sipped my drink.

She was quiet for a while. There were a thousand odd events she could have been replaying in her mind. Like, the time I said I wanted Jason Ward to ask me to the homecoming dance, and he was waiting by my locker after class. Or, when I told her I had a bad feeling about our gym teacher, and we found out on Monday he had died of a heart attack over the weekend. Finally, she looked at me again. "You know I wouldn't believe a word of this if I hadn't known you for so long."

I nodded. "I don't believe it most of the time myself."

"When you say you 'know' people. What do you know? Like, do you know that guy?" She pointed at the bartender.

I laughed. "No. It's just a sense I get. I can tell you he's an OK guy, but I'm not a mind reader."

She drummed her long nails on the countertop. "So you're psychic?"

"No, I don't think so. I just seem to be able to read people really well."

She leaned toward me and dramatically fanned her fingers like a magician. "And make people suddenly appear!"

"Shhhh!" I looked cautiously around.

Luke, who was waiting nearby, caught my eye and started in our direction.

Adrianne extended her long arm to stop him. "Not so fast, you little eager beaver."

I laughed, and the tension finally started to drain from my shoulders. After a moment, I gripped her arm. "You're not gonna get all freaked out on me now, are you? I haven't told anyone about this since I was old enough to know better."

Her head snapped back with surprise. "Old enough to know better?"

I ran my fingers across the faint scar just above my right eyebrow. "Kids can be pretty cruel when they find out you're different. When I was eight and we still lived in Florida, one of them threw a big rock at me during recess."

She gasped. "That's horrible!"

I nodded. "After that, Mom and Dad decided it would be best to move."

"So they know about what you can do?" she asked.

I shook my head. "Not exactly. Whatever is wrong with me can't be explained by science, so I think it scares them to talk about it. They haven't brought it up once since we moved here." I touched my scar again. "And seven stitches in the face taught me to keep my mouth shut."

She squeezed my hand, her eyes no longer judgmental. "Well, I'm not going to freak out, and I'm not going to tell anyone."

I sighed. "Thank you."

She grinned over the top of her glass. "No one would believe me anyway."

"I know."

Suddenly, she perked up with a wild smile. "What about Brad Pitt?"

I raised my eyebrows. "What about him?"

"Can you get him here?"

I laughed. "That's not the way it works!"

She crossed her arms over her chest. "How do you know?"

I smiled. "Because I've already tried."

2.

IT HAD BEEN several years since that night when I finally told Adrianne the truth about me. She had spent that entire weekend hounding me with ridiculous questions:

Can you read people's minds?

If you can sense bad people, why did you let me date Bobby?

How do you get people to come when you call their name?

ARE YOU a witch??

I couldn't blame her. Adrianne knew about as much as I did about whatever powers or abilities I possessed. After that weekend, however, she calmed down, and our friendship returned to being as it had been before I told her—maybe even better.

I finished college that year at the University of North Carolina at Chapel Hill and graduated with a degree in public relations much to the dismay of my father. He was a geriatrics physician who had wanted me to follow in the family footsteps of a long line of doctors in the Jordan family history. Specifically he wanted me to become an obstetrician so we could, as he would like to joke, 'bookend the family practice with one doctor to bring 'em into this world and another doctor to take 'em out!' He was a funny man, my dad.

It had been my mother's idea for me to put my impeccable people skills to use and pursue a career in public relations. I had interned with the Buncombe County media department during college, and when I graduated they offered me a full-time job in the communications office. After two years, I had been promoted to Public Information Officer, which was a fancy title for a publicist. It hadn't proven to be the most glamorous job in the world, but it was fairly easy, close to home, and it paid really well.

Settling in Asheville after college made sense. Most of my life had been centered around that weird little town. Asheville had somehow slid straight from the 70's into the new millennium, pausing in the time shift only long enough to pick up a few Goth kids from the 90's. It was the only city I knew of where one could pay homage to a war memorial, open an investment account, befriend a vampire, visit a fine art gallery, and pick up a new bong—all on the same street. In 2000, Rolling Stone magazine christened Asheville as 'America's New Freak Capital' which reaffirmed my decision to put down permanent roots there.

Over the years, I got better at using my ability and at hiding it. Talking about someone and having them make an appearance had almost become routine. I still couldn't summon just anyone at will, but I had noticed that if I was talking about someone and picturing them in my mind at the same time, they were much more likely to show up. It still hadn't proven true with Johnny Depp or Brad Pitt, however.

The leaves had just begun their colorful transformation in the fall when my workday began at the sheriff's office rather than at my office in the county building. I was to attend the swearing in of two new deputies at nine in the morning and prepare a press release. Before I left my house, I checked my purse to make sure I had remembered to bring my Xanax. I took a half of one as a preemptive strike against the anxiety attack I knew was coming. The sheriff was headquartered at the county jail. I hated going to the jail. A place packed with that many bad people was a panic incubator for a girl like me.

I arrived on time and checked my reflection in the glass doors as I approached the sheriff's office entrance. My white blouse was tucked in all the way around, and my black slacks weren't showing any panty lines. I reached for the door handle, but before I could pull on it, the sheriff himself swung it open and stepped aside for me to enter.

The lobby was full, and I suspected the entire bunch had just watched me check out my own ass in the mirrored glass. "Wonderful," I muttered.

"Nice to see you, Ms. Jordan," Sheriff Davis said with a grin.

I shook his extended hand. "You too, sir."

"We were about to head to my conference room," he said.

I nodded, ducking my head with embarrassment as I fell in line with the group.

As we shuffled through the lobby, the nerve endings at the base of my neck began to tingle. I sucked in a sharp breath and held it. On the count of three, I blew it out slowly and reminded myself that the walls weren't really humming with evil. It was only my imagination. I needed to think about something else. Anything else.

My eyes scanned the room of county officials before landing on the two new officers who were being deputized. One, in particular, was certainly an adequate distraction. He was about my age and a little taller than me in the heels I was wearing. He had short blond hair, and his black police uniform fit so well over his sculpted torso that I would've believed it had been custom made had I not known the county was too cheap for such a luxury. A polished brass name tag was pinned to his chest that I had to squint to read. "N. McNamara" could have been Mr. January on the Buncombe County Hot Cop Calendar if one existed.

"Good morning, Sloan," a familiar, squeaky voice said behind me, snapping me out of my hormone infused daze.

Mary Travers, a petite woman with mousy brown hair and a face smushed like a Pug's, was shuffling to match my stride. I smiled down at her. I liked Mary a lot. She was old enough to be my mother and was one of the most genuinely kind people I'd ever encountered. As the county manager, Mary was also my boss.

"Hey, Mary. How are you today?" I asked.

She pushed her bifocals up the bridge of her stubby nose. "Busy as a bee." She looked up at me. "Are we going to be ready to have the newsletter out by Friday?"

"I'm confident I'll have it done by Thursday," I answered with a smile.

She hugged the armload of file folders she was carrying. "And you'll take the pictures today and get the statement posted on the website and on the Facebook and Twitter thing?"

"Yes, ma'am. I've got it all under control."

She patted my arm like a grandmother praising a child. "Good girl."

The whole group was coming to a slow stop at the locked, heavy metal door to get inside the heart of the facility. All of the doors were secured electronically and were only able to be opened by whoever was running the master control desk. I suspected, given our halted status, that Virginia Claybrooks was working master control.

The sheriff rang the buzzer for a second time, impatiently trying to see through the double-sided mirror beside the door. There was no answer. He pressed the buzzer again.

A loud woman belted over the loudspeaker. "Who keeps blowin' up my door? I'll get to you when I get to you! I've only got two hands, ya know?"

Yep. It was Ms. Claybrooks.

The sheriff let out an exasperated sigh. "Ms. Claybrooks, it's Sheriff Davis. Can you please open the door?"

"Uh...Oh, oh," she stammered over the loudspeaker. Her voice shifted from shrill and threatening to syrupy sweet. "Sheriff, you shoulda said somethin'. C'mon in."

He closed his eyes and silently shook his head as the door slid open. "Thank you, Ms. Claybrooks," he said to her as we passed by her office door.

She stood up and gave him a small wave and a wide, toothy smile.

Ms. Claybrooks, a black lady from southern Georgia, was barely five feet tall and almost as wide. Her bosom was narrowly confined to the sheriff's office button-up shirt she was stuffed into. She wore bright red lipstick and a short bobbed wig. I would guess she was in her mid-fifties. Ms. Claybrooks was one of my favorite people on the planet and almost made it worthwhile for me to face my fears and visit the sheriff's office more often.

She peeked around the corner as the group of us filed in. "Dang, Sheriff Davis! How many people you bringin' through my door today?"

He didn't answer.

I smiled at her. "Hey, Ms. Claybrooks."

Her face shifted into a tilted look of confusion. She planted her feet and put her hand on her wide hip. "How 'you know my name? Do I know you?"

"Everyone knows your name," Mary added with a sweet smile.

"Well, hi there, Mary!" Ms. Claybrooks cheered. "Let's do lunch soon, m'kay?"

Mary nodded and waved to her. "Maybe later this week!"

Ms. Claybrooks swung around into her office and plopped down in the master control chair before picking up her radio and barking into it again. "I told you to hold your damn horses!" she shouted at another unfortunate soul.

I giggled. "I absolutely love that woman."

Mary nodded. "She definitely brightens the mood around this dreary place."

That was the truest statement I had heard all week, but dreary wasn't the word I would've chosen. Before I started to obsess over the heebie jeebies that were creeping in on me, I changed the subject. I leaned down so only Mary could hear me as we filed into the conference room. "Did everyone see me looking at my backside in the window?"

She nodded and chuckled silently. "Everybody."

I groaned.

The swearing in ceremony consisted of oaths, pictures, and paperwork. The hot Mr. January officer was from Raleigh, and he was a detective with an impressive resume. His name was Nathan McNamara. Unfortunately, hanging around to meet him after the ceremony would require spending more time at the jail than I was willing to, no matter how good he looked in his uniform.

Mary insisted on us getting an early lunch together before returning to our office, so she rode with me down the street to the Tupelo Honey Cafe.

"It was a good ceremony today," I said as we sat down at a wooden table that overlooked the street.

She shrugged her shoulders. "Wasn't much of a ceremony if you ask me." She opened up the brunch menu and adjusted her glasses as she carefully scanned the page. "What do you like here?"

"The craft martinis," I replied.

She laughed.

"What do you think about the new officers?" I asked.

"They seem satisfactory," she said, void of any emotion.

I pushed my menu away from me and folded my hands together on the table. "Just satisfactory?"

"Well, the one was really handsome." She was grinning behind her menu.

I perked up. "The cute blond one from Raleigh?"

She pursed her lips and shook her head. "No. The older one who came here from Knoxville. He was a fox."

In my opinion, with his red hair and ultra long nose, he could have been a fox—an actual fox—maybe in a previous lifetime. I grimaced. "No. I meant Detective McNamara. I wouldn't mind getting on a first name basis with him."

She smiled. "Oh, to be young. You never told me what is good to eat here," she said, signaling the end of our boy talk.

My shoulders sank, and I looked out of the window to the busy downtown street. "The goat cheese grits are amazing."

It had been over a year and a half since I had been in an actual relationship with a man. Getting dates wasn't a problem because I enjoyed meeting new people. The problem was my ability to see the grime on the souls of everyone I went out with. That, and the constant worry that men were simply attracted to me because of my power. The longest romance I had ever entertained was with Luke Burcham, the waiter from Alejandro's. Our relationship lasted long distance for a total of three and a half months while I was in college. Elvis broke up with me because he felt like I was hiding something from him. If he only knew.

After lunch, I returned to my office in the Buncombe County building. It was a cozy space with calming gray walls and black and white photos of places I had never visited. The large window behind my desk framed the view of the national forest that was beginning to pop with the colors of autumn. Asheville tourism advice was one of my biggest responsibilities as nature lovers from all over the country flocked to the colorful North Carolina mountains in the fall.

For a few hours, I worked on the county e-mail newsletter before remembering the unedited photos on my camera from that morning. As I ejected the memory card, it catapulted from its slot into the furthest corner under my desk. After an unsuccessful attempt to retrieve it blindly with my toes, I crawled under my desk.

There was a knock at my door.

Startled, I smacked my skull against the underside of my keyboard tray.

When I popped my head up after scrambling backward on my hands and knees, Detective Nathan McNamara was wide-eyed and standing in my doorway with his hand still posed in the knocking position.

"I'm sorry." He cautiously stepped into the room and looked

around. "I didn't mean to frighten you. Are you Ms. Jordan?"

In an instant, I forgot about my possible skull fracture and broke out in an involuntary smile. I stood up and extended my hand. "Call me Sloan," I answered as he squeezed my hand. "You're Detective McNamara, correct?"

He shook his head. "Just Nathan or Nate, please."

I smiled again and motioned to the two empty chairs in front of my desk. "Nathan, what can I do for you?"

He had changed out of his formal uniform and was wearing a black polo shirt and black tactical cargos. He wore an olive drab ball cap with a grayscale American flag patch on the front. He had a badge pinned to his belt that I couldn't even look at for fear of getting too distracted. It was the first time I had seen him up close. His eyes were the color of cold gray steel. I had to remind myself he was talking to me and I probably should pay attention so I could respond.

"I have a press release about a missing person." He handed me a sheet of paper before settling into a chair.

Blame it on the tantalizing belt or the eyes, but after glancing at the middle-aged man's photo, without thinking I blurted out "he's dead" as mindlessly as I would've said "thank you" or "yes, I'll go out with you!"

His eyes widened. "Excuse me?" He drew out each syllable.

I slowly sank down behind my desk and cleared my throat as I scrambled for a recovery. "It's just my guess." I shrugged my shoulders like it was no big deal that I had just sounded at best calloused and uncaring, or at worst—crazy.

He studied my face until I thought my heart would pound out of my chest. I couldn't even bring myself to look him in the eye.

Forcing a smile, I placed the sheet carefully in front of my computer screen. "I'll take care of it right away." I hoped he would leave so I could have a proper meltdown, but he looked too puzzled to move. I decided to change the subject. "How did you get stuck bringing me press releases on your first day?"

His shoulders relaxed. "Rookie grunt work, I guess. I think some people aren't too happy that I lateraled straight over to detective."

My heart rate was beginning to slow to normal. "Probably not. Welcome to the department, by the way. You're from Raleigh, right?"

"Yes, ma'am. Technically, I'm from—"

I cut him off, laughing and waving my hand in his direction. "Watch it with the 'ma'am' stuff. I'm pretty sure you're older than me, and I would rather be unprofessional than feel old."

He laughed. "Sorry. I transferred here from Raleigh, but I grew up closer to Durham."

"No kidding?" I asked. "I went to college at UNC."

He reclined in the seat and grimaced. "Ahhh...I'm a State fan."

I crossed my fingers like the letter X. "Boo." I leaned against my desk and frowned. "Oh, that's so sad. I thought I was really going to like you!"

He laughed. "Sucks for me, I guess."

Grinning, I folded my hands in my lap. "Too bad."

Nathan rose from his seat. "Well, I've injured you, insulted you, and I like NC State. I'd better take off before you hate me any more than you already do."

"I'm glad you stopped by, Nathan," I said.

He smiled and I felt a little dizzy. "Me too." He paused at the door. "I'll see you around, Sloan."

I thought about telling him to just fax over missing persons' reports in the future, but I just nodded and enjoyed watching him leave. Interdepartmental efficiency be damned; I wasn't going to let a fax machine stand in the way of another possible visit from Detective McNamara.

When he was gone, I dropped my forehead onto my desk and groaned. After a moment of sulking and one hell of a scolding internal monologue, I typed out the pointless press release.

The cops weren't looking for a person anymore. They were looking for a corpse.

* * *

After work, I drove to my parents' mountainside chalet for dinner like I did almost every Monday night.

Robert and Audrey Jordan were actually my adoptive parents but few people knew it. Audrey had been a twenty-two year old nursing student in Florida when she found me wrapped in a pink blanket on a park bench outside of the hospital where she worked. I was only a couple of days old. Even though she was unmarried and only working as an intern, she fought the courts for custody of me and won. My adoption was finalized shortly after she married the man who would become my dad. She had often joked that Robert only married her because he loved me so much, but I knew that wasn't true. They never had any other children.

Even though they were amazing parents, I often wondered if their love for me was completely real, or if it was some kind of supernatural manipulation that obligated them to me.

"Knock knock!" I called as I pushed the front door open.

Mom was in the kitchen with her hands covered in flour. "Hey, honey," she called over her shoulder. My mother was about a foot shorter than me and almost too thin. She had cropped brown hair that was showing more gray every time I saw her. However, even at fifty, she still jogged three miles every day and taught yoga at the local senior center.

"Where's Dad?" I jerked my thumb in the direction of the driveway. "His car isn't here."

"Oh, he's running late at the office. He'll be home soon," she said.

I sat down on a stool at the kitchen breakfast bar. "Can I help with anything?" I already knew what her answer would be.

She shook her head. "Nope. I'm almost done. How was work today?"

I recalled the look on Detective McNamara's face and slumped in my seat. I groaned and dropped my face into my hands. "Ugh. I made an idiot out of myself twice today."

She chuckled. "What did you do?"

"Well, I had to go the sheriff's office this morning for a meeting, and before I walked inside I checked myself out very thoroughly in the reflection of the mirrored glass. Little did I know that half the county was in the lobby watching me check my butt for panty lines."

She covered her mouth with her hand and laughed.

I cringed. "And I said something really stupid to this cute new detective at work."

"Oh really?" Her voice slid up an octave. She was clearly more interested in the cute guy than me embarrassing myself. My mother wanted grandkids.

I sighed. "Yeah. I probably blew my chances with him."

Her laugh was full of sarcasm. "You know better than that."

With Nathan McNamara, I wasn't so sure. He had seen a bit of my circus freak side that day.

"Do you like him?" she asked, recalling my attention to the conversation.

I drew circles with my finger on the countertop. "Well, he's really,

really attractive and he seems like a pretty good guy, but I only met him today, so I don't know yet."

She nodded and motioned toward the television in the den behind me. "Honey, can you turn on the news?"

I got up and found the remote on the coffee table. I switched on the TV and surfed to the local news station. On the screen, a man in a ridiculous blue suit was waving his arms and pacing around a used car lot. "Commercials." I sat back down at the counter.

"I want to see the weather. I've put together a running group for tomorrow morning," she said. "You should join us."

I laughed. "No thanks."

She leaned over the counter and squeezed my forearm. "Chasing boys around the office isn't exercise, Sloan."

I felt an uneasy nudge in the back of my brain. It was a twinge akin to having a tiny pebble trapped under the lining of a tennis shoe. I pulled away and looked at my mom. There were lines I had never noticed before at the creases of her eyes.

"Are you feeling all right?" I asked.

She looked at me curiously and laughed. "I'd be better if I knew my daughter was taking better care of herself."

The door from the garage opened, and my dad walked in pulling his rolling briefcase behind him. He was thin and wiry like my mother. His brown hair was graying around the ears, but it was still thick with a distinctive wave toward the back. He had the lightest blue eyes I had ever seen. My father could have been a movie star. "Hey, sweetheart," he said when he saw me.

"Hey, Daddy." I smiled over at him. "How was work?"

"Exhausting." He groaned and parked his briefcase by the wall. "I had one patient break a hip in my waiting room, and another dementia patient wandered into my office and fell asleep on my sofa."

I laughed.

He sighed. "I should've gone into pediatrics."

My mother helped him pull his coat off and laughed as she folded it over her arm. "Then you could've had babies spitting up on your sport coat and toddlers peeing in your office."

He gave her a soft peck on the lips. "I missed you today." My mother was still a nurse, and she worked in my dad's office.

She patted his chest. "I'm sorry, honey. I don't know what I was thinking. I completely planned my days wrong this week and forgot you said you needed me today. I hope you weren't too shorthanded."

The sound of the news station anchorwoman caught my attention. *"Breaking news in Buncombe County…"*

Dad gave me a side hug. "How was your day, Sloan?"

I held up my hand to silence him and then grabbed the remote. I turned up the volume on the television. "Just a sec, Dad."

The man's photo from the press release was splashed across the screen. *"The body of missing BB&C executive Byron Milstaf was found today at his sister's lake home in Tuxedo, North Carolina. Milstaf has been missing since Saturday from his home in Asheville. Police say it was an apparent suicide, and no foul play is suspected. In other news…"*

"Are you all right?" My dad was peering down at me. "Did you know that man?"

I looked out the window toward the mountains. "Sort of."

* * *

A few times during the week, I had briefly considered making up an excuse to visit the sheriff's office so I could bump into Detective McNamara again. However, those urges were overridden by my fear of the jail. I had also considered phoning in some sort of detective-necessary issue but couldn't justify missing pens from the supply closet as a reason to call the police. So I was pleasantly surprised when I came into work the following Monday to find Nathan leaning against my office door with a stack of paperwork in his hand.

"Good morning, Detective. Are they still sticking you with the office grunt work?" I batted my eyelashes up at him as I fumbled for the key to my office.

"No," he said. "I came on my own. I was hoping to talk to you."

When the door was opened, he followed me inside and closed the door behind us. I eyed him suspiciously as I walked around my desk and placed my briefcase on the floor. He wore black cargos and a dark gray t-shirt with his badge on a chain around his neck. His American flag ball cap was pulled down low over his eyes. He wasn't doing office work that day. His rigid stance made me a little nervous.

"Talk to me about what?" I sat down in my chair and pressed the power button on my computer.

He folded his arms across his chest, tucking the papers against his side. "How did you know that Byron Milstaf was dead?"

It was my hope to never revisit that conversation.

I turned my palms up. "I told you. It was a guess."

He shook his head. "I don't believe that. I'm an interview and interrogation specialist. I know when people are lying."

Laughing, I cocked my head to the side. "Are you planning on interrogating me, Nathan?"

A muscle worked in his jaw. "No, ma'am. I would just appreciate you telling me the truth."

I pointed to the chairs and narrowed my eyes. "Have a seat, Detective." Any flirtatious desire was suddenly quelled.

My icy tone caused his eyebrows to lift. He sat in the chair and rested the ankle of his tactical boot on top of his knee. His stare was expectant, and his perfect lips were shut.

Leaning forward, I rested my elbows on the desk. "First of all, I don't appreciate being clotheslined at my office door with accusations about being dishonest. I especially don't like it when it comes from a detective who is apparently suspicious about a deceased victim. Don't barge in here and shut my door and demand answers from me without telling me why you're here." I splayed my palms face down and leaned toward him. "I may be young and I may be a woman, but I'm not going to be bullied by anyone. Not even you."

For a moment, he was speechless.

His tense shoulders relaxed a bit. He leaned forward and dropped his stack of papers on my desk. On the top was a report sheet with a photo stapled to it. It was a picture of a child, a little girl. She had blond ringlets and a bright, cheerful smile. Her eyes were captivating; one was blue and one was bright green. My stomach twisted in knots.

"What is this?" I looked at him instead of at the photograph.

He tapped his finger on the picture. "This is Kayleigh Marie Neeland. Last night, there was a raid on a suspected meth operation in Leicester. Her mom's boyfriend, Ray Whitmore, panicked when the cops busted down the door. He grabbed Kayleigh and held a Taurus 9mm to her head, using her as a shield to escape. At 3:19 this morning, we found his abandoned car in Haywood County with blood on the back seat."

I was horrified but determined to keep a clear head. I sat back in my chair and turned my hands up in question. "What do you want from me?"

I could tell he wasn't sure exactly what he expected to find out in my office, but it was obvious this wasn't an excuse for a social call. "I guess I want your opinion," he replied.

I pushed the papers toward him. "My opinion is that you should do your job, Detective McNamara, and stop wasting your time in the office of the department publicist."

He let out a frustrated huff and stood up so fast his chair threatened to topple backwards. He reached into the velcro pocket on his thigh and slammed down a business card before picking up the stack of papers. He cut his eyes at me. "Kayleigh is about to turn six. For her birthday she wants a Prince Charming to go with the Sleeping Beauty doll she got from her Nana at Christmas. She hasn't put down that doll all year until she dropped it in the driveway as she was being dragged away. If you think of anything, Sloan, give me a call." Without waiting for a response, he turned on his heel and stormed out of my office.

I picked up his business card and flicked it against my fingertips as my brain scrambled to make sense of what had just happened. Why had he come to my office that morning? What did he think I might know? The bigger question was, what was I going to do?

Kayleigh Neeland was still alive and I knew it.

3.

ADRIANNE AGREED TO meet me for lunch on her break from her job at the Merrimon Avenue Salon. My head was throbbing as I sat in the corner booth waiting for her at the Mellow Mushroom. She walked in with fresh new highlights and pink high heels that were so tall I wasn't sure how she cleared the doorway without ducking. She slid into the bench across from me and pushed her sunglasses up on top of her head. "Hey weirdo," she said with a wink.

I forced a smile and rubbed my temples. "Do you have anything for a headache?"

She retrieved a bottle of ibuprofen from her purse and slid it across the table toward me. "You all right?"

I grimaced. "Rough day."

She glanced down at her silver watch. "It's only eleven."

I closed my eyes and pinched the bridge of my nose. "I know."

The waiter appeared and took her drink order. When he was gone, she scanned the menu and then looked up at me. "What's up? You sounded really stressed on the phone."

I sighed. "I've got a big problem at work." She waited expectantly, and I leaned on my elbow to support my throbbing head. "There's this new guy, a detective, at the department. I sort of slipped up the other day and told him I knew that a missing person was dead."

She straightened in her seat. "Who was dead?"

"Some random guy he wanted me to do a press release about."

"How did you know he was dead?"

I just glared at her with a raised eyebrow.

"Oh."

"Well, I played it off, and he hasn't said another word about it until today. He met me at my office this morning asking questions," I said.

Her lips sank into a frown. "Uh oh."

The waiter returned with her water and we ordered a pizza to share.

"What did he want to know?" she asked.

I thought that was obvious. "Well, the guy turned up dead in another county, and the detective wanted to know how I knew."

"And what did you say?"

"I played dumb. I insisted it was a guess," I said.

She shifted uneasily in her seat. "Does he think you were involved? Like, are you a suspect or something?"

I shook my head. "No. It was a suicide, but he suspects something because he came to my office asking me about a little girl who was kidnapped at gunpoint. They think she might be dead."

"Is she dead?"

"No."

She raised an eyebrow. "Do you know where she is?"

I shook my head. "It doesn't really work like that. I can't find people."

"But people can find you," she said. "What's her name?"

"Kayleigh Neeland." I knew what Adrianne was trying to do. She wanted to see if I could summon the girl. "I don't think I can summon someone I don't know. If I could, I would have found my birth mom years ago."

"I heard about that kid on the news this morning. What are you going to do? Are you going to tell him you know she's alive?" Adrianne was mindlessly tearing her straw paper to bits.

I had been asking myself the same question all morning. "It's only going to make him ask more questions that I can't answer. Adrianne, I think I have seriously screwed up my perfect job."

She thought about it for a second. "Or maybe you've found a way to really do your job well." She lowered her voice. "Sloan, what's the purpose of being…whatever you are, if you're not supposed to use it to help people?"

"This isn't exactly the kind of news people process well. I can't even get my parents to believe me. You know that, Adrianne."

She nodded. "But what do you do? Keep your mouth shut when you're the only person who knows this little girl is still alive?"

I squeezed my eyes closed. "That's why I have a headache."

Her eyebrows scrunched together. "Not to sound like a bitch or anything, Sloan, but I think you're being pretty selfish. This is a little kid we're talking about. You have the power to help her, but you're worried what questions about you that it might raise."

She was right.

"I know. It's completely selfish. There's just going to be a whole lot of blowback from this that I'm not sure I'm ready to deal with," I said.

She smirked. "Poor you." She leaned forward. "Are you ready to deal with the guilt you're going to feel if that little girl winds up dead, and you didn't say anything?"

I hated it when Adrianne was right.

After lunch I took the rest of the day off and went home to the stillness of my house. I stretched out on my white sofa that was trendy and stylish but absolutely uncomfortable. In an attempt to relax, I kicked off my black heels and covered my eyes with my forearm.

The details of Kayleigh's abduction replayed over and over in my mind. I envisioned that Sleeping Beauty doll discarded in the driveway and realized Nathan McNamara was a better manipulator than I could ever be. I picked up my cell phone, punched in his phone number, and sent a one line text message.

She's alive. - Sloan

A reply came less than ten seconds later. *Where are you?*

When I didn't respond, he tried to call me.

I hit ignore and tapped out another message. *I can't help you any more than that. I promise, that's all I know.*

I hadn't lied to Adrianne. I had no way of finding the girl even if I wanted to. I wasn't omniscient, and I couldn't see anything that a detective couldn't. The only thing I had to offer was more confusion, and that was exactly the reason I chose to stay out of the affairs of others. I wasn't hero material.

The little bit of help I could offer obviously wasn't enough for the good detective. Twenty minutes later, my doorbell rang.

The hardwood floor was cold against my bare feet as I trudged across the room to the entrance foyer. I pulled open the front door and leaned my head against it. "You looked up my home address?"

"Can I come in?" Nathan's ball cap was still pulled low over his eyes, but I could still see they were bloodshot from stress and lack of sleep.

Rolling my eyes, I stepped out of his way. "Be my guest."

This wasn't exactly what I had in mind when I dreamed of Nathan McNamara's first invitation into my house. I felt like a criminal watching him wipe his boots on my welcome mat. "Nathan, I told you I can't help you with anything else. All I know is that, yes, Kayleigh is still alive."

He followed me to the couch and sat down next to me. "Do you know where she is?"

I folded my arms across my chest and narrowed my eyes. "Do you not understand the version of English that I speak?"

He tightened his hand into a fist, clenched his jaw, and squeezed his eyes closed for a split second before throwing both hands in the air in frustration. "Can you not, for one second, put yourself in my shoes here?" He was almost shouting.

"You?" I spat at him. "You keep pushing and prying into things that aren't any of your business!"

He jabbed his thumb into the center of his chest. "This is my job!"

I held my hands up. "I'm not your witness! I'm not involved in this thing at all, and I don't want to be! You're pinning all your hopes and dreams of finding this kid on a feeling I have that I can't explain to myself, much less to you or a judge or the freaking media!" Tears were beginning to prickle my eyes.

He dropped his head and took a few deep breaths before he finally placed his hand on my knee. He blew out a slow sigh. "I'm sorry."

Nervously raking all my fingers through my hair, I tried to exhale all of the anxiety and adrenaline that was pumping through my veins. After a few beats of awkward silence, I looked over at him. His head was down, but his face was bent toward me.

"I'm sorry too," I whispered.

He placed his hand on my back for a second and then stood. "I appreciate you letting me know, Sloan."

I nodded, and he backed out of the room. When I heard the front door open, despite my better judgement, I called out to him. "Wait."

I turned around, and he looked over his shoulder. He closed the door.

"Just wait." I dropped my face into my hands, and when I looked up again, he was seated on my coffee table in front of me. "I don't know where she is. It's just a feeling I get. I know she's alive."

He leaned forward, resting his elbows on his knees. "What do you mean, it's a feeling? Do you get feelings about everyone?"

I nodded. "Yes."

"Is it just a dead or alive thing or what?"

I sighed. "It's more than that. I know things about people."

His face was inscrutable. "What do you know?"

"Like, I know you're a pretty decent guy who has lived a clean life. However, I have another feeling that I may regret ever having met you."

He thought for a moment. "What if you talked to Kayleigh's mother? Would you know if she was lying to me?"

I raised an eyebrow. "I thought you were the interrogation specialist? I thought you could tell when people are lying?"

His head tilted to the side. "Will you help me?"

"I will talk to the mother, but that's it." I pointed my finger at him. "I mean it, Nathan."

He quickly stood so I wouldn't have a chance to change my mind. He pulled his keys out of his pocket. "I'll drive."

In the passenger's seat of Nathan's county-issued tan SUV, I wondered what on earth I was getting myself into. I could see before me the proverbial can of worms that was about to be cracked wide open. My entire life, I had dedicated myself to trying to be like everyone else, and there I was headed at forty-five miles per hour toward never being normal again.

Nathan was angled back in his seat with one hand on the steering wheel. "Thanks for doing this." He slowly merged onto the interstate.

I just nodded.

He looked over his shoulder at me. "You know I'm going to have a hell of a lot of questions when this is all over with."

My index fingernail was bloody from my nervous chewing. "Why did you come to my office this morning?"

After a few quiet seconds, I cut my eyes over at him. He was grinning. "I guess I just had a *feeling*."

"Jerk."

He laughed.

Desperate for a new topic of conversation, I forced a change of subject. "What's your story, Nathan? How did you wind up here? Why Asheville?"

He sucked in a deep breath. "My girlfriend lives here."

The day kept getting better and better.

Nodding, I prayed he wouldn't continue. He did.

"She's a reporter for WKNC."

"Of course she is," I grumbled under my breath. I probably knew his girlfriend through work.

He leaned his ear toward me. "What'd you say?"

I examined my bloody fingernail again. "I didn't say anything."

"What about you?" he asked. "Have you always lived here?"

I nodded. "Other than college and the time I spent being probed by the aliens on the mothership, yes."

He laughed again.

"I actually grew up about five minutes away from here. If you ever visit the Grove Park Inn, you will pass my parents' house on the way up the mountain," I said.

He took the exit onto College Street. "I hear that hotel is really nice."

Sitting up straight, I looked out my window. "Where are we going?"

"The jail. The mom was arrested last night during the raid," he said.

I dropped my face into the palm of my hand and groaned.

"Is that a problem?"

I forced a smile. "Nope."

He pointed at me. "You're lying."

I shuddered. "I hate the jail. It gives me the creeps."

He focused on the road ahead. "I won't let anything get to you."

His words would have made me feel all warm and tingly inside, had the thoughts of prison rapists and murderers—and his reporter girlfriend—not squelched the moment. I waved my hands in the air and rolled my eyes. "Yay."

He chuckled and playfully shoved me in the shoulder.

We pulled into the parking lot in front of the drab green building, and I contorted my shoulders to try to relieve some of the tension that was building in my spine. I reached for my purse, pulled out my prescription bottle, and popped half of a chalky tablet under my tongue.

He looked at me surprised. "What are you taking?"

"Xanax, nosy," I said.

"You should probably leave your purse in here," he said.

I had never actually been in the guts of the jail side of the building. For a moment I considered taking the other half of my anxiety pill, but I was afraid I might end up drooling on his leather seat during the drive home. We parked in a parking spot that was labeled with his name, and I shoved my purse under my seat.

I matched Nathan step for step as we approached the front door. He paused and looked at me when we reached the landing at the top of the stairs. I looked around in confusion. "What are you doing?"

He motioned toward the door. "I wasn't sure if you needed to check out your ass in the window or not."

Smacking him hard in the chest, I genuinely laughed for the first time all day.

When we entered, the lobby was empty. We walked up to the sliding door and he pressed the buzzer. No response. He shook his head and pressed the buzzer again, this time letting his finger linger on the button.

"Press that button again!" Ms. Claybrooks yelled over the speaker. "Press it again! I'll come atch'you with razor blades and lemon juice!"

His wide eyes spun around to meet mine. I covered my mouth to keep from laughing too loudly. He pointed at the door. "Is she always like this?"

I nodded. "Every time I've ever been here."

"Razor blades and lemon juice?" He chuckled. "What the hell?"

"Who's callin'?" she finally barked over the intercom.

"Detective McNamara," he answered.

"Do I know you?"

He rested his hand on his hip and sighed. "Ms. Claybrooks, I've been here for a few weeks now."

"Ohhhhh," she purred. "You're one of the new boys, huh? Are you the red head or the cute little blond boy?"

He laughed and dropped his head. "I guess I'm the cute little blond boy."

"You come on in, cutie pie." The door slid open.

Laughing, I squeezed his arm. "I love her so much."

My heart was pounding as I followed him through a maze of concrete walls and metal doors. Just when I was certain I would never find my way out, we entered a small office, and he dropped his keys on the desk. "You OK?" he asked.

I imagined that my face was white, and I could feel sweat beading across my forehead. "Yeah, I'm good. Let's get this over with."

He picked up the phone and pressed a few buttons. "This is Detective McNamara. I need Rebecca Neeland in CID." He hung up the phone and pulled his shirt up over his waistband. I darted my eyes away as he unholstered his handgun.

I caught my reflection in the glass of a framed certificate on his wall. I smoothed my hair down and swiped some smudged mascara out from under my eyes. "What's CID?"

"Criminal Investigations Division." He pulled open the bottom drawer of the desk. "Do you have anything in your pockets I should lock up? Pens, knives, scissors, fingernail file?"

I ran my hands over the smooth fabric of my black, slim-line skirt. "Nope, I think I left all of my knives and nail files in my other skirt."

He chuckled.

We left the office and walked down to another room. I recognized it as an interrogation room from television, except the mirrored glass was a disappointingly small window instead of the whole wall. I guessed the Buncombe County jail didn't have the budget Hollywood did. I looked around at the bleak gray walls and shuddered.

"How do you want to do this?" he asked.

"Can I talk to her alone?"

He shook his head. "Absolutely not."

I scrunched up my nose. "Well, can you at least try to not be so intimidating? Maybe smile a little bit?"

"I smile," he argued.

"Not when you're in interrogator mode. I saw *that guy* this morning, remember?" I gestured toward him and tried hard not to roll my eyes.

He smiled and nodded his head.

I took a step in his direction and lowered my voice so no one else could hear. "Nathan, please keep in mind that I really don't know exactly what I'm doing here, so please don't put too much hope in this."

He squeezed my shoulder. "We have over two dozen officers knocking down doors as we speak. We are doing everything we can on our end. This woman was really uncooperative when we brought her in, and she was tweaked out of her mind on crystal meth. I appreciate you just trying to help."

"Have you told anyone about our conversations today?" I asked.

"Not a soul."

I relaxed a little.

There was a knock on the doorframe, and we both turned around. A bedraggled woman, about my age, was being led into the room by a female deputy. It was obvious Rebecca Neeland was, at one time, a stunning girl. She had thick, naturally highlighted blond hair and striking green eyes. But her hair was weighed down with straggly dead ends, and her eyes were cloaked in dark circles. Her full lips were dry and cracked, and her sallow skin was thin, blistered, and stretched over high cheekbones and a perfectly shaped button nose. She scowled at us before casting her gaze at the tile floor beneath her orange sandals.

"Thank you, Deputy," Nathan said. "I'll take it from here."

"I'll be outside," the deputy answered. She pulled the door closed behind her as she stepped into the hallway.

"Have a seat, Rebecca." He motioned toward the armless chair at the table. "I'm Detective McNamara and this is Ms. Jordan. Can I get you something to drink? Some water or—"

She cut him off. "No. What do you want?" she snapped. "Have you found my baby yet?"

I studied her face. Rebecca Neeland wasn't a victim, but she wasn't necessarily a villain either. She had certainly made some bad choices, and I couldn't tell if she would ever right her path or not, but she wasn't evil. I slipped into the seat across from her. "Hey. Is it Rebecca? Or Becky maybe?"

Her eyes darted to the table. "Becca," she muttered.

"Hey, Becca. I'm Sloan," I said.

"Who are you?" she asked.

I laughed. "I'm nobody."

She glanced skeptically down at my white buttoned blouse and cocked her head to the side. "You don't look like nobody."

"Well, I'm not a cop. Or a lawyer." I turned my palms face-up on the table. "I'm actually a publicist."

Her eyebrows scrunched together. "A publicist?"

"Yeah, I work with news people and stuff. It's very boring," I said.

"What are you doin' here? Am I gonna be on TV or somethin'?" she asked.

I shook my head. "No. I just want to help. My buddy, Nathan, over there came by my office this morning with this picture of Kayleigh, and it broke my heart. She's really cute." I pushed the photograph of her daughter in her direction.

Her eyes teared up, and she quickly swiped at them with the sleeve of her orange jumpsuit.

I placed my hand on top of hers. "Do you have any idea where we can look for her?"

She jerked her hand away. "I already told 'em, I don't know where Ray went."

"How long have you and Ray been together?" I asked.

"Since I moved here from Greensboro. What's it matter?" she snipped.

I shrugged my shoulders. "Just curious because if my friend up and disappeared right now, I would have a good idea where to go looking for him, and we haven't been together that long." I lowered my voice and cut my eyes at her with mock sympathy. "Does Ray keep secrets from you?"

She scowled. "Ray don't keep nothin' from me."

"But, obviously, you must not know him very well." I took a deep breath. "Or, Ray doesn't trust you to keep quiet, and he doesn't tell you everything."

She tapped her finger against the table. "Ray knows I can keep my mouth shut."

"So you do know where he goes?"

"Of course I do!"

My eyes widened. So did hers.

I lowered my voice again. "Rebecca, I'm not a legal genius here, but I'm pretty sure if you don't tell us what you know, then you're going to make things a lot worse for yourself in here. You'll get a lot more time stacked up on you in this hell hole, and you'll lose your daughter, maybe forever."

She just stared at me.

I tapped my chest. "I'm going to go and get Kayleigh. I'm not going to arrest Ray. I just want to make sure your little girl is safe."

Her eyes widened with curiosity. "You're going to go get her?"

I nodded. "Yes. Me. I'm going to go."

She shifted in her seat. Her eyes darted nervously around the room before settling on the picture of Kayleigh. She leaned forward. "There's an abandoned house at the end of the road on Clarksdale.

Ray goes there sometimes," she whispered.

I smiled. "Thank you."

I looked over my shoulder to where Nathan was leaned against the wall with his mouth hanging open. I pushed my chair back and stood up. "Let's go."

Rebecca jumped out of her chair. "But you said you was gonna go! Not him!"

I nodded and held my hands up in defense. "I said I was going to get Kayleigh and not arrest Ray. That's the truth. I'm just a publicist."

She shouted a few obscenities, and the deputy outside rushed in as Nathan and I walked out of the room.

"How did you do that?" he asked as he jerked his radio off of his tactical belt.

It was hard to keep up with his pace; I was practically jogging in my heels. "I guess I know how to talk to people."

He was on his radio the whole way out to the car. When I ran over to the passenger's side and grabbed the door handle, he stopped and pointed at me over the hood of the vehicle. "Oh, no. You're not going."

"Oh yes I am! You're not leaving me here!" I shouted. "There's not enough Xanax in the world, buddy."

He must have accurately assumed it would be pointless to try and argue with me, so he got in and started the SUV. I buckled my seatbelt as he peeled out of the parking lot with his blue lights flashing. "When we get there you have to stay in the damn car."

I held my hands up in resignation. "Oh, I don't want to be a hero. I'll stay."

It was a short drive through an older residential part of town. The houses along Clarksdale were sixties style homes that looked as though they hadn't been cared for since the sixties. The house at the end was a foreclosure covered in graffiti and no trespassing signs. Given the state of the area, it was doubtful that any of the neighboring residents would have noticed—or, much less, reported—any unusual activity at the end of the street.

Two other patrol cars had beaten us there by seconds. There were police officers in the street with their weapons drawn, slowly approaching the house. Nathan practically leapt from the car before he even slid the transmission into park.

I watched in silence as Nathan directed the officers around the sides and back of the house. After a few minutes, he kicked in the front door. My knuckles went white as I clenched the dashboard looking for any sign of activity from within the dilapidated home. After a few minutes, a news van from Channel 2 and two other police officers pulled in behind us. I rolled my window down enough to hear what was being said. I could hear over the radio someone's voice requesting a body bag.

An over-groomed female reporter from News Channel 2 was swatting her brown bangs out of her eyes as the cameraman was getting his equipment ready. After a moment of straightening her suit, she began her spiel. "We are here at the scene of the possible location of missing five-year-old, Kayleigh Neeland. Kayleigh was abducted by her mother's boyfriend during a meth lab raid last night in Leicester. Information from an unidentified source has led officers to this address on Clarksdale Avenue in West Asheville…" She paused, and I turned to see Nathan standing in the doorway with his hands up.

"She's not here!" he called to me.

The reporter strained to see who he was talking to. I wanted to cower down and throw a blanket or something over my head, but I knew it was too late for that. I pushed my door open. "Is it safe for me to get out?" I yelled.

He nodded and I crossed the lawn. He met me in the tall grass and lowered his voice. "Ray is dead inside. It looks like someone got to him before we did. Kayleigh isn't here," he said. "We searched the entire house."

I shook my head. "She's not dead."

He shielded me with his arm, moving me away from the crowd that was growing in front of the house. "I'm running out of ideas here, Sloan."

"Take me inside. I want to check," I said.

He narrowed his eyes. "That's not a good idea."

"Do you have a better one?" I asked.

He jerked his head toward the house and put his hand on the small of my back. "Come on."

I followed him in the front door, and the stench almost knocked me to my knees. The room was sour with mildew, and the walls had gaping holes where the wiring had been stripped out. Melted puddles of wax from half-burnt candles were cemented into the dingy, torn carpet and trash was everywhere. A mattress was beneath the window and stained with...I didn't even want to know what. In the doorway of the kitchen was a body that I assumed belonged to the recently departed Ray Whitmore. His eyes were open and covered in a milky film.

Oddly, dead bodies didn't bother me. Dead bodies were just discarded shells. I would forever be more fearful of the living than the dead.

A familiar sensation came over me, and I carefully scanned the room again. "We're not alone, Nathan."

His gun was drawn. "She's here?"

"Someone is." I stumbled over a pile of trash. "I can feel it."

My eyes searched the room for any sign that a child had ever been there. I shuddered at such a thought. "Come on, Kayleigh, where are you?" I mumbled.

Nathan's head jerked up. "Did you hear that?"

I was completely clueless. "Hear what?"

Then I heard it. A very faint sliding sound was over our heads. "Nathan, she's in the attic!"

We both began scanning the crumbling popcorn ceiling for an opening. I stepped over a pile of beer cans and rags and peeked around the doorway to the hall. "It's in here!" I lunged forward to grasp the string to the attic pull-down door.

Nathan clotheslined me with his forearm. "No. Let me."

He pulled on the string, lowering the stairs to the floor. Once it was open, we could hear a muffled whimper. With his flashlight in one hand and his gun in the other, he carefully maneuvered his way up the ladder.

I chewed on my nails. "Be careful."

"Oh, God," he said once his head was through to the attic. "Sloan, I'm going to need you up here to hold the flashlight."

I hoisted myself up the rickety steps, and when my eyes adjusted to the dim light above, I saw her. Kayleigh Neeland was curled up on her side in her Dora the Explorer pajamas. Her ankles and wrists were tied together with what looked to be fishing line. A wide piece of duct tape covered her mouth. She had soiled herself, and her face was covered in dried blood from a cut across her tiny forehead. Her exhausted eyes were terrified. It was all I could do to not scream at the horror.

Nathan passed me his flashlight and tucked his gun into his holster.

He held out his hands for her to see. "Kayleigh, I'm not going to hurt you. I'm a policeman, and I'm here to help you." She blinked her eyes at him. "I need to get my knife so I can cut those ties off of your hands, OK? But I promise I won't hurt you."

Slowly, he pulled out a tactical knife and carefully cut the line holding her hands together. As gently as he could, he peeled away the strands that had sliced into her delicate skin. She cried out in pain as he freed her bloody hands.

"I'm so sorry," he said over and over, his voice quavering as he tried to maintain his composure.

Even from a few feet away with hardly any light, I could see Kayleigh was trembling. He severed the lines around her feet and, though she was weak, she scrambled toward him. Nathan sat all the way down and scooped her up in his lap. Gently, he rocked her and smoothed her matted blond hair. "Shh...it's all over." He kissed the top of her head. "Shhh."

When she saw me standing halfway up the ladder, she stretched out her arms. I thrust the flashlight at Nathan and reached for her. Carefully, I lifted her up, and she clung to me like I was a lone buoy afloat in the wide ocean.

"Nathan, get the tape off." I turned around so he could work the tape on her mouth over my shoulder. After a moment and a few whimpers, he wadded up the duct tape and tossed it on the floor with the rest of the trash. She buried her face in my shoulder.

Two officers had appeared at the bottom of the steps. "Hand her down, ma'am," one of them said.

I shook my head. "No. Just help me get down without falling."

"Get the paramedics in here!" Nathan shouted.

When I finally descended the ladder, I sat down against the steps with her still in my arms. "We've got you. You're safe now. You don't have to be afraid anymore." Tears streamed down my cheeks.

"Don't let me go," she whispered.

4.

AS PROMISED, I didn't let Kayleigh go. I rode with her to the hospital and tried to help the police shield her from the crowd of media when we got out of the ambulance. I knew some of the reporters from my work at the county office, so everyone knew my name by the time we arrived.

"Sloan Jordan, what is your involvement here?"

"Are you related to the victim?"

"How did you help the police find Kayleigh?"

Their shouts and questions rattled around in my skull as we fought our way through the ambulance bay doors.

A team of emergency room staff ushered us straight to triage when we entered, and I held her hand as they surveyed her injuries. A nurse, who reminded me a lot of my mother, carefully cleaned her face exposing a lot of bruising and swelling around the site of the large gash in her forehead. "Sweetie, do you remember how this happened?" she asked.

Kayleigh shook her head. Her eyes were leaking uncontrollable tears, but she wasn't audibly crying.

The nurse looked up at me. "My guess is she was knocked unconscious."

I cringed.

I wasn't sure how much time had passed when Nathan eventually came through the door carrying a bundle in his arms, but I was half asleep in the chair next to Kayleigh's bed. After being poked, prodded, x-rayed, and questioned, she was finally sleeping somewhat peacefully.

"Hey," he said. He knelt down beside me and placed his hand on my forearm. "How's she doing?"

I leaned out of the way so he could see the bruising for himself as Kayleigh slept. His jaw tightened, and he let out a slow puff of air. "Her grandparents were notified and they just got here from Greensboro. They are on their way back here now," he said.

I sighed. "That's good. She's been asking me to call her Nana, and I didn't know what to tell her."

He turned his attention to me. "How are you holding up? I brought you a sweatshirt from my car. It's not exactly clean, but I figured you might want to change." He shook the sweatshirt out straight in front of him.

I offered him a weak smile. "You have no idea how grateful I am." I looked down at my dingy blouse; it had been white when I left my house that morning.

Just then, a couple in their late sixties came in with a doctor. "Oh, my sweet baby!" the woman exclaimed as she rushed to the bedside.

Kayleigh's eyes fluttered open and then darted around the room in confusion. I reached for her hand. When her eyes settled on the couple rushing toward her, Kayleigh scrambled up in the bed and reached out for the woman. "Nana!"

The grandfather was in tears, but he stopped to shake Nathan's hand. "Thank you, Detective. Thank you."

Nathan just nodded.

When the grandmother finally released the child, she grabbed me around the neck and squeezed me so tight I thought she might cut off the circulation to my head. "Thank you so much," she cried. "God bless you."

When she finally released me, I stepped closer to Kayleigh's bedside and surveyed her tiny, battered face. "Hey Kayleigh, is it OK if I step out for a little bit now that your Nana is here?"

She nodded.

I leaned down and pressed a kiss to the top her head. I gently raked my fingers through her blond curls. "I promise I'll check on you in a little bit, OK?"

"OK," she whispered.

I felt Nathan's hand at the small of my back as he turned me toward the door. Once we were around the corner, out of sight, I crumbled. Uncontrollable sobs, that I'd been holding in for hours, erupted without warning so violently that I doubled over and had to grasp my knees. Nathan's arms wrapped around me, and his fingers tangled in my hair as he pulled my head to his chest. I could feel his warm breath on my neck as he breathed. "Shhhh..."

When I regained my composure, I pulled away and looked at him. I was still gripping his forearms for support. "I'm sorry."

He cupped my face in his hands and swiped away what I was sure was a mess of mascara with his thumbs. "Are you kidding? There is absolutely no reason for you to be apologizing. I couldn't have done this without you. You saved that little girl's life."

I took a deep breath and let it out slowly. "What do we do now?"

He handed me the sweatshirt and pointed to the bathroom behind us. "First, you change."

In the bathroom, I scrubbed my hands clean and splashed my face with cold water a few times. I unbuttoned my blouse and, though it was probably washable, shoved it in the wastebasket. I washed my hands again before pulling the black hooded sweatshirt, with the letters S.W.A.T. across the back, over my head. The strong smell of Nathan's cologne and sweat about made my eyes roll backward. It was the only pleasant feeling I had experienced all day. I combed my fingers through my hair and retied my mangled ponytail before leaving the bathroom.

Nathan was leaned against the wall making notes in a small black notebook. He looked me up and down. "Did you forget your shirt?"

I shook my head. "I trashed it. I'm never wearing that thing again."

He nodded. "Come on, let's try and sneak out of here and find some food. I don't know about you, but I'm starving."

I pointed toward the entrance to the emergency room. "I assume the waiting room is full of reporters?"

"Yep. You definitely don't want to go out there." He held the door at the end of the hall open for me.

I hugged my arms to my chest as we passed down the fluorescent lit hallway that reeked of antiseptic and sickness. "What are they saying?" I asked.

He looked over at me with an expression that made it clear he was worried I might either cry or punch him in the face. "They're talking about you quite a bit. Apparently, News Channel 2 is replaying some video of you carrying Kayleigh out of the house. Everyone wants to know why you were there."

I sighed. "Honestly, right now I don't even care. I'm just glad it's over."

As we followed the signs to the hospital cafeteria, his cell phone rang. I realized my purse, along with my wallet and phone, was still under the seat of his car. If my mother had seen the news she was probably frantic with worry. My voicemail inbox was probably full.

As Nathan talked, I couldn't help but listen in on his conversation. "Hey. Yeah, it's over. The guy was dead when we got there, and we found the little girl in the attic." He paused for a few seconds and then looked over at me. "Yeah, she works in public relations for the county. I just, uh, happened to be in her office when I got the call, and she wanted to tag along."

I rolled my eyes. "You're a terrible liar."

He ignored me. "Yeah, I'm going to have a late night. A ton of paperwork, ya know," he continued. "I'll grab dinner on my own. Probably at the office. I'll try and call you later if it's not too late." He paused and listened again. "Yeah, me too. Bye."

I tsked my tongue against the roof of my mouth. "Lying to your girlfriend already? That's not a good sign."

"What was I supposed to tell her? That you're psychic or something?" he asked.

"Then we would both sound crazy," I said.

We finally reached the bustling cafeteria. The smell reminded me of elementary school lunch trays and cartons of milk. He stopped at the vending machine and looked at me. "You hungry?"

"No, but I would love a Diet Coke if you could spot me the change. My purse is still in your car," I said.

"I'm sorry. I meant to grab it for you and I totally forgot. I can run out and get it if you want," he said.

I waved my hand. "I'll get it when we leave. I don't have the headspace to deal with the phone calls right now anyway."

He fed a dollar bill into the drink machine. "I'm pretty sure a Diet Coke is the least I can do for you."

When he handed me my drink, I watched him buy a bag of Skittles, a Snickers bar, and pack of Nerds. I looked at his toned physique and then cocked my head sideways. "I had you pegged for a health nut or something."

He shrugged. "I'm a candy freak. I just have to run twice as far."

I laughed.

He motioned to an empty table near the door and we sat down. He ripped open the wrapper around the Snickers bar. "It's question time."

I pointed at him. "No questions."

He leaned forward. "Sloan, I have to come up with some really brilliant reason why you are on that police report from today. You've got to give me something."

I rested my elbows on the table and propped my chin up in my hands. I studied his face for a moment. "Give me a serious answer as to why you came to my office asking me about Kayleigh."

He thought for a second, biding his time by chewing on a bite of his candy bar. He squinted his eyes enough to indicate he was seriously attempting to answer my question. "There was something about the way you said 'he's dead' when you saw that missing person's report on Milstaf. I am always analyzing how people phrase things, their body language, and the inflection in their voice to judge if they are being honest or not. You might as well have been telling me the sun was shining outside. You weren't speculating—you *knew*." He sat back in his seat. "It stuck with me."

After a moment of staring at him and racking my brain for what to say next, I sighed and turned my palms up. "I don't know how I know these things. I just do."

"Are you ever wrong?"

"Not in twenty-seven years," I answered.

I could almost hear the gears turning in his mind. "Can you tell with everyone? Like, I have a sister. Is she alive or dead?" he asked.

I shrugged. "I would have to see a photograph of her."

He seemed to be making mental notes as I talked. He drummed his fingers on the table. "You also knew we weren't alone in that house. You knew Kayleigh was there."

"No. I knew *someone* was there. We got lucky that it was Kayleigh."

He thought it over. "How? Is it like hearing a heartbeat?"

"It's more like feeling a pulse," I explained.

That seemed to make sense to him. "Could it have been a rat? Or a dog?"

"No. I only feel humans. Animals must operate on a different system than we do," I said.

"Is that all you can do?" he asked. I glanced up at the ceiling, and he pointed at me again. "You're about to tell me a lie," he said.

"Quit using your interrogation crap on me!"

He laughed. "Tell me the truth. I swear it won't leave this table."

There was a boulder of anxiety forming in the pit of my stomach. He kept staring at me, waiting for an answer I didn't want to give. I opened my mouth and closed it several times before finally being able to form words. "I seem to be able to call people to me, like, subconsciously."

He closed his eyes and turned his ear toward me, like he was certain he had misheard something. "What?"

I thought for a second. "You know when we were in the house and you heard Kayleigh move in the attic?" He nodded. I looked at him seriously. "I had just said her name out loud."

"And you think you made me find her?"

I shook my head. "No. I made her be found."

He just stared at me without chewing the bite in his mouth. Finally, he started laughing. "Ha, you're good. That's pretty funny. You almost had me."

I wasn't laughing.

In slow motion, I could see the humor dripping from his face and fear surfacing underneath. I sank down in my chair, bracing for the blowback.

"You're not joking are you?" he asked a moment later.

I shook my head again.

He shifted uneasily in his seat. "How do you do it?"

"No idea," I said. "I just have this sense about other people. Like, I already know them before I meet them and somehow they are drawn to me like magnets."

"And no one knows you can do this? That you can make people magically appear by talking about them?" His eyes were wide with disbelief.

"Well, my best friend knows and now you know," I said.

He swallowed a bite. "Your parents?"

"Oh no. My dad's a doctor and my mother is a nurse. I'm pretty sure they would have me committed."

"Huh," he mumbled. He finished off his candy bar and chewed in silence for what felt like an eternity.

The tension was killing me. "Are you going to freak out?"

His eyes settled on me again. "No," he said. "I'm not going to freak out. This is nuts though."

"I know."

He grabbed his Skittles and Nerds and tucked them into his jacket pocket. "We should probably head back to the emergency room. I know you want to check on the girl before I take you home, and we've got to deal with the media sooner or later."

"What are you going to put in your report?" I cringed as I waited for his answer.

He pressed his eyes closed. "That I knew this thing would be a media nightmare, so I thought it would be smart to bring PR along."

I turned toward him and frowned, putting my hand on my hip. "You didn't need to know my secret to come up with that explanation."

He smiled and gave me a mischievous wink. "I know."

I punched him in the shoulder.

Nathan had already briefed Sheriff Davis about my presence at the scene, and the sheriff was in the lobby with the media when we returned to that side of the hospital. He had assumed I already had a speech prepared for him for the ten o'clock news. I didn't, but I faked it pretty well as I went over his notes with him. When he finished detailing the events for the broadcast, the female reporter I had seen at the house on Clarksdale, raised her hand with a question.

When she was acknowledged, she looked at me. I looked down at my ragged outfit as several news cameras panned in my direction. "Sloan Jordan was at the scene today and was videoed carrying Kayleigh Neeland from the house. What was Ms. Jordan's involvement with this case?"

The sheriff was a little surprised by the question, but he handled it like a true politician. "Ms. Jordan, as you know, is the county's publicist, and she was there for the sake of the media when our officers needed help with the frightened child. That was Ms. Jordan's only involvement."

I wish.

It was after dark when Nathan finally pulled up to the curb in front of my house. To my surprise, he turned off the engine and walked with me to the door. I put my keys in the lock and turned the handle. "Do you want to come in? I've got coffee…and Jack Daniels," I added with an exhausted laugh.

He smiled. "No. I'd better get home. I can't thank you enough for today, Sloan."

I shook my head. "Stop thanking me. She's safe and that's all that matters."

He nodded.

"I can change out of your shirt if you'll give me a minute," I offered.

He tugged on the hem. "Just keep it for a while. I'll get it from you soon."

His smooth voice gave me chills.

He lingered for a moment. I wondered if he was thinking of changing his mind about my invitation inside. Finally, he turned toward my steps. "I'll see you at work."

"Goodnight, Nathan."

5.

I SLEPT IN the next morning and called out of work for the day. When I finally talked myself into getting out of bed, I returned all of the missed calls from my mother, my dad, and Adrianne. My parents wanted to check on me after being put through such a traumatic ordeal. Adrianne wanted to know what the hell I was thinking appearing on the news in a black hoodie and no makeup.

I was still wearing the hoodie when my doorbell rang just before noon. I had taken a shower before bed, but couldn't help myself when I thought of how nice it would be to fall asleep to the smell of that shirt. I cursed the decision when I opened the door to Nathan standing there holding a to-go bag from Tupelo Honey.

He looked me up and down and smiled. I died a little on the inside.

I leaned against the door. "What are you doing here?"

He stepped inside and laughed. "I guess I didn't come by to get my shirt back."

I rolled my eyes and closed the door behind him.

"I went by your office, but you weren't there. Your boss said you had taken a comp day, so I decided to bring you lunch. She suggested goat cheese grits." He held up the plastic bag.

I laughed and accepted it. "Thanks. Come sit down." I returned to my spot on the couch and pulled my fleece blanket up over my bare legs.

He sat on the loveseat caddy-cornered to the couch and laid a thick file folder on the coffee table. I looked at it and then at him. My eyes widened and I shook my head. "Oh no," I said. "I'm not doing anymore police work. Do you hear me? I am not going to be your secret, silent partner helping you crack cold-cases and solve murder mysteries."

He laughed and flipped the folder open. "It's not that, I promise."

I relaxed a little and pulled the plastic bowl of steaming grits out of the bag. He had also gotten me some type of sandwich.

Nathan passed me a worn 8x10 photograph of a football player and a cheerleader. The number fifty-four was printed on his jersey and drawn on the girl's cheek in blue paint and glitter. The football player with the tousled blond hair and crooked smile was a younger, less stern version of Nathan. The girl on his arm held a bouquet of red roses and had a blue ribbon tied in her long, dark hair. She was strikingly beautiful.

She was also dead.

I tapped my finger on the picture and looked up at him. "Who is this girl?"

"My little sister, Ashley."

I deflated a little. "How did she die?"

He took a deep breath and leaned his elbows on his knees. He cast his gaze to the carpet. He had been forewarned about my ability, but that hadn't lessened the shock of it.

After a moment, he sat back against the seat. "She went missing two weeks after this photo was taken after a different football game." He looked at the picture for a moment before tucking it back into the folder. "I didn't know until just now that she was really dead."

Gasping with shock and trying to swallow wasn't a good combination. I sucked a spoonful of grits down my throat, then coughed and sprayed them all over my lap. I yanked a napkin out of the paper bag, wiped my mouth, and put the food on the coffee table. I covered his hands with my own. "I'm sorry, Nathan. I really had no idea. I assumed—"

He cut me off with a wave of his hand. "It's OK. I've believed she was dead for a very long time now, but they never found her body."

I gulped and slowly retreated to my side of the sofa. "Is this why you went into police work?"

He forced a smile, but it was full of pain. "I was planning to be an engineer."

"What happened to her?"

He laid his head back and stared at the ceiling. "She was a junior in high school when she disappeared. I was a senior and the captain of the football team. Ashley was a cheerleader. She was supposed to ride with me to a party after a game we won, but our coach took an extra-long time during the end of the game meeting. I couldn't find her when we broke out. I assumed she had ridden with some of her friends, but she never showed up at the party. The last time anyone saw her, she was putting her gym bag in the back seat of my car in the parking lot."

"So instead of becoming an engineer, you became a cop," I said.

He nodded. "When I got out of high school, I did my two years at the community college studying criminal justice and enrolled in the police academy."

"So you could protect people?"

He shook his head. "No. So I could find the person who took my sister."

I hugged my knees to my chest and tugged the blanket down over my feet. "And nothing ever turned up?"

He sat forward again and reached for the folder. "Not on my sister's case." He pulled out more photographs. "There have been eleven disappearances very similar to hers since then. All of them happened in different cities between Asheville and Raleigh."

I sat up and looked at the faces of the girls smiling up from their pictures.

I looked up at him. "You think they are related?"

He shrugged. "If not, it's a pretty big coincidence."

My skin began to crawl. I really hated the word 'coincidence'. "Why are you telling me all of this?" I asked.

He leaned toward me. "Because you can help me."

"No offense, Nathan, I realize this is your sister we are talking about, but you just promised me that you're not trying to pull me into criminal investigation," I reminded him.

"I know, I lied to get you to listen to me," he admitted. "Sloan, what if this is a serial killer?"

I pushed the photos toward him. "Then I really don't want anything at all to do with it!"

"Can you just tell me if they are alive or dead?" He picked up the photos and moved to the seat next to me before fanning them out on the coffee table. "That's all I'm asking for."

I cut my eyes at him for several moments before begrudgingly leaning forward and taking a closer look. My eyes moved slowly from face to face until I settled on one that was very familiar. I tapped her picture. "I went to school with this girl." I said. "I remember Adrianne telling me about someone we went to school with who disappeared while I was away at college."

He nodded his head. "Leslie Ann Bryson. She disappeared in 2009 after getting off work at Chili's Bar and Grill."

I shuddered. "Are there any more girls from around here?"

He shook his head and pulled out a legal sized sheet of ledger paper. It was a timeline. A map was glued to the bottom of the sheet with red "X" marks and numbers scrawled on it. There had been two disappearances in Raleigh, two in Greensboro, two in Hickory, two around Winston-Salem, two around Statesville, and Leslie Ann Bryson in Asheville.

A light bulb flickered on in my brain.

I pointed at him. "You didn't move here for your girlfriend," I said. "You moved here because you believe the next victim is going to be from around here!"

He just stared at me.

I raised an eyebrow. "Why isn't this the FBI's problem?"

He closed the folder. "Well, the FBI just recently started looking into this as these cases being possibly related."

I closed my eyes and pressed my palms over them in frustration. "Nathan, why the hell did you have to come to Asheville? My life was so much less complicated before you showed up! Do you even have a girlfriend?"

"Yes. I didn't lie about that."

I smirked and shoved him hard in the shoulder. "Does she know you're using her as an alibi to be some kind of vigilante with a badge?"

"I'm not using her," he argued. "And I did move here for her. I don't know the next abduction will happen here. I don't even know if these crimes were all committed by the same person."

I pointed at him. "But you suspect it and you are using her. And now, you're trying to use me." I got to my feet and began to stalk across the room.

He followed and grabbed me around the waist before I could throw the front door open and insist that he leave. He pulled me against his body and rested the side of his face against my hair. "Sloan, I'm just asking you to think about it," he said quietly in my ear.

His pheromones were making my head foggy and I suspected he knew it. I wrenched his arm off of my mid-section and pulled on the front door handle. "Go away, Nathan," I said as I pointed to the street.

His shoulders slumped and he moved toward the door.

"Wait," I said.

Out of the corner of my eye, I saw his shoulders straighten and his eyes widen with hope. I returned to the living room, gathered up his files, and closed the folder. I rejoined him at the door and shoved the folder into his chest, forcing him backward over the threshold.

"Now, go away." I slammed the door in his face and tumbled the deadbolt.

* * *

Surprisingly, I didn't see Nathan at all the rest of the week. I thought for sure he would be waiting at my office door when I arrived for work the morning after I expelled him from my house, but he wasn't. He didn't call or text either. Not that I was disappointed.

On Friday after work, I met Adrianne at 12 Bones Smokehouse for dinner and drinks. She was waiting at the bar and flirting with the bartender when I arrived. Like me, it seemed Adrianne would be eternally single, but it wasn't for lack of suitors. Adrianne became more and more exotic with age. I felt sloppy in my work blouse, black pants, and heels next to her mile-long legs and eyelet lace party dress.

I slid onto the barstool next to her. "I hate you."

She laughed and tossed her hair over her shoulder. "What did I do?"

"Look at you." I motioned to her evening outfit. "I look like I came from a meeting with the school board."

She nudged me with her elbow. "*Did* you come from a meeting with the school board?"

"No. That was on Monday."

We both laughed.

The bartender walked toward us. "What are you drinking tonight, Sloan?"

"Beer," I answered. "Rebel IPA if you've got it on tap this week.

Thanks, Gary."

He nodded and turned away.

"Drinking the hard stuff tonight?" She traced her finger around the rim of her martini and waited expectantly for a reason.

I groaned. "It's been a week from hell."

"I figured as much. I haven't heard from you in days," she said.

I sighed as the bartender placed the frothy amber liquid in front of me. "I know. I'm sorry. I've been so swamped and so stressed out."

She lifted the skewered olive from her glass and popped it between her cherry lips. "Why? What's going on?"

I took a long swig of ice cold beer. "So, obviously, I helped the detective find that little kid. Then, the very next day, he showed up at my house with this huge folder full of a bunch of missing girls. He wants me to help him with the case. He thinks it might be a serial killer."

She blinked in disbelief. "He wants you to investigate a serial killer?"

I gripped the frosty glass. "Pretty much."

"What did you tell him?"

I laughed and took another long drink. "Oh, I kicked him out of my house."

She nodded. "Good girl. You don't need to get involved in that stuff."

I dropped my face into my hands and whined. "But he makes it so hard! I'm so freaking attracted to this man it's infuriating. And"—I gripped her arm—"one of the victims is his sister. His *sister*, Adrianne!"

She raised an eyebrow and turned toward me on her seat. "You didn't tell me you had a thing for him."

I dropped my face into my hands again. "I don't want to have a thing for him, but I *sooooo* do."

"What's his name?" she asked.

I straightened and looked at her. "Detective Nathan McNamara," I said. "Even his stupid name is sexy."

She laughed and her eyes widened. "Oh yeah. He's the blond guy who was standing next to you on the news."

I sighed. "Yes."

"He is hot. *Super* hot." She sipped her drink. "Are you sleeping with him?"

"No!"

She shrugged her shoulders and laughed. "I would be."

"This has been the worst week ever." I groaned as I raked my fingers through my hair.

"So the hot cop wants you to hunt down a serial killer," she said. "How would you even do that?"

I shook my head. "I *can't* do that."

"Are you sure? You didn't think you could find that little girl either, but you did. Maybe you can find a serial killer too and you just don't know it," she said.

I pointed at her. "Just two seconds ago, you told me to stay away from it."

She shrugged. "That was before I knew all the facts."

"There is another fact." I tilted my glass toward her. "Remember that girl from our school who went missing a few years ago?"

Her eyebrows lifted. "She's one of them?"

I nodded.

"Is she dead?"

I leaned my elbows on the bar top and cradled my face in my hands. "Adrianne, they're all dead."

She shifted uncomfortably on her barstool. "That's big."

"I know," I said.

"What are you going to do?"

I shook my head. "Nothing. I'm not going to do anything. I'm going to drink my beer and enjoy my peaceful, quiet little life."

She laughed and drained the last of her martini. "Finish your beer. We're getting out of here."

"Where are we going?" I looked at my watch. It wasn't even eight o'clock.

She pointed to my outfit. "We are going to your house so you can change into proper Friday night clothes, and then we are going out."

"We are out, and I need to get some food in my stomach," I argued.

She shook her head and signaled the bartender for our check. "No, ma'am. We are going out and getting your mind off of dead girls, serial killers, and the hot detective."

After several wardrobe changes and having my hair yanked and pulled till my scalp nearly bled, we arrived at The Social Lounge. It was the closest thing Asheville had to a swanky, upscale bar. My dress, which looked like a black satin garbage bag cinched at the waist with a jeweled belt, kept sneaking its way up my backside. Adrianne had given me the dress two birthdays prior, and it had hung in my closet ever since. My heels were too tall and my makeup was too thick, but my hair did look amazing. Sometimes it was a really good thing to have a top hair stylist for a best friend.

We made our way up to the rooftop and navigated through what appeared to be Manhattan transplants until we found two empty bar stools at the bar. When our drinks were delivered, I looked at my Rebel IPA and at her martini and scowled. "I don't see the difference here as opposed to an hour ago when we were paying a lot less for the same drinks, and I was a *lot* more comfortable."

She winked at me over the rim of her glass as she tilted it up to her glossy lips. "You look so good now our drinks might end up being free." She nodded toward the other side of the bar. "Those guys are cute."

I followed the path of her eyes. At the far left end of the bar, two thirty-something-year-old frat boys were speaking in hushed tones as they stared at us—no, as they stared at Adrianne. One was tall and wiry with blond hair and a chiseled face. The other was shorter with dark, wavy hair and overly perfect teeth. He gave me the creeps.

I shook my head. "No. Absolutely not."

She rolled her eyes. "They're cute, and they look like they could afford to pay our tab at the end of the night." She smiled over at them.

I sighed and drank my beer.

"I'll have what she's having," a voice said to the bartender from behind me. I saw Adrianne's eyes widen and then dart away. "A beer girl, huh?" Nathan wedged his body between my chair and the older man seated next to me.

I covered my eyes with my hand. "Seriously?"

"You called him here," Adrianne teased as she nudged me with her elbow.

His lips spread into a wide smile. "You were talking about me, huh?"

I smirked. "Oh, it wasn't flattering." I drained half of my glass before putting it down.

He leaned down close to my ear. "I'm kinda surprised I haven't heard from you this week."

His voice disturbed the butterflies that had taken up residence in my stomach since he had moved to town, but I refused to let him know it.

I glanced up at him. "Was I not clear enough for you the other day when I slammed my front door in your face?"

The bartender placed a beer in front of Nathan. "Do you want to start a tab?"

Nathan shook his head and put a twenty dollar bill on the counter. "No thanks. Take care of these three drinks and keep the change."

"I'm not inviting you to join us," I told him.

He shook his head. "I wasn't expecting you to."

Adrianne reached across me and offered him her hand. "I'm Adrianne. Sloan's best friend. You're Detective McNamara."

"Just Nathan or Nate," he said as he shook her hand. "It's nice to meet you."

"You can join us," she said with a smile. "My invitation."

He laughed and looked at me. "As tempting as that sounds, I can't. Thank you though." He looked back and waved to someone. I knew it was his girlfriend before I even turned around.

Shannon Green, the girl I had wished syphilis on in high school, was walking toward us when I spun around in my chair.

I looked at Adrianne. "Is this really happening right now?"

"Sloan?" Shannon hesitated as she approached.

Nathan's eyes darted between us. "You two know each other?"

I laughed and crossed my legs. "Oh yes. We know each other very well." I pointed at her. "This is your girlfriend?"

"Uh oh," I heard Adrianne mumble next to me.

"Yes," Shannon answered, so bubbly I wanted to smack her. She draped her arms around Nathan's neck and leaned her body into his. "Isn't he wonderful?"

"He's actually a pain in the ass." I looked at him. "I thought you said your girlfriend was a reporter?"

Shannon tossed her hair over her shoulder. "I am a reporter."

Adrianne laughed. "You're the traffic girl!"

Shannon put her hand on her hip. "I'm not *just* the traffic girl!" she protested. She started counting on her fingers. "I have to put together news stories, and interview people, and lots of stuff."

Adrianne nodded, sarcasm dripping from her eyes. "I'm sure that it's very challenging to keep up with the traffic of the Asheville metropolis."

Shannon wanted to speak, but her mouth couldn't find any words. Her eyes darted from Adrianne to me and then back at Nathan. He was doing his best to try and look offended on her behalf, but he wasn't very successful. Finally, Shannon turned and stalked off.

I chuckled quietly to myself and turned around in my seat. I picked up what was left of my beer and tipped it toward Nathan. "Thanks for the drink, Detective."

When they were gone, Adrianne gripped my bicep so hard she left fingerprints. "Hold up. Wait a second. He's dating Shannon Green? Out of all the women in this city, *that's* his girlfriend?" She was laughing so hard she doubled over in her seat.

"Apparently so." I sighed and shook my head.

Tears leaked from her eyes as she slapped the bar and laughed next to me. "How does this stuff happen to you? That's the funniest thing I've ever seen in my life!"

I buried my face in my hands and couldn't help but laugh. "I have the worst luck in the history of the world." I finished off my glass and held it up so the bartender would see I desperately needed another one.

Adrianne draped her arm across my shoulders. "Well, look on the bright side," she said. "You finally have an opportunity for payback. Now you have the chance to hook up with *her* boyfriend."

"When you said, 'you're the traffic girl' I about died," I said, trying to control my giggles.

She made a serious face with overly pouty lips. "She really is a serious news reporter."

I nodded and grinned at her over my glass. "I know I couldn't get to work without her in the mornings."

The laughter erupted all over again.

"What's so funny?" someone asked from behind.

"I'm afraid to even turn around," I grumbled.

It was the two guys from the other end of the bar. Between their heads, I caught Nathan watching from across the room. I turned a sultry smile toward the blond guy, since he seemed to be less creepy than the guy with the offensively white teeth. "Hi there," I purred.

He leaned toward me. "Can we buy you ladies a round?"

Nathan was still watching.

"Absolutely."

* * *

I woke up the next morning to the sound of the phone ringing. I looked at the caller ID. It was my dad. I pressed the answer button and rubbed my tired eyes. "Hello?"

"Hey, sweetheart. Did I wake you?" he asked.

I yawned. "Yeah. I had a bit of a late night last night. What's up?"

"Mom wanted me to call and tell you that she made biscuits and gravy for breakfast and that you should come over since you missed dinner this week," he said.

I groaned. "What time is it?"

"It's after nine."

"I'll be there soon if I can drag myself out of bed. Don't let breakfast get cold if it takes me a little bit. Go ahead and eat without me," I said.

"OK. Be careful. Love you," he said.

"Love you too, Dad." I disconnected the call and looked at notifications screen on my phone. I had a text message from Nathan that I had missed about an hour before.

Did you make it home OK last night?

I decided to let him wonder and didn't respond.

The smell of sausage billowed out of the front door when I walked into my parents' house. My stomach immediately rumbled. "Oh my gosh, it smells like heaven in here," I said as I walked into the kitchen.

Dad was at the breakfast bar with a cup of coffee and the newspaper. Mom was in her housecoat and slippers at the stove. I kissed him on the cheek. "Morning, Daddy."

He looked up from his paper. "Morning, sleepyhead."

Mom turned around with a coffee mug in her hand. "The coffee's fresh." She kissed my cheek as she handed me the empty mug.

I shuffled toward the coffee pot, filled my cup full, and pulled up a seat next to my father. He was reading the obituaries. "Are you looking for a hole in your patient load?" I asked.

"Sloan," he scolded. "That's not funny."

I winked at him. "It's a little funny."

He just grinned.

"How was your week?" I tilted the steaming cup of life-giving caffeine up to my lips.

He turned in his seat toward me. "Not as interesting as yours, I hear," he said. "You've been on the news all week."

"Still?" I asked.

Mom turned around and pointed a spatula at me. "Your Aunt Betty saw the broadcast all the way up in Lexington."

I sipped my coffee. "Really? I can't believe people are still talking about it."

Dad looked curiously over at me. "One reporter said that she heard you say the girl wasn't dead before anyone even knew she was in the house."

I rolled my eyes. "That's crazy. How would I know that?"

He was eyeing me with blatant skepticism.

I shrugged my shoulders. "There was a lot of commotion. She probably misheard something."

I could tell my father didn't believe me, but he didn't push the subject. My parents enjoyed their state of voluntary ignorance concerning the oddities that always seemed to follow me. If they didn't bring it up, they knew I wouldn't, and our mutual silence on the matter would allow them to keep on believing there wasn't anything medically or psychologically unsound about their only child.

"The detective who was at the hospital with you and the sheriff, is he the one you told me about the other day?" Mom asked.

I nodded. "That would be him."

A small, teasing, smile played at the corners of her lips. "He's very handsome."

My father perked up. "Are you dating someone?"

I laughed. "No."

My mother turned with her hand on her hip. "Why is that funny?"

I shrugged. "I just haven't met anyone worth dating."

"What's wrong with the detective?" she asked.

"A lot," I said. "And he has a girlfriend. Guess who it is. Shannon Green."

My mother gasped and her mouth fell open. "No!"

I cupped the warm mug with both hands. "Yep."

"The traffic girl?" my dad asked.

"That's the one," I replied.

"What's wrong with the traffic girl?" he asked, confused. "I thought the two of you were friends."

"*Were*," Mom said. "Till that hussy went and stole Sloan's boyfriend. You don't remember? Sloan cried for a month."

I groaned. "Let's not relive it, Mom."

"Well, sweetie, you can do better," she assured me. "You don't want any guy who would stoop to so low of a standard."

I nodded and rolled my eyes. "I know." I looked at Dad, desperate to change the subject. "Tell me about your week."

He thought for a moment. "Well, it doesn't compare with finding a missing little girl, but I did find another missing Alzheimer's patient of mine serenading people on the elevator with *Your Mama Don't Dance and Your Daddy Don't Rock and Roll*."

I almost spat out my coffee. "That's pitiful!"

He nodded. "And pretty humorous. Especially when she got me to sing it with her on our ride back up." He smiled. "I think God has to allow us a little laughter because it's such an awful disease."

I sighed. "Your job is never boring, is it?"

He shook his head. "Never."

I looked over at Mom. "Speaking of missing people, weren't you friends with that Bryson woman whose daughter disappeared a few years ago?"

She thought for a moment. "I worked with her at the hospital, but she ended up quitting. She was really devastated after her daughter went missing."

"They never found out what happened to her?" I asked.

She shook her head. "No. The Brysons spent all their savings on private investigators and everything. I don't suppose anything ever turned up. I can't imagine something happening and not knowing whether your child is alive or dead. It's turned their whole family upside down, I think."

"That's so sad," I said.

"What brought that up?" Dad asked.

"Someone at work mentioned the case. They thought I might have heard of it," I said. "No real reason."

"I know it made me want to hold on to you a little tighter," Mom said to me. "And you were off at college. I was sick over it."

I shuddered and stood up from my seat. "Dad, can I use your computer?" I asked. "I need to check my email."

"Sure, it's turned on in my office." He motioned toward the steps that led to the second floor.

"Make it fast," Mom called after me. "Breakfast will be ready in two minutes."

Dad's office always reminded me of something out of a Norman Rockwell painting. The shelves were covered with medical books, papers were neatly arranged on the desk, and the brown shutters were always halfway open because he liked to see the birds outside his window. I sat down at his computer and clicked on the Internet icon. I wasn't sure what I hoped to accomplish, but I typed "Leslie Bryson Asheville Disappearance" into the search bar and clicked on the first article.

For the longest time, I sat and stared at her picture. I was pretty sure she and I had shared a class—maybe art or Spanish. Finally, I skimmed the article. Her family had offered a huge reward for her return, but the police never found anything. I looked at the photo of her mother holding a "Bring Leslie Home" sign. I thought of my own mother and nearly burst into tears.

"Sloan, the biscuits are done!" Mom called from the bottom of the stairs.

I closed the browser window and stood up. "Coming!"

* * *

When I pulled up in front of my house, there was a family waiting on my porch. I parked and got out of my car and recognized them immediately when the little girl ran down my steps toward me. Kayleigh Neeland looked like a completely different child wearing a pink dress, sparkly shoes, and carrying her Sleeping Beauty doll by the hand.

I teared up as I dropped my keys on the sidewalk and knelt down to her level. She threw her little arms around my neck.

"What a wonderful surprise!" I squealed as I hugged her. After a moment, I pulled away to see the bruising had almost completely faded, and the stitches had been removed from her forehead. "You look so pretty, Kayleigh."

She swayed back and forth, the thick tulle under her skirt giving off a light swooshing sound as she batted her eyelashes. "Do you like my dress? My Nana made it for me."

I had to wipe tears from my eyes. "I love it. You look like a princess!" I kissed her tiny cheek.

Her grandparents made their way down the steps to meet me. I stood up and Kayleigh clung to my leg. Her Nana reached out to hug me. "Ms. Jordan, I can't thank you enough for what you did for my grandbaby."

I ran my fingers through Kayleigh's blond curls. "I'm so thankful for a happy ending."

"So are we," the woman's husband added. He pointed to the door. "We rang the bell, but no one answered. Kayleigh wouldn't let us leave so we waited for a few minutes to see if you came home."

I laughed. "I'm so glad you did!"

Kayleigh tugged on the leg of my sweatpants. "Miss Sloan, I got you a present." She looked up at her grandmother. "Give it to her, Nana."

Her grandmother held out a small box and a folded sheet of pink construction paper.

I knelt down next to Kayleigh again and opened the paper to a crayon drawing inside. I smiled at her. "Did you make me a card too?"

She nodded with a bright smile.

It was a picture of two figures holding hands. "Is this you?" I asked, pointing to the smaller figure in a pink dress who had one blue eye and one green eye.

She nodded furiously again. She pointed to the other figure. "And that's you!"

I looked at it sideways. "Do I have wings?" I asked, laughing.

"Yes! 'Cause you're an angel and angels have wings!" she said.

I had to sit all the way down on my backside. She fell into my lap, and I tried desperately to choke back huge, bear-sized sobs. I hugged her around the shoulders.

She pried the small box from my hands. "Here, I'll open it for you!"

After a moment of fighting with the tape and ripping the pink wrapping paper, she wrenched open the box displaying a small, silver angel pin. She thrust it toward my face. "It's an angel, just like you!"

I covered my face with my hand and tried to regain my composure. "I love it," I cried.

"Now, you can wear it and think of me!" She blinked her bright blue and green eyes up at me.

I kissed the top of her head. "I will wear it every single day," I wept. I hugged her tight again. "Thank you so much."

Her grandfather offered me a hand up. Once I was on my feet, I straightened my outfit and hugged both of them again. "Thank you for coming to see me," I said. "You've made my whole year."

"The gratitude is all ours. You gave us our whole world back," he said.

I wiped my nose with the back of my hand and looked down at Kayleigh again. "I hope you'll come see me again soon."

Her eyes widened. "I'll try, but I gotta go to kindergarten, Nana says, in a few days, so I might get kinda busy."

More tears spilled onto my cheeks. "You'll be great."

"I know," she said with more confidence than I had ever had.

When they were gone, I sank to the steps of my front porch. Holding my angel pin in one hand and my cell phone in the other, I typed out a message to Nathan. *Bring your folder. I'll be home all day.*

My phone buzzed before I made it to the front door. *I'll come by and pick you up.*

6.

"WHERE ARE WE going?" I asked as I buckled my seatbelt. "Don't you dare say the jail."

Nathan pulled away from the curb. "My place."

Normally an answer like that would take my breath in a good way. This time, I choked on the air. "Is Shannon going to be there?"

"She's at her house. I don't live with Shannon." He looked over at me, his eyes dancing under the brim of his ball cap as he tried not to laugh. "She didn't tell me she knew you. I wonder why?"

"Because if I had a mortal enemy, it would be Shannon Green."

He burst out laughing. "What? Come on."

"We used to be friends. Really close friends, actually. We were on the cheerleading squad together and the soccer team. Then, one day after cheerleading practice I went to the field house to look for our coach, and I found her making out with my boyfriend, Jason Ward, in the locker room." I shook my head and watched the building pass outside of my window. "I've hated her ever since."

He chuckled and stared up ahead. "She's not too crazy about you either."

I leaned against the window. "I'll bet not. I convinced our whole school she had syphilis."

He cackled again. "Seriously?"

I nodded. "Yep."

He shook his head. "You're evil."

"She deserved it. You don't do that to a friend." I looked out the window. "I can't believe you're dating her."

He grinned over his shoulder. "Is that why you agreed to help me?"

I thought about it. "Not entirely, but that's definitely part of it."

"Why else then?" he asked.

I held out the card Kayleigh had made for me. I hadn't been able to leave it at home when he picked me up. "Kayleigh Neeland and her grandparents came by my house today, and she brought me this. She called me an angel. The thought crossed my mind, what if I hadn't agreed to help you and that little girl died alone in that attic? I wouldn't have been able to live with myself."

I took a deep breath. "Adrianne said to me recently, 'what's the point of being what you are if you can't use it to help people?' She was right. So I should, at least, try." My eyes glazed over, staring out the windshield. "All of those girls are dead, Nathan."

Nathan just nodded and kept driving.

Just outside of the city, in a smaller suburb called Arden, Nathan lived in a third floor apartment. I followed him inside and bit down on my lips to keep from laughing. The white walls of the room were bare, save for a large nail by the door. The few pieces of furniture—a futon couch and a recliner—were centered around the largest flat screen television I had ever seen. The only decor consisted of the black devices attached to the TV, a ridiculous collection of DVDs, and a family portrait that was leaning against the wall.

Nathan hung his keyring on the nail by the door and glanced around the room. "It's not much."

"That's the understatement of the year," I teased. "You don't even have a dining table. Where do you eat?"

He smiled. "Downtown."

I laughed and dropped my purse on the floor.

He turned toward the hallway. "Follow me."

At the end of the hall, a small bedroom had been converted into an office. It had more stuff crammed into it than the rest of the apartment combined. It was an impressive setup with a desk and a computer, a chair, a pin-board filled with paperwork and photographs, two filing cabinets, and a coffee pot.

On the desk lay the American flag patch I had seen on his ball cap. I looked up at his hat and noticed a different patch was on the front. It had a picture of an assault rifle and the caption 'I Plead the 2nd' below it. I laughed and picked the flag up off the desk. "It's velcro?" I asked.

He nodded and took the flag from my fingers. "The flag is my work patch."

I pointed at his hat. "And the assault rifle?"

He grinned. "I'm off work today."

I laughed and nodded my head. "That's cute."

His face scrunched in disgust. "It's not *cute*. It's rugged and funny, not cute."

I rolled my eyes. "Whatever you say, Nathan." I walked over and studied the timeline of the murders on the board. "Does Sheriff Davis know you're investigating this?"

He nodded and stepped over behind me. "Yeah. It's part of the reason he hired me," he said. "Raleigh didn't want me to leave because I've put so much time into the case."

I looked at his sister's picture on the board. "Isn't it sort of a conflict of interest, since you are so close to it personally?"

He shrugged his shoulders. "I suppose, but I don't think the reason really matters when you put in ten times the hours of any other investigator."

He sat down in the office chair and turned on the computer. I leaned over his shoulder and saw a photo of him and Shannon together on the desk. I reached over him and turned it face-down on the table. He laughed.

"Have a seat," he said.

I looked around the room. "On the floor?"

"Crap. I'm sorry." He stood up and offered me his chair. "I'll get some more furniture before you come over again."

"Already planning the second date, huh?" I joked as I sat down in his chair.

He smiled and knelt down beside me so he could open files on the computer.

The first two disappearances happened fairly close together in 2000. Melissa Jennings, like Nathan's sister, disappeared after a high school football game. Police and volunteers canvassed the area for weeks, but no sign of her was ever found. She was seventeen. Three weeks later, Nathan's sister Ashley vanished. At the time, police suspected the two cases may have been related, but no evidence to support the theory was ever found.

The next similar disappearance was almost a full year later in 2001. Angela Kearn, a nineteen year old student at Lenoir-Rhyne, went to her morning classes but returned to her dorm to change books for her afternoon classes and wasn't seen again.

Angela's disappearance seemed to be the beginning of a pattern. Each disappearance after Angela happened in an almost calculated timeframe. Every twelve to fifteen months, another girl would go missing from a very public place and never be seen or heard from again.

Many of the cases had gone cold over the years, but the most recent of the victims were still being actively investigated. The face of Joelle Lawson, a twenty-one year old nursing student from Winston-Salem, had been plastered on billboards all along I-40 since she disappeared in 2011. She had been at a fraternity party on October 2nd where she became sick from drinking too much alcohol and decided to call her roommate for a ride home. She was last seen waiting near the curb for her ride. When her roommate arrived, Joelle wasn't to be found. She assumed Joelle had changed her mind and returned to the party. The next day, when she didn't come home, her roommate called Joelle's family, who notified the police.

Colleen Webster, the most recent victim from Statesville, had been the subject of a couple of my press releases for a collaboration effort between our sheriff's office and that of Iredell County. Colleen was twenty-five and last seen on November 21st outside of a sports bar she frequented. She was laughing with the driver of a silver sedan, so no one suspected foul play. Two days later, her car was discovered in the driveway at the house where she lived alone. Her purse, phone, and keys were on the passenger's seat.

All of the victims were close in age, ranging from seventeen to twenty-five, and they were all attractive and from similar backgrounds. From looking at Nathan's map, I could see why he wondered if the next victim might be from Asheville. Like with the timeline, the murders seemed to be located in a pattern along the I-40 route through North Carolina.

I was chewing on a pen cap, staring at his elaborate pin-board. I put my feet up on the desk and reclined in the office chair. "What do we know about the killer?"

He looked around the room. "Hold up," he said. He went to the closet and pulled out a long piece of thick poster board. He rested it on the tray of the pin-board so I could see. It was covered in large, yellow sticky notes.

A few facts were written in thick black marker. He pointed to them. "Here's what the victims say about him: Number one. He blends in well with a crowd and seems to go unnoticed because no one reported seeing anyone remarkable at any of the locations. Number two. He's approachable and not threatening because there were no reports or signs of struggles at any of the crime scenes."

I raised my hand. "Out of all eleven cases, no one noticed anything out of the ordinary?"

He shook his head. "Not really."

I raised my hand again and held my pen over the pad I was using to take notes.

He leaned toward me. "This isn't a middle school history class. You don't have to raise your hand."

I stuck my tongue out at him. "Give me the ages of the victims in the order in which they were taken."

He straightened up and pointed to the board as he rattled off numbers and I wrote them down. "17, 16, 19, 18, 22, 19, 23, 24, 24, 21, 25."

I tapped my paper with the pen. "He's about their age. He's growing up with his victims."

He frowned at me. "If you would wait, that was point number three."

I put my hands up and bowed my head in apology. "Continue."

He turned toward the board. "I think the killer is likely from the Raleigh area and that he attended one of the metro schools. Both of the football games where my sister and Melissa disappeared were in the same district. The killer probably has some kind of ties to the different areas." He used his pen to point to the different cities on the maps.

I shrugged. "Or, he kidnaps them away from home and takes them to wherever he comes from."

He nodded. "That's a possibility too."

I squeezed my temples. "How is it even possible for someone to get away with this now with forensics, video surveillance, and crime scene investigation being as robust as they are? This person doesn't leave any evidence? No DNA? Fingerprints? Tire tread marks?" I found the whole thing incredibly implausible.

He almost laughed. "You watch too much television."

"I'm serious! And why hasn't anyone else picked up on these possibly being related?" I asked. "It seems pretty obvious to me and I'm not a cop."

He sat down on the edge of the desk. "The first two happened so close in proximity and time that the police *did* think they were related, but all the rest have been spread out over the state and over so much time that it was hard to connect them together. There are over 10,000 missing person reports filed each year in the state of North Carolina alone. I've done a lot of eliminating to come up with this list. Imagine if you were looking at it among hundreds of thousands of reports."

I sighed. "I guess so. I just can't believe this is still even possible. You don't hear about serial killers anymore."

"That doesn't mean they don't exist. They just don't get the attention they did in the days of Bundy and Dahmer. Terrorists and school-shootings are the big media shockers now," he pointed out.

"Have there been any suspects?"

"There have been plenty of suspects." He pulled another file out of the cabinet and handed it to me before sitting down again. "But these are the only serious leads that have been pursued."

I opened it and found a few groupings of paperwork and photos. I pulled all of the stacks out and laid them in front of me. There were photos of four different men. I tapped my finger on the first mugshot of a middle-aged man with a thick brown mustache and a long scar over his right eye. "This guy is creepy, but he doesn't fit your profile at all."

He leaned over the paperwork. "That's Roger Watson," he said. "He was originally brought in for questioning because his prints were on my car when my sister disappeared. He was a teacher at our school and had been on security duty in the parking lot during the football game. He was never charged with anything."

"Then why does he have a mugshot?" I asked.

"Well, because it turns out you're right. He is a creep. He was arrested two years later for the sexual abuse of two boys on the basketball team. He's serving twenty-four years in federal prison," he explained.

"So he was in prison for most of the murders," I said.

Nathan nodded.

I looked at the other photos. I pointed to the one at the end—a twenty-something-year-old who looked like a Ken doll. "Well, if it's handsome here, then you have nothing to worry about. He's dead."

"I know," Nathan said. "He was killed in a car accident in 2010."

"And the other two?" I was carefully examining the remaining photos.

"These two have only been suspects in the individual disappearances of the respective victims in their areas, but I find them interesting enough that they are being watched." He pointed at the blonde on the left. "Logan Allen was the boyfriend of Christy Dumas who disappeared from her home in Hickory a couple of days after Christmas in 2005. He has two priors for domestic violence and a pretty nasty meth problem. He also has a grandmother in Winston-Salem and a sister who lives in Hendersonville."

I looked at the other guy who appeared to be the right age. He was attractive and obviously strong enough to easily subdue the small-framed victims, but he didn't get the sense that he was a horrible person. "This doesn't feel like a bad guy."

Nathan looked at me. "What do you mean?"

I remembered I hadn't told Nathan everything about my ability. "I have a really keen sense about people. Kind of like how I know if someone is alive or dead by looking at a picture, I sort of have an evil radar that goes off when someone is a rotten human being."

He looked up like he had just solved a great mystery. "That's why you don't like going to the jail."

I shuddered. "That's why I have to take sedatives before going to the jail. I can feel the evil radiating out of that place."

"Can you detect a person's tendencies?" he asked.

I leaned back in the chair. "Not exactly. There are a lot of good people who make really bad decisions. They don't seem evil to me at all, just lost."

"So you're saying that a person's decisions determine who they are?" he asked.

"I think what I'm saying is that you shouldn't put too much stock in feelings I get," I said. "You're not going to be able to convict people based on if they give the county publicist the heebie jeebies or not."

He nodded and stared at me for a moment. His gray eyes had flecks of blue in them that I hadn't noticed before. Finally, he put his finger on the picture. "Scott Bonham is the most likely suspect we have. He's thirty-two years old and was fired from the police force in Cary after being a cop for two years. He graduated from the same high school where Melissa attended and has family in Asheville. He hasn't held a stable job since he was fired in 2002 and has had residences in Raleigh, Asheville, and Winston-Salem."

"Is he in custody?" I asked.

"Nope. Again, not enough evidence," he said.

I thought for a moment. "Why was he fired?"

"For gross misconduct and sexual harassment. He was accused of groping two women during a routine traffic stop," he answered.

"But he wasn't arrested?" I asked.

He shook his head. "They decided not to press charges. He was let go among a flurry of embarrassing news reports."

"Where is he now?"

"Police in Winston-Salem try and keep tabs on him. That's his last known residence," he said.

Nathan's cell phone rang. He pulled it out of his pocket and answered it. "Hey," he said. "I'm working at home. What are you doing?" He listened for a moment. "No, I think I'm going to stay in today...No, don't come over. Maybe we will go to dinner tomorrow... Sure, church in the morning would be fine."

I laughed.

"Yep, OK. You too," he said and disconnected the call.

I folded my arms across my chest. "Are you going to church to repent for lying—again—to your girlfriend?"

"I didn't lie," he said with a pitch of offense in his voice.

"You didn't tell her I was here. That's lying by omission," I said.

He shook his head. "Nope. That was bypassing extra details for the benefit of everyone."

"What's with you saying 'you too'?" I asked.

"What?"

I cocked an eyebrow. "I'm pretty sure she says 'I love you' and you say 'you too'. What's up with that?"

He shifted uncomfortably on the desk. "I'm not sure that's any of your business."

I laughed. "Oh, it's not my business. I'm just curious. Are you in love with her?"

He stood up. "Sloan, that's a really inappropriate question."

"Why won't you answer it?" I asked, grinning up at him.

"Why are you so hung up on me and Shannon?" He folded his arms across his chest. "It didn't seem to bother you much when you and your friend left the bar last night with those two guys."

I laughed. "Now who's being inappropriate?"

Nathan walked out of the room. "Do you want something to drink?"

I got up and followed him to the kitchen. "You're completely blowing me off."

"Yep," he replied as he opened the refrigerator. "I've got beer and water."

I hoisted myself up onto his kitchen counter and tapped my fingers quizzically against my lips. "You say you're not using her, but you won't say you love her either."

He turned around and offered me a bottle of beer and a bottle of water. I took the water. He opened the beer and tipped it up to his lips. "Ready to get back to work?"

I kicked him lightly in the thigh. "Come on," I said. "You have forced me to get super personal with you in the past few weeks. I've told you stuff I haven't even told my mother."

"I didn't force you," he argued.

I cocked my head to the side. "Really?"

He shrugged. "I persuaded you."

"How did you meet her? How long have you been together?" I asked.

He groaned. "I met Shannon about six months ago when I was here researching the murder of Leslie Bryson," he said. "Some of the guys from the department here took me out for drinks, and I met her at the bar. We've been dating long distance ever since. Are you satisfied?" He turned and walked down the hall toward the office.

I jumped off the counter and followed him. "No. It's Shannon Green," I grumbled.

"She's not that bad," he said.

"She's high maintenance, spoiled, and has absolutely no loyalty."

He rounded on me and he wasn't laughing. "Let it go, Sloan."

I rolled my eyes and sat down in the chair. "Fine." I huffed and looked up at the board. "Tell me about Leslie Bryson."

Nathan cleared his throat. "Leslie worked at Chili's as a bartender. About twenty minutes after she clocked out at 10pm, she sent a text message to her roommate saying she was going to be late and to not wait up for her. She never came home."

"No other numbers on her phone?"

He shook his head. "None that were suspect."

"What about camera footage from the parking lot?" I asked. "Maybe she ran into the killer outside before she left."

He shrugged. "Maybe so, but there were no cameras."

"That's frustrating," I said. "What about GPS tracking on her phone?"

"Her purse and phone were found in her car which was abandoned at the Texaco gas station off of Tunnel Road," he answered.

I thought for a moment. "No one saw anything? That's a really crowded area."

He shook his head. "No witnesses."

I looked at the photos of the women and shook my head. "I still don't understand why there isn't some sort of public service announcement about this," I said. "It seems like the public should be made aware that there is a serial killer on the loose."

He sat down on the corner of the desk in front of me. "Well, I just found out a few days ago that all of these girls are dead. No bodies, remember? And there has been a lot of news coverage on all the kidnappings, just not all lumped together."

"I don't watch the news," I told him.

"You're a publicist," he said, surprised.

"The last thing I want to do at the end of my workday is come home and watch news stories about murders, missing people, and violence." I tapped my finger on the desk. "You know, all the stuff you've been throwing at me since we first met."

His smile was genuine and apologetic. "I really do appreciate your help."

"I know," I mumbled. I looked around the room at all of the work he had done, practically all on his own. "How are you going to convince the FBI that there is a serial killer involved? I don't think 'my publicist friend told me they're dead' is going to cut it with the Feds."

He chuckled. "They've been exploring it as a possibility for a while now. We've also considered it might be linked to human trafficking. Now I know which direction to focus on. It would really help if I could find the bodies."

I shook my head. "I'm not a cadaver dog."

He laughed. "I know."

"What do we do now? Just wait for someone else to go missing?" I asked.

He shrugged his shoulders. "Well, it helps now that I know that all of the victims are actually dead. Maybe you and I can find something that will help connect the dots." He kicked the side of the desk with his heel. "You know, even without your supernatural abilities, you're actually really good at this. Have you ever considered being a cop?"

I doubled over. "Me? Around criminals all the time? Seriously?"

He laughed and nodded his head. "Yeah, I didn't think about it that way."

"Supernatural, huh?" I asked.

"What do you call it?" he replied.

I rolled my eyes. "Lately, thanks to you, I call it a pain in my ass."

7.

IT WAS BUSINESS as usual when I returned to work on Monday. The entire week was extraordinarily boring in comparison to the weekend as I hammered out the county newsletter; warned the citizens of West Asheville of a sewage backup off of Haywood Avenue; and reminded the city to not drink and drive during the upcoming Brewgrass Festival at Memorial Stadium. Most of the city would turn out for the festival, Adrianne and I included. It was my favorite event around the city all year.

I spent my downtime in the office and most of my evenings at home reading through some files Nathan had sent home with me. I found it difficult to believe that all of the women simply vanished without a trace of evidence and their bodies never surfaced, even by accident. I called Nathan at home on Thursday night to tell him as much, but he didn't answer. I hung up when the call went to his voicemail.

I got a text message from him a moment later. *On a call. What's up?*

I responded. *Nothing that can't wait, just brainstorming.*

I think I'm almost done here. Can I swing by on my way home?

The clock on the wall said it was almost 10 pm and I wasn't feeling sleepy yet. I tapped out a reply. *Yep.*

On my coffee table, I spread out each of the victims' summary sheets in the order in which they disappeared. Though I was sure that Nathan had already done the same thing, I searched for even the smallest similarities between the girls. After about a half hour of reading, the dates seemed to come together: all of the girls had been abducted during the fall and winter months. There weren't any that occurred in the spring or the summer. I jotted a list down in my notebook of the dates chronologically. They spanned from September 22nd to December 28th.

There was a knock at my door. When I opened it, Nathan was pulling off a pair of muddy boots. He was splattered in dried mud all the way up to his belly button. I looked at him sideways. "Have you been spelunking?"

He braced himself against my doorframe as he fought to free his foot from his left steel-toed boot. "Practically. I responded to a burglary call and ended up chasing a guy through a storm culvert."

I looked at the mud and then inside at my white furniture. "Why didn't you go home and take a shower?"

"Because I'm tired, and if I had gone home, I wouldn't have left again," he explained.

I thought about offering him a shower at my house, but I was pretty sure I wouldn't get any work done after knowing he had been naked in my bathroom. "Let's talk out here," I suggested.

He looked down at his ruined pants. "That's probably a good idea."

"One sec." I jogged to the living room to grab my notebook and tooth-mangled pen.

When I returned, he was sitting on the top of the steps, so I sat down beside him.

"What's up?" he asked.

I showed him my list. "Have you noticed the dates?"

"Yeah," he answered. "September through December."

"Don't you find that strange?" I asked. "Why just the cold months?"

"I've asked that question a lot. He could live seasonally in this area," he said.

I scowled and shook my head. "People live seasonally around here in the summer. They go to Florida for the winter."

"Older people go to Florida," he pointed out.

"Why would anyone live seasonally here when it's cold?" I asked.

"The leaves?" he suggested. "Tourist season starts here around what? September?"

I nodded. "Here, yes. But not in Raleigh, and it certainly doesn't last till December. Besides, do you really think anyone could be impressed by dying leaves so much that they would make a life change out of it? Particularly a guy in his twenties?"

"Good point," he said.

"Retail jobs are very seasonal," I said. "That's the same time that businesses start hiring for holiday help."

He thought about it. "Maybe. It could be how he finds his victims too."

I frowned and put a hand on my hip. "Are you suggesting that all women are shoppers?"

He laughed. "Yes."

I elbowed him in the side. "We're not all like Shannon."

He smiled. "It has to be more specific than retail though. You can do that anywhere in the country. Why here?"

"Because he's native to the area?" I offered.

"Perhaps, but a retail clerk moonlighting as a serial killer still seems pretty unlikely. It's too public. Someone would have suspected something," he said. "You got anything else?"

"Why were the bodies never found? It seems like it would be pretty hard to hide a body and get away with it," I said. "Where would you hide a body?"

He laughed. "I'm not sure I like where you're going with this."

"I'm serious. How do you make one disappear?" I asked.

He considered it. "I would incinerate it," he said. "Burn it to dust, then scatter and cover the evidence."

My nose wrinkled. "The smell would be suspicious."

He shrugged. "Not necessarily in this area. Moonshiners hide their smoke pretty well."

"How's a serial killer gonna tote an incinerator all over the state?" I shook my head. "You're not much help."

He laughed. "Probably because I'm tired. Let's continue this over the weekend."

"I'm going to the Brewgrass Festival this weekend at Memorial Stadium," I said.

"Oh, yeah. I've heard a lot about it. It's a good time, huh?" he asked.

I smiled. "If you like beer."

He stood up. "You know I do."

"So I'll see you there?" I asked.

"Maybe." He reached out his hand and pulled me to my feet. "I'm going to go home and pass out before I have to do this crap all over again tomorrow. I'm exhausted."

He picked up his boots and carried them down the stairs. As he stepped onto the sidewalk, the sound of rustling leaves between my house and the house next door caught both of our attention. Nathan grabbed a flashlight off his belt and I closed my eyes.

"There's no one there. Must be a cat or something." I leaned against the front handrail of my porch.

He panned the flashlight around the side of the house and then looked up at me. "How do you know?"

I smiled. "Maybe I'm a witch."

He shook his head and rolled his eyes. He yanked his driver's side door open and grumbled as he climbed inside. "I'm never going to get used to this. Goodnight, Sloan."

I waved to him. "Goodnight, Nathan."

* * *

When Saturday finally rolled around, I drove to Adrianne's townhouse to pick her up. She had on sunglasses that were bigger than her face. "You look ridiculous," I said as she got into my car.

She scowled over the top of her glasses at my black "This Girl Needs a Beer" tee and blue jeans. "Oh, you're the fashion expert now?" She noticed the angel pin on my shirt. "What's this?"

As I drove, I told her all about Kayleigh surprising me at home. When I finished, she slapped my leg. "See? Doesn't that feel good?" she asked.

I smiled. "Better than any feeling I've ever had before."

"And I've always thought you were a witch. Maybe you are an angel instead," she said.

I smirked. "You're so funny."

"How are things with the hot detective?" she asked.

I shrugged and turned toward the stadium. "Well, I agreed to help him with the serial killer case. We spent almost all day Saturday working on it." I looked over at her. "I want you to promise me you'll be careful, Adrianne."

She nodded. "No serial killers for me," she said. "I'm going to run every guy I talk to by you first."

"You have done that for the past several years and you *never* listen to me," I said.

"Well, you're a little overprotective. You need to tell me, 'that guy's a serial killer, Adrianne' and I won't go out with him," she assured me.

"They don't come with references and a background check," I said. "If I tell you I'm getting bad vibes, that should be enough."

She floated her hand through the air signaling she was bored with the conversation. "You've got our tickets?" she asked.

"They are in the bag next to the chairs," I said.

Memorial Stadium was already overflowing with people when we pulled into the grassy parking lot. "I hope you don't mind," Adrianne said as we got out and began unloading my trunk, "but I told Mark that we were going to be here today, and he said that he and Colin might come by."

"Who?" I pulled out a camping chair and slung it over my shoulder.

She retrieved the other chair. "Colin and Mark, the guys from the bar last weekend."

I groaned and leaned against my bumper. "Seriously, Adrianne? Case in point of you not listening to me. Please tell me that you're joking."

She shrugged. "They were cute and they paid our tabs."

"They were obnoxious. Especially Mark. And Colin was so full of himself I wanted to hit him over the head with my beer." I draped my backpack over my other shoulder.

We started toward the stadium. "You didn't like them because you're so hung up on that detective."

I adjusted my sunglasses against the mid-morning sun. "I didn't like them because they were jerks."

She looked over at me. "Is your boy coming today?"

"Nathan is not my boy, and I haven't talked to him in a few days. He said he would probably be here though," I said.

"With Shannon?" she asked.

My face twisted into a sour frown. "If I know my crappy luck, I'm sure she'll be with him."

She started laughing again. "She may have to cover a *serious* news situation."

I smiled. "Gridlock and drunk driving at the beer festival."

We found an open spot on the field, and I set up our chairs while Adrianne went to find our first beers of the day. A band was playing in what was normally the end zone of the football field, and a few people were dancing around the twenty yard line. Local breweries had tents set up all around the sidelines, offering samples and full-sized drafts of their craft brews.

The fragrant mix of sunshine, patchouli oil, booze, and cannabis floated through the fall sky, reminding me I was at home in America's 'Freak Capital.' There were guys wearing broomstick skirts and girls with dreadlocks and facial piercings. In other groups, the boys wore tight pants and Buddy Holly glasses. Some people were dressed ready for Broadway, while others were dressed for a Renaissance festival. Scottish kilts seemed to be popular, and one man even carried a set of bagpipes. I looked down at my outfit and felt almost out of place. The Brewgrass Festival was people watching at its best.

My eyes scanned the crowd until they fell on someone, or some *thing*, that made my stomach leap into my throat. I coughed and blinked my eyes.

A man, tall with broad shoulders and shoulder-length black hair pulled back into ponytail, was watching me near a group of tents about fifty yards away. He had dark eyes set above high cheekbones and a square jaw. His gaze fixed on me when we locked eyes; it was like staring into the center of a black hole.

For the first time in my life, I sensed something I never had before. A stranger.

"Oktoberfest is out early this year!" Adrianne sang as she lowered a plastic cup over my head from behind. "Aren't you excited?"

I accepted the cup and she moved in front of me. When she had passed, the stranger was gone. Adrianne followed my gaze across the field. When she didn't see anything peculiar, she waved her hand in front of my face. "Yo, Sloan!"

I blinked again and focused on her face. She was still waving. "Huh?"

She leaned toward me. "What's up? You look like you've seen a ghost. You're all pale and stuff."

Sweat prickled on my forehead despite the autumn chill. "I think I have."

Seeing a ghost was *exactly* what it felt like. It was reminiscent of seeing Ray Whitmore lying in the doorway of the kitchen on Clarksdale. The dark man could have been an animated corpse. There was nothing in him for me to read.

"Hey!" Adrianne shouted, snapping me back to reality again. "What the hell?" She kept looking around and then at me.

I pointed across the field. "There was a guy over there. A guy I didn't know." I strained again to see if I could find him.

She laughed. "There are thousands of people here you don't know."

I shook my head and stood up, craning my neck and searching through the crowds. "No. I mean I didn't *know* him."

"What?" She was looking at me like I had spoken in Mandarin.

I sat down. "Remember me telling you that I—"

"Hey, hey, hey!" someone cheered, stepping into our circle. It was Mark and Colin.

Adrianne stood up and hugged Mark, the guy with the ridiculously perfect teeth and the douchebag personality. She put her hand on his chest. "I thought you would be here later!"

Mark draped his arm across Adrianne's shoulders and held up the cup in his hand. "Oh no. We got here early and decided to try and make it through all forty brew stations before the day is over."

I rolled my eyes. "Of course you did."

"Hey, Sloan." Colin opened up an NC State folding chair and plopped it down on the grass next to me. "Whatcha drinkin'?"

I looked in my cup and realized I couldn't remember. I looked at Adrianne for help.

"Oktoberfest from Brevard Brewing," she answered. "Earth to Sloan."

I shook my head and stood up. "Excuse me for a second," I said. "I'll be right back."

Adrianne followed me and grabbed my arm. "What are you doing?"

I squeezed her hand in frustration. "I don't think you grasp exactly how big this is for me. I've never seen anyone I don't recognize. Ever. In all my life!"

Her face melted from irritation to worry. "What are you going to do?"

"I'm just going to walk around. I'll be back soon and I have my phone in my pocket."

"I'm coming with you," she said.

I shook my head. "No because Dumb and Dumber will follow. Just stay here and entertain. I'll be back in a second."

Her brow wrinkled with worry. "Please be careful."

"Of course," I assured her.

I took off in the direction of the tents before she could protest again. I sipped my beer as my eyes darted from face to face. Halfway around the field, I heard someone call my name. I turned to see Nathan walking hand in hand with Shannon toward me.

I had just passed a guy wearing a fur toga and a Viking helmet on his head, and then there was Shannon dressed in a silky sundress and high heels. Her heels kept sinking into the football field turf with each step that she took. *And I thought I wasn't dressed for the occasion,* I laughed to myself.

Nathan was in his standard tactical attire, except he was wearing a shirt that said "Conserve Water. Drink Beer" and the patch on the front of his hat said "Drinks Well With Others".

"I was wondering if we would bump into each other in this swarm of drunks," he said as they approached.

I held up my cup and forced a smile. "You found me."

"You need another beer," he said. "Let's go take care of that."

Shannon looked annoyed, so I agreed.

We walked toward the tents. "Let's see," he said. "Will it be Wicked Weed or Greenman?"

I looked at both tents. "I haven't tried Wicked Weed," I said.

He stepped toward the vendor leaving me alone with Shannon. "Nice dress," I said to break the uncomfortable silence.

She flipped her blond hair over her shoulder and angled her face toward the sky. "It's a LULUS exclusive."

I didn't know or care what that meant, so I went back to searching the crowd for the guy with the ponytail.

"Here you go." Nathan handed me a new full cup. "It's called the Freak of Nature Double IPA. It seemed appropriate for you."

I laughed and shoved him in the shoulder. "Hey!"

"Haha." He sipped on his beer. "This festival is pretty great. Do you come every year?"

I nodded. "Every year since they started it."

He laughed. "I had to drag Shannon here."

A smug "imagine that" slipped out before I could stop myself.

She huffed and crossed her arms across her chest.

"You looked like you were searching for someone," he said. "Are you lost?"

There was more than one reason I wished Shannon wasn't there. I really wanted to talk to him alone. "I saw this guy that was really strange to me," I said, trying to use words that Nathan would pick up on.

"Are you kidding?" Shannon asked. "Everyone here is strange."

Nathan nodded toward her. "She has a point."

"This guy was different." I cut my eyes at him, urging him to catch on to what I was trying to say.

We locked gazes for a moment. "What's he look like? I'll let you know if I see him."

"He's about your age and he's really tall. Maybe 6'2. He was wearing a dark blue shirt and blue jeans, and his hair was black, probably shoulder length or so in a ponytail."

Nathan was making mental notes. He took a quick look around. "I'll let you know if we see him."

I smiled. "Thanks. We are somewhere around the fifty yard line if you want to come by."

"Oh, we won't be here much longer," Shannon snapped.

I couldn't help myself. "Is there an important lane closure on I-40 that you need to go report?"

Her mouth fell open.

"I'll call you later," Nathan said, trying to sound defensive but not doing a convincing job of it.

I held up my beer as they walked away. "Y'all be careful, and stay away from 3rd South Street. I heard on the news that it's going to be blocked off all day for parking."

Nathan shot me a scowl over his shoulder and I laughed.

"Thanks for the beer!" I called after him.

"You're welcome," he replied. "Quit wandering around alone!"

I finished my lap around the field with no sign of the stranger. His face hung in my mind, like it was going to be permanently fixed there for a long time. Adrianne was at her intoxication stage of giggling by the time I returned. My cup was once again empty.

Colin stood up. "We were about to send a search party after you."

"Find anything?" Adrianne asked.

I shook my head.

"I'm about to get another beer. Want one?" Colin asked.

"Sure. Surprise me." I handed him my empty cup and plopped down into my seat.

He looked disappointed that I didn't offer to join him, but I didn't care.

I closed my eyes and pictured the stranger's dark eyes again. No matter how hard I searched the memory of his face with my gift, I couldn't register his soul. Thinking of the way he had watched me sent chills up my spine. There was some kind of connection there that my brain couldn't fit together.

Adrianne snapped her fingers in front of my nose. "Hey!"

My eyes popped open and settled on her. Mark had his arm across the back of her chair.

"Do you want to go to a dodgeball game tomorrow?" she asked.

"Um. What?" I asked.

"Adult dodgeball," she repeated.

I cocked an eyebrow. "Does that even exist?"

Mark nodded. "Yeah. Parks and Rec has a league. Colin and I play. We have a tournament tomorrow."

I looked at Adrianne. Her eyes were pleading. I didn't want to go but only slightly less than I wanted her to go anywhere alone with Mark. I didn't trust him. "Sure. What time?"

Adrianne smiled.

"It's at eleven in the morning," he said. "We'll come by and pick you up."

"No, we'll meet you there. Adrianne promised to go with me to the mall tomorrow, so we can swing by after," I said.

She tugged on his arm. "Oh yeah. Sorry, I forgot."

"That's cool, babe." He was a little closer to her face than I was comfortable with.

My cellphone buzzed in my pocket. I pulled it out to see a message from Nathan. It said, *Is this him?* A moment later a photo of the guy from behind appeared on my phone.

I dialed Nathan's number and he picked up on the first ring. "Yes! Where is he?"

"Gone," he replied. "I saw him ahead of us going toward the parking lot. He got into a black Dodge Challenger and took off. North Carolina tags and I got the plate number. Want me to run it?"

"Isn't that illegal?" I asked.

He chuckled. "I'll let you know what I find out," he said and disconnected.

Colin returned with my beer as I dropped the phone into the cup holder on my chair. Mark was whispering in Adrianne's ear.

"Hey Mark, what's your last name?" I asked.

"Higgins," he answered. "Why?"

I shrugged. "Just wondering." I was just wondering because I really didn't like Mark Higgins. Maybe I could convince Nathan to run him too.

* * *

When I roused myself from a restless sleep the next morning, my brain was still churning with thoughts of the soulless man from the day before. His face had haunted my dreams, taunting me with questions I couldn't answer. Who was he? *What* was he?

I might have spent all day lying there obsessing over him, had Adrianne not begun texting me to see if I was up and ready to go. I prayed that I could talk her out of going to the dodgeball game during shopping, but I failed. After a short trip to the mall, I drove to the downtown recreation gym, and for an hour, we watched grown men throw red rubber balls at each other.

I gestured toward the concession stand. "I'm going to go get a drink," I said. "You thirsty?"

"I'll take a Diet Coke," she replied.

I navigated the sideline to the concession window and got the attention of the girl behind the counter. "What can I get'cha?" she asked, chomping on a piece of bubblegum.

It was very unfortunate that the state restricted beer sales until after two o'clock on Sundays. Alcohol would be the only thing to make adult dodgeball more interesting. "Two Diet Cokes, please."

My phone rang. It was Nathan. "Where are you?" he asked.

"Dodgeball game," I answered over the sound of grown men screaming and the distinct squeak of tennis shoe soles on a gym floor.

There was silence on the other end of the line. "Did you say dodgeball?" he asked.

"Yep."

"Swing by my apartment when you're done," he said. "I went by your house and you weren't home."

"OK. Hopefully it won't be too long, but I have to take Adrianne home," I said.

"K," he said and disconnected.

I carried the drinks to the bleachers and realized the game must have ended since the two teams were shaking hands. I said a silent prayer of thanksgiving. I handed her the plastic cup. "Is it over?"

"Yep. They lost," she replied.

I smirked. "Shocker."

She threw a discarded piece of popcorn at me. "Be nice!"

Mark and Colin finally came out of the locker room carrying their gym bags. They had both showered and changed into fresh clothes. Mark had more product in his hair than Adrianne and I combined. He dropped his bag on the bleacher seat in front of us and smiled at me. "Who's hungry?" he asked.

"I'm hungry," Adrianne said.

"Me too," Colin added.

I bumped my friend with my shoulder. "I've got to go into work. No time for food."

"I'll take you home," Mark said to her.

I rolled my eyes and stared at Adrianne with blatant disapproval.

She raised an eyebrow at me. "You don't work on Sundays."

"I need to today. I promise. I've got to go and meet with Nathan," I told her.

"Well, then go. I'll ride with them," she said. "No worries."

But I was worried and she knew it.

She put her hand on my arm and stood up, slinging her purse strap over her shoulder. "I'll be fine. I'll call you tonight."

I knew there was no point in arguing with her. Adrianne always did what she wanted no matter my opinion or anyone else's. I sighed and followed them down the bleachers and out of the gym.

Before I stopped at my car, I grabbed her arm. "Seriously call me tonight," I said.

She smiled and hooked her arm through Mark's. "I promise," she said.

Obvious rejection was etched across Colin's face. "Are you sure you can't come, even if just for a little while?"

I opened my car door and sat down in the driver's seat. "Yeah, sorry. You guys have fun."

I watched them for a moment, unable to dismiss the nausea I felt over letting her go with them. All the way to Nathan's apartment, I reminded myself that I wasn't Adrianne's mother and that she was twenty-seven and fully capable of taking care of herself. I still felt sick though; staring at victims of a serial killer for hours on end had that effect.

There was no answer at Nathan's door when I knocked on it. I looked around the parking lot and his SUV was parked in his spot. I called his phone. He was out of breath when he answered. "Hello?"

"I'm at your door," I said.

"Oh. I thought you were going to be a while. I went for a run. Sit tight and I'll be right there," he said.

I ended the call and sank down on his welcome mat. His apartment building was built on a hill, so at least I had a decent view of the Blue Ridge mountains which were now thoroughly speckled with red, orange, and gold. The fall scenery was one of the things I loved most about the mountains of Western North Carolina. However, I couldn't help but be reminded that the killing season had just opened for our murderer.

As I sat there, I realized that the case was already tainting just about every area of my life, and I had only been involved for a handful of days. I wasn't sure how Nathan had lived with it for so many years.

After about five minutes, he appeared running up the hill in the parking lot. I stood up and brushed crumbled leaves off the seat of my yoga pants. A moment later, he was taking the steps two at a time up to the landing. He had on a white dry-fit shirt and a pair of black gym shorts. He had perfect calves.

He pulled his earbud speakers out of his ears and reached into his waistband for his keys. "I'm sorry. I thought I had plenty of time."

"Adrianne decided to go out and eat with the guys," I said.

He pushed the door open. "What guys?"

I followed him inside. "The ones we met at The Social Lounge."

He turned and looked at me. "You didn't go with them?"

I grimaced. "With Captain Douchebag Veneers and his side kick? No thank you."

He laughed as he wiped the beaded sweat off his forehead. "What was up with that guy's teeth?"

I threw my arms in the air. "I don't know. It looks like they were whitened with a nuclear agent."

He laughed and went to the kitchen. "Want some water?"

"Sure," I replied.

He came out and handed me a bottle of water. "I'm gonna take a quick shower. Make yourself at home."

"Ok."

He walked down the hallway and I sat down in the lone recliner in the living room. I studied the oversized remote before pressing the red ON button. Unfortunately, that was as far as I got. After pressing all of the other buttons, turning on a zombie video game, and possibly calling his mother on video chat, I gave up and turned the set off.

I walked to his office and found a new brown leather loveseat against the back wall. The couch was endearing, like it was a gift specifically put there for me. I stretched out across it and stared at the ceiling willing myself to think of anything except the sound of the shower running in the adjacent room.

After a few minutes, steam poured out of the bathroom door as it opened, and Nathan stepped into the hallway without a shirt on. I leaned a little too far over and fell off the couch with a loud thud.

"You all right?" he called from his bedroom.

"Fine!" I scrambled to my seat. I could feel my face pulsing with embarrassment, but he didn't seem to notice when he joined me a moment later. Thankfully, he was dressed in sweatpants and a t-shirt.

"You like the couch?" he asked.

"Very much."

"Did you fall off the couch?" he asked with a grin.

"Shut up."

While chuckling to himself, he looked under a pad on his desk and pulled out a sheet of paper. "I found your guy. He's clean." He handed me the paper and plopped down in the office chair.

I looked at the sheet. There was an identification photo in the top left corner. It was the guy I had seen at the festival. "Where'd you get this?"

He shrugged. "I have friends in important places."

I stared at the DMV photograph. "Nothing," I said out loud. "Absolutely nothing."

"Nothing?" he asked, confused.

I slapped the paper. "I don't get anything off this guy! If I didn't know any better, I would say he's dead." I raked my nails through my hair, tugging it in frustration. "This is so weird."

I scanned the paper. "Warren Michael Parish. Aliases: Shadow, Parish. Date of birth: August 27th, 1984. Lives in New Hope, NC. Honorable discharge from the Marines in 2010. No criminal records." I looked up at Nathan. "Who is this guy?"

"If he's in New Hope with a Marine background, I would assume he's with Claymore," he said.

"What's Claymore?" I asked.

"Hired mercenaries," he replied. "They go into high combat zones for the US and some of our allies, but they aren't governed by the Geneva Convention."

"That's scary. Why is a mercenary following me?" I asked.

He shrugged his shoulders. "That's a good question. How are you so sure he was concerned with you?"

"He was looking right at me," I said.

He laughed. "You're an attractive female. Of course he was looking at you."

I stood and began to slowly pace the room. "No. He was staring at me. He was staring at me like I was staring at him, but I couldn't tell anything about this guy. He was like...a void. I didn't know him at all."

"That's rare?" he asked.

I stopped and turned toward him. "That's non-existent."

He raised his eyebrows in doubt. "That never happens?"

"Never, Nathan. Unless someone is dead. That was the feeling I got from him. Like he was a corpse or a shell," I said.

He pondered my words for a while. I expected him to laugh or look at me like I was crazy. He never did. "*Was* the guy dead?" he finally asked.

"He was staring right at me," I said. "How could he be dead? It's impossible."

He leaned forward on the chair and rested his elbows on his knees. "Sloan, how can you tell if a person is alive or dead by looking at their photograph?" He leveled his gaze at me. "I'm beginning to think that less and less stuff is really impossible."

I sat down. "Good point."

"And you're sure he was staring at you? Could he have been just looking in your direction?" he asked.

"He was staring at me. No doubt about it," I said.

He was quiet again. "Do you have a carry permit?"

"Like a gun permit?" I asked.

"Yeah."

I laughed. "No. I've never shot a gun in my life."

He scowled and cocked his head to the side. "Seriously?"

"Never even touched one," I added.

He dropped his face into his hands. "But you're a mountain girl."

"What does that have to do with anything?" I asked.

"I thought it was like a rule or something, by nature, that you had to learn how to shoot if you live here," he said.

I was puzzled. "My dad's a doctor, not a hunter. Half the people of this city are granola vegetarians. Where would you get an idea like that?"

He groaned in exasperation and rubbed his palms over his eyes. "Well, I'm going to teach you," he said.

I looked around the room. "Right now?"

"No. Not right now. It will be dark soon," he said. "Maybe we can go—"

There was a noise in the front of the apartment. The door opened and we heard Shannon's voice. "Knock knock!"

"Uh oh," I said. I looked up to catch Nathan's surprised glance down the hallway in the direction of the front door. I tried to stifle a laugh as he darted from the room.

I didn't move.

"Hey," he said. "What are you doing here?"

"Since you blew me off all day, I decided to come by and bring you dinner," Shannon purred.

"You should've called," he said.

"I tried to call, but you haven't been answering your cell phone," she said. "What have you been doing all day?"

"Working," he answered. After a beat he added, "Sloan is here."

There was a distinct pause. "Sloan *Jordan* is here?" she asked like my name was some profane word that offended her to say. "Where? In your bedroom?"

I clapped my hand over my mouth to keep myself from bursting out in laughter.

"In my office," he clarified. "Sloan, can you come out here, please?"

Obediently, I got up and walked to the doorway of the office.

Shannon was poised with her hand on her hip by the kitchen. She was pissed. "What the hell are you doing here?" she shouted at me.

I couldn't contain my giggles any longer.

"We're working," he said again.

She forced a cough. "On what? Are you going to be on the six o'clock news, Nathan? She's a publicist, not a cop!"

She started to take a step in my direction, but he put his arm out to stop her. "Shannon, please go home. I'm sorry. I'll call you later."

She pointed an angry acrylic nail at me. "Tell *her* to go home!"

"She was invited," he snapped back.

That shut her up.

She stared at him with her mouth hanging open before slinging her purse over her shoulder and stalking to the front door. She looked to see if he would stop her. He didn't. She slammed the door on her way out.

He was frozen with his back to me. His hands were resting on his hipbones and he dropped his head and blew out a long huff of frustration. Finally, he turned around. I tried not to smile, but I couldn't help myself.

He walked to the office. "Oh, shut up."

"Trouble in paradise?" I asked as he brushed by me.

He plopped down in his chair. "Sometimes she makes me crazy."

"We have a club. Would you like a membership card?" I asked.

He scowled at me.

I hovered in the doorway. "Should I go so you can patch things up with her?" I asked, but I wasn't sure why.

He shook his head. "No. She needs to cool down anyway." Hesitantly, I walked to the loveseat and sat down. "Where were we?" he asked.

I folded my legs under me. "Gun range."

He nodded. "Tomorrow over lunch."

8.

AFTER FINALIZING OUR plans for bullets and targets over my lunch hour the next day, I said goodnight to Nathan and drove home. The sun had just finished sinking behind the horizon when I turned onto my street and found a black Dodge Challenger parked in front of my house. I slammed on my brakes.

Warren Parish heard the gravel shifting under my tires and looked up from where he was leaning against my front porch handrail.

"Dang it! I should have known!" I yelled at myself.

Quickly, I yanked out my cell phone and called Nathan.

The dark stranger was slowly walking toward me with his hands up in the surrender position. I knew I should put the car in reverse to get the hell out of there as fast as possible, but my insatiable curiosity got the best of me. I inched my car forward.

Nathan's voicemail picked up, so I left a message. "Hey. That guy, Warren Parish, is at my house. Thought you should know in case I turn up missing. I know it's probably not a smart idea, but I have to see why he's here."

I stopped behind his car in the middle of the street near the front of my house. I didn't put the car in park in case I needed to make a quick getaway. Warren stayed on the curb with his hands still raised. His black hair was pulled back and he was wearing a fitted white t-shirt and black jeans. I was terrified out of my wits, otherwise I probably would have been drooling. If Warren Parish was a corpse, death suited him.

I studied him for a moment before inching down my window enough to speak. "Who are you?" I snapped.

He slowly lowered his hands to his sides. "Warren." His voice was as deep as the void I felt when he spoke.

I was wringing the steering wheel with my sweaty hands. "I know you've been following me. What do you want?"

He gave an awkward laugh. "I'm not a hundred percent sure, other than I want to talk to you." After a pause, he lowered his face and cut his eyes up at me. "And I'm pretty sure you want to talk to me too."

I did want to talk to him. Desperately.

"How do I know you're not some lunatic who is trying to kill me?" I asked.

He cracked a smile. "I have an idea." He held his hands up again. "I'm going to give you my gun. It's loaded and ready to fire. All you have to do is pull the trigger and kill me if I even move too suddenly."

Oh geez. He's armed. My eyes narrowed. "You're crazy."

He nodded. "Probably so."

Slowly, he pulled his shirt up to display a black holster on his side. "I'm going to take it out and hand it to you. I won't move too fast."

My foot was poised and ready to slip from the brake to the gas pedal. My knuckles were white from my death grip on the steering wheel. He lifted the gun out of the holster and turned it around in his hand. He eased forward and passed it to me by the handle.

"Please don't shoot me," he said. "I promise I won't give you a reason to."

My hand was shaking as I took the gun through the open portion of the window. He stepped backward to the sidewalk again. I took a deep breath and slid the transmission into park without pulling the car over. I figured that I could only benefit from completely blocking the street with my car. I left the engine running and carefully got out.

His gun was shaking in my hand. "What are you doing here?" I asked.

He seemed to relax a little. "I saw you on the news. You helped save that little girl."

"And?" I asked.

He hesitated for a moment. "And I couldn't read you."

For a second, I thought my heart had stopped beating.

"I've never met anyone I couldn't read," he added. We stared at each other in loaded silence for what felt like an eternity. Finally, he spoke again. "What are you?"

"A publicist."

He laughed. "That's not what I meant."

I couldn't laugh if I had wanted to. "I know what you meant, but I don't have an answer for you. I don't know what I am. What are you?"

He shook his head. "I don't know either."

"I can't tell if you're good or evil," I admitted.

He laughed again. "Sometimes, I can't either."

I cut my eyes at him and studied his face in the light of the streetlamp. "Are you a serial killer?"

His eyes widened. "Are you?"

"No," I answered.

"Would you tell me if you were?" he asked.

"Probably not," I replied.

He shrugged again. "Then I guess it doesn't matter what I say, but I'm not a serial killer, and I promise I'm not here to hurt you. I just needed to meet you. Can we please talk?"

I thought about the stack of photographs of dead girls I had in my briefcase. "This isn't a really good time in my life to be talking to strangers."

He was quiet for a moment and then raised his hands again. "How about this? I'm going to empty my pockets and give you everything I have. I have a knife, and I'm going to open and close it, and then it's yours. Again, I promise I won't make any sudden moves."

Nervously, I nodded and raised the gun slightly.

He reached into his pockets and retrieved a large pocket knife from one and a set of keys from the other. He left his pockets turned out. He tossed the keys at my feet then pulled his wallet out of his back pocket and tossed it over. Next, he took the knife, opened it, and pricked his finger with the tip. He closed it again and slid it across the concrete toward me. "I'm going to walk to the front of your car," he said.

I was puzzled, but nodded again.

Slowly, with his hands still raised and blood trickling down his left index finger, he crossed in front of me to my front bumper. He wiped the blood on the hood of my car and then spat on it.

My mind raced trying to make sense of what was happening.

He raised his hands again and returned to the sidewalk. "Now you have my gun, my identification, my knife, my getaway keys, and enough of my DNA to clone me. Do you think we can relax and you can at least put my gun down on your car or something? You're shaking so bad that I'm afraid you might shoot yourself in the foot."

The tension began to leave my shoulders. Slowly, I placed the gun on the lid of my trunk.

He pointed to it. "Would you mind spinning the barrel away from us?"

I turned the gun so that it pointed down the street. He let out a deep sigh of relief.

I stretched my sweaty hands for a moment and took several deep breaths.

He sat down on the curb and looked up at me. "You OK?"

"Yeah." I sighed and looked down at him, but I was still unwilling to move from my spot. "Why did you come here?"

He shrugged his shoulders and draped his long arms over his knees. "Curiosity, I guess," he answered. "I've been all around the world a few times and have never encountered anything like you."

He was verbalizing my thoughts. "A stranger," I finally said.

"Yes!" He pointed at me. "That's exactly it!"

I nodded. "I feel the same way about you."

We studied each other. Finally, he spoke. "I know when people are alive or dead."

I narrowed my eyes. "Prove it."

He looked around the empty street. "How?"

My briefcase was in my house, but Nathan had given me the files of the suspects that evening. They were in the car. I pointed at him. "Don't move." He lifted his hands in the air again. I reached into my car and retrieved the folders from the passenger's seat. I pulled out the four photos of the suspects.

I looked at him from my car for a moment before taking a bold step forward. "Don't try anything," I warned him.

"You have my word," he said.

I sank down on the curb next to him and offered him the pictures. His hand brushed against mine and a jolt, like a warm, gentle buzz of electricity shot through me. Our eyes locked. He felt it too.

"That was weird," he said, wide-eyed with genuine surprise.

"Very weird," I agreed. "What was it?"

He shook his head and smiled a little. "I don't know, but it didn't hurt."

After a moment of letting the air settle down, I nodded to the pictures. "Tell me."

He flipped through them. "This guy is alive. This guy is alive. This guy is dead. And this guy is alive."

Slowly, my eyes met his. "You're like me."

The realization of what I had just said spread over his face. "Do you think that's why we can't sense each other?" he asked.

"Has to be," I said.

He raked the few strands of loose hair that had fallen around his face back toward his ponytail. "What the hell?" Suddenly, he began to laugh. "What are we?"

Within the span of seconds, I felt more understood by this random, seemingly menacing man than I had by anyone else in my entire life. I couldn't help but laugh with him. "I have no idea."

He looked at me with a handsome smile. "You're laughing," he said. "You're not afraid of me?"

I shook my head and looked up at the starry night sky. "Not anymore." I quickly pointed at him. "But don't prove me wrong!"

"I won't," he said as he nudged me with his shoulder.

I felt the buzz of energy again and it sent chills down my spine. "I don't think that's static electricity," I said.

He looked at me. "I don't think so either."

We both sat there in silence. There were frogs singing from the creek behind my house. After a while, he shifted his heels in the gravel. "People are always afraid of me," he said.

I chuckled. "You're kind of a big, scary dude with your black hair and your black car."

He shook his head. "No, I mean like *really* scared around me. I don't have a lot of friends."

"Hmm." I looked over at him. "That's different. People seem to like me for no reason at all. I'm way more popular than I should be."

He smirked. "You're hot and obviously pretty smart, and based on that little jitter dance you did holding my Glock, you're not intimidating *at all*."

I whined and buried my face in my knees. "That's the first time in my life I've ever touched a gun."

He burst out laughing. "Seriously?" He shook his head. "I'm glad you didn't kill us both, then."

"I'm supposed to learn to shoot tomorrow."

He chuckled a little. "Then I will certainly be on guard the next time we meet."

"Where are you from?" I asked.

"I live in New Hope, NC right now, working as a contractor for Claymore. Before that, I was all over the place with the Marines. Iraq, Kuwait, Afghanistan. I grew up in south Chicago," he said.

"Chicago," I repeated.

"Well, I don't know if I was born in Chicago. I really have no idea where I'm from originally," he added.

I sat up straight. "You're adopted?"

He shook his head. "Orphaned. Grew up in the system."

I blinked my eyes at him. "I'm adopted. I was a few days old when my mother found me. Maybe we're related!"

He looked at me out of the corner of his eye with a sly smile. "God, I hope not."

I blushed and laughed again. "You're going to feel really sleazy about that if it turns out that you're my brother."

We were quiet again. "What else can you do?" he finally asked.

I thought about where to begin, but before I could answer, an SUV —with blue lights ripping through the dark—screamed around the corner. "Oh no," I said. I jumped to my feet.

Warren didn't move. "You called the cops?"

I bit my lower lip. "Sort of. I'll handle it." I hesitated for a moment. "You don't need to, like, escape or anything do you?"

He laughed and shook his head. "No."

Nathan's SUV slid to a stop behind my car. I held my hands up as he ripped his driver's side door open. "It's OK!" I shouted. "It's OK. I'm fine!"

He stepped cautiously around his door with his hand on the gun at his side. "Sir, would you mind standing up, please? Keep your hands where I can see them."

Warren obediently stood with his hands raised over his head.

I stepped into his path and tried to block him with my body. "Nathan, you don't have to do this."

"Get out of my way, Sloan," he said.

I growled and moved out of his way.

"Please turn around," he said to Warren.

When Warren turned, Nathan carefully patted him down. While he searched, he carefully surveyed our surroundings. "Why is there a gun on your trunk, Sloan?" he asked without looking at me.

"I put it there," I said. "Seriously, it's OK."

"It's my gun, Officer—" Warren began, but he was cut off.

"I'm talking to her," Nathan barked.

I put my hands on his forearms. "Nathan, listen to me. I'm fine. I'm sorry I know I frightened you, but Warren and I have been talking and everything is—"

He cut me off. "Have you not been listening to a damn word I've been saying for the past couple of weeks? Do you want to get yourself killed?" There was genuine panic in his voice.

I looked around when a light flickered on outside of one of the neighboring houses. "Can we calm down and go inside, please?" I asked.

His eyes were still wide as he took a step away from Warren. "Do you mind if I see your information, buddy?" he asked.

Warren nodded to me. "She's got my wallet."

"Oh yeah." I dashed to the rear of my car to retrieve it. "He gave me everything in his pockets, including his gun." Nathan's eyes were dancing with confusion. I handed him the wallet. "Oh, and he wiped blood on my car so there would be DNA evidence if he hurt me."

Nathan blew out an angry huff and turned toward my car, but not before telling Warren not to move.

I looked at Warren. "I'm so sorry."

"Don't apologize. You can't be too careful," he said with a smile. "If you are my sister, I would expect no less from you."

Nathan perked up in the driver's seat and looked out at both of us. "Sister?"

"It's a long story," I said to him.

He finally stepped out of my car and handed Warren the wallet. "Here you go," he said. "Is that gun loaded?"

"Yes," Warren answered.

"Mind if I *unload* it?" Nathan asked.

Warren shook his head. "Go ahead."

Nathan picked up the gun, removed the magazine, and cleared the chamber. When he was done, he looked at Warren again. "Mind if I hold onto it while I'm here?" he asked.

Warren turned his hands out. "Be my guest."

"Sloan, you wanna move your car to the curb?" Nathan asked.

"Sure," I said. "I'm just gonna pull in my driveway, m'kay?"

"Fine," Nathan answered.

By the time we got our vehicles out of the road, two different neighbors were on their porches watching the ordeal. I waved to them as the three of us walked up the steps to my front door. "Sorry folks! Everything is OK. Nothing to see here!"

Mrs. Wilson, who lived across from me, was in her nightgown. She shook her head in disgust before disappearing inside. I groaned and unlocked the door. Warren and Nathan followed me.

When the door was closed, Nathan folded his arms over his chest. "Do you mind telling me what the hell is going on here?"

I urged him toward the living room. "Come on. We're not barbarians. Let's sit down and talk like civilized people," I said.

I sat on the couch, Warren took the loveseat, and Nathan scowled as he sat on the edge of the seat beside me.

Warren leaned forward, resting his elbows on his knees. "I'm really sorry I scared the shit out of everyone tonight. I couldn't bring myself to leave town without saying something."

"Saying what?" Nathan snapped.

I put my hand on his leg. "Simmer down. We're all friends here."

"No we're not," he said through a clenched jaw.

I realized I hadn't made introductions. "Warren, this is Detective Nathan McNamara. Nathan, you already know Mr. Parish," I said. "I'm sorry, Warren. Nathan and I have been through a lot here recently. We're both a little on edge."

"I told you, you don't have to apologize," Warren said.

"No! You *don't* have to apologize," Nathan barked at both of us. He cut his eyes at Warren. "Why were you here, waiting in the dark at her doorstep for her to come home alone?" he shouted across the room.

Warren shook his head. "I didn't know that she would be alone," he reasoned. "I tried to be as non-threatening as possible. I stayed outside of my car in the streetlight. I let all the neighbors get a good look at me—"

Nathan cut him off again. "It's bullshit! What are you doing here?"

"I wanted to talk to Sloan," he said.

"Why?"

Warren looked to me for help. I nodded my head. "It's OK. He knows," I assured him. I looked at Nathan and tried to get him to focus on my face. "He's like me."

That seemed to take Nathan back. He swallowed hard. "What do you mean? He's psychic?"

Warren cringed. "I hate that word."

"Me too!" I laughed, completely forgetting the seriousness of the moment.

Nathan wasn't laughing. "I don't like this, Sloan."

I patted his hand. "I know."

"Why are you stalking her?" Nathan asked.

Warren shook his head. "I wasn't trying to stalk her. I was actually trying to figure out how to approach her."

"And at night, at her house was your solution?" Nathan asked.

Warren shrugged. "It was a now or never moment. I've got to head home."

"To Claymore?" Nathan asked.

Warren nodded.

Nathan stood up and pointed at the front door. "Good. Go!"

"Whoa ho ho. Wait a minute." I reached out and grabbed Nathan by a belt loop. "You don't order people in and out of my house. This is *my* house and Warren can stay for as long as he likes."

Nathan was grinding his teeth, looking down at me. "Can I talk to you in private for a minute?"

I stood up.

Warren thrust his hand toward us. "By all means, say it to my face, bro," he said.

Nathan's face was burning with anger. "I'm not your 'bro' and I *will* say it to your face! I don't like you. I sure as hell don't trust you." He looked at me. "I can't even begin to explain how bad of an idea this is. You don't know this guy."

I smiled at the thought. "You're right. I don't know him. For the first time in my life I don't know someone!"

Nathan was looking at me like I was growing another nose on my face.

I put my hands on Nathan's arms which were flexed and not in a good way. "Do you have any idea how exhausting it is to see people everywhere you go and think, 'Hmm. Do I really know that person or do I just think I do because I'm a freak?' or 'I might know that woman, should I talk to her or will she think I'm a lunatic?' or even worse, 'That guy is terrifying! I wonder if he's planning to eat my face off!'"

I realized I was close to shouting, so I stopped and took a deep breath.

His hand shot out toward Warren. "But this—"

I cut him off. "*This* is not your business!" I forced him to look at me. "I know you think this is crazy, but crazy or not, he's here and he's not going anywhere until he wants to or I want him to."

Nathan's gray eyes were frantic.

Gently, I put my hands against his cheeks. "I've never in my life met anyone that understands as much about me as this guy. Not Adrianne, not my parents, and certainly not you. I sincerely appreciate you being so protective over me—I love it really, I do—but this isn't your call. This is something I can't ignore, even if it might get me killed."

That seemed to disarm Nathan ever so slightly. His jaw was working overtime, but his eyes relaxed a little. "All right," he forced out.

Nathan sucked in a deep breath and pulled the gun and clip out of his pocket. He handed it to Warren, but Warren shook his head. "Take the clip, man," he insisted.

After an awkward pause, Nathan placed the gun on the coffee table and then pointed a daring finger at Warren. "I swear to God, if you lay a finger on her, I will choke you to death on your own nutsack."

Warren pressed his lips together like I do when I'm trying not to laugh. "I promise she's safe."

I tugged on Nathan's sleeve and then wrapped my hand around his. "Come on. I'll walk you out."

We went to the front door and I opened it. He turned toward me, ran his hand up my jaw and pulled my ear to his lips. "Please don't do this," he begged.

I pulled back. "Nathan, trust me."

He shook his head. Then, out of nowhere, his lips crashed down on mine. As suddenly as he kissed me, he released me and walked out of the door. I was so stunned that I froze to the floor.

When he was halfway to his car, I shouted at him. "Wait! We're kissing now??"

He didn't respond, but he looked at me for a long second before getting in the SUV and starting the engine.

I groaned and closed the door.

When I returned to the living room, Warren was relaxed in the corner of the loveseat. "Well, that was very interesting," he said.

I sighed and fell onto the couch. "You have no idea." I sighed, staring at the ceiling. "I'm sorry, are you thirsty? Can I get you something to eat?"

He smiled and sat forward. "Some water would be great."

He followed me into the kitchen. I liked my kitchen, even if I rarely went into it. I had top of the line, shiny, stainless steel appliances, but the only one that ever got used was the coffee pot. I reached into the refrigerator and pulled out two bottles of water. I handed one to Warren and opened my own.

I tipped the bottle up to my lips and took a swig. "I hope Nathan doesn't call my parents."

He leaned against the white cabinets and motioned with his water bottle toward the door. "He loves you."

I choked on my water. "Ha. No, he doesn't. He just likes me because that's what people do—they like me." I shook my head. "And he was in RoboCop mode just now. We've been working on a really stressful case together and we're both really keyed up about it."

He raised an eyebrow. "A case? I thought I read that you were in public relations for the county."

I shrugged. "I'm pulling double duty these days ever since I slipped up and let the good detective know about my ability. Unpaid double duty," I added.

"Is that how you found that little girl? She was missing and you knew she was alive?" he asked.

I nodded. "You heard about that all the way out in New Hope?" I asked, astonished.

"Yep. Saw the video, on some news station website, of you carrying her out and everything. It went pretty viral," he said.

I rolled my eyes. "What did we ever do before the Internet? We all just stayed closed off in our neat little bubbles."

He shrugged his shoulders. "Relatively neat."

My phone rang. I pulled it out of my pocket, expecting it to be Nathan. It was my mother, of course. I hit the answer button. "Hi Mom," I said, looking at Warren with I-told-you-so eyes.

He laughed.

"Hi honey," she said. "Just calling to check in. I haven't heard from you all weekend."

"I'm good, Mom. Did Detective McNamara call you?" I asked.

"Who?" she replied.

"Never mind," I said. "I actually have company over. Can I call you tomorrow?"

"Sure. Are you coming by for dinner tomorrow night?" she asked.

"Yep. I'll be there after work," I answered.

"OK, sweetie. I love you," she said.

"I love you, too," I replied and disconnected the call.

I held the phone out toward Warren. "Can you do that?"

He raised his eyebrows. "Talk to your mother?"

I walked toward the living room, sat down, and propped my feet up on the coffee table. "Summon people," I clarified.

Warren sat down next to me. "Summon people?" he asked.

I folded my legs under me and put my water bottle on the floor. "I seem to be able to call out for people and make them show up."

"Like, just now with your Mom calling?"

I nodded.

"You think you caused that?" he asked.

I shrugged. "It happens enough around me that I'm pretty convinced of it. Like, I had this long conversation with that detective about you this afternoon and then came home and you were at my house."

"I'm pretty sure I came all on my own," he said.

"You'll see for yourself if you hang around long enough," I told him.

He stretched his arm across the couch toward me and tapped the seat cushion between us with his fingers. "It's not that I don't believe you. Trust me. I believe you." He took a deep breath. "You make people show up; I make people disappear."

I turned my whole body toward him. "You what?"

He shrugged. "I don't know how."

"Like *'poof'* disappear?" Thoughts of a magician in a top hat with a bunny and a cloud of smoke came to mind.

He shook his head. "No. Like, if I had really wanted your buddy McNamara gone, I could have made it happen without having to say a word."

I didn't doubt him, but I was intrigued by what he meant. I rubbed my forehead. "This is all so crazy."

He nodded in agreement.

I looked over at him. "Does anyone else know about what you can do?" I asked.

He leaned against the armrest. "Not anymore. Well, not until tonight anyway. I told this girl one time, but she died a long time ago."

"I'm sorry," I said. "You know, I don't think I've ever known anyone who's died."

"Really?" he asked, surprised.

I thought about it and shook my head. "Not personally."

He was quiet for a while, seemingly lost in a memory that I wasn't privy to. "I think you and I have a lot more differences than we do similarities," he finally said.

"Do you get a sense if people are good or evil just by looking at them?" I asked.

"Yep," he said. "That was part of the reason I was so interested in you. I couldn't even tell if you were alive or dead. I kept waiting for the news to announce your death, but they never did, so I checked for myself. I've never seen anyone like you."

"Me too!" I said. "That's exactly what I told the detective about you. Of course, he sort of looked at me like I was crazy, and I'm pretty sure he wondered if you might be a zombie or something, but..."

He leaned toward me and lowered his voice. "Can I tell you something else?"

"Sure," I replied.

He thought for a moment. "Do you promise you won't get really freaked out about it?"

I smiled. "That's usually my line."

He smiled, but it quickly faded away. "When I say 'I make people disappear', what I mean is…I can kill people."

I blinked. "Kill people?" I tried to mute the panic in my voice as best I could.

He nodded.

I pulled my head back. "How?"

He turned his palms up and dropped them onto his lap. "Just by looking at them."

Suddenly, I realized that maybe Nathan had been right. Maybe this was a very bad idea. My eyes floated aimlessly around the room and settled on the unused, but beautifully decorated fireplace in the corner. My parents wedding picture was resting on the mantle. I briefly wondered if I would ever see them again. My mind was racing with a thousand different fears.

"I'm sorry. I've frightened you." Warren reached over and put his hand on my leg.

All at once, a calming warmth spread through me. My eyes closed, my pounding heart began to settle, and without thinking, I wrapped my fingers around his. I was quiet while my breathing returned to normal.

"You did," I admitted. "But I'm OK now." I squeezed his hand.

I wasn't sure what was happening whenever we touched, but it was magnetic. The man had just admitted he could end my life if he wanted to, and still, the sensation surging through me was so deliciously addicting that I never wanted to release him.

He looked down at our hands and then into my eyes. "I could stay here forever," he whispered.

"I don't know what this feeling is, but I don't want you to ever leave," I confessed. "A lot of really strange stuff has always happened around me, but this is by far the strangest."

For a long time we sat there, some unseen bond holding us together. I couldn't explain it, but I also didn't care. I felt like a lightning rod in the middle of a thunderstorm, completely content to soak up all the energy in the atmosphere.

He took in a slow deep breath and locked his eyes with mine. His eyes were so dark that I could hardly distinguish his pupils from the irises, save for a faint light halo of gold around the pupils. "I'm going to have to leave or I'm going to get really inappropriately close to you," he admitted. "This is like heroin."

He broke the connection of our hands and pushed himself up off the couch. It was like the room suddenly dropped ten degrees in temperature. I wanted to cry, but I didn't know why.

"I have a seven hour drive home." He sighed and stretched his arms over his head. "And I have to work tomorrow."

I stood up as he gathered his gun and keys from the table. I wanted to physically block his path to the door, but I didn't.

At the front door, he stopped and looked down at me for a several seconds before laughing. "I'm actually afraid to hug you goodbye. I might not leave."

I smiled and felt my face flush red. "Will I see you again?" I was almost afraid to hear his answer.

He sighed and twisted a strand of my hair around his finger. "Sooner than you think."

I pulled out my phone and brought up a new message. "What's your number? I'll text you mine."

He told me his phone number and I sent him a message.

"Let me know that you've made it home safely," I said as his phone beeped in his pocket.

He nodded. "I will." He drew in a deep breath. "Thanks for letting me in, Sloan."

Unable to stand our proximity without touching any longer, I stretched my arms up around his neck. I let out the breath I hadn't realized I was holding. "Thanks for finding me."

Enveloped in his dizzying embrace, I was sure that touching Warren was like connecting with destiny. In his arms was exactly where I was supposed to be.

9.

I LOCKED THE door behind Warren and watched from the window till he got in his sports car and drove away. When he was gone, I turned around and leaned against the door. I closed my eyes and desperately tried to hold on to the feeling of his presence for as long as possible. The buzz faded with every second.

When I opened my eyes again, the room seemed brighter than usual. Even stranger, my dining room was missing. I blinked a few times and then looked straight at the dining room table. It was there, but to the right of it, the kitchen had disappeared. I pressed my palms to my eyes and walked forward, tripping over a fake flower arrangement that sat in the foyer. I turned toward the kitchen and saw it, but the wall to my right was gone. My heart was pounding so hard that I could feel my pulse throbbing in the side of my neck.

My phone was still in my hand, so I sent Nathan a message. *Warren is gone. I'm not feeling well, so I'm going to bed. I'll call you tomorrow.*

I turned toward the steps that led upstairs, but I was so dizzy I had to grasp the handrail for support. Each step of the staircase seemed to be broken. I couldn't see the right side of any of the steps before me.

By some miracle, I made it to my room but bumped into my bed before falling on top of it. Something was wrong. My phone buzzed in my hand. I looked down at the message on the screen, but most of the words and letters were missing. It was impossible to read. I tapped out a response the best I could and hit send just as it seemed that an invisible ice pick was jammed into the side of my skull. I crumpled onto the covers.

My phone rang. I knew I had to answer it. "Hello?" I drew my knees to my chest and rolled onto my side.

"Are you OK? Your messages aren't making any sense. Half of the words are missing or are misspelled," Nathan said.

I cringed. It was like he was screaming at me over the phone.

"I'm not OK," I said. "Something's wrong. I feel like my brain is bleeding."

"I'm on my way," he said. "Where are you in the house?"

"In my bed," I answered. "I can't see to make it back down the stairs and I locked the door."

There was a lot of noise on his end of the line. I held the phone away from my ear. "How can I get in? Do you have a key hidden?"

"Stop screaming," I begged.

"Sloan, I'm not screaming," he insisted.

I was rolling back and forth in pain. "No key," I choked out.

"Stay with me. I'm on my way."

I was in and out of consciousness, but sometime later I felt Nathan lift me off my bed. He was shouting at someone as he carried me down the stairs. There were bright lights flashing red and white, and each flash felt like a butcher knife to my brain. He laid me down and someone strapped a belt around my middle. Everyone was screaming.

"Shhh..." I cried. I covered my eyes with my arm to block out as much light as possible.

Someone was holding my hand. Whatever I was lying on felt like it was being knocked into walls and slammed against the ground. I tried to roll over onto my side, but the belt around my waist prevented it. "Sick," I mumbled.

"Are you going to be sick?" someone shouted as I began throwing up uncontrollably.

Everything went black.

* * *

When I opened my eyes again, I was in a dimly lit hospital room. My mother was seated next to me on the bed. Nathan was asleep in a chair in the corner. I heard my father's voice some distance away. I tried to raise my arm, but there was an IV in my hand that hurt like I had been shot. My head was throbbing with pain.

I tried to blink away the hazy film that covered my eyeballs. "What happened?"

My mother turned and leaned toward me. Nathan bolted out of his seat like he had been fired from a cannon.

Mom smoothed my hair gently with her hand. "How are you feeling?" she whispered.

Nathan came around to the other side of my bed and wrapped his hand around mine.

"Head hurts," I replied with a voice so raspy I hardly recognized it as my own. "What's wrong with me?" I asked as another figure appeared in the room.

It was my dad. Mom got up and moved out of the way so he could sit down beside me. "Hey, sweetheart," he said as he leaned down to kiss my forehead.

"Am I dying?"

He laughed softly. "No. You're not dying. You had a really severe migraine."

"A migraine? I'm in the hospital with a headache?" I groaned with embarrassment.

Dad rubbed my arm. "Sloan, you experienced a hemiplegic migraine. One of the most severe and serious forms of any migraine headache. You were paralyzed on your right side and couldn't speak," he said. "Nathan was right to call an ambulance and get you here."

Nathan squeezed my hand. "I thought you had been poisoned or that you were having a stroke or an aneurysm. You scared me to death."

I offered him a weak smile. "I'm sorry."

He kissed my fingers and held them against his lips. "I'm just glad you're OK."

"We already did a CT scan and it was clear. I'm thinking of ordering an MRI to be on the safe side," Dad explained.

"Did the hospital call you?" I asked.

He shook his head. "No. Nathan did."

"I took your phone and called them on our way to the hospital," he said.

"Thank you," I whispered. "Can you let Mary know I won't be at work tomorrow?"

"Today," he corrected me. "It's almost 11 am."

I looked around the room. "What? Seriously?"

"You've been asleep for a while," Mom said.

"Part of it is the drugs. Part of it is just the headache," Dad explained.

I groaned. "Nathan, shouldn't you be at work?"

He shook his head. "They can live without me for one day. You're much more important right now."

I squeezed his hand.

The hospital released me with a prescription for a migraine medication that I was instructed to keep with me at all times in case another headache began. They said that the ripples and holes in my vision that I experienced was usually the first sign of the onset of a migraine. Dad gave me strict orders to spend the day in bed. He and Mom drove Nathan and me to my house, since Nathan had left his car there to ride with me in the ambulance. Dad went to his office, and Mom decided to spend the day as my personal nurse.

Nathan kept his arm tight around me the whole way up to my bed. I was feeling better, but my knees wobbled all the way up the stairs. Dad said it was the drugs still in my system.

I stretched out across the bed, and Nathan sat down next to me. My mom stood in the doorway. He gently brushed a loose strand of hair off my cheek and smiled at me. "Are you going to be OK?"

I nodded and reached for his arm. "Thank you for everything." I tugged on his sleeve. "I don't know what would have happened to me if you hadn't shown up."

He bent over me and kissed my forehead. "You may not be so thankful when you see what I did to your back door."

I laughed, but it hurt my head. "I don't even care."

"I'll come by and fix it later," he promised. "Or do you want me to stay? I can. We can curl up right here and watch movies or just sleep. I don't have anywhere else to be."

I shook my head. "I know you've got work to do, and you've been up all night, I'm sure." I glanced at my mother who was still waiting quietly by the door. "I'm in good hands."

He nodded, but he looked a little disappointed. If my mother hadn't been supervising, I might have changed my mind and invited him to crawl under my covers with me. He reached into the pocket of his fleece pullover and handed me my phone. "Will you call me if you need anything at all?"

I forced a smile as he laid the phone beside my pillow. "I will."

He leaned down and kissed my forehead again before getting up and walking across the room.

My mother hugged him at the door. "Thank you so much, Nathan," she said.

He shook his head. "No thanks needed, ma'am."

When he was gone, she looked at me. "If you don't marry that boy, I will disown you and cut you out of the will."

I had two missed calls and a text message from Warren. *Finally made it home. Had a pretty messed up night. Call me when you can.*

Later, while my mother was downstairs, I dialed his number.

He picked up on the first ring. "Hello?" He sounded a lot like I did.

"Hey, sorry I missed your calls," I said. "I've been in the hospital since last night."

"What? Are you OK?"

"I had this really debilitating migraine after you left. I was paralyzed and everything," I said.

"So did I," he said. "I actually blacked out when I stopped at a rest area."

"Oh my gosh, me too." I draped my arm across my forehead. "What is going on?"

"I have no idea," he said. "I've been sick all day. Feeling better now, but I never made it to work today. I guess I could've stayed another day with you."

"Do you think we would've gotten sick together?" I asked.

"I don't know," he said. "But it felt like I was detoxing off of you or something."

He was right. That's exactly what it felt like, though the only thing I had ever detoxed off of was caffeine. This was exponentially worse. "Warren, what do you think this means?"

He was quiet. "Either it means that we shouldn't be apart or that we never should have met in the first place. I don't know about you, but I'm pretty pissed that we haven't met until now."

"Me too," I agreed.

He sighed. "I think I need to pass out for a couple more hours. Can I call you later?" he asked.

"You don't have to ask," I said.

"OK," he said. "Take it easy and get some rest."

"You too," I said and hung up the phone.

The ceiling fan blades were spinning slowly overhead. I still felt like hell, but I knew I would rather feel that horrible for the rest of my life than to never feel the sensation of Warren's presence ever again. I had an even bigger problem than the migraine when I considered the events of the night before. What was going on with Nathan McNamara?

10.

THERE WAS A smiley face balloon and a smiley face coffee mug full of chocolate candy on my desk when I returned to work the next day. Along with them was a note from my boss. *Hope you're feeling better. You gave us all quite the scare. - Mary.*

I smiled and sat down at my desk. A dull pain still throbbed in my skull, but my dad said it was normal and that it might take a couple of days to completely subside. My email inbox was full, and my voicemail light was showing nine new messages. I groaned and started sorting through the emails.

About halfway down the list was a bulletin from Catawba County. The subject line caught my attention. *Human Remains Discovered May Be That of Missing Hickory Woman.* I clicked the email open and read it aloud.

"Human remains were discovered on Monday underneath the home of Myrtle Allen, 82, of Hickory, N.C. Air conditioning contractors, working in a previously sealed off section of the home's crawl space, unearthed pieces of a human skeleton. Police believe that the remains may be that of Crystal Jennifer Dumas, a local woman who disappeared in 2005. Dumas was the girlfriend of Myrtle Allen's grandson, Logan Allen, 32, also of Hickory."

I picked up my phone and dialed Nathan's cell. A phone rang down the hallway, and a moment later he appeared in my office holding his phone. "You rang?" he asked.

I ended the call and pointed at the screen. "Come here. Have you seen this?"

He sat down in one of my chairs and put his feet up on the edge of my desk. "Christy Dumas?"

"Yes!"

He nodded. "Yep. I've seen it. They arrested Logan last night. I was coming by to see if you were up for a little road trip."

My eyes widened. "Nathan, I've got so much work to catch up on."

He pointed to the balloon. "I think Mary would understand if you said you still weren't feeling well." He plucked one of the chocolates out of the smiley face mug, unwrapped it, and popped it into his mouth.

I shook my head. "You're going to get me fired."

He leaned forward with his palms on my desk. He lowered his voice. "Do a little catch up work till lunch, and then tell her you're not feeling well and take the rest of the day off." He knocked his knuckles against my desk. "I'll pick you up at your house at"—he looked at his watch—"two o'clock."

He was gone before I could protest.

At five minutes till two I was sitting on my front porch steps feeling terribly guilty as I waited on Nathan. It was the first time I had ever lied to my boss to get out of work.

My phone rang. "Hello?" I answered.

"Hey, it's Warren."

"Hey there." I quickly forgot about my guilt and broke out into a smile. "What are you up to today?"

"I was wondering if you had plans this weekend," he said.

I thought for a moment. "I don't think so. What did you have in mind?"

"I was thinking about making another trip to Asheville," he said.

An uncontrollable giggle bubbled out before I could stop it. "I think that is a brilliant idea. You can stay with me as long as you promise to not tell my mother. I have a guest room."

He laughed. "OK. I promise not to tell your mother. I'm usually done with work by noon on Fridays, so I should be there around five or six."

"That's perfect," I said. "I get off at five."

"Are you working today?" he asked.

"Uhh, sort of," I said. "I went to work this morning, but now I'm on my way to Hickory to find a serial killer."

There was a pause. "You're doing what?"

I adjusted my sunglasses on my face. "Remember me telling you that I was working on a case with the detective? Well, they caught a guy in Hickory that we think is a suspect for a bunch of other murders."

"You didn't tell me it was a serial murder case." He started laughing. "No wonder that cop was so pissed off the other night."

"Yeah," I said.

"Do you want my help?" he asked.

I was surprised. "How can you help?"

Nathan's SUV turned onto my street.

"The stack of photos you quizzed me on the other night. Was that your group of suspects?" he asked.

"Yeah, why?" I asked.

"None of the guys you showed me in that stack are serial killers," he said. "One of them has murdered someone, but only that one person."

"Which guy?" I asked.

"Blonde hair with a goatee," he said.

"Logan Allen. That's who we are going to see today," I told him. "How do you know he's only killed one person?"

"I just know. It's kind of like people who have killed have death attached to them. Like they carry it with them," he said. "I can tell exactly how many there are and that Logan guy only has one."

Nathan rolled to a stop in front of the curb, and I got up and walked around the front of the vehicle.

"I never get anything that specific," I said to Warren. "I only get an impression if someone is good or not."

"Hmm. I find evil and death really well. Goodness, not so much," he said. "I wonder if it's because I've been around it more and have paid more attention to it."

"I don't know. Maybe. I've been pretty sheltered," I admitted. I got in the passenger's seat of the SUV and fastened my seatbelt. "What do you mean by you can find death?" I asked. "Like, can you find corpses?"

Nathan looked over at me, catching the tail end of my question.

"Sure. If I know where to look," Warren said.

I turned the thought over in my mind. "When I was in the house where we found that little girl, there was a dead body in there and I didn't feel anything. I knew Kayleigh—or someone else who was alive —was there, but I didn't get anything off the corpse."

"Sloan, I do the opposite," he said.

I swallowed hard. "Huh."

"We'll talk more about it later," he said. "I've got to get back to work."

"Ok," I said.

When I disconnected the call, I sat there in stunned silence till Nathan punched me in the shoulder. "What was all that about?" he asked.

I turned in my seat to look at him. "Warren can find dead bodies."

"Really?" He pulled away from the curb. "Tell him I'm looking for ten more."

I stared out of the window. "He said he would have to know where to look, like a general area I guess."

"That dude is weird," he said.

I looked at him. "I'm weird."

He nodded. "Yes you are."

I sat back against my seat. "You know, a month ago my life was pretty dang normal. Then you showed up and turned everything— absolutely everything—upside down."

His ball cap, with the American flag in place, was pulled down close over his eyes. One arm was draped over the steering wheel. "No offense, but I don't think anything about your life has ever been exactly normal."

I pointed at him. "No, but it was peaceful. I went to work. I hung out with my friends. I had dinner with my parents on Mondays. Now look at me. I'm lying to my boss, skipping work, and I'm on my way to Hickory to meet a guy that murdered his girlfriend and shoved her under his granny's house."

"And maybe a lot of other girls," he added.

I shook my head. "Warren doesn't think so. He said Logan Allen has only killed one person. He's not a serial killer."

He looked at me with a raised eyebrow. "I think I would rather investigate it for myself than just take Warren's word for it."

I folded my arms across my chest. "How come you're so certain about things that I tell you, but you have no faith in what he says?"

"Because I think Warren is a con. I think that he's dangerous, and I don't think you should be involved with him at all," he said.

I frowned. "A con? How could he possibly be conning me? No one knows about what I can do except for you and Adrianne. Now, unless one of you has posted some tell-all about me that I'm unaware of, I don't see how he could know as much as he does unless he was telling the truth."

"I don't like him," he said.

I nodded. "Obviously, but you'd better start getting used to him being in the picture if we're going to keep working together."

He glanced over. "Why?"

"Because he's coming again on Friday," I said.

"Why? Are you dating him now?" he asked, his voice jumping up a few decibels.

"If I was, it wouldn't be any of your business," I reminded him.

"None of my business? This guy stalks you, shows up at your house, and I wind up carrying you to an ambulance when he leaves, and you don't think this is any of my business?" He was close to shouting.

I leaned toward him and narrowed my eyes. "Let's call Shannon and see if she agrees that this is your business."

He was gripping the steering wheel so tight I was afraid he might break it off the column and send us careening off the highway. I sat back in my seat again and stared at the road ahead. He was leaning against his door with his hand over his mouth. We rode in complete silence until we crossed out of Buncombe County.

Finally, he spoke. "I'm sorry. I don't want to fight with you this whole trip."

"I'm sorry too," I said, still staring straight ahead.

After another moment, I looked over at him. "Why did you kiss me the other night?"

He dragged his knuckles over his bottom lip, then turned his hand up and shrugged. "I thought there might be a good chance I wouldn't see you again. Warren gives off really bad vibes."

"He's supposed to," I said.

His eyebrows scrunched together. "What?"

I shrugged. "He gives off bad vibes like I give off good vibes," I said. "People like me and people hate him."

Nathan cracked a smile for the first time in thirty miles. "Shannon doesn't like you."

I laughed. "Touché."

"If he gives off bad vibes, why doesn't he bother you?" he asked.

"I don't feel him giving off anything. I told you, I don't read anything on him at all," I said.

"Can he read you?" he asked.

I shook my head. "No, and I think it's one of the reasons why I like him so much," I admitted. "I always wonder if people really want to be around me or if they are just attracted to whatever power it is that I give off. Like, I wonder if it forces people to like me. I don't worry about that with Warren."

Nathan looked over his shoulder at me. "Do you worry about that with me? Do you think I only want to be around you because of the vibes you give off?"

I laughed and shook my head. "Nathan McNamara, I can't figure out a damn thing about you."

When we passed into Hickory, I looked over at him. "How close are we?"

"About five minutes," he answered.

I nodded and pulled out my purse. I retrieved my bottle of Xanax and put a half of a tablet under my tongue.

He watched me tuck the pill bottle back into my purse. "Do you do that every time?"

"Every time I visit a jail? Yes," I said.

"When you go in there, what's it like exactly?" he asked.

I shook my head. "You wouldn't understand."

"Help me understand," he said.

I thought for a moment. "Were you ever afraid of the dark when you were a kid?" I asked.

"No," he answered quickly.

I looked at him with a raised eyebrow.

"Maybe. Shut up," he whined.

"It's like that. It's like walking into the blackest, most all-consuming darkness you can imagine. It's that feeling that you're trapped in the dark, unable to find the light switch, and that at any second, whatever is hiding in the darkness is going to rip you apart." I shuddered. "And it's frustrating because I know I'm safe, like I know nothing can really hurt me, but I just can't feel safe. It gets so bad sometimes that I can't even breathe."

"Damn. That sucks," he said.

I nodded. "Sucks doesn't cover it. My dad put me on anti-anxiety meds when I was in the seventh grade because I started having panic attacks at school. It turned out that my math teacher was a pedophile, and once he was removed from the school, I was fine again."

He shook his head. "That's nuts."

"Yep," I agreed. "I'm a walking, talking evil barometer."

He reached over and put his hand on my knee. "Well, we will make this as quick as we can. If, at any point, you need to leave, you just say so and we're out. No questions asked."

I smiled at him and squeezed his hand. "Thanks, Nathan."

It turned out that our trip to the Catawba County Jail wasn't as bad as I had feared that it would be. Without a doubt, Logan Allen had a dark soul, but Warren had been right—he wasn't a serial killer.

Nathan and I walked out into the setting sun. "Well, that was a complete waste of a sick day," I said.

"You never know," Nathan said. "He might still be our guy."

I stopped and turned to look at him. "He was in there bawling like a toddler. You saw the look on his face when you started asking about the other girls. He's *not* our guy."

Nathan slapped the file folder he was carrying against his thigh and groaned. "Oh well," he said. "I'm hungry. Let's go eat."

We went to the Bleachers Sports Bar & Restaurant that we had passed on our way into town and ordered burgers. Nathan ordered a Snickers pie as an appetizer.

When the waitress walked away from the table, I looked at him sideways. "How in the hell do you stay in such good shape eating like that all the time?" I asked. "I honestly don't think I've ever seen you eat anything that's remotely healthy."

He laughed and shrugged his shoulders. "I have good genes, I guess."

I shook my head. "I'm so jealous. In fact, I hate you a little bit."

He winked at me from across the table. "You can't hate me. I'm the 'cute little blond boy', remember?"

I laughed and rolled my eyes.

The waitress returned with Nathan's slice of pie and he picked up his fork. "How are you feeling after yesterday?"

"Pretty good now. I still have a little dull pain, but nothing like it was," I said. "I really can't thank you enough for what you did."

He put his hand to his forehead. "You scared me to death. I literally thought I was watching you die. I was sure he had poisoned you."

"He didn't poison me," I said.

"Well, I know that now," he said. "I made them run a blood test to check for toxins."

"Really?"

He nodded. "Oh yeah."

I was eyeballing Nathan's pie and wishing I had ordered a slice for myself. "I want a bite." I opened my mouth wide.

He cut off a forkful and held it to my lips. "One bite," he said with a hint of warning in his tone.

The sweet cold chocolate and cream almost made my eyes roll back in my head. I licked my lips. When I looked at Nathan again, he was staring at me with the fork still frozen in the air. I covered my mouth and laughed.

He cast his eyes down at his plate and cleared his throat. "What were we talking about?"

"Migraines and poisoning," I reminded him. "Warren actually got really sick too. Same thing happened to him on the way home."

"Good," Nathan mumbled. He picked a piece of candy bar off of the top of his pie and dropped it into his mouth.

I wadded up my napkin and threw it at him.

My phone rang. "Lo and behold." I turned my phone around so he could see that it was Warren.

He shook his head and shoveled another forkful of pie into his mouth. "You're a creepy chick," he said with his mouth full.

I answered the call. "Hey. I was just talking about you."

"And here I am," he said, laughing. "What are you doing?"

"I am sitting at a sports bar in Hickory with Nathan. What are you doing?" I asked.

"I am watching football at home. How'd it go at the jail?" he asked.

"Not our guy," I said.

"I told you," he said.

I nodded. "I know you did."

Nathan nudged me with his foot under the table. "Ask him what he needs to find someone."

"What you were saying earlier about finding bodies, how do you do that?" I asked.

"I guess the same way you found that kid. You knew where to look and when you got there, you knew she was there," he said.

"Well, I knew someone was there. I didn't necessarily know it was Kayleigh," I clarified.

"Same thing with me," he said.

I made a sour face. "You can sense dead bodies anywhere? That seems like it would get exhausting."

"Ehh, no more so than you being around people and sensing life all the time," he said. "You get kind of used to it."

"I guess that makes sense. What kind of radius are we talking about here as far as a search area goes?" I asked.

"It depends. Where do you think they are?" he asked.

I bit the tip of my index finger. "Between Asheville and Raleigh."

He laughed. "Yeah, I need it to be a little more specific than that. Like maybe the size of a football field," he said.

I nodded. "OK. I don't know that much."

"We'll talk more about it this weekend," he said. "You sure you don't mind if I come?"

"Are you kidding?" I laughed. "I can't wait."

"Me either. Well, I'll let you get back to whatever you're doing. Give my regards to the detective," he said.

I laughed. "I will. I'll text you later." I hung up and looked at Nathan. "He said to tell you hello."

"Yay," he said, feigning interest.

"When we get home, we need to go over the map again," I said.

"How come?" he asked.

"Warren said if we could narrow down the area, he can tell us if anything is there," I told him.

"How does he do it?"

I wiggled my fingers in front of his face. "Magic."

He smiled and wiped his mouth.

On our ride home, I looked over at him. "You never told me what happened with Shannon after I left your house the other night."

"Well, she was pissed," he said. "I actually didn't call her back until last night. That didn't help things much."

"Seriously?" I asked.

He shrugged. "Well, I was going to call her, but then I got your message saying that some stalker was at your house, so I took off. Then, I was so mad when I left your place that I didn't want to talk to anyone. After that I was at the hospital with you all night. I didn't really have the time."

"I so would have dumped you," I said, shaking my head.

He nodded. "I know you would have."

"Did you fix things with her?" I asked.

"I guess. I don't really know if I even want to fix things with her. Dating her long distance is quite different than it being a full-time gig," he said.

"Ladies and Gentlemen, he's finally making some sense," I teased.

"Shut up," he said.

"You know, without Christy Dumas being a part of the group anymore, your theory about the next victim being from Asheville is completely shot to hell," I pointed out.

He nodded. "I know. I already thought of that."

I rolled my head against the headrest to face him. "And if you dump your girlfriend, you really have no reason to be here anymore,"

He looked over at me. "You don't think so?" It was a loaded question. He was curious about a lot more than my opinion.

I felt my cheeks flush, and I looked out the window without giving him an answer.

"Hey," he said.

I looked toward him again.

He was still staring at me over the arm that was resting on the steering wheel. "I can promise you, it's more than your vibes, Sloan."

I swallowed hard. "You don't know that."

He raised his eyebrows. "Don't I?"

I looked away, signaling the end of the conversation. With Warren suddenly in the picture, the timing couldn't be any worse for a heart-to-heart conversation about romance with Nathan.

He was quiet for a moment. "I can always go back to Raleigh."

I wasn't sure where my heart landed on that idea. I was just starting to get used to having him around. I certainly wouldn't tell him that, so I decided to change the subject.

"We should've gone by Lenoir-Rhyne University before we left Hickory," I said. "I would've liked to look around where the other girl was taken."

"Angela Kearn," he said.

I kicked off my shoes and put my feet up on his dashboard. "You really have lived, slept, and breathed this stuff, haven't you?"

"Wouldn't you?" he asked.

"Probably." I looked out of my window up at the night sky. "But I've never had any siblings."

"I didn't know that," he said.

"My parents couldn't have any children of their own," I said.

He looked over at me surprised. "You're adopted?"

I nodded. "I was abandoned at the hospital. You know what's weird?"

He raised his eyebrows in question.

"Warren's adopted. Well, orphaned. He was given away by his birth parents too," I said.

He looked ahead. "That is weird. You both have these crazy abilities and neither of you know your birth parents."

"I keep wondering if we might be related," I said. "Maybe we are brother and sister."

"That would explain a lot." He was silent for a moment, and then he laughed. "I'll keep my fingers crossed."

I pointed at him and smiled. "Don't get your hopes up."

He reached out and playfully grabbed my finger. He held onto it for a little longer than was appropriate, but I didn't stop him.

When we got to my house, he walked me inside and took a look around. The back door was boarded up and held closed with nails. "I haven't forgotten that I promised to fix that," he said.

I laughed as we walked to the front door. "Maybe I'll hold your shirt for ransom till it gets fixed."

He reached up and ran his thumb over the angel pin on my collar. "Keep the shirt. It looks better on you anyway."

He studied my face in the moonlight for a long moment. I might have had the ability to read Nathan's soul, but I had no idea what was on his mind. Gently, he pulled on my collar and touched his lips to mine. Without another word, he was gone.

11.

BY FRIDAY I was caught up on the work that had piled up at the beginning of the week. I wasn't exactly sure how I got it done because my mind seemed to be everywhere else except in the county building. Between Nathan and Warren, I had so much confusion and excitement rolling around in my head that I could hardly think straight.

Just before five o'clock, Nathan walked into my office dressed in black from head to toe. I was a little surprised to see him. "Hey, Nathan."

"Hey," he said. "I know you've got a full weekend, but I was wondering if you wanted to grab a beer before you went home."

I looked up at the clock. "I'm sorry. I don't have time. Do you need something?"

"I was hoping to talk some sense into you, I guess." He was looking at the ground and lightly kicking the toe of his boot against the leg of my desk.

I walked around my desk and pinched his nose. "You're so cute when you're worried," I said in a munchkin voice. "Stop being so paranoid. I will be fine."

He caught me by the arm and looked at me seriously. "The last time you said that, I had to sleep in a chair listening to your IV machine beep all night."

I squeezed his hand. "I'm going to be fine."

As I turned to pick up my purse, he grabbed me by the arm and pulled me back. "We need to talk."

"Then you should've come by earlier. I'm going to be late," I told him.

"Don't go with him, Sloan."

I laughed. "That's not an option, Nathan."

He slid his hand down my arm and tangled his fingers with mine. "Yes, it is an option. Have I been misreading everything with you for the past few weeks?" He took another half-step closer to me and lowered his voice. "I want to be with you."

The space between us was dangerously close, and his eyes were fixed on my mouth. I took a deep breath and backed away from him. "Damn it, Nathan. I can't do this right now! A week ago, yes. A week from now, maybe, but I can't do this today!"

He stepped back and leaned against the wall. "So it's him."

I pulled on his arm. "I don't know if it's him, but I do know that you're with Shannon and I just met Warren. The Shannon thing I could probably overlook—actually, I know I could forget about Shannon—but I *can't* forget about Warren. He is, literally, a once in a lifetime thing for me. It's not fair to anyone if you and I try to do this now and you know it."

He nodded his head, but his jaw was set.

I picked up my purse and stopped in front of him. "Please don't be mad at me."

"I'm not mad at you," he said.

I touched his forearm. "I'm really sorry." And I meant it.

He nodded, but he wasn't happy about it. I locked my office and we walked down the hallway together in silence. He held open the back door and when we walked outside, Warren was leaning against the hood of his muscle car.

Nathan shook his head and slipped on his sunglasses. "Have a good weekend, Sloan," he said and took off in the opposite direction. My shoulders slumped as I watched him jog down the steps and cross the parking lot.

I shook my head and made my way down the steps.

Warren stood and smiled as I approached. His missing soul was still as shocking to me as if he wasn't wearing pants. He was wearing pants, however, blue jeans and a black button-up shirt. His hair was parted just off center and hanging loose to his shoulders.

"I thought you were going to meet me at home," I said when I reached him.

He shrugged. "I got here a little early and I didn't want to wait."

I stepped into his open arms and into the magnetic surge. Every nerve ending inside me began to tingle. Never in my life had I experimented with drugs, but if being with Warren was anything like being high, I had a newfound sympathy for addicts and junkies. I took a deep whiff of his faint cologne. "I'm so glad you're here."

He rested his chin on the top of my head as he held me. "I'm glad you let me come back."

It was hard to pull away from him, but I had to or we would never make it out of the parking lot. I stepped away, but he still gently held onto my wrist. I looked up at him against the setting sun. "Well, what do you want to do this weekend?"

He shrugged and laughed. "I don't know. Know anywhere open on the weekends that does DNA testing?"

I laughed, but it quickly faded. I looked at my watch. "Actually, I do," I said with wide eyes. "Get in the car. We have to go now."

"I was joking," he said.

I shook my head. "I'm not. Come on. My dad's office is open until six, but we've got to hurry."

He opened the passenger side door, and I slid into the warm, black leather seat. The car was immaculate. I thought of the Diet Coke cans and junk mail that littered my car and felt ashamed. He got in and cranked up the engine. The machine roared to life under me. "Where to?" he asked.

"Turn left out of the lot," I said.

He rolled out of the spot and toward the exit.

I trailed my fingers along the soft leather. "This car is awesome."

He smiled. "Yes." He turned left onto the street. "I traded my truck in for it a few months ago."

I scrunched up my nose. "I'm kinda jealous."

He grinned at me. "Where are we going?"

"My father's a doctor. His office is part of a larger medical facility that's associated with the hospital. I know they have a lab somewhere in the building," I said. "Turn right at the light."

Warren looked over at me. "I'm meeting your dad?"

My eyes doubled in size. "Is that OK?"

He laughed. "It's fine with me," he said. "Just be warned, he's not going to approve."

Nervously, I squished my mouth to one side. "My mom will probably be there too."

"OK." He started laughing. "This is an interesting way to start the weekend."

Realizing that I may have just gone way too far way too fast, I reached over and touched his forearm that was stretched toward the gear stick. "We don't have to do this," I said. "Not if you don't want to."

He looked down at my hand and then covered it with his own. "No, I want to know. The sooner the better." He winked an eye at me.

My father's office was located on the third floor of a five story building adjacent to the hospital. When we went inside and walked onto the elevator, Warren leaned against the wall and stared at the floor.

I leaned next to him. "You look nervous."

"I don't like hospitals. I don't like being around dying people," he said. "It feels like it sucks the life out of me."

I looked at my watch again. "They shouldn't be taking any more patients, so it's probably close to empty in there."

With a mechanical ding, the doors opened to the bright and airy hallway. I reached for Warren's hand and exchanged a smile with him at the tingle. I tugged him down the hall. "Come on. It's this way."

I pushed the door open and the petite, brunette receptionist smiled. "Hi, can I help you?" she asked.

"I'm here to see Dr. Jordan," I said.

She looked puzzled and glanced up at the clock on the wall. "Do you have an appointment?"

"I'm his daughter."

She covered her eyes, embarrassed. "Of course you are. I know you from the pictures that your dad has all over his office. I'll let him know you're here."

"Is my mom in today?" I asked.

"She is." She disappeared through the door behind her.

I turned around and Warren raised an eyebrow. "Your dad's secretary doesn't know who you are?" he asked.

"I try to avoid coming here. I had to come a lot when I was a kid, but these old people flock to me and it always makes me uncomfortable," I explained.

"That's interesting," he said.

A moment later, the receptionist reappeared. "Come on back, Sloan," she said.

I nodded and pulled the door in front of us open. My mom was walking toward us wearing white scrubs covered in pink breast cancer ribbons. "Hey, Mom."

Her eyes were puzzled. "Hi, honey. Is everything OK?"

I nodded. "Yeah. I just need a little help with something. Can I talk to Dad?"

"In a minute. He's finishing up with his last patient." She looked at Warren then at me. "Who's your friend?"

"Mom, this is Warren Parish," I said. "Warren, this is my mom, Audrey."

He smiled and offered his hand. "Hi, Mrs. Jordan," he said.

She looked confused, but her smile was genuine. "Nice to meet you, Warren." She looked at me again. "Can I talk to you a second?" she asked, her voice a little higher than usual.

Warren nudged me. "Go ahead. I'm fine."

I stepped across the room and behind a partition near my father's office door. "Who is that?" she asked with wide eyes.

"A new friend of mine. Isn't he cute?" I whispered.

She cocked her head to the side. "Yes, he's handsome, but who is he? And what about Detective McNamara?"

I sighed. "Mom, I'm not dating Nathan."

She put her hands on her hips. "Well, you could have fooled me by the way that boy hovered over you all night at the hospital."

Just then, my dad's office door swung open. A small white-haired woman, with thick pink-framed glasses and blue polyester pants pulled up almost to her chin, stepped out into the hall. A younger woman held her carefully by the arm as she shuffled forward. The old woman saw me and her face lit up.

She stepped toward me with her hands stretched out. She was smiling from ear to ear. "Sloan Jordan!"

My mouth smiled, but my eyes danced with bewilderment and worry. "Hi there."

She took my hands and squeezed them. "You are just as beautiful as you are on the television screen. We saw you carrying that little girl out of that house on the news last week. Your parents must be so proud of you!"

My mother leaned close to the woman's ear. "We are very proud of her!" My mother was over enunciating and almost shouting.

The woman looked at her, obviously annoyed. "Goodness gracious, you don't have to yell, Audrey."

My mother exchanged a puzzled glance with the woman's daughter.

"It's very nice to meet you," I said, stumbling over the end of my sentence because I had no idea how this woman knew me.

She tapped her chest. "I'm Geraldine Flynn. This is my daughter, Ann. It's been wonderful to meet you as well."

My dad's head was peeking around his door. His eyes were wide and glancing between the old woman and my mother. He looked as confused as I felt.

I patted her shoulder politely. "You have a good day now, Mrs. Flynn."

She nodded and Ann took her by the arm and led her across the room.

When she was a few feet away, my mom looked at my dad. "Did you hear that, Robert?"

The old woman stopped short of the door when she neared Warren. She looked back at us. "My ride's here, doctor!" she shouted. "I'm going home with handsome here!"

My father was scratching his head. "Well, that was unusual."

Mom touched the sleeve of his white lab coat. "Did you hear her talking to Sloan?"

"I caught bits and pieces of it," he said.

I looked back and forth at them. "What's going on?"

"I can't tell you because of confidentiality reasons, but she's practically deaf and I haven't heard her that lucid in a very long time," he said.

"Years," my mother added.

Dad shrugged his shoulders, then stepped out of his office and hugged me. "This is a surprise. How are you feeling?"

"I'm fine now. I actually have a reason for being here and it's sort of time-sensitive," I said.

"I assumed you wouldn't show up without needing something," he said with a teasing wink. "What do you need?"

"Can the lab here do DNA testing?" I asked.

He looked puzzled again. "They would have to send it to the hospital, but yes. Why? And who is that man?"

I wished I had prepared more for this conversation. "It's kind of hard to explain, but his name is Warren and we just met recently. Because of some really big similarities, I'm curious to see if he and I might be related to each other."

"Biologically?" he asked surprised.

My mother's mouth fell open. "You want to do a DNA test?"

I nodded. "Yeah. Is that possible? I'll pay whatever it costs."

Dad's brow furrowed. "Why do you think you might be related?"

I shrugged. "We have a lot in common. We both have dark hair and similar skin tone, and he was abandoned when he was a baby a couple of years before I was."

They exchanged awkward looks.

I grabbed my dad's arm. "I know this seems really crazy, but it's really important to me. I need to know, and we've got to do it today because he's only in town for the weekend."

Dad patted my hand. "The results aren't immediate. They will take a few days, but I'll order the test."

I stretched up on my tiptoes and kissed his cheek. "Thank you, Daddy."

He nodded toward Warren. "Well, introduce me at least."

I tugged on his sleeve and Warren met us halfway across the office. My dad extended his hand and Warren shook it. "Warren, is it?" he asked.

Warren nodded. "Yes, you must be Dr. Jordan. Sloan's father."

My dad shook his head. "Call me Robert."

Warren smiled.

Dad looked at the clock. "If you want to make it to the lab, you had better hurry. Your mom will call them on your way."

Mom smiled in agreement.

I kissed his cheek again.

Warren nodded. "Thank you, sir."

Dad looked at me. "Well, my daughter doesn't ask for much, and this must be pretty important to her, so no thanks needed. The lab is on the second floor, on your left when you get off the elevator. Warren, perhaps we will see you again soon."

Warren smiled down at me. "I certainly hope so," he said.

I hooked my arm through Warren's. "Thanks," I said to my parents.

"I'll call you later!"

They both nodded and stared curiously as we left the office.

When we were in the hallway, Warren looked down at me. "Well, that was easy."

I smiled up at him. "I'm a bit of a daddy's girl."

The elevator doors opened and we stepped inside. "He seems like a really good man," he said.

I nodded and punched the button for floor two. "He's the best."

We walked into the lab and a nurse was waiting for us. She was a heavyset black woman who reminded me a bit of Ms. Claybrooks at the jail. "Sloan?" she asked.

"Yes," I said.

She held the door open for us. "Come on back. My name is Joyce. Your mother called to let me know you were on your way up here."

We followed her down the hallway to a sterile white room with a padded blue chair and a large collection of syringes and specimen bottles. Joyce rubbed her hands together. "Who am I sticking first?" she asked.

I looked at Warren. "I'll go first," he said with a touch of reluctance. He unbuttoned his black shirt revealing a white ribbed tank top underneath.

He handed me the shirt and sat down in the chair. She sat down on the office chair in front of him and pulled on some purple rubber gloves. He extended his toned arm out on the armrest and she grabbed it with both hands.

She pulled his arm forwards and gasped with glee. "Look at those beautiful veins!"

He cut his eyes up at her. "So it will be easy?"

She smiled and shook her head in amazement. "Honey, this is like nurse porn right here."

I laughed. "Nurse porn?"

"Heck yeah, girl. I could do this with my eyes closed." She prepared the needle and rubbed alcohol across the bend in his arm.

"Please keep your eyes open," he begged, his voice cracking a little bit.

I stuck out my lower lip. "Oh, are you scared of needles?"

"Shut up," he said, not looking up at me.

The nurse slid the needle into his vein. He cringed and she shook her head. "It's always the big tough ones who freak out on me the most." As the vial was filling, she tapped her finger on the black tribal tattoo that was wound around his bicep and shoulder before it disappeared under his tank top. "Men, all day long, sit through huge tattoos like this but one tiny little stick for blood and they become the biggest babies."

"I'm not a baby," he protested.

I laughed.

She removed the needle and capped the lid on the vial. "All done," she said. "Was that so terrible?" She covered the spot with a cotton ball and a Band-Aid.

"No," he said, but didn't mean it.

Warren got up and I handed him his shirt. He shrugged into it and started securing the buttons as I pushed up the sleeve of my sweater and sat down.

"You're Dr. Jordan's daughter?" Joyce asked.

I nodded. "Yes. My name is Sloan. Can I ask you a question?"

"Sure, honey," she said as she tied a tourniquet above my elbow.

"How accurate is DNA testing?" I asked.

"Depends on what kind. Paternity?" she asked.

I shook my head. "Sibling."

She shrugged. "Pretty accurate. Science is so advanced these days, they can even tell if you're half-siblings or full ones," she said. "Why? Are you two related?"

"We don't know," I answered.

She stuck the needle in my arm and then looked from Warren's face to mine while my blood drained out into her vial. "Nah," she said. "I'd place money on it."

He leaned his shoulder against the wall and crossed one black boot over the other. "You don't think so?" he asked.

She shook her head. "I mean, I don't know for sure, but everything's different. Bone structure, eyes, nose, mouth. Nah. I don't think so."

He stuffed his hands into the pockets on his blue jeans and smiled over at me. "I'm really hoping not."

She smiled. "Oh, I see. Y'all have some Days of our Lives stuff going on."

He laughed. "More like Stephen King stuff."

She removed the needle from my arm and patched me up. "All done. I'll send it over before I leave for the day. I got your information from your mother. I just need his. What's your name, sir?"

"Warren Parish," he said.

"Date of birth?" she asked.

"August 27th, 1984," he answered.

She nodded. "I'm gonna put the same address and phone number." She filled in the blanks on the paperwork in front of her. "I think that's all I need."

I tugged my sleeve down and stood up. "Thank you so much."

She smiled. "Y'all have a good weekend."

We walked out of the office. Warren glanced down at this watch. "Well, I've been here for an hour, and I've met your parents and had my blood taken. This is shaping up to be a very interesting weekend."

I laughed as we got on the elevator. "You hungry?" I asked.

"Starving actually," he answered.

"I say we grab some food to go and find a spot by the river somewhere that we can talk in private," I suggested.

He nodded. "That's a perfect idea."

We picked up fast food sandwiches and drinks and drove out to a picnic area by the French Broad River. There was a father and son fishing from the bank, but other than that we were alone. I sat down on the picnic table and he straddled the bench.

He looked out over the wide river. "This looks like something off of a postcard."

I laughed. "I'm sure this very scene is on many postcards, actually."

Towering red oaks and orange and yellow maple trees dotted the mountains that confined the rushing waters of the river. The water was deep, but just up ahead, huge rocks formed a series of churning rapids. The sun was setting over the jagged Carolina horizon, casting pink and purple streaks across the blue sky.

"What river is this?" he asked.

"The French Broad," I answered. "They say it's the third oldest river in the world."

He looked up at me and cocked an eyebrow. "How do they know that?"

I shrugged my shoulders. "Not a clue."

He laughed and looked out over the water. "Well, it's really pretty."

I nodded and sucked on my straw. "It looks pretty, but don't get in it." I pointed just offshore. "Adrianne and I once saw a cow's head floating right by here."

"Nice." He laughed and took a bite of his sandwich. "Who's Adrianne?"

"She's been my best friend for forever. I'm sure you'll meet her soon." My phone began to ring in my pocket. "Wanna take bets?" I asked with a smile.

"No," he said.

I pulled out the phone and showed him Adrianne's face that was lit up on the screen.

He shook his head and picked up his drink. "That's crazy."

I ignored her call and tucked my phone back into my pocket. "I know."

"How does it work?" he asked.

I shrugged. "I'm not really sure. I figured out a few years ago that it happens more often when I mention someone while picturing them in my mind. It doesn't always happen, but it's becoming more and more frequent that they show up in some way."

"So it's not always in person?" he asked.

"No. Sometimes it's just a phone call or email or on Facebook. Other times, I don't get anything," I said. "I'm not sure why it seems that sometimes I make it happen and other times I can't do it at all."

He thought for a second. "I think whatever we can do is like working out. The more we use our muscles, the stronger they get."

I nodded. "That makes sense. It began getting a whole lot stronger after I finally opened up about it."

He pointed the straw from his drink at me. "You accepted it."

"Yeah."

"Do your parents know?" he asked.

I leaned forward against my knees and told him about what had happened when I was eight. "It was pretty traumatic," I explained. "I learned not to bring it up after all that happened."

He reached up and lightly ran his thumb over the scar on my eyebrow. "I don't blame you." He shifted on the bench. "Only your friend and the detective know?"

"And now you," I added.

He nodded. "I have to ask. What's going on with you and the detective?"

I laughed. "I really don't want to talk about him. We don't need him showing up here right now."

He didn't laugh. "You know we have to talk about him. The two of you seem to have a lot of history."

"Oh no." I feverishly shook my head. "We don't have any history at all. I just met him like a month ago."

His head snapped back with surprise. "Really?"

"Really," I said. "He sort of walked into my life and turned it all upside down."

"He's into you," he said.

"I know. Well, he's been interested in me since you showed up anyway. I think it's a territorial thing," I said. "He has a girlfriend."

"Do you like him?" he asked.

I took a deep breath. "I'm not going to lie to you about it. I've liked him since I met him, but then you showed up."

He nodded. "And complicated things."

I squeezed my eyes closed and smiled. "Definitely complicated things."

He looked up at me and shrugged. "But it might turn out that I'm your brother and that would make things easier for you."

I laughed and threw a pickle at him. "You're not my brother."

He smiled and put his straw to his lips. "I know I'm not."

I finished off the last of my sandwich just as he did, and I got up and carried our trash to the garbage can. As I walked back to the table, he turned around backward on his seat and reached his arms out toward me. I took his hands, and he pulled me close and rested his head against my stomach. I couldn't help but run my fingers through his silky smooth hair as I stood in front of him. His touch was absolutely intoxicating.

"What do you think this is?" He looked up at me, resting his chin on my belly button. "It's like I can't get close enough to you."

I pushed his hair behind his ears. "It's like we're magnets," I said. "I'm the positive. You're the negative. We're drawn together."

He nodded. "That makes a lot of sense actually. We're the same, but we have different purposes."

"And it's really hard to separate us," I added.

He pulled away. "Isn't it? What was up with the headaches?"

I sat down next to him. "I have no idea, but I thought I was dying. My dad said it's called a hemiplegic migraine. The most severe kind there is. I couldn't move or talk for hours."

He shook his head. "Me either, and I was on the interstate. I ended up sleeping in my car for a while."

I shuddered. "I can't even imagine. Nathan called an ambulance to come and get me."

"I hope it's not like that every time I leave," he said. "That will be very problematic till my contract with Claymore ends."

"What do you do exactly?" I asked.

"I'm transitioning out of being a High Threat Personal Security Contractor for Claymore Worldwide Security," he said.

My eyes glazed over. "A what?"

He smiled. "It's a private military company. We're contracted by the US Government and other governments for doing things the regular military can't do," he explained.

"Mercenaries?"

He cringed. "That makes us sound like traitors."

"And you do what exactly?" I asked.

He took a deep breath. "Well, I was just a hired gun when I was recruited in 2010, but two years ago I became a team leader. I just got back from Afghanistan, and I'm filling in as an instructor until my contract ends." He sighed and shook his head. "I'm done with being deployed."

"What did you do in the Marines?" I asked.

"I was a sniper," he answered.

I raised an eyebrow. "Seems a little ironic being what you are, doesn't it?"

He laughed. "I guess it does."

"I want to hear about *that*, too," I said.

"You will. That's more of a 'behind closed doors' conversation, you know?" he said.

I nodded. "Oh, I know."

He looked at me sideways. "That doesn't scare you?"

"It did at first," I admitted. "But people who live in glass houses shouldn't throw stones."

He pointed at me. "You save people. That's quite a bit different."

I smiled and showed him the angel pin on my lapel. "The little girl I pulled out of that attic told me I was her angel."

"Huh." He stood and tugged up his shirt and tank top, displaying the gun on his hip. He pushed his waistband down, and under the holster, tattooed on his side, was the word *Azrael*.

Without thinking, my fingers traced the letters. I looked up at him. "The Angel of Death."

12.

WE LEFT MY car at the office for the evening and went straight to my house. I unlocked the front door and we walked inside. "Home sweet home," I announced.

He stopped at the end of the foyer and looked across the room. "What happened to your back door?"

"That night when I had the migraine, the detective broke it down to get to me," I said. "He patched it up for now."

"I'll fix it before I leave," he said.

I tugged on his arm. "Come on, I'll show you to your room." He followed me toward the stairs.

At the top of the steps was a small hallway. I pointed to the right. "This is my room." I turned to the left. "And this is the guest room and bathroom." I flipped on the light to the small guest bedroom that I had decorated in pastel blues and greens. It reminded me of the beach.

He walked to the queen sized bed and put his tactical black bag on top of the seashell comforter. "It's a nice house," he said.

I leaned against the doorframe. "I like it. I've lived here for a couple of years now. It was the first thing I ever bought that made me feel like a grownup." I motioned toward my room. "I'm going to go change out of my work clothes. Do you think you might want to go out again tonight, or am I safe changing into my comfy clothes?"

He smiled at me. "I didn't come here to see the city, so I would be perfectly happy staying in tonight if that's what you want to do."

"Great." I backed out of the room and into the hallway. "Make yourself at home."

He nodded and I went to my room.

I kicked off my heels, stripped out of my slacks and sweater, and pulled on a pair of blue Victoria's Secret sweatpants, a sports bra, and a black tank top. I stopped in the bathroom to fix my ponytail and brush my teeth before rejoining him downstairs.

Warren was standing in front of my refrigerator laughing when I walked in. He looked at me. "Your fridge looks like mine. Water, cheese, and beer."

"Don't tell my mom." I reached around him and retrieved a beer.

He grabbed one too and followed me to the living room. He nodded to the fireplace. "Want me to build a fire?"

I hesitated. "Ehhh...I haven't used that thing since I moved in. It might burn the house down."

He laughed and picked up the couple of pieces of wood that I brought inside just for looks. "We'll call the fire department if we need to."

I sat down on the sofa and watched him as I drank my beer. He had pulled his hair back and taken off the black shirt, but he was still in the same tank top and blue jeans. His shoulder tattoo apparently went down his arm and completely down his side. I could see a hint of black on his skin through his shirt.

After a few minutes, a flicker of fire began to dance between the logs. He got up and dusted his hands off on his jeans. "See, that wasn't hard." He picked up his beer and joined me on the couch.

"Have you always had long hair?" I asked.

"Oh no. I had to keep it within military regulations for eight years." He gripped his ponytail. "I think this is still out of rebellion."

I laughed. "Makes sense. I like it. It looks really good on you."

"Thanks." He tipped the beer bottle up to his lips then looked over at me. His face was serious. "Are you ready for the conversation to get heavy?"

I tucked my feet under me. "Yes."

"You're sure? He raised an eyebrow. "I've never told anyone what I'm about to tell you."

I swallowed hard but nodded with confidence. "I'm sure." A strange mix of fear and excitement seemed to bubble inside of me.

"And you promise what I say here doesn't leave this room?" he asked. "This is some really bad stuff that I'm getting ready to admit to."

I held out my little finger. "Pinky swear."

He hooked his little finger with mine, spurring another small electric shock. It made him jump a little and he laughed. "I'm not sure I'll ever get used to that."

I rubbed my finger. "Me either."

He blew out a deep breath. "OK. Here goes," he said. "When I was eight, I was in the foster system. Me and this other girl who was seven were living with a couple in the suburbs of Chicago. The woman was all right, but the man gave me nightmares. Just evil at the core. You know what I'm talking about."

I nodded and shivered with familiarity. "Yes."

"The little girl's name was Alice. She and I were in the system together for a while. She was a little slow and had a speech impediment, but she was really nice to me when a lot of the other kids weren't. After we had been there for about a month, the man started picking us up from school. We would go to the house and he would take her into his room," he said.

I put my hand over my mouth and closed my eyes.

"Well, you can guess," he said. "I didn't know what was happening, but I knew this guy was a monster. Alice began to shut down. She cried a lot and wouldn't talk to me or play with me anymore."

My heart was pounding, and my stomach churned with nausea.

"One day, we came home from school, and he started to take her to his room. She started crying. I yelled and told him to stop. He said that he might have to make me come too. I started crying. Alice was sobbing. I just knew, even at eight, that he shouldn't be allowed to be alive. I screamed, and there was a crack that reverberated around the room. It sounded like lightning striking a tree. The guy fell to his knees and face-planted on the carpet. I took Alice by the hand and we ran to the neighbor's house." He paused and took a deep breath.

"He was dead?" I asked.

He nodded. "His heart stopped."

I sat back and rolled my head against the cushion. "That's horrific."

"I knew, even then, I had done it," he said. "I tried to tell my caseworker I had caused it, but of course he didn't believe me."

"Of course," I said.

"After that, Alice and I were split up and sent to different foster homes. Then when I was fourteen, I was sent to a group home in the city," he said. "No families ever kept me for longer than six months because everyone seemed to be afraid of me."

I rested my head on my hand. "That must have been traumatic."

He nodded. "In a way, but there was this huge part of me that was so fiercely protective of other people. I knew I wasn't a bad person. I never felt like a bad kid." He took another long sip from the bottle. "Then, when I was sixteen, me and a couple of the other boys from the group home went to the movies. They embodied all the horror stories you hear about system kids. Smoking, drinking, drugs, gangs... you name it. But they were the only people that didn't seem to mind being around me.

"After the movie was over, we were supposed to walk home, but they decided to follow this girl who had left alone. I think she must have lived close by. They cornered her in this alley. I grabbed one of them, this kid named Rex, by his hair and threw him backward. The other guy, Travis, lunged at the girl and shoved her into the corner of this dumpster. It split her head open pretty bad. Travis jumped on top of her and pounded her in the face. Rex had me by the back of the shirt, but I was focused on Travis. He was going to kill that girl if I didn't stop him. Then there was another crack like lightning."

"And it stopped his heart," I said.

He nodded. "Rex was so shocked that he backed off. When I turned toward him, he took off running."

"What happened to the girl?" I asked.

"I picked her up and carried her to the gas station around the corner. They called 911, and I took off into the streets before the police arrived. I'm pretty sure she lived though," he said.

I rubbed my hands over my face. "Wow."

He finished his beer and placed the empty bottle on the floor beside him. "I made it on the streets till I turned eighteen and could join the military. That was my only way out."

"And you became a sniper," I said.

He shrugged his shoulders. "I was already a killer."

I shook my head. "No you weren't. You were a savior."

He turned his palms up. "It doesn't feel that way when you know you've stopped a beating heart."

I let out a long puff of air. "How many times have you done it?"

"Nine times," he said. "Three of them at once in Iraq in 2006."

"I guess that ability comes in handy during wartime," I said.

He nodded. "Yes, it does."

"How does it work? Can you do it at will now?" I asked.

"I wouldn't say 'at will' exactly, but I can do it when I have no other choice," he said.

"Whatever happened to Alice?" I asked.

He took a deep breath and leaned his head back on the couch. After a moment of awkward silence it became clear that he didn't want to talk about her.

I put my hand on his. "It's OK. You don't have to tell me."

He sighed and shook his head. "No, I need to tell you," he said. "Alice is dead."

My head snapped back with surprise. "How?"

He was silent again. He looked down at his hands and then back up at me. There were tears brimming along the edges of his dark eyes. "I killed her."

I swallowed hard but didn't release his hand. "How did it happen?"

"I didn't see her again until after I ran away from the group home. When I found her, she was holed up in a crack house on the wrong side of the city. I stayed with her for a while and tried to help get her cleaned up, but one night I came back from buying us food and she was overdosing on something. I still don't know what she took." He dropped his head.

His hand was sweaty in mine.

"She was choking to death on her own vomit and convulsing. I tried to clear her airway, but there was too much," he said. "I could feel her slipping away, and I knew she was in pain. I didn't have a phone to call for help. No one else was there. So I stopped it."

I put my arms around his neck and pulled him close to me. I didn't know if he was crying, but his breaths were rapid and shallow. Uncontrollable tears were dripping off my cheeks. "You didn't kill her." I shook my head. "You helped her find peace. No one should die in that much pain."

He didn't move for the longest time. Neither did I. I just raked my nails through his hair, till his breathing returned to normal. He was just a kid when Alice died. She had been his only semblance of family.

Suddenly, I felt guilty for having such a charmed life growing up. Warren and I may have had our similarities, but he had lived through things worse than anything I could even imagine.

Finally, he straightened and wiped at his eyes. "She was the one I told about what I could do. She was the only person until now who ever knew."

I tucked his hair behind his ear. "Warren, I'm so sorry."

He nodded. "I am too. I've always felt so responsible for her. I should've protected her when we were in that awful house together. I should've been able to save her when she died." He sniffed.

I shook my head. "It wasn't your responsibility."

"Wasn't it?" he asked, his voice full of sincere doubt.

"No," I said. "You were a kid. No kid should carry that much."

He nodded, but he wasn't convinced. Perhaps he never would be.

After a while, his shoulders seemed to relax. "Wow, I've never told that stuff to anyone."

"It will never leave this room," I promised.

He smiled. "I know." He stared at me for a minute. "All this time, I thought I was all alone. I thought I would always be alone, carrying this shit around with me."

I tangled my fingers with his and remembered the sting of my face being split open on the third grade play ground. I kissed his knuckles and whispered, "Never again."

Our conversation took a lighter turn after that and I told him about growing up in Asheville and about college at UNC. I told him about Ms. Claybrooks at the jail and about wishing syphilis on Nathan's girlfriend. We laughed and talked until almost two in the morning.

Finally, he yawned and he shook his head. "I don't want to, but I have to go to bed. I've been up since four this morning." He looked down at the large black watch encircling his wrist. "That's almost twenty-four hours ago."

"You're right. I don't want to sleep the day away tomorrow," I said.

He stood up and offered me his hand. "What's on the agenda for tomorrow?"

I shrugged. "I don't know. Maybe matching tattoos or running away to Mexico."

He laughed and pulled me to my feet. "I would go with you to Mexico."

I smiled and he followed me upstairs. When we reached the top, I turned toward him. "Well, goodnight, Warren."

He leaned down and pressed a kiss to my forehead. "Goodnight, Sloan."

I went to my room and left the door cracked open. I brushed my teeth and climbed under the sheets and the down blanket. My brain was spinning, sleep nowhere to be found. My body twisted under the covers. I hugged my pillow and pushed it aside. I rolled to the other side of the mattress. I kicked my blanket off only to wrap it around my legs again.

My Xanax was in my purse downstairs. A full tablet would lull me into a coma. As I contemplated the hangover it would cause the next morning, my bedroom door creaked open, and Warren crept inside.

"You OK?" I asked across the moonlit room.

"Yeah." He was slowly walking toward me. "I'm coming to ask your forgiveness."

I watched over my shoulder as he stopped at the edge of my bed. "Ask my forgiveness for what?"

He lifted the covers and lay down behind me. His arm slipped around my waist, and he rested his head on my pillow. "You're going to have to forgive me for climbing into your bed," he whispered. He pulled me tight against his body, making the bed hum with electricity.

I hadn't slept that well in years.

* * *

The sound of a hammer downstairs jarred me from a deep sleep the next morning. I was alone in my bed. While our 'sleeping together' was confined to the very literal sense of the phrase, my body was so exhaustively satisfied that my brain couldn't help but wander to all sorts of 'what if' fantasies. My toes curled at the thought.

The scent of fresh coffee urged my unwilling body parts out of the bed, and my legs wobbled as I took the first step toward the bathroom. My muscles felt like Jell-O.

Downstairs, Warren was pounding nails into a new door frame around my back door. "Where did you get the tools?" I asked at the bottom of the steps.

He looked up and smiled. "I had to go buy them, but I rented the saw. Good morning," he said.

"Good morning. How long have you been up?" I crossed the room toward the kitchen.

"I slept in and got up around seven," he said.

I laughed. "Seven is sleeping in?"

"I'm always up by four," he replied.

I shook my head and pulled a coffee mug out of the cabinet. "And you made coffee? I could get used to this."

I carried the coffee to the living room and stretched out on the couch. He was in his white tank top, and I admired watching his biceps flex as he used the hammer.

He caught me grinning. "What are you doing?" he asked.

I blushed over the rim of my mug. "Enjoying the view."

He laughed. "I had to get you a new door. The other one was broken beyond repair. McNamara must have kicked it in."

"Probably. He's like a bull in a china shop sometimes," I said. "Let me know how much I owe you, and I'll pay you back."

"Shut up." He swung the door back and forth. "How did you sleep?"

I moaned and stretched my head back. "Better than I ever have in my life."

He smiled. "Me too."

The doorbell rang. I sat up to answer it, but he held out his hand to stop me. "I can get it."

He opened the door, and Adrianne froze when she saw Warren. "Uh, who are you?" she asked with wide eyes.

"It's OK!" I called out to her. "I'm in here."

She looked Warren up and down as she crept past him.

"Warren, that's my best friend Adrianne," I said. "Adrianne, that's Warren."

He shook her hand. "I've heard a lot about you," he said.

Her mouth was hanging open. "I haven't heard a word about you." She looked at me for an answer.

"Sure you have!" She slowly sank down on the couch beside my feet and I leaned toward her. "He's the guy I was looking for at the festival last weekend."

"The one that you said reminded you of a corpse? Now he's here installing a door." She dropped her head to one side, her eyes bewildered. "I'm so freaking confused right now."

"I tried to call you Wednesday night to explain, but you didn't answer or call me back," I said. "A lot has happened since Sunday."

Warren laughed and returned to fixing the door. "That's an understatement."

She put her purse on the coffee table and crossed her legs. "Please catch me up," she begged.

"I met Warren last Sunday. Remember me trying to explain to you at the festival that I couldn't read him?" I asked.

"Yeah," she said.

I nudged her in the thigh with my toe. "He's like me. That's why I couldn't tell anything about him."

"He can do your weird voodoo stuff?" she asked.

"Yeah. More or less," I said.

She rubbed her forehead. "I'm so lost."

I took a deep breath. "Let me see if I can sum this all up. Warren lives near the beach. He saw me on the news. He couldn't read me, like I couldn't read him, so he came here to find me. On Sunday night, I came home and he was here."

She looked at Warren. "Did you break in her house?" She pointed to the door.

I shook my head. "No, Nathan did."

"The detective? Why did he break in your house?" she asked, her voice jumping up an octave.

"To take me to the hospital," I said.

"Hospital?!" she shrieked.

I looked at Warren who was leaning against the door laughing.

"This really isn't making any sense is it?" I asked him.

He shook his head. "The more you talk, the crazier you sound."

Adrianne picked up her keys and shook her head. "Maybe I should leave and come again later. I was just stopping by to see if you wanted to grab breakfast. My brain is not nearly awake enough to handle this kind of information."

I laughed. "No. Stay," I said trying to hold her with my feet.

"I'm assuming he stayed here last night?" she asked, pointing to my pajamas.

"Yes."

"Are you like *together* now?" she asked.

Warren lost his composure and burst out laughing again. "Not until we find out if I'm her brother!"

I doubled over and buried my face in my knees. "Ha!"

She stood up. "I've got to be in the wrong house."

I reached out and grabbed her by the arm. "I'm sorry. This sounds a whole lot worse than it really is."

"I hope so," she said as I pulled her back to the couch.

I rested my head on her shoulder. "He's really great and you're going to love him."

She looked down at me and then over at Warren. "You're talking about him like he's a puppy."

He shook his head. "I am certainly not a puppy." He knocked his knuckles against the door. "I'm going to clean this mess up and jump in the shower. Maybe that will give you enough time to fill Adrianne in."

"OK," I said. He winked at me before he walked outside.

In a slower version, I recapped the events of the week for my friend until she finally understood some of what I was saying. When I was done, she shook her head. "You're such a freak. Only this kind of crap happens to you."

I nodded. "I know."

"When do you find out the DNA test results?" She pointed up the stairs. "Because if he is your brother, I'm totally going to ask him out."

"He's hot, isn't he?" I asked.

"Smoking hot," she said. "What does he do?"

"He's a sniper," I said with a wild, excited smile.

She sighed and rolled her eyes. "Of course he is."

"Oh, guess what else?" I asked.

She held up her palms and shook her head. "There is absolutely no telling."

I punched her in the shoulder. "In the past week, the hot detective kissed me *twice*." I waved two fingers in front of her face. "Twice, Adrianne!"

She laughed. "No way."

"Yep. He is crazy jealous," I said.

"So you already have a backup plan."

"Nathan isn't a backup plan," I said. "I really don't think Warren and I are related."

She smiled. "For your sake, I hope not. For my sake, I'm going to pray that you are."

I laughed and kicked her in the thigh.

Warren came down a few minutes later with wet hair, wearing a fitted gray thermal shirt and jeans. He sat down on the love seat and placed his black boots on the floor beside him. "Did you ladies get everything figured out?"

"I think so." Adrianne sighed. "That's a pretty unbelievable story."

He laughed. "Which part?"

"All of it." She stood up and slung her purse over her shoulder. "Well, I'm going to take off. Warren, it was really great to meet you."

Warren and I stood up. He wrapped his arms around me from behind. "You too, Adrianne. I'm sure I'll be seeing you again soon," he said.

She smiled. "I'm sure you will." She pointed at me. "You and I are having lunch on Monday, and I want every detail of how the rest of this weekend plays out."

Warren looked from her down at me. "What's happening the rest of the weekend?"

Adrianne shook her head. "With this girl, you never know. She's a complete freak of nature."

"Bye," I said with a little wave. "I'll call you later."

When she was gone, I sat down and Warren stretched out on the sofa, resting his head in my lap.

"You're all wet," I said, running my nails through his hair.

He smiled up at me. "You don't care."

He was right.

I looked down at him. "You know, I think you're wrong."

He angled his neck to look at me. "Wrong about what?"

"About nobody liking you. Neither Mom, Dad, or Adrianne seemed freaked out by you at all. Adrianne even says she's going to ask you out if it turns out we're related."

He laughed. "Really?"

"Yup," I said.

"I think it's really strange. Everyone I've met with you has made me feel...normal. They don't automatically dislike me," he said. "Except Detective McNamara. He clearly doesn't like me."

I laughed. "That's a testosterone issue."

"That's probably part of it," he agreed.

"You know, I wonder if we sort of neutralize each other. Like, maybe you're more likable around me," I said.

"People don't seem to like you any less with me around," he said.

"That's because I'm adorable." I said as I batted my eyelashes down at him.

He chuckled. "That you are." He closed his eyes. "Tell me about this serial killer case. We haven't discussed that subject much."

It took a while, but I relayed all of the information that Nathan had given me.

"I've heard about some of those missing girls," he said. "I wasn't aware they were related to anything else."

"Well, that's just all coming together now," I said.

"So they are all about the same age, race, and similar appearance. Anything else?" he asked.

"Yes. They were all kidnapped—and I assume killed—during the fall and winter months. September through December," I said.

"Huh. That's interesting," he said.

"It's very interesting," I agreed. "Have you ever met a serial killer in person?"

He shrugged. "That's a pretty vague definition. I've met many people who have murdered more than one person."

"No, I mean like the sick and twisted Ted Bundy type," I said.

He thought for a moment. "There was one guy over in Afghanistan. He went nuts and killed a bunch of civilians while I was doing private security work. He was pretty twisted," he said.

"Do you think that killing someone always reads the same when we look at them?" I asked.

He shrugged. "Considering how many people I've taken out, I certainly hope not. I do know there's a big difference between me looking at my comrades who have fought and killed in war and a guy that shot a bunch of kids in their sleep."

I thought about it. "I've always assumed that it is something to do with the soul that I can detect. The actual essence of a person that thinks, makes decisions, and experiences emotions."

"I can get on board with that theory, but I don't think that people are born good or evil. I think their choices determine which side of the moral divide they fall on," he said. "I've never met a little kid who felt dark."

"Me either," I agreed.

"So the choices people make taint their souls," I said.

He nodded. "I think so because some people are definitely more evil than others."

Warren continued. "And some people that I've known for several years have become more evil over time."

"Yeah, I'm beginning to notice that more and more," I said.

He looked up at me. "Because you're paying more attention and trying to figure it out now. I told you, it's like exercise."

"That's why you're so much better at everything than I am?" I asked. "You've been practicing it longer?"

"Having the power to end someone's life kinda makes you want to work at mastering it," he said. "You don't want that kind of loose cannon flailing around."

"Makes sense," I said.

He pointed at me. "Here's a bigger question. If it is their souls that we can see, does that mean you and I don't have souls since we can't read each other?"

I raised my eyebrows. "That's scary."

He smiled. "I wouldn't be surprised if I didn't have a soul."

I shook my head. "Shut up." I drummed my nails on his chest, and my thoughts returned to the girls who were missing. "Do you really think that if we found a suspected area that you could tell if there was a dead body there?"

He closed his eyes as I played with his hair. "Absolutely."

I shuddered at the thought of feeling death everywhere I went. "I know you said it isn't a big deal, but that has to be creepy."

"I'm pretty used to it," he said.

I scrunched up my nose. "I'll bet you freak out around cemeteries."

He laughed. "Not exactly."

I shook my head. "I don't want to talk about murders and death anymore. What do you want to do today?"

He didn't open his eyes. "I'm doing it right now."

I rubbed my hands down his chest. "I say, we go get some food, maybe pick up some movies from Redbox, and then spend the rest of the day doing exactly this."

He smiled and pushed himself up. "I can get on board with that plan."

We drove to the Sunnyside Cafe for breakfast, and on the way home, we stopped at the gas station near my house to pick up some movies from Redbox. "I think I'm going to get some more beer. What do you want?" I asked.

He was pulling the movies out of the kiosk. "Hold on, I'll come with you."

The door chimed as we walked into the store. I retrieved a six pack of Highland Brewing's Pale Ale, grabbed a bag of Doritos, and followed Warren to the counter. A burly man wearing camouflage pants with suspenders was ahead of us in line.

Warren leaned down close to my ear. "Do you think if I moved up here, I could pull off wearing those pants?" he whispered.

I honestly thought Warren could pull off a burlap sack if he really wanted to. I motioned toward the window, drawing his attention to the camouflage truck parked at the gas pump. "Only if you get the truck to go with them," I said.

He laughed.

I cut my eyes at him. "More important than the pants, what is this you say about moving here?"

He shrugged his broad shoulders. "It's just a thought. I don't wanna keep driving back and forth forever."

I smiled but didn't say anything.

"What's there to do around here?" he asked. "Sell me on Asheville, and don't talk about the leaves changing colors. I don't give a shit about leaves."

I laughed. "Well, the only things to do around here in the fall, besides looking at leaves, are hunting and watching football. If you're not into either of those, you're screwed in the fall and the winter."

A bell *dinged* in my mind.

"I thought you guys have some ski slopes around here—" he began.

I held up my hand to silence him. "Hold on. When is hunting season?"

His face twisted with confusion. "What?"

I tugged on his sleeve. "Seriously! When is hunting season?"

"Well, it depends on what you're hunting. Deer season is the biggest sport, and it usually runs from September to January depending on what weapon you're using and where you are in the state. Why?"

My eyes widened. I put the beer on the counter and gripped his forearms. "September to December!" I almost shouted at him. "The murders happen during deer season! The killer is a hunter!"

13.

"NATHAN, ARE YOU at home?" I shouted into the phone as I buckled my seatbelt.

"I just got back. Why?" he asked. "Are you all right?"

"Warren and I are on our way to your house." I looked at Warren and moved the phone away from my mouth. "Turn right."

"Umm...excuse me?" Nathan asked.

"Nathan, I know what the connection is with the dates," I said. "The killer is a hunter! These girls are buried in the woods. I need a topographical map and a list of hunting areas. We'll be there in ten minutes." I disconnected the call before he had the chance to object.

I looked over at Warren. "Are you sure you don't mind?" I asked. "I wouldn't do this if it weren't a big deal."

He shook his head. "No, I get it. I'm not sure if McNamara is going to let me in the house though."

"He will if he wants my help," I said. "Take the next left."

Nathan was brooding when he answered the door, but he nodded hello to Warren and let us inside. He motioned toward the office. "Come on back."

He had a topographical map up on the board with pins stuck in the areas where the girls disappeared. "Did you get the list?" I asked.

He nodded. "It's on the computer," he said. "What is all this about?"

"Remember how we said all this time that this killer is seasonal?" I reminded him. He nodded and I gripped his forearm. "Hunting season is during the same time frame. That's the only thing that has made any sense to me so far about this whole case!"

He laughed and crossed his arms over his chest. "That's a long shot, Sloan."

"Maybe," I agreed, looking down at the computer screen. "But it's better than any other lead we've had."

Nathan stepped over behind me. "But deer season is the busiest time of the year in those woods. Why would the killer hide bodies during such a high time of traffic? And how would he do it without being seen?" Nathan shook his head. "That doesn't make sense."

"I think the idea has some merit," Warren said. "If I were going to bury bodies in the woods, I would do it when I knew a lot of different tracks were going to be covering up mine. Also, the wildlife service makes sure the woods are cleared of poachers every day at sundown, so witnesses wouldn't be likely."

Nathan turned and shot him a hateful glare "Given this a lot of thought, have you?"

I punched him in the arm. "Shut up. He's just trying to help."

"He shouldn't be here," Nathan mumbled.

That was it. I whirled around at him. "OK. I'm putting an end to this crap right now!" I pointed at Warren who was sitting on the couch eating my bag of Doritos. "Let me remind you, Detective, that this man wouldn't be here if it weren't for *you*. You put me in the middle of the media spotlight and he saw me. That's not his fault. And neither of us are here because this is what we want to be doing right now. As much as I like you, Nathan, I would really rather be working on my own mystery that I've been trying to solve all my life —figuring out what I am! We are here because you begged for my help on this case. So you can either stop being a jackass right now, or I'm walking and you're on your own."

By the end of my rant, both of their mouths were hanging open.

I leaned toward him. "Do we understand each other?"

He nodded, snapping his mouth shut.

I put my hands on my hips and looked back at the map. "Now, where was I?"

"Poachers," Warren answered with a mouthful of chips.

"Right." I tapped my fingernail on the computer screen. "If we try and narrow these down to a small search field, we can check it out and see what we find."

"You don't want to start here in Asheville," Nathan said. "There's way too much hunting ground here to cover."

I looked at the map. "Which of these areas where girls went missing has the least amount of hunting land?"

"Raleigh," they said at the same time.

I looked at Nathan. "Where can you hunt around Raleigh?"

"Private or public?" he asked.

"Public," Warren answered. "If it's the same guy, nobody has access to private hunting land all over the state."

Nathan squeezed his eyes shut. "OK, public game lands would be Jordan Lake or Butner-Falls around Raleigh." He grabbed a marker and circled the areas on the map. "Butner-Falls would be closest to the murders, but we're talking about an area of about ten square miles."

"Minus the water," I said. "Wait. Could the bodies have been dumped in the water?" I looked between the two of them as I waited for an answer.

Warren shook his head. "Very doubtful. I imagine that river system has a really fluctuating current. Even if someone weighed down the body, chances are still high that it would eventually surface when it was swept to the smaller waterways."

"So, ten square miles minus the water," I said.

Warren crossed the ankle of his boot over his knee. "We could cover that in a day. We won't need to hike all of it."

"We?" Nathan asked, surprised.

Warren shrugged. "You can't exactly call in a search team with our unreasonable suspicion. So yeah, I'll do it if you want my help."

I leaned against the desk. "Warren, is there any kind of time limit on these bodies? The ones in Raleigh disappeared about thirteen years ago."

He shook his head. "There's no expiration date on death."

Nathan and I both halted at his statement. "Good point," Nathan finally said.

"I'm heading that way tomorrow. If you guys want to come, you can ride back together, and I can go on home," Warren offered.

I held my hands up in the air. "We're doing this?"

Nathan put his hands on his hips and shook his head. "This is such a long shot."

"I think she's on to something," Warren said.

I wrung my hands. "I'm right. I know I am."

Nathan sighed. "Yeah. Let's do it. One big happy family going on a hike in the woods."

I clapped my hands together and squealed.

"We're going to need some supplies if we're going to be trekking through the woods all day," Warren said. "I didn't bring any gear with me."

"I've got a couple of packs we can take," Nathan said. "Sloan, do you have any hiking boots?"

I laughed. "Nope."

"Where is a sporting store around here?" Warren asked.

"River Hills," I answered.

"Good. We'll need some hunter safety orange this time of year too," Warren said.

"We can go do some shopping on the way home," I told him.

Nathan leaned against his desk. "What time do you want to head out tomorrow?"

Warren shrugged. "I'm up at four."

"Five, then?" Nathan asked. "That would put us there by nine."

I frowned. "Five in the morning?"

"I promise you'll live, babe," Warren said. He stood up and offered his hand to Nathan. "See you in the morning, then?"

Nathan hesitated for a moment looking down at Warren's outstretched hand. I elbowed him in the ribs, and he finally shook it. "Yeah. See you in the morning. Thanks," he said.

Warren and I left Nathan's house and went shopping for hiking supplies before picking up dinner and returning to my house. "I'm sorry our day on the couch got pretty screwed up," I said as we lugged bags up my front steps.

"I'm here. That's all that matters," he said.

I unlocked the front door and smiled at him. "You're pretty remarkable."

He smirked. "No, I'm not."

"Yes, you are. You hardly know me, and yet you're willing to go to all this trouble for me and another guy that you don't even like. That's really impressive." We walked inside and I flipped on the light.

He placed the bags in his hands behind the sofa and carried the beer to the refrigerator. "I think even though it's only technically been a week, I know you pretty well." He smiled over at me. "And this is important to you and you're important to me."

"Just know I really appreciate it," I said. "Nathan does too, even if he's kind of an ass about it."

He started laughing as we went to the living room. "Holy crap, you went off on him back there. That was one of the sexiest things I've ever seen in my life."

I put the movies we had picked out on top of the DVD player. "He deserved it. Everything that has happened here recently really is all of his doing."

He groaned and hooked a finger in my belt loop, turning me around to face him. "Oh, don't say that. I don't want to have to be grateful to him at all for bringing us together when I know he's trying to work his way in here when I'm not around."

I put my hands on his strong chest. "Nobody is going to be doing anything when you're not around." I looked up at him and motioned between us. "This is different."

He nodded and rested his forehead against mine. "*Different* doesn't even begin to cover what this is."

I closed my eyes and mindlessly traced my fingernails up his forearms. "We've still got to take this really slow until we know for sure."

"Sloan." His voice was commanding.

I looked at him.

He cupped my face in his strong hands.

When his lips touched mine, the rest of the world was obliterated. Every nerve in my body pulsed with energy as I melted into him. His fingers tangled in my hair and pulled my head back, forcing my mouth to open for him. I could no longer tell where his lips ended and mine began.

After what felt like an eternity that could never last long enough, he broke the kiss. The break in energy was like a shower of ice water. We were both breathless.

His deep voice was rough and desperate. "If we don't stop now, I'm not going to be able to."

"That was…"

"I know," he whispered.

* * *

Warren didn't sleep in my bed that night. We possessed superpowers, but defying temptation after that kiss wasn't one of them. There was a fine line between 'playing it safe' and 'who cares if it might be incest', and that line was sandwiched between Warren Parish's perfect lips. That mind-blowing kiss was the first thought in my head when I woke up to the sound of a knock at my door the next morning.

"You awake?" Warren asked.

He was already showered and dressed in the tactical pants and black and bright orange pullover he had purchased the night before. I groaned and rolled over away from him. His boots clunked against the hardwood as he crossed my bedroom.

"What time is it?" I asked into the dark.

"4:15," he answered. "I let you sleep in a little longer."

"Fifteen minutes. You're not very generous," I whined.

The bed sank under his weight, and he ran his hand along my back. "How did you sleep?" he asked.

"Terribly." I thought of how well I had slept in his arms before. "You ruined me."

"I slept like crap too." He began massaging the muscles around my spine. "Come on. I made coffee."

I felt him move to get up, so I twisted my arm around and grabbed a handful of the front of his shirt. I pulled him toward me and he leaned down over my back.

His hand slid along the length of my arm till his fingers tangled with mine underneath my cushy pillow. "This is a bad idea," he moaned.

His warm breath dampened my skin as he dragged his lips across my neck.

"I don't care," I said.

For a second, I felt his weight press into me, but he quickly pushed himself off the bed. I rolled onto my back and looked up at him. He put his hands on his hips and shook his head. "You've got to get out of that bed, *right now.*"

I smiled.

He pointed at me. "Get up. I'm going downstairs." He turned on his heel and left my room before I could tempt him any further.

When I came downstairs, ten minutes later, he was leaning against the kitchen counter drinking a cup of coffee. He smiled over the top of the mug. "Good morning, you evil woman."

I yawned and reached for an empty mug. "There is no such thing as a good morning."

He wrapped his arms around my waist from behind. "That's not entirely true. For a moment there, I was very tempted to make this a really good morning," he said, his lips against my ear.

I poured my coffee and smiled over my shoulder. "You know, it's not too late to say screw it all and go back to bed."

He pulled away and pointed at me again. "Don't even start."

I laughed and looked at the clock on the oven. "I'm surprised Nathan isn't here yet."

The doorbell rang. Warren shook his head and pushed passed me, smacking me on the backside as he went. "Adrianne's right. You are a freak."

"Those are big words coming from the guy who can sniff out dead bodies," I teased.

Warren chuckled as he pulled the front door open. "Morning," he said, stepping aside.

Nathan walked in. "Morning." He wiped the bottom of his boots on the welcome mat. "It's pouring out there."

Warren followed him to the kitchen. "I checked the weather in Raleigh. This storm will be there by the time we get there," he said.

I frowned. "Ugh."

"It will be better for us. There won't be as many hunters in the woods," Warren said. "I'd rather get wet than get shot."

Nathan laughed. "For real." Nathan's eyes fell on my new back door. He put his hand on his hip and glared in my direction. Under the brim of his ball cap his eyes echoed the patch on his hat that read, 'Whiskey. Tango. Foxtrot.'

"Want some coffee?" I asked, smiling like I was oblivious to the insult that had just occurred.

He shook his head. "Thanks. I've got some in my truck." He produced a large paper book from his jacket. "I talked to some buddies of mine last night and asked them where the most heavily tracked parts of the game land are. I figured those should be the last places we should check. I also picked up this book of hunting maps last night."

Warren nodded. "That's good." He pointed to the book. "May I?"

Nathan handed it to him. "Have you been there before?"

Warren shook his head. "No, but I'm no stranger to the woods."

I raised my hand. "I have a question. What are we going to do if we actually find something today? We can't exactly say we were out hiking in the rain and happened upon it." I looked at Nathan. "Not with you being so close to the case."

Warren flipped through the book. "I figured that out last night," he said. "I can call it in after you guys leave. I will say I was on my way home from visiting my girlfriend and was scouting the woods for escape and evasion drills in the spring."

Nathan crossed his arms over his chest. "Your girlfriend or your sister?"

I pointed at Nathan. "Don't start."

Warren was smiling down at the book.

I pushed away from the counter and stretched my arms up over my head. "Come on boys. I didn't get up before the sun to stand around chatting in my kitchen. If we hang out here much longer, I'm going back to bed."

It was a four hour drive to Raleigh. It rained the entire way. Thankfully, when we pulled into a parking area at Butner-Falls, the storm had minimized to a drizzle. The parking lot was almost empty. Nathan pulled his blue four-door truck up beside us, and we got out of the car. When we stopped in Winston-Salem, Warren let me drive the Challenger the rest of the distance. I didn't think I would ever be satisfied with my car again.

Warren spread out the map on the hood of Nathan's truck. "I went over this on the way here. I think we should hit these areas first." He was pointing to three red circles he had drawn on the map. "Coupled with the list you provided, these areas are the most secluded. There are few trails for hikers to come stumbling through, and they are heavily wooded with lots of ground covering."

I adjusted the ball cap I had stolen out of the back seat of Nathan's truck. "If there aren't any trails, how are we going to find our way through the woods and back again?"

Warren and Nathan looked at each other and smiled for the first time ever at each other. "I think we'll be OK," Nathan said.

Warren made some notes on the map, and we started off into the woods.

I shook my head. "This feels like the set up to a really bad, B-rated horror movie. 'A sniper, a detective, and a publicist go into the woods…'"

Nathan laughed behind me. "Or a really bad joke."

I peeked over my shoulder at him. "Speaking of really bad jokes, how's your girlfriend?"

He stuck his middle finger up in the air and I laughed.

"Who do we think is buried out here anyway?" Warren asked over his shoulder.

"My sister," Nathan answered.

Warren turned around so suddenly that I slammed into his chest. "Oh shit. Seriously?" he asked.

Nathan nodded. "She's been missing for almost thirteen years."

"Man, I'm sorry. I had no idea." Warren shook his head and turned away again. "I was wondering why you are working on a case in Raleigh when you live in Asheville."

"He's been working on it his whole career," I said.

"Haven't had any good information until I met Sloan," Nathan said. "We didn't even know they were all dead."

"But you still don't know that they are all connected, right?" Warren asked.

"No, but it seems that they are," Nathan said.

"Follow your gut, man. If I've learned anything being whatever it is that I am, it's to follow your gut," Warren said.

After a half an hour of walking seemingly nowhere, I asked, "How big is that circle?" All I could see were trees in every direction.

"About a hundred and fifty acres," Warren answered over his shoulder.

"Um, I'm no expert, but I'm pretty sure that's a little bigger than a football field," I said.

"It's about a hundred football fields," Nathan said.

My mind flashed back to grueling laps around the football field during high school cheerleading practice. Back then, the terrain was flat and there were cute football players to discuss with Adrianne. Butner-Falls was cold and wet and without a level concrete path. The eye candy was definitely sufficient, but even the view of Warren from behind wasn't able to distract me from the dread of trekking through a hundred mountainous football fields in the rain. I wondered how much sweet-talking it would take to get one of my companions to give me a piggy-back ride.

I was really beginning to doubt myself and my theory about the murders when Warren finally stopped in a clearing with a view of the lake and shook his head. "There's nothing here," he said. "It's not this section."

I almost burst into tears.

"How do you know?" Nathan asked.

Warren turned and took my hand as he led me past Nathan. "The same way Sloan knew those girls were dead."

"You just know?" Nathan asked with an arrogant tone.

"I just know," Warren repeated.

"Sloan, why can't you do this?" Nathan asked.

I shrugged my shoulders. "I don't know. Why can't you do it?"

He smirked. "Funny," he said. "You know, not too long ago I was a real detective who did real police work. Now I'm wandering around the woods in the rain looking for dead bodies with two psychics."

"Ick," I said. "Don't use that word."

"I hate it." Warren laughed and looked down at me. "It always makes me want to break out singing, 'That's What Friends are For' by Dionne Warwick."

"That singer with the Psychic Friends Network?" Nathan asked.

"Ha! Yes," I answered. I smiled up at Warren. "And I think you should sing."

"I second that," Nathan agreed.

Warren was shaking his head. "Singing it in my head is bad enough."

We stopped for a sandwich when we got to the parking lot, and then we drove to the second spot Warren had circled. I didn't like the sight of it from the road. The incline was steep, and it went on for farther than my legs were willing to go. We parked in a grassy spot near a guardrail, and I got out and looked up. Straight up.

"I think I'm going to sit this one out, boys. I'll wait in the car with the heater and the radio on," I said.

Warren slung his backpack over his shoulders. He raised an eyebrow. "We're out here looking for the body of two dead girls who we believe were murdered by a serial killer in this vicinity, and you want to stay in the car alone?"

"I could wait with her," Nathan suggested with a sneaky grin.

Warren smiled and cut his eyes over at Nathan. "Then they might have to look for three bodies."

I groaned and re-tied my shoelaces. "Who would bury bodies on this cliff? That's stupid."

Warren looked at the map. "If the bodies are here, they will be on the other side of this hill. We could hike in from the access road on the other side, it's not as steep, but it is about eight times as far, and we would have to cross a river. The hill is our fastest route."

I looked down at my drenched clothes. "I don't think the river is a deterrent at this point. And stop calling that thing a hill." I pointed at the incline. "That's a mountain."

Warren shoved the map into his back pocket and offered me his hand. "Come on. It's not as bad as it looks," he said. "We'll be there before you know it."

I put my hand in his, and the three of us walked down into a creek before starting up the mountain on the other side. Some parts were so steep that we had to pull ourselves upward using tree roots that poked out of the ground. Halfway to the top, the sky opened up and the rain poured down once again.

"This is every single bit as bad as it looks, Warren," I whined as he helped me up onto a boulder near the top.

Nathan hoisted himself up after me. "I would like to take this opportunity to remind you, Sloan: this was *your* brilliant idea."

Warren put his backpack down and pulled out the map. I plopped down next to the pack and pulled out a water bottle. I offered it to Nathan. He took it and then stepped closer to look over Warren's shoulder. My wet hair was matted to my face, and my teeth were chattering. Cold rain drizzled down the bridge of my nose like a freshwater spring.

The other side of the mountain leveled off after a small decline from where we were. I could see the lake in the distance.

"It was a brilliant idea," Warren finally said. He was straining his eyes out over the view. "This is it."

I jumped up, causing water to squish out of my new boots in every direction. "What did you just say?"

Nathan stepped forward. "Where?"

Warren held his hand out. "That direction," he said, reaching for his pack. "Come on."

I had initially hoped that knowing we were on the right track would renew my strength, but the screaming pain in my legs proved otherwise. The only thing that improved was the rain finally let up again. Still, I didn't want to take another step. "OK, I'm done." I was dragging my heavy feet through the fallen leaves and the mud. "Who wants to carry me?"

"We're almost there," Warren insisted.

I tossed my head back over my shoulder. "Nathan, you wanna carry me?"

"No he doesn't," Warren said.

"This time, he's right," Nathan agreed.

We walked for another half a mile to an area thick with twisted mountain laurel and kudzu. Warren stopped so suddenly that I slammed into his backpack once again.

I rubbed my head where it smacked into a piece of the pack's hard plastic. "You've got to start warning me before you do that," I griped. "Maybe get a set of brake lights."

"There's a body buried under there." He was pointing to a spot on the ground, just beyond a fallen tree covered with moss and mushrooms.

My head snapped up. I looked around him for confirmation but didn't see anything suspicious in the mess of woodland brush. All I saw was a patch of decaying flowers and a mulberry bush.

Warren spun around to his left and started walking again.

"How can you tell?" I asked. "Can you describe it?"

He thought for a moment. "It kind of feels like the sucking force of a vacuum. Like the spot is swallowing up the life around it."

"That actually makes a lot of sense. I always know when a person is nearby because it seems like they are pulsing with energy and I can sense the vibrations," I said.

Nathan looked puzzled.

I put my hand on his arm. "It's OK. You wouldn't get it."

Warren began walking a wide circle, leaving Nathan and me watching him like he might sprout a long nose and a tail at any moment. He was like a six-foot-two bloodhound scouring the ground with his eyes.

About forty feet away from us, he finally looked in our direction. "There's another one this way." He took a few more steps to his left. "This one is easier to get to." He started toward a wild rhododendron.

"Should we disturb it?" I asked when we got closer.

Warren looked up at me. "How am I going to convince anyone there is a body up here if I don't have something to show them?" he reminded me. "I'll say I was scoping out areas for foxholes. I'll dig up some other places too."

He put his pack down and pulled out a large knife. I started to go with him, but Nathan blocked me with his arm. "Stay back. You and I should keep our distance. We aren't supposed to be here."

Warren ducked under the rhododendron and fought his way through more kudzu before he knelt down and began scraping at the ground with his blade. A few minutes passed and he finally stopped. "Bingo," he said.

I dug my nails into Nathan's arm.

Warren's hand came up, and resting on his fingers was a piece of bone that was hooked like the letter *J*. It was four or five inches long. He raised his eyebrows.

"Oh god," Nathan moaned. He folded his arms over top of his head and began to pace around.

"What is it?" I asked as Warren stood up still examining it.

Nathan paced the other direction and groaned. "It's a jawbone."

14.

EVEN THOUGH WE had been talking about it for two days, Nathan obviously wasn't prepared to actually find his sister's remains. If he hadn't been so worried about tainting the crime scene, I was sure he would've been vomiting. It wasn't the first time he had seen human bones, but it was the first bones that carried the probability of being his baby sister.

Warren carefully walked over and put the bone into a zip lock bag he had brought along. He turned it over in his hand so I could see the teeth that were still attached. I felt my stomach do a backflip. I turned and covered my mouth with the back of my hand.

He nodded toward Nathan who had wandered farther away. "Go check on him," he mouthed.

Cautiously, I crossed the grass. "Nathan? You OK?"

He nodded, but didn't answer. His eyes were closed as he paced.

"Why don't you sit down?" I suggested. "Have a drink of water."

He shook his head furiously and walked away rubbing his hands over his face.

Warren caught up with us. The bone was tucked securely somewhere in his pack. "Let's get him out of here," he said quietly. He walked over and clapped Nathan on his back. "Hey man, we've got to get out of here before you and Sloan leave too much of your presence behind."

Nathan blew out a hard puff of air and nodded. His hands were visibly shaking. He shoved his arms through the arm holes of his pack and turned in the direction of the cliff we had just scaled.

Warren let him lead the way back to the car. I was pretty sure it was to keep Nathan completely focused on where he was putting his feet instead of on what Warren was toting down with us. If that was his reason, it worked. Nathan was more himself when we reached the bottom, but he still went directly to his truck and climbed in the cab without saying a word. He sat there with his head on the steering wheel while I walked with Warren to the Challenger.

"What do we do now?" I asked him.

Warren carefully put the pack in the back seat. "You and Nathan need to get on the road. The sooner he gets home the better because I'm sure the cops around here are going to be blowing up his phone when they find out about it. I'm going to give you a few minutes head start so he's not recognized by some of the local law enforcement. I just can't wait too long because they won't be able to do anything if it gets dark."

I nodded. "OK."

He pointed over at Nathan. "Make sure he goes straight to Asheville. He's probably going to want to be with his family, but he needs to get home," he said.

I frowned. "I just realized this is going to be a really abrupt goodbye."

He draped his forearms over my shoulders. "I know. It sucks, but at least it's for a good reason," he said. "I'm glad we were able to find them."

I nodded. "Me too." I put my arms around his waist and my head on his chest. "Thank you so much, Warren."

He kissed the top of my head. "I'm glad I could help."

I looked up at him. "When will I see you again?"

"Next weekend. I'll come to you or I can fly you to New Hope," he suggested.

"Let's see how this week goes and we will figure it out," I said. "I'm sorry it's been such a crazy weekend."

He smiled. "Something tells me we're going to be having a lot of those."

I stretched up on my toes and kissed him quickly, knowing that I couldn't linger too long without us both of us being catapulted into the stratosphere and losing all track of time. "I'm going to miss you," I said.

"I miss you already," he said. "Come on. I'll put your things in Nate's truck."

Nathan was still face down on the steering wheel when we approached the truck. Warren opened the back door and put my bag inside. When he closed it, Nathan sat up. He looked a little better than he had at the top of the mountain, but his face was pale and his eyes were bloodshot. He stepped out of the truck and offered his hand to Warren.

"I can't thank you enough, Warren," he said.

Warren shook his hand and squeezed his arm. "I'm really sorry about all this, but I hope it helps."

Nathan nodded. "It does."

Warren put his hand on my shoulder. "You guys need to get out of here. I've got to call this in before it gets too late in the day, but I want you long gone before they start coming this direction."

"Why don't you let me drive?" I asked Nathan.

He shook his head. "Nah, I'm good. I can drive. Are you ready to go?"

I nodded. "Yeah."

Warren walked me around to the passenger's side and opened the door. "Keep me updated on where you guys are. Please be careful," he said.

I smiled. "I promise. Call me in a little while."

He pressed a kiss to my forehead and lingered for a moment. "I will."

Nathan and I drove for miles in complete silence. I couldn't imagine what was going on inside his head, and I certainly didn't know what to say, so I just rested my hand on the back of his neck. I watched the road ahead, lost in my thoughts, until the right side of my vision became a little blurred. Soon, the entire right side of the road was missing from my field of vision.

I groaned. "Oh no."

Nathan looked over at me. "What's the matter?"

I bent forward and opened my backpack. Thankfully, I had remembered to pack the medicine they gave me at the hospital. "Another migraine is starting." I fumbled through the pack. "Nathan,

I need your help."

"Hold on." He flipped on his emergency lights and jerked the truck over into the emergency lane on the side of the interstate.

My hands were beginning to tremble. "I can't find my medicine. It's a white box with a prescription label. I can't see to find it!"

He slammed the truck into park and yanked my bag up onto the seat. He dumped its entire contents before finding the small white box. "Here, here!" He ripped the packaging open and popped the seal around the capsules inside their plastic. "It says you're supposed to take two at the onset." He thrust two pills into my hand.

I took some deep breaths and dropped the pills into my mouth without waiting for water to swallow them. He put a bottle of water up to my lips and instructed me to drink.

I laid my head against my seat. "Oh god, this is going to be bad."

"Should I find a hospital?" he asked.

I covered my face with my hands. "No. No. Just drive home. We need to get out of here." I felt dizzy, and the pain was beginning like a pinprick in my skull just above the top of my ear.

"Where's your phone?" he asked.

I handed it to him.

A moment later, I heard his voice. "Warren, it's Nate. Sloan is getting another migraine. Really?" I felt his hand on my shoulder. "He's getting one too. He wants to know if he should meet us somewhere."

I reached toward him, grasping for the phone with my eyes clamped shut. "Let me talk." I pressed the phone to my ear. "Hey."

"Where are you guys? I'll come to you."

"No. We need to get home. Are you OK?" I asked.

"I'm getting worse by the second," he admitted. "I'm hoping they will be done with questioning me soon. I'm at the police station now."

"Nathan, drive," I said.

"It might stop if I come to you," Warren argued.

"You said it yourself. No stopping. We've got to get back to Asheville. I took the meds they gave me at the hospital. I'm hoping that will lessen the blow," I said.

"Ok," he said. "I'll call in and check on you."

"Please be careful, Warren." I was unable to imagine how he could begin to cope with dealing with the police in this state.

"Let me talk to Nate," he said.

I handed Nathan the phone as the car rolled onto smooth pavement. "Yeah?" Nathan asked. "OK. Of course. I've got her phone."

The medicine certainly helped. At the very least, I wasn't paralyzed or vomiting all over the truck. I was, however, slumped over the seat with my head in Nathan's lap for the rest of the drive. I also had his jacket shrouding my head to prevent the pangs from the headlights of oncoming cars. I cried the entire last fifty miles of the trip.

It didn't help that Nathan's phone started ringing non-stop by the time we crossed into Buncombe County. Though Nathan switched his phone to vibrate and tried to talk as quietly as possible, every word I heard was like an axe being driven into my skull. Even the silent buzz from his phone felt like a jackhammer. Finally, he turned his phone off when he realized my writhing intensified whenever he was on a call.

When we got to my house, I sat up and fumbled for the passenger side door.

"Wait, I've got it," he said.

He came around to my side of the truck and opened the door. "I'm going to get your keys and open up the house. Sit tight and I'll come back for you."

Sitting up was apparently a bad idea, and before he had gotten farther than a few steps away I started hurling, thankfully, onto the street. He held my ponytail out of the way and kept a firm hand on my shoulder to ensure that I didn't flop forward and crash into the asphalt.

When the puking subsided, he rubbed my back. "Can I take you to the hospital now?"

"No. Take me to bed, please," I begged.

He unlocked the door and carried me into the house. I held onto his neck until we got to my room and he carefully placed me on my bed. "I'll be right back," he whispered.

I reached for him. "No, Nathan. Go home. I'm fine."

"You're a terrible liar. I'm not leaving," he said.

I closed my eyes and tried to ignore the pounding of his footsteps against the hardwood floor. He turned on the water in the bathroom, and a moment later, my side of the bed dipped down under his weight. A cool washcloth touched my cheek. It felt like a kiss from heaven.

"I'm going to put this over your eyes to block out the light. They did it at the hospital and it seemed to help," he said. A moment later, the cool cloth was resting over my eyes.

His hands went to work on my boots and he carefully placed each of them on the floor. Next, he stripped off my socks and then tugged my blanket up around my waist. I felt his hand on my thigh.

"I've got to make some phone calls, but I'll be back. I put a trashcan by the bed in case you've got anything left in your stomach."

I fumbled around until I found his fingers. "Thank you," I whispered.

He squeezed my hand, and then he was gone.

The next morning I woke up to the sound of an alarm I didn't recognize. My headache had calmed to a dull throb. I looked over to see Nathan reaching for his cell phone on my nightstand. The early morning sun filled the room.

I rubbed my hand over my face. "What happened?"

He silenced the alarm and rolled onto his side to face me. He was in a white t-shirt and what I assumed were a pair of blue, plaid boxer shorts.

"Are you in your underwear?" I asked.

He grimaced. "Well, you puked all over my pants."

I groaned and draped my arms over my face.

"And my boots," he added.

"Oh, this is so embarrassing."

He laughed softly. "How are you feeling?"

"My head hurts, but better." I looked over at him. "You stayed with me all night?"

He winked an eye at me. "And slept in your bed."

"Warren's going to be so pissed," I told him.

"Warren threatened my life if I left you alone," he said.

"Really?" I asked surprised.

He laughed and nodded his head. "Yeah. First, I threatened to kill him. Now he's threatened to kill me. I think we've reached the first level of friendship."

I raised an eyebrow. "Friendship?"

He laughed. "OK, maybe not exactly."

"What time is it?" I asked.

"Six," he said. "Do you think you'll go into work today?"

I groaned. "I have to. I have a feeling this is going to be a crazy week for all of us."

He nodded and sat up. "I'm sure it is. I'm probably going to head to Raleigh today."

"What happened last night? I could hear you talking on the phone, but I couldn't make sense of anything because of the pain," I said.

He swung his legs off the bed and wrapped the bed sheet around his waist for the sake of decency. He walked to my bathroom and rinsed out his mouth with my mouthwash.

"Well, some of my buddies in Raleigh called to tell me that some guy found a skeleton at Buckner-Falls. They said they thought it might be a young female, but they wouldn't know for certain until they heard from the medical examiner. I told them I had a theory about the suspect being an avid hunter and that they should canvass the area with cadaver dogs. They said they were going to today. My story sounded plausible enough, I guess."

I pushed myself up in the bed. "How are you doing with it all?" Nathan had removed my hiking boots and socks, but I was still dressed in my jeans and even my rain-resistant, bright orange pullover.

He splashed water on his face. "I'm all right. It was a pretty big shock yesterday, but I feel better knowing we found her, if in fact it is her," he said.

"Have you talked to Warren? Did he make it home?" I asked.

"He was in pretty bad shape when he was threatening my life. They questioned him for a few hours but released him without any suspicion. I think he was going to stop and rest for a while before trying to drive," he said.

I walked into the bathroom behind him and grabbed my toothbrush. "Where are your clothes?"

"In the dryer. I washed them last night while you were passed out," he said. "I hope that's OK."

I laughed and squeezed toothpaste onto the brush. "I puked all over you. The least I can do is let you wash your clothes." I looked up at our reflections in the bathroom mirror. My hair was halfway in and out of my ponytail, my face was black with mascara and dirt, and my eyes were swollen and puffy. "Well, I look awesome."

He laughed. "Like a princess."

I spat toothpaste into the sink and stuck my tongue out at him.

He smiled and left the bathroom. A few minutes later, I turned on the shower and he walked into my bedroom fully dressed as I was picking out an outfit for work. He strapped on his tactical belt and checked his gun before tucking into his side holster.

"I've got to run home and change and head to the department. Call me later and let me know how you're doing," he said.

I walked across the room and put my arms around his neck. "Thank you so much, Nathan."

He was smiling when he pulled back, and he wiped a smudge of black out from under my eye. "Anytime, Sloan."

* * *

A couple of pain pills knocked out what was left of my headache on my drive into work. Still, the world seemed a little too bright, and my brain seemed to be half a step behind in processing thoughts and paperwork. It was like having a hangover without having the good time the night before.

The morning was exceptionally mundane except for the news articles that kept coming through my email from the state capital. By that afternoon police had located the other body in the woods, and the medical examiner confirmed that the first skeleton was that of a teenage female. The police and the media were all speculating that the remains were of Ashley McNamara and Melissa Jennings, and some reporters were already saying the murders may be the work of a serial killer.

I didn't hear from Nathan again that day other than a text message to check on how I was feeling.

I had called Warren that morning before leaving the house. He was awake but still in a great deal of pain. He promised to call me later, after he figured out if he was going to make it to work. When his name popped up on my caller ID again, I was sitting in my office with my feet propped up on my desk, eating a bag of pretzels and drinking a Diet Coke out of the vending machine.

I pressed the answer button and held the phone to my ear. "Hello."

"Hey," Warren said.

I popped another pretzel into my mouth. "Hey. How are you feeling?"

He groaned. "Like someone took a battle axe to my skull last night. I came into work, but I'm counting the seconds till I can leave and go home."

"You should stop leaving me," I said.

"I agree," he said. "Did the meds help you last night? Was it any better this time?"

"It was definitely better, but I still ended up puking all over Nathan," I said.

He chuckled softly. "So I heard."

"Did you also hear that he slept in my bed last night?" I asked.

His end of the line was quiet for a beat. "No," he finally said. "I asked him to stay with you, but that's not exactly what I meant."

I smiled. "Not to worry. I woke up in my blue jeans and rain coat."

"Still," he grumbled and blew out a sigh. "What are you going to do tonight?"

"It's Monday," I said. "I have dinner with my parents on Monday nights."

"Do you think your dad has had a chance to get the results of our blood test?" he asked.

"That's what I'm hoping to find out," I said.

"Well, call me as soon as you can if you find anything out. I've got to get back to work," he said.

"I promise."

I was lost in my office. Putting together announcements about road closures and the submissions deadline for the county online cookbook almost seemed insulting after discovering a human jawbone the day before. I was thankful when five o'clock came and I could head to my parents' house for dinner. I didn't feel like going. I really wanted to go home and climb back into my bed. That desire, however, was trumped by my curiosity to know if Dad had heard anything from the lab about the DNA test.

I was surprised to find Dad's car in the driveway when I got to their house. Dinner was already on the table, and Mom was filling three glasses with sweet tea when I walked in and put my purse down on the counter. "Hey," I said. "Where's Dad?"

"Upstairs," she answered as I leaned over to give her a welcoming kiss on the cheek. "He will be down in a minute."

Looking at my mother, something snagged my attention once again. I couldn't put my finger on what it was, but something felt strange about her. I studied her face until she sheepishly blushed.

She touched her cheek. "What?"

I smiled. "Nothing. Can I help with dinner?"

She shook her head and smiled. "I've got it," she replied. "How was your day?"

"Better than my night," I groaned.

"What happened last night?" she asked.

I leaned against the counter. "Another migraine."

She put the tea pitcher down and walked over to me. "You should've called me," she said. "Or you should've gone to the emergency room."

"Mom, I can't go to the ER every time I have a headache," I said.

She pointed at me. "You shouldn't be alone when those things hit you. That's pretty dangerous."

I shook my head. "I wasn't alone. Detective McNamara stayed with me."

She raised her eyebrows and smiled. "Oh really?"

"Yes, but stop looking at me like that. There is nothing going on with me and Nathan," I said.

Her smile grew and she shook her head. "I'm not so sure about that."

I rolled my eyes and laughed. To be honest, I wasn't so sure either.

Dad appeared in the kitchen. He came over and gave me a hug. "Hi, sweetheart."

"Hi, Daddy," I answered. "How was work?"

He smiled. "Not too bad. I left a little early today at your mother's insistence, so I'm not complaining. How are you?"

Mom squeezed my shoulder. "Your daughter had another migraine last night."

His brow wrinkled. "Really?"

I nodded. "Yes. I took the medicine though, so it wasn't as severe."

He shook his head. "I don't like this, Sloan. I think we should schedule some more tests. Maybe it's time to meet with a neurologist."

"No, Dad," I objected. My eyes brightened. "But...speaking of tests?"

A thin smile spread across his lips and he lifted an envelope in his right hand.

I beamed at him, but he shook his head and motioned to the table. "Let's sit so the food doesn't get cold."

The tone of his voice sounded ominous. The DNA test results were in that envelope. I knew it.

We all sat down to three steaming plates of meatloaf, mashed potatoes, green beans, and bread. Monday night dinner was usually the only homemade meal of the week that I ever had. When I put a forkful of buttery mashed potatoes in my mouth, I regretted not paying attention more when my mother cooked.

The table was silent for a few minutes. My father looked lost in thought as he chewed his food and my mother looked nervous. I wiped my mouth and put my napkin on the table. "OK, what is going on? You guys are killing me."

My dad reached for my mother's hand and gave it a reassuring squeeze. "The lab rushed your test results for me and I have them."

I sat forward on the edge of my seat. "Well, what does it say?"

Dad shook his head. "I don't know. It would be illegal for me, as your father, to look at them without your permission."

I shot my hand out. "Well, *gimme!*"

He slid the envelope toward me, but pressed his fingers down to prevent me from picking it up. "Sloan, your mother and I want you to know that no matter what, you will always be our little girl, even if you do want to know who your birth family is."

I focused on their faces. My mother looked like she might melt into a puddle of tears at any second. I had been insensitive with my vague explanations of how this had all transpired. I took my hand off the envelope and pushed my plate back. "Mom, Dad, of course I've always been curious as to where I came from, but I'm not on a quest to replace you. I met Warren by accident and we had a lot of similarities and I got curious. That's all this is. I promise."

"Well," my mother began, "if he is your brother, we want you to know we are truly happy for you, and we will always do whatever we can to support you. Even in finding your birth family."

I smiled. "Thank you."

She seemed to relax a little.

Dad released the envelope and I snatched it up. I tore it open and pulled out the letter inside which contained a spreadsheet full of letters and numbers that I didn't understand. The results might as well have been written in hieroglyphics. "Uh, what is this?"

"If you're looking for a green check mark or a red letter 'x' you're not going to find it." My dad was grinning. "Want me to have a look?"

I handed it to him and sat on my hands to keep them from shaking completely off of the ends of my arms. "Please."

He examined the paper for a moment. My mother was leaning toward him. He adjusted his glasses. "Well, sibling tests done without a sample from at least the mother are very difficult to determine. This is actually two different tests. One of them assumes you have the same mother and the other assumes you do not. You and Warren do share some of the same alleles, but both tests fall on the probable side that you are not siblings. The percentages and odds are extremely low."

"He's not my brother?"

Dad handed me the piece of paper. "No one can say with absolute certainty, but the DNA test says most likely not."

I sat back in my seat. My mother reached across the table and squeezed my hand. Her smile was sympathetic. "I'm sorry, honey."

I laughed. "I'm not."

She looked surprised, and she glanced from me to my father.

"You weren't hoping you had found your brother?" Dad asked with a raised eyebrow.

"No." I laughed and shook my head. "I mean, it would have been nice to know I had a brother out there and maybe finally get some answers to questions I've had all my life, but no. I was really, *really* hoping Warren wasn't related to me."

Dad's shoulders relaxed like he had been preparing for me to have a meltdown. "Well, congratulations are in order, then!"

I laughed with relief. "Do you mind if I excuse myself for a moment? I need to call Warren."

"Go ahead, honey," Mom answered.

I grabbed my phone from my purse and carried it out onto the back porch. I looked out over the light-speckled mountains which suddenly seemed full of hope and possibilities. I dialed Warren's number.

"Hey." His voice was groggy.

"Were you sleeping?" I asked.

"A little. I came in and fell asleep on my couch right after work. It's been a rough day," he said.

"Are you ready for it to get a whole lot better?" I asked.

After a beat of silence his voice came over the line much more coherent than it had been before. "I told you I wasn't your brother."

* * *

A blue truck was parked at my curb when I got home. Nathan looked up from his cell phone as I slowly drove by. I waved and pulled into my driveway. He was standing under the streetlight on the sidewalk when I made it around to the front.

"Hey." I fumbled through my keyring. "What are you doing here?

Returning for another slumber party?"

He laughed and followed me up the front porch steps. "I don't know. Is that an invitation?"

I grinned at him over my shoulder as I used my key to tumble the deadbolt. "Come on in," I said as I pushed the door open. "Have you been here long?"

He shook his head as we stepped inside. "I had just pulled up when you came home."

I turned on the light switch. "You should have called me."

He stripped off his ball cap and placed it with his keys on the table in my foyer. "I was on my way home and decided to drop by."

"You don't live anywhere near here." I smiled at him as I shrugged out of my jacket and hung it on the hook near the door.

He winked a steel gray eye at me. "I decided to take the long way home."

I smiled and flipped on the light in the living room. "Fair enough."

He followed me to the living room. "I was surprised you weren't home when I got here. I came by assuming you would be in your pajamas by now."

I looked over my shoulder at him. "Well, I thought I would be too, but it's Monday and that means it's dinner night with my parents. I didn't want to cancel it because my dad had some really big news to tell me."

"News?" he asked.

"Yeah. Warren and I had a DNA test done last week, and Dad got the results in today," I answered.

Nathan faltered a step as we walked into the living room. "Really? Can I ask what it said?"

I sat down in the corner of the sofa and tucked my legs underneath me. "We're not related."

He sank down on the edge of the seat next to me. He nodded and forced a smile. "Well, I guess I should congratulate you."

I lowered my gaze at him. "I know you wouldn't mean it."

He shrugged his shoulders. "I want you to be happy, Sloan, and I get why you're with him. He's got an edge nobody can compete with."

It was really hard for me to know that my happiness was unintentionally painful for Nathan. I cared about him so much, but he was right; there wasn't anyone who could compete with the connection I had with Warren. Still, I felt Nathan deserved my apology. "Can you keep a secret?" I asked.

He raised his eyebrows in question.

I leaned toward him. "From the moment I saw you at the sheriff's office during your oath ceremony, I had the biggest crush on you. I was so devastated when you told me you had a girlfriend that I almost cried in your car."

He laughed. "Really?"

"True story," I answered.

He looked down at his hands. "I'm really sorry about that."

I reached over and squeezed his forearm. "I'm sorry about this now."

"I know," he replied.

I nudged him. "Different subject. Why did you come by here on your 'long way home'?" I asked. "I wasn't expecting to see you again tonight."

He leaned forward, resting his elbows on his knees. "I wanted to stop by to see how you were feeling and to tell you goodbye. I'm leaving in the morning and don't know how long I'll be gone."

"Raleigh?"

He nodded. "Yeah. My mom is pretty hysterical, understandably so. And if it is Ashley, then we will have to make a lot of arrangements for her body."

My stomach felt queasy thinking about the jawbone Warren had found. "How long will it take them to know for sure if it's her or not?"

He shrugged his shoulders. "I'm sure it will at least be a few weeks," he said. "The investigation will go on for a while, but we will eventually have a burial service for her, I guess. We already had a memorial service a couple of years after she disappeared."

I groaned. "That sucks. Will you keep me updated on what's going on out there? And, certainly, let me know if there's anything I can do to help."

"Of course." He raked his fingers through his hair. "You know, we've been through a hell of a lot together in a really short time."

I laughed. "You can say that again."

He pushed himself up off the couch and offered his hand to help me up. When he pulled me to my feet, he looked down to where his hand was wrapped around mine. "Can you keep a secret?" he asked quietly.

I smiled. "Yeah."

He tugged on my hand and stepped toward me. His free hand slipped behind my head as he brought his lips down onto mine. Nathan tasted like Skittles.

15.

WARREN SAID HE would be late on Friday, but that he was coming for the weekend. He had a meeting on Friday afternoon, and he said he would leave as soon as he was able. I was at home waiting for him that night when there was a knock at my door around nine o'clock.

It was Adrianne, wearing a party dress and enough makeup to be in a televised beauty pageant. "You haven't been answering your phone," she said.

I stepped aside to let her in. "I've been busy and didn't have time to talk."

She looked around my living room. "Where's your boy toy?"

"He's on his way. What are you doing here?"

"I had to run over to the salon because I ran out of bobby pins." She framed her hands around her formal updo. "Like my hair?"

It was spectacular, as usual. "It's gorgeous."

She pointed at me. "Since you've forgotten how to use a phone, I came by to kidnap you for this party." She looked up and down at my blue jeans and black V-neck sweater. "But you need to change."

I looked down at my outfit. "What's wrong with my clothes? I thought I looked pretty good." I had actually spent over an hour getting redressed after work.

She tugged on the hem of my sweater. "You can't go to a party like that."

I pushed her hand away. "I'm not going to a party at all." I sat down on the couch. "Warren will be here soon, and we are spending the night at home."

She smiled and leaned against the armrest with a mischievous grin. "Like, spending the night at home or *spending the night at home?*"

My face flushed. "He and I have a lot to talk about."

She laughed. "Yes. I'm sure there will be plenty of talking."

"Either way, we're not going out," I said. "What party is it?"

"Mark and I are going to the opening of a new club on Merrimon Avenue. It's called Crush. Everybody's been talking about it," she said.

With all that had happened in the past week, I had almost forgotten that Mark Higgins even existed. I choked back the bit of nausea that seemed to accompany thoughts of him and put my feet up on the coffee table. "I guess I've been too wrapped up in skeletons and boy problems to hear about the latest buzz in the Asheville nightlife."

"How's the detective doing since they identified his sister?" she asked.

The thought of Nathan's kiss resurfaced in my memory, triggering a mix of butterflies and guilt in the pit of my stomach. I hadn't told anyone about that night.

I pushed the thought away and shrugged my shoulders. "I don't really know. He's been in Raleigh all week with his family."

Adrianne sighed. "That's so sad."

"Yep, but at least I think they have some closure now," I said. "I think not knowing is worse."

Her phone beeped. She looked down at the screen and then up at me. "I've got to run. Mark's going to pick me up at my house in five minutes."

I stood up and walked with her to the door. "Are you dating Mark now?"

She laughed and waved her hand toward me. "Just having fun," she said. "It's nothing serious. Maybe we can double date sometime soon."

"Sure. I would *love* to hear Warren's opinion about him," I said with a smirk.

I opened the front door just as Warren had raised his hand to knock.

Adrianne shook her head and looked at me. "I don't think I'm ever going to get used to you being such a freak." She kissed me on the cheek. "Call me if you change your mind. Hey, Warren!"

"Hi, Adrianne," he replied.

"I'm not going to change my mind!" I called after her as she walked out.

She giggled as she carefully maneuvered her way down the stairs in her heels. "Have fun you crazy kids."

"You have fun, and be careful!" I shouted.

I looked up at Warren, and my breath caught in my throat. "You're finally here!"

He stepped inside. "I'm sorry I'm so late." He put his bag down by the door and reached for my hand. "I had a really important meeting at work."

"About what?" I asked.

He pulled me to him. "I'll tell you in a minute." He bent and covered my mouth with his. He pushed the front door closed and moved me back against it. When he finally released me, I would have fallen to the floor had he not had his arms around me.

I laughed as he rested his forehead against mine and the world seemed to swirl back into place. "I'm almost afraid for us to go any further than that," I admitted. "I worry my heart might stop or my brain might explode."

He smiled against my cheek. "That would be a hell of a way to go out." He pulled away and looked at me as he bit his lower lip. "I plan on testing it out very soon, but I want to talk to you first."

I exhaled slowly, still trying to catch my breath. "Talk to me about what?"

He tugged on my hand, and I followed him to the living room. "What did Adrianne want?"

"She wanted us to go to a party with her and this creep, Mark, tonight. I told her no."

He sat down on the sofa and pulled me down next to him. "Do you want to go?"

I laughed and leaned into him. "Hell no."

He draped his arm over my shoulders, and I reached up to hold onto his hand.

"Have you heard from Nathan?" he asked.

The guilt returned. "I got a text from him this morning saying he convinced the FBI and the state to send search teams into the game lands around the areas where the girls disappeared."

He nodded. "That's good. Did he say if they positively identified the bodies?"

I shook my head. "He's pretty sure it's his sister and the other girl, but he said it could take a while to get anything from the medical examiner. Before he left, he told me they are planning to do a burial service for his sister sometime, but they can't till the state has finished with her remains."

He wove his fingers in and out of mine. "Are you going to the service?"

"Probably so," I said. "I can't imagine how hard this has to be for him."

Warren kissed my temple. "I can't either. I may hate him, but Nate's not a bad guy."

I smiled over my shoulder at him. "You don't hate Nathan."

"If I hadn't been as sick as I was on Monday, I would've driven back over here and kicked his ass for sleeping in your bed," he said.

I laughed. "You told him to stay."

He nodded. "He could've slept on the floor."

It felt like an angel and a demon were arguing on my shoulders about whether or not I should tell Warren about Nathan kissing me. Nathan had asked me to keep it a secret, but it felt wrong. "He stopped by before he went to Raleigh, and I told him the DNA results said we aren't related." Silently, I gave one point to the good angel on my left shoulder who was urging me to be honest.

"How did that go?"

I sighed. "He was pretty obviously disappointed, but he said he understood why you and I are together. He even said, 'congratulations'."

Warren chuckled. "That's bullshit."

"Maybe," I agreed.

"Not 'maybe'. Nathan is in love with you," he said.

I kissed his fingertips. "But I'm with you now," I said, and I knew I meant it.

I sighed and decided to give a point to the demon on my right shoulder by changing the subject before the conversation about Nathan went any further. "What did you want to talk to me about? I know it's not about Nathan McNamara."

He nodded and turned in his seat. I turned around sideways so I could look at him, folding my legs under me. He tucked his hair behind his ears. "You know how I'm a contractor for Claymore, right?"

I nodded.

He took my hands and rested them on my lap. "So you understand that it's only for a contracted period of time with no guarantees for a continuation after the contract is over, correct?"

I nodded. "Yes."

He sucked in a deep breath. "Well, they offered me a permanent position with them today. That's what the meeting was about."

"Really?" I asked surprised. "That's a good thing, right?"

He moved his head from side to side. "Well, the money is great. So are the benefits."

I raised an eyebrow. "But?"

He looked down at my hands. "The job is in Oregon."

My mouth dropped open. "Wow."

He nodded. "Yeah. It's a pretty big deal."

"What did you tell them?" I asked.

He sighed. "I told them I would have to think about it. I said I had some reservations about moving that far."

"What are your reservations?" I asked.

He squeezed my hands. "You. You are my only reservation."

I took in a slow, deep breath and then blew it out even slower. "Wow. OK," I said. "So if I weren't in the picture, you would take this job."

He nodded. "In a heartbeat."

It was like the weight of the world fell onto my chest. My shoulders sank down, and I balanced my elbows on my knees for support. It was a lot of pressure, especially considering I had cheese in my refrigerator that had been around longer than Warren.

He put his finger under my chin to lift my eyes to meet his. "I know this is a lot to put on you. We've technically only known each other for what? Twelve, thirteen days maybe?"

I laughed. "Yeah."

He pulled my fingers up to his lips and kissed them. "Sloan, I don't know about you, but I feel like I am finally where I'm supposed to be for the first time in my life. When I'm with you, it's just...right. It's like gravity has aligned when we are together."

I knew what he was talking about. There was something there. Something between us that couldn't be seen or explained or probably understood by anyone else in the world. It wasn't necessarily love; in many ways, it felt much bigger than that. Whatever it was seemed to be a cosmic or even supernatural desperation to be connected. I had never been one to believe in fate or predestination... not until I first brushed the hand of Warren Parish.

He shook his head. "I don't know what to tell them."

"When do you have to give them an answer?" I asked.

He gave a reluctant smile. "That's kind of good news. They gave me the next week off to really think about it and come to a decision."

"What happens if you accept?"

"Then I would be on the West Coast by mid-October," he said.

"That's just a few weeks away," I said.

He nodded. "I know."

"And if you turn it down?" I asked.

He shrugged. "Then they probably won't offer me another contract when mine runs out at the end of the month. Or, maybe they will. I don't know for sure."

I rubbed my face over my hands. "Wow. That's big."

He dropped his head. "I know. I'm sorry. This is way too much, way too fast, but I couldn't make this decision without talking to you first."

My mind was racing. "What are you asking me, Warren?"

He brushed a loose strand of hair out of my face. "I realize this is absolutely crazy, but would you ever consider going with me to Oregon?"

My mouth dropped open again. I laughed. "Really? Seriously? Are you asking me to move to the other side of the country?"

He turned his hands over. "I need to know if it's a possibility."

I thought of Adrianne and our lunches with martinis and goat cheese grits. I thought about Monday night dinners with my parents and the fact that I still didn't know how to make her mashed potatoes. I even thought of Nathan McNamara leaning against the wall in my office. "Warren, I've got my Mom and Dad here and Adrianne. I've got my career and my house—"

He nodded. "I know. That's why I'm asking."

My phone rang. Adrianne's face was on the screen. I hit ignore and put the phone on silent before placing it on the coffee table.

I turned my palms up. "I can't make this decision for you, Warren. If you want to go, we will just have to figure it out."

"Sloan, you don't understand." He pressed his eyes closed and then opened them. "If you won't even consider it, then I'm turning the job down. End of story. I can't stand being on the opposite side of the state from you, I can't imagine how much harder it would be if I were on the other side of the country."

"You're going to turn it down?" I asked.

He wrapped his fingers around mine. "I'm not asking you for some big commitment or anything, but I do know that no matter whether or not you and I end up together, I can't be that far away from you."

"But what will you do?" I asked. "Where will you work?"

He laughed. "I'm a marksman. This is probably the easiest place in the US for me to get a job. It may not pay six figures a year, but it would be near you."

"Six figures?" I asked.

He nodded. "Yeah. Does that change your mind?"

I laughed and shook my head. "No. I can't leave my family. At least not in a few weeks. But I don't want to be without you either." I clasped my hands over my heart. "Is that really selfish of me? That I want to stand in the way of a really great opportunity for you?"

He ran his fingers through my hair. "Do you realize that no one ever in my life has been selfish for me? I would give up all the money in the world to be wanted that badly."

He hooked his finger inside the collar of my sweater and pulled me close. His lips touched mine, sending sparks through my body. He pulled back and smiled. "Did we just decide I'm moving here?"

I giggled. "I think we did."

He grinned and stood up, offering me his hand. When I was on my feet, he tucked my hair behind my ear and trailed his knuckles down the side of my neck. His eyes, dancing with mischief, glanced to the stairs behind me. "Can I take you upstairs and try to kill us both now?"

I laughed. "Please!"

Without another word, he bent down and grabbed me around my thighs. He slung me over his shoulder, and I laughed all the way up the stairs. When he returned me to my feet at the foot of my bed, I nearly fell over from all the blood rushing from my head. He smiled and smoothed my hair into place. His dark eyes searched mine and my giggles quickly faded.

I bit my lip as he slowly reached for the top button on his white shirt. When all of the buttons were undone, I pushed his shirt off of his shoulders. Underneath was a black, fitted t-shirt with a distressed picture of the Grim Reaper on the front. I looked up at him in silence as I untucked the shirt and pulled it up. When I couldn't reach any higher, he tugged the shirt off over his head.

For the first time, I could see the full length of his tribal tattoo. I traced the lines with my fingertips. There was a claw that came down the center of his chest and curved to a point toward his ribcage. The lines came up along his left collarbone and spread wide over his shoulder and down to his elbow. He slowly turned to show me the back. There were three more large claws that stretched from his shoulder to halfway down his spine. It was a talon, like that of a massive eagle, gripping his body from above.

"Wow," I whispered.

He turned back around and slid his hands up the curve of my jaw. He tipped my face up and slowly brought his lips down to meet mine. His touch was gentle at first, but as his fingers twisted into my hair, the kiss deepened until he released every reservation he had held each time before. With one smooth motion, my sweater was on the floor and his hands were working at the clasp of my bra. He pulled my body against his as he slipped the straps off my shoulders. I pressed my teeth into his salty skin at the bend of his neck and heard my name.

But…my name wasn't coming from Warren.

"Sloan?" I heard again, closer this time. I broke free from him.

"That's my mother!" I said in a panicked whisper.

"Sloa…oh oh!" Mom nearly choked on my name as she staggered backward as soon as she walked into my room.

"Mom!" I snatched up the closest discarded shred of clothing my fingers found and wrapped it around my chest.

She had stumbled out of my room to the hallway. Warren sat down on the edge of the bed, laughing.

I looked around the corner to see my mom panting and gripping her chest. She was leaning against the wall. "Mom, what are you doing in my house?"

"I used my key. You didn't answer when I rang!"

"I didn't hear the doorbell!"

She threw her hands in the air. "Obviously." She was still panting. "I'm sorry. I didn't know you had company."

"What do you want?"

Her face sobered. "You need to get dressed. Your father just called me from the hospital. It's Adrianne. There's been an accident!"

Warren stood and I darted out into the hall and grabbed my mother by the arm. "What?"

"Your dad called and said they brought her in by ambulance. It's bad. You need to go," she said.

I pressed my eyes closed and reached out into the world with my gift to find my best friend. She was alive, but that was all I knew.

Warren came out in his black t-shirt and handed me my sweater. "Let's go," he said.

16.

MARK HIGGINS HAD been drunk when he came by to pick up Adrianne. They never made it to the party because he had driven his Jeep off an extra high road shoulder, flipping it. As is the case with most drunk drivers, Mark was practically unscathed; Adrianne, however, had been ejected.

My father had been on call and was at the hospital with a patient when they brought her in. He had tried to call me several times, but my phone had been on silent. When the three of us got to the hospital, I ran to the emergency room's waiting area.

Her mother, Gloria, who was like a second mom to me, crossed the room when we walked in. She started crying, and she gripped me so tight I feared my head might pop off.

"How is she?" I asked as I pushed her back enough to search her bloodshot eyes.

She sniffed and wiped her runny nose on the cuff of her sleeve. "I don't know," she cried. "They had to take her into emergency surgery because of swelling on her brain."

My father came in right behind us and slipped his arm around my shoulders giving me a gentle squeeze. "Hey, sweetheart."

"Do you know anything?" I asked frantically.

He shook his head. "Not much. She wasn't conscious when they brought her in, and she didn't look good. They said she had a lot of obvious broken bones, but the head trauma was their biggest concern. I'm trying to get any information I can, but unfortunately, we just have to wait." He looked over at my mother. "I've got to finish up with my patient, but I'll come back here when I'm done."

I turned toward Warren and buried my face in his chest and cried. He kissed the top of my head and rubbed my back, but even his magical touch brought little comfort. Adrianne had called me, and I had ignored her.

After a couple of hours in the waiting room with Adrianne's parents and mine, the doctor walked in, hugging a clipboard to his chest. "She's stable," he began. "There was very severe swelling from a head injury, so we placed a monitoring device in her skull to gauge the pressure in her brain cavity. We are giving her medicine to keep her sedated. It will give her body some time to repair itself. The next few hours are very critical. I'm not going to lie. This is very serious." His face was grim. "It will be a miracle if she makes it through the night, but it's still a possibility."

It felt like invisible hands were squeezing and twisting my heart like a dishrag inside my chest. There didn't seem to be enough oxygen in the waiting room anymore. Warren's hand rested on my hip, and I remembered to inhale.

I took a step toward the doctor. "Can we see her?"

He nodded his head but held up his hand. "Once we get her settled and stable in the ICU, two visitors at a time will be allowed in. It will still be a little while before anyone can go back." He sucked in a deep breath. "Please understand she has severe lacerations and bruising on her face. She's intubated, very swollen, and her head is in a stabilizer. It can be a very disturbing sight."

"What else did you find?" Adrianne's mother asked.

The doctor sighed and glanced down at his clipboard. "Besides the brain injury, she has a broken arm, a cracked shoulder blade, three broken ribs, two broken fingers, a broken leg in three places, and more stitches than we could keep track of." He looked up again. "The head trauma is the only thing potentially life-threatening at this point, but she's very banged up."

"Where's the jackass who put her in here?" I nearly shouted at him.

The doctor took a cautious step backward. "The driver of the Jeep was taken into police custody after being treated for minor injuries.

That's all I know."

I wished I had Warren's ability to stop a beating heart.

I looked up at my dad. "Do you think she's going to make it?"

He slipped his arm around my shoulders. "Tonight will be the real test," he said. "The odds of her recovery will increase exponentially in the morning."

Tears rolled down my cheeks, and I quickly brushed them away with my sleeve.

I choose to distract myself with anger. "Do you know what happened to Mark Higgins, the driver she was with?"

Dad lowered his voice. "The driver had six stitches above his left eye and a bruised sternum, but you're not supposed to know that. I'm sure he's at the county jail by now."

Anger boiled inside of me.

He squeezed my arm. "I'm going to take your mother home. Are you going to stay here for the night?"

I nodded. "Yeah," I said. "I can't leave."

"I'll stay with her." Warren stood up and offered his hand to my father.

My dad shook it. "I'm glad you're here, son."

I wondered if that would remain true if Mom decided to tell Dad what she had interrupted earlier at my house. I hugged my mother. "Thanks for coming to get me." I dropped my voice to a whisper in her ear. "And I'm really sorry."

She gave me an awkward smile. "Call us if anything changes. Do you want me to bring you some more comfortable clothes?"

Warren stepped forward. "I'll go by the house and get some for her," he said. "Thank you, Mrs. Jordan."

Her smile was even more awkward with him. "Thank you, Warren."

They left, and I sat down beside Gloria. Warren knelt down in front of me. "What do you want from the house? I'm going to go change and grab you some clothes."

I tried to think. "Just some sweats or something," I said. "They are in the tall chest of drawers on the bottom."

He nodded. "Do you need anything else?"

I shook my head and kissed his lips. "No, thank you."

While he was gone, Adrianne's parents were allowed in to see her. When they returned, I was permitted to go in. Adrianne's mom came with me. I froze once I stepped behind the curtain in ICU. There were more tubes going in and out of my best friend than I had ever seen in my life. Her face was so badly injured that I wouldn't have recognized her. Even with the bandaging, I could see they had to partially shave off her beautiful hair.

A doctor stepped in and asked to speak with Mrs. Marx. Before she left, she touched my arm. "Are you all right?" Her eyes were puffy and bloodshot.

I nodded, and she walked out into the hallway with the doctor.

I went to Adrianne's bedside and picked up her left hand. It was unmangled, unlike her right, and still perfectly manicured. I bent down and cried as I grasped her fingers. The machines around us beeped and wheezed, buzzed and clacked. I kissed her nails. "Please fight," I whispered. "Please stay with me."

A moment later, a nurse bustled into the room, and I straightened and wiped my eyes on the back of my sleeve again. "How is she?" I asked.

The small framed woman made some notes on a piece of paper and checked the readout on the machine that was beeping in rhythm with Adrianne's heart. "Her heart rate is increasing. That's a good sign," she said.

I rubbed my best friend's cool fingers as they laid lifeless in my hand. "She's going to beat this." I sniffed. "She's going to come through."

"We're all pulling for her and praying," the nurse said with a sympathetic smile.

Praying, I thought. I had never been much of a praying type of girl, mainly because I had big doubts about a god that could be in control over the entire universe and allow some of the wickedness I had seen and felt in people. If a deity did exist, I wasn't even sure how to pray to him—or her. But for Adrianne, I would try anything. I pressed my eyes closed. *God, if you're listening. I need a favor...*

For a long time, I watched the changing numbers on the machines around the room. I didn't know much about blood pressure, but I knew numbers like 56/40 weren't good. Slowly, the numbers inched up and with each minute increase, I nearly broke out in cheers. When the nurses came in to check her vitals again, I trudged to the waiting room.

Warren was sitting with our little group, slowly swinging the backpack I had carried on our hiking trip between his knees. He stood up when he saw me, and I walked into his arms and buried my face in his chest. "Shh…" he said as I began to sob. He tucked me under his arm and turned me toward to the door. "Come on. Let's take a walk."

We stepped out of the waiting room into the hallway. Once we were away from Adrianne's family, he pulled me in close and let me weep in his arms. "She looks so bad," I cried.

He kissed the top of my head. "You heard the doctor. There's still a chance. Don't give up on her yet."

I gathered the fabric of his shirt in my fists and cried until I ran out of tears. When the sobbing subsided he nodded toward the door. "I brought you some clothes and a couple of pillows. Why don't you change and get more comfortable? This is going to be a long night."

I wiped my nose on my sleeve and nodded. I followed him inside, and he handed me the backpack. "Thank you," I said.

He nodded toward the bathroom and nudged my elbow. "Go change."

The single bathroom was empty when I walked in and locked the door. It was the same bathroom where I had changed after bringing Kayleigh Neeland to the hospital. I splashed water on my face before stripping off my sweater and reaching into the bag. I pulled out my blue Victoria's Secret sweatpants and a black S.W.A.T. hoodie I had never even washed.

* * *

The next morning, I awoke in a puddle of my own drool on Warren's lap. I had been up and down all night checking on Adrianne but had slept for a couple of hours stretched out across him and three of the plastic chairs in the waiting room.

"Morning," he said as I sat up and wiped the drool off my chin. He was grinning.

If I hadn't been so exhausted, I would have been mortified. "Good morning. Did you sleep at all?" I asked through a yawn.

He gave a weak smile. "A little."

"Have you heard any updates?" I looked down at the time on my phone. It was just after eight in the morning.

He straightened in his seat. "They said she steadily improved overnight and the swelling has decreased significantly. Her mom said you can go and see her whenever you wake up."

"Do you want to come with me?" I asked.

He frowned and shook his head. "It's not a good idea for me to be around critical people. They always seem to get worse."

"Really?" I asked.

He nodded. "Unfortunately," he said. "You go see her, and I'll go get us some breakfast."

He started to get up, but I stopped him and put my arms around his neck. "I'm so sorry that, once again, our time together hasn't worked out."

He laughed. "Shut up. I'm here. That's all I need. Go see your friend. I'll be here when you get back."

I kissed him and walked toward the ICU.

Mrs. Marx went with me into the ICU room, but stayed to the side so I could get close to Adrianne. I traced my finger along her hand, careful to not disrupt her I.V. "She looks the same."

"They say the worst of it is over," Mrs. Marx said. "The swelling has gone down and her vitals look much better than they did last night."

I let out a deep breath and kissed her hand again. Her fingers flinched under my lips. I sat up and looked at her face. Her eyes were fluttering. Her left eye, which wasn't as swollen as the right, flickered open briefly. "Adrianne?" I leaned down close to her face.

Her mother stepped close to the other side of her bed.

Adrianne's eye flickered again, and I could see a hint of hazel. "Adrianne?" I repeated.

Her fingers slightly curved around mine, and for an instant, she looked at me. I cried again and looked up at her mom. "Gloria, did you see that?"

"I did. Adrianne, can you hear us?" she asked.

Adrianne's fingers bent slightly again.

"She's trying to squeeze my hand," I said. "Come here!"

I stepped aside and let her mother take hold of her fingers. Her eye opened again and she looked at her mother. Gloria began to cry and I covered my mouth with my hands. Another nurse, a male one, came into the room. "What's going on?" he asked.

"She's waking up," I said.

He shook his head and stepped to her bedside. "That's impossible. It's probably nerve endings firing at rand—"

He stopped in the middle of his sentence when he checked her eyes and Adrianne looked right at him. Without thought, I grabbed his shoulder and almost shook his arm from the socket. "Did you see that?" I shouted.

He leaned closer to her. "Adrianne, if you can hear me, I want you to try and blink."

I leaned in close behind him. Adrianne forced her eye closed and then reopened it.

"I'll be damned," he said.

Gloria Marx was about to collapse onto the floor.

The nurse stepped out of the room. "Jamie, call Dr. Wilson. Adrianne Marx is awake."

"Awake?" another voice asked.

"You heard me," he said.

I practically ran to the waiting room. When I went through the door, I slid to a stop so fast I almost lost my footing. Warren—and Nathan—stood up. Nathan looked down at my shirt, raised an eyebrow, and scrunched his mouth over to the side.

My eyes doubled in size as I cautiously moved forward. "Hey," I said. "You're back."

Nathan nodded. "I got in last night. I heard about Adrianne this morning, so I thought I would stop by and see if you were here." He held up a bag from McDonald's. "I brought breakfast."

I smiled and stopped in front of him. "Thanks."

He looked down at the shirt again and back up. His eyes were asking, *Really?*

Warren folded his arms over his chest and nodded toward Nathan. "I filled him in while you were gone."

"Oh my gosh. She opened her eyes. Like, just now while I was in there!" I clapped my hands together. "The nurse said it was impossible, but she did it! She actually did it!"

"That's awesome," Nathan said.

Warren bit his lower lip and looked up at the ceiling.

"What is it?" I asked.

He nodded toward the corner. "Come over here."

"All of us?" Nathan asked.

"Sure. Why not?" Warren said.

We stepped to the empty corner of the room.

I folded my arms across my chest. "What's up?"

Warren ducked his head and lowered his voice. "Do you remember what I said earlier about not wanting to visit her?" His eyes narrowed. "About how I might make her worse?"

I nodded.

"I think this might be one of those situations where you do the opposite," he said.

Nathan's eyes darted with confusion from me to Warren. "Huh?"

"Do you think I'm healing her?" I asked.

Warren shrugged, but his eyes were affirmative.

Nathan held up his hand and stared at me. "Wait. Now you can heal people?"

I turned my palms up.

Nathan pointed at Warren. "Are you saying you make people sick?"

I elbowed him in the side. "Keep your voice down."

"You certainly make me sick," Nathan grumbled.

Warren laughed and I elbowed Nathan again.

Warren shrugged. "I think it's an idea worth exploring."

Nathan shook his head and walked across the room to our seats. "I haven't had enough coffee for this shit."

We followed him, and he handed me a cup of coffee as I plopped down in the seat between them.

"Thanks," I said. The coffee burned my throat. "How are things going with the case?"

Warren passed me a sausage biscuit out of the greasy paper bag.

"Really good," Nathan said. "Search teams are starting to look today in the game lands close to where the abductions happened."

"I hope they find the rest of them," I said. "You guys aren't dragging me through the woods again."

"I thought you did pretty well," Warren said.

"Minus the whining, complaining, and constantly trying to con us into carrying you," Nathan said.

I shot him a glare and pointed my finger at him. "You know, you're pretty hateful considering you'd still be sitting in your office with your thumb up your butt in front of that bulletin board if I hadn't come along. The FBI must think you're a genius for coming up with the hunter thing."

He laughed. "They actually do. They're talking about bringing me on."

I straightened. "Really?"

He crossed his boot over his knee. "Yeah. If we solve this thing, I may be moving again."

"Warren got offered a new job too," I said. "Everyone is trying to run away from me, I think."

Nathan looked across me to Warren. "What's the job?"

"Permanent field training position out in Oregon," he said.

Nathan perked up. "You gonna take it?"

Warren sipped his coffee. "I doubt it."

"It sounds like a good opportunity," Nathan said.

Warren cracked a smile. "For me or for you?"

I jumped in to redirect the conversation before it escalated. "What's Shannon think about the FBI thing?"

"I haven't told her yet." He paused. "She probably won't be too excited since she hated my stories about being on the *S.W.A.T. team*," he said, adding more emphasis to his words than necessary.

I tried to sit back against the seat, but Warren grabbed the back of the sweatshirt I was wearing.

He looked at Nathan, tugging on the hoodie. "This is yours?"

I dropped my head.

Nathan smiled. "It looks good on her, doesn't it?"

Warren slid his hand across my shoulders. "I must have thought so because I picked it out for her *in her bedroom* this morning."

I covered my face with my hands. "Will you two stop it? I'm about to make you both yank out your junk and having a pissing contest right here in the waiting room."

An older couple a few seats down from us turned their wide eyes our direction. I gave them an apologetic smile.

Nathan got up and stretched his arms. "I'm going to take off anyway. Give Adrianne my best. Keep me posted."

"Thanks for the breakfast, Nathan," I said as he walked across the room.

"No prob," he replied.

"Later, Nate," Warren called.

Nathan gave him the finger before walking out of the room.

Adrianne kept improving throughout the day, particularly when I was in the room with her, so Warren and I went home that evening. I was so tired my brain felt like it was fogged with tear gas. We both fell onto my bed in unison.

I groaned and tugged the comforter over my legs. "I don't think I've ever been so exhausted in all my life."

He flopped back against the pillows and draped his arm across his eyes. "You think you're tired? I've been up since four yesterday."

I rolled over toward him and rested my head on his chest. He wrapped his arm around my back and then shook his head. "Nope. This isn't going to work," he said. "Sit up."

"What?"

He pushed me off of him. "Sit up."

We both sat up in the bed.

"Arms up," he instructed.

I put my arms in the air and he pulled off Nathan's shirt and sent it flying across the room. He pulled me down against his chest. "Now, you can go to sleep," he said.

I laughed and closed my eyes.

17.

I WOKE UP alone again in my bed the next morning. The alarm clock read 8:07 in the morning. Rolling over and sleeping for another hour was a tempting idea, but I wanted to check on Adrianne, and I could smell fresh coffee downstairs. Before sitting up, I grabbed my phone off the nightstand and saw a new message from Adrianne's mom.

She's off the ventilator. Vitals are good.

I closed my eyes and smiled.

Reluctantly, I pushed myself off the bed and shuffled to the bathroom. Warren's toothbrush was in the holder next to mine. With butterflies fluttering in my stomach, I brushed my teeth and then my hair. I applied a light coat of lip gloss before heading downstairs in my sweat pants and sports bra.

Warren looked up from the couch where he was watching television. He was showered and dressed for the day. He put the remote control down on the cushion beside him and smiled. "Good morning, sexy."

I wrapped my arms around his neck from behind. "Am I always going to wake up alone?"

He looked at his watch. "If you always sleep in till eight, most likely."

I shook my head. "I don't like it."

He pulled me around in front of him and down onto his lap. A mischievous grin slowly crept across his chiseled face. "Trust me, I lay there for a very long time before I finally got up. I kept contemplating seriously disrupting your peaceful sleep."

I put my arms around his neck and pulled his ponytail holder out. His black hair fell around his shoulders. "Why didn't you? I would have had no objection." I ran my fingers through his hair which was still slightly damp from the shower.

He squeezed my knee. "Well, I knew you would wake up wondering about how your best friend is doing. Call me sentimental, but I don't want you to be thinking of anything else the first time we are together. That's why I left the bed."

"Oh, that's actually really sweet." I rubbed my nose against his.

He shrugged. "I'm a big softie. What can I say?"

I laughed. "Right."

He rubbed his hand up my thigh. "Get dressed. Let's go check on your friend."

I smiled. "I need a shower. Want to join?"

He dropped his head backward and groaned. "I try to be a good guy with you, and you go and say crap like that."

I pushed myself up. "Fine. Fine," I said. "Give me ten minutes."

"Hey!" He grabbed my arm and pulled me down. He kissed me, then released me. "Now you can go."

I smiled and skipped upstairs.

When we got to the hospital, Gloria Marx and my Dad were talking in the waiting room.

They both stood up when we walked in. "Hey Sloan," she said smiling.

"Hi, Gloria. Hey, Dad. What are you doing here?" I asked as I stepped underneath his outstretched arm.

Dad smiled. "I came by to see how she's doing. I admitted a patient last night, so I was here this morning anyway. Hi again, Warren."

Warren waved hello.

I looked between Gloria and my dad with wide eyes. "How is she this morning?"

She nodded. "I was just telling your dad she's doing really well. They took her off the ventilator late last night because she kept trying to wake up. So far, so good. They are talking about maybe even moving her out of ICU later today and into critical care."

"Really?" I asked surprised.

"Yep. I swear it's a miracle," she said. "You can go on to see her if you want."

I smiled. "Thanks."

"Gloria, I'm going to go with Sloan if you don't mind," Dad said.

"Of course not. I need to make some quick phone calls," she said.

I looked up at Warren. "Are you going to wait out here?"

He nodded. "Yeah. I'll be here when you get back."

I gave him a quick peck on the lips and walked with my father down the hallway.

When we were out of earshot, Dad leaned down close to me and lowered his voice. "Is it safe to say I can reasonably assume why you were happy Warren wasn't your brother?"

I felt my face turn red. "Yes, I think you can assume correctly." I hoped he wouldn't push the topic any further.

"Well, I do hope you bring him over to the house soon so we can get to know him better. He's kinda fallen out of the sky as far as we're concerned," he said.

"I will, Dad. Soon," I said.

When we got to Adrianne's room, a nurse was changing out one of her I.V. bags. I was amazed at the difference in Adrianne's appearance. A lot of the machines were gone, some of the tubes had been removed, and her cheeks were a more natural pink. "Wow, she looks so much better," I said to my dad.

"Well, with her blood pressure being so low before, and with the drugs they give to keep the pressure on her brain down, it sort of sucks the life out of a person. The pressure in her brain has significantly decreased, so everything in her body is working much better than before. It's a drastic improvement in two days, really. I'm very surprised," he said.

I walked over and touched her hand. She felt much warmer than she had the two days before.

Her eyes opened ever so slightly and she tried to contort her mouth into a smile. "Witch," she whispered.

I laughed. "You almost die and the first thing you say to me is call me a witch?" I asked. "That's some crap."

She wiggled her fingers in my hand.

"How are you feeling?" I asked.

She slightly shook her head and closed her eyes. Tears rolled back onto her pillow. I wiped them away while fighting my own.

"Well, my dad is here and even he can't believe how well you're doing. You're going to be fine, Adrianne. The worst of this is over. Well, maybe not..." I scrunched up my nose. "They screwed up your hair pretty bad. You're going to be pissed."

She tried to laugh, but it was obviously too painful for her.

"Stay," she whispered.

I smiled down at her and lowered my face toward her. "I'm not going anywhere."

Dad stepped over by the bed. "Hi, Adrianne. Sloan is right. You're doing incredibly well. Each day it's going to get better." He patted her leg—the one that wasn't in a full cast. "I'm going to check on you every time I'm at the hospital and make sure they are taking the best care of you."

She didn't respond, but she followed him with her eyes.

He put his hand on my shoulder. "She's going to have a hard time talking because her throat is really sore from the ventilator, but she's surprisingly coherent."

"Did you hear that? Dad says you're coherent, but you can't talk. That means you have to listen to me and for once keep your mouth shut," I said.

Dad was chuckling to himself. "I'm going to let you girls talk." He leaned over and kissed me on the head. "I love you, Sloan."

"Love you too, Daddy," I said.

When he was gone, I gently sat down on the edge of her bed and held her hand. "You're not going to believe what you did," I said. "I was half naked in my bedroom with Warren—for the very first time, mind you—when my *mother* showed up and barged in on us to tell me your ass was in the hospital. Who's really the witch here?" My eyebrow rose with skepticism.

She tried to smile again.

I folded my arms across my chest. "I really hate you, you know?"

She reached her hand toward my face and I bent to meet her fingertips. "Love," she whispered.

I grasped her hand and kissed it. "I love you, too."

* * *

Warren and I left the hospital around lunchtime and went to Papa's and Beer Mexican restaurant to eat. I frowned at him over my fajitas.

"I just realized I have to go to work tomorrow. Today is Sunday."

He nodded. "All day long."

I thought it over. "It's impossible for me to take vacation time tomorrow, but I could try and take off toward the end of the week."

"Do what you've got to do, babe. I'll be fine," he said.

"What are you going to do while I'm at work?" I asked.

He sipped his water. "I dunno. I thought about maybe heading up in the mountains and looking around for a few hours. I came a little more prepared with gear this time than I did last weekend."

"You're going to look for the girl who went missing around here?" I asked.

"Maybe," he replied.

"Well, tomorrow I'll probably go see Adrianne over lunch if you want to join me," I said.

"Yeah, we'll see where I'm at when you're ready to go," he said.

I sighed. "I'm glad the worst of this is all over. I hope it is anyway," I said. "I don't know what I would ever do without her."

"I think she's going to be all right," he said. "You actually got her to talk."

"Do you really think I can heal?" I asked.

He nodded. "I think so," he said. "You seem to literally be my better half. Sick people get sicker around me, so it only makes sense they would get better around you."

I dug around with my fork on my fajita skillet looking for another piece of grilled chicken. "I wish I could figure out how to do this stuff on purpose."

"You've got to work at it," he said. "Exercise it till you get better."

"How do I exercise it?" I asked.

"The summoning thing is pretty obvious. You just need to figure out what works and what doesn't," he said. "We could try together."

I pointed my fork at him. "OK. Let me try and summon Mark Higgins, and then you can take him out."

He laughed and pointed at me. "Interesting idea but not exactly what I meant."

"Then what did you mean?" I asked as I bit into a piece of chicken.

"When was a specific time it happened?" he asked.

I thought about it for a second. "The very first time you showed up at my house after I left Nathan's."

He narrowed his eyes at me. "Are you sure that wasn't a

coincidence? Because I'm certain I was going there anyway, and I know you didn't call me there on purpose."

I waved a small chunk of a green pepper in his direction. "That seems to be how it happens most of the time. I don't do it on purpose. You didn't feel anything weird?"

He shook his head. "No. I just knew I had to see you."

I shrugged "I don't know, then."

"Have you ever tried to do it on purpose?" he asked.

I nodded. "Sure. I tried for years when I was younger to summon my birth mom," I said. "And maybe a few cute boys."

He rolled his eyes. "But were you serious about it?"

"My birth mom? Absolutely." I shook my head. "I don't think I have to be serious about it. Did I ever tell you about the night I told Adrianne?"

"No," he said.

"I was home from college and we were at this restaurant not too far from here. She was always teasing me because she thought it was funny how people would randomly show up after I had mentioned them. That night, she was begging me to try and summon this guy she was crushing on," I said.

He slid his empty plate across the blue tile tabletop. "What did you do?"

"I pretended I was meditating. I pushed my chair back, crossed my legs, and everything. Then, she started throwing stuff at me and she made me repeat 'Billy Stewart' after her three times."

"And?" he asked.

"And when we walked out of the restaurant, maybe ten minutes later, he drove by. It scared the crap out of both of us because we knew he was supposed to be in a completely different town at work."

He thought for a moment, then tapped his finger on the table. "When I do, *what I do*"—he looked at me with knowing eyes—"it's almost like I speak to them. I see it in my mind before it happens, and I will it on them."

"I did not see Billy Stewart in my mind sitting outside of that Italian joint," I said.

He pointed at me and leaned against the chair next to him. "Maybe not, but I'll bet you wondered what would happen if Adrianne saw him there. I'll bet it crossed your mind what would happen with her if Billy did show up."

I sat back in my chair. "I've never thought about that. That makes sense. I'm sure I probably did."

"I'm also pretty sure your curiosity about me was the same as mine about you that night you were talking to Nate about me," he said. "You wanted to meet me."

"That's true," I said.

"So try to do it now," he said.

"You want me to summon Billy Stewart here? Right now?" I asked.

He shook his head. "No. Try someone else. What's something else you need to do?"

I thought for a moment. "I need to talk to my boss, Mary Travers, about taking the rest of the week off."

He nodded. "That should work."

I pressed my eyes closed and pictured my boss with her mousy brown bob and her smushed face. "Mary Travers."

When I opened my eyes, he was grinning at me.

I laughed and threw a green pepper at him. "You just made me feel like an idiot!"

He laughed. "That was kind of funny." He turned his hand over. "But you never know. It might work."

I rolled my eyes. "Shut up," I said. "Finish your food. I wanna get out of here and actually do something with you today before the week gets crazy."

"I'm trying to figure out if your life is ever not crazy," he teased.

"It's certainly been very crazy lately." I pointed at him. "It's been straight up chaos ever since I met Nathan McNamara."

My phone rang. Warren and I looked at each other.

"If this is my boss, I'm going to go and check myself into the psych ward right now," I said.

He smiled.

I looked down at my phone and then showed Warren. It was Nathan. "I should check myself in anyway," I muttered. I shook my head and answered the phone. "Hey."

"Hey, what are you doing?" he asked.

"Practicing voodoo with Warren." I wiped my mouth with a napkin and then dropped it onto my skillet. "What's up?"

"I wanted to give you a heads up that Mark Higgins, the guy who was driving Adrianne, just bonded out of jail," he said.

My mouth fell open. "Are you serious?"

"Yep."

"How did that happen?" I asked.

"That's how the system works, Sloan. Go to jail, bond out, and wait for your court date," he said.

"That's completely unacceptable!" I slammed my palm down on the table. "I guess I'm going to have to handle it myself!"

"What are you going to do?" he asked, obviously trying to contain his amusement at my outburst.

I pushed my chair away from the table. "I can go find Mark Higgins!" I said and disconnected the call.

"What was that about?" Warren asked.

"Come on," I said. "It's time to go inflict some street justice."

He laughed. "What?"

I shot up out of my chair. "That guy—that creep—who was driving drunk with Adrianne bonded out of jail."

He looked up at me. "What are you going to do about it?"

"I'm going to go find him and kick his ass!"

He laughed and dropped a twenty dollar bill on the table before standing up. He wrapped his hand around mine. "You're so sexy when you're a raving lunatic. Let's go."

I pulled him toward the door and threw it open. A group of Sunday morning churchgoers almost went flying through the parking lot as I stormed outside. When I looked down, I realized that one of the tiny women I had plowed into was my boss.

I stumbled backward into Warren.

"Hi Sloan!" she cheered. "Where are you off to in such a rush? Who's your friend?"

I tried to make my mouth form words but only disjointed syllables came out. "I, uh…the, uh—"

Warren reached around me. "Hi, I'm Warren."

She extended her tiny hand to meet his, smiling brightly. "Hello, Warren. I'm Mary. Sloan and I work together at the county office."

Warren laughed. "No shit?" he said just loud enough for me to hear.

I went into a coughing fit and covered my face with my hands.

Mary grabbed my arm. "Are you OK?"

"I'm fine," I choked out. "I'll see you tomorrow, Mary."

Warren ushered me toward the car. "Well, congratulations, Ms. Jordan, you have mastered your superpower."

"That's crazy!" I jabbed my thumb into the center of my chest. "I'm crazy!"

He held the door to the Challenger open for me and gripped my jaw in his hand. "You're not crazy. You're just not exactly normal."

I huffed and sat down in the car.

He got in and started the engine. "Do you still feel like going and kicking some ass?"

I leaned against the door and covered my eyes with my hand. "No. Just take me home. I need a drink, and I need to lie down."

"I think that's probably a good idea," he said, backing out of the parking space. "I think all the stress and exhaustion is starting to get to you a little bit."

Warren stopped at the grocery store on the way home. He put the car in park but left the engine running. "I'm going to run in and get some beer and food to make for dinner."

I groaned and sank down in my seat. "I don't cook, Warren."

He winked at me. "I do."

I sighed and rolled my head toward him. "Will you marry me?"

He blinked at me and laughed. "Sloan, you're putting a lot of pressure on me."

I rolled my eyes. "You started it."

When we reached my house, I opened a beer in the driveway.

While he put the groceries in the kitchen, I flopped down on the sofa and put my feet up on the coffee table. I pinched the bridge of my nose and prayed my head would stop hurting.

"You didn't ask your boss for your vacation time," he reminded me.

"Oh, I'm sorry." I smirked. "I was a little bit distracted."

He came into the living room and clinked his beer bottle with mine before sitting down on the coffee table so he could face me. "I think it's pretty cool what you can do," he said as he tipped the bottle up to his lips.

I frowned. "Of course you do. You can kill people."

He laughed. "Think about it. It's a pretty spectacular gift, Sloan."

I shook my head. "Nobody cares about your opinion."

He smiled and leaned toward me. "Why don't you go upstairs, take a nice hot bath, and drink your beer in the tub? Try and clear your head for a little bit. You've had a pretty big weekend all the way around."

I sighed. "What are you going to do?"

He smiled and gave me a gentle peck on the lips. "It's a Sunday in September. I'm going to watch football."

Obediently, I did as he said and went and finished my beer in the hot bath tub. My brain hurt because it was so full of everything that had transpired in the past month. I wasn't sure how much more I could stand. I laid my head against the wall and closed my eyes. *What am I?* I asked over and over again.

Just when I was about to drift off to sleep, there was a gentle knock at the door. I opened my lazy eyes and smiled at Warren who was standing in the doorway.

"Feel better?" he asked.

I nodded. "Much better."

"I think you must have been talking about me..." He slowly crossed the bathroom floor and picked up a towel off the rack. "Because I had this supernatural urge to come up here."

I smiled. "Oh really?"

He nodded his head and smiled. "Yes. It had absolutely nothing to do with the fact that you were wet and naked in the bathtub."

I laughed and reached for the towel he was holding. "Well, I have to get out, so turn around."

He shook his head. "No."

"No?"

"No." His deep tone signaled he wasn't joking.

My heart started to pound in my chest as he towered over me. More than just physically, I was certain Warren had reached heights of experience I had never dreamed of. For me, each romantic encounter left me with a feeling of emptiness, like each lover had been cosmically coerced into my bed. Warren was different. There was no compulsion to his desire. It was raw and genuine and dripping from his eyes as he watched me stand up.

The towel slid from his fingers and fell to the floor as he closed the distance between us. This time, when his lips connected with mine, there was no interruption. There was no holding back. He carried me to my bedroom and covered my body with his own, obliterating every thought of everything else outside of the powerful force of our connection. When it was over, and his sweat was mixed with mine, I was certain of one thing:

I had died in that bed...a couple of times.

18.

WARREN WAS ASLEEP next to me when I woke up the next morning. I was sure it was an occurrence that wouldn't soon be repeated. I smiled and studied the way his silky black hair fell across his perfect face as his muscular arm curled around his pillow. "I feel your eyes on me, Sloan." He didn't even crack a smile.

"I thought you were asleep," I said, tangling my legs with his under the covers.

His lips spread into a thin smile. "I've been thinking of different ways to wake you up since four." His arm slipped under the covers and grasped my bare hip. He pulled my body into his, and his eyes fluttered open.

I pushed his hair off his face. "I'm not sure my legs are going to function today."

He shook his head as his fingers trailed down my spine. "That's OK. You don't need them."

I groaned. "I have to go to work."

He rolled on top of me, his full weight pressing my body into the mattress. "Are you sure?"

"Yes." No.

He pinned my hands over my head and nibbled at the side of my neck. I squirmed underneath him. "I'm going to be late."

"I don't really care."

A half an hour later, I pulled on his t-shirt and my wobbly legs carried me to the bathroom. "What are you going to do today?" I asked as he watched me, smiling, from the bed.

He folded his arms behind his head. "I'm probably going to go scout out the woods and look for that girl from here."

"Leslie Bryson," I said, sticking my toothbrush into my mouth.

"Yep. Maybe I'll meet you at your office and take you out to dinner tonight," he said.

I turned to look at him. My cream colored bed sheet was wound around one of his legs and barely tugged up to his bellybutton. I dribbled toothpaste down the front of his shirt and forgot what I was going to say.

He smiled. "Don't go to work."

I groaned and spit in the sink. "I have to." I grabbed the bathroom doorknob. "And I'm never going to get there with you watching me like that." He laughed, and I slammed the door.

* * *

Warren had made me a to-go cup of coffee before I left the house, but my travel mug was empty by the time I reached my office. For the first time in my life, I understood why so many people hated Mondays. The weekend hadn't been long enough, and my mind was still at home in bed. The last thing I wanted to do was send out tourism specials for all of Asheville's leaf-enthusiasts. Warren had been right; leaves were stupid.

To add insult to injury, I had an email waiting from the sheriff when I turned on my computer. They were going to have to shut down the public forests in the middle of hunting season, and he would have to make a statement to the press during the five o'clock news hour. That meant I had to make a trip to the jail, and I had forgotten my Xanax due to Warren's distraction that morning.

Very reluctantly, I left my office and drove to the jail around eleven a.m. Knowing he would be out of the office for the day, I parked in Nathan's parking spot when I pulled into the lot. Anxiety began to pulse through my veins the moment I stepped out of my car.

Ms. Claybrooks wasn't even working at the master control desk to distract me. As I walked down the hallway to the sheriff's office, I nervously wrung my hands and practiced deep breathing exercises. I tried to replay the steamy events of my morning and the night before in my head, but even that wasn't enough to dilute the evil which seemed to envelope me from every direction.

"Are you all right?" Sheriff Davis asked with wide eyes when I walked into his office.

I nodded and sat down across from him. "Just a bit of a headache. I'll be fine."

In record time, I hammered out an apology to the hunters of Western North Carolina. The wildlife game lands would close that day at dusk and would reopen as soon as the area had been thoroughly investigated. I made the necessary phone calls to the media from the sheriff's office, and then I promised to meet him for the broadcast on the front steps of the sheriff's office right after lunch. When he was satisfied with his announcement, I made a bee-line for the exit. My heart rate had to be registering somewhere between cheetah and drumroll.

As I bolted through the final door that would lead to the lobby, I slammed face-first into a green and gold uniform. "Oh, I'm so sorry!" I looked up into the face of Billy Stewart.

He cocked his head to the side and laughed. "Sloan Jordan?"

Billy Stewart was as handsome as he had been when we were kids. He was carrying about twenty more pounds on him and had a few new lines around his eyes, but I could still see why Adrianne had always liked him so much.

Even in the midst of my panic attack, I laughed. "Billy, I was just talking about you over lunch yesterday and here you are!"

"Talking about me?" he asked surprised. "I don't think I've seen you in what? Ten years or more?"

"At least!" I was gripping my chest.

"Are you all right?" he asked.

I nodded. "Yeah, I'm fine," I lied.

"Hey, I heard about your friend Adrianne being in the hospital. That's terrible what happened to her." He crossed his strong arms over his chest. "How's she doing?"

I nodded. "She's getting better every day. I was just on my way to see her."

He raised his eyebrows. "I've been thinking about dropping by there myself. Mind if I tag along?"

Adrianne would kill me if I let Billy Stewart show up with her in the condition she was in, so I smiled. "Sure, but I'm heading out right now though."

He shrugged. "Not a problem. I've got to come back here afterward anyway. Wanna ride on the county's dime?"

I smiled. "Sure." I was desperate to get out of that building as quickly as possible. "How have you been? How's your family?" I asked, begging for conversation to distract me as we crossed the lobby.

He nodded. "Well, my dad passed in '09, and my mom moved to Statesville to be near her sister, but she's doing pretty well."

"Oh, I'm sorry to hear that."

"It was a heart attack. It happened fast and to be honest, he was an asshole anyway," he said. "How about your folks? Your dad still at the hospital?"

I nodded as he held open the door. It was all I could do not to run from the building like my hair was on fire. "Yeah. He's doing a lot of Alzheimer's research these days. Mom and Dad are both doing well."

"That's good to hear," he said. We reached the bottom of the steps and he nodded toward a green truck with the county emblem on the door. "This is me."

I got in the passenger's seat, and he put the files he was carrying in the back seat before getting behind the wheel. I took a series of deep breaths as he pulled away from the curb and gripped the handle on the door to help ease the shaking I couldn't control in my arms.

"What are you doing up this way today?" I asked.

"Had to drop off some paperwork about this search effort they are starting up in the morning."

I nodded. "I was just meeting with the sheriff about it."

He shook his head and chuckled. "There's gonna be a lot of pissed off rednecks 'round here."

He pulled out onto the street and straight into the sunlight. I shielded my eyes as I saw something move out of the corner of my eye. A sharp jab in my thigh caused me to shriek and grab for my leg. As we passed under the shade of an orange oak tree I could see Billy scowling at me. "Why were you talking about me yesterday, Sloan?"

"What?" I asked. I was still trying to inspect my thigh. Whatever it had been had gone straight through my pant leg and into my skin. That's when I saw Billy drop a syringe down between his seat and his door. My brain was scrambling to catch up.

"Why were you talking about me?" he demanded.

"What did you do?" I cried. A wave of dizziness washed over me.

"Don't worry," he said. "Pentobarbital only takes a minute."

"Pentobarbital?" I asked confused.

"Large animal sedative," he explained. "That's one of the perks of being a game warden."

After that, the world swirled out of view.

* * *

When I awoke, I was handcuffed to a radiator in a musty cabin with dirty wooden floors. There were holes in the baseboards from small woodland squatters. My head was throbbing and my stomach felt sick. Pain was pulsing through my knees and there was dried blood down my forearms. I looked around at the one room hunting cabin. The sun was low in the sky and casting a warm glow through the chilly room. I had been unconscious for hours.

It appeared as though I was alone, but I knew better. I could sense Billy's presence nearby. On the floor, just out of my reach, the photos of the missing girls were splayed across the floor. My briefcase was open lying next to them.

Oh god. I panicked as the realization of what was happening settled in.

I pressed my eyes closed. "Warren Parish...Nathan McNamara... Warren Parish...Nathan McNamara," I repeated quietly.

"They ain't gonna help you now." Billy stepped inside from the front door with a large hunting knife strapped to his side and his gun on the other hip. He wasn't wearing his uniform anymore. He was in dark camouflage.

"Billy, what are you doing?"

"Waiting for the sun to set. Then I'm going to show you my special place," he said with wild eyes.

"Why are you doing this?"

He smiled as his heavy boots clunked across the wooden planks toward me. "You know, for a minute there, I wondered if you had figured it out. You know, when you said you were talking about me. Then you got into the truck like a damn fool, and I knew better." He laughed and rubbed his calloused palms together. "I guess this is my lucky day."

"What are you going to do with me?" I asked.

He knelt down in front of me and began to count on his fingers. "Well, I'm going to rape you. Then I'm going to kill you. Then I'll probably rape you some more before I dig you a nice warm hole in the ground."

I shuddered and twisted against my restraints.

He laughed again. "Government steel, honey. You ain't gettin' loose."

"You'll never get away with this," I said. "They're onto you now. Police and volunteers are going to be all over this place tomorrow, and they will find you."

He leaned so close to my face I could smell the rancid chewing tobacco on his hot breath. "I'm heading up the search team. How else are they gonna know where someone might hide a body away from all the tree stands, the deer beds, and the watering holes?"

I thought I might throw up, but I wouldn't give him the satisfaction of seeing me panic.

He leaned over the pile of pictures and took a knee beside them. "You know what's funny about all this?" He started sorting through the photographs. "I was actually lookin' for you the night I killed this one." He spun the picture of Leslie Bryson across the floor toward me.

I looked down at Leslie's face and details started snapping together like building blocks. 2009. Billy Stewart. Chili's Bar and Grill, where Leslie was a waitress, was a block over from Alejandro's. I had summoned Billy that night, and he had been planning to kill me.

He scratched his forehead with dirt-caked fingernails. "Never found you that night, so I chose someone else." A grin, oozing with evil, spread across his lips. "But I've found you now."

I shook my head. "No. You screwed up taking me. You finally made a stupid mistake. Detective McNamara is already searching this area, and you'd better believe he's keeping a close eye on me. If I go missing, he'll burn the forest to hunt you down."

He grabbed me by my hair and pulled till I screamed. "He won't burn it before you're nothing but a pile of body parts," he said, showering my face with spit. He shoved me toward the floor, and I hit my head on the radiator.

He crossed the room and picked up a small box off the wooden table. He flipped it open as he walked toward me. I scrambled away from him as he produced another syringe. "Don't worry," he said. "This will make you woozy for a little bit, and then you'll sleep till we get there."

He slid the needle carefully into a vein in my arm and pressed down on the plunger. Then he tucked the needle back into the box and walked away.

I looked to where my hands were cuffed. My mom's older sister had a radiator like it when I was a kid. Even then, Aunt Joan's was so old that it hadn't worked in years. I wasn't sure how old the rusty piece of metal was, but I was sure it wasn't as strong as the handcuffs. I pulled and tugged and pounded the edge of the handcuffs into the radiator bars but nothing cracked. The cuffs were biting into the sensitive crevices between the bones in my wrists, and my thumbs and pinky fingers were going numb.

He laughed on the other side of the room. "Good luck with that. You're not the first bitch that's tried to break that thing."

I slumped against the radiator. My scalp felt warm and sticky with blood against the cold metal. The chill seeped into my skin, making my body tingle.

"Warren, where are you?" I cried, barely above a whisper.

"Oh, are you praying? Are you calling out for help?" Billy whimpered, teasing me. "It's OK, Sloan. It will all be over soon."

When I awoke again, it felt like I was being drawn and quartered, only I was being dragged, literally, by my arms across the rough terrain of the mountain. I didn't need to be able to see to know that my body was bloody and broken. My legs screamed like the skin was being peeled away with a jigsaw. Something was shoved into my mouth that I couldn't expel because of the strong tape that was stretched tight across my lips. It was almost completely dark, and I knew if I didn't put up a fight soon, I was going to quickly run out of chances.

Desperate, I scrambled to get my feet under me. My bare and lacerated toes tried to fight for a foothold into the cold, hard earth beneath my feet. Billy spun around and backhanded me across the face. "Calm the hell down, you dumb whore! You're making this a lot worse for yourself!"

I tried to claw at him, but my fingers couldn't find his skin.

Wrecked with exhaustion and agony, the fight left my arms. Billy continued to drag me about a hundred more feet over dirt, rocks, and tree roots that stuck out of the ground like tire spikes. I thought of the day in the woods when I had wanted Warren or Nathan to carry me. I remembered the terrified look on Nathan's face when Warren produced the jawbone from the dirt. I remembered trying to imagine

Warren singing along with Dionne Warwick. *It's funny the things that flash through your mind when you know you're about to die.* I swear I could hear Warren singing...

Billy stopped walking. Billy heard Warren singing too. I hadn't imagined it. Nathan and Warren had already found the 'special place' where Billy was planning to hide my body along with Leslie Bryson's corpse.

"What was that?" I heard Nathan's voice say. "I heard movement up there."

I tried to look around, and for a split second I thought I could see a light flash up in the distance. Billy knelt down and grabbed me by my right arm and my right thigh and hoisted me over his shoulder like a lame sheep. He was turning around and heading back the way we came.

He was retreating because Warren and Nathan were really there!

I tried to struggle, but I was dangling upside down. Then I saw it. Billy's hunting knife was just within my grasp. He was moving too quickly and with too much panic to notice when my fingers unsnapped the leather that was holding it. With the nerve damage in my hands it was difficult to hold onto the knife, but somehow I managed to cut him in the side deep enough to make him yelp with pain and stumble.

It was enough to cause a stir of leaves in the woods behind us. "Who's there?" I heard Nathan shout.

Flashlights were going wild through the trees. I looked up to see salvation coming. There was just enough daylight for me to make out two figures rushing toward us as Billy tried to run. I stabbed at him again. This time, he dumped me off his shoulder and made a run for it. I felt my ribs crash into the unearthed roots of a large tree and thorns tore through the flesh I had left along my right thigh.

I rolled over enough to see Billy lunge for the driver's side door of his truck. As he yanked it open, Warren fired a bullet into the door spinning Billy around and slamming him face-first into the dirt.

Warren cautiously approached as Billy reoriented and tried to get to his knees. "Get your hands up!" he ordered with a voice so dark and menacing that it seemed to add to the darkness of the forest.

Billy began to rise up slowly as Nathan shined his flashlight in my direction. His eyes locked on me and fear flashed through him. "Sloan!" he shouted.

Distracted by the sound of my name, Warren looked away for a split second. I couldn't even scream when I saw Billy raise his gun and fire wildly into the air. The gun fired again and Nathan dove in front of me. His airborne body seemed to explode in a different direction and land just out of my reach.

Behind him, Warren was down on one knee when he fired twice, sending Billy Stewart flying backward through the air.

I scrambled toward Nathan and used both cuffed hands to roll him onto his back. "Sloan," he sputtered, splattering my face with blood. His eyes were terrified.

I couldn't even scream.

"Nate, you all right?" Warren yelled as he approached Billy cautiously. "I need your 'cuffs. This guy's not dead. Sloan, can you hear me?"

I tried to scream but couldn't.

I yanked Nathan's shirt up and found a bloody exit wound a few inches below his collarbone. I pressed my hands to it and looked desperately around for Warren.

He had his knee pressed into Billy's throat as he unloaded Billy's gun. "Nathan!" he yelled again. Finally, when he had no other choice, Warren reached into Billy's truck and pulled the keys out of the ignition. He locked the doors and slammed it closed. Then he shot Billy again in the foot before running across the road.

When he reached me, visible panic washed over him. "Holy shit!" he yelled as he dropped down next to me. My eyes begged him to help Nathan first, but instead, he peeled off the sticky tape that covered my mouth. I fought to spit out the wad of fabric that I was beginning to suck down my windpipe.

"Help him, Warren! He's been shot. In the back or the side. I'm not sure," I screamed.

"Back, near my ribs," Nathan sputtered.

"We've got to move you to the road," Warren said as he grabbed Nathan under his armpits. Nathan tried to help push with his feet, but he was having a hard time breathing.

When we made it to more level ground, Warren produced a knife and cut Nathan's shirt away. He rolled him until he found the bloody hole in Nathan's back. "Sloan, get me that tape," he instructed.

I grabbed Nathan's flashlight and scrambled to the grass. I found the discarded scrap of duct tape and carried it to Warren. He was shredding Nathan's shirt with his knife. "Nate, I need you to exhale all the way." He handed me a strip of fabric. "Sloan, wad this up and seal off that hole in the front the best you can."

The hole in the front of Nathan's chest was producing foamy, gurgling blood. I looked into Nathan's eyes and he nodded. "Do it," he whispered. Blood was drizzling out of the corners of his mouth.

"Don't you die on me," I threatened.

"Exhale," Warren told him.

When he had, Warren covered the fabric with tape. Then, he did the same thing on his back. "It's hit your lung, man," he said. "We've got to get you out of here."

"Really, Warren? No shit," Nathan gurgled.

I scowled. "This is not the time for a smart mouth, Nathan McNamara."

Warren searched for Nathan's handcuff keys, then finally freed my hands. I couldn't feel my fingers at all. "Are you OK?" he asked me.

I wiped mud and sticky wet blood off my face. "The game warden. It's him. It's Billy Stewart. He's the killer."

Warren's head jerked with recognition. "Billy Stewart?"

I nodded furiously. "Yes!"

"Other than the obvious, did he hurt you?" he asked.

I shook my head.

Billy was attempting to crawl away from the truck when Warren and I carried Nathan over. "Do you want me to shoot you again?" Warren shouted. Of course Billy kept going.

Warren unlocked the truck and we carefully laid Nathan across the back seat. Then he looked over at me. "I'm going to need your help with the game warden."

I nodded.

Billy had made it to the side of the road, leaving a thick trail of blood behind him. Warren kicked him in the side, toppling him over onto his back. He coughed up blood, spewing it in my direction as I painfully knelt down next to him. My ribs and every inch of my torn skin were screaming with pain.

Warren put his muddy boot down on Billy's throat.

I wanted to smack him across the face, but I couldn't feel my fingers. "OK, asshole. It's truth time," I said.

He gasped. "I'm dying here."

I put my knee square on the center of one of the bloody holes in his chest, making him squirm in agony. "I certainly hope so," I hissed. "But right now, you're going to talk and tell me the truth."

"I'm not telling you shit!" He gurgled and spat blood on me.

Warren kicked him in the face.

"Warren, can you tell how many victims this guy has on him?" I asked looking up to where Warren stood over us both.

Warren studied Billy's face for a moment before finally looking at me. "Twelve."

We had only been aware of ten missing girls, not twelve. "We know about the ones between here and Raleigh. Where are the others?" I pressed my knee harder into Billy's chest.

"Toccoa, Georgia," he whispered.

I looked at Warren. "Think that's it?"

He nodded. Warren's eyes were fierce and his jaw was set. "Should we let him bleed out?" he asked.

I struggled to my feet. "No. I don't want to take any chances. Finish him."

Billy began to scramble as I turned toward the truck and Warren leaned down close to him.

There was a loud crack of lightning, but I didn't even flinch.

19.

WARREN FOLDED DOWN the front passenger's seat of Billy's truck, and I sat on top of it as we navigated our way down the obscure mountain access road. I held pressure against Nathan's chest. His breathing was shallow and uneven. His face was pale and he was sweating, but he was alive.

"Sloan, are you OK?" His voice was weak and raspy.

I shivered with the release of adrenaline through my veins. My chin had begun to quiver with shock. I did my best to force a smile. "I'm not as bad as you."

"Would you mind filling me in on what the hell just happened?" he struggled to ask.

"That was the game warden. He's your serial killer." I pointed out the window where we had left Billy Stewart's body lying by the road. "He kidnapped me this afternoon. What were you guys doing up here?"

Nathan coughed. "Warren called me and—"

"Let me do the talking, Nate," Warren interrupted, looking over his shoulder. "I found another body up here today. I called Nate, and he met me at the bottom of the mountain. We hiked in together and had just gotten here when we heard someone coming up behind us. Surprise, surprise. It turns out it was you and the serial killer."

"How did he kidnap you?" Nathan wheezed.

"He's an old friend of Adrianne's. We all went to high school together," I explained. "I ran into him at the jail today and invited him to come with me to see her. He offered to drive because he said he had to come back to the sheriff's office after lunch."

"You went with him willingly?" Warren asked surprised. "Could you not feel how dark he was? That dude was exactly what I imagined a serial killer would feel like."

I shuddered with a sickening chill. "I ran into him at the jail, so I really didn't notice. I was already mid-panic attack, and I wanted to get out of there as fast as possible."

"But you knew him before, right? Didn't he freak you out before?" Nathan asked.

I shook my head. "No. I mean, we were kids then."

"Before he committed his first murder," Warren said almost to himself.

I nodded. "It had to have been. I'm pretty sure Adrianne told me he went to NC State to study forestry after he graduated from our high school."

"In Raleigh," Nathan wheezed.

I looked down at him. "I told you NC State was terrible."

He pointed at me with a blood-stained frown. "Hey!"

Warren glanced back at me. "But you told me yesterday you saw him when you were in college. You didn't sense the evil then?"

I thought back to the night with Adrianne at Alejandro's. "I only saw his truck from a distance."

"Damn," Warren said.

"Anyway, once we were in the truck, he injected me with some kind of animal tranquilizer. Check in the door pocket next to you, Warren. I'll bet it's still there," I said.

Warren flipped on the light in the cab and searched between the door and his seat. He steered the truck with one hand as he carefully reached down and picked up a long, metal syringe. He flinched just looking at it.

"I passed out in the passenger's seat and when I woke up, I was chained to a radiator in an old cabin somewhere up in the woods," I said. "I was there for hours."

"He was waiting till dark when the woods were cleared, just like Warren said he would," Nathan said. "He was going to bury you there with Leslie Bryson."

"He was going to do a lot more than that." I thought I might vomit.

"You're sure you're all right?" Warren asked again. He reached back to touch my shoulder.

"Oh, I'm very far from all right considering I was just nearly raped and murdered." Another chill shot down my spine. "I'm sure my ribs are broken, and I doubt I'll be wearing shorts this summer."

"You've got to get checked out," he insisted.

I nodded. "I will." I looked at Nathan. "He said there were twelve girls altogether and that the other two are buried in Toccoa, Georgia."

"A team from Hickory found Colleen Webster just outside of Statesville today," he said.

"His mother lives in Statesville," I told him.

He nodded. "Is he dead?" Nathan asked.

"I'm pretty sure he bled out before we left," I lied.

He sighed and closed his eyes. "Good."

After a moment, I looked at Warren. "Weren't you wondering why you hadn't heard from me?" I asked.

"Well, when I got off the mountain, I called but got your voicemail. I assumed you were busy. Then I hiked up here with Nate and didn't have cell service," he said. "Honestly, I wasn't worried about you. I was afraid you were going to be mad at me for being gone all day."

"Well, I am a little mad at you." I pouted. "I was kidnapped and you weren't even worried."

"I was worried about you," Nathan croaked and winked up at me.

Warren and I would have laughed if it hadn't been so serious.

"We do have a problem," Nathan said.

"How to explain me being there...again?" Warren asked.

"Yep."

"Maybe we'll luck out and Raleigh and Asheville won't connect the dots?" I offered.

Nathan shook his head.

"No babe. This is going to be big," Warren said.

My shoulders sank. "The West Coast is sounding pretty good about now."

Warren smiled over his shoulder at me. "We'll figure it out. We are going to have to tell them I was in those woods last week on purpose."

We rode for a while in silence. My hands felt each breath that

Nathan struggled to take. I knew he was going to live, but I knew it was because of me that he almost didn't. If I had been right when I suggested to Warren that I might have a neutralizing effect on people's hatred of him, then the same had to be true for me. That night, Nathan McNamara dove in front of a bullet to save me. I wasn't sure how much truer love could get than that. Nathan rested his hand on top of mine and closed his eyes.

Part of Nathan's lung had collapsed by the time we got to the hospital, so they took him immediately into surgery. I also got to see the extent of my injuries when I was rolled into triage. Apparently when I got out of the car at the emergency room, everyone thought I was the patient. I looked a bit like something out of a zombie movie. Warren stayed with me the whole time, and the hospital staff called my parents.

The majority of the sheriff's office was waiting when we arrived at the hospital. That seemed to be standard protocol whenever a detective calls in his own 'officer down' distress over the radio. The sheriff himself walked into my triage room with his hands on his hips.

"Miss Jordan, do we have you on the wrong payroll list? You keep showing up at my crime scenes," he said.

I raised an eyebrow and settled against my hospital pillow. "If I am on the wrong payroll, you certainly don't pay me enough, Sheriff."

He laughed and shook his head. "I was worried when you didn't show up for the press conference today, but I would never have imagined this would be the reason."

"Well, I was really worried about all the disappointed hunters in the area, so I decided to speed the case along," I said with a smile.

He rolled his eyes. "Well, mission accomplished."

"Did your guys go up to Pisgah?" I asked.

He nodded. "We're up there, the state is up there, and the feds. You're going to have a lot of work to do when you get out of here."

I groaned. "Well, I have nerve damage in my hands from being thrown around in handcuffs, so there may not be a whole lot of typing in my future for a while. I may have to dictate your news stories."

"What else did the doctors say, if you don't mind me asking?" he asked.

"I have a concussion, two broken ribs, and I'm missing enough skin on my legs from being dragged that they asked if I had been pulled behind a car."

He cringed with sympathy.

"I keep trying to figure out if this is workman's comp related since I was kidnapped from work by an officer of the state and bludgeoned half to death," I said.

He laughed. "Well, I think, at the very least, the county can afford you some time off."

I shook my head. "I'm already working on the press release in my head. I'll get someone else to type it."

The sheriff noticed Warren in the corner. "You must be the big hero."

"Sheriff Davis, this is my boyfriend, Warren," I said.

They shook hands and Warren smiled. "I just happened to be at the right place at the right time."

The sheriff cocked his eyebrow. "That seems to be happening around you a lot these days."

Warren shrugged. "McNamara is a friend of Sloan's, and he told me the disappearances might be related. Because of my background in human tracking with the military, he asked for my help. Yesterday, we decided to scope out some similar places to where I found that girl last weekend. Everything else is all a really lucky coincidence."

"I'll say. It's a huge lucky coincidence," he said. "I'm sure we'll be talking with each other some more."

Warren nodded. "Whatever you need, sir."

The sheriff pointed at me. "You get to feeling better, Sloan." He turned to leave, but stopped in the doorway. "And please try and stay out of trouble."

When he had gone, Warren stretched out on the bed beside me. "How are you feeling?"

"Like an MMA champ," I said.

He shook his head and laughed. "I wouldn't say 'champ' exactly." He traced his fingers along my arm. "Seriously, how are you doing?"

I rolled my face toward him. "I'm going to have nightmares for a while. He was going to kill me. If you and Nathan hadn't been there, I would be lying next to Leslie Bryson's bones right now."

He rested his forehead against mine. "But we *were* there, and you're not buried in the woods. Thank God." He pressed his lips to my temple.

I shuddered remembering the feeling of being dragged along that wooded path. "Thank God," I agreed.

Across the room, a shimmer of light reflected off of my discarded clothes that were laying on the table near the door. Kayleigh's angel pin had somehow survived the ordeal in much better condition than the bedraggled blouse it was still attached to. A thought that I couldn't quite piece together rolled around in my brain. Perhaps it was the morphine.

"Warren, can I ask you a serious question?"

He sat up a little and looked at me with concern. "Of course. What?"

"Do you think we will ever figure out what we are? Why we can do the things we do?" I dropped my head back and stared at the fluorescent lights above.

He reclined against my pillow and rolled his head toward mine. "The answer is out there somewhere. Maybe someday we'll find it. I think we're off to a pretty good start."

I blew out a deep sigh. "Can I ask you something else?"

"Anything," he whispered and closed his eyes.

I cut my eyes at him. "Were you really singing 'That's What Friends are For?' with Nathan in the woods?"

He burst out laughing and planted a kiss on my lips.

20.

TWO WEEKS LATER, I was sitting on Warren's lap with my heavily bandaged legs resting on the edge of Adrianne's hospital bed. We were sharing a tub of popcorn. Nathan was on the other side of the bed popping Skittles into his mouth. Adrianne was wearing a hat and sitting up as she slurped on some purple jello.

"Oh, this is it!" I squealed. I reached for the television remote on Adrianne's bed but winced with pain from my ribcage and drew my hand back.

Warren shook his head. "Please let me do it." He picked up the remote and turned up the volume.

Shannon Green's face appeared on the television set. She was dressed in a bright yellow suit with freshly whitened teeth and enough hairspray to set the city ablaze.

Adrianne scrunched up her nose. "What's going on with her hair?"

"I was afraid she might get too close to the stage lighting and blow us all up." Nathan laughed gingerly, still with a bit of rasp to his voice.

Shannon smiled at the television screen and began her monologue. "Some are calling it the luckiest break in criminal history. Others are calling it nothing short of a miracle. I am Shannon Green with WKNC News coming to you from our studio with an exclusive interview with two people at the center of one of the most fascinating crime cases in our state's history. We are here with Detective Nathan

McNamara and Buncombe County Public Information Officer, Sloan Jordan."

I leaned into Warren. "I love this part."

The camera panned to Nathan, who carefully shifted toward Shannon in his seat. He was wearing a suit. "Thank you for having us, Shannon. We are delighted to be here," he said and smiled at the camera.

We all laughed and Nathan launched a red Skittle at my head. "Shut up!"

"Oh, it gets better," I assured them.

Shannon folded her hands over her knee. "Twelve girls have gone missing in North Carolina and Georgia. Gone without a trace. One of the first of them was your sister, Nathan, and she disappeared almost thirteen years ago. How is it, that such an unlikely pair could solve a case that has had police and investigators across the nation puzzled for well over a decade?" she asked.

Nathan smiled at the camera again. "Well, Shannon, Miss Jordan and I met by chance on another case recently where she brought some very valuable insight and opinions to the..."

Warren squeezed my thigh. "My girl? Opinionated? No..."

I tried to clamp my hand over Warren's mouth. "Shhh…"

"She is actually the one who found the link between the disappearances and the hunting season." Nathan smiled at the camera again.

"Why do you keep smiling like that?" Adrianne asked. "You look like a demented Ken doll."

We all laughed again.

Shannon forced a smile on screen. "You two must have been spending an awful lot of time together to be able to come up with such an elaborate conclusion." Her voice was squeaky and more high-pitched than normal.

The camera moved to me. "Over the course of a few weeks, Detective McNamara and I did spend almost every waking hour together."

Nathan shook his head. "You're mean, Sloan."

I smiled at Warren and then looked back at the television.

"We did a lot of traveling and interviewing people. We employed the help of a friend who was able to track and locate the bodies that were found in Raleigh and ultimately the one that was found here in Asheville. That discovery also led to the demise of the killer himself," I explained.

Shannon leaned forward in her chair toward me on screen. "I believe the question of the century is, how is it that you came by the information that led to the discovery of the first two bodies in Raleigh? What caused you to look in the exact spot where the bodies had been overlooked for so many years?"

On screen I turned and smiled at Nathan (who then turned and smiled at the camera) before I continued. "*We did a very thorough process of elimination of different areas, and I guess there was a bit of a woman's intuition at play, Shannon.*"

Warren shifted to look at me. "A 'woman's intuition'? Did you really just say that?"

I laughed. "I couldn't exactly say my boyfriend is somewhat of a cadaver dog, now could I?"

"*What about this mystery hero that located three of the girls without any aid from standard search equipment?*" *Shannon asked me.*

I smiled. "*Well, he has wished to remain anonymous, but I can tell you he is a bit of a bad(BLEEP) who has had the best tracking training and experience in the world.*"

Adrianne reached over and nudged my arm. "Check you out, Sloan! You got bleeped out on television!"

I laughed and squeezed her hand.

"*Sloan, this was a particularly terrifying ordeal for you as you were almost the next victim. Is it true you were kidnapped and tortured before the assailant was apprehended?*" *She was smiling a little bit too much for the words she was saying.*

"Would you say we actually 'apprehended' him?" Warren asked.

I giggled. "Shh...I'm on TV!"

"*I was actually taken from the sheriff's office building by someone I believed I knew fairly well. I trusted him and it almost got me killed. I think it should be a good reminder that we can never be too careful, ladies,*" *I said directly into the camera.*

Nathan was shaking his head on the other side of the hospital bed. "Just like a publicist to squeeze in a good public service announcement."

"Hey! I could be saving lives!"

He laughed and dumped the rest of the bag of Skittles into his mouth.

"*After being held for over six hours, I was taken into the woods where Detective McNamara and our other companion had already discovered the remains of Leslie Bryson. They were still on the scene, and they were able to stop Game Warden William Stewart and save my life,*" *I said.*

"*Detective, this is when you were shot during the struggle?*" *Shannon asked.*

Nathan smiled at the camera.

We all laughed.

"*Yes. I was shot in the back while I was attempting to shield Ms. Jordan from gunfire,*" *he said.*

Adrianne pointed to the television. "Look at her face!"

Shannon's mouth was smiling, but her eyes could have been burning holes in Nathan's skull. I was a little surprised his head wasn't smoking.

I held up my hand in suspense. "Oh, wait for it."

Shannon leaned forward in her seat toward Nathan. "Does it hurt, Detective? Does it hurt very badly?"

We all howled in laughter at the television.

"Does it hurt very badly?" Warren mimicked.

Nathan shook his head. "You guys suck."

"It could have been a lot worse. Thank you for asking," he said.

"Sloan, what are your plans for the future now? Do you plan on getting involved with any more crime solving mysteries?" she asked me.

I laughed. "No, Shannon. I think I'm going to try and stick with writing the news instead of living it."

"Fantastic. Well, we are thankful this nightmare is over for everyone, and we appreciate you both taking the time to talk with us here. I am Shannon Green with WKNC, Six O'clock News."

I held up my hands. "Wait, wait!"

The camera panned to Nathan. "Stay safe, Asheville," he said with a smile—and a wink—into the camera.

The room erupted into hysterics again.

"'Stay safe, Asheville'? What the hell is that about?" Warren laughed.

"Personally, I like the wink," Adrianne said, doing her best to wink at him.

Nathan got up, flinching slightly with pain and slammed his candy wrapper in the trash. "I hate you all."

"I think you've missed your calling in show business, man," Warren teased.

"Hey, Warren, I hear American Idol is doing auditions soon!" Nathan fired back.

I laughed and kissed Warren on the forehead.

When the laughter died down, Adrianne adjusted the incline of her bed. "Do you guys think anyone bought that bullshit?"

Nathan sat down and shook his head. "Not a chance."

"I've already had a call from the CIA and the Pentagon," Warren grumbled.

I kissed Warren again, this time on the lips. "We can always run to

Mexico."

"I think that's a wonderful idea." He kissed me again.

Nathan groaned. "I'm getting out of here before I start puking like Sloan with a migraine."

I laughed and stood up carefully. I grabbed Warren's hand for support as the blood rushed down to my throbbing legs. "Come on, guys. Let's get out of here," I said.

We paused at Adrianne's bedside to say our goodbyes for the night. She reached for my hand. "So have you two decided if you are going to use your powers for good or evil?" she asked.

I smiled down at her. "I still plan on using them for evil when I get my hands on Mark Higgins."

She laughed.

I slowly leaned over and kissed her on the forehead. "I love you, friend. I'll come by tomorrow."

She squeezed my hand. "I love you, too."

I turned toward Warren and Nathan. "You boys ready to go?"

"Yep. Lead the way. Bye, Adrianne," Warren said.

Nathan waved. "See you later, girl."

She smiled.

Warren draped his arm over my shoulders as they walked—and I limped—down the hallway.

Nathan looked at Warren when we got on the elevator. "So, the Pentagon? Really?"

Warren nodded and pressed the button for the first floor. "Yeah," he said. "Apparently they want to fly me up to Washington sometime, maybe next week. They didn't tell me much more about it."

I looked up at him. "Do I get to come?"

He tensed and gave a doubtful smile. "I don't think it's a 'bring a friend' deal."

I gave him a sheepish smile. "But I'm a celebrity now."

Nathan smirked looking up to watch the floors countdown. "Yes, I'm sure Hollywood will be calling for the movie rights any day now."

The door to the elevator opened.

Mark Higgins was holding a bouquet of bright yellow daisies.

With one punch, I knocked two shiny, veneered front teeth to the floor.

THE SIREN

ELICIA HYDER

BOOK TWO OF
THE SOUL SUMMONER SERIES

This one's for Taffy…
You've always believed in me.
My sister. My best friend.

1.

WHOMP WHOMP WHOMP WHOMP WHOMP. CLACK, CLACK. EEEENG! EEEENG! EEEENG!

"This is a test. This is only a test of the Emergency Broadcast System." I was practicing my best radio announcer's voice.

"Sloan, stop talking," my father said through his microphone. "And please, lie still."

Lying still was becoming increasingly more difficult with each second that passed. I had been trapped inside the deafening MRI machine for more than twenty minutes. My father had insisted on the test after my last hemiplegic migraine, but I knew its results would be as useless as the last two CT scans he had ordered. There was nothing wrong with my brain, and there was nothing wrong with me...except it seemed I had the power to read and control people's souls. That, however, had nothing to do with my migraines that I was aware of.

The trigger for my latest headache was the same as the others: Warren Parish had left town. He and I seemed to be bound together by an electrifying force, and when we were apart, paralyzing migraines were the penalty.

The MRI was going to be inconclusive.

When the machine stopped whirring and knocking like the inside of a drag racer's engine, I wiggled my feet from side to side. "Are we done yet?"

"All done," Dad said. The MRI table slid slowly out of the electronic cave I had been confined to.

My father was fascinated and terribly worried by my new development of headaches, but I knew telling him the truth wouldn't help. My adoptive parents were incredibly loving and supportive, but they were also medical professionals who believed everything had a scientific explanation. Being that my father was a geriatric physician who specialized in dementia, I knew what his diagnosis would be—mental instability.

Dad walked into the room as I sat up on the table and adjusted my twisted gown. Even in his fifties, he was still movie-star handsome with the brightest blue eyes I'd ever seen. He was looking down at a sheet of paper in his hand. "You can get dressed."

I held the back of my gown closed while I stood up. "What did the test show? Is it all sawdust and rocks up there?"

Dad rolled his eyes. "Nothing stood out to me, but I'm going to have a friend of mine in neurology look over it to be sure."

I put my hand on his arm and looked up at him. "Dad, I'm fine."

He kissed my forehead. "I can't be too careful with you. You're the only Sloan I've got." He started toward the door. "Do you want to grab lunch before you head to work? I have another hour or so before my first patient of the afternoon."

I looked at the clock on the wall. I had told my boss that I would be in around noon, and it was already after eleven. "Will you be terribly heartbroken if I skip lunch this time? I want to pop in and check on Adrianne before I go to the office, if that's OK."

He smiled. "Of course. Give her my love, and tell her I'll drop in to see her sometime this week," he said. "I'll see you at dinner tonight?"

I nodded. "I'll be there."

"Will Warren be joining us?" he called as I shuffled toward the door in my socks.

I looked back and shrugged. "I'm not sure. He's flying in from D.C. sometime today, but I can't remember when his flight lands. I'll let Mom know if he gets here in time."

"All right, sweetheart. We'll see you later," he said.

Adrianne Marx, my best friend, had been a patient at the hospital for almost three weeks since the guy she was dating decided to drive drunk and flip his Jeep into a highway guard rail. I had knocked out his front teeth in return and none of us had seen him since.

When I got to her room, she was reading a trashy tabloid magazine and munching on potato chips. Her hair was starting to regrow from where they had to shave it, and aside from the pink scars left by the stitches, her face looked almost back to normal.

I rapped my knuckles against the open door. "Knock, knock."

She looked up and smiled. "Hey, weirdo." She shifted against her mound of pillows as I crossed in front of her feet and plopped down in the chair by her bed. "What are you doing here?"

"I had an MRI upstairs. I thought I would swing by and say hello before I went to work."

She sat up in her bed. "An MRI? I thought you just had a few broken bones and some stitches."

Barely two weeks before, Warren and I had helped Detective Nathan McNamara take down a serial killer who had been murdering women across the state of North Carolina for over a decade. Billy Stewart had drugged me, beaten me, and then dragged me to his Bundy-style, secret body-stashing spot where he planned on raping and burying me in the woods. Thanks to Warren's ability to track down dead bodies and Nathan's protective instincts, I walked away with only a few broken ribs, nerve damage in my hands, and enough gashes on my arms and legs to potentially keep me in pants for the rest of my life.

I shook my head. "Dad wanted the MRI because he's worried about my migraines. I had another really bad one on Sunday."

Her head tilted to the side. "So Warren is gone?"

"Yeah. He had to go to Washington for a meeting at the Pentagon."

She folded the open end of her bag of chips and laid it on the bedside table. "That sounds alarming. What do they want with him?"

I shrugged. "I'm sure they want to know how he tracked down those missing girls."

Her eyes widened. "I wonder how he's going to explain that."

I laughed, though I was more worried than amused. "I don't know, but I don't think telling them he can *feel death* is going to cut it."

"Probably not," she agreed. "When he left, did you puke all over the detective again?"

Heat rose in my cheeks at either the embarrassing memory of my last migraine or at the simple thought of Nathan McNamara. I wasn't sure which. My endocrine system had been thoroughly confused since

Warren and Nathan came to town. "No. I was with my parents, and I didn't puke on anyone this time."

"How is Nathan?" she asked.

I leaned against the armrest. "I guess he's doing OK. I haven't seen him in a few days. This week he's in Greensboro looking for Billy's last victim on our list who hasn't been found."

"Which one is she?" she asked.

"Rachel Smith. She was reported missing by her co-workers in 2008. She didn't have any known relatives, so her case went cold pretty fast. She was a social worker," I said.

Adrianne shook her head. "That's so sad."

"Let's talk about something else, please." I was desperate to change the subject. Talking about the whole case still made me feel squeamish.

She nodded. "OK. How's the boy drama?"

"Oh, it's still drama." I sighed. "Warren finished moving his stuff into my house this week. He put his furniture in storage over in West Asheville, but his clothes and his many weapons are at my house. My guest room looks like a freaking armory."

She looked at me sideways. "Are you planning on living together, like long term?"

I laughed and shrugged my shoulders. "I haven't planned anything with Warren up until this point, and life hasn't exactly allowed for a lot of forethought and decision-making. I don't know what we're doing."

She raised an eyebrow. "What does Nathan think about it?"

I sat back in my seat. "I have no idea. It's not like we have heart-to-heart discussions on the subject. He still comes by the house and my office all the time, so I guess it hasn't fazed him too much."

"Is he still dating Shannon?" she asked.

The muscles tensed in my jaw at the mention of Nathan's girlfriend because if I had a nemesis, Shannon Green would be it. But that bitterness was rooted a lot deeper than in just her relationship with Nathan. His presence only added fuel to embers that had been smoldering for over a decade.

I rolled my eyes. "I guess they're still together, but you would never know it. He's always around, and she's never with him, and he doesn't talk about her."

Adrianne held out her hands. "Why is he with her?"

"I've been asking the same thing for a while now."

"What does Warren say about Nathan showing up all the time?" she asked.

"He doesn't say much. They actually spend more time together than Nathan and I do these days. Warren's been helping recover the missing victims, and aside from their constant ping-ponging of insults back and forth, they've actually become pretty good friends. They love to hate each other."

"I've noticed," she said. "To be honest, I kind of feel bad for Nate. He's crazy about you, and then Warren showed up and it was over with you guys before it even got started."

I nodded. "I know. Warren came into town like a hurricane." I chewed on my pinky nail. "Wanna hear a secret?"

She scooted forward in her bed. "Of course."

I pointed a warning finger at her. "Do you promise to take it to the grave?"

She crossed her heart. "I swear."

I lowered my voice. "I keep thinking about that night in the woods when Nathan dove in front of that bullet for me. He could have died trying to save me. That's love on a whole different level."

"Are you having second thoughts about you and Warren?" she asked.

I shook my head. "No. That's what makes it so hard. I genuinely care about them both, but it's too different with Warren for there to even be a competition. He's like gravity or oxygen. I can't *not* be with him."

"You guys are really intense," she said.

I tapped my finger against my forehead. "Intense enough for migraines." I laughed. "Enough about my supernatural soap opera. How are you doing?"

"I'm doing OK. I started physical therapy yesterday, which sucked more than you could ever imagine," she said with a groan. "They are talking like I'll be able to go home maybe tomorrow or the next day."

"That's awesome," I said.

She nodded. "Yeah. Everyone is pretty shocked at how fast I've recovered. Most of nurses didn't think I would live, much less be walking out of here anytime soon." She eyed me suspiciously from the bed. "I'm pretty sure I have you to thank for that."

I shrugged. "Who knows?"

"Sloan, you're the only one I remember being here during the beginning of all this. I remember you being in my room when I still couldn't even talk," she said. "It was like I could feel you right here next to me."

"Really?" I asked, surprised.

She smiled. "Yeah. I think Warren is on to something. I think you healed me."

"Well, I wouldn't say 'healed' necessarily." I laughed. "Have you seen your hair today?"

She threw a pillow at me. "Shut up."

"So, what are you going to do when you get out of here? Go to your apartment?" I asked.

She shook her head. "Not for a while. I can't get up and down the stairs yet. I'll probably stay with my parents till I'm fully recuperated."

"What about work?" I asked.

She shrugged. "They're holding my booth at the salon, but it will probably be a while before I can be on my feet all day again."

I leaned forward and put my hand on her broken leg.

"Are you putting your voodoo on me?" she asked with a smile.

I winked at her. "It can't hurt."

* * *

It was noon when I got to my office at the county building downtown. Most everyone was gone to lunch, leaving the halls unnervingly quiet. As I hurried to my office, I kept a careful watch over my shoulder. My father would call it PTSD from my recent attack. I would call it common sense after all I'd been through. In my rush to unlock the door, I almost missed the yellow sticky note attached just above eye-level. *Call me when you get in. -Sheriff Davis.*

I pulled the note down as I walked into my office. "That's odd."

After tucking my briefcase under my desk and turning on my computer, I dialed the direct line to the sheriff's office at the jail. I prayed he wasn't going to ask me to come by. My gift never felt more like a curse than when I was in that building. The jail, with all the dark souls locked inside it, was a panic incubator for a girl like me.

"Sheriff Davis." His gruff voice was more like a bark than a greeting.

I sat back in my office chair. "Hey, Sheriff. It's Sloan. I got the sticky note you left on my door."

"Hello, Sloan. How are you feeling?" he asked.

I smiled. "I'm healing up pretty well. I still have a few itchy scars on my legs, and the feeling hasn't completely returned to my hands, but it could be a lot worse." Billy Stewart had dragged me by a pair of steel handcuffs through the woods, causing extensive nerve damage in my hands. The doctors said the numbness and tingling could last for up to a year.

"Well, I'm glad to hear you're on the mend. Listen, I've been trying to get in touch with Detective McNamara all morning. You seem to always know where he's at, even though *I'm* his boss. Got any idea where I can find him?" he asked.

I thought for a second. "I talked to him yesterday, and he said he would be up in the woods all day in Greensboro. He probably doesn't have cell phone service."

"Yeah, that's what I figured," he said. "I thought you might both want to know a report came across my desk this morning that they found a third body on Billy Stewart's property in Stephens County, Georgia. They believe it's a twenty-three-year-old female who disappeared from a camping trip last year."

My mouth fell open. "You're joking?"

"This isn't really a joking subject, Sloan."

"I know it isn't. That just means we were wrong about the last victim—the one who is still missing on our list." I thought of Nathan and his team who were still trudging through the forest looking for a body that wasn't there.

"Either that or there are more victims than we initially thought," he said.

I knew for a fact there were only twelve victims. It was part of Warren's gift. Of course, I couldn't explain that to Sheriff Davis without sounding like a lunatic.

"Perhaps you're right, Sheriff."

"Tell McNamara to call me," he said.

"I will." He hung up his phone before I could say goodbye.

I yanked my cell phone out of my purse and dialed Nathan's number. It went straight to voicemail, so I left a message. "Hey, it's Sloan. You can come home. You're not going to find a body in Greensboro. The sheriff called and said they recovered a third body on Billy Stewart's property in Georgia, so she must be victim number twelve, not Rachel Smith. Call your boss. Bye."

I ended the call and dialed Warren's number. He answered on the first ring. "Perfect timing. I just got off the plane," he said by way of a greeting.

"In Asheville?" I asked.

"Charlotte. I have an hour layover, and then I'll be home."

Home. It was strange to hear him say it out loud.

"How are you?" he asked. "Did you sleep better last night?"

"I'll sleep better once you're back." That was the truth. I'd had nightmares about my abduction almost every night Warren had been gone.

"I'll be there tonight," he said. "Are you at work?"

"Yep. I just got here," I said. "I had that stupid MRI this morning."

"How did that go?"

"Oh, it was long and very boring. Dad said he didn't see anything wrong, but he's going to have some more doctors look at it."

"Are you ever going to tell him the truth?" he asked.

"I don't know. Dad believes so much in modern medicine he would never accept this is beyond explanation. He would probably have me committed to the psych ward."

Warren laughed. "That's highly unlikely. He loves you and he's worried. I think you should tell him."

I scrunched up my nose at the idea. He was right and I knew it, but just the thought of that conversation was daunting, no matter how loving I knew my parents were. "I'll think about it." I drummed my nails on my desk. "What time will you be here?"

"My flight lands sometime around three, so I should be there before you get off work at five," he said.

I smiled. "Great! We're having dinner at my parents' house tonight."

He groaned. "Do we have to? I was planning on us staying at home. We've got a lot to talk about."

The tone of his voice was alarming. I didn't like it at all. "We do?"

"This wasn't a leisure trip, babe," he said.

My blood pressure jumped up a few points. I decided avoidance was the best course of action. "Well, it's gonna have to wait. I promised my parents I would come because I haven't been since you moved in, and they keep badgering me about when you're coming to see them again."

He sighed. "OK. I'll go to the house and change when I get in town. You can pick me up on your way."

"All right," I said. "Guess what."

"What?"

"Rachel Smith wasn't Billy's victim. They found a third body in Georgia."

"Interesting," he said. "So that's all of them, then?"

Leaning back in my chair, I stared at the halogen light above my desk. "That's all of them."

"Did you let Nate know?"

"I tried, but the call went to voicemail. Have you talked to him?" I asked.

He chuckled. "Sure. He called earlier to ask how my trip was going and what the weather was like in Washington and if I'd gotten a good night's sleep…"

I rolled my eyes. "Oh, shut up."

"I'll see you in a few hours, Sloan."

"Bye." I disconnected the call.

On the desktop of my computer, I clicked open the missing persons file Nathan had sent me. It contained all the victims we had originally believed had been murdered by Billy Stewart. I found Rachel Smith's folder and opened it. I printed off her picture and her missing report which had been filed in 2008. She was twenty-four when she disappeared, beautiful with long, dark hair and light brown eyes. Her co-workers at Child Protective Services in Greensboro, North Carolina reported her missing. There was a note that no family had been found or notified of her disappearance.

For a moment, I stared out the window behind my desk and wondered what had become of her. The upper side of downtown Asheville was poised against the colorful fall backdrop of the North Carolina mountain range. The forest in the distance was popping with gold, orange, and bright red trees.

It reminded me I had work to do.

The fall tourist season was in full swing in Asheville, and the Buncombe County event calendar needed to be updated. I tucked Rachel's sheets into my briefcase and turned toward my keyboard to attempt to type with the few fingers I still had control over.

* * *

Warren was waiting on my front porch when I pulled up to the curb after work. He had showered, and his shoulder-length black hair was still wet and tied in a ponytail. He was six-foot-three with oh-point-no body fat, and he had a chiseled tan face and killer black eyes—literally.

He shared a lot of my strange abilities, but his gift was more specific, practiced, and frightening than mine. I could summon the living; he could find the dead. I had the ability to heal people, and he could kill them with a glance.

Warren was like antifreeze: effective, delicious, and absolutely deadly.

I felt a little dizzy watching him come down my steps.

When he opened the passenger side door and angled inside, my eyes nearly rolled back in my head as his ice cool cologne filled my car. "Gah, you smell good."

He leaned over and gave me a welcoming kiss on the lips. The familiar buzz of his touch zinged through me. "I've missed you," he said, smiling when he pulled away.

I savored the taste of his kiss. "I don't wanna go see my parents now."

He laughed and moved his seat back as far as it would go to accommodate his long legs. "You said we had to."

I laid my head against the headrest. "We do have to, or I'll never hear the end of it." I put the car in drive and pulled away from the curb before I could talk myself out of going. "What did they want with you in Washington?"

He didn't look at me. "Too much to tell for a short car ride. We'll talk about it later."

I frowned. "Should I be worried?"

Reaching across the car, he squeezed my shoulder. "Of course not, babe. How was work today?"

I relaxed in my seat. "Boring. After hunting down missing people and serial killers, I'm not sure how I'll ever be satisfied with county newsletters and press releases again."

With his long arm still draped across the back of my neck, he began twisting strands of my long brown hair around his fingers. "Maybe we should go into private investigating," he suggested. "We could work together."

I raised my eyebrows. "The only problem is none of our tactics would ever be explainable in court," I said. "I would love to see the look on a judge's face when I say 'my boyfriend is sort of like a human cadaver dog.' That's totally plausible, right?"

He stopped twisting my hair and grinned at me.

"What?"

He shrugged. "I like it when you call me your boyfriend."

Rolling my eyes, I shook my head. "You know, for you being such a badass, you're more of a girl than I am sometimes."

He laughed, but he withdrew his arm and shoved me playfully in the shoulder. "So, what's on the agenda at your folks' house tonight?" he asked.

I shook my head as I turned onto the main highway. "Nothing special. Just Monday night dinner."

His head whipped toward me. "It's Tuesday."

I grinned. "I think Mom moved it on purpose because she knew you'd be gone."

The house smelled like roast beef and Mom's secret-ingredient mashed potatoes when Warren and I walked through the front door. It smelled so good I could have licked the air. Mom had once promised to divulge the secret if I ever took the time to learn how to cook. My cooking skill set extended to being able to burn toast and make coffee. Someday I knew I would make time, but until then I would have Monday night dinners at their house, and I had Warren at home. He was almost as good a cook as my mother.

"Hello! Hello!" I called from the foyer.

Mom's gray head peeked around the corner of the kitchen. "Hey! Come on in! Hi, Warren!"

Warren wiped his shoes on the welcome mat. "Hello, Mrs. Jordan."

She put a hand on her hip and shot him a teasing smirk. "How many times do I have to tell you to call me Audrey?"

He laughed. "A few more, Mrs. Jordan."

Tugging on Warren's hand, I led him to the kitchen. Dad stood up from the table where he was reading a thick book. I walked over and gave him a kiss on the cheek. "Hi, Daddy."

"Hey, sweetheart." He shook Warren's hand. "It's good to see you again, Warren."

"Thank you, sir. It's good to see you as well." Warren smiled politely. "Thanks for letting me crash dinner."

"Nonsense. You're always welcome here," Dad said. "How was your trip?"

I couldn't discern Warren's face. The man could make a killing at poker.

He cleared his throat. "It's cold in Washington."

Mom laughed. "I'm sure it is." She stepped over to give him a sidearm hug. My tiny mother fit neatly under the hook of Warren's strong arm. It made me smile.

"Whatcha readin', Dad?" I asked as I pulled out a chair next to his.

He held up the book so I could see the cover. "Hemiplegic Migraine Symptoms, Pathogenesis, and Treatments," he read aloud.

Warren caught my eye and cocked an eyebrow.

My shoulders slumped. "Dad, we need to talk."

He took off his reading glasses. "About what, sweetheart?"

I reached over and closed the book. "You're not going to find the answer to my headaches in here."

"How can you be so sure?" he asked.

My mother put the roast on the table. "Come and sit down. You two can talk while we eat. I don't want dinner to get cold."

When our places were set and our plates were full, my father looked to me for an explanation. "Now, back to the headaches. What did you want to tell me?"

Warren reached over and gave my hand a reassuring squeeze.

My mother noticed his show of support, and she put her fork down. "Is everything OK?"

I nodded before drawing in a deep breath. I carefully looked at both my parents. "It's not a tumor. It's not weak blood vessels that are going to rupture. And it's not an injury. You're not going to find the answer in a book or on a CT scan or on an MRI image."

My parents exchanged confused glances.

"Then what is it?" Dad asked.

"It's something supernatural."

2.

CERTAIN MEMORIES WILL always be crystal clear in my mind. Watching the jets crash into the World Trade Center is one. Seeing Warren for the first time and wondering if he was actually dead is another. But even international terrorism and an animated corpse could never compare to seeing the look on my father's face when I chose the word *supernatural* to explain my migraines. I was pretty certain I would've gotten the same reaction had I told him I could burp rainbows and spit out golden coins.

Beside me, Warren snickered.

"Supernatural?" my mother repeated, to be sure she had heard me correctly.

I looked to Warren for help, but he put his hands up in resignation and chuckled. "You're on your own here."

Dad leaned forward on his elbows and pushed his untouched dinner plate out of the way. "Please explain, dear."

My palms were starting to sweat. "You guys love me, right?"

"Of course we do," Mom said.

"And I'm not prone to lying or hallucinations or being dramatic, right?"

Dad shook his head. "No."

I looked at both of them. "Do you remember why we left Florida when I was eight?"

Simultaneously, their expressions melted.

My eyebrows rose. "I think it's time we talk about it."

Mom's mouth was smiling, but her eyes were not. "We moved because your father got a job here."

I leveled my gaze at her. "We moved because I was attacked on the playground." I rubbed the scar over my eyebrow. "We moved because people were figuring out I was different."

Dad held up his hand. "Sloan, you were having problems at school, but let's not dramatize it. We did believe a change of setting would be beneficial for you, but we didn't move here just because the other kids were giving you a hard time."

I cut my eyes toward him and held both hands up in question. "You never sent me back to that school, and we packed up and moved a week later."

He shook his head. "It's still not the whole reason we moved." He folded his arms on top of the table. "Don't you think we love you enough to at least talk to you about it if we were *that* worried?"

For that, I didn't have an answer. "Didn't you ever wonder what was wrong with me?"

His brow scrunched together, and his lips bent in a deep frown. "Sweetheart, there's nothing wrong with you, but I do have some good friends at the hospital if you want to talk to—"

Cutting Dad off, I pointed at him and looked at Warren. "See? I told you he'd try to have me committed."

Warren covered his face with his hands, his shoulders shaking with silent laughter.

Dad was clearly not as amused as we were. "I'm not trying to have you committed."

I smiled. "I know." I leaned on my elbow. "Do you want to hear what I have to say or are we going to pretend that this, too, never happened?"

He looked like he wanted to argue or berate me for the snide remark, but he didn't. He gave a slight nod instead. "Please continue. Tell me about your supernatural headaches."

Here goes nothing...

I sucked in a deep breath. "I have some sort of sixth sense. I *know* people before I meet them. It's kind of like when you see someone at the grocery store who looks familiar, but you can't remember their name or how you met them. You know what I'm talking about?"

My mother nodded hesitantly.

"Well, I'm like that with everyone. I don't meet strangers. It's like I can already see a person for who they really are on the inside before I ever even speak to them." I turned my palms up on the table. "I think I have the ability to see people's souls."

All the blood drained from my father's handsome face, and I'm pretty sure Mom almost fainted.

I shifted uneasily on my chair. "Anyway, it's how I found that little girl, Kayleigh Neeland, and it's how I helped find that serial killer and those missing girls. I knew they were dead as soon as Detective McNamara showed me their pictures."

Neither of them spoke.

"I know this sounds crazy, but the headaches aren't explainable, except it has something to do with Warren and me being separated. Every time he's left town, it has happened to both of us," I said.

They turned their puzzled eyes on Warren who, in turn, scooted his chair back a few inches. He cautiously raised his hands in defense. "She's right, but I'm not causing it."

My mother rolled her eyes. "That's preposterous."

"It happens every single time, Mom. I swear."

Her mouth was still gaping. "That's highly coincidental then."

"Mom, it's not a coincidence," I said. "Tell her, Warren."

Warren shook his head. "I'm staying out of this."

My dad looked like *he* was getting a migraine. "So, Warren, do you have this sixth sense as well?"

Warren hesitated. "Yes, sir." I doubted he would be willing to elaborate on the differences between his gift and mine. I was right. Warren didn't say another word.

My mother was staring at her plate like it might get up and walk right off the table. Dad took off his glasses and pinched the bridge of his nose, pressing his eyes shut. Warren, whose mouth was clamped closed so tight that his lips turned white, appeared to be counting the number of steps to the closest exit.

I put my hands in my lap. "I know this is a lot to take in. I just don't want you worrying that I'm going to have an aneurysm and die or anything. It's not normal, but I don't think it's life-threatening." I looked at my father. "Dad, I'm not crazy."

He slowly opened his eyes and focused on me. His expression was inscrutable, but he reached out and squeezed my shoulder. "I know." He sat back in his seat and looked at my mother. "This is just a little hard to..." His voice faded as he searched for the right word.

"Believe," I said, filling in the blank.

He shook his head adamantly. "No. It's a lot to process, Sloan, but I'll never doubt you." He nodded toward Mom. "We've always known you were special."

Mom's shoulders seemed to relax a bit. She nodded in agreement but didn't elaborate.

For several moments, the table was quiet. It wasn't awkward or tense, but I was desperate to know what my parents were thinking about.

Finally, Mom's gentle laugh broke the silence. "You terrified me as a child," she said. "We would go to the grocery store or the mall, and you would take off and start talking to people."

Dad chuckled. "I remember that. The stranger-danger talk with you was completely pointless."

Mom put her hand on Dad's arm. "Robert, do you remember Mean Santa?"

Laughing, Dad dropped his face into his hands. "How could I forget?"

I had no idea what they were talking about. "Mean Santa?"

Mom leaned forward. "You were maybe four or five, I guess, and we took you to the annual Christmas party with the hospital staff. Every year, they had a Santa there for the kids to have their picture taken with. Naturally, we waited in line with you so you could sit on Santa's lap. When it was your turn, your dad lifted you up and put you on Santa's knee." She paused and covered her mouth to stifle a giggle. "You looked right at the man and said, 'You're not Santa.' When he tried to argue, you fired right back, wagging a finger in his face and everything. You told him, 'Santa is jolly and you are not jolly. You're a mean Santa.'"

I laughed. "Really?"

Dad nodded. "You were right. I had to work with that Santa for a few years, and he's one of the most hateful men I've ever met."

I shook my head. "I don't remember that at all."

Mom's laughter slowly subsided, and she reached across the table to take my hand. "Like your dad said, we've always known you were special, in the very best way."

Tears prickled the corners of my eyes. "Thank you."

Dad held up a finger. "And while we did not leave Florida just over the incident at your school, we did believe you'd be better off growing up in a smaller town." His eyes softened. "We probably should have tried harder to talk to you about all this, but you must understand that we really didn't know what we were dealing with. To us, you were simply very outgoing and intuitive. Your behavior was different but not alarming, so we agreed to not press the issue as long as you seemed healthy and happy. I hope we weren't wrong in that decision."

I shook my head. "Honestly, I'm kind of glad you didn't make a bigger deal out of it. I already felt like enough of a freak."

Warren's arm slid across my shoulders. "I, for one, think she turned out just fine."

We exchanged smiles and a quick kiss.

Mom's eyes widened and she pointed at us. "This is why you had the blood test done! This is why you wondered if you were related."

I nodded.

Dad's eyes narrowed. "I know how you met, but how did you ever find each other?"

Warren leaned into me. "I saw her on the news when she saved that little girl. Like she said, we have a sense about people just by looking at them. I couldn't read her at all."

I looked at him. "And I thought Warren was a zombie when he first showed up in town."

Mom shuddered.

I smiled. "It's not as creepy as it sounds."

"So, who else knows about this?" Dad asked.

I looked around the table. "Adrianne and Nathan."

Mom's head snapped back in surprise. "The detective knows?"

I nodded. "Yeah. I sort of let it slip when we first met."

"That's a hell of a slip, isn't it?" Dad asked.

"A life-changing one," I agreed.

Dad's expression softened. "Maybe it was time."

Warren squeezed my hand.

I smiled. "Maybe it was."

* * *

"Well, that went better than I expected," Warren said when we walked out of the house after dinner. As we walked to the driveway, he wrapped his arm around my waist, hooking his thumb into one of my belt loops. "Not nearly as bad as you have feared all these years, correct?"

I shook my head. "Not at all."

He glanced toward the house. "They're pretty great, you know?"

A warm tingle of gratitude rippled through me. "*Great* doesn't do them justice."

He looked down at me. "What exactly happened when you got that scar? It seems odd to me that other kids wouldn't like you."

I nodded. "I know. I've always thought it was weird, but there was this one kid, Ivan Moots, who always picked on me. I'll never forget him. He's the one who threw the rock and split my face open."

"Why?"

I shrugged my shoulders. "Don't know, really. I kind of had a meltdown one day at school because of this horrible substitute teacher who was put in my classroom." Looking up at him, I widened my eyes. "She was so scary my parents had to come and get me. The next day on the playground, Ivan was worse than ever, teasing me and calling me names. He and a couple of his friends started throwing rocks at me while I was on the swings." I touched my brow. "He hit his target."

"Seriously?" We reached the car, and he turned to face me. "That's horrible."

"Yep. Knocked me off backward." My body shuddered. "It was awful."

"Want me to hunt the bastard down?" He was grinning as he looked down at me.

I relaxed and smiled. "No, but thank you anyway."

He pulled me close and pressed a kiss into my hair. "I say we go home, open a bottle of wine, and take a bubble bath."

I rested my head against his chest. "That sounds like heaven."

He held out his hand. "Give me the keys. I drive faster than you."

Laughing, I kissed his perfect lips.

When he turned onto my street, a familiar tan SUV was parked in front of my house. Completely against my will, butterflies took flight in my stomach.

I looked at Warren. "Did you know he was coming?"

Warren laughed. "Do I ever?"

We parked in the driveway, and when we walked around front, Nathan McNamara was waiting on the sidewalk. He wore camouflage pants and a black fitted shirt. On his blond head was an olive green ball cap that had a space on the front for interchangeable embroidered patches to suit his mood. That day, the patch was a grayscale American flag signaling he was on duty.

"What are you doing here?" I asked as we approached.

He spread out his arms. "I haven't seen you all week and that's the kind of greeting I get?"

I nodded and walked past him up the stairs. "Yes, when you show up uninvited and unannounced."

"Sloan, you know you've missed me." He followed Warren and me up the stairs. "Warren, I'm a little surprised to see you back from Washington so soon. I figured they would have found you a nice warm bed in Area 51 by now."

"Sorry. You're not that lucky." Warren handed me my keychain and added some dramatic flair while pulling out his own keys from his pocket. "I've got the door, babe."

Nathan noticed. "Do you have a quota of times per day you need to remind me you live here now?"

I huffed. "Not this again. Don't even start, Nathan." Warren was smiling, and I pointed at him. "And you quit trying to stir up crap!"

Warren laughed and pushed the door open.

There was a fine line between admiration and loathing between Warren and Nathan. They secretly liked each other, but with me in the middle, they would never admit it. Warren and I were together, but there was a very gray area with Nathan McNamara. And everyone knew it.

After kicking off my shoes at the front door, I walked around to my white sofa. I plopped down and put my socked feet up on the coffee table. "What's up, Nathan?"

Warren went to the kitchen, and Nathan sat down next to me. He leaned forward and rested his elbows on his knees, locking his fingers in front of him. "I got your message today about Rachel Smith."

I frowned. "You could have told me that in a text message."

He smiled. "I thought you should know I'm going to continue to investigate her disappearance."

"Good for you," I said and closed my eyes.

He nudged my leg with his knee. "You know you want to help me."

I shook my head but refused to look at him. "No, I don't. I'm done with police work and missing people and murderers—"

He cut me off. "You want to sit behind a desk and exchange emails with reporters and government officials all day? Keep working on the county online cookbook?"

I rolled my eyes toward him. "I have to eat and pay the bills around here. You've used up my personal and sick time for the next ten years."

He opened the folder in his hand and passed me the same picture of Rachel Smith I had printed in my office earlier that day.

I passed it right back to him. "Not to sound harsh or anything, but why do you want to go chase down another dead girl? She's not even in your jurisdiction."

He cocked an eyebrow in question, a curious smile playing on his lips. "What if she's not dead?"

I glared at him. "I've been looking at this photograph for months. She's dead."

He pulled another piece of paper from the folder and put it on my lap. It was a still image from the video surveillance system of a convenience store. The image was date-stamped just two days before. The exact same girl was looking directly into the camera.

"Are you sure she's dead?" Nathan asked with a smile.

3.

WARREN WALKED BEHIND the couch and looked over my shoulder as I sat up and examined every detail about the woman's appearance. As if reading my mind, Nathan handed me the photo from her missing report again, and I compared them side by side. "This is impossible," I said, knowing exactly how wrong I was.

Nathan tapped the picture with his finger. "Is she alive or dead?"

"Dead," Warren and I answered at the same time.

One side of Nathan's mouth tipped up in a half-cocked smile. "This was taken two days ago. Didn't you think she was dead before then?"

"This must be someone who looks like Rachel Smith," I reasoned.

Nathan frowned. "You know it's the same woman."

"I hate to say it, Sloan"—Warren shook his head—"but I think Nathan's right. They're the same."

Nathan laughed and turned to look at him. "How did those words taste coming out of your mouth?"

"Don't get used to it," Warren said.

Nathan leaned against the armrest of the sofa and angled his head to look at me sideways. "Do you remember saying you felt like Warren was dead when you first saw him?" Nathan jabbed his thumb toward Warren behind me. "Yet here he is, alive and irritating and—"

"And living here with Sloan," Warren interrupted with an evil grin.

I gave them both dirty looks. "Stop it." I returned my attention to the two photos of Rachel Smith in my hands. Finally, I looked up at Warren. "Do you really think this is possible?"

Nathan laughed. "No offense, but how can the two of you be possible?"

Warren walked around the couch and sat on the coffee table in front of us. "I guess we aren't alone," he said. "I've always wondered if there might be more people like us out there."

I held up the new picture and looked at Nathan. "How did you get this?"

Nathan sat back with an annoying amount of satisfaction. "The FBI sent it over while I was gone to Greensboro. Rachel Smith—or whoever this woman really is—isn't dead."

I handed the photos back to him. "Good. Case closed."

Warren and Nathan both stared at me, and as if on cue, they crossed their arms over their chests in unison.

I blew out a deep sigh and looked between them. "You seriously want to go and hunt this woman down?" They both smiled. I groaned and dropped my face into my hands. "The two of you are going to end up getting me fired."

Nathan clapped his hands together with excitement.

Warren winked at me.

I pointed at them both. "If we do this, I'm laying down some ground rules. I'm not refereeing the two of you the whole time, and I'm not doing any more hiking trips searching for dead bodies."

They both laughed.

Warren reached toward Nathan for the photograph. "Where was this picture taken?"

Nathan passed it to him. "San Antonio, Texas."

I thought it over. "I like San Antonio. Good food, good shopping..."

Warren smiled at me. "Road trip?"

I shook my head. "I don't drive anywhere over six hours. That's why God created airplanes."

"Is that a yes?" he asked.

I put up my hand. "Hold up." I looked over at Nathan. "This isn't related to your work. Why are you so interested in this?"

He shrugged and flashed me one of his tantalizing grins. "I guess since you helped me solve my big mystery, it's time for me to return the favor and help solve yours."

"This isn't exactly police work. How will you get the time off?" I asked.

"Vacation time?" he suggested.

Frowning, I scrunched my eyebrows together. "You've been at the department for two months. You don't have vacation time."

He pulled a half-eaten bag of Skittles out of his pocket. "I just solved the biggest case in North Carolina's history. I don't think the Sheriff's going to object."

I cleared my throat. "Correction: *we*"—I pointed between Warren and myself—"just solved the biggest case in North Carolina's history."

Nathan popped a handful of candy into his mouth. "You helped," he said with a wink.

Warren rubbed his palms together and looked at us both. "So, we're doing this?"

"I'm in," Nathan said. "Sloan?"

They were watching me expectantly.

With a huff, I dropped my shoulders in resignation. "Let's go to Texas."

* * *

The next morning, as I brushed my teeth in front of the mirror, Warren came into the bathroom and wrapped his arms around my waist from behind. A dizzying current of electricity flowed through me as he dragged his warm lips down the side of my neck. For a second, my eyes rolled backward. Only Warren Parish could turn dental hygiene into foreplay.

I spat out my toothpaste because moaning is much less seductive when foaming at the mouth. "Mmm...Good morning."

"Good morning." His voice was low and rough. "How did you sleep?"

I squirmed against him. "When you *let me* sleep, it was peaceful." I leaned over to rinse my mouth out with water, and I could almost feel his blood pressure rise. I straightened and smiled at him in the mirror. "This is nice. You being here when I wake up."

He slipped the strap of my tank-top down and kissed my shoulder. "You just like that I make coffee," he said, smiling against my skin.

"And you can cook," I added as I wiped my mouth with the hand towel.

His hands slid across my hip bones. "Stay home today."

"You're seriously going to get me fired," I said, laughing.

He rested his head on my shoulder. "That's OK. I'll take care of you."

I looked over at him. "You don't have a job, remember?"

"Good point."

I put my toothbrush in its holder and turned around in his arms. "I tell you what. I'm going to go to the office and turn in my vacation paperwork. Then I'm going to work really hard to get done early today, and tonight, we can stay home. Just us. No parents. No Nathan. No interruptions."

"I like that idea, but I like the idea of carrying you back to bed right now even more." He leaned in to kiss me, but I blocked his lips with my hand. His eyes popped open and then narrowed in frustration.

I shook my head. "Don't even go there," I said. "I can't walk into work late and then ask for paid time off."

Warren growled and bit the palm of my hand. "Well, you'd better hurry up and get out of here before I decide to not let you leave." He tightened his arms around me. "We didn't get to have our talk last night."

I held up my hands. "That was Nathan's fault. Not mine." After successfully wrenching myself free from his grip, I walked to my closet. "Do you want to talk about it while I get ready?"

Shaking his head, he returned to the bedroom. "No. We'll talk about it tonight."

"What are you going to do today?" I asked over my shoulder.

The bedsprings squeaked under his weight. "I guess I'll look into flights and hotels for our trip."

I pulled a white blouse and a pencil-line black skirt down off their hangers. "Do you want me to leave my credit card so you can book them?"

He laughed. "I may be out of a job, but that doesn't mean I need your credit card."

I picked up a pair of black high heels off the floor. "I have $172 in my bank account to last me till payday. I wouldn't be able to eat without a job."

I carried the day's wardrobe to my room and stumbled a bit as I took in the sight of the shirtless mercenary who was reclined against my fluffy pillows.

Warren was oblivious to my stupor. "I have a tad bit more than that in savings. I banked my combat pay over the years in case I ever needed it." He winked at me, almost recovering my full attention to what he was saying. "I think we'll be OK."

A part of me—the shallow part that liked to buy shoes—wanted to ask how much money we were talking about, but I didn't dare. The other part of me was so distracted by the Adonis stretched across my comforter that I dropped my clothes onto the floor when I meant to put them on the bed.

He chuckled. "You missed."

"Shut up." I bent and gathered them up.

Refusing to look at my boyfriend—or his perfect set of abs—I spread my outfit across the foot of the bed before turning toward my dresser. Inside the top drawer, where I stashed my mostly-fake jewelry, I found the silver angel pin Kayleigh Neeland had given me after Nathan and I rescued her. Like a talisman to keep me safe, I fixed it to my blouse, as I did every morning.

When my clothes were in order, I retrieved some clean underwear from the dresser before returning to the bathroom and turning on the shower. I stuck my head into the bedroom and looked at Warren. "I'm locking this door."

"You don't trust me?"

I laughed. "Not even a little bit."

* * *

My brain was everywhere but on my work that day, and the minutes seemed to be ticking backward each time I glanced at the clock. I thought about Rachel Smith. I thought about Texas with Nathan and Warren. And, most of all, I thought about whatever big talk Warren was planning for that evening. I worked through lunch in hopes of leaving early, and despite all my mental wandering, I had everything completed by four. As I packed up my things, my boss stepped into my office.

Mary Travers was waving a sheet of paper in her tiny hand like a surrender flag. "Vacation request, huh?"

I smiled from behind my desk. "Yeah. I'm heading to Texas for a little break."

She handed me the paper that was stamped APPROVED in bright red letters. "You should be aware, there's a rumor going around Human Resources that Detective McNamara asked for next week off as well. There's speculation that it may be more than a coincidence." She was grinning as she peered at me over her brown glasses.

I laughed and put the paper on top of the stack in my inbox. "Detective McNamara is going with me, but I can assure you it's nothing to gossip about. We're just friends."

She put a hand on her hip. "I may be old enough to be your mother, but I'm not senile or blind. You've had a thing for that boy since the first day he started work here."

I folded my hands on my desk. "My boyfriend, Warren, is going with us," I said. "Do you remember him? I introduced you at the Mexican restaurant a while ago."

"Tall, dark, and handsome?" she asked.

I nodded. "That's Warren."

"I heard my name," Warren said, walking into my office behind Mary.

She spun around so fast I thought she might fall down. She clasped her hands over her heart. "You startled me!"

I laughed and covered my mouth with my hand.

Warren smiled and squeezed her shoulder. "I apologize," he said. "It's good to see you again, Ms. Travers."

"The same to you, Warren." She looked back over her shoulder. "Have a good night, Sloan."

I waved. "You too," I called out as she left.

Warren leaned over my desk and pressed his lips to mine. My heart fluttered. "Hey, gorgeous," he said when he pulled away.

"What are you doing here?" I asked.

He sat down in one of the chairs opposite my desk and relaxed with his arms on the armrests. "Can I not come see you at work?"

I tilted my head to the side. "Of course you can, but you never do. What's up?"

He looked down at his watch. "I was in the neighborhood, so I thought I would come by and pressure you to leave early."

I smiled. "Well, you're in luck. I was just getting ready to head out of here." I pushed my chair back. "Do you want to go out?"

He shook his head. "No. I want to go home." He was looking out the window.

"Are you OK?" I asked.

His eyes snapped to mine. "Yeah. I'm OK." He stood up. "You ready now?"

I nodded. "Yes, sir." I stood and picked up my laptop case and purse. "What about dinner?"

He took my bag from me and winked. "I'll worry about dinner."

I kissed his lips again. "Best roommate ever."

When we got home, I changed into sweats while he started cooking. In the few minutes it took me to swap out my clothes, the first floor of my house was flooded with the savory aroma of curry mixed with cinnamon. I shuffled barefoot into the kitchen and slipped my arms around Warren's waist. I stretched on my tip-toes to peek over his shoulder. "Want some help?"

He was chopping up vegetables. "You can get me a beer out of the fridge."

"I can do that." I released him and walked to the refrigerator. "Oh, you got the good stuff." I pulled out two Green Man IPAs.

He looked over at me. "I love this city."

I smiled and reached for the bottle opener. "Beer capital of the US." I opened one and handed it to him.

"Thank you," he said, tipping it up to his lips.

I opened my beer and hopped on top of the counter, a safe distance away from the cutting board. "What did you do today?"

He didn't look up from the plump potato he was butchering.

I nudged him with my toe. "Earth to Warren."

"Huh?" His head whipped toward me, and he blinked like he was trying to reset his thoughts.

I laughed and took a sip of my beer. "What's with you?"

He put the knife down and took a deep breath, nervously knocking his knuckles against the counter. "I'm being reactivated with the Marines."

My heels hit the counter beneath me with a thud. "What?"

He crossed his arms over his chest and cut his eyes up at me. "That's what the whole trip to Washington was about."

My pulse began to pick up speed. "But you're out. You're not in the Marines anymore."

He dropped his head back and looked at the ceiling. "I screwed up when I signed my contract seven years ago. They offered me more money to take four more years of active duty and then four years on IRR if I chose to get out."

"IRR?" I asked, confused.

"Inactive Ready Reserve," he said. "It means I'm out, but for four years they can recall me for any reason they want. I have one year left before I'm completely free and clear of the military."

I put my beer down. "What does this mean?"

"It means I have to report to MEPS in Charlotte in thirty days—well, twenty-nine days now."

I shook my head. "So many acronyms. What's MEPS?"

"Military Entrance Processing Station," he said. "I'll do a lot of paperwork, have a bunch of medical tests and shots, and then they'll ship me out."

"Ship you where?"

He shrugged. "The Middle East most likely, but they haven't told me."

Tears began tickling the corners of my eyes, and he must have noticed because he closed the space between us before the tears hit my cheeks. Sandwiching his torso between my legs, he ran his strong hands down my arms. "I'm so sorry," he said. "This is my fault."

I sniffed. "It's not your fault. It's *my* fault."

He laughed with surprise. "How do you figure?"

"I pulled you into the case with the missing girls. I put you on the government's radar when we landed on the news," I said.

He tucked my hair behind my ears. "No, you didn't. I should never have agreed to that many years on IRR. I got greedy, I guess. At the time I didn't have any good reason to turn the money down for a shorter term. Now I do." He tipped my chin up to look in my eyes.

"How long will you be gone?"

He shrugged. "I don't know. It could be up to a year."

A boulder dropped into my stomach. "A year?"

He moved his head from side to side. "It will probably be more like nine months. Maybe shorter if it's just a mission they want me on. It won't be longer than a year though."

I put my head on his shoulder. "A week is too long."

He stroked my hair. "We'll get through this, I promise. I'll always come back for you."

His words gave me chills rather than comfort. Statements like that were more ominous than anything, but I didn't ruin the sentiment with my fears. I pulled back and looked at him. "What about our trip to Texas?"

He smiled. "We can still go. I've got a whole month. In fact, I booked our tickets before I left the house, and I got us a nice suite at the Hyatt Regency right on the River Walk. The room overlooks the river."

"What about Nathan?" I asked.

He dropped his head and cut his eyes up at me. "I will do anything in this world for you, but I draw the line at sharing our hotel room with another man."

I laughed and wiped my eyes with the cuff of my sleeve, smearing mascara on the cuff. "That's not what I meant."

"God, I hope not." He tugged on the strings of my hoodie. "I texted Nate and told him where we're staying. He can stay where he wants. Our flight is Saturday at 7:45."

"In the morning?"

He chuckled. "Yes. In the morning, and you're going to be pleasant and grateful."

Frowning, I looked up at him. "You're asking a lot."

He gathered my hair behind my head and looked at me seriously again. "I am really sorry, Sloan."

I laced my hands together behind his neck, and he rested his forehead against mine. "Warren, I don't want you to leave." I teared up again.

"Shh." He kissed my eyes. "We're not going to worry about that till we have to. You never know, they could call it off between now and then."

Deep down, I knew our luck wasn't that good, but I nodded like I believed him. I looked up into his deep, black eyes that had faint halos around the pupils. After a lifetime of seeing into the souls of everyone around me, it was still a refreshing surprise that this man was so much a mystery.

"I love you," I blurted out.

He pulled back, his eyes wide with shock.

I covered my mouth with my hands and laughed with embarrassment. "I've never said that to anyone other than family or Adrianne before."

He smiled. "Really?"

I bit my lip. "Never."

Warren closed his eyes and shook his head.

Panic washed over me. *Oh no. It's too soon. What have I done?*

"Sloan." His voice was barely above a whisper. When he looked at me again, tears sparkled in his eyes. "No one has ever said that to me *at all."*

The magnitude of his statement could have been calculated on the Richter scale. Tightening my arms around him, I pulled him close. "I love you, Warren," I said again.

Quietly in my ear he replied, "I love you, too."

4.

"NO." IN PROTEST, I pulled the covers up over my head and rolled to cocoon myself in the blankets of my warm bed.

"Sloan, it's 4:30. I let you sleep an extra half hour." Warren kicked the side of the bed frame with his boot.

"I don't want to go to Texas anymore," I whined into my pillow.

"Don't make me get mean," he warned.

I ignored him.

A moment later, I was hurled across the bed, unwinding from my swirl of covers like a spinning top being flung across the mattress. Stunned, I landed on my back against Warren's pillows. He was holding my comforter in both hands.

He pointed at me. "If you go back to sleep I'm going to break out ice water and fog horns."

I frowned. "I love you a little less in moments like this."

He was still pointing at me. "We're about to have our first fight, woman." He walked to the door and flipped on the light. It scalded my eyeballs. "We're leaving in twenty minutes if you want to stop at your parents' house on the way to the airport." He turned before I could object, and I heard his heavy footfalls on the stairs.

Apparently, I was wrong to believe that once I became a fully-functioning adult, my internal alarm clock would awaken and, like my mother, I would begin bounding happily out of bed at sunrise. Perhaps my hatred of mornings was further proof I was adopted.

Warren was probably right that our first fight would likely happen over our morning schedules. He was always awake at four like clockwork, and I believed it was ungodly to be up before the sun. On the rare occasions when I was forced to wake up with his alarm, he was so dang perky before coffee that I wanted to slap him till he felt as terrible as I did. I groaned and pushed myself off the bed.

Thankfully, I had showered and packed the night before, so there wasn't much to do besides brush my teeth and pile my hair onto the top of my head in a messy bun. Twenty minutes later, I trudged to the car in my sweats, dragging my bags behind me. The October chill of the North Carolina mountains nipped at my face, but it still wasn't enough to rouse me from my sleepy stupor.

Warren shook his head with grief from where he waited at the trunk of his black Dodge Challenger.

I held up a finger in warning. "Not one word." I rubbed my eyes, blindly handing him my toiletries bag and my makeup case that I hadn't opened that morning.

"Here," he said as he handed me a travel mug full of coffee.

"Bless you," I whispered. I walked to the passenger side door, wrenched it open, and climbed into the already-warm car.

After he got in and fastened his seatbelt, he looked over at me before putting the car in drive. "We'll have about fifteen minutes to spend at your mom's. We need to be at the airport pretty soon."

I looked at the clock. It was five minutes till five. "Our flight isn't for three hours."

He pulled away from the curb. "Yes, but we've got to park, check our bags, go through security, and get to the gate on time."

I pulled my knees up to my chest and sipped my coffee. "It's the Asheville Regional Airport, Warren. Not Chicago/O'Hare. They have one terminal and only seven gates. I think we can manage."

He reached over and pushed my feet off his black leather seat. "Has anyone ever told you that you're kind of a bitch before nine a.m.?"

I nodded. "Yes."

He laughed and shook his head.

We drove to my parents' house in blessed silence. I envied the houses that were dark and untouched by the cruelty of morning, their undisturbed inhabitants still dreaming in bed. Such was not the case at the Jordan homestead, however. Every light in my parents' house was on. Knowing my mother, I was certain the coffee was fresh, breakfast was on the stove, and that she'd already been for a morning jog around the neighborhood.

Yes. There was no doubt I was adopted.

My mother met us at the door. "You look terrible," she said, stepping aside as we entered.

I smirked as I slipped off my winter coat. "Love you too, Mom."

Mom squeezed Warren's arm. "You're an angel, dear boy."

He laughed. "Has she always been like this?"

Mom nodded. "Since the day I brought her home." She put her arm around my shoulders. "Do you need some more coffee, sweetie?"

I shook my head. "I'm good."

A familiar, uncomfortable sensation came over me that I was noticing more and more only around my mother. It was like something unseen was pulling at my attention, but I couldn't figure out what it was. I turned and studied her face. "What's wrong with you?" I asked, not meaning for the words to come out the way they did.

Her eyebrows lifted. "She's pleasant, isn't she?" Mom asked, looking up at Warren and shaking her head.

Warren pinched my side so hard I flinched. "What's the matter with you?"

I held up my hands in defense as we followed her to the kitchen. "I didn't mean it like that."

Dad came down the stairs already dressed for the day. He looked me up and down. "Is it Christmas morning and I forgot? You're never here this early without the promise of presents and food." He walked over to give me a hug. Over my shoulder, he spoke to Warren. "You're a brave man, son."

"Or a very stupid one," Warren said.

Dad laughed. "To what do we owe the pleasure of your company this morning?"

"We're going to Texas for a vacation, so I wanted to tell you goodbye before we left," I said.

Dad crossed his arms over his chest. "What's in Texas?"

"Sand," I answered as I plopped down on a stool at the bar.

Warren leaned against the counter. "We're going to San Antonio for a little while. We found another woman who might be like us."

Dad's eyes widened. "Someone with your same gifts?"

"Maybe. That's what we want to find out," Warren said. "Hopefully, it will be a little bit of a vacation as well. I just found I'll be deployed next month."

"Deployed?" Mom asked.

Warren nodded. "The Marines are recalling me. I'm not sure why, but I assume they will be sending me back to Iraq or Afghanistan."

My dad shook his head with a frown. "I'm sorry to hear it. We were just getting used to having you around."

Warren sighed and rolled his eyes. "Trust me. You aren't as sorry as I am."

"So, will it just be the two of you in Texas?" Mom asked. "That sounds very romantic."

"And Nathan," I added over the rim of my coffee cup.

My mother cocked her head to the side. "Really?"

I was sure my mother's mind was spinning with confusion and excitement. She really liked Warren, and she was truly happy for me, but Audrey Jordan had picked out Nathan McNamara as her new son-in-law the very first time she laid eyes on him.

"We've all become really good friends," Warren said.

I raised an eyebrow. "Liar."

He chuckled.

My mother put a bowl of fruit down in front of me along with a fresh, steaming blueberry muffin from the oven. "Eat something, dear. It will raise your blood sugar and possibly make you a little more tolerable."

I fished a green grape from the bowl. "Thanks," I grumbled, popping it into my mouth.

"Warren, would you like some breakfast?" Mom asked, holding up the basket of muffins.

He shook his head. "No thank you, ma'am. I ate at the house before we left."

I rolled my eyes, pointing in his direction. "Warren eats healthy crap that tastes like horse feed and grass in the mornings."

Mom gently shook my shoulder. "Maybe you should follow his lead. I like this man more and more as I get to know him."

I did too, but I was too grumpy to agree with her or make Warren feel good about himself.

"I will take some more coffee, if you don't mind, Mrs. Jordan,"

Warren said.

"Certainly, Mr. Parish." My mother's tone was mocking as she took his travel mug.

My father leaned against the counter with his coffee cup. "Parish? Like the church?" he asked.

Warren nodded. "Exactly like the church. When I was a baby, I was found outside of St. Peter's Parish in Chicago. No one knew my name, or even if I ever had one, so the caseworker who came and got me named me Warren after her father, I believe, and Parish after the church."

I looked up. "I didn't know that."

My mother handed him the refilled mug. "That's fascinating."

Warren shrugged and screwed the lid on his cup. "And pretty sad."

My mother patted Warren's cheek. "Not sad at all. I think it's remarkable how you have lived your life despite such a mysterious beginning."

He smiled at her. "Thank you."

She squeezed his hand. "No matter how heinous our daughter can be in the mornings, I hope you know you have a family now."

"I'm not heinous," I protested.

Warren slipped his arm around my shoulders from behind and kissed the top of my head. "Yes, you are, but it's OK. I love you anyway. Are you about ready to go? We need to get to the airport."

I groaned and stood up. "Can I have alcohol on the plane?"

My mother shook her head and sighed.

I gave her another hug. "I love you, Mom. I'll see you when we get home."

"Have a wonderful time. Tell the detective we said hello," she said.

"I will."

I hugged my dad. "I love you, Dad. Maybe I'll bring you a cactus or a ten-gallon hat."

He winked at me. "I'll wear it with pride. I'm sure my patients would love it." He grabbed my hand as I turned to leave. "Did you remember to pack your meds? Your headache prescription and your Xanax?"

I nodded. "Yeah, don't worry. I've got them, and Warren's going to be with me the whole time, so I'm sure I'll be fine."

Dad shook Warren's hand. "Have fun. Take care of my little girl and enjoy your downtime."

"I will. Thank you, sir," Warren said.

We walked out of the house, and on the way to the car, Warren looked at me. "You take Xanax? For anxiety or what?"

I nodded. "Usually only when I know I'm going to be around really bad people. Like, the jail causes me to go into hysterics."

"That's interesting."

"Why?"

He shrugged. "I tend to be sharper, more focused around bad people. Not anxious."

I looked up at him. "That is interesting."

When we reached the car, he opened my door. "I like your parents a lot."

"Yeah, they're great," I said without emotion, still hugging my coffee.

He shook his head. "Maybe you need Prozac in the morning."

I got in the car and looked up at him. "Maybe you shouldn't talk so much."

He laughed and shut my door.

As we pulled out of the driveway, I turned in my seat to look at him. "Does my mom give off anything weird to you?"

"What do you mean?" he asked.

I shrugged. "I don't know. For the past few months I've gotten this really strange feeling around her."

He laughed. "Is that why you snapped at her back there?"

"Yeah, but I didn't mean it as hateful as it sounded," I said.

He shook his head. "I haven't picked up on anything. What's it feel like?"

I thought for a moment. "Do you know that fairytale called the Princess and the Pea?"

His head turned in my direction. "Really? Do I look like a fairytale kind of guy to you?"

I laughed. "It's about this princess who can feel a pea at the bottom of twenty mattresses."

"What the hell?" he asked, laughing as he turned onto the highway.

"There's this girl who claims she's a princess, and this old woman hides a pea under twenty mattresses that the girl is going to sleep on —"

He interrupted me. "Who the hell sleeps on twenty mattresses?"

"Pay attention!" I snapped. "In the morning, they asked the

princess how she slept, and she said she slept terribly because there was a pea under her mattress," I explained. "They knew she was a real princess because she could feel the pea hidden at the bottom."

"Fairytales are stupid. That makes no sense." He glowered over at me. "I'll bet you couldn't feel a pea. You're definitely not a princess."

"You're missing the point, Warren."

"What's the point?" he asked.

I was getting frustrated, and he was grinning because he knew it. "That's what it feels like with my mom. There's something there that's hidden, but I can still feel it." I held up my hands in question. "You don't sense anything strange around her?"

"Peas?" He shook his head. "No peas."

I rolled my eyes. "You're impossible."

He reached over and put his hand on my knee. "I'm sorry. I'll pay more attention when we see her again."

I sighed. "Thank you."

The airport was almost empty when we arrived. We checked our bags, declared the arsenal Warren had brought along with us, and made it through security with well over an hour to spare. I wanted to say *I told you so*, but I kept my mouth shut. I stretched out on the sandpaper-esque carpet near the gate and used my carryon bag as a pillow. Warren sat in a chair with a newspaper.

"Did Nathan book the same flight?" I asked.

"I thought so, but he should be here by now," he said.

I closed my eyes and felt the rumble of planes on the tarmac outside. "He's probably still in bed asleep like a normal person," I mumbled.

"What?" Warren asked.

"Nothing."

I woke up sometime later with the toe of Warren's boot nudging me in the ribs. I opened my eyes.

"Feel better?" he asked.

I yawned. "A little." I struggled to my feet while Warren picked up my bag. I looked around to see that Nathan still hadn't shown up. "Do you think I have time to get more coffee?"

"They'll have coffee on the plane," he said.

To my surprise, the flight was nearly full. In our row of three seats, I took the middle so Warren could wedge his six-foot-three frame into the aisle seat.

I rested my head against his shoulder. "How long is the flight?"

He looked down at the large tactical watch encircling his wrist. "We should be there by noon. We have to change planes in Atlanta."

I nodded and closed my eyes again, this time enjoying the scent of Warren's cologne. It was strong and masculine, but it reminded me of the ocean breeze and moonlight. The peaceful hum of electricity between us was enough to lull me to sleep again despite the chatter and fumbling of luggage around me.

"Uh oh," he said, jarring me awake.

I sat up and looked at him. "Uh oh, what?" I followed the direction of his gaze.

Nathan was shoving a large red carry-on into an overhead compartment six rows ahead of ours. He waved when he saw us. I smiled and returned the gesture, but when he stepped out of the narrow aisle, my smile quickly faded and my stomach did a backflip.

Shannon Green was standing right behind him.

5.

"YOU HAVE GOT to be freaking kidding me!" I shouted, causing the older gentleman in front of us to turn around in his seat and look at me.

Warren gripped my hand and squeezed. "Keep your voice down."

"Did you know he was bringing her?" My voice was a squealing whisper, like an emphysemic banshee.

He shook his head. "No, I didn't."

I sat back hard in my seat. "What was he thinking?"

Warren turned toward me. "He was probably thinking he didn't want to be the third wheel here with us," he said. "Would you want to be tagging along with another couple by yourself?"

Yanking my hand from his, I folded my arms over my chest. "I would be by myself for eternity before I would even go to the grocery store with that woman. I'm certainly not going to Texas with her." I furiously shook my head. "No. No. No."

He angled his shoulders to face me. "So, what are you going to do? Get off the plane?" It was obvious Warren's patience was wearing very thin.

"Do you have any idea how much I can't stand her?" I jabbed my thumb into the center of my chest. "Do you know how hard this is for me?"

He narrowed his eyes, and for the first time ever, he looked angry with me. "Let's think about that for a second." He pointed over the top of the seats toward Nathan. "That guy up there more than obviously has a thing for you. You work together, you hang out together, and he's even stayed the night at your house—in your bed—at least once. I don't think you've slept with him, but he's kissed you before, and if he had half a chance he would edge me out of the picture without a moment's pause." He was fighting to maintain control of the volume of his voice. "Still, you don't see me yelling on the plane because he's here."

"That's not the same."

He blinked with surprise. "How's it different?"

"Nathan only thinks he has a thing for me. You know, people fear you and they love me." I gestured between us. "It's part of...whatever *this* is."

"Right, Sloan! Because a dude falling for his hot co-worker is so out of the ordinary!"

I pressed my lips together and shrank down into my seat. "But I—"

He held up his index finger, daring me to continue my protest. "Enough."

I stared at the blue seat back in front of me and picked at a loose thread from the fabric. "I can't promise I'm going to be nice to her."

He didn't say anything more. He just opened up the *SkyMall* magazine and began thumbing through the pages, not pausing long enough to read any of it. He was definitely mad.

I needed to get a grip. Fast. I had chosen to be with Warren which forfeited any right I had to a temper tantrum over Nathan being with someone else but damn it was hard. And of all people...Shannon? Talk about salt in an open wound.

Still, it didn't change the fact that I was wrong.

"I'm sorry." And I was.

Warren didn't even flinch in acknowledgement.

After a moment of being ignored, I leaned into him. "How did you know Nathan kissed me?"

He didn't look up from his book as he continued to flip through the pages. "I was there."

My brain scrambled. "You were there?"

"At your house, the first night I met you. He kissed you at the door and stormed out." His eyes slowly rolled toward me. "Why? What kiss are you thinking about?"

Crap.

My shoulders sank, and I tried to squelch the guilt churning in my stomach even though, technically, I hadn't done anything wrong. "It was before you and I got serious."

"When?"

Every muscle in my body tensed. "The last time, it was—"

He cut me off and closed the magazine. "The *last* time? How many times have there been?"

I cringed. "Three." He didn't respond, so I continued. "The last time was the night after we found his sister's body in Raleigh. The night I got our DNA test results."

His teeth were audibly grinding, and he turned his gaze toward the seat. I half-expected it to start smoking. "That was the last time?"

I put my hand on his arm. "I swear it was."

He nodded, but still didn't look at me. "I already knew about that."

My head snapped back in surprise. "You did?"

"Nathan told me when we were out looking for bodies a couple of weeks ago." He seemed to relax a bit.

My jaw went slack. "Why didn't you say something?"

"There was nothing to say. You were right. It was before we got serious."

His leniency and patience creeped me out. Rather than coming across as being a bit of a doormat, his steel resolve to be objective and understanding was unnerving. It was scary to think what would happen if Warren was pushed past his limit. I certainly didn't want to find out.

"I haven't slept with him ever," I added, quickly and with conviction.

"OK." He returned his attention to the magazine.

I shuddered.

My cell phone buzzed on my lap. It was a text message from Nathan. *Good morning, sunshine. Surprise.*

I tapped out a reply with my thumbs. *I hate you.*

A moment later, another message came. *I know.*

It was a short flight to Atlanta, and we didn't have much of a layover. Nathan and Shannon exited the plane first but waited for us in the terminal. I tried to look pleasant as we approached.

Shannon's blond hair was neatly framed around her face, she was wearing a black pant suit, and—unlike me—she had opened her makeup bag that morning. She was ready for the six o'clock news; I was ready for a cardboard box under a bridge.

She was looking at me with an equal amount of disgust.

I forced a smile. "Good morning."

"Don't you look lovely?" Nathan laughed as his eyes scanned me up and down. He nodded toward my head. "Your hair looks like a bird's nest."

I cut my eyes at him and looped my arm through Warren's. "Well, your face is stupid."

Nathan laughed.

"You guys barely made it, didn't you?" Warren asked.

Shannon flipped her hair over her shoulder. "I had to do the news at five this morning." She giggled and put her hand on Nathan's arm. "We had to literally run down the terminal!"

I glanced down at her four-inch high heels. "In those shoes, and you didn't break your neck?"

Warren nudged me with his arm.

I looked at Nathan. The patch on his ball cap read *Shitstarter*. I pointed to it and smirked. "That's appropriate. I didn't know you were bringing a friend."

Shannon laughed. "I certainly wouldn't classify me as a friend."

I shook my head. "I wouldn't either."

Her mouth twisted into a deep frown.

Warren cut his eyes down at me, but the corners of his mouth were twitching as he tried to suppress a smile. He looked at her and extended his hand. "You must be Shannon. I've heard a lot about you. I'm Warren Parish."

She blinked her bright green eyes up at him and smiled so big I wondered if she might get a face cramp. "I've heard a lot about you too." She was still holding onto his hand. "It's nice to finally put a face with your name."

I pulled his hand away from her. "That's enough of the pleasantries. We've got a plane to catch."

I pushed my way past them, and Warren did a double-step to catch up with me. "Did I just detect a hint of jealousy, Ms. Jordan?" He was smiling wildly down at me.

"No," I answered.

He laughed and hooked his arm around my waist. "I think you were a tiny bit possessive for a moment."

I bumped him with my hip. "Don't let it go to your head, Mr. Parish."

He kissed my cheek as we walked. "I like it when you get territorial."

"Do you want me to pee on your leg or something?" I asked.

He laughed. "Nah. Dirty looks and snide remarks are enough."

When we landed in San Antonio and walked outside to get our rental car, the heat almost reduced me to a puddle on the sidewalk. It had been forty-two degrees when we left Asheville, and even before noon in Texas, it was already pushing ninety. All four of us were severely overdressed. On the curb outside the airport, I stripped off my coat. Unfortunately, I was still wearing a hooded sweatshirt.

Shannon, in her black pants and suit jacket, looked like she was seriously rethinking her decision to tag along on our trip. "We have got to find some air conditioning." She panted as she fanned herself with what appeared to be an unused barf bag from the plane.

Nathan slipped on his sunglasses. "Let's get the car and go to the hotel. We'll figure out the rest of the day after that."

A bead of sweat drizzled down my spine. "I'm going to need a shower."

Warren was looking at the rental car signs. "Which way are we headed, Nate?"

"Budget," Nathan answered, pointing to the left.

I looked up at Warren. "We're sharing a rental car?"

He nodded as we followed Nathan and Shannon. "Yeah. Is that a problem?"

Cautiously, I lowered my voice and slowed my pace to put some distance between us and them. "I promise I'm not trying to be whiney or difficult, but have you considered how we are going to go searching for Rachel Smith with Shannon tagging along?" I asked. "You don't think Nathan told her about us, do you?"

He shook his head. "I doubt it. Maybe he plans on letting her play at the spa all day while we are combing the city. She seems like a spa kind of girl."

I giggled.

He laughed, looking down at me. "I'm so glad you're not high maintenance. I would honestly prefer your hot mess over that nonsense any day."

"What? You don't want to see me in four inch heels?" I asked, smiling.

He flashed me a devilish grin and lowered his face toward mine. "I don't know. Would you be wearing anything else?"

I poked him in the ribs. He wrapped his hand around mine as we walked. In front of us, Shannon was throwing her hips from side to side as she navigated the sidewalk. I sighed. "This is going to be an interesting trip."

He laughed. "Just think of it as a personal growth opportunity for you."

I groaned.

* * *

The Hyatt Regency on the River Walk in downtown San Antonio was undoubtedly the nicest hotel I had ever been in. The grand lobby stretched high above our heads with balconies lining the walls that looked over the sparkling reflecting pool in front of us. Even Shannon seemed impressed as we walked to the check-in desk.

While Warren got our keys, I walked over to the small bridge that stretched across the water and looked out of the massive window that framed the view of the San Antonio River Walk. A gondola full of tourists was floating by, and there were bistro tables covered with colorful umbrellas that stretched along the water's edge. The tables were full of smiling patrons nibbling pretentious looking edibles.

A moment later, Warren was at my side. "You like it?" he asked with a raised eyebrow.

I laughed and leaned against the railing. "I feel like total white trash right now. Why did you let me show up at this nice hotel looking like a hobo?"

His jaw dropped. "Like you would have listened to me!"

I couldn't really argue.

Nodding toward the floors above, he offered me his arm. "You ready to go upstairs?"

I hooked my arm around his elbow. "Heck yeah, I am!"

We rode the glass elevator to the seventh floor, and I followed him down the hallway to our room. He opened the door to a spacious suite with a fluffy, white, king-sized bed centered between a leather couch and a massive window that overlooked the city. The flat-panel television hanging on the wall dwarfed the one I had at home. I stepped inside and inhaled the scent of green apples and Clorox.

"This is ridiculous." I laughed and dropped my bag on the bed. I walked to the window and pulled the curtains the rest of the way open, displaying the peaceful San Antonio River and restaurants below.

He walked up behind me and encircled me with his arms. "Did I do well?"

"You did crazy well. This is gorgeous." I was buzzing from his energy and from excitement. "I may not want to ever go home."

He kissed the side of my neck and let me go. "I'm going to change into something lighter. Are you going to take a shower?"

"Yeah." I walked to the bed and unzipped my suitcase. "What's the plan for today?"

Warren pulled his shirt over his head, and I forgot what I was doing. It was like his torso had been sculpted out of cream cheese. A large talon shaped tattoo stretched over the right half of his body, both front and back, with hooked claws like that of an eagle snatching him away from above. He had the word *Azrael*, meaning the Angel of Death, inked in script just below where his right side holster normally rested on his hip.

I bit my lower lip.

"I told Nate we would meet them for lunch in an hour." He stopped rifling through his bag when he noticed me staring at him. "What?"

I felt my cheeks flush red. "You're very distracting."

He smiled. "I'm glad I'm not the only one who gets distracted in this relationship."

I walked over and pushed his suitcase back and sat down in front of where he stood. I ran my fingers across the tattoo peeking out from the waistband of his jeans. "Why Azrael?" I asked. "You've never told me."

His chest expanded with a deep breath. "When I was in Iraq about five years ago, we had to clear a section of Baghdad around an Islamic mosque. We entered into this building where, I guess, some Shiite leaders were meeting. This one guy with a long white beard looked at me and freaked out. I mean, we were all dressed in our cammies, carrying M-4s and everyone was pretty nervous, but this guy was looking just at me. I thought he might jump out the window."

"Really?" I asked.

He nodded. "He had these crazy eyes, and he pointed at me and said the word *Azrael*. I didn't know what it meant at the time, but I asked our translator. He said it's the name some Islamics use to refer to the angel of death or the angel of retribution."

"So you had it tattooed on your hip?" I asked.

He shrugged. "If the shoe fits."

"Do you think that guy knew who you were—or *what* you were?" I traced my finger over the word again.

He sighed and shook his head. "If not, it's one hell of a coincidence."

The angel pin little Kayleigh had given to me was attached to the front of the pocket on my jeans. I ran my finger across it. "I don't believe in coincidences anymore." I looked up at him. "Do you think whatever we are could be linked to angels?"

He sat down next to me and laughed. "No." He turned his palms up. "Then again, who knows? I certainly haven't come up with any other reasonable explanations."

"Do you believe in angels? Or God for that matter?" I asked.

He blew out a deep sigh. "I don't know. It's hard for me to wrap my brain around the notion of some loving, all-powerful being with the hell I've seen over the years. However, I do believe there is more out there than just what everyone thinks. You and I are proof of that."

I nodded. "Yeah. I agree."

He pushed himself up and leaned on his arms over me. His perfect face was inches from mine. "I do know one thing for sure."

I grinned. "What's that?"

He shook his head. "You are no angel before nine in the morning." He laughed and kissed the tip of my nose.

* * *

Nathan and Shannon were waiting at a table at Paesano's restaurant on the River Walk, just down from our hotel, when Warren and I caught up with them. Warren, Nathan, and I were dressed in jeans and t-shirts. Shannon had changed into a green sundress and a hat that was nearly as big as the umbrella over our table.

I adjusted my sunglasses and looked up at Warren as we walked toward them. "I'll play nice, but there are no guarantees I won't push her into the river."

He laughed and tucked his fingers into my back pocket.

Warren pulled out my chair, and I sat down between him and

Shannon at the square table. Nathan was across from me, sipping on a beer, wearing aviator sunglasses underneath his Shitstarter ball cap.

"What are you drinking?" I asked him.

"Peroni." He held the glass toward me. "Wanna try it?"

I shook my head. "I've had it before. I think I'll order one too." I picked up a menu. "This place is delicious. I ate here when I came for a conference last year."

Shannon was fanning herself with the wine list. "I don't know why anyone would come here. It's too hot," she griped. "We should have gotten a table indoors where there's air conditioning."

I blinked my eyes in question at Nathan, wondering what he was thinking in bringing her along. He just grinned at me.

Shitstarter is right, I thought.

After we'd ordered and our beers were delivered, Warren split a glance between me and Nathan. "So, what's our game plan while we're here?"

Nathan sat up in his chair. "Well, we can't do a whole lot of work until Monday, but I was able to get my hands on some records for caseworkers in the city, females with the last name of Smith."

I tipped my beer up to my lips. "What if she's not a caseworker now? Or what if she's not going by Smith anymore?"

"Who?" Shannon asked.

"The woman we are here looking for." I turned my attention back to Nathan. "What if her name never was Rachel Smith?"

He shrugged his shoulders. "We've got to start somewhere. I also got the information for the convenience store where she was last seen. That should help narrow the list down a bit."

"How far is it from here?" Warren asked.

"Just a few miles east," Nathan said, nodding in the direction away from where the sun was sinking lower in the sky. "We can cruise over that way this afternoon and look around if you want."

I shook my head. "Let's have some downtime for the weekend. We can work on Monday."

Shannon laughed. "Sloan and I actually agree on something."

I leaned my elbows on the table and glared at Nathan. "What's Shannon going to do while we're working?"

"I'll come along, of course," she answered.

I cut my eyes across the table. "Nathan?"

"I can answer for myself, thank you very much," Shannon snipped.

I blinked at Nathan again.

He put his hand on hers. "It might be best if you stay at the hotel while we're gone. The case we're working on is classified."

She laughed and turned her nose up in my direction. "Classified? I don't think Sloan has any kind of secret clearance."

He pulled down his sunglasses enough to make direct eye-contact with her. "Shannon, we talked about this. I told you if you wanted to come, you were going to have to be on your own some." He leaned toward her. "What we're doing might be dangerous."

"Then why does she get to go?" Shannon was pointing her finger at me, and for a moment I considered reaching out and breaking it off.

I held my hands up and pushed away from the table. "OK. We need to get a few things straight here." I looked her square in the face. "We're not just here for some kind of double-date vacation. Nathan is helping Warren and me with finding someone we need to talk to. This is business. So don't think you and I are going to be part of some kind of wives' club that gets our nails done while the boys go to work."

Shannon's mouth fell open. I was becoming accustomed to that expression from her.

Nathan reached over and took her hand. "I'm sorry, but I told you this when you asked me to come along. Sloan's right. You've got to sit this one out."

She pushed her chair back and stood, tossing her hair dramatically over her shoulder. "Well, maybe I should sit lunch out too then!"

"Don't leave." Nathan sat back hard in his seat and folded his arms over his head in frustration.

She turned on her stiletto and stalked down the sidewalk, her heels click-clacking as she marched. He started to get up, but I held out my hand to stop him. "No, let me," I insisted.

Warren caught my arm. "You play nice."

I rolled my eyes and yanked my arm free from his grip. I jogged to catch up with her. "Shannon, wait!"

She spun around with her finger in my face. "You know, everything was perfect before you showed up!"

I reared my head in surprise. "Me?"

"Yes, you! It's like I haven't even had a boyfriend since he met you!" She stamped her foot on the brick sidewalk.

The river behind her looked terribly tempting. *Just one little shove…*

I took a deep breath, to calm my temper. "Shannon, listen. I don't know what's going on with you and Nathan, but it's not about me."

"Don't lie to me, Sloan! You may have your hunk of a boyfriend over there, but that doesn't mean there's nothing between you and Nathan." Her voice cracked with emotion.

My jaw was clenched so tight I thought my teeth might break. "Did you come here to babysit us?"

She didn't respond.

I shook my head. "Look, I honestly don't know what Nathan sees in you, but you are going to lose him if you keep acting like a jealous, self-centered wench. I'm sorry if your relationship is on the rocks, but I can promise you if it is, you're probably the problem. Maybe you should stop worrying so much about me and start taking a little better care of him. God knows, you don't deserve him."

"Why do you hate me so much?" She yanked off her oversized sunglasses. "Because I hooked up with Jason Ward in high school? That was a million years ago!"

I took a step toward her and kept my hands at my sides so I didn't punch her in the face. "No, Shannon. It's because I trusted you! I thought you were my friend, and you betrayed me!"

She threw her hands into the air. "You told the entire school I had syphilis!"

I laughed. "Yes. I did! But only because you hurt me. There, I said it. You were my friend and you hurt me."

Her eyes widened, but she didn't respond.

I let out a deep sigh. "Now, I'm not going to pretend I like you because you know I don't, but I'm willing to try and get along since I don't have much of a choice. So, will you please stop acting like the drama queen you are and come back and sit down at the damn table for lunch?"

She pressed her lips together and shifted her weight from one foot to the other.

I offered her my hand. "Truce?"

She eyed it, and then looked at me. Her shoulders sank, and she huffed as she shook my hand. "Truce."

6.

AFTER LUNCH, THE four of us walked along the river, visiting the shops and acting like a group of normal friends. Shannon insisted we go on a gondola ride, so we did. I settled under Warren's arm at the rear of the boat. The sun was dipping lower and lower on the horizon, and the heat was starting to taper off for the day. The gondola driver was giving a detailed history of the area, and Shannon was listening intently with Nathan a few rows ahead of us. I stared up at the deep blue sky and enjoyed the feeling of my head against Warren's shoulder.

He nodded toward Shannon up ahead. "So, did the two of you kiss and make up?"

I shrugged. "I called a truce. You're right. I don't want to be miserable the whole time we're here. I can go back to hating her with full force when we get home."

He laughed. "That's my girl."

"Sorry I was so bitchy this morning," I added.

He pulled off his black sunglasses and hooked them on the front collar of his shirt. "I'm getting more used to it, but I don't think we're ever going to get along in the mornings."

I scraped my fingernails down his thigh. "We get along just fine when I wake up with you still in my bed."

He chuckled. "How many times has that happened? Maybe twice?"

I dragged my nails back up. "Maybe, but wasn't it very well worth it on both occasions?"

He tightened his arm around my shoulders. "You start talking like that and I'm going to make him turn this boat around."

I settled against him. "It wouldn't be the worst thing."

He looked down at me. "Can you believe we've only known each other for six weeks?"

My head fell to the side. "Six weeks? Are you sure that's all?"

"Crazy isn't it?" He motioned down to his watch. "I've been counting. This is the longest relationship I've ever been in."

I laughed. "Seriously?"

He nodded. "Yeah. I guess it's a by-product of emanating fear to everyone you meet. I mean, the bad-boy thing kinda works for me for a while, but it doesn't last." He smiled. "It's nice to be treated like a normal person when I'm with you."

"What is normal?" I laughed as we passed under an arched, stone bridge.

"True." He leaned his head against mine. "Can we talk seriously for a sec?"

I rolled my head to look at him. "Sure, I guess. Talk about what?"

"If it's all right with you, I'm going to leave my stuff at your place when I leave next month," he said.

I frowned. "I don't want to talk about that."

He was drawing circles on my shoulder with his finger. "We have to talk about it sooner or later. I'd rather get it over with."

"Of course you can leave your stuff at my house. You know that." I perked up a bit. "Wait, even the car?"

He nodded. "Even the car. Please don't wreck it."

"I promise I won't." I crossed my heart.

"Also, before I leave I'll have to update my paperwork with the government. I'm going to make you my power of attorney, and if something were to happen to me while I'm gone, everything will be left to you."

My heart felt like it forgot to beat for a second. "I *really* don't want to talk about *that*," I said, poking out my lower lip.

"Sloan, they wouldn't be recalling me if this wasn't for something major. This is probably going to be really dangerous, and I want you to be prepared for worst case scenario."

"You're going to make me cry again," I warned.

He shook his head. "No more crying." He squeezed my shoulder. "I also want you to know, if something does happen to me, you should stick close to Nathan. He knows about what you can do and the weight it brings. He'll take care of you."

My mouth fell open. "Are you seriously giving me your blessing to be with Nathan if you die?"

"Hell no." He laughed. "If you end up with him after I'm dead, I'm going to haunt the shit out of both of you."

"You promised you're going to come home to me," I reminded him.

He pressed a kiss to my temple. "Always."

I crumpled a little in my seat at the thought of a world without Warren in it. Even in such a short amount of time, I realized how completely dependent on him I had become. Being with Warren was like needing to breathe oxygen. Considering the migraines, I was beginning to wonder if it was even physically possible for me to go on without him.

I reached over the side of the boat and cupped a handful of cool water. I splashed it on my face and laughed. "Geez, I'm going to need to get off this boat and do some serious drinking." I flicked the rest of the droplets onto his face.

"I could get on board with that plan." He sat up straight and craned his neck to see over the people in front of us. "Hey, Nate!"

Nathan turned to look at us.

"We did your girl's boat ride. After this, my girl wants to go to a bar!" Warren called out.

Nathan smiled and gave us a thumbs-up.

* * *

An hour later, we were at Durty Nelly's Irish Pub. Nathan and I were drinking beer, Warren was drinking straight whiskey, and Shannon was sipping a cosmopolitan that had seemed to offend the bartender to make. Thank God she had taken off her ridiculous hat because it might not have fit in the crowded room. We were huddled around a small wooden table near the bar that backed up to a piano where a man was singing Irish drinking songs.

"Anybody else think it's weird to have a bar this Irish next to the Alamo?" Nathan asked, holding up a napkin with a bright green shamrock on it.

Warren laughed, and I looked around at them confused. "Who

fought at the Alamo?"

Nathan's eyes rolled toward the ceiling like he was searching his memory.

Warren pressed his lips together as he stared at the back of the piano.

Shannon's head fell to the side. "The British?"

I shook my head as I finished the last of my second beer. "That's definitely not it."

"You want another one?" Warren asked, nodding to my empty glass.

"Please," I said and gave him a peck on the lips.

He stood up and walked to the bar.

Nathan was still thinking. "Davy Crockett was there, but I'll admit I only know that because of the Disney movies."

"Maybe we should tour the Alamo tomorrow and find out!" Shannon shouted over the music.

I leaned back in my chair. "I was thinking about going to that really pretty Catholic church we passed down the street on our way to the hotel."

Nathan's head tilted in surprise. "Are you serious? I didn't know you went to church."

"And you're not Catholic," Shannon said.

I shrugged. "I have a theory I want to explore."

"What kind of theory?" he asked.

I drummed my hands on the table. It was sticky. "I want to see what someone there can tell me about angels."

Nathan's eyes widened, and he straightened in his seat. "Really?"

"Angels? Why?" Shannon asked.

"I'm just curious." It wasn't a lie. "I have some questions."

Warren placed another frosty mug of amber beer in front of me. "Questions about what?" he asked.

I looked over at him as he sat down with another tumbler of Jameson. "I was telling them I think I might go by that cathedral we passed earlier today and see if I can talk to a priest or something about angels."

"A priest." He nodded his head. "That could be interesting."

"What do you want to know?" Shannon asked. "I'm not Catholic, but I am Baptist, and I've heard about angels all my life."

I was surprised at her willingness to talk to me and actually try to be helpful. Perhaps it was the vodka. "What do you know about them?" I asked.

She shrugged. "Well, the Bible says they are beautiful and they sing and they announced the birth of baby Jesus."

I looked at Warren. "Well, that theory is out. Your singing sucks."

"Amen to that," Nathan said, raising his beer.

Warren laughed and sipped from his glass.

Shannon finished off the last of her drink. "The angels in the Bible are like messengers. They told Mary she was going to have Jesus. They told the shepherds in the field when Jesus was born, and they told Mary Magdalene that Jesus had risen from the dead."

"How did they tell them?" I asked.

Shannon pushed her chair back and used her hands for wide gesturing. "They came down from the sky, dressed in white and shining like the sun, and they said 'Fear not! I have come with good news for all people!'"

The people in the bar were staring at her.

"Fear not," I repeated. I looked curiously up at Warren before turning back to Shannon. "Were they scary?"

She shrugged. "I dunno. A man walking out of the sky would scare the bejeezus outta me."

I leaned into Warren and lowered my voice. "Fear seems to fit with you."

"But not with you," he added.

She started counting on her fingers. "There were angels who guarded the Garden of Eden when Adam and Eve got kicked out. There was also the Passover angel who killed the first-born sons in Egypt and the angels who protected Daniel in the lion's den."

"So angels have different jobs?" I asked.

She tossed her hands up. "Beats me. That's all I know."

"Thanks, Shannon." The words felt strange as they left my mouth.

She smiled. "Sure."

Nathan leaned toward Warren and pointed his finger between me and Shannon. "Did a pleasant exchange just really happen here or am I drunk?"

Warren laughed. "The world might be coming to an end, man."

I elbowed my boyfriend. "Shut up."

Nathan waved to our waitress. "I think this is cause for celebration." The waitress stepped over to our table. "Can we get four Irish Car Bombs?" He held up four fingers.

"Oh no." I shook my head as she walked away. "Liquor and I are not friends."

Nathan shook his head. "You and Shannon aren't friends either, but obviously anything is possible."

I laughed. "Yes, anything is possible. Me dancing on tables and picking fights with strangers is certainly possible." I tipped my beer up to my lips again.

Shannon shoved Nathan in the shoulder a little harder than she obviously intended and sloshed his beer onto his lap. "Did you tell them your good news?"

He sighed as he sopped up his lap with a napkin.

I glanced at Warren who seemed as clueless as I was. I looked at Nathan again. "Good news?"

He shifted uncomfortably in his seat and wadded up the napkin. He drummed his fingers on the sides of his glass. "Yeah. The FBI officially offered me a job."

"Really?" Warren asked. "That's awesome, man."

"Where is it?" I asked.

He looked down at his beer. "I'll do training in Virginia, and then I'll probably be working out of Charlotte."

My heart sank a few inches. "You're moving again?"

He shrugged his shoulders. "Well, I don't know yet. I haven't given them a definite answer."

My lower lip protruded. "Everybody's leaving me."

Warren squeezed the back of my neck.

Nathan looked at Warren and pointed at him. "Are you leaving?"

It was Warren's turn to appear uncomfortable. He nodded. "Yeah. In a few weeks. I'm being involuntarily recalled to the Marines."

"You're joking?" Nathan said, pushing his beer away from him.

Warren shook his head. "Unfortunately, not."

"What do they want you for?" Nathan asked.

Warren turned his palm up. "Who knows? I'm pretty sure they are sending me to a combat zone for something. They hinted they're looking for someone specific, but I'm not certain who it is."

"Have you checked the most wanted list? Even if it's global terrorism, the FBI might have them listed," Nathan said.

Warren shrugged. "No, I haven't checked. All I know is they want me back and I don't have a choice in the matter."

"I hate to hear that," Nathan said.

I wasn't so sure that was true.

Unable to think any longer about Warren leaving, I looked at Shannon. "What will you do if Nathan takes the job in Charlotte?"

She shrugged and smiled at Nathan. "We haven't decided yet." She reached over and squeezed his hand. "I might be able to transfer to a station out there, but we haven't seriously talked it over."

Nathan looked grateful when the waitress reappeared with a tray of four dark beers and four milky shot glasses. She passed them around. I looked at the drinks in front of me. "You've all been warned that I might get belligerent, and Warren, I hope you're prepared to carry me to the hotel."

He smiled and leaned down to kiss me. "Gladly."

* * *

Forty-five minutes and another round of shots later, the bar was beginning to swirl in and out of focus. Shannon had convinced Nathan to dance, and I had decided to sit in Warren's lap instead of on my chair. I looped my arms around his neck. "I'm dizzy."

He smiled up at me. "I can tell. I'm wondering if I might actually have to carry you out of here."

I narrowed my eyes. "I'm not that drunk."

"That's what all drunks say."

I tugged on his nose. "You're pretty cute, you know?" I said. "In a cute and scary kind of way."

He laughed. "Cute and scary, huh?"

I held my thumb and index finger millimeters apart. "A little bit scary."

Warren pointed at Nathan who was twirling Shannon around a non-existent dance floor. "How much has he had to drink? He doesn't strike me as a dancing kind of guy."

I laughed. "Nathan, you look ridiculous!"

Upon hearing his name, Nathan stopped dancing and came over and grabbed my hand. "Can I borrow her for a second, Warren?"

"Bring her back in one piece," Warren said. "And watch where you put your hands. I've got my eye on you."

Nathan pulled me to my feet and spun me under his arm toward the piano.

Shannon sat down at the table, obviously drunk because she wasn't even mad she had been jilted for me.

"You think I look ridiculous, huh?" Nathan asked.

I laughed as he twirled me around. "You can't dance."

"Maybe not, but you can't either!" He dipped me back so far that I almost toppled over, taking him down with me. He straightened up and rested his forehead against mine, laughing.

Warren was snapping his fingers in our direction. "Hey! Leave room for the Holy Spirit there, McNamara."

Nathan laughed and took a step away from me. He started hopping from one foot to the other like a drunken leprechaun.

I laughed and grabbed his forearms. "Let's go get more drinks. I'm thirsty."

He stopped hopping. "OK. Hey, Warren! Shannon!" he called out. "Want another round?"

"Yes!" Shannon squealed.

Warren held up his half-full glass. "No thanks. I'm good."

Arm in arm, Nathan and I supported each other as we pushed our way across the room. His eyes were still dancing, and he had sweat trickling out from under his cap. He laughed as he tried to catch his breath.

We leaned against the glossy, wooden bar, and he looked around for the bartender.

I bumped him with my hip. "I'm pretty mad at you, you know."

He laughed. "I know."

"I'm serious."

He looked over at me and his laughter faded. "What was I supposed to do though? Not bring a date and hang out with you sitting on his lap all weekend? That's not me."

I looked back to the table where Shannon was giggling something to Warren and sitting a little closer to him than I was comfortable with. My raging hypocrisy surprised me as I realized I was still clutching Nathan's arm. I released him. "Are you serious about her?"

He shook his head. "No."

"So, you're not going to move her to Charlotte if you take the job?"

He frowned and raised an eyebrow at me.

I laughed. "I didn't think so. You should probably tell her though. It's not fair. Not fair even for Shannon Green."

He nudged me with his elbow. "I think you're starting to like her."

I smirked. "Hardly."

The bartender stopped in front of us with an expectant stare.

Nathan leaned forward. "Two Smithwick's and another damn

cosmopolitan, please."

I laughed when the bartender rolled his eyes.

We turned around as we waited. Shannon was talking to Warren with dramatic and flailing arms like she was cheating at a game of charades. He looked at us with wide, pleading eyes, begging for our quick return.

Nathan looked over at me. "What are you going to do when he leaves?"

My face fell. "I've been asking myself that since the minute he told me. Survive, I guess."

He shook his head. "I can't imagine the migraine that will come as a result of him leaving the country. I might as well book your hospital room now."

Nathan had been there the first time Warren left and I developed my first hemiplegic migraine. He had actually broken through my back door and carried me to the ambulance. Then he slept in a chair all night beside me at the hospital. The second time it happened, I was with him again. That night, I puked down the front of his pants and ruined his tactical boots.

"I don't know what I'm going to do. Especially if you're in Charlotte and not there to let me throw up all over you." I smiled at him.

He grimaced. "That was the most disgusting night of my life. I don't even want to think about it."

I laughed and felt my cheeks flush. "Well, you've repaid me by letting Shannon crash my vacation."

He shook his head. "Not even remotely close."

The bartender brought us our drinks. I picked up my beer and Nathan followed me to our table. Warren looked bewildered as I leaned down in front of him. "You OK?" I asked.

"I don't think she has an off button." He jerked his thumb toward her. "Getting her drunk was a very bad, bad idea."

I laughed and kissed him. "I'm going to run to the bathroom."

"Sloan, wait!" Shannon called as I walked toward the bathroom. I stopped and she nearly plowed into me.

She hooked her arm through mine, and I turned around in time to see Warren and Nathan sharing a laugh at my expense. I stuck out my tongue at both of them.

After using the restroom, I washed my hands while Shannon

slathered on a new layer of lipstick like a fat-fingered kindergartner using a red crayon for the first time. To keep from laughing, I bit the insides of my lips.

The water ran cold over my hands, and a chill zinged down my spine. I shuddered. The room looked brighter. The music seemed louder. For a second, I felt lightheaded. *No more booze for me.* I shut off the water and reached for a paper towel.

"Your boyfriend is hot, Sloan." Her speech was slurred, and she staggered as she stepped back and smacked her red lips together.

"I know he is." I pointed at her. "You stay away from him."

She laughed. "That was a long time ago. I was jealous of you."

"Jealous?"

She waved her arm toward me and nearly fell into the sink. "Yeah. You won homecoming and you were the captain of the cheerleading squad, even though you're uncoordinated as shit," she confessed. "I secretly hated you."

I smirked. "That's good to know."

"I am really sorry though. I was a bitch." She was making a serious attempt at a pouty face.

I nodded. "You've got that right."

She grabbed me by the shoulders. "I mean it, Sloan. I'm really sorry."

Rolling my eyes, I took her by the wrist. "Come on, blondie."

When I hauled her out of the bathroom and turned toward our table, I slammed face-first into the blackest soul I'd ever seen.

7.

"OH, EXCUSE ME." The man's moist breath hit my face, reeking of bad scotch and stale cigarettes.

I would have screamed had I been able to breathe.

He ran a calloused hand over his oily black hair and brushed against my arm as he walked past. I thought my skin might peel away from the bone.

The room began spinning out of control. My legs crumpled under me, my knees landing with a thud on the scuffed and sticky hardwood floor.

"Sloan? You all right?" Shannon's voice sounded far away.

The only response I could muster was shaking my head.

A calming wave washed over me as Warren's strong arms closed around my waist. He hoisted me to my feet, and for the first time in almost a full minute, I inhaled. My hands were shaking, and sweat was prickling my forehead.

"Sloan, what is it?" He turned me around and studied my eyes.

"Men's room" was all I could choke out.

Warren spun his head around. "Nate!" he shouted and pointed at me.

Shannon grabbed my hand when Warren stepped away, and Nathan caught me in his arms before my knees buckled again.

"Outside." I was beginning to hyperventilate. "Take me out."

Nathan hooked his arm around me. "Shannon, tell the waitress we'll be right back. I'm going to take her out for some air."

"What's wrong?" The panic in her voice was evident to everyone who could hear. Other patrons were looking around with alarm.

"Outside," I said again, digging my nails into his arm.

"Just go!" Nathan shouted at Shannon.

I put my arm around his shoulders as he helped me across the crowded room toward the front door.

When we were outside in the warm night air, I gasped, sucking deep into my lungs every molecule of oxygen I could. It was too much, and I puked in the planter on the sidewalk.

Once again, Nathan held back my hair.

When I was finished, he steered me away from the door to a park bench nearby. I collapsed onto it the second we were close enough.

He dropped to a knee in front of me, but he wobbled a bit and had to catch himself before falling over. "What happened?"

Shaking my head, I continued to focus on breathing. To be honest, I wasn't exactly sure what had happened inside the bar. "There was a guy." I was still panting, but I could finally speak. "Oh God, he's bad. He's done something really horrific."

"Where?"

"He went into the bathroom," I said.

He started to get up, but I grabbed his hand. "No. Please stay with me. Warren went to check it out."

Nathan nodded and sat down next to me. He rubbed my back. "I don't think I've ever seen you freak out quite like that."

I took another deep breath and blew it out with forced control. I held up my hand so he could see it violently shaking in the air. "Now you know why I take Xanax when I go to your office."

He clasped his hands over mine and held them still.

A moment later, Shannon came outside with a glass of water. "Here." She spilled a little as she offered it to me.

For the first time maybe ever, I was sincerely grateful for Shannon Green. "Thank you."

She pointed toward the building, but the motion threw her off balance and she stumbled a bit. "I'm assuming the party's over and it's time to go home," she said. "I'll go in and settle our tab."

I nodded and drank the water. I wanted to get as far away from

Durty Nelly's as humanly possible.

On her way inside, she knocked shoulders with Warren as they passed in the doorway. He didn't even notice. His eyes were dark and dangerous. There was a quickness to his step that he hadn't had all day.

"What *was* that?" I asked.

He shook his head. "I haven't had that feeling since I was eight." He flashed a loaded glance in my direction.

When Warren was eight years old, he and another girl were placed in the home of a child molester who had somehow made it into the foster system. It was the first time Warren had ever used his power to kill someone.

I had only seen him do it once to end Billy Stewart, and at that moment, I wanted him to do it again.

"I felt"—I swallowed hard—"I felt weird in the bathroom. I thought it was the alcohol. Then I came out and he was right there."

Warren's face was set like stone. The muscles in his forearms were rigid as he clenched his fists at his sides. "I felt it too. Then I saw you hit the floor."

The door to the bar opened and the man came outside. I put my head between my knees and willed myself to not start throwing up again. Alcohol plus a panic attack was a bad combination.

Warren knelt down in front of me. "I'm going to follow him and see where he goes." He looked at Nathan. "Are you sober enough to get her to the hotel?"

Nathan nodded. "Yeah, I'll be fine. Are you sure you don't want me to come with you?"

Warren shook his head as he stood. "No. Some things need to be done in the absence of the law." He kissed the top of my head. "Breathe. I'll be back as soon as I can. You stay with Nathan."

We watched until Warren disappeared out of sight down the River Walk. Beside me, Nathan was gently slapping his cheeks to sober up. I handed him what was left of my water.

"Thank you," he said before draining the glass.

Shannon came out a few minutes later with my purse and hers. "We're settled up. Where's Warren?" she asked, looking around.

"He's going to meet us at the hotel. Sloan, can you walk?" Nathan asked, offering me his hand.

I nodded and he helped me to my feet.

"What was that about?" Shannon teetered on her heels as we turned in the direction of the Hyatt.

I patted my chest over where my heart was slowly beginning to settle down. "It's a long story."

Nathan didn't let go of my hand until we had crossed the bridge and I realized it was awkward. I pulled my hand away. He was still watching me like I might keel over at any second. I was a little worried it was with good reason.

When we reached the elevator inside our hotel, he pressed the number five button for their floor. I reached over and pushed the number seven.

"Just come with us," he said. "Even Warren said for you to stick with me."

I shook my head as the doors closed and we began to ascend. "No, thanks. I'm going to go to my room and lie down."

He frowned. "You don't look so good. I don't think you being by yourself is a good idea. We'll stay with you till Warren gets here."

I put my hand on his arm. "I'm OK. Seriously."

The doors opened on the fifth floor and they stepped out. Nathan blocked the doors with his arm and leaned in. His eyes were slightly bloodshot. "I'm worried about you," he said, lowering his voice.

"Don't be," I said. "I'll be fine."

He pointed at me as the doors began to close. "Call me."

"I will. Goodnight, guys. Shannon, we'll pay you back," I called to her.

"No worries. Goodnight, Sloan!" She bumped into a planter in the hallway.

The doors shut, and I leaned against the glass. I took a few more deep breaths and closed my eyes. When I got to my room, it felt much smaller than before. I tried to open the window, but it was sealed closed. I thought about taking my medicine, but I worried about it mixing with the alcohol.

My cell phone beeped. It was a text message from Warren. *Jumped in a cab to see where he goes. Be back soon. Don't worry.*

I put my purse on the bed and tapped out a response. *I may go to the pool to try and clear my head. Please be safe. I love you.*

Love you, he replied a moment later.

I flipped through the concierge book and found out the pool was located on the roof, and it was open till midnight. I sighed with relief. The open air of a rooftop sounded like paradise. I changed into the black bathing suit I had thrown into my suitcase and put on one of Warren's t-shirts and my flip-flops.

As I walked toward the door, I caught sight of myself in the full-length mirror. I stopped and examined my arms and legs, quickly remembering the night I was dragged through the woods by Billy Stewart. My right leg looked like I had been mauled by a tiger. Silvery pink scars stretched up the side of my calf and up my thigh. The rest of my limbs hadn't fared much better.

It occurred to me, I was about to go out of my room at night alone. If the walls hadn't felt like they might suffocate me, I might have just crawled into—or under—the bed. Instead, I slung a towel over my shoulder and walked out the door before I could change my mind.

On the elevator ride to the roof, I sent Nathan a message telling him not to worry and that I was going to the pool. For a moment, I considered asking him to join me, but decided that was in no one's best interest.

When I opened the door to the rooftop, the long, rectangular swimming pool was sparkling in the moonlight. Tension began to leave my neck and shoulders just at the sight. There was a couple curled up together on a lounge chair, but the pool was empty. Jazz music floated up from the streets below along with the distant hum of the San Antonio nightlife.

I placed my phone, room key, and towel on a lounge chair and stripped off Warren's shirt. After kicking off my shoes, I walked to the edge of the deep end. Looking at the still water, I sucked in a calming breath before diving in headfirst. The cool water flowed over my body as I dolphin kicked to the surface. I rolled to my back and kicked my feet up in front of me, till I was completely horizontal and floating.

There were more stars than I should have been able to see in the city.

When Kayleigh Neeland was kidnapped, Adrianne had convinced me that my ability must have been given to me to serve some kind of purpose, but as I floated on top of the water, feeling the adrenaline diffusing in my bloodstream, my powers felt like a curse. It was commonplace to encounter bad people, but every once in a while, I encountered someone who was truly evil. I shuddered at the mere thought of that man's eyes.

I swam to the edge and pushed off the side and began swimming slow laps across the pool to push the sickening thoughts out of my mind. As I finished lap eight and opened my eyes under water to look for the wall, I saw a pair of perfect calves and bare feet dangling in front of me. I stopped swimming and picked up my head to wipe my eyes.

Nathan was at the edge of the pool, wearing only a pair of red and black swimming trunks.

I reached for the ledge of the concrete beside him and looked around. "Where's your girlfriend?"

He laughed. "Passed the hell out. She didn't even take off her clothes or makeup before she collapsed onto the bed. I've never seen her drink that much."

"I think we were all headed in the same direction before the evening took a nosedive," I said.

He laughed. "Probably so. Hell, I'm still a little buzzed."

"Wonder what Shannon would think about you being up here?" I asked, raising a skeptical eyebrow.

He eased down into the water. "At this point, I'm sure she wouldn't be surprised."

A bright pink circular scar was gleaming on his chest. That hole had been put there to save my life. I gently pushed on his shoulder. "Turn around and let me see your back."

He turned so I could see the entry wound scar. Nathan had been shot in the back as he dove between me and Billy Stewart's Smith & Wesson. His lung had collapsed when the bullet tore through both sides of his ribcage.

"At least you got some cool scars out of it," I said, smiling as I gently ran my finger across the smooth scar tissue.

He laughed as he turned around to face me. "Heck yeah. Chicks dig scars."

I held up my forearms and slowly turned them over to display the spots where the nurses had to dig gravel and splinters out of my skin. "Do guys dig scars too?" I scrunched up my nose with disgust.

He winked at me. "You could be missing your arms completely and you'd still be hot."

A half-hearted smile crept across my face. "Thanks."

I turned around and rested my back against the side of the pool, sinking down till the cool water touched my chin.

Nathan leaned on his elbows and looked over at me. "Are you

feeling better now?"

I blew out a deep breath and shuddered. "That was bad. That guy was terrifying."

He looked up at the stars. "I wish I knew what it felt like."

I shook my head. "No, you don't."

"Who do you think he was?" he asked.

I shrugged my shoulders. "I have absolutely no idea. Warren sent me a text and said he was taking a cab to follow him and see where the guy goes."

Nathan nudged my leg with his foot under the water and grinned with the soft rippled light from the pool reflecting off his face. "It must be bad for him to leave you at a hotel with me."

I laughed for the first time since we had left the Irish pub.

"Other than the ending, did you have a good time tonight?" he asked.

"Yeah. I have to admit that even hanging out with your obnoxious and belligerent girlfriend was even a little fun. She actually apologized to me in the bathroom for what she did in high school."

"No shit?"

"No shit."

"Are you going to let it go?"

I shook my head. "Not a chance."

He chuckled.

"Did you enjoy yourself?" I asked.

He nodded. "Yeah, I haven't had that much fun in quite a while." He sank down to my level in the pool. "What's new with you these days? We don't talk much since Warren moved in."

I smirked at him. "I talk to you more than I talk to my own mother, even with Warren around."

He looked sad. "It's not like it was before though."

He was right. Before Warren moved to Asheville, I spent so much time at Nathan's house that he had bought a leather loveseat to put in his home office for me to have a comfortable place to sit. Much of that time was dedicated to pouring over the investigation of missing girls across the state, but we did enjoy our time enough that it made Shannon extremely jealous.

I thought about those days in stark contrast to my new life with Warren. "There's not much to tell. I'm pretty boring, Nathan."

He laughed. "Aside from the superpowers and all."

"Aside from that." I laughed. "Oh, I did finally tell my parents about it."

"Really?"

I dropped my head back and pressed my eyes closed. "It was kind of hilarious. I sort of blurted it out. We were talking about headaches, and I told them my headaches were supernaturally related to Warren's absence."

He cracked up laughing. "Supernaturally related? And you're not locked in the looney bin? I'm shocked!"

I smiled. "They actually handled it spectacularly well."

He shook his head. "I'm not surprised. Your parents are great."

"Oh, that reminds me. My mother said to tell you hello."

"Your mom loves me, you know," he said.

I nodded. "Oh, I know."

He smiled. "When she came to visit me in the hospital after my surgery, she asked me to dump Shannon and marry you."

I gasped. "No, she didn't!"

"Wanna bet?" He sank under the water to soak his blond head. Then he came back up and raked his fingers through his hair, leaving it spiked in different directions.

"Well, my mom loves Warren now too," I said.

He looked over at me. "Do you?"

I was stunned by his candor. "Do I love Warren?"

He nodded.

"Yes. I love him very much."

He looked up at the sky. I felt like I wanted to apologize, but I knew it would only make everything worse. I stared at the water droplets drizzling down the side of his face until he looked at me with questioning eyes.

"What are you thinking about?" he asked quietly.

"You, me, Warren," I admitted.

He turned toward me. "What do you think would have happened if he had never shown up?"

I had asked that same question a lot since the Friday afternoon when Nathan cornered me in my office and confessed he wanted to be with me. But there, face-to-face in the pool with him while Warren was gone, was not the time to be daydreaming about what might have been. It felt wrong to even be entertaining the question.

I sucked in a deep breath and blew it out nervously as I searched for the right words to say.

"Sloan."

While I had been lost in thought, Nathan had closed some of the distance between us. The moonlight bounced off his dangerously tempting gray eyes that were fixed on my lips. The jazz music from the streets below was nearly drowned out by my pounding heart, and every nerve ending in my body began to tingle. His face was inches from my own.

Then the moment was gone.

The door to the building opened, and Warren walked outside. His step faltered as if he could sense the tension on the rooftop.

I snapped out of my daze as he slowly walked over. "Hey," I said.

Nathan rolled his shoulders back and exhaled before turning around.

Warren looked down at us both. It was obvious he wanted to ask what was going on, but he didn't.

"What did you find out?" Nathan asked, avoiding direct eye contact with either of us.

Warren knelt down at the edge of the pool. "Well, I followed him to a house on the west side of town, not too far from here. I got the address." He tapped his chest pocket and looked down at Nathan. "Do you think you can work some magic and figure out who he is?"

Nathan nodded. "Yeah. I can make some calls in the morning and see if I can find a name and some information."

"What did you get off of him?" I asked.

"Well, he hasn't killed anyone." He turned his palms up. "Not in the literal sense anyway. I'm sure he's ended plenty of lives though."

I reached up for his hand. "Are you all right?"

He kissed my knuckles. "Yeah. Not exactly how I wanted to end such a fun night, though. Are you feeling OK now?"

"Yeah," I said. "Swimming and the night air helps. Nathan's been a good nursemaid like always."

Nathan laughed and then looked at Warren. He rested his arms on the side of the pool. "So, do you want to go after this guy?"

"Oh, I'm going to go after this guy." Warren's response had no hesitation. "There's no question about it."

"You realize there is zero probable cause here," Nathan pointed out.

A thin smile spread across Warren's lips, and he cut his eyes down at

Nathan. "You realize I'm not a cop, right? That I have all the probable cause I need?"

Nathan laughed. "All right, man. Just leave my name out of it."

Warren looked at me. "You ready to get out?"

I nodded. "Yes."

He tightened his hand around mine and pulled me up onto the deck. Nathan got out behind me.

Warren looked around the roof. "Where's Shannon?"

"The girl can't handle her alcohol." Nathan laughed and dried off with the towel he had deposited next to my flip-flops. "I told Sloan she passed out as soon as I opened the door to the hotel room."

Warren laughed as I retrieved my things off the lounge chair. "She's so loud when she's drunk, and she doesn't shut up."

I wrapped the towel around me as we walked inside. "Does she shut up when she's sober?"

Nathan laughed, but he hung his head and shook it sadly.

When the elevator stopped at our floor, I looked at Nathan. "Are you coming to Mass with us in the morning?"

His head snapped back with surprise. "You're really going?"

"Yeah," I said.

He shook his head. "No. Probably not. I'm pretty sure I'm going to have to babysit someone with a really severe hangover."

"Probably," I agreed. "I don't envy either of you."

"We'll catch up with you after," he said. "Maybe we can grab lunch. I wouldn't mind visiting the pool in the sunshine."

"That sounds good to me. Goodnight, Nathan," I told him.

"Night, guys," he said as the doors closed behind us.

Warren and I walked to our room. He looked down at the black bundle in my arms. "Is that my shirt?"

"Maybe," I answered as he slipped the room key into the slot.

We went inside and he locked the door behind us. I turned around to look at him. "Tell me the truth. Did you kill that guy?"

He shook his head. "No, but I thought about it."

"Why didn't you?"

He emptied his pockets onto the desk. "I've learned it's best to have all the facts before making a decision like that. What if he's got hostages or something stashed somewhere?"

He was right, but I didn't like it. I touched his arm. "Are you sure you're OK? I know how badly he got to me tonight, and it seemed to hit really close to home for you."

He tugged on my towel and pulled me close. "Yeah. I'm sorry he screwed up a pretty fun night." He pushed my wet hair off my shoulders. "Who would've ever thought we would enjoy a night out with Nathan McNamara and the syphilis princess."

I laughed. "I know."

"So, church in the morning?" he asked with questioning eyes.

"Yes," I said. "You don't have to go, but I'm going to stop in and see if I can find someone to talk to."

He shrugged. "I'll go. God knows I've got a lot of repenting to do."

I giggled. "Are you going to go to confession?"

Warren's fingers found the knot in my bathing suit ties at the back of my neck. He worked the strings loose and smiled as the straps came down. "Maybe, and I might have a few more things to add to the list before morning."

8.

IN ALL MY life, I had attended church exactly three times. It was an impressive—or sad—record, considering I grew up in a town with a steeple on about every street corner. I went once with my mom's sister around Christmas, once for Easter because the Presbyterians were having an egg hunt, and once because a distant cousin was being baptized. None of those churches were Catholic. All I knew about Catholicism was what I learned from television: they had a Pope, they liked Mother Mary, they were allowed to drink alcohol, and priests wore white collars and black suits.

The nicest outfit I had packed was a floral sundress with spaghetti straps. I guessed it was hardly appropriate for church, but I was certain it was better than blue jeans. I was slipping on my flip-flops when Warren walked out of the bathroom. A cloud of steam rolled through the door with him, like his own personal stage production. I half-expected spotlights and the sound of angels singing.

"You look great," I said. He was in dark jeans that clung to all the right muscle groups and a simple, black button-up shirt. I scrunched up my nose. "But I'm afraid you're going to burn up in the sun."

"It's Texas. I'm going to burn up regardless." He walked over and tugged on the hem of my dress. "You look cute."

"Thanks. Are you ready to go?"

He looked a little nervous. "As ready as I'll ever be."

Outside the hotel, directly across the busy street, was the stone face of the Alamo. I pointed to it as Warren took my hand. "You know, it still doesn't seem right that the Alamo is in the middle of the city. You think Alamo, you think desert."

He laughed, squinting his eyes against the sun as he slipped on his black sunglasses. "I think Alamo and I think of rental cars and steak houses."

It was going to be another hot day in Texas. I thought of the swimming pool on our roof. "What do you want to do this afternoon?"

He didn't hesitate with his answer. "Go disembowel that guy we saw last night."

"Well, that's gruesome." I shuddered at the thought of the night before. "That was such an awful feeling. I wonder who he is."

"I don't know who he is, but I have an idea of what he's up to," he said.

I shook my head. "I don't want to know. Let's talk about something else. We could go look for Rachel Smith this afternoon. At least cruise through the area around the convenience store and see if anything looks interesting."

"We can if you want," he said. "I wonder how long the service will last."

"I have no clue," I said. "I've never attended Mass before."

"I've never been inside of any church that I can remember," he admitted.

I looked up at him with wide eyes. "I wonder if you might burst into flames."

He laughed. "I wouldn't be surprised."

The San Fernando Cathedral was impressive. Two high, Gothic-style stone pillars were adorned with crosses on each side and weathered by three hundred years of Texas sunshine. In the middle, there were three arched, heavy wooden doorways that sat below circular windows framed in peaks that resembled royal crowns. There was certainly nothing architecturally comparable to it in the mountains of Asheville. It looked like it belonged on a hill in Italy, not at the corner of Main and South Flores in downtown San Antonio, Texas. A sign out front stated the church had been founded in 1738, and it was the oldest church in the state.

We followed a group of people inside. Mass was already in progress. A choir was singing with a piano at the front of the elaborate sanctuary. One soprano was slightly off-key and singing a little bit louder than the rest. The song was in Spanish, or maybe it was Latin. I wasn't enough of an expert in either language to be sure.

There were no seats left in the pews, so Warren and I stood with the other latecomers in the back of the room. The inside of the church was long and narrow with a high arched ceiling and massive arched columns dividing the room in thirds with the main section straight down the middle. The middle section ended at the far end of the sanctuary with a podium in front of the largest crucifix I had ever seen. Jesus was crucified between enough elaborate stained glass and gold leaflet to pay off my mortgage at least twice over.

Warren leaned down close to my ear. "There's a dead body in here. Maybe more than one."

My breath caught in my chest. "Are you sure?"

"Positive," he replied.

I looked around the room. Behind a group standing in the corner was a large marble box on the wall. I tugged on his hand, and we inched our way over to it. I read the bronze plaque on the side: *Here lie the remains of Travis, Crockett, Bowie, and other Alamo heroes.*

"You're really weird," I whispered up at Warren.

He winked. "So are you."

When the music ended, a man in a long green robe stepped behind the podium and began to read, in what I was sure was Spanish. He was swinging an elaborate steel pot from a chain, pouring smoke in every direction. I looked at Warren. He shrugged his shoulders. I scanned the entrance way, hoping to find a *Catholic Mass for Dummies* book. The next person who got up to speak was also speaking Spanish.

I leaned over to him. "I think we've come to the wrong service. I can't understand a word," I whispered. "This is pointless."

He motioned toward the door we had come in. "You wanna go?"

I nodded.

Once we were outside, I slipped on my sunglasses and shook my head. "That's not the way the Presbyterians do church."

He laughed and followed me across the stone courtyard. I sat down at a small metal bistro table, and he pulled a chair over next to mine. On either side of us were water fountains shooting up out of the ground like the splash pad at the Buncombe County water park. I doubted these weren't frequented by toddlers in swimming diapers though.

He scanned the courtyard. "Well, what do you want to do now?"

I looked up at the elaborate building. "This was a complete bust. I really wanted to talk to a priest or something." I also felt a little defeated that I didn't last more than five minutes in church.

"Do you want to wait till the service is over and try to find someone? Maybe they have people you can talk to when it's over."

I shrugged and slumped my shoulders. "I don't know. That's a long time to sit here and wait in the hot sun."

A large shadow crept over our table. "May I help you?" a man behind us asked.

I turned to see an old man with thick glasses and a dentured smile that was as welcoming as it was contagious. His bald head was covered in sunspots, several of which came together to perfectly form an outline of South America. He was wearing a black suit with a white collar, and a gold cross dangled around his wrinkled neck.

I smiled and jerked my thumb toward the cathedral. "Do you work here?"

"I have been here for many more years than I can count. May I be of some assistance? You seem a little lost." He was supporting himself on the back of an empty chair.

"I don't want to trouble you if you're busy." I squinted up at him against the sunlight which seemed to form a halo around him. "I had some questions."

He nodded to the table. "May I join you?"

"Please." I slid my chair away from the table a few inches.

Warren rose from his seat and pulled out a chair for the priest. The old man grimaced as he eased down into the chair as if every joint between his head and his toes ached with age and arthritis. He had to be pushing ninety. Warren sat back down next to me and leaned his elbows on the table.

Behind the priest's coke-bottle-thick lenses, his eyes were fascinating. They were brown, but the right eye seemed to be split down the middle. Half of it was brown, the other half green.

I offered him my hand and he shook it. "My name is Sloan. This is my boyfriend, Warren. We are down here visiting from North Carolina."

He smiled. "North Carolina is a beautiful state. I love the mountains there. I haven't been in some time, but it is a spectacular piece of God's handiwork, particularly this time of year." He chuckled a bit like Santa Claus. "Not to mention it's a lot cooler there than here."

I laughed and nodded my head. "That's for sure. Can I ask your name?"

"Father John Michaels, but I am old and nontraditional with no need for formalities. You can call me John if you'd like." He had lowered his voice like he was telling us a great secret.

"Father John, can you tell me anything about angels?" I asked.

He studied my face for a moment and then suddenly broke into laughter. "Most questions I get are about Mass or Jesus or Mary."

I laughed. "Well, I have lots of questions about Mass as well. They really need a cheat sheet in there."

He smiled. "I agree. What would you like to know about angels?"

"Do you think they are real?" I asked.

"Of course I do." He chuckled again and folded his hands over his belly.

"Are they here on Earth? Like, could they be walking around here with us?" I asked, gesturing with my hand toward the courtyard.

He nodded. "Absolutely. The Bible makes that very clear. The book of Hebrews, chapter thirteen verse two, reminds us to 'not neglect hospitality, for through it some have unknowingly entertained angels.'"

"Really?" I looked over at Warren and then at the priest. "Here's a weird question." I hesitated for a moment. "Do you know if they can have children? Or maybe reproduce with humans?"

He considered my query. "I believe so, though some others in The Church do not. The Old Testament, the book of Genesis specifically, speaks of the Nephilim, who were the children born to the sons of God and the daughters of men. However, it has been greatly debated that they were the actual offspring of angels."

Warren leaned toward him. "Do you know anything about Azrael?"

The priest's eyes widened. "Azrael is not mentioned in the Christian Bible, but in other texts, Azrael is said to be an angel of death. The Bible does speak of an angel of death, but he is not named. I believe Azrael is derived from the teachings of Judaism and, perhaps, Islam."

Warren nodded and looked off into the distance.

"You've studied up on this quite a lot, haven't you?" I asked.

He smiled and spread his hands on the table. "I admit I've always had a touch of fascination with the angelic." He looked between us. "May I ask what has stirred your curiosity on the subject?"

Warren and I exchanged glances. I scrambled for an answer. "We have a friend who we believe could have some kind of supernatural gifts. We were curious as to where those gifts might have come from. Does that sound crazy?"

He smiled and shook his head. "No, dear. It doesn't sound crazy at all. God puts us all here with different gifts and abilities to further His kingdom."

I was skeptical. "What if our friend doesn't share your beliefs about God's kingdom?" I was a little afraid of his answer. "What if she's not sure God even exists at all?"

He smiled and lowered his voice again. "God is still God, despite what we believe about him."

Warren chuckled.

I reached for the old man's wrinkled hand. "Thank you, Father John. You don't know how helpful you've been."

He squeezed my fingers. "It is my pleasure. I will pray you find the answers you seek." He smiled warmly and sunlight glistened off his glasses. "And remember, even if you don't believe in God, he still believes in you. Ask and you shall receive. Seek and you shall find. Knock and the door will be opened unto you."

I had no idea what he meant, but I smiled as if I did and stood up.

"Thank you," Warren said. He shook the priest's hand and then helped him to his feet.

I smiled at Father John. "I'm glad we stopped by, even if we didn't understand a thing about Mass. I hope you have a good rest of your day."

Warren put his hand on my back as we turned to leave. Church bells rang out from the cathedral tower, disturbing a flock of black birds.

"Sloan." The priest grabbed my arm, pulling us to a stop.

We turned toward him.

"I feel like I should give you a word of caution," he said. "Not all angels are good. The fallen angels of Heaven were banished here to Earth when they rebelled against God. If you are on a quest seeking angels, take great care. Even Satan himself masquerades as an angel of the light."

9.

"WELL, THAT WAS terrifying." I was laughing as we crossed the street but didn't exactly think it was funny. "I've got my hands full worrying about murderers and child molesters. Now I've got to worry about Satan himself?"

Warren laced his fingers with mine. "A lot of what he said seems to fit with your theory."

"Yeah. Maybe it's true then," I said.

"How do we know for sure though?" he asked.

"I think finding Rachel Smith would be a good start," I answered.

He laughed. "Unless she's as clueless as we are."

"True."

He patted his flat stomach. "I'm getting hungry."

I nodded. "Me too. I wonder what Nathan and Shannon are doing."

My cell phone buzzed in my hand. I looked at the screen. Of course, it was a message from Nathan.

Warren looked down at my phone and shook his head. "That's still pretty creepy."

"I know." I read Nathan's message aloud. "Having lunch at the pool. Where are you guys? Did Warren get struck by lightning when he walked into church?" I laughed.

"Jerk," Warren grumbled.

I looked up and tugged on his hand. "Do you want to have lunch at the pool and cool off for a bit in this heat? I know you must be sweltering in that black shirt."

He smiled down at me. "You gonna wear that bathing suit again?"

"Maybe," I answered. "Do you think it looks bad with my hideous scars?"

He stopped walking so suddenly that I stumbled backward when his hand jerked mine to a stop. "Are you serious?" he asked.

I turned and looked at him. "Of course I'm serious." I held out my arms and then pulled up the hem of my skirt to show him my leg. "I promise I'm not feigning modesty here. I look like I lost a death match with a cheese grater."

He pulled me close to him. "Sloan, you looked so hot last night, I was a little pissed off you were in the pool with Nate." He tucked my hair behind my ear. "You have absolutely nothing to be embarrassed or ashamed about."

I blushed. "OK. I'll wear it then. Thank you."

He smiled and draped his arm across my shoulders. "We will definitely go to the pool."

Later at the hotel, as Warren and I left our room, I realized worrying about what I looked like really didn't matter. Warren didn't wear a shirt to the pool, so no one was looking at me anyway. On our walk through the building, he caused an old lady to drop her purse and a cleaning woman to run her cart into a wall. When we reached the top floor, every head on the rooftop turned in our direction.

I noticed two college-age girls pointing and giggling near the bar. I shook my head and looked up at him. "I'm about to make you cover up."

He laughed and smacked me on the butt.

Nathan waved from a table between the water and the bar. He was shirtless again, a detail I refused to focus on, and Shannon was wearing her enormous hat and sunglasses. Her face was pale, and she was leaning on her elbow for support.

"Is someone having a rough day?" I teased as I put my towel down on the chair next to her.

"I feel like I was run over by a bus." She groaned. "All I wanna do is sleep, and Nathan dragged me up here."

Nathan pointed at Warren's chest. "Nice ink, man. What is it?"

Warren turned to show the rest on his back. "It's a dragon's claw."

I laughed. "I always thought it was a bird."

Warren sat down and shook his head. "Nope. It's a dragon. Why the hell would I get a bird?"

Shannon looked over the top of her glasses with bloodshot eyes. "Why would you get a dragon?" she mumbled.

Warren smiled and wiggled his fingers in front of my face. "Maybe it's a demon trying to carry me away."

I slapped his hand down. "Ugh. Given our present circumstance, that's not very funny."

"How was church?" Nathan asked Warren.

Warren shook his head. "Confusing."

"Did you find out anything?" Nathan asked.

I nodded and stripped off Warren's t-shirt that I had worn again. "Yeah. We found this adorable old priest outside, and he talked to us for a little while."

"And?" Nathan asked.

"And we still don't know anything for sure, but a lot of what he said made sense," I answered.

Warren looked around toward the bar. "I'm going to go up there and order some food. What do you want?"

I looked at Nathan's grilled sandwich. "Bring me something like that," I said. "I'd like kettle chips instead of fries if they have them. Thank you."

Warren nodded and walked off toward the bar.

There was a file folder on the table in front of Nathan. I tapped my finger on it. "What's this?"

"Oh, it's that list I told you about. Female child protective services caseworkers in San Antonio named Smith," he said. "It has the addresses where they work."

I shook my head. "The government is a scary beast."

He laughed. "No kidding. You should see what pops up when I run your name through the computer."

Rolling my eyes, I opened the folder. Quickly, I skimmed down the list. It was a total of two pages long. "This isn't as bad as I feared it would be."

He stuck a french fry in his mouth. "It's not too bad *if* she's still going by Smith." He pointed at me. "And if she's still a caseworker."

I groaned. "Good point. Well, there are two Rachel Smiths on this list, so I guess that's our starting point."

"Why would a social worker do anything under a fake name?" Shannon asked.

She'd been so quiet, I had forgotten she was still at the table. "That's actually a good question."

Nathan shrugged. "She's hiding."

"From what?" I asked.

"Could be anything. An abusive spouse, criminal charges, the IRS. Who knows?" he said.

I pulled off my sunglasses and chewed on the tip. "How would you get a job, multiple jobs for that matter, in the government with a fake name? That seems like it would be a hard thing to do."

He nodded. "It's impossible to do. I'm sure they fingerprint and do background searches and everything for those kinds of positions."

"So how could she be getting away with it?" I asked. "You can change your name, but you can't change your fingerprints."

He shrugged again. "That's a good question. My guess is she doesn't work for the government anymore. Maybe she's working for a private company or a non-profit. Hell, she could be working at McDonalds for all we know."

I looked at the list. "There has to be a better way of doing this."

"Can't you find her?" Nathan asked.

I looked at Shannon and then gave Nathan a warning with my eyes.

He held up his hands and mouthed the word "sorry."

I flipped through the file and found Rachel's picture. I stared at it for a long time and wondered if there was any way I could find her with my ability. I closed my eyes and pictured her face. "Where are you Rachel Smith?"

When I opened my eyes, Nathan was scanning the roof expectantly.

I shook my head. "That's not how it works." Just in case, I glanced around the roof as well.

The two college girls were talking to Warren at the bar. Both were in bikinis and both were spilling out of their tops. The blonde was tracing her finger along the tattooed lines on his shoulder. He waved to get my attention, then pointed at me and spoke to them. Judging by their suddenly smug expressions, he was turning down some sort of proposition.

I frowned. "He's such a chick magnet."

"Yes, he is," Shannon agreed, unable to suppress a weak smile.

Nathan balled up his napkin and threw it at her. "Not you, too!"

She just shrugged her shoulders.

By the time Warren returned to the table with our plates, Shannon had found a nearby empty lounge chair and appeared to be asleep with a white towel completely covering her head. Every now and then she would moan in pain. Nathan was on his cell phone.

I looked over at Warren. "Thanks for lunch."

"Of course," he replied, unrolling his silverware.

I jerked my thumb in the direction of the bar. "Did you enjoy your little fan club over there?"

He blinked with surprise. "My fan club?"

I smirked. "Don't play dumb with me, Warren Parish. You may not have a lot of relationship experience, but you know those talking breasts over there were flirting with you."

He chuckled. "No idea what you're talking about."

I threw a potato chip at him.

He caught the chip in his mouth. "It's your fault," he said as he chewed.

"My fault?"

He held his hands up. "If you weren't here, they'd run from me."

I scowled. "I doubt that."

He held up two fingers in front of my face. "That's twice in two days you've gotten jealous. I like it."

I pushed his hand away. "Shut up."

Across the table, Nathan ended his call and put the phone down along with the pen he was holding. "That was my buddy in Charlotte."

Warren straightened in his seat.

Nathan leaned on his elbows. "He found the guy from last night and is emailing me his rap sheet." He looked down at the paper in front of him. "The guy's name is Larry Mendez. He's a convicted felon on robbery, assault, and drug charges. He's out on parole."

I was shocked. "That's it?"

Warren caught my eye. "That's just all he's been convicted of. That's certainly not all he's done."

I crunched on a potato chip and nodded my head. "Yeah. There's way more than robbery, assault, and drugs going on with that guy."

"Definitely," Warren agreed. "I'm going to go back out there tonight and look for him again. I want to see if he's at home."

"What are you going to do?" Nathan asked.

"I don't know. See what he's up to for now," Warren said.

Nathan's brow wrinkled with concern. "Don't go and get yourself arrested on stalking charges while we're down here. I really don't want to have to come and bail your ass out of jail."

Warren smirked. "I'll do my best."

"What time should we leave?" I asked.

Warren waved his fork at me. "I want you to stay here," he said. "You can hang out with Nathan and Shannon. We both know how dangerous this guy is."

I folded my arms across my chest. "Yes. We both *do* know how dangerous this guy is, and because of that, I don't want you going out there alone."

He looked insulted. "Have you met me? Do you not think I can handle him?"

Realizing he was right, I changed tactics. "Well, what if he's not there? You'll need me to find him. I'm coming along."

He shook his head. "No."

I widened my eyes at him and tilted my head to the side. "No?"

"Uh oh," Nathan said. He scooted back a few inches from the table with pure amusement splashed across his face.

Warren leaned forward and put his hand on the back of my chair. "This is too dangerous. It's a bad part of town, and I'm not going to let you—"

"*Let* me?" My voice jumped up an octave. "I don't remember ever giving you the authority to decide what I can and cannot do, Warren Parish."

Like watching a volley being returned across the net, Nathan's head whipped toward Warren.

Warren's eyes narrowed. "What if we find him and you have another meltdown like you did last night? Then what are you going to do?"

Nathan looked at me.

"I'll have my Xanax, and I'll stay clear of the guy," I said. "I'm a big girl. I can handle myself. I think I've proven that."

"Nate, tell her what a bad idea this is," Warren said. He picked up a french fry off his plate and dunked it into a pile of ketchup.

Nathan held his hands up and shook his head. "You're on your own, brother. I'm just enjoying the show."

I sat back in my chair. "Warren, if I don't go, you don't go."

Warren stared at me in stunned silence for a moment before

shaking his head and picking up his sandwich, signaling the end of the conversation.

Satisfied with my victory, I looked at Nathan. "Are you coming with us?"

"Heck yeah, I'm coming. I don't want to miss seeing how this plays out."

"What about Shannon?" Warren nodded to where she was sprawled across the chair a few feet away.

Nathan laughed. "I don't think Shannon will have any interest in leaving the hotel today."

I picked up another potato chip. "I don't think I've ever been that hung over."

"Me either. I have a feeling she won't be drinking again anytime soon," Nathan said smiling.

* * *

Late in the afternoon, after we had showered from the pool, I came out of the bathroom dressed in a pair of black tactical cargo pants and a black t-shirt. I had purchased the ensemble for such an occasion when Warren and I started dating.

He was watching television on the bed when I walked into the room. He shook his head when he saw me. "Well, you certainly *look* the part." He was not amused. He was pissed.

I put my hands on my hips. "Are you going to be mad at me all night?"

He nodded. "Probably."

I kicked the side of the bed with my boot. "Well, get over it."

His eyes were dark and glaring up at me. "Sloan, you can't defend yourself if something happens out there. You can't carry a gun or even shoot one. What happens if we get into something bad and I can't get to you in time?"

"Warren, I think I can handle a simple stakeout. I've been kidnapped, beaten, and shot at, remember?"

He sat up. "Yeah. I remember. That's exactly why I don't want you going. There's no telling what we might encounter out there, and I don't want to put you in harm's way if I don't have to."

I sat down on the edge of the bed and put my hand on his cheek. "I sincerely appreciate you worrying about me, but you're going to need my help with this whether you want it or not. What if you can't find Larry Mendez and he hurts or kills someone when I could have prevented it? I would rather take the risk and help stop this guy, than sit here safe in my hotel room."

He dropped his forehead onto my shoulder. "You're going to cause me to have anxiety."

I kissed the top of his head. "Well, I've got plenty of Xanax for both of us. Come on. Nathan's probably waiting."

There was a knock at our door.

I smiled as I stood, and Warren shook his head.

When I swung the door open, Nathan looked me up and down. "Uh, hi." He awkwardly looked at my outfit and then down at his own black pants and t-shirt.

We both laughed and walked into the room side by side.

Warren rolled his eyes. "Geez," he said. "Should I change? I feel like I don't fit in with the mob squad." He was wearing jeans and a blue t-shirt.

Nathan tugged on the brim of his ball cap. It still said *Shitstarter* across the front. "All you need is a hat."

"And a bunch of inappropriate patches," I said, smiling. "I feel like we need a dynamic duo name. Maybe Cagney and Lacey."

He shook his head. "Nah. Mulder and Scully."

Warren pushed himself up off the bed. "More like Lucy and Ethel."

"I get to be Ethel." Nathan smiled. "Are you guys ready to go?"

"Almost," Warren said.

He walked to the closet and pulled out the huge black gun case he had brought on the trip. He placed it carefully on the bed and used a key to open the lock. I had never even seen what he carried in it. Nathan stepped over beside him as he opened the lid. Inside, a sniper rifle and two black, semiautomatic handguns were encased in dark gray foam.

Nathan surveyed the rifle while Warren strapped a double shoulder holster over his t-shirt and attached the straps to his belt.

"Is that a Remington MSR?" Nathan asked.

Warren nodded. "Yeah. It's awesome. One of the best rifles I've ever owned."

While Nathan drooled over the gun case, Warren loaded both handguns and tucked them into the holster. It seemed excessive.

I crossed my arms and looked at him sideways. "Why do you carry two guns?"

They both looked over at me. Warren's mouth was agape, and his eyes were genuinely puzzled. "Because I don't have three hands," he answered.

Nathan laughed.

Warren shrugged into a vintage blue plaid button up to conceal the holster, and he adjusted his belt. He smoothed the front of his shirt with his hands and looked over at me. "Now, I'm ready."

Warren carried the rifle case to the door.

"You're bringing that thing with us?" I asked.

He looked at me confused. "Of course I am."

At first, Warren carrying guns perplexed me since he had the ability to inflict death with a single glance. It finally made sense the night he shot the serial killer in the woods. He shot Billy three times without killing him because he knew we needed more information. Guns, to Warren, were just a stopping force. Warren himself was the lethal weapon.

"We should find a range while we're here," Nathan said as we walked to the elevator. "I want to shoot that rifle."

Warren pointed at me. "I agree we should find a range, because *she* needs to learn."

Nathan nodded in agreement. "Especially if she's going to dress like that."

I punched him in the shoulder.

* * *

It was almost dark by the time we reached the west side of town. Warren had stopped protesting my coming along, but he made me ride in the back seat of the SUV. We rolled slowly down a street lined with older, one-story, vinyl-siding houses where half the owners did their best to keep up their homes, while the other half did not. Rusted chain-link fences divided most of the properties, and there was graffiti covering the broken sidewalks. An old Hispanic man appeared to be reading a Bible on the porch of one house, while a group of teenagers were drinking forties and passing around a joint on the porch next door.

Warren slowed down as he pointed to a house on the left side of the street. "This is it."

At one time the house had been blue, but most of the paint had peeled away. It had a stone front porch lined with fractures and a swing that was only hanging from one side. Most of the windows were dark, except for the main one in the front that flickered with the light from a television screen.

"Is he home?" I asked.

Warren shook his head and looked up and down the street. "I don't think so. Last night he was driving a maroon truck and he parked on the curb. It's not here."

Nathan looked over at him. "Can't you use your laser vision and see if he's inside?"

Warren scowled. "I don't have laser vision, and that's not even close to how it works." He jerked his thumb toward me. "Besides, Sloan's better at that anyway."

Leaning forward, I cupped my hand around my ear. "What was that? What did you just say?"

He didn't turn to look at me. "Oh, shut up."

I chuckled.

Over the past month, Warren and I had been practicing my ability to summon people. The power was definitely getting stronger, but I still only had a certain amount of control over it. Sometimes it worked. Sometimes it didn't. I sat back in my seat and closed my eyes. Even though it made me a little queasy, I pictured Larry Mendez's terrifying face and his black soul hidden behind his thick glasses. "Where are you, Larry Mendez?" I asked out loud.

When I opened my eyes, Nathan was peering out of his side window. "I keep thinking someone is going to fall out of the sky when she does that."

"Turn left," I told Warren.

He looked at me in the rearview mirror. "Why?"

I shrugged. "It just feels like you should go left."

"You're the boss." He obediently turned left onto Blaine Avenue.

Nathan turned around in his seat and looked at me. "Since when can you find people like that?"

"Warren's been teaching me," I told him.

Warren was better than any bloodhound when it came to tracking down human remains. In total, he had found six of Billy Stewart's missing victims without any aid or equipment at all. Two of them had been dead and missing for well over a decade. His theory was I could apply his same techniques to my connection with the living. My powers were still faulty, but I was getting better.

After a few minutes, I closed my eyes. "Turn right."

We rolled down another street that forked a few blocks ahead.

"Now where?" Warren asked.

"Right again."

The street curved in a semicircle around a gas station at the end of the block, and it stopped at a three-way stop sign. "Go right," I said.

Nathan clapped his hands. "Congratulations, we have almost completed a circle."

"Look!" Warren pointed down the street.

A dark red pickup truck pulled out in front of us a few blocks up ahead.

Nathan straightened in his seat, then looked at me with wide eyes. "No shit."

I clapped my hands together. "I did it!"

"Good job, babe." Warren pulled over to the right curb and turned off the headlights.

We watched in silence as Larry Mendez got out of his truck and carried a brown paper bag to his front door. He was talking on a cell phone and didn't notice the brand new, sparkling white SUV parked a block down the street.

I took a deep breath as I felt my chest begin to tighten with panic, but I didn't dare complain and risk igniting a series of I-told-you-sos from my boyfriend.

"I'll bet he's got beer in that bag," Nathan said. "He probably went to that gas station we passed to get booze for the night. I doubt he's leaving again."

Warren nodded. "You're probably right. Let's give him a minute, and if he doesn't leave again, we'll take off."

After six boring minutes of zero activity at the Mendez home, I pulled out my cell phone and started playing Candy Crush. After successfully completing two levels, I decided to text Adrianne to see how she was feeling. She didn't answer, so I sent a message to my mom.

Mom replied after a few seconds. *Not feeling so great. Gone to bed early. Hope you're having fun in Texas. XOXO.*

After that, I sent a group message to Warren and Nathan. *I'm bored.*

Their cell phones beeped at the same time. They exchanged puzzled looks before checking their messages.

"Very funny, Sloan," Nathan said, tucking his phone into his jacket.

Warren straightened in the driver's seat and dropped his phone on the console. "Well, what do we have here?" He pointed out the windshield.

I looked up and followed the direction of his finger. A young girl, with long dark hair and light brown skin, was walking up the concrete steps to Larry's front door. She couldn't have been older than fifteen or sixteen. She used a key to open the front door and disappeared inside.

"Could it be his daughter?" I asked.

Nathan snatched up the papers off the dashboard where he had deposited them and flipped through the stapled pages. "It doesn't say he has any kids."

"Huh," I said. "I don't like it."

Warren grunted. "I don't like it either."

We waited for another twenty minutes, but there was no other movement at the house. I was half-asleep with my head propped against the glass.

"Call it a night?" Warren asked, looking around the car.

I leaned in between the two front seats and looked at him. "Can't you just go break down the door and drag him outside?"

Nathan answered first. "No, he can't."

"Well, technically I *could*," Warren said.

Nathan shook his head. "We'll keep an eye on him. If he's the monster you two think he is, we'll get to the bottom of it without getting ourselves killed or worse, arrested."

Warren grinned. "I can't believe you're such a rule follower."

Nathan rolled his eyes. "And I can't believe you're any kind of angel. Let's go."

10.

"TAKE THE GUN."

Warren pushed the unloaded handgun against my chest as he glared down at me.

I scrunched up my nose and looked around the dusty wooden shelter on the pistol range. It was hot, but sweat wasn't rolling down my spine just because of the Texas sunshine. The thought of firing the gun that Warren kept thrusting in my direction had me sweating like a turkey on Thanksgiving.

"Sloan," he said again, snapping his fingers in front of my face to get my attention. "If you don't do this, I'm going to leave you at the hotel with Shannon for the rest of the time we are here."

I pressed my lips together and took the gun, holding it with two fingers out in front of me like it was contaminated with some dreadful disease.

He frowned and brought my other hand up to support it. "Hold it correctly." He tapped the side of the barrel with his finger. "See this lever? This is the safety. If you see red, the safety is off." He flipped it and a red mark appeared. He looked at me seriously. "Red is dead. Say it."

"Red is dead," I echoed.

He put the safety back on before putting his hands on my shoulders and turning me around to face the gray and black silhouette target downrange. Stepping up close behind me, he extended his arms along mine and looked over my shoulder.

I took a deep breath and sighed. A wave of dizziness washed over me, partly because I was bordering on hysterics but mostly because of the effect he always had on me. I looked over at him. "For future reference, you're not allowed to wear cologne when I'm handling firearms."

"Pay attention." He began repositioning my fingers around the gun. "Keep your finger off the trigger and along the side of the barrel till you're ready to fire. Point it at the target or down, but never point it at another person unless you plan on killing them." He moved my arms down, pointing the gun at the ground, and then up toward the target. "Don't forget and start waving this thing around."

I nodded. "OK. Don't point it at you unless I'm ready to shoot you. I got it."

Warren didn't laugh.

"Now, pull it in, keeping the barrel pointed away, and remove the empty magazine," he said.

Obediently, I pulled the gun close to my chest.

He moved my thumb over a small button on the side. "This is the button to release the magazine."

I pressed it, and a metal piece slipped out of the bottom. Warren quickly moved and caught it. He shook his head.

I beamed at him. "I did it!"

He handed me the magazine. "Shove it back in there and try it again. This time, *you* catch it."

I pushed the magazine up into the handle, but it slipped down again.

He shook his head. "Don't baby it. That's a good way to jam the gun. It won't break. Really slam it in there."

I slammed it hard the second time, nearly knocking the gun out of my other hand.

He smiled. "Better, but don't have butterfingers either." He nodded toward the gun. "Now, drop the magazine again."

I hit the button again and dropped the magazine into my left hand.

"Good." He took the magazine out of my hand and laid it on the table. "Now, pull the slide back to clear the chamber."

I pulled on the slide at the top of the gun, but it wasn't as easy as

Warren made it look.

He scowled. "Stop being a baby."

"It's hard!" I whined. "I have nerve damage in my fingers, remember?"

He ignored me. "Yank it back."

I pulled as hard as I could, and it slid into a locked position. "Hey, I got it!"

"Good job." He put his hands on top of mine again. "Now, push it forward to look down the barrel, and then pull it back to look down the barrel the other way. You've got to make sure it's clear in both directions." He did the motion again. "Push. Pull."

I obeyed, and he nodded with satisfaction. He handed me a loose bullet. "Now, put this in the clip to load the gun."

"So many steps," I grumbled.

I put the gun down and picked up the magazine. I pressed the bullet into it. There was a little resistance, but I did it without invoking more scowls from my beautiful, frustrated teacher. He actually looked pleased. Then he handed me the heavy box of ammo. "Now, load it full."

"I hate you."

"I know."

One by one I pushed the ammo into the magazine, but with every bullet the task became harder and harder. "Geez! How many times do I have to do this?"

"It holds fifteen rounds." His smile was getting wider as I struggled.

I stopped counting somewhere around twelve, and as I neared the end, loading more bullets was next to impossible. The last bullet simply wouldn't fit.

"Help me," I whimpered.

He shook his head. "Nope. If you can't load it, you can't shoot it."

I put my hand on my hip. "I don't want to shoot it!"

He nodded and held out his hand for the gun. "OK. Let's go to the hotel and I'll book you and Shannon manicures at the spa."

I huffed and turned away from him. "Damn you."

He chuckled as I went back to trying to press the bullet into the magazine. After what seemed like an eternity, I got it to go in.

Warren nodded. "Now take them out and do it again."

My mouth fell open.

He cracked up and took a step toward me. "I'm kidding." He picked up the gun off the table and handed it to me. "Pop the magazine back in. Hard."

With all the strength I had left, I slammed the magazine in. By some miracle, it locked into place on the first try.

"OK. Now pull the slide back to put a round in the chamber."

I yanked the slide back hard and released it.

"Nice! It's ready to fire." He pointed at the target. "Now aim and shoot."

I frowned. "I don't wanna."

"Sloan." His tone was a warning.

I groaned and turned toward the target.

"Hold on." He stepped forward and slid noise-canceling ear protectors over my head. Then he put on his own. After that, his mouth was moving, but I couldn't hear what he was saying.

I leaned toward him and shouted, "What?"

He laughed and pulled the ear protection away from my left ear. "Take off the safety, look down the site to where you want to shoot, and pull the trigger."

He released the ear covering, and it slammed against my ear. "Ow!"

He pointed at the target and took a step backward.

I pulled the gun up straight in front of me, looked down the barrel, and aimed the notch at the top at the center of the black body outline. I pulled the trigger.

Bang!

The recoil knocked me back a few steps.

"Jesus, Mary, and Joseph!" I screamed.

I put the gun on the table and turned to see Warren doubled over, laughing with his hands on his knees. I ripped off my headset. "Why didn't you warn me?" I shouted, stepping over and punching him square in the chest.

He was still laughing. "I thought you knew there would be some kickback."

"There's no kickback in the movies!"

The man two stalls down from us was watching and laughing as well.

I folded my arms over my chest and kicked Warren in the shin.

He straightened and put his arms around me. "You did well though! I'm proud of you." He kissed the side of my head and turned me toward the target.

There were no holes in it.

My head dropped in defeat. "I didn't even hit it."

He squeezed my shoulder. "But you didn't kill anyone either."

I glared at him. "Yet."

He smiled. "Do it again. Empty the clip." He pointed down at my tennis shoes. "Plant your feet this time and try to not let it knock you over." He chuckled, and I stuck out my tongue.

I turned toward the target and put my ear protection on. I picked up the gun and fired again, this time not caught so much by surprise. Dust *poofed* up on the embankment behind the target which was still left untouched.

Aiming again, I tried to hold my shaking hands steady. I fired and saw more dust.

Slowly, I blew out a deep breath and squeezed the trigger a third time. This time, the target moved. A small hole was ripped in the top right corner.

I put the gun on the table, then clapped my hands as I spun around toward Warren. "I did it! I did it!"

He laughed. "Congratulations."

Nathan and Shannon walked across the wooden floor toward us. They had been inside looking at the selection of guns the place had for sale.

"How's it going?" Nathan asked as they approached.

I grabbed his arm and pointed at the target. "Look! I hit it!"

He chuckled and patted me on the back. "Congrats. That's practically a kill shot."

I smiled. "I hit it though!"

He nodded. "Yes, you did."

Warren nudged me with his knuckles. "Finish."

I put my headset on and turned back to the target. With more confidence than before, I didn't stop firing until the magazine was empty. Most of the shots hit the bank, but two more bullets hit in the white space of the paper, and one actually pierced the silhouette target's shoulder. I turned around and smiled with satisfaction.

Warren clapped his hands before handing me the box of ammunition again. "Now reload it and practice some more."

I frowned and lowered my voice so only he could hear me as I accepted the box of bullets. "You're never getting sex from me ever again."

He laughed and rolled his eyes. "*Sure.*"

While I struggled with the magazine, Nathan and Shannon got ready to shoot in the stall right beside us. Without instruction, Shannon loaded a small handgun and slipped on a pair of pink ear protectors.

I looked at Warren. He was curiously watching her as well.

Nathan took a step back beside him and leaned toward his ear. "Watch this."

We covered our ears as Shannon raised her pistol. Like a pro on the hunting channel on TV, she aimed and popped off one bullet after another. The paper target rattled furiously till she stopped and put the gun down.

My mouth dropped open.

Warren clapped his hands—for much longer than he had clapped for me—and laughed. "I did *not* see that coming at all!"

In my head I was screaming, *Oh hell no!* But I kept my mouth shut. Almost every shot Shannon had fired pierced the inner part of the target's body. Furiously, I began cramming bullets into the magazine.

Shannon turned, smiling with pride.

Nathan kissed her and put his arm around her shoulders. He had never done that in front of me before.

She shrugged. "My daddy started teaching me when I was ten."

"*My daddy started teaching me when I was ten,*" I mimicked under my breath.

Warren was nodding his head. "I have to say, I'm pretty impressed."

I rolled my eyes and turned away from everyone.

Shannon came over and put her hand on my shoulder. "Don't worry, Sloan. You'll get better with practice."

I thought about punching her in the face.

Forty-five minutes later, I was a little better, but I still couldn't shoot like Shannon Green. I was, however, able to shoot and not feel like I might pee all over myself.

Warren put his arms around my waist after he'd packed up his guns. "I'm proud of you," he said, pressing a kiss to my forehead.

I groaned. "Thanks."

He smiled and tightened his grasp on me. "I mean it. And, you look smoking hot holding that thing."

I rolled my eyes.

"Mind if we go to the rifle range for a bit?" he asked.

I shook my head. "I don't mind."

We packed up what was left of our ammo and cleaned up the stall. Warren picked up his rifle case and we headed across the complex. Aside from the range master, who was there to observe and enforce safety, we were the only people at the rifle range. It was much longer than the pistol range we had just left. There were three sets of targets, one at a hundred yards, one at two hundred, and one at three hundred.

I leaned against the wooden support post and watched Warren pull the huge rifle out of its case. As he attached the scope, I realized I had only seen guns like his in video games and action movies.

The gun rested on a stand on the table. Warren straddled the bench sideways behind it and looked down the scope. He was wearing a fitted gray t-shirt that stretched tight over his biceps when he positioned himself behind the gun.

Shannon was practically drooling next to me.

Warren stood up and looked at Nathan. "Go on, man. It's ready to fire."

Surprised, Nathan smiled. "Thanks."

Warren leaned against the wall beside me and folded his arms across his chest. "You need any help?" Warren asked him as he slipped his ear protection on.

Nathan shook his head and sat down on the bench. "Nah, I'm good."

"Good luck, baby," Shannon said, blowing Nathan a kiss while she covered her ears.

My hands tightened into fists at my sides as I glared at her.

Nathan began firing, and I screamed and clasped my hands over my ears. He stopped shooting and looked back at me while Warren laughed and pulled my ear protectors up from around my neck. My head was ringing, Shannon was giggling, and Nathan was shaking his head.

I hung my head and ducked under Warren's arm, a victim of my own bad karma.

Once Nathan was certain my ears were secured, he fired off a bunch of rounds, but the target was too far away to see how he had done. When he stopped shooting, he looked through the scope. "Six kill shots out of ten. Not too bad." He turned and looked at us.

Warren had a sly smile on his face as he looked through a pair of binoculars. "Not bad at all. Not excellent, but not bad."

Nathan smirked. "You can do better?"

I wasn't sure what Nathan was thinking. Warren was a sniper for the Marines. Surely, he knew that.

Rolling my eyes, I looked at Shannon. "Men and their balls."

She laughed.

Warren pushed himself off the wall when Nathan stood up and moved out of the way. Warren pressed the binoculars into Nathan's hand as they passed. Without a word, he straddled the bench, swapped out the magazine, and looked around with the scope for a moment. Then he pulled on his ear protection and slipped on his black sunglasses before settling over the weapon. A few seconds later, he fired off three evenly spaced shots.

Pow!

Pow!

Pow!

When he stopped, he looked through the scope, and then sat up and cracked his knuckles.

Nathan had the binoculars squashed over his eyes. He laughed. "You didn't even touch it! The target didn't move!"

Warren stood up and walked in front of Nathan. He shifted Nathan and the binoculars a little bit to the left. "That's because you're looking at one hundred yards and not three hundred."

After a second, Nathan's jaw went slack. "Holy shit." He started laughing again, this time in awe.

I smacked Nathan in the stomach. "Let me see!"

He handed me the binoculars, and I searched the three hundred range. Warren's target had three holes in the face. I pulled the binoculars down and laughed. "That's the sexiest thing I've ever seen in my life!"

He smiled as I passed Shannon the binoculars and then draped my arms around his neck.

Nathan shook his head, resting his hands on his hips. "I can see why the Marine Corps wants you back."

When we left, I carried Warren's target proudly to the car. "I think I'm going to frame this and hang it over my bed at home."

Nathan laughed. "You're not going to hang your shoulder shot over your bed?"

I whipped my head around toward him. "Don't make me have my boyfriend shoot you in the face."

"Where are we going next?" Warren asked as he loaded his gun case into the back of the SUV.

I rubbed my hands together with a renewed sense of hope. "Let's go find Rachel Smith."

11.

RACHEL SMITH WASN'T easy to find.

We spent the better part of that week driving all over San Antonio with no sign of her and without gathering any more evidence on Larry Mendez. I was beginning to think the whole trip might be a bust.

On Friday morning, I rolled toward Warren in the bed with a crystal clear defeat on my face. "This sucks." I rested my head on his chest and traced my finger along his tattoo. "Maybe we should call it quits and fly home when Shannon leaves on Sunday."

"You want to go home?" he asked surprised.

"I don't know. I kinda miss Adrianne."

He kissed the top of my head and tightened his arm around me. "We'll do whatever you want."

I pushed up on my elbows next to him. "I want to lie by the pool again for a while today. I'm going to miss the warmth when we go home to the mountains."

"We can do that." He brushed my hair away from my face. "Then maybe we can take one more crack at Rachel Smith this afternoon."

I nodded. "Yeah. We might as well try. We've covered Nathan's entire list though. I don't know where else we could even look. She could have been passing through San Antonio, you know? She might not have even lived here at all."

"That's true," he agreed.

"I mean, we might have wasted an entire week here for nothing," I said.

Under the covers, he slid his hand up my bare side and smiled. "I wouldn't quite say that any of this week has been a waste. I've had a pretty good time here in Texas."

"I would say you have. You've stayed in bed with me every morning we've been here." I smiled and bit my lower lip. "For that reason alone, I don't want to return to the real world."

His hand ran down my back. "I'm trying to convince you to be a morning person by making them extra good."

Laughing, I leaned over and kissed his cheek. "You're doing a good job of it. I think getting away from everything was exactly what I needed. The nightmares have stopped, and I don't feel so nervous all the time. You must be a good influence on me."

He rolled over on top of me and pinned my arms down over my head. "You're not sick of me yet?"

"Not even a little bit." I smiled and squirmed underneath the weight of his body.

He nodded. "That's good because I'm not going anywhere," he said, "for the rest of your life." He buried his face in the crook of my neck and nipped at my skin.

I giggled as his hair fell into my face. "Well, if that's true, my daddy is going to insist that you marry me. He's pretty old-fashioned like that."

He pulled back and smiled down at me. "I know. I already talked to him about it."

Wait.

I turned my head and cut my eyes at him. "You what?" The volume of my voice was a little louder than I intended.

He was still grinning. "I might have bounced an idea off him before I came by to see you at work last week."

"Well, bounce it off of me, would ya?" I pushed him away and sat up on my elbows.

He rolled onto his side, propping his head up on his arm. "I just asked him what he thought about letting his only daughter marry a guy who has no job and no family and no history with you at all."

"Are you serious?" I was laughing with an uneasy mix of nerves and excitement.

"Yeah. Why wouldn't I be?" he asked. "You didn't think this was some kind of random fling for me, did you?"

Everything had transpired so quickly, I wasn't sure what I thought. "No, but I didn't think you were talking to my dad about marriage either." I jerked the sheet up over my body. "Are you proposing to me right now?"

He opened his mouth and widened his eyes like he was about to say, *Surprise!* Instead, he laughed. "No."

Strangely enough, I was disappointed. "No?"

He shook his head. "No."

"Why not? Do you want to marry me?" I asked.

He raised an eyebrow. "Are *you* proposing now?"

I smirked. "No."

He cupped my chin in his large hand and pulled on my lower lip with his thumb. His eyes fell to my mouth. "I'm going to marry you, but not just yet."

My brow wrinkled. "What are you waiting for?"

He gave me a half-smile and slid his hand down to my arm. "I guess I'm waiting until I don't wonder where your mind goes sometimes."

I twisted my head in confusion. "What?"

He just stared at me till a light bulb flickered on in my mind and I realized what he was talking about. It felt like my stomach had fallen through the mattress. "Nathan McNamara."

He nodded, and there was a knock at our door.

He sighed. "Speak of the devil."

Warren flung the covers to the side and pushed himself off the bed. As he walked to the door, he slipped on the jeans he'd discarded the night before. Around the corner, I heard the door open.

"Morning," Nathan said. "You guys up?"

"Yeah, but we're not ready yet."

"We're heading up to the pool for breakfast if you want to join us," Nathan said.

"Sounds good. Give us a few," Warren answered.

When he returned, he didn't rejoin me in the bed. "You hungry?" he asked.

It was obvious the subjects of marriage—and Nathan McNamara —were no longer open for discussion. My brain was firing in a thousand different directions. I got up, and we both dressed in awkward silence.

Everything was happening so fast, and for the first time since we'd been together, I felt really overwhelmed. I loved him, but he was right. My mind was still prone to wandering. My ears had been ringing from noise damage all week to prove it.

The silence continued when we got up to the roof. Nathan and Shannon both noticed over breakfast. Nathan pointed his fork at both of us. "What's with you two?"

"It's none of your business," Shannon scolded him from underneath her ridiculous hat.

That was both true and untrue.

I shifted in my seat. "We've been trying to decide this morning if we should stay for a few more days or not. We haven't accomplished anything at all," I said. "Not with Rachel Smith or with Larry Mendez."

Nathan's head snapped back in surprise. "You're thinking about going home early?"

I shrugged. "I don't know. Probably, if we don't start getting somewhere pretty fast."

Nathan looked at Warren. "You're just going to walk away from Mendez?"

Warren didn't look up from his omelet. "I might go kill him before we leave and neutralize the problem."

Nathan stared at him with an awkward smile, like he wasn't sure if Warren was joking or if he was serious. To be honest, I wasn't sure if Warren was serious or not either.

My phone rang, and I jumped at the chance to escape from the table and answer it. I looked at the screen. "It's my dad. Excuse me." I stood up and walked to the edge of the roof.

"Hey, Dad," I answered. I leaned my elbows on the chest-high concrete wall that surrounded the area.

"Hey, sweetheart. How's the Lone Star state?" he asked.

I groaned. "A little tense at the moment. Did Warren talk to you about us getting married?"

There was a beat of silence on the other end of the phone. "Why? Did he propose?"

"No, but he said he talked to you."

"He did. He came by my office last week," he said. "Is everything OK?"

I sighed. "It will be. How are you?"

"Well, I'm fine. Your mother, however, isn't feeling too well," he said. "I'm trying to convince her to go to the hospital for some tests, but of course she's being stubborn. If she isn't any better today, I'm going to drag her there if I have to."

"What's wrong with her?" I asked.

"Well, it started with a mild headache. Then a few days ago she started getting dizzy and throwing up. She thinks it's an inner ear infection, but I'm not convinced. She started on antibiotics three days ago and still isn't any better. I don't think it's anything serious. I just wanted you to know before someone called you and said your mother was at the hospital."

"Yeah. Thanks for letting me know. Keep me posted on how she's feeling and what you find out. Tell her I said to quit being stubborn and go to the hospital and listen to you," I said.

He laughed. "She hasn't listened to me in twenty-seven years. I'm not sure why she would start now."

I laughed. "Give her my love, OK?"

"I will," he said.

"Love you, Dad."

"I love you too," he said and disconnected.

Warren looked up with concern as I approached the table. "Is everything OK?"

I nodded and sat back down. "Mom is pretty sick, and Dad wanted me to know he's trying to get her to go to the hospital for some tests. He's going to keep me updated. What are you guys discussing?"

"Nathan thinks we should go back to the gas station, where the photo was taken, and see if anyone recognizes Rachel," Warren answered.

"I'm kinda surprised we haven't already thought to do that," I said.

Shannon raised her hand. "What's so special about this Rachel person anyway? Why have you spent all week looking for someone you don't even know?"

"It's complicated," Nathan said.

She put her fork on her plate. "I think I can keep up."

Nathan looked at me for an answer.

A bright idea popped into my head. "You remember how I'm adopted, right?"

Shannon nodded.

"Well, Rachel Smith might know something about my birth parents and where I came from."

She adjusted her hat. "Right, because she's a social worker."

Nathan's eyes widened at me. "Yes," he said. "That's exactly correct."

"Well, that doesn't sound too dangerous. Mind if I tag along?" she asked. "I've been in every shop on the River Walk at least twice, and I don't think I can stand another day of being left behind and cooped up in this hotel."

I thought about it. Shannon really hadn't been a pain in the ass all week about staying at the hotel while we went out like I had expected she would. She had actually almost been pleasant to be around. I also knew the chances were very slim we would even find Rachel, so I decided to throw Shannon a bone. "Sure. Come with us."

Warren looked up at me but didn't say anything.

Shannon clapped her hands together and squealed. "Yay! Thank you! I promise I won't get in the way. I'll be as quiet as a church mouse."

I doubted that.

We hung out at the pool until families with a lot of young children showed up just after noon. We decided to go get changed and grab lunch on our way toward what we assumed was Rachel's neighborhood.

When Warren and I got to the room, I grabbed him by the hand. "Can we talk a sec?"

He turned toward me and nodded. "Sure."

"What you were saying this morning." I shifted uneasily on my feet. "Do you worry about me and Nathan?"

He shook his head. "No. I don't think you would cheat on me, if that's what you're asking. But I also know if I weren't in the picture, the two of you would be together."

"He's with Shannon."

He crossed his arms and frowned down at me.

I sighed. "OK. Yes, we probably would be together, but we aren't because I love you, and I've chosen to be with you."

He put his hands on my shoulders. "I know that, Sloan, and I'm not mad at you. I want to make sure you're in this 100 percent before we start making permanent plans together. Not 99 percent or 99.9 percent. I don't want the majority of you. I want all of you."

"Do you want me to not be friends with him anymore?" I asked.

"I would never ask you to do that. I just think we need to give it some time to make sure you're never going to look back." His eyes became very serious. "I don't want to be walking in on my wife someday looking at him the way you were looking at him the other night in the pool."

His words were like a knife to the chest. "Nothing happened in the pool."

"Maybe nothing physical." His eyebrows were raised, daring me to argue. I didn't. "I told you, I'm not angry about it. I'm not happy about it either, but I trust you."

I cast my eyes down at his feet. "I'm sorry, Warren."

He shook his head. "There are a lot of layers to this relationship, Sloan. This whole thing with you and me blew up overnight, taking everyone by surprise, including us. You've still got some things to figure out, whether you want to admit it or not."

I opened my mouth to protest, but he kissed me to shut me up. When he let me go, he smiled like the whole conversation hadn't even happened. "Get dressed."

* * *

We drove to the gas station where the surveillance photo was captured and showed both clerks who were there the picture of Rachel Smith. Neither of them recognized her.

When we got back in the SUV, I slammed my door shut. "The clerks at the Texaco near my house would at least recognize my face," I said. "She doesn't live here."

Warren nodded and started the engine. "You're probably right."

I felt a hand on my shoulder from behind. It was Shannon. "I'm really sorry, Sloan."

I nodded. "Thanks."

Warren looked over at me. "Well, you wanna cruise by Mendez's house again before we completely call everything quits?"

I looked up at the sky. "It isn't dark yet." I glanced at Nathan. "What do you think?"

He leaned against his door and shrugged. "It's your call."

"It wouldn't hurt to take one more look," I said.

Across town, the maroon pickup was parked at the curb outside of Larry Mendez's house. All the lights inside appeared to be on. We parked a block away and watched.

"Who is this guy? What do you want with him?" Shannon asked.

"He gives me the creeps," I said. "I want to figure out why."

She laughed. "Lots of people creep me out, but I don't sit outside their houses like a stalker."

A blue car that was missing the front fender pulled up behind the truck. Nathan leaned forward between the front seats for a better view. The car doors opened and two men got out and stepped onto the sidewalk. One was a white guy wearing a white tank top and baggy jeans. The other was Hispanic, wearing a red polo and a lot of gold jewelry. They were both covered in tattoos, and they were both about our age.

Warren leaned over the steering wheel and ripped off his sunglasses. He strained his eyes. "That's impossible," he muttered.

I looked over at him. "What's impossible?"

He pointed. "The guy in the white shirt. I think I know him."

"What?" Nathan asked.

"Who is it?" I asked.

Warren cocked his head to the side. "Sloan, do you remember me telling you about the two guys who attacked that girl at the dumpster in Chicago? One died and one got away."

Warren had told me the story. It had been the second time he had ever used his power. He killed a guy from his group home who was trying to rape a girl in an alleyway near a movie theater. "Yeah. I remember."

"I could be wrong, but I'm pretty damn certain that's the one who escaped. That's Rex," he said.

My mouth fell open. "You're kidding? We're a bazillion miles away from Chicago."

Nathan shook his head. "That would be a huge coincidence."

I groaned and felt my heart start to pound. The word *coincidence* was becoming a verbal red flag. True coincidences never seemed to happen around me. I looked at Warren. "What do you want to do?"

He reclined in his seat and rested his hand over the steering wheel. He tapped his fingers on the dash. "Let's see what they do."

The two men talked for a moment on the curb, and then the Hispanic guy made a phone call. A moment later, they scanned the street, then walked up the stairs and knocked on the door. They disappeared inside. After a few short minutes, the Hispanic guy came out first holding his car keys. He scanned the street again before signaling to the front door.

Nathan chuckled. "Not so good as a lookout, is he? Big white SUV right here."

I laughed. Warren didn't.

Rex and Larry Mendez came outside, holding onto the arms of two young Hispanic girls. One was the teenage girl we had seen earlier that week and the other was much younger. They both looked sluggish, like they had been drugged, as they were led to the car.

I gasped and covered my mouth with my hand.

"They're trafficking," Nathan said. He moved to reach for his door handle.

Warren reached out and grabbed him by the back of his shirt. "Hold up. Hold up. We should follow them and see where they go."

"I agree with Nathan," I said. "I think we should take them down before this escalates any further."

"No, Warren's right. We need to see where the hub of this thing is." Nathan sat back and put his seatbelt on.

"What about Shannon?" I asked. "This isn't safe."

Warren put the car in drive and chuckled to himself. "I'll give her my gun and she can protect you."

"Hey!" I shouted and punched him in the shoulder.

Larry Mendez turned and walked back to his house as the car rolled away from the curb. Warren followed at quite a distance behind as it moved through the streets of west San Antonio. We twisted and turned through the city until the car reached the on-ramp for Interstate 10. We were stopped at a red light, but Warren was able to find them again on the interstate. The car was cruising at a safe speed, right at the speed limit.

After about ten minutes of driving, I looked over at Warren. "I don't think they are planning on staying in San Antonio. What if they're going to Houston?"

"Or Mexico?" Shannon asked.

"Do you ladies have somewhere else you need to be?" Warren asked.

I shrugged my shoulders. "I guess not."

"They're not going to Mexico. At least not if that's Rex in the car. I doubt he could even fill out an application for a passport," Warren said.

"Do you really think it could be him?" I asked.

Warren turned his palm up on the top of the steering wheel. "If it isn't, then there are two of him."

"What are you going to do when they stop?" Shannon asked.

Nathan laughed. "Wing it."

I turned in my seat. "Seriously, what are we going to do?"

Warren looked over his shoulder at me. "I really have no idea."

I rubbed my hands over my face and groaned. "That's great. Just great."

Nathan pointed to the car as it was easing its way toward an off ramp. "They're getting off the interstate."

I sat forward in my seat as Warren slowly moved to the right lane. The blue car was three cars ahead of us. "They're going north, Warren," I said, nudging his arm.

"Yep. Turn left," Nathan added.

"Will you two shut up and let me drive?" Warren snapped.

We headed north on a main highway, winding around till we reached the northeast side. It was an industrial area that had been neglected by the wealth of San Antonio for some time. Buildings were crumbling into disrepair, and there was an unsightly mix of rundown strip malls and gas stations with bars on the windows. The blue car pulled into an alleyway between a two-story building and a warehouse. Warren parked across the street at a liquor store.

"What is this place?" I looked up at the building and noticed the number of broken windows and the flashing red neon OPEN sign near the front door.

"Must be a brothel," Nathan said.

"I believe it might be called a *cantina*. There are lots of them around Texas," Shannon said from the back seat.

At the same time, the three of us turned to look at her, all with the same baffled expression. What in the world could the Baptist traffic reporter from North Carolina know about prostitution in Texas?

Shannon shrugged, noting our skeptical faces. "I've watched a lot of television while you guys have been gone all week. The city has raided a lot of these kinds of places lately. They are bars where girls are bought and sold for prostitution."

"I'll be damned." Warren shook his head and laughed. "Anything else we should know?"

She nodded. "They usually have a lookout posted outside to watch for police."

We turned to scan the building.

Nathan pointed. "Up there on the roof."

Sure enough, there was a man in a white lawn chair perched on the roof, carefully watching the streets.

I looked at Shannon in amazement. "I have to say, I'm kinda glad we brought you along."

"How should we do this, Nate?" Warren asked.

"Well, we can't exactly go in there with guns blazing. We'll wind up getting ourselves killed," Nathan said.

"Can we call the cops?" I asked.

Nathan rubbed his chin. "I'm sure the cops already know this place exists. They can't just come in either. They would need someone to investigate and get proof, and then they would have to go through a judge to get a no-knock search warrant. It's a pretty lengthy process."

"Should one of us go in?" I asked.

"Well, I can't go in because if that is Rex, he'll recognize me," Warren said. "And Nate, you can't go in because everything about you screams law enforcement."

"I'll go in," I said, surprising myself as much as I surprised everyone else in the car.

Warren said "absolutely not" and Nathan said "hell no" at the exact same time.

"We can't sit here and do nothing. Those girls were just kids!" I reasoned.

Warren shook his head. "You can be hard headed and argue all you want, but there's no way I'm letting you out of this car to go in there. I will tie you to the seat if I have to."

Nathan reached up and squeezed my shoulder. "We'll figure something out."

"Maybe no one has to go in," Shannon said. She leaned forward quickly and pointed out the window. "Look!"

Two San Antonio police cars and a police van with blue lights flashing screamed to a stop in front of the front door. Two unmarked SUVs parked along the sides of the building. Cops, some in uniform and others in all black, rushed out of the cars with their guns drawn.

"Holy shit," Nathan said, laughing. "Sloan, did you summon a police force?"

I scratched my head. "I don't think so."

We watched the police break down the front door and rush in. Like cockroaches scattering, people began to pour out of the building from all kinds of disguised doors and openings. Two of those people were Rex and the man in the red polo shirt. They darted behind the black SUV, took off across the street, and jumped a fence about fifty yards away from us.

"Oh, hell no," Warren said. He wrenched his door open and took off after them.

Nathan followed.

I looked at Shannon, who was cowering in her seat. "What do we do?" I asked.

"You couldn't pay me enough to get out of this car," she said.

Shannon was right. Gun fire exploded inside the building. I hit the lock button on the door and sank down in my seat. A few nail-biting minutes later, Nathan came through a gate in the fence, leading the guy in the red polo shirt by one handcuffed arm. A second after him, Warren appeared, dragging Rex by his blond hair, his arms flailing and his legs trying to keep up. His face was covered in blood—so were Warren's knuckles.

We watched from the car as Warren and Nathan delivered the two to the police officers on the curb. After talking with the officers for a moment, Warren waved for us to come over. Hesitantly, Shannon and I got out of the car. She gripped my arm so hard I winced as we crossed the street. Nathan was still talking to one of the officers. Warren caught my eye and nodded toward the front door.

Scantily dressed girls, some as young as ten or eleven, were being ushered outside and led to a large white police van. Tears prickled my eyes as they shuffled along the curb with their shoulders slumped and their empty stares fixed on the ground. Some of them were bloody and bruised, and others looked drugged or drunk out of their wits.

My heart shattered.

Then, as I watched them, my eyes fell on the woman guiding the girls from the building. She was wearing a gray pants suit and had long dark hair tied up in a no-nonsense ponytail. There was a deep and empty void where I should have sensed her soul.

It was Rachel Smith.

12.

RACHEL'S EYES LOCKED on mine with the same bewildered expression I was sure was on my face. She tried to refocus on her task of loading up the girls, but her eyes kept glancing in my direction. When she finally closed the door to the van, she said something to a uniformed officer, then walked down the sidewalk toward me.

"Rachel Smith?" I asked as she approached.

She turned her head slightly and narrowed her eyes. "*Abigail* Smith," she said, tapping her name tag which was labeled with *Morning Star Ministries* in bright green letters. She lowered her voice. "I haven't gone by Rachel in years. Who are you?" Then she pointed at Warren. "And who is he?"

"We're like you," I said just above a whisper. I blinked my eyes like they were delivering a secret message.

She laughed. "No, you're not."

I was jolted by surprise. When Warren and I first saw each other, time stood still. Our realization that we weren't alone in the world had been cosmically astounding. Mistakenly, I had expected a similar reaction from Rachel Smith, and this woman was laughing at me like I'd told a knock-knock joke.

"Can we talk?" I asked, looking around. "In private?"

She gestured toward the commotion around us. "As you can tell,

I'm pretty busy right now." She reached into her purse and produced a business card. "But here's my information. Come by my office in a couple of hours. I'll be there all night."

I smiled. "Thank you."

She stared at me for another moment, and I studied her carefully while I had the chance. She was even more beautiful in person than in her photos. We were about the same age and height, but she was wearing heels. There was an emptiness in her dark brown eyes that I had only ever seen inside of Warren.

She nodded like she was answering a question I didn't ask. "Yes. Definitely come by my office later."

"I will."

Without another word, she turned and walked toward the police van. Before she got into the passenger's seat, she glanced over her shoulder to where I was still watching, mesmerized. She waved and gave a slight smile. I waved back as the van pulled away.

Warren stepped up behind me. "Well?"

"She wants us to come by her office later."

Confounded and shaking his head, he crossed his arms over his chest. "Well, two birds, one stone."

Nathan and Shannon walked up beside us. "Was that who I think it was?" He was pointing in the direction the van had gone.

With the two of them flanking me, and Shannon clutching Nathan's arm, we turned toward our SUV. I nodded as we crossed the street. "It sure was."

"Who are you talking about?" Shannon asked.

Nathan jerked his head back toward the building. "That woman in the gray suit who Sloan was talking to is the woman we've been looking for all week."

"Seriously?" Shannon asked in amazement. She looked around Nathan at me. "That's a crazy coincidence. Did you talk to her? Was she able to tell you anything?"

I shrugged. "Not yet, but we're going to meet her at her office in a little while."

Warren looked over at us as we reached the car. "The cop told me she's the head of a big human trafficking rescue mission here in Texas. Apparently, she's got a couple of homes here. One in San Antonio and one in Houston."

"That explains why we couldn't find her working for the

government," I said as I pulled open my car door.

We all got in.

Nathan was still shaking his head as he fastened his seatbelt. "You know, I don't think I'm ever going to get used to the crazy shit that seems to follow the two of you around."

I grabbed Warren's forearm. "Speaking of crazy, was that the guy from Chicago?"

He laughed as he started the engine and put the SUV in reverse to exit the lot. "Yes, ma'am. What are the odds of that?"

My brain was spinning like a mental Rolodex full of questions as I stared out my window. "Impossible odds."

Behind us, Nathan chuckled. "We should go to Vegas."

I looked at Warren. "Did he say what he was doing here or how long he's been in Texas?"

Nathan poked his head between our seats. "He didn't have a chance to speak. He was kind of busy having his face rearranged." He slapped Warren on the shoulder. "This guy beat the hell out of him."

I blinked. "I'm surprised you didn't kill him."

He stared straight at the road ahead. "Trust me. I thought about it."

"What will happen to Larry Mendez?" I asked.

"Nathan told the cops we were in Mendez's neighborhood because we got lost, and we saw them leaving the house with the two girls. He said we thought it looked suspicious so we followed them. He gave them Mendez's address."

I laughed and looked back at Nathan. "You told them we were lost, and they bought it?"

Nathan shrugged. "They seemed grateful we saved them a lot of work."

"So they'll go arrest him?"

He nodded, exchanging a glance with Warren in the rearview mirror. "They should have enough to take him into custody, but we may get called in to testify at some point."

I relaxed in my seat. "Good."

"Where to now?" Warren asked.

"Take me and Shannon to the hotel and drop us off," Nathan said.

I looked at him. "You don't want to come talk to Rachel with us?"

He smiled at me. "No. You go and get to the bottom of all this. I've done my part."

"Thank you, Nathan." I reached to the back seat and squeezed his hand.

He squeezed my hand in return. "You're welcome, Sloan."

We took Shannon and Nathan to the Hyatt before heading across town to the address of Morning Star Ministries. Night was falling over San Antonio, but the city was so bright it was almost unnecessary to burn our headlights. My vision blurred in and out of focus as we drove through the city. The passing lights left trails behind them as my mind wandered.

We were on the cusp of something big. The answers we had sought our entire lives were dangling right in front of us. There were a thousand possibilities, but one thing was certain: everything was about to change.

Warren reached over and took my hand. "You seem tense."

"I don't know why, but I'm a little nervous, and I'm excited." I looked at him. "She's not clueless like us. I told her we were like her, and she laughed and said we're not. She had this certainty in her voice."

"That's interesting," he said.

"I thought so too."

Morning Star Ministries was located next door to a large brick church on the west side of town. Warren parked at the curb, and I sat and looked out the window. It was a nice two story building that was relatively new with two large double glass doors out front. The sign bearing the name had a fresh coat of paint, and orange and yellow mums were blooming at its base.

Warren turned toward me in his seat. "You ready?"

I took a deep breath. "Yep."

Inside the front lobby, there was a receptionist desk to our right, secured behind a large glass window. In front of us was a huge living room, and a restaurant-size kitchen was to our left. The second story walkway looked down on the lobby, and there was a young Hispanic girl watching us. She wore a San Antonio Spurs sweatshirt and blue jeans, and even from where we stood, I could see a large gold and jade cross hanging around her neck. She appeared to be around seventeen years old.

A young blonde in casual dress clothes peeked out from the receptionist area. "Can I help you?"

"We're here to see Abigail. She told us to come by tonight." I held up Abigail's business card.

The woman nodded. "Can I tell her your name?"

"Sloan Jordan," I answered.

She smiled. "You can have a seat," she said, nodding to a padded bench behind us.

We sat down, and Warren held my hand. "This place is nice." He was looking around at the newly tiled floors and professional paint job.

Two girls walked by us, speaking Spanish, and disappeared into the kitchen.

I lowered my voice. "I think it's a home for them. A home for the girls they rescue."

"Looks that way," he said. "Can you imagine going from that dilapidated cantina to this?"

I shook my head and sighed. "This place is giving them their lives back."

On a table next to us were some brochures. I picked one up and read it aloud. "Morning Star Ministries was founded in 2011 by Abigail Smith." I scanned through the rest of it. "They bring in girls rescued from human trafficking rings around San Antonio," I told him. "This is the main office. The one in Houston is smaller."

The click-clack of heels against the tile announced Abigail's entrance as she came around the corner, obviously looking for us. We both stood when she saw us. "Hi. I'm glad you came by. Both of you." She smiled warmly as she stretched out her hand. "Sloan, is it?"

When her fingers touched mine, I jumped from the jolt. Every nerve ending from my scalp to my toes sizzled. "Whoa!" I looked down at my finger, almost expecting it to be singed.

She chuckled. "Sorry, I should've warned you."

Still rubbing the tip of my finger, I looked up at Warren. "Abigail, this is my boyfriend, Warren Parish."

Cautiously this time, she offered him her hand.

His eyes doubled in size when he shook it, but he didn't freak out like me. "It's nice to meet you," he said.

"The pleasure is all mine." She nodded toward the hallway. "Let's go to my office where we can talk and have a bit of privacy."

We followed her around the corner and down a long, carpeted hallway. There were plain white doors in groups of two all the way down to the end.

"This is a pretty impressive place you have here," I said as we walked.

She smiled over her shoulder. "We have sixty beds in this home. We run at capacity all year long. The girls who were brought out of the cantina earlier will be on this floor till they receive proper medical attention. Then, once their physical needs are met, we will start dealing with their emotional ones."

"What happens to them?" I asked. "When they leave here?"

"Most of them are returned to their families, the ones whose families we are able to locate. Others will remain in our care until they can be placed through the foster system," she said.

"So this a government agency?" I asked as we walked into a humble but nice office.

She shook her head. "We work with the local government, but we are strictly funded through private donations. Once you start accepting government money, you become subject to government red tape. I vowed when I began this ministry that we would operate as an independent agency only." She closed the door and motioned to the two chairs opposite her desk. "Please, have a seat."

Warren and I sat down in the chairs. "Thanks for seeing us. We've looked all over for you," I said.

As she settled behind the cherry wood desk, her eyes widened. "Why were you looking for me?"

I exchanged a glance with Warren. "We actually thought you were murdered by a serial killer we helped take down a few weeks ago."

She laughed and leaned back against her chair. "A serial killer? Where?"

"In Asheville, North Carolina," I replied.

Her head tilted with confusion. "Why would you think I was murdered in Asheville?"

I shook my head. "We actually thought you were murdered in Greensboro. You were reported missing from your job there, and you seemed to fit with the profile of all the other victims." I looked at Warren again. "We assumed you were dead because—"

"Because when you looked at my photograph, you didn't see my soul?" she interrupted.

I swallowed hard. "Yes."

She leaned forward over her desk and rested her chin on her hands. She carefully studied our faces. "That's because I don't have a soul."

Her answer knocked the breath out of me like a baseball bat to the chest.

"Are you human?" Warren asked.

A thin smile spread across her lips as she tugged at the skin on her hand. "This is human."

The whole scene was a little unnerving. Had I not been so curious and fascinated, I probably would have been terrified. Instead, I was desperate to know more. "Are you an angel?"

She nodded slowly. Then she pointed at us. "And you *are not*."

Warren looked at me as if to say, *I told you so*.

I ran my fingers through my hair and blew out a deep sigh. "Do you know what we are?" I asked.

She tapped her fingers on her lips. "You are Seramorta."

"Seramorta?" I had never heard the term before, and from the look on Warren's face, he hadn't either. I turned back to Abigail. "What does that mean?"

She leaned on her armrest. "You are half-angel, half-mortal."

I had known for quite a while that there was something supernaturally different about me and the hunky man sitting at my side, but I was fully unprepared to have it confirmed out loud by someone in the know. I burst out laughing. Loud, crazy-person laughter.

Abigail's eyes widened. "This amuses you?"

I reined in my cackles, pressing my palms against the sides of my head. "It's just so…"

"Unbelievable," Warren finished. He rubbed his forehead and squeezed his eyes shut. "So what happened? We had a mortal mother who got knocked up by an angel?"

Her head tilted. "Or a mortal father."

I narrowed my eyes and wagged my finger between Warren and myself. "So, we had angel parents who abandoned us both to figure all this out for ourselves?"

She shifted in her chair. "They didn't have a choice. It is forbidden for angels to raise their offspring."

I folded my arms across my chest. "Forbidden by who? God?"

She gave a noncommittal shrug. "More so forbidden by nature. The human mind is a fragile thing, especially during its developmental years. The prolonged physical contact of an angel in the early life of a Seramorta would have dire consequences for the child."

I thought of what it felt like when she touched my hand. "Could it kill them?"

She shook her head. "No, but it can cause insanity of the worst kind."

I pinched the bridge of my nose. "This is a lot to take in."

"I can imagine." She looked over at me. "How old are you?"

"I'm twenty-seven. He's twenty-nine," I answered.

Warren leaned back and rested the ankle of his boot on his knee. "Why do Sloan and I have different abilities?"

"Because of your lineage. Much like the human race, you inherit different traits from your parents." She studied his face. "For example, you, Warren, have the power to end life, don't you?"

His eyes widened.

She pointed at him. "That's because you're the son of an Angel of Death."

I looked at him. "Well, you were right about that."

"So, am I evil?" he asked.

She laughed. "No one, angel nor human, is inherently evil. We are all given a choice."

"What about me?" I asked. "Do you know what I am? I seem to be able to talk about people and make them show up."

She nodded. "That's a summoning power, shared by the Angels of Life. You have the power to influence the paths of others around you."

I raised my hand. "Angels of Life?"

"The second choir in Heaven."

I had no idea what that meant.

"She can heal people too," Warren added.

"That's not exactly been proven," I said. "People do seem to get better around me though."

Her face was curious as she nodded. "That's part of your gift."

I pointed at Warren. "He and I can't see each other's souls. Does that mean we don't have them either?"

She shifted on her chair. "What you call a soul is your eternal spirit that lives in the body on this earth and then lives forever in eternity. Human spirits and angelic ones are entirely different, and you were born with both. Your human spirit and your angelic spirit are so closely knit together that you are blind to each other because your mortality doesn't allow you to see the angelic."

"So, that's why we can't see you?" I asked.

She nodded. "Yes, but your angelic spirit—which is stronger—allows you to see the human souls of others, as can I."

I sighed and closed my eyes. "My brain hurts."

"That's another thing." Warren leaned forward. "Whenever Sloan and I are away from each other—"

She cut him off. "You get a headache?"

"Yes," we answered at the same time.

She smiled. "The connection you have on a spiritual level affects your human physiology. When you remove that connection, your body is starved for that flow of spiritual energy."

"You were right, Warren." I looked over at him. "It's like detoxing off of each other."

Abigail nodded. "That's exactly what it is."

I looked at her seriously. "Is it dangerous?"

She shrugged. "It could be dangerous if your body is already compromised for some reason. Humans die all the time from complications of detoxing."

"Does it just happen with me and Sloan?" Warren asked.

She shook her head. "No. It happens with all angels who walk among humans. Some angels stay exclusively with other angels, while others, like me, prefer to be alone. I will suffer when you leave town."

"You'll have a migraine?" Warren asked.

She nodded. "Yes."

I rubbed my face. "That's fascinating, and I'm really sorry."

The telephone on her desk beeped. "Abigail, Mr. Parker is on line two for you."

"Thank you. Ask him to hold for a moment," Abigail replied. She glanced down at her watch before looking at us again. "I hope I have been of some help. I would like to speak with you more, but I'm sure you understand how busy I am right now."

I nodded. "Of course. Thank you for meeting with us."

She offered me her hand and I shook it, this time less jarred by her powerful energy. "Call me anytime." She examined my face carefully. "I mean it."

I smiled. "Thanks. I probably will." I pointed toward the door. "We will see ourselves out."

Abigail turned and picked up her telephone as we walked out of the office, and Warren quietly closed the door behind us. "Well, that went well," he said.

I looped my arm through his. "We're angels."

He laughed. "You called it," he said. "Are you happy to have some answers now?"

I sighed and rested my head against his shoulder. "So happy I could cry!"

He held the front door open, and we walked out into the warm night air. He squeezed my hand. "I say we go somewhere and celebrate."

I gripped his arm. "I want to go to the hotel and get Nathan. We've got to tell him the good news!"

He stopped and looked at me. Then he shook his head and laughed.

"What?" I asked as he opened my car door.

He rolled his eyes. "Nothing. Let's go find Nate."

Nathan met us at the bar in the hotel lobby when we got back. Per my request, Shannon wasn't with him. "How'd it go?" he asked as we settled into a booth in the corner.

I shuddered with happiness. "It was awesome." I leaned across the table toward him. "Guess what?"

He produced a bag of Skittles from his pocket and poured a handful. "What?"

"We're angels." I dramatically dropped my jaw.

Nathan laughed and a green Skittle tumbled off his lip. "Sure you are." He tapped his chest. "Hell, so am I."

I threw a sugar packet at his head. "Do you want to hear this or not?"

"Tell me," he said, smiling around a mouthful of candy.

Before I began, a waiter stopped at our table and Warren ordered us all a round of beers. When he was out of earshot, I lowered my voice. "She said we are Seramorta."

Nathan blinked. "Sera-whatta?"

"Seramorta," I said. "Half-angel, half-human."

He started chuckling again. "Are you going to sprout wings?"

I ignored him. "She said Warren is the son of an Angel of Death and I was born from an Angel of Life. I have the power to influence the paths of the people around me."

Nathan nodded and looked at Warren. "That's the truest thing I've ever heard. Wouldn't you agree?"

"Absolutely," Warren said and they slapped a high five across the table.

The waiter delivered our drinks, and Nathan held his high in the air like he was about to propose a toast. Instead, he said, "You're welcome."

My head fell to the side. "Huh?"

He placed his glass on the table. "Well, if it weren't for me being such a pain in your ass, as you constantly tell me, you never would have known Abigail even existed. So, you're welcome."

I smiled and held my glass toward him. "Thank you, Nathan."

He clinked his beer with mine and winked. "I'm happy for you both."

Warren squeezed my shoulder.

In my purse, my cell phone rang. I pulled it out and saw my father's picture on the screen. It was nearly midnight in North Carolina. "That's weird." I answered the call. "Hey, Dad."

"Sloan," he said, his voice cracking.

"Are you OK?" I asked. "It's really late."

"Sloan, it's your mother."

13.

THE TONE OF my father's voice alarmed me even more than his words. "What's wrong with Mom?"

He cleared his throat. "I think it would be a good idea if you came home as soon as you can."

I sat forward on the edge of my seat. "Why? What's going on?"

Concerned, Warren leaned in close.

Dad sighed over the phone. "Maybe we should talk about it when you get home."

"Dad, there's no way I can get a flight home tonight. You have to tell me what's happened!" I demanded.

There was another pause. "It's a tumor, Sloan, in her brain. It's very serious."

I gasped and covered my mouth. "What?"

His voice was shaky. "I've never seen anything this aggressive. The growth rate alone shows it has to be malignant. We are making plans to do surgery to try and remove it as soon as possible, hopefully first thing in the morning. There isn't any other choice."

I closed my eyes and took a deep breath. "OK. I'm going to figure out how to get home," I said. "Can I talk to her?"

"She's not conscious anymore, sweetheart. She fell asleep about an hour ago, and we haven't been able to wake her up," he said.

Tears spilled down my cheeks. "Dad, no!"

"Please come home as quickly as you can, but please be careful," he said. "I promise I'll call you if anything else changes. I love you, Sloan."

"I love you too," I said and disconnected the phone.

"What's going on?" Warren asked.

My mouth was hanging open in shock. "My mom has a brain tumor. It's really, really bad," I said. "She's unconscious, and they are going to try and remove the tumor tomorrow. We have to go." I pushed myself up from the table. "I need you to take me to the airport."

Warren reached for my arm. "You said it yourself. There aren't any more flights out tonight."

"Then we need to start driving!" I cried.

"It's at least a fifteen hour drive, Sloan," Nathan said. "You can sleep and fly home faster than you could drive there."

Warren pulled me under his arm. "We will call the airline and get on the first flight out in the morning," he said. "If we catch the five a.m. flight, we can be home before lunch."

I melted into his chest and sobbed. He rubbed my back and let me cry for several minutes. Then, he finally suggested we go to our room.

When we stopped at Nathan's floor, he hugged me. "I'm so sorry. Call me in the middle of the night if you hear anything."

I nodded and the doors closed behind him.

When we got to our room, I sat down on the bed, and Warren put my purse on my lap. "Take one of your pills so you can relax and get some sleep. You're going to need it. I'm going to call the airlines and figure out what flight we can get on."

"OK," I whispered. My hands were shaking as I rifled through my purse.

While I waited for the anti-anxiety medicine to seep into my bloodstream, I called Adrianne and then packed my suitcase. Warren was on the phone with the airline. I kept picturing my mother in my mind. She was alive, and I could still sense her presence, and that was the only thing that remotely consoled me.

I was still awake when Warren stretched out next to me. "We're on the five-ten flight on American Airlines in the morning. That's the first flight out."

"Was it expensive?" I asked.

He smiled. "Not at all."

"You're a rotten liar."

"Come here." He pulled me into his arms and pressed his lips against the side of my head.

Tears leaked from my eyes onto his bare chest. "This is my fault."

"That's crazy. No, it isn't." He ran his fingers through my hair.

"I told you before we left that I knew something was wrong with her. The tumor has been there all this time. I've felt it for a few months. I just didn't know what it was. I've been keeping her healthy by just being around, and I didn't know it. Why else would she get so bad so quickly right after we left?"

"Shh," he said. "This is a tumor. You didn't cause this."

"You know I'm right," I whispered into the dark.

He was quiet for a moment. "If you were keeping her healthy, then you prolonged her life, Sloan. It's not your fault. We'll get you home and you'll make her better again. You'll see."

I sniffed and nodded my head. The Xanax was kicking in and my eyes were getting heavy. Before long, with my mother still in the forefront of my mind, I was fast asleep.

* * *

The sound of my mother's voice rattled me from a deep sleep. "Sloan," I heard her say.

I opened my eyes. The hotel room was still dark. The clock on the nightstand read two-fourteen. I pictured my mother and felt nothing but a deep void. I sat up and tried harder, but again, I felt nothing. Uncontrollable sobs welled up inside me as I tried, over and over, to find her presence in the dark.

My mother was gone.

* * *

The flight to Asheville was excruciating. I had called my father in the middle of the night, and he told me they had put mom on a ventilator because she was having trouble breathing on her own. I didn't have the heart to tell him the machines were only keeping her organs functional.

I knew it. Warren knew it. My mother wasn't going to wake up.

Adrianne was in a wheelchair in the waiting room with her father when we got to the hospital. It was the same room where I had slept for several nights when she was in intensive care after the car wreck.

I stopped to hug her. "You should be at home in bed," I said.

She squeezed my hand. "You know I wouldn't be anywhere else."

I wiped my eyes.

"Your dad is down the hall," she said, pointing through the door. "He came out and talked to us a few minutes ago."

My Aunt Joan, Mom's sister, was talking with Dad in the hallway when we walked through the door. Aunt Joan looked a lot like my mom, except she had more gray hair and was probably thirty pounds heavier. Mom had been extremely health conscious and was an avid jogger. She had always been the healthiest person I knew. It made the whole scenario very ironic.

I released Warren's hand and ran to my dad when he saw me. I cried all over again in his arms. Tears soaked my hair as he wept holding me.

He pulled away. "She's stable, but she's still on the ventilator. Do you want to go in and see her?"

I sniffed and nodded my head.

Warren squeezed my arm. "I'll wait out here."

Dad and I walked down the hall and behind a curtain in ICU. My mother was tethered to every life-sustaining machine in the room, but I knew it was pointless. I cried as I took her cold hand and kissed it.

My father's hand came to rest on my back. "The results of the tests we did this morning weren't good," he said. "It's grown in such a way that there's not much hope they'll be able to get it all. They are still going to attempt the surgery, but I asked them to wait until you got here because there is a good chance she might not come out of it."

I sucked in a deep breath and leaned down to push some stray gray hairs away from my mother's smooth, peaceful face. "Don't do the surgery, Dad."

He took a step toward me. "It's the only option we—"

I cut him off. "Mom's gone. These machines are making her heart and her lungs work, but she left early this morning."

The blood drained from my father's handsome face. His blue eyes were bloodshot from worry and lack of sleep. They filled up with tears again. "How do you know?"

"Because her soul isn't here. This is only a shell." For the first time in my life, I didn't care that I sounded like a lunatic. "She's gone, Dad."

My father crumpled into the chair beside the bed. I went over and knelt down beside him as he wailed. "I'm not ready," he cried. "I can't let her go."

My mother was the first experience I had ever had with death, not counting Billy Stewart. I wondered if something about me had extended the lives of others without me realizing it. Holding her hand on that bed, one thing occurred to me: the word dead was the wrong word. My mother's body may have been lifeless, but my mother, herself, was just gone. I had no idea where she was gone to, but I was certain I didn't have the power to summon her back.

Over the next hour, my dad had to convince my aunt and my mom's doctors to not attempt the brain surgery. He signed a medical release stating he didn't want any more excessive measures to keep her body alive. The doctors turned off the machines. Even though I knew she wasn't there, something about hearing the finality of my mother's last heartbeat devastated me all over again. Warren held me as I sobbed with my dad at her bedside.

Blindly, I walked to the waiting room and sat down next to Adrianne. She reached over and took my hand and rested her head on my arm. "I'm so sorry, friend," she said. "I love you."

I nodded. "I love you too."

My dad walked into the waiting room. Aunt Joan was with him. Warren got up from beside me and offered Dad his seat. "The funeral home is sending someone to pick her up," he said. "We'll need to go down there at some point today or tomorrow and make the arrangements."

"OK," I said, unsure of what else to say.

"Do you want to come to the house? We are going to head that way since there's nothing left for us to do here," he said.

I squeezed his hand. "Of course, Daddy. We'll be there."

"All right." He pressed a kiss to my knuckles.

Warren hugged my dad. "I'm so sorry, Dr. Jordan."

Dad patted Warren on the shoulder. "Call me Dad, son."

When he was gone, we waited for Adrianne's dad to bring the car around, and Warren helped her into the front seat. "Let me know when the service will be. Come over and have a beer if you need to get away." She held my hand through the car window.

I smiled. "Thank you."

When they were gone, Warren put his arms around me, hiding me from the chill of the mountains. As I shivered against his warm chest, I deeply regretted not wearing a jacket.

His hands rubbed my bare arms. "We need to get you home so you can change. Are you ready to go?" he asked.

"I need to get my phone. I left it in the waiting room." I pulled away from him and turned back toward the hospital.

A tall black man was standing in the doorway of the waiting room. He matched Warren in size and had a shiny bald head. He was wearing blue hospital scrubs and an I.D. name tag. His eyes sparkled like gold nuggets, but there was nothing behind them. I knew exactly who he was.

An angel of death.

14.

LIKE A BULL being released from a rodeo pen, I charged at the man and slammed my fist into his face as hard as I could. The jolt from touching him nearly knocked me off my feet. He barely flinched, but I recoiled, grabbing my hand and cursing in pain. Warren took hold of my arms and pulled me under his control. Without a word, the man wiped a trickle of blood from his bottom lip.

"It was you!" Undeterred by the possibility of fractured fingers, I fought as hard as I could to free myself from Warren's tight grip. "You took her!"

The man held up his hands in defense and took a half-step away from me. "Yes, I took her." His voice was calm and even.

I lunged at him again, but Warren kept me from reaching him. He shook me and put his lips close to my ear. "Sloan, you need to calm down."

"Shall we talk inside?" The man nodded toward the building behind him.

Without waiting for us to agree, he turned and walked through the door. After exchanging a worried glance with each other, Warren and I followed. Once we were inside the waiting room, the man raised his large hand and waved it toward the doors. They slammed shut without being touched, and I heard their heavy locks tumble.

Beside me, Warren froze. Had I not been blind with rage, I probably would have been frozen in awe and fear as well.

"Who are you?" I demanded.

He tapped his name tag and looked at it upside down. "Today I am David Miller."

I narrowed my eyes. "Who are you really?"

He bowed his head and touched his fingertips together. "My name is Samael."

I shoved him in the shoulder. "Why did you kill my mother, Samael?"

Warren bent down to look at me in the face. "The dude just slammed the doors in the room without touching them and locked us in here. Please stop putting your hands on him."

Samael held up his hand and smiled, clearly amused by my weak show of hostility. "It's OK. I was warned she could be a little volatile if provoked, particularly early in the day."

I was puzzled but still furious. "Who told you that?"

"Your mother." He smiled. "Her exact instructions were to not try and approach you until at least ten in the morning, unless I bring coffee, at the risk of physical assault." He touched his lower lip. "Maybe I should have waited a few hours more."

I cut my eyes at him. "What do you mean my mother told you?"

He motioned to the chairs behind us. "Shall we sit?"

Warren pushed me down into a chair and pulled one over next to me. Samael moved a chair around to face us and carefully sat down. I massaged my sore knuckles.

"I'm Warren, by the way," Warren said, extending his hand.

Samael shook it. "It is my pleasure to meet you both. I am very sorry it is under these circumstances."

I pointed a finger at him. "Cut the pleasantries and start explaining to me why you killed my mother."

He leveled his gaze at me. "I did not kill your mother, Sloan. Mortality destroyed her body. I simply freed her from this world and escorted her into mine."

Warren eyed Samael skeptically. "No offense, but I've killed plenty of people, and there has never been an angel there to take them anywhere."

Samael slowly pointed at him. "You were there."

That was sobering.

Warren sat back in his seat, his jaw a little slack.

Samael had a small smile on his face. "You using your power is a little more..." He paused like he was searching for the right word. "Explosive."

Explosive was a good way to describe what Warren could do. He was still speechless and even a little pale.

Samael looked at us both. "Typically, when we are present, we are unseen, hidden just beyond the veil of what your mortal eyes can see. I only came here today as you see me"—he motioned down at his body—"because of my conversation with your mother. Are you aware of what you are?"

"Seramorta," I answered.

Samael nodded. "You are very rare, and two of you together, even more so. I had to see for myself if it was true." His finger moved slowly between me and Warren. "This pairing is quite curious."

I looked over at Warren. He cocked an eyebrow but didn't comment.

Frustrated, I rubbed my hands down my face. "Two angels in two days. Now this." I groaned. "I'm not sure how much more I can stand."

Samael perked in his seat, his golden eyes wide with intrigue. "You met another angel?"

Warren nodded. "A woman named Abigail in Texas."

Samael shook his head. "There is no *Abigail* in our world."

I crossed my arms over my chest and smirked. "You know everyone in your world?"

"Yes. We have been together from the beginning of time," he said.

Warren nudged me with his elbow. "Abigail probably isn't her real name. Remember, we originally thought her name was Rachel."

I shrugged. "Yeah, I'll bet you're right. I didn't even think to ask."

Samael smiled. "We rarely go by our real names when we walk among you. Their obscurity makes us more conspicuous than we would prefer, and you can rarely pronounce them properly. Samael is my real name."

Warren shifted in his seat. "Abigail said I was the son of a death angel. Could you be...?" He was cringing.

Samael laughed. "I am not the only angel in charge over the dead, and I have no children. If I did, I would not be able to cross the spirit line."

"Why not?" I asked.

"Having a child on Earth binds the spirit here. While the child lives, the parent cannot leave," he said.

My eyes widened. "So our parents are still here?"

He nodded. "Absolutely."

I sat forward in my chair. "Do you know who they are or where we might find them?"

He looked at us both carefully before shaking his head. "I'm sorry. I cannot say that I know."

Warren crossed his arms. "So, what do you want from us, Samael?"

"Nothing," Samael answered. "I wanted to see if it could be true."

There was a note of wonder in his voice that made me a bit nervous, though I wasn't sure why.

He pointed at both of us again. "This is not a likely occurrence."

I groaned and looked at Warren. "In other words, it's not likely a *coincidence.*"

Samael had a knowing smile. "The mortal often dismiss too much as coincidence."

I rolled my eyes. "Tell me something I don't know."

"My time here must come to an end." Samael slowly rose and extended his hand to me. "I am truly sorry for your loss, Ms. Sloan. But please know your mother no longer suffers, and she is not far away."

"So, it's real?" I asked. "Heaven is real?"

"More real than this very room."

The notion was only mildly comforting. I wanted my mother in *my* world, no matter how glorious the other side was. "Can you give her a message?" I asked.

He nodded.

"Tell her I love her and I'm sorry I didn't get here in time to make this right," I said.

Like a grandfather comforting a child, he put his hand under my chin. "It was time for her suffering to end, Sloan. Someday you will understand."

Something about his words brought me a strange sense of comfort. I believed him and I doubted him in equal portions.

Warren and I stood, and Samael waved his hand and reopened the doors. A nurse stuck her head into the room as if trying to figure out what had happened in the waiting area, but she quickly disappeared again.

Samael paused before walking outside and looked at us with a serious expression. "I must implore you to exercise extreme caution. There are some to whom you will be a great threat, and they will do everything in their power to overtake you or destroy you."

Chills ran down my spine. "Why?"

"Because you are more special than you realize."

My shoulders slumped. "I don't want to be special."

With a smile, he bowed his head. "Until we meet again." Without another word, he disappeared through the door outside.

I pointed toward the exit. "Warren, did that really just happen, or am I so stressed out and exhausted that I'm hallucinating?"

He wrapped his hand around mine. "That really just happened."

We walked outside, but Samael was nowhere to be seen. "Do you think he was being honest? Do you think he really talked to my mom?"

Warren slipped on his sunglasses and pulled the car keys out of his pocket. "I don't see why he would have any reason to lie about it," he said. "And I'm pretty sure lying is a sin and angels can't sin, right?"

I leaned my head against his arm. "Please take me home and lock me away before anything else weird happens. I've had enough supernatural crap in the last twenty-four hours to last a lifetime."

"Are we going to your dad's?" he asked.

"Yeah. There's going to be a whole lot of stuff that needs to be taken care of, and I don't want him to be alone."

We drove in silence to my parents' house. My brain ran through the events that had transpired like a horror movie reel that I was unable to stop. We helped take down a human trafficking ring. We found Rachel Smith and she was an angel named Abigail. She informed us we were angel half-breeds. My mother died and crossed into the spirit world. And we met an Angel of Death who told us some other angels might try and kill us. My head was beginning to throb. I longed for the morning before when we were enjoying omelets by the pool and my biggest concern was a marriage proposal.

We rolled to a stop on the cobblestone driveway next to Aunt Joan's sedan, and it occurred to me it would be the first time in as long as I could remember that I would walk into the house and not smell anything delicious coming from the kitchen. I had never learned how to make Mom's mashed potatoes. My heart sank and tears would have flowed had my eyes not been all cried out. It's the little things that hurt the most when the most important things are suddenly gone.

I looked at the house, pausing with my hand on the car door handle. "I never should have gone to Texas." I sighed and pushed the door open with my shoulder.

Anticipating at least a one night stay, Warren carried our suitcases into the house. Aunt Joan was at the bar in the kitchen when we came in, and she looked at us and pressed her finger over her lips. We quietly walked in and she nodded to the den where my dad was stretched out across the leather sofa.

I gave her a side hug and lowered my voice to a whisper. "How long has he been asleep?"

"About ten minutes." She looked up at Warren and stuck out her hand. "I'm Joan Thornton. Audrey's older sister."

"Warren Parish," he answered.

I touched her arm. "Sorry, Aunt Joan. This is my boyfriend."

She nodded. "I assumed so. Audrey mentioned him a time or two. You're a detective for the county."

I hung my head and felt Warren gently squeeze the back of my neck. "No, ma'am," he answered quietly. "You're thinking of Detective McNamara."

She smacked her forehead. "Oh, I'm sorry. You're the other one. Military is it?"

"Yes, formerly," he replied and kissed my forehead.

Her cheeks were flushed with embarrassment, and she flashed me an apologetic, wincing smile. "Please forgive me."

He shook his head. "Don't worry about it."

Desperate to change the subject, I tapped my watch. "Do you know what the plan is for the day?"

She sighed. "I don't think we are going to try and do anything today. Your father was up all night long and has been very worried all week. I called the funeral home, and they suggested we come first thing in the morning to make the arrangements. We'll need to talk about what you and your dad want for the service. A pastor, flowers, and such. I'm just guessing, but I think we will try and have the funeral on Tuesday."

I had never been to a funeral before.

She held up her cell phone. "I've been making calls to everyone who needs to know."

I picked up the list she had scribbled on the back of a receipt. "Can

I help you?"

She patted my hand. "Go lie down, sweetie. I know you've not gotten much sleep either. I can take care of this. You're going to need your rest. It's going to be a trying few days ahead."

I hugged her again. "Thank you for being here."

She sniffed and rubbed my forearm. "I just can't believe how fast this happened. A week ago we were at the farmer's market picking out pumpkins and now she's gone."

I wanted to apologize, but that would sound crazy. "I can't believe it either," I said. "I can't imagine what Dad is going through."

She shook her head. "Or what he will go through in the days ahead. Those two have been inseparable since the day they first met."

My eyes turned toward my father who was on his back with his arm draped over his eyes. Mom had not only been his wife of twenty-seven years, but she was also the head nurse in his office, his cook, his bookkeeper, housecleaner, and grocery shopper. I wondered if Dad even knew where to begin with paying bills at home or keeping up with the accounting at work. My heart broke for him all over again.

"I'll have to start taking better care of him myself," I said.

She smiled. "We'll all pitch in."

I kissed the top of her gray head. "I'm going to try and rest for a while. We'll be up in my old room if you need me."

"OK, sweetie. I'll come get you if necessary," she said.

Warren and I walked upstairs to my former bedroom that mom had converted to a guest room when I moved out after college. I sank down on the edge of the magnolia print comforter, and Warren gently sat down next to me. I dropped my head and a rogue tear slipped down my cheek. "I can't believe she's gone."

He turned toward me and gathered me into his arms. "Come here," he said.

I silently cried against his chest, listening to the even thump of his heartbeat and savoring the warm buzz of energy that flowed between us. I wanted to lose myself in him and hide from the pain that threatened to consume me. In his arms, he gently rocked me as his fingers trailed up and down my spine. Warren was my safe haven from the horrors outside of that very moment. I pulled away to look up at him.

His eyes were soft and pleading for a way to remove my burden, and we both knew he would if it were possible. Instead, he cradled my face in his hands and leaned his forehead against mine. "I'm sorry," he whispered, his thumbs stroking my cheeks.

Please, was the only coherent thought in my head as I stretched up until my lips met his. My fingers tangled in his hair as his mouth parted and moved against mine.

Perhaps Warren was as desperate as I was to escape from reality together because there was no pause for foreplay as his hand slid up the inside of my thigh underneath my skirt. As he bent over me and pressed me back against the pillows, his fingers slid my panties down my legs. A moment later, my skirt was pushed up around my waist and he was inside me. He hadn't even kicked off his boots.

My vision went in and out of focus until I closed my eyes and melted into the intoxicating surge of our connection. The world went black around me, and the chaos that had fueled everything leading up to that moment was squelched by his touch. I dug my nails into his back, gathering the fabric of the shirt he was still wearing.

"I love you, Warren."

His black hair spilled down across my face as he rocked against me. "I love you too."

15.

THE ENSUING DAYS were a nauseating blur, like a week-long hangover from the world's worst party. There was a visitation and a service at the funeral home where I met more people than I had ever seen in my life. Between countless patients of my father and at least half of the staff at the hospital, people and flowers spilled into every crevice of the building. My dad would have casseroles in his freezer until the apocalypse.

During the service, the pastor rattled on about comfort and grief and encouraged us to not waste the days we are granted. Considering the amount of people who had shown up to offer their condolences, it was comforting to know not one second of my mom's life had been squandered. The impression she had made on the world was immeasurable, and even greater was the void she left behind.

After the minister shared a final prayer, we rode in a black town car to the graveside. There, they placed my mother's mahogany casket in the ground. It was surreal, like I was stuck in a nightmare that even the bitter cold couldn't shake me from.

When the formalities were over, a large group of people gathered at my parents' house where the staff from the hospital brought over enough food to feed the entirety of downtown Asheville. Nathan, Adrianne, and even Shannon came over. Warren and I sat on the porch swing with them on the deck that overlooked the sparkling city. Warren held my hand and gently swung us back and forth.

"Are you going to stay here with your dad for a while?" Adrianne asked.

I looked inside to where my father sat at the table with a few of his friends. His mouth was smiling, but his eyes were sad and tired. I nodded. "I'm probably going to stay till he kicks me out," I said. "This was so sudden. He had no time to prepare for it at all."

"I'm really sorry, Sloan," Shannon said gently.

Nathan came over and knelt down in front of me. He placed his hands over mine. "You want some good news?"

I sighed. "I would love some good news."

"I made a call to Houston today. They rescued nineteen girls total out of that trafficking ring, and they arrested Larry Mendez," he said.

I forced a half-smile. "That is good news."

He squeezed my hands. "We're going to take off. Will you call me if you need anything at all?"

Nodding, I rose to my feet. I put my arms around his neck and hugged him for a tad bit longer than was probably appropriate. "Thanks for being here, Nathan."

He rested his cheek against mine and spoke softly in my ear. "I wish I could fix it."

I smiled. "I know."

Shannon stepped over and hugged me also. "I'll be praying for you and your family," she said as we embraced.

When they were gone, I sat back down by Warren and put my head on his shoulder.

Adrianne rolled her wheelchair closer and pointed at me. "You just hugged Shannon Green."

"And neither of them burst into flames. Aren't you shocked?" Warren teased.

I tried to laugh, but it came out as a throaty cough.

Adrianne leaned on her elbow. "You want some more good news?"

I straightened and looked at her. "Absolutely."

Biting her lower lip, she put her hands on the armrests of her wheelchair. She locked the wheels and pushed herself up.

"Whoa, whoa, whoa!" Warren shouted as he jumped up to grab her arm.

She swatted his hand away. "Don't touch me."

He kept his hands close just in case, and I sat forward on the swing and watched her as she straightened all the way up. I covered my mouth with my hands and teared up again. I stood and put my arms around her. "Congratulations!"

She laughed and pushed me away. "I can't stand up forever." Warren and I helped her settle into her chair.

"But you can stand!" I cheered.

"I took five steps at physical therapy yesterday without holding on to anything." She smiled with pride. "I'll be wearing my stilettos and dancing again before you know it."

Genuinely happy for the first time in days, I leaned over and hugged her. "I can't wait! I'll let you dress me up like a paper doll and put as much makeup on me as you want. We'll dance until we're dizzy."

She squeezed me. "I love you so much."

I smiled. "I love you too."

* * *

The next morning when I came downstairs, I smelled coffee and sausage cooking in the kitchen. For a split second, I completely forgot Mom was gone. I stepped around the corner and saw Warren at the stove. I walked over and put my arms around his waist and rested my head against his back.

He rubbed my forearms and looked around at me. "Good morning," he said. "The coffee is ready."

I squeezed his waist, then crossed the kitchen to retrieve a coffee mug. "Have you seen Dad yet this morning?" I asked.

He shook his head. "He's not up yet."

Glancing up at the clock, I put the mug down next to the coffee maker. It was after nine. "That's strange. I'm going to go and check on him."

"OK."

I walked out of the kitchen and down the hall past the stairs to the door of the master bedroom. Gently rapping my knuckles against it, I pushed it open just a crack. Dad was sitting on the edge of the bed in his flannel pajama pants and a white t-shirt, staring at the carpet. I pushed the door open farther. "Dad?"

He looked up. His eyes were red, and there were dark circles beneath them. I walked over and sat down beside him, looping my arm through his. For a while, neither of us spoke because there was absolutely nothing to say.

Finally, Dad sucked in a deep breath. "It's just so hard to even get up in the morning now." He was shaking as tears streamed down his cheeks.

I turned and put my arms around him, our roles for once reversed.

After a moment, his weeping subsided and he pulled away. Wiping his eyes on the back of his hand, he shook his head. "I'm sorry. I'm trying to keep it together," he said. "I never even thought about a life without her in it."

On the nightstand was a box of tissues. I grabbed one for Dad and one for myself. "Me either."

He sighed and stood up, dabbing his eyes with the tissue to dry them. "Come on. Let's get some coffee. I'm going to need it. I've got to figure out how to pay the mortgage today."

* * *

The fourth day of what I had dubbed *Dad Intervention Week* was laundry day. When I returned to his house after putting in a few hours at the office, we spent ten minutes discussing the importance of sorting the colors from the whites and figuring out which buttons did what on the washing machine. While Dad gathered the laundry from the house to practice, Warren carried boxes of Mom's stuff to the garage.

When we passed in the hallway, I grabbed Warren by the arm. "How do you think he's doing?"

He nodded his head. "He told me a dirty senior citizen joke over breakfast this morning, so I would say he's doing better."

I squeezed his forearm. "Thank you for staying with him so I don't get fired."

He shook his head. "Stop thanking me." His eyes widened. "Guess what today is."

"Laundry day?"

He smiled. "Halloween."

"Oh geez. We'd better get candy today," I said.

He nodded. "Remind me and we'll pick some up on our way home from dinner."

"Sloan, honey! Can you come up here please?" Dad shouted down the stairs.

"Coming!" I called and headed up the steps. When I got to the top, I looked into his office, but it was empty. "Where are you?"

"Your room," he answered.

I walked down the hall and found my father sitting on my bed, holding a file folder. "What's up?" I asked.

He held up the photograph of Abigail Smith. "I found this on top of your clothes. Do you know this woman?"

Puzzled by his intrigue, I walked over and peered over his shoulder. "Yeah. Her name is Abigail. I met her in Texas. Why?"

He looked out the window and rubbed his hand over his mouth. Finally, he snapped the folder shut and looked at me. "Nothing, honey. She just looks really familiar." He put the folder in my suitcase.

"She was a missing person in Greensboro for a while, but we located her in San Antonio," I explained. "You might have seen her on the news."

"That must be it." He stood up. "Excuse me for a second."

He walked out of the room and left the laundry on the bed. "Dad, you forgot—"

The sound of his office door closing cut me off.

I looked down at the clothes and at the file folder, then scratched my head. "That was weird."

A half hour later, Dad was still in his office, and because I'd skipped lunch to leave early, I was starving. I went back upstairs and knocked on his door. "Dad, we're going to go out and get some food, do you want anything?" I shouted through the wooden door.

"No, thank you!"

"Are you all right in there?" I called.

"Just fine!"

I shook my head and galloped down the stairs. Warren was holding my jacket at the bottom. "He's not coming?" he asked.

"Nope," I answered, shrugging into the black coat. "He's acting really strange."

"How so?" He opened the front door and stepped aside to let me exit first.

The brisk October air slapped me in the face. "Brrr." I zipped my jacket closed and shoved my fists into my pockets. "I don't know what's up with him. He saw that picture of Abigail up in our room earlier, and he's been locked in his office ever since. He looked like he had seen a ghost or something."

"Do you think he knows her?" he asked.

I looked up at him and tried to hide my face behind the collar of my jacket. "How would he?"

"I don't know." He clicked the button to unlock the Challenger.

I held out my hand. "Can I drive? I haven't driven a car in weeks."

He hesitated for a second. "Will you be careful?"

With a hand on my hip, I reached for the keys. He held them up away from me, his eyes demanding I answer the question.

"Yes, I'll be careful!"

He laughed and handed them to me.

When we climbed inside, I sank down in the leather driver's seat and moved it up so I could reach the pedals with my feet. My eyes closed involuntarily as I started the engine and felt the beast roar to life underneath me. An unstoppable moan slipped out.

When I looked over at Warren, he was frowning. "Please don't make me jealous of my own car."

I laughed and put the transmission in reverse. "Oh, I love driving this thing."

He pointed at me. "No hot-rodding it while I'm gone."

Gone.

The word reverberated in my skull like a clanging cymbal inside a racquetball court.

I slammed my foot down on the brakes, and my hands released the steering wheel in shock. "Oh my gosh! With everything going on, I completely forgot you're leaving. When is it again?"

"Seven days."

I muttered the worst of all curse words and pressed my temple against the ice cold window. "What am I going to do?"

He reached over and put his hand on my thigh, and I realized an entire year without the calming zing of his touch was going to feel like an eternity.

"I'm sorry. I shouldn't have brought it up," he said.

"No, I'm glad you reminded me. Seriously, what am I going to do while you're gone?" Panic was pushing my voice a full octave higher.

"You could take up knitting," he suggested.

My eyebrows scrunched together. "The Angel of Death is suggesting I adopt knitting as a hobby?"

Warren's shoulders shook with silent laughter.

I stared out the windshield. "Maybe I'll stay with Dad for a while. Maybe till you come home," I said. "I don't think either of us are going to be able to tolerate being alone."

He stretched his arm over the back of my seat. "I would feel better if you weren't in the house by yourself."

"Can't you tell the military to buzz off?"

He laughed. "Sure, I can. Then I'll wind up in the brig and we still won't be able to see each other."

I looked both ways before backing the car out of the driveway and turning down the hill. "You still have no idea why they're recalling you?"

"No, but I'll start digging more in the media this week to see if I can figure out any leads," he said.

"Did you ever check the FBI's Most Wanted list like Nathan suggested?" I asked.

"I actually forgot about it." He pulled out his phone. "I'll do it right now."

I drove as Warren searched the Internet on his cell phone.

The houses in the neighborhood were decked out with pumpkins, tombstones, and ghosts made out of bedsheets. I had always loved Halloween—the dressing up, the plethora of chocolate, and the thrill of haunted houses and scary movies. Almost every year since high school, Adrianne and I had celebrated with an *Exorcist* movie marathon before dressing up and hitting the hottest costume parties in town. The year before, we'd been a pair of severely underdressed angels. The irony was not lost on me. Along with so many other things in my world, Halloween would never be the same.

After a few minutes of driving, I pulled the Challenger into a parking space at the Sunny Point Cafe just down the road.

Warren was flipping through web pages on the screen with his index finger. "Huh," he said as I turned off the engine.

"What is it?" I asked.

He handed me his phone. "Check this out."

In my hand was a mugshot of a Middle Eastern man, with more thick black hair in his beard and eyebrows than on his balding head. There was emptiness behind his eyes. "Is he alive?" I asked.

Warren shrugged. "I don't know. Normally, I would say no, but we were wrong about Abigail, so I'm not sure."

An interesting thought occurred to me. All my life I'd seen photos and videos of people I assumed were dead. I suddenly wondered how many times I'd been wrong.

Warren was still reading. "He's wanted for terrorist attacks in Palestine and threats against the U.S. as recent as two days ago. It says he's responsible for the deaths of over 1,500 Israeli civilians."

I cocked my head to the side as I tried unsuccessfully to pronounce the series of S's, A's, B's, and K's. "How do you say his name?"

He shrugged his shoulders. "Beats me." He looked at me, the sides of his mouth dipping into a deep frown. "What do you want to bet this freak-show is my dad?"

I laughed, but it wasn't exactly funny. I examined Warren's face and shook my head. "You don't look Palestinian to me."

He laughed. "I'm not sure genetics works the same with supernatural creatures, and I could have taken after my mother."

A sickening feeling settled in my stomach. "Oh no." I groaned. "What if you're right and genetics with angels doesn't work the same? What if the DNA test we had done was faulty? Even Dad said they aren't absolutely accurate as it is. What if we really are related?"

His face twisted with disgust, and he wrenched his car door open. "Why, Sloan? Why would you go there again?" he shouted as he angled out of the car.

I got out and skipped around to meet him. "Eww…what if you've been sleeping with your sister all this time?" I squealed.

He grabbed me by my collar and jerked me under his arm. "You're not my sister."

I laughed and clicked the lock button on the Challenger's remote. "You'd better hope not or that's sick."

The cafe was buzzing with early bird diners when we walked inside. We followed the hostess to an empty table by the window and sat down across from each other. I opened my menu and looked it over. I settled on my usual, a sweet potato waffle and a side of chipotle cheese grits, and placed the menu down in front of me.

I folded my hands under my chin and leaned on my elbows. "So, *brother*, I'm thinking they might send you to Palestine or Israel instead of Iraq or Afghanistan."

He bit his lower lip and playfully smacked me across the head with his menu. "No more talk of war or incest. I'm hungry and you're killing my appetite!"

The sun was setting when we got back to the house after stopping at the store to stock up on candy for the inevitable flood of trick-or-treaters. My father was sitting in the kitchen with my file folder on Abigail Smith spread out before him when we walked inside. Perplexed, I dropped our Halloween haul on the table and leaned against his chair. "OK, Dad. Why are you so fascinated by this?"

Warren plopped down on the couch in the den and turned on the television.

Dad tapped his finger on the bottom corner of the surveillance photo. "Is this date correct?"

I nodded. "It was taken a few weeks ago."

He looked up at me. "And you met this woman?"

"Yeah. We met her the night you called me in Texas and said to come home. Why?" I asked.

He dropped his head into his hands. "It would be impossible," he mumbled.

I squeezed his shoulders. "I'm learning there isn't much in this world that is truly impossible."

"You being pleasant in the morning is impossible!" Warren called from the den.

Dad and I both laughed, but I was rolling my eyes. "Dad, what do you know about Abigail Smith?"

He turned around in his seat to look at me. "You're going to think I've lost my mind."

I gave him a reassuring smile. "Try me."

His mouth fell open, but it took him a moment to form words on his lips. Finally, he spoke. "If this is who I think it is…this woman might be your biological mother."

16.

LOOKING AT MY dad, I was keenly aware of how others must feel when I reveal I can see and manipulate souls. I stumbled back a few steps till I slammed into the kitchen bar. Warren was on his feet and suddenly standing next to us. I gripped the counter for support as my mind struggled to process what my dad had just said.

Dad pushed himself up out of his chair and paced the kitchen, wringing his hands over and over. "When I knew her, her name was Sarah. She was a nurse at the hospital where we worked. I remember her well because she was such a likable person. Everyone loved her. She got pregnant while she was there and stayed through most of her pregnancy, but one day she didn't show up for work. The hospital received a letter by mail that she was relocating to be closer to her family."

He turned to look at me from across the kitchen. "About three days later is when Audrey found you outside the hospital. Even then, your mother and I wondered if you might be Sarah's child because of the timing of her disappearance and your arrival, but no one could ever locate her. We tried for a while."

I looked to Warren for help, and he shook his head. "It can't be," he said. "Abigail can't be much older than you are right now, and we're talking about twenty-seven years that have passed. Nobody ages that well."

Dad stopped pacing and leaned against the countertop. He tapped his finger on the granite. "I'm as certain as I am standing here that the woman in the photograph is the same woman I worked with at the hospital in the early eighties." He walked to the table and picked up the folder. Underneath it was another photograph of a large group. "Here. This was taken at our department Christmas party."

I had seen the photograph before. My parents, just in their twenties at the time, were at the front of the group, standing together. Dad reached over and tapped his finger in the middle of the picture. Abigail Smith was smiling in the center.

My breath caught in my chest, and my eyes slowly rose to meet Warren's. "That's her. That's her, Warren!" My voice was slightly frantic. "I remember seeing this photo when I was a kid. I told Mom the lady was dead, and she completely freaked out on me."

Dad nodded. "Audrey told me about that when it happened, and we both talked about it again the night you came over and told us you were different." He held up the photo. "She was pregnant when this was taken."

Perhaps fearing I might pass out, Warren grabbed my arm. His eyes were as wide as mine. "Whoa," we said at the same time.

After a moment, Dad looked up at us with imploring eyes. "Who— or what—is Sarah? I mean Abigail...or whoever she is."

Scrunching up my nose, I looked at my dad sideways. "She's a social worker."

He cut his eyes at me over the rim of his glasses and frowned. "Sloan, tell me the truth."

Warren stepped in between us. "She's an angel. When we met her, she told us that Sloan and I are like angel hybrids. Part angel, part human. In the angel world, we are called the Seramorta."

Dad sucked in a deep breath and held it in his mouth, causing his cheeks to puff out. Finally, he released it slowly, like hot air leaving a balloon. "Angel hybrids, huh?"

I held my hands up cautiously. "Don't freak out."

He shook his head. "I'm not freaking out." His shocked eyes glanced around the kitchen. "I do, however, need a drink."

"Me too," I agreed.

"Let's all have a drink." Warren moved to the cabinet where Dad had stashed a bottle of Tennessee Honey Jack Daniels. I'd only ever seen him drink it when he was sick with severe chest congestion. Warren poured three tumblers and passed them out to us. Dad's was gone before my glass even touched my lips.

The warm whiskey burned its way down my throat, making me cough. Warren chuckled as he poured my dad a second share.

"Shut up," I said.

Still laughing, he shook his head. "I didn't say anything."

I began to pace around the room, tapping the rim of the glass against my bottom lip. I stopped and looked at Warren. "If this is possible, how do you explain the age thing?"

He shrugged. "You said it yourself. Maybe angel genetics are different."

"Don't you think Abigail would have mentioned she might be my mother? I mean, if she suspected I might be her daughter, she would have brought it up, *right?*"

Warren drank a big gulp of whiskey. "Maybe she was as surprised by it as you are right now. We did kind of broadside her by showing up out of nowhere like we did."

"That's true, but still." I tossed my free hand up in the air with a frustrated huff.

"Call her. You've got her number," he reminded me.

My eyes widened, and I handed him my glass before I ran out of the kitchen. I took the stairs two at a time and jogged till I reached our bedroom. Abigail's business card was tucked into the front pocket of my suitcase. I dialed the number as I walked back downstairs.

A woman answered as I reached the kitchen. "Morning Star Ministries, how may I direct your call?"

My heart was pounding in my chest. "Hi. Can I speak with Abigail, please?"

"I'm sorry. Abigail is out of town on business. May I direct you to her voicemail?" she asked.

I resumed my nervous shuffling around the kitchen. "Do you know when she might be in the office, or do you know of another way I might contact her? I really need to talk to her."

"May I ask who is calling?" the woman asked.

"Sloan Jordan."

"Oh! Hello, Ms. Jordan." Her tone had completely changed. "Ms. Smith directed me to give you her cell phone number if you happened to call here looking for her while she was away."

"Great! What is it?"

I scribbled the number down on the corner of an old newspaper and thanked the woman profusely before ending the call. Staring at the number on the paper, I froze. I hadn't paused to think about it before, but I was about to potentially find out the identity of my birth mother. This day had been on the back burner of my mind for as long as I could remember.

Warren must have noticed the shift in my demeanor. "Are you OK?" he asked.

Slowly, I sank down onto the barstool. "This is just...*huge*."

He crossed his arms over his chest. "You don't have to do it."

Yes, I do.

I dialed Abigail's cell phone number before I could change my mind. As the line rang, I gnawed on a hangnail.

She answered on the fourth ring. "Hello?" Her voice was smooth and melodic, nothing like my own.

"Abigail, it's Sloan."

"Hello, Sloan. I've been hoping to hear from you again," she said.

My finger started bleeding. "Are you my mother?" The words were out of my mouth before I could stop them.

There was silence on her end of the line. "Perhaps this is a conversation you and I should have in person."

Her response wasn't a confirmation nor a denial.

"I know you've already left Texas," she continued, "but do you think you could return for the weekend? I'll be back in town in the morning. I would be happy to pay for your plane ticket."

Caught off guard by her proposition, my brain scrambled for a response. "I'll have to talk to Warren, but maybe. I don't know. You didn't answer my question."

"I will clear my schedule for you if you can come," she said.

My frustration was growing. "Abigail! I'm not hanging up this phone before you tell me the truth. Are you my mother?"

Silence.

"I am."

My phone slipped from my grip, bouncing off the counter before clattering onto the kitchen tile. I was paralyzed by shock.

Warren spread his hands out in front of him. "Babe, you're kind of leaving us hanging here."

Finally, I picked up my glass and finished off my whiskey with one painful gulp. "It's her."

Their jaws fell slack in unison.

"Holy shit." My father's words came out slowly. I had never heard him curse before.

Suddenly, I felt dizzy. "I might fall off my chair."

Warren crossed the room in two steps and put both of his strong hands on my shoulders to steady me. I slumped over the counter and thumped my head on the countertop. I rolled my forehead back and forth against the cool stone. "I'm losing it. I'm officially losing my mind." I watched the granite swirl in and out of focus an inch below my eyes.

His hand came to rest on my back, and I trained my attention on the warm buzz of comforting energy it transmitted. I slowly lifted my head as my nerve endings settled into place.

"This is impossible," my father stammered again. He made a few laps around the kitchen island before he turned on his heel and walked to the table. He picked up Abigail's photo again and thrust it toward me. "She has to be at least my age now!"

Warren groaned. "Dr. Jordan, something tells me she's been looking at your age in the rearview mirror for quite some time."

Everything made sense. Abigail was an Angel of Life. She had a very attractive personality. Everyone loved her. I was found at the hospital, and Abigail disappeared because angels are forbidden to raise their offspring. If I was a summoner, then Abigail was too. All this time, all the coincidences...

"She was summoning me."

Warren's eyes snapped to meet mine. "Oh my god. Do you think so?"

I held out my hands. "How else do you explain the crazy stuff that's happened lately?"

He didn't have an answer.

I took a step toward him. "Why wouldn't she tell me? I think if I were sitting across the room from my daughter, I would say something!"

He was quiet for a while. "I don't know." He shook his head. "I don't know about any of it. We need more information before we start making big assumptions."

I rubbed my hands over my face. "This is too much. I can't process this."

Dad leaned over the counter toward me and raked his fingers through his hair so hard the tendons in his hands strained with tension. "You don't think *you* can process this? How do you think I feel? You've had a chance to get used to this supernatural stuff, and I'm still trying to get my head around the news that you can see people's souls!" He sounded a bit maniacal.

He must have realized he was starting to go a little Jack-from-The-Shining on us, and he walked over and pulled me into a tight hug. "I'm sorry. I'm rattled right now. We'll figure this thing out together. What can I do for you?"

"Will you be all right here for a couple of days if I go to Texas again? She wants me to come talk to her about it in person. Or, you can come with me?" I suggested.

He shook his head. "No, sweetheart. I think I need to sit this one out. This is a lot for an old man to handle. You and Warren go. I'll be fine."

My heart was torn between desperately wanting to talk to Abigail and not wanting to leave my father alone. I also felt guilty that this revelation had come so soon after my mother's death, like she might be looking down on me and fearing I had already found her replacement.

Maybe my father heard my anxious thoughts. "This is something you need to do, Sloan. Honestly, I want to hear what this Abigail woman has to say."

I smiled and nodded my head. "OK."

Warren refilled my father's empty glass for a third time and looked over at me. "When do you want to go?"

I turned my palms up. "She said she'll be home tomorrow. Could we leave right after I get off work?"

He shrugged his shoulders. "I'll get online and look at flights tonight."

My eyes widened. "You'll come with me, won't you?"

He smiled. "You don't really think I would let you go alone, do you?"

I shook my head. "I hope not."

My dad's arm was still around my shoulders. He seemed to be leaning, ever so lightly, on me for support as he sipped his drink. He held his glass toward Warren. "Sloan, I really like this young man. You need to get your act together and marry him."

Laughing, and a little bit embarrassed, I patted his chest. "I like him too, Dad. Have you eaten today? You wouldn't let me bring you dinner."

He shook his head. "Nope." The word popped off his lips.

I patted his hand and then pried the tumbler from his grip. "No more whiskey till you've got some food in your system. Daughter's orders."

I prepared a turkey and provolone sandwich and put a bag of chips on the plate. Dad was sitting next to Warren at the counter. "Here," I said, placing the sandwich in front of him. "Eat this before you get sick."

"Buzzkill," he grumbled with a smile.

After a moment of looking around for my phone, I realized I had never picked it up off the floor. When I retrieved it, the screen was cracked. "Damn it."

Warren looked over. "Uh oh. Does it still work?"

"Yeah. I'll have to replace it soon though. It's busted pretty bad." I turned it around to show him the spider-webbed glass on the front.

He shrugged his shoulders. "You can have my phone switched to your number. I won't be needing it for a while."

I frowned. "You'll need it while you're still in the States," I said. "I'll get a new one when we get home from Texas. I have insurance on it, so it's not a big deal."

My dad picked up his sandwich and put it back down again. "I forgot you're leaving us," he said, looking at Warren. "I don't like that at all."

I kissed Dad's cheek. "I don't like it either."

I pulled up a new group text message on my phone and put in Nathan's phone number and Adrianne's. *Here's a spooky Halloween story for you: Abigail Smith is my biological MOTHER.*

Adrianne called first. "You're kidding me?" she asked without saying hello when I answered the phone.

"Nope. Dad figured it out. Get this, she used to work with my parents at the hospital in Florida," I told her. "And she hasn't aged a day. Apparently angels don't age."

She laughed. "*You* age. I'm going to have to start covering up gray in your hair soon if you don't cool it with all the intergalactic drama you seem to get yourself into."

"That's the freaking truth." I sighed. "How was physical therapy today?"

My phone beeped with an incoming call. It was Nathan, so I ignored it.

"You just found out your biological mother is an angel and you want to hear about me doing leg lifts and squats?" she asked.

"Of course I do. You're still more important."

"Physical therapy was fine, but I want to talk about you. What are you going to do?" she asked.

"I think Warren and I are going to try to fly to Texas tomorrow and meet with her. She asked me to come so we can talk in person," I said.

"The bitch dropped you off outside a hospital as a newborn. She could at least fly to you."

I laughed. "I hadn't really thought about it that way. She did offer to buy me a plane ticket."

My phone beeped again, and again it was Nathan.

I sighed. "Nathan's blowing up my phone. I'll call you later."

She laughed. "Bye, freak."

I swapped calls on my phone. "I was on the other line. You know I'll call you back," I told him without a greeting.

"You can't send a message like that and then not answer your phone!" He was shouting. "How did you figure it out?"

"I didn't. My dad did," I said. "Her name was Sarah when he knew her. They worked together at the hospital in the eighties. Isn't that the craziest thing you've ever heard?"

"It's right up there with everything else I've ever heard from you, Sloan. How is it possible she's the same person? She would have been maybe two years old when you were born," he said.

I sat down on Warren's lap at the counter. "Nathan, weren't you the one who originally asked how any of this is possible? Why are you still asking that question?"

"Good point," he said. "Are you going back down there?"

"We are going to try and go tomorrow. You wanna come with us?" I asked.

"As intriguing as it sounds, some of us have to go to work to pay the bills," he said.

"It's just for the weekend," I told him. "We'll be home in plenty of time for you to go to work on Monday."

"Three's a crowd, babe," he responded.

Warren leaned his mouth close to the microphone. "I heard that.

You're not allowed to call her *babe*, Nate."

"Hi, Warren," Nathan said. "Sloan, let me know how it goes." He raised his voice. "Maybe you can come over when you get back and tell me about it over dinner and a bottle of wine!"

"I'll bring the dessert!" Warren replied.

I rolled my eyes. "I'll talk to you later, Nathan." I laughed and disconnected the call.

The doorbell rang. I pushed myself up and crossed the room, grabbing the giant bag of candy on my way to the front door. When I pulled the door open, a small girl and her even smaller brother were dressed as an angel and a devil respectively. "Trick or treat!" they sang together, holding up their plastic pumpkin buckets.

A chill ran down my spine.

Truly, Halloween would never be the same again.

17.

FOR THE FIRST time—and probably the last time—I was out of bed and getting dressed before Warren the next morning. At four a.m. he walked into the bathroom in his boxer shorts, sleepily rubbing his eyes. I had already showered, dressed, and put on my makeup.

He squinted at me. "Did I wake up in the wrong house?"

I brushed my long hair up into a ponytail and wound an elastic band around it. "I couldn't sleep last night."

He shook his head and pointed his toothbrush at me. "I think the stress lately is taking its toll on you. Are you cracking up on me?"

I put my arms around his waist as he brushed his teeth. "We are so close to answers, Warren! Aren't you excited?"

He paused, watching me carefully in the mirror. "I'm more terrified of you right now than I am on normal mornings when you're hateful and sadistic."

I hopped up on the edge of the counter and swung my boots off the side as he finished brushing. "I think I should get a reward for beating you out of bed."

He shook his head. "It doesn't count if you never went to sleep. Besides, I don't get rewards when I sleep in with you."

I winked at him. "Yes, you do."

He laughed. "Touché."

I kicked my heels against the cabinet beneath me. "Are you going to pick me up at the office since I'm closer to the airport?"

"Yes. Are you sure it won't be a problem for you to leave at noon?" he asked.

"I'm sure. Most everyone leaves early on Fridays anyway."

He nodded. "Good. We need enough time so I can check my guns at the baggage counter."

I narrowed my eyes. "Why do you need guns this time? This is a social visit, not a man hunt."

He packed up his travel case. "Babe, you should go ahead and get used to the fact I'm going to be carrying heat no matter where we go. It's what I do."

I sighed. "It just seems like a big, unnecessary hassle."

"Was it worth it when I took Billy Stewart down in the woods?" he asked.

I crossed my arms over my chest. "That was different."

He reached in the shower and turned the water on steaming hot. "Hope for the best, but have your guns locked and loaded for the worst." He leaned over and gave me a minty kiss.

I drummed my nails on the counter and smiled as he dropped his shorts and stepped under the water.

He wiped the fog off the glass shower door and looked at me. "Should I charge admission for this?"

I bit down on my lower lip. "You'd make a killing if you did." After a moment of enjoying the show, I pushed myself up. "I'm going to go make breakfast."

He shook his head. "We didn't remember to pick up cereal at the store yesterday."

"I'll cook something then," I said.

"Oh God. Does your dad have a fire extinguisher handy?"

I laughed. "Shut up!"

The house was still and quiet downstairs. Dad was still sleeping. I started a pot of coffee, then yanked open the refrigerator and immediately regretted we hadn't made a list before going shopping the day before. I wondered what Dad was going to eat while we were gone. I pulled out the carton of eggs and carried it to the stove.

The cabinet above the cooktop was where mom kept her small, brown Rubbermaid file box full of her recipes. I was sure the box was older than I was. Inside were hundreds of index cards, most were yellowed with age. I found the breakfast tab and searched for scrambled eggs. I pulled out the entire stack of cards and couldn't find it anywhere. Frustrated, I slammed the cards back into the section.

Then I noticed another tab labeled "For Sloan." I carried the cards over to the kitchen island and sat down on a barstool. Dad's bottle of Tennessee Honey was still on the counter and significantly more empty than it had been the day before. I pushed it out of the way and pulled the index cards from the section.

My mother's handwriting, the familiar curve of her S's and the peculiar cursive style of her E's, brought tears to my eyes. I stroked the paper with my thumb like I was touching her very hand. The first card was the detailed recipe for sausage gravy with step-by-step instructions she knew I would need. The second was for made-from-scratch biscuits. The third was for her roast beef, and the next one was for her secret-recipe mashed potatoes. There was an asterisk by the ingredient—cream cheese. I dropped my face into my hand and cried.

After a moment, I felt a hand on my shoulder. I looked up at my father's sympathetic smile. He leaned down and gave me a side hug. "She wrote them down because she knew you were never coming to learn in person. She figured someday you might want to cook for someone else."

I wiped mascara on my knuckles and covered my dad's hand with my own. I sniffed and glanced up at him again. "There aren't any recipes for eggs."

He nudged me with his arm and smiled. "Come on. Your old man can handle that one without a recipe card."

He pulled a glass bowl out of the cabinet and picked up the eggs.

I snatched the carton right back from him. "I can crack them."

"OK. Go ahead and crack eight into the bowl. Warren strikes me as a man who can eat more than two," he said with a chuckle.

I smiled over at him. "I think Warren could eat the whole dozen."

"Well, then crack the whole dozen," he said as he walked to the refrigerator.

As I worked on the eggs, he carried butter and sour cream back to the stove. I shot him a quizzical glance. "Sour cream?"

He nodded. "Your mother swears a tablespoon of sour cream makes them fluffier."

When I finished cracking the last egg, he put a huge dollop of sour cream into the bowl. He handed me the salt and pepper. "Sprinkle them with just a little." After I added the seasoning, he handed me a large metal whisk. "Now, whip them around till it's mixed and frothy."

He pulled out a large frying pan and put it on the stove. He cut off a hunk of butter and dropped it in the pan.

"How much butter are you putting in there?" I asked.

He grinned and winked at me. "The more, the better."

I wagged a finger at him. "I don't think doctors are supposed to say that."

He laughed as he turned the stove up to just higher than medium heat. He tapped the temperature dial. "Don't turn it too high or you'll burn them. Wait until the butter starts to melt, then swirl it around to coat the bottom. Once it sizzles a tad, pour the eggs in and keep stirring till they're done."

Dad poured us two cups of coffee while I followed his directions. I dumped the contents of the bowl on top of the melted butter and grabbed a wooden spoon. When the eggs were solid, he turned off the stove.

"See? That wasn't so hard." He kissed my forehead. "Now put some bread in the toaster and we'll have a real, bona fide breakfast."

I turned around and Warren was leaning in the doorway to the kitchen smiling. He winked at me before coming over and pouring himself a cup of coffee. "I was prepared to call the fire department," he said over his shoulder.

"Shut your face," I said.

Dad put a jar of peach preserves on the table along with the butter. "What time does your flight land in Texas?"

"Around six," Warren answered.

I dished out three small plates full of scrambled eggs, giving Warren the largest portion. "Dad, are you sure you're going to be all right here for the weekend?"

Dad sat down at the table with his newspaper. "Sloan, I really appreciate your concern, but I am a fifty-five-year-old renowned physician. I think I can handle a weekend alone in my own home."

I flashed him a coy grin. "Two days ago I had to show you where the toilet paper is kept."

He nodded and pushed his reading glasses higher up on the bridge of his nose. "And now that I know where it is, I'm sure I'll be fine."

I kissed the top of his head and sat down next to him.

He tasted the eggs and nodded with approval. "They're perfect."

Warren swallowed a forkful. "Best eggs I've ever had," he agreed.

I laughed and launched a napkin across the table at him.

Dad's expression melted into seriousness. "Sloan, are you holding up all right? You have been hit with a lot of huge, life-changing stressors in a very, very short period of time."

I sighed and sipped my coffee. "I try not to over-think it, Dad. That's the only way I'm still functioning. If I stop long enough to consider the whirlwind that has become my life, I'm afraid I would be sucked up in it and spat out somewhere in the stratosphere."

He pointed his fork at me. "Well, be sure to find some time to relax. That much stress—good or bad—will wreak havoc on your body if you aren't careful. You might wind up making yourself very sick."

"I'll be fine, Dad," I insisted. "When I get home, life will revert to the same old same old. I'll go back to work cranking out press releases and preparing the county newsletter, and I'll be having dinner with you on Mondays. Maybe we can even tag team the cooking duty."

He smiled. "I would like that."

* * *

Instead of staying at the Hyatt on the River Walk again, we checked into a hotel closer to Abigail's neighborhood. I called her from the room once we got settled, and she answered on the first ring. "Hello?"

"Hey, it's Sloan. I wanted to let you know we're in town. We're staying at the Holiday Inn Express near your ministry."

"Wonderful." She sounded anything but wonderful herself. "How was your trip?" she asked.

I sat down on the bed. "It was uneventful, which is always good when you're on an airplane. Are you all right? You don't sound well."

"I'm fine. Just a bit of a headache from traveling," she said. "And I'm swamped trying to get a number of our girls transferred to our home in Houston. Tomorrow, however, I have blocked out the entire day for us. Would you like to come over to my house around lunch?"

An involuntary smile crept across my face. "I would love that."

"Wonderful. I'll text you my address," she said.

"Great."

"I'll see you tomorrow then?" she asked.

"Yes. See you tomorrow," I replied and disconnected the call.

Warren came out of the bathroom and stretched out on the bed next to me. "Tomorrow, huh?"

I nodded. "Yeah. She's busy today, but she's open all day tomorrow.

She wants me to come to her house. Are you going to come with me?"

He shrugged his shoulders. "I think it would be good for you to spend some time with her on your own. I'm sure you have a ton of questions."

"Well, yeah, but what are you going to do?" I asked.

"I was thinking of trying to get on the visitation list at the jail tomorrow. I'd like to go have a chat with Rex and make sure Mendez is locked up. Of course, if you really want me to stay with you, I will."

I patted his arm. "No, I'll be fine. You can drop me off at her house and do what you need to do," I said. "Why do you want to go and talk to Rex?"

He laughed. "I don't know. Morbid curiosity, maybe."

He rolled over enough to work his cell phone out of his blue jeans pocket. He searched on the Internet before dialing a phone number and pressing the phone to his ear. When his call was answered, he sat up a little. "Yeah, I'd like to find out how I can get on the visitation list to see an inmate you have. His name is Rex Parker." He waited for a few moments and then cocked his head to the side as he listened to the person on the other end of the line. "Really?" he asked with surprise. "OK. Thank you. How about a Larry Mendez? Is he still in custody?" There was another pause, and I watched his face darken. "No records?"

My stomach twisted in a knot at the thought of Mendez out on the street.

"Thanks anyway for checking." He disconnected the call and dropped the phone onto the mattress.

I pulled my knees up to my chest and peered down at him. "What is it?"

"Neither of them are in jail," he said. "Rex bonded out and they haven't had Mendez at all."

"Are you serious?" I asked. "Nathan said they arrested Mendez."

He shrugged. "He must have gotten released somehow."

"I hate the justice system."

He nodded. "I should have killed Mendez when I had the chance." He looked up, lost in thought. "I wonder what the hell happened."

I wondered the same thing.

"Well, do you want to go out and look for them tonight? I can find them for you."

He reached for my hand, then held it against his chest. "No. Your dad was right about taking it easy. We both need a break. For one evening, I want to be normal and do some normal-people shit like go to the movies and out to dinner."

I laughed. "Have we ever done anything normal?"

He shook his head. "No."

I pulled out my cell phone and searched for things to do in San Antonio. "OK, here we go," I said. "Thirty Most Awesome Things to do in San Antonio."

"That sounds promising," Warren said.

"Number one on the list is the Six Flags theme park. Too bad we didn't get here earlier," I said. "Ooo, there's the San Antonio Botanical Gardens."

He chuckled. "Next."

My eyes skimmed the list. "What about a ghost tour? I've never done that before."

His brow wrinkled in confusion. "We're both part-angel and you want to go hear ghost stories?"

I smiled as I clicked on the tour website. "I think it sounds like fun."

"We'll do whatever you want to do, babe," he said.

I leaned down over him. "I really want to go to the botanical gardens."

He rolled his eyes. "We'll do anything but that."

I lay down on my stomach beside him and propped myself up on my arm. I twirled a strand of his long dark hair around my finger. "Do you think ghosts are real?"

He thought for a second. "Two weeks ago I didn't believe in angels. So, stranger things have already happened."

"I wonder if human spirits can cross back into our world. Maybe they can walk around on Earth like angels do," I said.

He offered a sympathetic smile. "Are you thinking about your mom?"

Releasing his hair, my hand flopped onto the mattress. "I'm always thinking about my mom." The words seemed to trip some emotional wire in my brain, and before I could stop them, tears spilled out as I pressed my eyes closed.

He quickly rolled toward me and touched my arm. "I'm sorry. I didn't mean to make you cry."

Unable to hold back, I buried my face in the pillow and cried. Warren curled into me, but even his touch couldn't ease the pain that was twisting my heart into knots.

"Let it out." His voice was gentle as he rubbed my back.

When my muffled wailing subsided, I turned my face on the wet pillow to look at him. We were nose to nose. "I'm sorry," I whispered.

He tucked my hair behind my ear. "Don't apologize. God knows, if anyone needs a good cry, it's you."

My lip quivered as I nodded.

"You've been through so much. Adrianne's accident, Billy Stewart, all the shit with me and Nate, then your mom…" His hand rested against my face. "It's more than anyone should have to survive."

I covered his hand with my own.

He leaned over and kissed my forehead. "I'm here anytime you need fall apart."

I squeezed his fingers. "Why are you so good to me?"

"Because you're everything to me. I don't have a choice in the matter."

I closed my eyes again. "Talk about something else before I start crying again." I managed a depressing chuckle.

He sat up on his elbow, and I rolled onto my side to look at him.

After a moment, he spoke. "You should start making a list of questions to ask Abigail tomorrow."

I sniffed and dried my eyes on the back of my hand. "That's not a bad idea. Maybe we could do it over dinner."

He looked at his watch. "What time is the tour?"

"Ten. Are we even going to have time to eat?"

He grimaced. "Not if we don't leave right now."

I turned my palm over. "Are you ready to go?"

He thought for a second, then smiled and shook his head. "Absolutely not."

"No?"

He leaned over me. "I haven't had you to myself in two weeks. We can be a little late." His eyes were twinkling with mischief as he untucked my t-shirt.

* * *

We caught up just in time with the ghost tour group behind the Alamo. There was one family with two small children, two other couples about our age, and a group of teenage girls who immediately began whispering and giggling when we approached. I looked up at the object of their attention and admired him as well.

Warren noticed me staring. "What?"

"You haven't shaved in a while," I said.

He rubbed his chin. "I'm enjoying the option of not shaving while I can," he said. "Do you hate it?"

"Are you kidding?" I shook my head. "It looks so hot on you, I'm thinking about not shaving myself."

His face melted into a frown. "Let's not get carried away."

I laughed and playfully backhanded his arm. He pulled me against him and pressed a kiss against my temple.

A tall man in his early forties approached our group. He had a thin black beard and thick black eyebrows. He was dressed in character, wearing a top-hat, black pants, a shiny red vest, and a Western necktie.

Warren looked down at me and frowned. "What the hell have you dragged us into?"

The man at the front of the group jumped up on top of a concrete planter that was built into the sidewalk. He cleared his throat, and a hush fell over our group. "Good evening, ladies and gentlemen. My name is Patrick Henry Jameson, and I invite you to walk with me tonight through a history of violent death and mass murder."

I leaned into Warren and lowered my voice. "Just another night in the office then."

I felt his body shake with laughter.

Patrick Henry continued his spiel. "Tonight, I implore you to stay close as we make our journey back in time, for we will, I guarantee you, brush elbows with the dead and come face to face with troubled spirits!"

"We paid forty bucks for this?" Warren asked.

I nudged him in the ribs with my elbow. "Shush."

Patrick Henry was making grand gestures toward the Alamo behind us. "As many as a thousand souls were lost right here on the ground where you stand." His voice dropped to a dramatically low octave as he swept through our small crowd. "Many of the decimated remains are still buried under your feet."

My eyes shot up at Warren. "True?"

"True," he said. "I could have told you that for free."

"And that doesn't creep you out, even a little bit?"

He shrugged. "I told you. You get used to it."

A chill ran down my spine and I shivered. "I don't think I could. Time really doesn't affect it? Like, can you feel prehistoric remains underground?"

"I don't know that I would go that far. Bodies disintegrate over time and, after a lot of time, it diminishes what I feel." He grinned down at me. "Whole bodies are much easier to find."

I shook my head. "You're such a freak."

He rolled his eyes with a grin. "Hi, Kettle. This is Pot. You're black."

I giggled and tugged on his arm. "Oh, shut up."

The rest of the tour was even less interesting than the Alamo. Warren was able to debunk most of the guy's claims, but he only told me. Patrick Henry said a woman was buried in the wall of a hotel. That wasn't true. He also said the body of an actress was buried under the floor of a theater. That wasn't true either.

Finally, I looked up at Warren. "Searching for Rex Parker would have been more fascinating than this."

"Wanna head to the car? Maybe stop somewhere for a drink?" he asked.

"Please," I begged.

We abandoned our group and returned to the Alamo. When we crossed into the square, an odd movement in the crowd caught my attention. Rex Parker had seen us and was running in the opposite direction down the street.

I released Warren's hand and took a step back, preparing for him to break into a sprint, but he didn't. I was puzzled. "You're not going after him?"

He shook his head and watched Rex dart down an alleyway. "I'll hunt him down tomorrow. Tonight I'm spending with you."

18.

ABIGAIL LIVED IN a nice neighborhood near the ministry where she worked. She had a beautiful two-story brick house with a two-car garage and elaborate stonework around the front entryway. The lot was professionally landscaped and water from the sprinkler system arched across the lawn. The house seemed big for just one person, but then it occurred to me that I didn't know if she lived alone or not. She could have an entire family inside that I knew nothing about.

"You look nervous." Warren reached over and gently squeezed the back of my neck as we sat in the car at the curb in front of her house.

I realized I was wringing my hands in my lap. I stretched out my tingly fingers which felt stiff with tension. I blew out a heavy sigh. "I guess I am. What if she doesn't like me?"

He laughed. "When has anyone in your life not liked you?"

"Shannon doesn't like me," I reminded him.

"I believe she likes you more than you think she does," he said. "Sloan, Abigail is going to love you. You're going to get the answers you have looked for your entire life. This is a good thing."

I nodded. "I know. OK, I'm ready."

We got out of the car and walked up the path to the front door. I rang the bell and a moment later, Abigail opened it.

"You made it!" she cheered as she stepped out to give me a hug.

When the initial shock from her embrace subsided, her arms felt awkward around me, like I was hugging a radioactive stranger in the supermarket. She pulled away and grasped my hands. "It's true. I can't believe this moment is here." She looked close to tears as she studied my face for a moment so long it creeped me out a bit.

I pulled my hands away.

She took a deep breath and let out a sing-song sigh as she stepped to the side. "Well, come on in."

I looked at Warren.

He brushed a loose strand of hair from my cheek. "You good?"

I nodded. "Yeah. You can go."

Abigail's eyes widened. "You're not staying?"

He shook his head. "No, ma'am. I think you two should have some girl time." He leaned over and kissed my lips. "Call me when you're about ready to go and I'll come pick you up."

"I love you," I said.

He squeezed my hand. "I love you too." He lowered his voice and whispered in my ear. "Relax."

When he turned to leave, I followed Abigail inside. The inside of the house was beautiful and very tastefully decorated in hues of blue and brown. She had the same formal dining table that I did, which made me laugh. I wondered if she didn't use hers either. There was a large, brown leather sectional sofa in her huge living room that faced a sixty inch television screen on the wall. The kitchen, with tall white cabinets and marble countertops, overlooked the living area.

I ran my hand over the soft leather of the sofa. "Your house is amazing."

"Thank you. I'm leasing it. I don't tend to stay in one place long enough to justify buying anything. I'm a bit of a vagabond." She walked into the kitchen. "Have you eaten lunch?"

I shook my head. "No, ma'am."

She waved her hand toward me and smiled. "You don't have to be formal. We're family."

Awkward.

I watched her move around the kitchen. She had long dark hair, the same as mine. Her skin tone was similar as well. We had the same thin frame, but I definitely hadn't inherited her boobs. They were ginormous.

"I made enough for your boyfriend. I hope he didn't feel like he would be imposing here. The invitation was certainly for both of you." She carried two green plates to the dinette table in the kitchen.

I walked to the table and placed my purse on the floor. "He had some things he wanted to do today, and he thought it would be best for us to spend some time alone."

She nodded. "Well, that was very thoughtful of him. We do have a lot to catch up on." She motioned to the table. "Shall we?"

I pulled out a chair and sat down. "Thank you. I know you're really busy, so I appreciate you taking the time to see me."

Abigail laughed and waved her hand in my direction. "Are you joking? I've been dreaming of this day for twenty-seven years."

I had too, but the fruition of the dream lacked the fireworks I'd always expected.

"I hope deli turkey is all right," she said. "I also have wine if you would like some."

I nodded to the full water glass to the right of my sandwich and kettle-cooked chips. "Water is fine."

She sat down across from me and stared for a moment. Her eyes were brown, but outside of that, I didn't see much semblance in our faces.

She smiled. "You're very beautiful, Sloan."

"Thank you," I said again.

"Have you enjoyed your time here in Texas?" she asked.

"We just got in yesterday. Last night we went on a ghost tour through the city, but it was pretty lame. My boyfriend has the ability to find dead bodies, so he kinda squelched the mystery of it all," I said.

She laughed. "I'm sure he did."

"Are ghosts real?" I asked, thinking of my mother.

She shook her head. "No. Human spirits do not come back across the spirit line." She must have noticed when my face fell. "Why do you ask?"

"My mother died last week," I said. "The day after I met you."

Abigail put her hands down on the table. "Oh, I am terribly sorry to hear that. Was she ill?"

I stared at my plate. "Not when I left to come here, but she got really sick while I was gone. The doctors found a brain tumor, and it was growing out of control. She was dead before I got home."

She reached over and took my hand. "I'm terribly sorry."

"I feel like it was my fault. That maybe if I hadn't left, she wouldn't have gotten so bad so quickly," I admitted.

"It's true you probably kept the cancer at bay. You would have inherited life and health promoting gifts from me. However, that doesn't mean it's your fault. Cancer destroyed her body. Not you." She smiled and squeezed my hand.

I sighed and crunched on a potato chip, still unconvinced of my responsibility in the matter. I blinked back tears. "I'm sorry. Can we talk about something else?"

She picked up her sandwich. "Of course we can. I'm sure you have a ton of questions for me. Where would you like to begin?"

I thought about it for a moment. There were so many questions floating around in my mind, and I was having trouble picking a starting point. Warren was right. I should have made a list. Finally, I blurted out the question that had been bugging me the most. "Did you know you were my mother when I was here the last time?"

She swallowed the bite in her mouth and slowly nodded her head. "Yes."

My jaw went slack. "Why didn't you tell me?"

She shook her head. "It wasn't the right time. You wouldn't have believed it."

With that, I really couldn't argue.

I inhaled a quick breath. "Did you summon me here?"

Her face was unreadable. "I planted the seed long ago for you to find me, but I didn't directly summon you here."

"I don't understand."

Abigail was thoughtful for a moment. "I have much more control over my summoning power than you do. I can use it in different ways. So yes, I summoned you many years ago, but in a way that was very gradual and natural."

I looked up at the ceiling. *Nothing about any of this is natural.*

She continued talking. "I created you for a purpose, Sloan. And as much as I hated having to leave you as a child, I knew someday the pieces would fall into place for you to find me again. In the meantime, I knew you would be well loved by whoever took you in. You would have inherited that from me as well. It's part of who we are."

"So, people liking me is part of this gift or whatever?" I asked. "I've always wondered about that."

She nodded. "People are attracted to the life power inside you. It can be a blessing and a curse at times."

I sighed. "That's the truth." I thought of Nathan. His attraction to me was cosmic coercion, after all.

"Would you like to know more about your gifts?" she asked.

My eyes widened. "Absolutely."

She straightened in her chair. "First, you must understand your powers are not as strong as mine because you are also human."

"Like with genetics, I only inherited part of your gifts?" I asked.

She shook her head. "Oh no. You inherited all of my gifts. Your humanity, though, limits what you can do with them."

"OK. So what can you do?" I asked.

She leaned toward me. "I am an Angel of Life. All angels of the second choir—"

I raised my hand. "Choir?" In my head, I envisioned the singing variety.

"It's a division of angels. There are seven different choirs, all with different jobs, if you will," she clarified.

I nodded.

"All angels of the second choir have the power to influence the human spirit. The human spirit—or what you call a soul—is like the powerhouse of the human body. Without the spirit, the body doesn't function."

The vision of my mother's body lying on the hospital bed came to mind. "The body is just a shell."

"Correct," she said. "In addition to being able to summon and heal, I can also prolong the lives of humans past their normal life expectancy."

"Is that why your body hasn't aged?" I asked.

She shook her head. "Aging happens as cell death begins to outpace cell reproduction. My body was created with a similar genetic makeup to yours, but my cells are programmed to continually reproduce. Therefore, I do not age."

I examined her face. "How old are you?"

A small smile played across her lips. "I'm twenty-nine and holding." She pointed to my empty glass. "Would you like some more water?"

I hadn't even realized that I had finished all of it. "Please."

She picked up the glass and walked to the refrigerator.

I leaned on my elbow. "So, the summoning thing…How does it work, exactly?"

She thought for a moment. "Close your eyes."

I hesitated.

Abigail laughed and put my water down in front of me. "Trust me."

Obediently, I closed my eyes.

"Picture that handsome boyfriend of yours," she said, settling in her seat.

I smiled. "That's easy."

"Now, imagine there is a string connecting you to him."

My eyebrow peaked with skepticism. "OK."

"Pull the string."

I couldn't help it—I laughed. My eyes popped open. "You want me to pull Warren's string?"

Frowning, she rolled her eyes and pointed at me. "This is exactly why you have a hard time controlling your gift."

I crossed my arms over my chest. "And you can do this at will?"

She nodded. "Absolutely. If I wanted your boyfriend to return right now, all I would have to do is call out to him, and he would be here as quickly as possible. I could summon him here from across the world if I so desired."

I shook my head. "My gift doesn't work that well. It's getting stronger, but most of the time it still feels a lot like coincidence."

She smiled. "It's certainly not coincidence."

"Warren thinks I'm getting better at using my power because I'm exercising it more. Is that true?"

"Yes, and just your exposure to him strengthens your ability to access your gifts. It's also a matter of discipline, and I can teach you."

That was an interesting prospect, but I doubted we would get to it over lunch. "Can you just summon humans?" I asked. "Or can you summon angels too?"

She shook her head. "Only human spirits."

I picked at a stray sliver of turkey. "Have you created anyone else? Do I have any brothers or sisters?"

She settled back in her seat. "No. We do not have the ability to create more than one offspring."

That settled the debate over whether or not Warren and I were related.

I sipped my water. "What about my father? Who is he?"

Abigail thought for a moment and closed her eyes like she was trying to remember. I found it offensive that she had to think about it, but I didn't say so. Her eyes fluttered beneath her eyelids. Finally, she looked at me. "He was a remarkable man. One of the most intelligent and resourceful humans I've ever encountered. I chose him because I wanted you to have the best genetic makeup possible from your human line."

Anticipation was compounding inside me by the second. "Who was he?"

She pressed her lips together and searched my face carefully. After a moment, she shook her head. "I don't believe you're ready to know."

I folded my arms across my chest and sat back hard in my seat. "Excuse me?"

She folded her hands in front of her. "Someday I'll tell you, perhaps. But not today."

My jaw went slack. "You're kidding, right?"

Her expression didn't change. "Sloan, there are many things about my world you can't comprehend. This is one of them."

I tossed my hands up in the air. "Does he know about me?"

She shook her head. "No. I doubt it would even be possible for him to remember the act of your conception."

Surely, I misheard her. "What?"

"I have full control over my summoning powers, Sloan. When I summon someone for a purpose, they often don't remember it."

"You raped him?"

She laughed and squeezed my arms from across the table. "Stop being so dramatic. It wasn't rape."

"How do you possibly arrive at that conclusion?" I started counting on my fingers. "You coerced him against his will, and he has no memory of it. Here in America, that's a felony!"

"I apologize if you're offended. You must understand, it's simply different in our world. Copulation is a means to an end, not an act of love." She forced a smile. "Let's change the subject. Tell me about your boyfriend."

It was hard to change the subject. I was confused and pissed off. Her rationalization of her actions baffled me. She could have just as casually been telling me why she chose turkey for our lunch.

I stared at her for a moment before deciding to let the issue of my birth father rest till later. "What do you want to know about Warren?"

She shrugged. "How did you meet? How long have you been together?"

"He saw me on the news rescuing a little girl out of a drug house.

He couldn't see my soul, so he came to Asheville to find me and figure out why. It was only a couple of months ago," I said.

She leaned forward on her elbow. "I wish you knew how unique your relationship is with him." She took a sip of water. "Are the two of you pretty serious, then?"

"Yeah. Certainly as serious as two people can become in such a short amount of time. He moved in with me a few weeks ago when his job ended out on the coast," I told her.

"What does he do?" she asked.

"He was a mercenary, and he's a sniper for the Marines," I said. "He's being deployed next week."

Abigail laughed and covered her mouth with a napkin. "Being an Angel of Death and being a sniper is a little heavy-handed, isn't it?"

My face broke a smile. "I think the same thing all the time."

"Where are they sending him?" she asked.

I shrugged my shoulders and pushed my half-eaten sandwich away from me. "They haven't told him yet."

"Well, I hope it works out for the best." With a long fingernail, she was drawing circles around the rim of her glass. "You should know, Sloan, there could be serious repercussions if you are committed to another Seramorta."

I frowned. "Another angel hinted at the same thing recently."

She stopped drawing circles. "Another angel?" Her eyes were wide and questioning.

"When my mother died, I met an angel named Samael. He warned me and Warren that we should be very careful," I said.

"Samael?" She sat forward on her chair. "Really? He doesn't come to this side of the spirit line very often."

"That reminds me, he didn't know who you were. What is your real name?" I asked.

She stared at me for a moment. Then, she relaxed. "My name is Kasyade."

"Kahh-See-Ahh-Day," I repeated. "That's very pretty."

"It means The Siren," she said.

My brow lifted. "Like the sirens in Greek mythology?"

She smiled. "Exactly." She leaned forward and lowered her voice. "Would you like to know the name I gave you?"

My eyes widened. "I have a different name?"

She nodded. "Of course."

I straightened in my seat. "Yeah, I guess."

"Praea," she answered.

The name fell flat. "Pray-yah," I echoed slowly.

She leaned close as if to tell me a great secret. "In my language, it means a gift."

"A gift? Really?"

"That's what you are, Sloan."

I turned my palms up in question. "What's the big deal about me and Warren? Why is everyone so fascinated by us being together?"

She hesitated for a moment. "Because there are billions of people on this planet and very few Seramorta. It's improbable that two of you would find each other in the time of a human lifespan. It's only ever happened a couple of times in history. Neither of those pairings combined the powers of life and death."

I giggled. "We'll be a power couple like Brad and Angelina."

Her eyes were serious, and when she gripped my arm, my skin began to crawl. "This no laughing matter, Praea."

I recoiled from her grasp, suddenly feeling hot and dizzy. "I'm sorry. Can I use your restroom?"

She nodded, still watching me carefully. "Certainly. I need to check in at the office anyway. The bathroom is down the hall, the third door on the left. Take all the time you need."

Forcing a smile, I stood up. "Thank you."

I picked up my purse and carried it down the hallway on the other side of the living room to the bathroom. The bathroom was painted a deep red, and it had elaborate golden fixtures. It felt like the walls were closing in as I braced myself against the sink. I pulled my cell phone out of my pocket and brought up a text message to Warren. *I think I'm ready to go. I know I'm cutting this terribly short, but it's too much for me, and I have a bad feeling I can't shake. Starting to feel sick.*

A moment later, my phone beeped with a response. *Be there in ten. Are you OK?*

Yes. Don't make a big deal out of it when you get here, I replied.

When I walked out of the bathroom, my feet froze outside the door. Something unseen was pulling at my attention, but I couldn't place what it was. A feeling of foreboding was growing inside my chest like a cancer running rampant. Then I heard it. Not exactly an audible voice, but a clear message from somewhere. *Go to the office.* It was as plain as I could hear Abigail on the phone in the kitchen.

Across from the bathroom was a home office. The room was dark, save for a small amount of light coming through the cracks in the blinds over the window. There was a large cherry desk, a desktop PC, and piles of neatly stacked paperwork. There were no pictures on the wall. It was as impersonal as a broom closet. I tiptoed across the carpet toward the desk, and right on top was a lone sheet of paper. Quietly, I turned it around so I could read it.

It was an invoice from The Law Offices of T.R. Shultz for the criminal representation of...Larry Mendez.

Oh hell.

My mind scrambled. Why would Abigail have an invoice for Larry Mendez's attorney? He had been linked with a human trafficking operation, and she had the largest human trafficking rescue mission in Texas. Nausea began to churn through my stomach. I backed out of the office as quietly as possible. Once I was safely in the hallway with my snooping undetected, I leaned against the wall and struggled to slow my rapid breathing.

My phone rang, causing me to jump. It was Warren. "Hey," I answered.

"Tell her the hotel found my guns and they need you to come and handle it because the room is booked in your name," he said. "My ETA is six minutes."

My shoulders relaxed. "You're brilliant. Hurry."

The line went dead in my hand.

Sucking in a brave, deep breath, I returned to the kitchen. Abigail was talking to someone about airfare when I returned. She held up her index finger indicating she was almost finished. When she ended the call, she let out a frustrated huff.

"Is everything all right?" I asked.

She rolled her eyes. "It's so hard to find good help, Sloan." She gestured toward me. "Perhaps now that we've found each other, someday you'll be interested in coming to work with me. I need someone I can trust to get things done right."

I laughed uneasily. "I've never been very good at keeping up with paperwork."

"I'll bet you would be better than the minions I have working for me now," she said.

I held up my phone before tucking it into my purse. "I just got some bad news. I'm going to have to run to the hotel. Warren insisted on bringing half of his arsenal with us on the trip, and the hotel cleaning staff apparently found it. They need me to come handle it because the room is in my name," I explained. "Could we maybe continue this over dinner tonight?"

She deflated. "Oh, I hate to hear that. Yes, dinner would be wonderful. There's a great Italian place not too far from here that would be perfect. Perhaps Warren could join us, and I can get to know him better."

I forced a smile. "That would be great." I already knew I wasn't going to make it to dinner. In that moment, I hoped to never see Abigail—Kasyade—ever again.

My heart fluttered with relief when the doorbell rang. I slung my purse over my shoulder. "That must be Warren," I said as we walked to the front door together.

She pulled the door open, and he was standing there with his hands stuffed in his pockets. I could have cried at the sight of him.

He rolled his eyes. "I'm really sorry I screwed up girls' day."

Abigail waved off the apology. "Things happen." She smiled brightly. "Sloan and I were talking about all of us getting together for dinner this evening."

He nodded. "Sounds good to me." His eyes locked on mine. "You ready?"

"Yes." I turned toward Abigail, and she pulled me in for a tight hug. I felt like I might barf over her shoulder.

"I'll call you about dinner plans. It was really wonderful spending some time with you today, even if it was cut short," she said.

When she released me, I stepped out of her personal space and into Warren's. "Me too. I'll call you later," I lied.

She watched us from the door as we walked to the car. I turned and waved when Warren opened the passenger side door for me. She waved back and stared at us from the doorway.

When he got in the car and started the engine, I whipped my eyes toward him. "Drive."

He pulled away from the curb as I buckled my seatbelt. "What happened?"

I turned to face him in the seat. "I have a really, really bad feeling about this. First, her name isn't Rachel or Sarah or Abigail. It's Kasyade. And guess what!"

He turned out of her neighborhood onto the main street. "What?"

"My real name is Praea."

He raised an eyebrow and shook his head. "Your real name is Sloan."

I had no desire to get philosophic about my name. "From the moment I walked into the house, I had a weird feeling. The conversation was all right until I asked about my biological father. She refused to tell me who he is."

He cut his eyes over at me. "Are you serious?"

I leaned toward him. "Oh yeah. She said I'm not *ready* to know, whatever that's supposed to mean. She said she 'chose' him for the purpose of getting pregnant, and he probably wouldn't even remember it. She talked about it like she was just visiting a sperm bank."

"Is that why you wanted to leave?" he asked.

I shook my head. "I wish. That's just the beginning of when things started to go downhill!"

He blew out a deep sigh.

"She asked some questions about me and you, and then she grabbed me and said how serious it is that we're together. It was the way she said it, like the world was going to end or something. I don't know. That's when I started to feel sick."

"Well, what do you want to do?" he asked.

I held my hands up and shook them furiously near his head. "Wait, I'm not done!"

"There's more?" he asked in disbelief.

"At that point in the conversation, I was ready to go. I snuck off to the bathroom and sent you the message to come and get me. Then, when I left the bathroom, I heard this voice in my head telling me to go into her office, so I did."

"You heard a voice?" he asked. "Whose voice?"

I shrugged. "I have no idea, but I know I did. Guess what I found in her office."

He looked at me with a raised eyebrow.

"An invoice from a criminal attorney for Larry Mendez," I said.

The car swerved, kicking up gravel from the shoulder of the highway. He brought the car to a screeching halt on the side of the road. "What?" he shouted.

"I saw it with my own eyes, Warren. She's the reason Mendez was released. She paid for his defense," I said. "That makes no sense!"

He stared out the window, lost in thought. "It only makes sense if he's working for her."

"What?" I asked.

He turned toward me. "Think about it. If Nate and I hadn't been there that day, Rex and the other guy would have gotten away. They were prepared to get out of that building and disappear. They had to have known the cops were coming to be able to slip out of there the way they did."

I squeezed my forehead. "Why hire criminals to sell girls to sex rings just to rescue them?" I asked. "If it's about money and getting donations, I don't think she has to create a human trafficking problem. There's already plenty of it."

His eyes widened. "What if she's not rescuing them at all? What if she's only shutting down her competition and selling them herself?"

My nausea returned. "You think she's monopolizing the industry?"

He nodded. "You're talking about a lot of girls with no families and no one who would miss them. Most of them don't even speak English, I would guess."

I covered my mouth as I began to connect the dots. "And she's not funded by the government, so she wouldn't be subject to their watchful eye. No one is checking up on her. She can send those girls right back out and claim they were released from the program because no one would follow up."

He gripped the steering wheel so tight his knuckles went white. "She releases some success stories, pulls in donations, and then sends these girls only God knows where." He looked over at me. "My guess is she bailed Rex Parker and his buddy out of jail too."

I gasped. "She's a monster."

The blood drained from Warren's face. "Do you remember what that old priest told us?"

Father John floated to my memory. I quoted his haunting words verbatim. "*If you are on a quest seeking angels, take great care. Even Satan himself masquerades as an angel of the light.*"

19.

MY FINGERS DIALED Nathan's phone so furiously the screen cracked even more, and a piece came off in my hand. The touchscreen was useless after that. I held out my hand toward Warren. "I need your phone to call Nathan. Mine is officially broken." I dropped the phone into the cubby between the front seats.

He adjusted in his seat and pulled his phone from his pocket. I found Nathan's number in his contact list and hit dial.

Nathan answered on the third ring. "Aww, it's my favorite Prince of Darkness. What's up?"

I rolled my eyes. "It's Sloan."

"Oh, hey," he said.

"I need your help."

"Sure. What's going on?"

"We're pretty sure Abigail is a fraud."

"She's not an angel?" He sounded confused.

"Oh, no. She is an angel. Actually, I'm starting to think she's a demon, if those are real too. You need to convince the FBI to investigate her. Larry Mendez is not in jail, and I found an invoice in her home office from his attorney."

"What?"

"You heard me." I gripped the phone tighter. "Nathan, we think she's using her ministry to sell those girls herself."

"Shit, seriously?" he asked.

"Seriously," I said.

His tongue was clicking on the other end of the line. "I'm going to need some kind of evidence to pursue this. Did you get a copy of that invoice?"

"No, of course not."

"Sloan, I can't go to the FBI with a hunch from *my friends the angels*."

I looked at Warren. "He needs evidence."

"I'll bring Rex to him," he said.

I spoke into the phone. "Rex Parker was bonded out of jail, probably by Abigail. Warren is going to bring him to you."

He was quiet for a moment. "If Rex is out on bond, he can't leave the state. I'll come to you," he said. "Let me see if I can get on a flight today. I'll call you when I've got something."

"Thanks, Nathan."

"I'll be in touch," he said and disconnected the line.

I looked at Warren. "What do we do now?"

He pointed to the road ahead. "I need you to find Rex Parker."

We caught up with Rex an hour later at a liquor store not far from the home of Larry Mendez. He took off running again when he saw Warren angling out of the rental car, but this time Warren didn't allow him to get away. Several people stopped and stared as Warren dragged him, again by the hair of his head, to our car. Rex wasn't a tiny guy, but you would have thought he was, judging by the ease with which Warren slung him around. Thankfully, we weren't in the type of neighborhood that would call the cops for a thug.

Warren opened the back door and tossed Rex in. "Babe, I'm going to need you to drive," he said.

I got out and ran around to the driver's side. Warren climbed in the back with Rex and pulled his gun out of his side holster.

Rex Parker looked like he had been run over by life a few times. His face was badly scarred from acne, and his nose looked like it had been broken more than once. A couple of cuts, one across his cheekbone and the other across his forehead, were still healing from the beating Warren had given him the week before.

"What the hell 'you want with me?" Rex shouted. He was hopelessly trying to open the child-locked back door. "This ain't cool."

I looked over my shoulder at Warren. "Where are we going?"

"Let's go to the hotel," he said.

I nodded and pulled out of the parking lot onto the highway.

"Who are you working for?" Warren demanded.

"Man, I'm not tellin' you shit. Why don't you tell me who *you're* workin' for? Why you keep poppin' up and beatin' the hell outta me?" Rex asked.

"Because you're still a no good piece of shit," Warren said. "Who are you working for?"

"I don't work for nobody." Rex spat at him.

Warren lowered his voice to a menacing octave. "Do you remember what happened to Travis? Do you really think it's wise to lie to me?"

"What the hell are you, man?" Rex asked, no longer able to hide his panic.

"Who are you working for?" Warren roared, making even me jump.

I swerved the car a little.

Like a frightened puppy being backed into a corner, Rex scrambled as far away from Warren as he could in the close confines of the back seat. "Shit man, calm down," Rex said, his voice trembling. "I work for that chick Abigail Smith."

"What do you do for her?" Warren asked.

"I'm a delivery guy," he said. "I'm her freakin' errand boy."

"Delivering little girls?" Warren asked.

Rex held his hands in front of his face. "And some older ones, man. Calm down!"

"She bonded you out of jail?" Warren asked.

He nodded. "Yeah, I'm supposed to be drivin' the van to Chicago tonight. She's gonna have me killed if I ain't there."

"Trust me. You shouldn't be worried about *her* killing you," Warren hissed. "Who are you taking to Chicago?"

"A few of the girls she's got ready to go," he answered. "All I do is pick 'em up and drop 'em off."

"So, she picks these girls up here in San Antonio and sends them to Chicago?" Warren asked.

"She gets 'em here and in Houston. Then she sends 'em to Chicago, LA, and New York," he said. "That's all I know, I swear. Warren, man, please let me go. We used to be like brothers!"

I could hear Rex's gold jewelry rattling behind me as he quivered with fear.

Warren laughed. "Brothers? I don't think so. And you're not going anywhere except on a little trip with us to talk to one of our friends."

"You're never gonna bust her. The cops around here think she shits rainbows," Rex said. "You're wastin' your time."

"We'll see about that," Warren said. "Sloan, when did you say our friend will be here?"

I turned my head to speak over my shoulder. "His flight gets in at 7:30. I told him I'd pick him up at the airport." I turned onto the interstate.

My cell phone rang. It was Abigail, but I couldn't answer it with the broken screen even if I had wanted to. And I didn't want to.

"Parker, you've got the next three hours to decide how this is going to go down," Warren said. "You either help us bring down your boss, or I won't be as merciful to you as I was to Travis in that alleyway. Do we understand each other?"

I glanced in the rearview mirror.

"She's gonna kill me," Rex said. I thought he might burst into tears. Warren shook his head and glared at him. "Not if I kill you first."

* * *

At 7:43 p.m., I rolled to a stop at the curb where Nathan was waiting outside the airport. I honked the horn, and he waved to me.

He opened the back door and tossed the backpack he was carrying onto the seat. He paused for a moment with his hand on the doorframe. "Is that blood?"

"Probably."

Groaning, he slammed the door. "Do I want to know?" he asked as he got in the passenger's seat.

"Nope."

He looked over, his gray eyes genuinely baffled. "You must be terrified to wake up every day. Just hanging out with you stresses the hell out of me."

I laughed. "It's getting that way. How was your flight?"

He pulled the seatbelt across his chest. "Expensive."

I cringed. "How much?"

"$1,498. The only seats left were first class."

"I'll pay you back." I did the math in my head. "By February."

He laughed.

"It's a good thing you find that funny because I was being serious."

He winked at me. "I know where you live."

I glanced up at the patch on his hat. It had a picture of a missile and the letter *F*. I shook my head and pointed at it. "I don't get it."

"F-Bomb."

I laughed and pulled away from the curb.

He sat back in his seat. "So, where is this guy?"

"Tied to a chair in our hotel room."

He turned his shoulders toward me. "You know that's illegal, right?"

I shrugged. "You know Warren doesn't care, right?"

"Well, if Warren goes to prison, I guess he doesn't have to worry about getting deployed."

My bottom lip poked out, but Nathan didn't notice.

"Don't use my name around this guy we're questioning. I don't want any of this shit blowing back on me and ruining my career," he said.

I shook my head. "We won't let it fall on you. Speaking of careers, what did you ever decide about the FBI?"

He shifted in his seat. "I turned them down."

"Really?"

He nodded. "Yeah, I told them I want to stay in Asheville because you're way more interesting than anything that could ever happen anywhere else." He laughed and stretched his arm across the back of my seat.

Sadly, he was probably right.

"I'll bet Shannon was excited you didn't take it."

He looked ahead down the road. "I broke it off with Shannon when we got home. You were right. I was using her and it wasn't fair."

My head snapped back in surprise. "Wow. That's huge. How did she take it?"

He laughed. "How do you think?"

I smiled over at him. "Well, I'm excited you're sticking around, even if I don't understand why you turned down the FBI."

"I'm glad I'm staying too. Although, you and I both know how much less complicated things would be if I left town."

My heart dropped a few inches. "Then why did you decide to stay? It would make life a lot less complicated for you too."

The corners of his mouth twitched. "You wouldn't believe me if I told you."

My eyes widened, and I looked over at him. "Don't tell me Warren asked you to stay."

He laughed. "OK, I won't tell you."

"What? Are you serious? Does he think I need a babysitter?"

"He's really worried about leaving you, with all that's going on." He looked out his window. "Hell, even I'm worried about him leaving."

I swallowed the lump in my throat. Warren always seemed to be a little more clued in on the happenings around us than I was. Perhaps it was because he'd always been an outsider, observing the world from a distance. Sure, Samael's warning had rattled me a bit, but if Warren was concerned enough to leave me in the care of Nathan McNamara, that was frightening on a whole different level.

"Personally, I don't know how you've not been locked up in the looney bin yet," Nathan was saying when I realized he was still talking. "Tell me the truth. Are you doing OK? Especially about your mom and all."

My hands twisted around the steering wheel. "I can't even think about it. In a way, I'm actually thankful for the drama in my life right now because I'm afraid if I slow down long enough to really process Mom being gone..." Tears threatened to spill.

He squeezed my shoulder. "I wish I could help."

I forced a smile. "Thanks." I needed to change the subject. There was no time for me to have a meltdown. "Warren must be really worried if he's entrusting me to you."

He nodded in agreement. "I definitely think this defines absolute desperation."

I pointed a finger at him. "I still hold you personally responsible for all this. My life was almost normal before you landed me on television. I distinctly remember telling you I wanted to stay out of it."

He looked out the window and took a deep breath. Surprisingly, his voice came out serious and somber. "I actually feel really bad about it, Sloan. Capturing Billy Stewart was huge, and we probably saved a lot more lives, but you're right. I got this huge boulder rolling, and now it seems like it's rolling right over you." He turned his eyes toward me. "I'm very sorry."

Suddenly, I felt bad for teasing him. "You had no way of knowing. Neither of us did. I just have to keep focusing on the good things like Kayleigh Neeland and the women we probably saved. We'll save a lot more when we stop Abigail."

"Can you even stop an angel?" he asked.

"We've got to try," I said. "This sex trafficking thing is a whole lot bigger than just the state of Texas. Warren's guy says she's moving the girls to Los Angeles, Chicago, and New York."

"No shit?" he asked.

I shook my head.

He started laughing. "Now, hopefully I can figure out a legal way to bring her down."

I shrugged. "Legal, schmegal."

He rolled his eyes. "You're starting to sound like Warren."

I laughed. "I guess I am."

"Does he really have this Rex guy tied to a chair?"

I shot him a knowing glare.

He sighed and shook his head. "Someday I'm going to be able to teach a training class on manipulating evidence and looking the other way."

When we got to the hotel room, I used my key and opened the door. Inside, Warren was stretched out on the bed watching football. Rex was facing the wall in the corner, his hands tied to the chair with strips of Warren's white t-shirt. The sight was pretty comical. Nathan shook his head and dropped his bag on the floor.

Warren clicked off the television and stood up to shake Nathan's hand. "Thanks for coming, man."

"I can't let you guys have all the fun without me." Nathan nodded to the corner. "So, you found him."

Warren nodded. "Let's just say I made a citizen's arrest."

Nathan sighed. "You make my job and my life very complicated," he said. "Is he ready to talk?"

"Oh, he'll talk, sing, tell you a joke...whatever you want him to do. Isn't that right, Rex?" Warren called over his shoulder.

The back of Rex's head nodded.

Nathan sat down at the table, and Warren spun Rex's chair around to face us. His eyes were wide with terror, and he had a tube sock shoved in his mouth. Nathan looked him over. "Well, at least he's not bloody this time."

Warren reached over and pulled the sock out of Rex's mouth, then he and I sat down on the edge of the bed.

"Who the hell are you?" Rex barked at Nathan.

Nathan scowled. "You'd better watch how you speak to me because I may be the only reason you walk out of this room instead of being carried out in a body bag. Do you understand?"

Rex withered a bit.

Nathan pulled a small notebook out of his pocket along with a small pen. "How long have you been working for Abigail Smith?"

"About three years," Rex answered.

"How did you meet her?" Nathan asked.

Rex shifted uncomfortably against his restraints, and looked up at Warren. "She worked for the state when we was kids, remember?"

Nathan and I both whipped our heads toward Warren. "What?" I asked.

Warren was looking at Rex like he'd sprouted a second nose on his pitted face. "What the hell are you talking about?"

Rex rolled his eyes. "Ms. Smith? They's no way you could forget her, dude." He huffed. "She was a caseworker for the group home."

Bewildered, Warren looked at us and shrugged. "I have no idea."

My eyes narrowed. "She was in Chicago?"

He held his arms up in question. "Not that I'm aware of. I would remember."

Rex looked pleased that he knew something we didn't. "I can't believe you don't remember her, dude."

Nathan leaned his elbow on the table. "You didn't notice anything strange about the way she looked after what, ten years?"

A sleazy grin spread across Rex's dry lips. He was missing a side tooth. "Man, I didn't notice nothin' except that bitch is fine as hell."

My skin was crawling.

Obviously frustrated, Nathan held up his hand. "Forget about it for now. How did you end up working for her?"

"She came back a few years ago, was volunteerin' at a rehab center downtown. She looked me and a few of the other guys up. Asked us if we wanted to do some work for her."

I was skeptical. "She pulled some random punks off the streets and put them to work trafficking girls across the country? She's not that stupid."

He shook his head. "Nah, bitch—"

Rex didn't get another word out before the back of Warren's fist slammed against the side of his head so hard it rocked the chair sideways. He yelped in pain. I expected Nathan to at least shoot Warren a reprimanding glare, but his fist was balled at the ready to go next.

I grabbed Nathan by the shoulder and Warren by the arm. "He's no use to us dead."

Warren pointed a sharp finger at Rex, and he flinched.

"Sorry, sorry!" Rex looked at me, his eyes a little off-center from the blow. "No, *ma'am*." He shook his head from side to side like he was trying to clear his muddled thoughts. "The work was legit at first. Me'n a few other guys was rehabbin' an old building in South Chicago. She said she was turnin' it into some kind of halfway house or somethin'."

"How did you wind up in Texas?" Nathan asked.

"When the place in Chicago was finished, she said she had some girls in San Antonio who needed to get outta town, and she was gonna move them into the building we just squared away. She sent me and another guy down here to drive 'em up to Illinois. He'd worked with her for a while," Rex explained.

Nathan was taking notes. "Who was the other guy?"

"Mendez," Rex said. "It wasn't till we brought the haul back from Texas that I realized what was really going on. Mendez is a pretty sick, twisted bastard. For a while, I thought he was playin' the broad and sellin' those girls behind her back. Then, he got busted for breakin' into his ex-wife's house in Texas and went to jail, and everything continued on just the same without him. I started making the runs with Tito."

"Who's in charge in Chicago?" Nathan asked.

"Tito's mom. This bitch named Marisol."

"What about New York and Los Angeles?" Warren asked.

"I don't know, man. It's not like we do company picnics and shit, ya know?" he said.

Nathan pointed his pen at Rex. "If you're running girls to Chicago for her, why were you taking girls from Larry Mendez to the cantina?"

"Since Larry's been on parole and can't leave the state, he's been workin' at pickin' up runaways and sellin' them to buyers around town. We gather intel on the buyers, and after a while, Abigail will claim that one of her girls ratted out another pimp somewhere. Then the cops bring it down, and Abigail is right there to bring the girls in."

I did the math in my head. "So, she makes money selling them, she gets them back for free, and then she pimps them out." I dropped my head into my hands. The whole thing was starting to make my head pound.

Warren looked at me. "She also doesn't have to do the leg work finding the girls and breaking them into the business."

"What is she planning on doing next?" Nathan asked.

Rex shifted in his seat and tipped his chin up defiantly at Nathan. "Are you gonna send me to jail or what? What the hell am I gettin' outta this?"

"You get to exist for a little longer," Warren interjected. "Answer the question."

Rex was clearly terrified of Warren. He looked at Nathan. "Me and Tito are supposed to be taking a haul back later tonight. She's been movin' almost all the girls out of Texas lately."

"Why?" I asked.

"Do I look like someone who sits at her conference table?" he asked. "I don't know what she's doin'."

"When are you supposed to leave tonight?" Nathan asked.

"We leave from the ministry at eleven," he said.

"Driving what?"

"A big white van with Morning Star on the side."

Nathan looked at us and then at Rex. "Sit tight." He grabbed the sock out of Warren's hand, wadded it up, and shoved it into Rex's mouth again.

Rex groaned and struggled again.

Nathan looked at Warren, then nodded toward the door. The three of us got up and walked outside. Once the door was closed, Nathan leaned against it. "We need to cut him loose," he said.

"What?" I asked, my voice cracking.

He nodded. "We need to let him make that haul. Once he crosses the state line, he will be in violation of his bond agreement, and it will become a federal offense. We can call in an anonymous tip. Maybe that will get the ball rolling with the FBI and give them enough probable cause to dig into this and bust Abigail and the rest of them," he explained. "I don't have anything else we can use. Everything he has said in that room would be inadmissible in court because you freaking kidnapped him."

Warren folded his arms over his chest. It was obvious he didn't like the thought of letting Rex go either. Finally, he sighed. "God, I hate it when you're right."

"How do we know he's not going to blab all this to Abigail as soon as you let him go?" I asked.

"I'll make sure he doesn't," Warren said.

When we went inside again, Warren sat down in front of Rex. "Are you listening to me?"

Rex nodded with frightful eyes.

Warren leaned in, inches from his face. "I'm going to let you go, but I'm going to be right on your ass. You're going to make that transport to Chicago, and I'm going to have my eyes on you the whole time. I have the ability to track you down, so you will not get away from me. Do you understand?"

Rex nodded again.

"I'm going to take down your boss, and if you get in my way or try to warn anyone involved in this, you will no longer have amnesty with me. What you saw me do to Travis fifteen years ago will be merciful compared to what I will do to you," Warren warned.

Rex's head furiously bobbed up and down.

Nathan leaned toward me and lowered his voice. "Who's Travis? What did Warren do to him?"

I just shook my head and closed my eyes.

He sighed and folded his arms over his chest.

Warren ripped the sock out of Rex's mouth, causing him to gasp for air.

"I'll keep my mouth shut. Swear to God," Rex said.

Warren took out his knife and cut the straps holding him to the chair. "God doesn't hear you anymore." He pointed the knife at Rex's neck. "Where are you supposed to meet them?"

"The van's already at the ministry." Frantic, he looked over at the alarm clock on the nightstand. "I'm supposed to be there in half an hour."

Warren stood and stepped out of his way. "Then I suggest you get a move on."

Rex bolted from the room like the devil himself was after him. My eyes settled on the door as it closed in his wake. "Think we can trust him?" I asked.

"Not a chance," Nathan said.

Warren shook his head. "I should have handled this myself."

"Ehh." Nathan shrugged his shoulders. "Even though they're scum, they're still entitled to a judge and jury."

Warren's gaze could have set the room on fire. "Someday, Nate, you're going to understand that I see guilt as clearly as you see skin color." He folded the blade of his knife into its handle. "Some villains don't need a justice system. They need an executioner."

20.

NATHAN AND I stood there, staring in stunned silence until Warren walked over to the window and peeked through the blinds. Out of the corner of my eye, I saw Nathan gulp.

"Is there a way to confirm if Abigail was actually in Chicago ten years ago?" Warren asked.

Nathan snapped out of his daze. "I can make some calls this week."

"Warren," I said.

He turned to look at me.

"I don't think he was lying."

He shook his head. "He wasn't. The question is, I was in that group home in '98. I didn't leave Chicago until 2002."

Nathan's head tilted. "That doesn't sound like a question."

Warren tapped his finger on his temple. "The migraines. There's no way we stayed within thirty miles of each other for that long, especially without me ever seeing her."

"Thirty miles?" Nathan asked.

Warren nodded toward me. "The migraines seem to start around the thirty mile mark. That's been roughly the distance we've been apart each time it's happened."

"What if they don't work the same with her?" Nathan asked.

I considered it. "No, she told us she'd have a migraine when we left town. We would have too had we not been together." I looked at Warren. "You never had migraines before me?"

He laughed with sarcasm. "No. I definitely wouldn't forget that."

"Interesting," Nathan said. "I'll see what I can dig up when we get home."

Warren nodded. "OK. How are we going to handle the current mess with the cops?"

Nathan blew out a sigh. "I'm not sure."

I sank down on the edge of the mattress. "An anonymous tip isn't going to work. You know Rex is right. The police and the community love her. They're going to need a solid reason to call her into question." My breath caught in my chest as I realized what we had to do. "I'm going to have to report this."

Warren didn't seem to hear me.

Nathan laughed. "What are you going to say? That the woman who is the same age as you is actually your mother and a demon?"

I frowned. "No, but I can tell them I met her that day at the bust and she invited me over to her house to talk about a job or something. I'll say I found the paperwork on Mendez by accident. That's all partially true."

Warren and Nathan exchanged glances.

Nathan pulled off his ball cap and scratched his head. "I don't know. That's a pretty unlikely story."

I smirked. "Not as unlikely as the truth. Do you have a better idea?"

He shook his head.

Warren looked at me. "I don't like it."

"We don't have another choice." I held out my hand toward Nathan. "Give me the phone number."

He pulled his phone from his pocket. "I'll call first and find out where the local office is here. This isn't the kind of thing you can usually do on the telephone." He walked out to the hallway.

Blood oozed into my mouth, and I realized I had nervously chewed a hole on the inside of my lower lip. I shuddered.

Warren walked over and sat down beside me. "You all right?"

My legs were bouncing. "We need a vacation to recover from this one."

He squeezed my knee. "I couldn't agree more, babe."

After a few minutes, Nathan reentered the room. "I gave them the short version and told them to be on the lookout for the van, but she's going to need to go in and make a formal statement in person." He held up a slip of paper. "We're supposed to ask for Agent Silvers."

My cheeks puffed out as I exhaled slowly.

Nathan looked at Warren. "I think I should take her. It would probably look weird to have a mercenary tagging along."

Warren's eyes narrowed. "I'm not a mercenary."

Nathan held up his hands in defense. "I'm sorry. It would look weird to have the Angel of Death tagging along."

We both laughed and it eased the unbearable tension in the room.

Warren looked over at me. "He's probably right, and he knows more about the legal process of this than I do. Will you be OK if I sit this one out?"

I sighed. "I just want to get it over with."

Nathan motioned toward the door. "Well, I'm ready to go when you are."

I covered Warren's hand with mine. "If I wind up in federal prison, I expect you to use your badass recon skills to get me out."

"I'll burn the jail down if I have to." He tucked my hair behind my ears.

I kissed him quickly and stood up. "All right, Detective. I'm all yours."

Nathan raised his eyebrows and grinned. "Really?"

Warren pointed at him. "Watch it."

Nathan glanced at the clock. "We should be finished in time to catch them before they leave the ministry at eleven. Do you want to try and follow them to see how this thing plays out?"

Warren shook his head. "As much as I would like to, I'm afraid we would be too conspicuous. All it would take is for one person to recognize us, and the whole thing could fall apart."

Nathan nodded. "You're probably right. We'll come back here once we are finished, then."

Warren stood up. "Please bring me some food. I forgot to eat today."

I kissed Warren once more before we walked outside to the car.

As we pulled out of the parking lot, Nathan looked over at me. "Are you nervous?"

I held up my hands. They were trembling. "I'm keeping the makers of Xanax in business this year by myself."

He laughed. "I'll bet. Don't be nervous though. You'll be fine."

"You'd better not leave me," I warned him.

He shook his head. "I wouldn't dream of it."

We rode most of the ten miles in silence. When we finally arrived, there were more lights on in the four story building than I expected for nine o'clock on a Saturday night. I stared out my window until I felt Nathan squeeze the back of my neck.

"Take a deep breath, Sloan."

I turned to face him and sucked in a huge gulp of air and blew it out slowly.

The confidence on his face was only mildly reassuring. "Remember, we're here for the weekend so you could talk to Abigail about a job."

I nodded and picked at my fingernail. "A job doing what?"

"I don't know. Publicity. That's what you do," he said.

It had been so long since I'd gone to work that I'd almost forgotten my job description. "Oh yeah."

"Just tell enough of the truth to make this all sound believable without bringing up the angels and demons stuff."

I swallowed the lump in my throat.

He smiled to ease the tension. "I'm going to tell them I'm your boyfriend if they ask."

I rolled my eyes. "Of course you are." I pointed a finger at him. "You'd better not let me wind up in jail."

He reached over and wrapped his hand around mine. "You're not going to wind up in jail. I promise."

I wasn't so sure I believed him.

When we walked in the front door, an armed security guard in the lobby stopped us. "Can I help you?" he asked.

I looked down at the notes Nathan had scribbled during his phone conversation earlier. "We're here to see Agent Silvers," I said.

He nodded and walked behind the desk. "Your name?"

"Sloan Jordan," I answered, but the name Praea came to mind.

He motioned toward an empty row of plastic gray chairs along the wall. "Have a seat."

When we sat down, Nathan put his arm around me and curled his body toward mine.

"What are you doing?" I whispered.

He smiled. "Playing the part."

"You said, 'if they ask,'" I reminded him.

He winked at me. "Gotta make it believable."

I shook my head. "I'm going to tell on you."

He chuckled but didn't remove his arm. Instead, he leaned in closer. "I have some news, but I didn't want to call you last week in the middle of everything with your mom."

"What is it?" I asked.

His eyes were fixed on the carpet. "They are finally releasing my sister's body to our family."

"Wow. Are you OK?"

After a second, he nodded. "Yeah. It's good to have some closure."

"Is there going to be a service?"

"Yeah. Mom is talking about doing it around Thanksgiving while the family is in town." He was still staring at the floor. "It will be small."

I nudged him with my shoulder. "Well, if you want me to come, I will."

He looked at me and smiled. "Thank you."

There was a loud buzz and the door behind the desk opened. A black woman in khaki pants and a blue polo shirt walked through it. She had a neatly edged bob and the most perfect, full red lips I had ever seen on another human. A blue and white lanyard hung around her neck with her FBI credentials.

She extended her hand as she approached. "I'm Agent Sharvel Silvers. Are you Sloan?"

I stood up and shook her hand. "Yes, ma'am."

She offered her hand to Nathan.

"Detective Nathan McNamara, her boyfriend," he said.

In any other situation, I would have rolled my eyes. Or maybe punched him.

Agent Silvers offered a polite smile. "Nice to meet you both. Let's go to my office."

We followed her through the door, down a bleak hallway lit up with painfully bright fluorescent lights. The walls were white and covered in plaques and department photographs. My stomach felt queasy, and I hugged my arms to my chest.

Agent Silvers' office was bland and impersonal. A half-dead plant was shedding its brown and shriveled leaves on the corner of her desk near the chairs where she motioned for us to sit. She sat down in her padded office chair, and the wheels squeaked as she rolled across the floor. "Detective McNamara, I read the report you called in earlier," she began. "We've alerted the state highway patrol to be looking for the van you described on the phone. If, in fact, it does cross into Oklahoma, they will stop it and see if the suspects are driving."

I sighed with relief. "Good."

She looked carefully at both of us. "I am very curious to know why you believe Morning Star Ministries is involved with human trafficking across state lines."

I looked at Nathan, and he reached over and wrapped his hand around mine. I cleared my throat. "I met Abigail Smith during a sting operation that we sort of fell into the middle of a few weeks ago."

"Fell into?" she asked.

Nathan leaned forward. "We helped capture a couple of guys who were escaping from a raid during a prostitution bust."

Agent Silvers was making notes. "Why were you at a prostitution bust? This says you're an officer in North Carolina."

He nodded. "That's correct. We were here on vacation, and we got turned around in the wrong neighborhood. It was there I noticed some odd behavior happening on the street. Because I'm a cop, I insisted on following two men who appeared to be transporting two underage girls." He squeezed my hand, signaling my turn to talk.

I looked at him. "We followed them to an old building and that's when the raid happened. Nathan and another friend of ours chased down two men who escaped through a side door."

"There's a report with the San Antonio police department with the details," he added.

My hand was sweating inside his. "Anyway, I met Abigail there. We talked for a while, and I expressed an interest in a job with her ministry. She invited me to her house for a lunch meeting earlier today."

She blinked up at me. "A business lunch at her private home?"

I smiled nervously. "Yes."

She looked skeptical, but she gestured toward me with her pen. "Then what happened?"

"I found an invoice from a lawyer representing Larry Mendez in her office. He's one of the men involved in the same raid where I met her. I believe she paid for his defense."

"You just happened to find it?" she asked.

I shrank down in my seat. "I was snooping." Her eyebrow twitched, but she didn't comment so I continued. "After that, I heard her on the phone making arrangements to have some girls sent to Chicago. She said Rex Parker was going to be taking them."

She was still writing down the details. "Who is Rex Parker?"

"One of the two guys my friend and I apprehended at the raid," Nathan said.

Agent Silvers put her pen down and massaged her temples. "Abigail Smith is a very highly respected member of this community who has been very proactive in taking girls out of sex slavery, and you're telling me you just happened to hear her detailing the specifics of an interstate sex trafficking exchange?"

I shrugged. "She thought I was in the bathroom."

Her smile was mocking. "What exactly did she say about Chicago?"

"I heard something about someone named Marisol and that a new group of girls would be arriving with Rex Parker soon. She said they were leaving for Chicago at eleven tonight. Then she wanted to know how much money had been brought in the night before."

Agent Silvers made a few more notes, then looked at Nathan. "Can you corroborate this story? Were you there?"

Nathan shook his head and leaned forward. "I wasn't there, but if you search her home office, you'll find the invoice for Larry Mendez. Also, I suspect if you dig further, you'll find that Rex Parker and Tito Juarez were both bonded out with cash."

She tapped the end of her pen against the desk. "You think she bonded them out of jail?"

Nathan turned his palm up. "It makes sense. She could kill two birds with one stone, if you ask me. Get the girls sent to Chicago and get the two of them out of the area to skip trial and not take the risk of them implicating her."

Agent Silvers folded her hands in her lap and raised her brow with blatant skepticism. "You think she would put up possibly hundreds of thousands of dollars in bond money and encourage them to go FTA?"

He nodded. "If this is true, you and I both know a few hundred grand is a drop in the bucket compared to what she's made off these girls."

She sighed and returned her attention to the papers. Finally, she leaned on her elbows over the desk and stared at me. "If this is true and we do find reason to indict her, are you willing to testify against her in court?"

Hesitantly, I nodded. "Yes."

"And you realize making a false statement is a felony criminal offense, correct?" she asked.

Nathan's hand tightened around mine.

I swallowed and nodded again. "Yes. I'll do whatever necessary to help stop her. I believe she's a very dangerous woman who definitely isn't the saint she has convinced everyone that she is."

After signing the paperwork, Nathan and I were allowed to leave. I dug my nails into his arm when we got outside and pulled him close to me. "I'm not tough enough to make it in prison," I said, just above a whisper.

He laughed and patted my arm. "You did the right thing."

I dug my nails in deeper, causing him to wince. "She doesn't believe me. You saw her face."

He shook his head. "It doesn't matter. You'll see. They'll take down the transport, get a search warrant for Abigail's house, and find that invoice. This will all be over very soon, and we can go home to your normal messed up life with boy problems, superpowers, and a boring day job."

I leaned into him. "Thanks for coming all the way down here. I do promise I'll pay you back."

He draped his arm around my neck and smiled down at me. "I'm starting a tab with you, Sloan. Someday I'm going to ask for a really huge favor."

Oh boy.

"I don't think I like being in your debt."

His grin made my stomach flip-flop. "I like it just fine."

* * *

The next morning, the shrill ring of the hotel phone jarred me from my sleep. The room was still dark, but light was peeking around the corners of the blackout curtains. I heard the shower running in the bathroom, and Warren wasn't in bed beside me. I rolled over and lifted the phone off the receiver. "Hello?"

"Morning, sunshine."

"Geez, Nathan. Do you know what time it is?"

"The FBI called."

I sat up straight in the bed. "Oh! What did they say?"

"The Oklahoma Highway Patrol stopped the Morning Star Ministries van early this morning near Ardmore. Rex Parker and Tito Juarez were arrested on violating the terms of their bond, and seven girls were taken into custody."

I let out a deep sigh. "Thank God. What about Abigail?"

"Silvers said they're moving forward with the case. She's going to try and get the search warrant for Abigail's house and business pushed through this morning."

"And Larry Mendez?" I asked.

"She didn't say, but at this point, I doubt they have any substantial reason to arrest him again, but maybe they'll dig something up during the investigation." He yawned on the other end of the line. "I'm going back to sleep for an hour. I'll see you downstairs for breakfast."

I hung up the phone and swung my legs off the bed. Twisting around to the right, I felt my spine crack all the way down to my tailbone. I got up and went to the bathroom, gently knocking before pushing the door open. Steam and light spilled out into the room.

Warren peeked around the shower curtain. "You're up early. Is the hotel on fire?"

I picked up my toothbrush and slathered it with paste. "Nathan woke me up. The FBI called."

"Really?"

"Uh huh." I brushed for a minute and spat toothpaste in the sink. "They caught Rex and Tito in Oklahoma this morning," I said and started brushing again.

"That's good news. Did they say when they are going after Abigail?" he asked.

I shrugged my shoulders.

"What about Mendez?"

I shrugged again.

His wet head tilted to the side. "Did you sleep in my shirt last night?"

Gripping the brush with my teeth, I glanced down at the black 5.11 Tactical t-shirt and dribbled toothpaste down the front of it. I turned my wide eyes toward him.

He shook his head. "I was going to wear that today."

"Sowwy," I said around the toothbrush.

I rinsed out my mouth and packed up my toiletry bag. Before leaving the bathroom, I pulled the shower curtain aside just enough to stick my face in. "Kiss me," I said. "I'm going to lie down till you get out."

Water trickled from his face onto mine as he kissed me. Then he reached out and hooked his wet arm around my waist, pulling me into the shower.

I laughed and pounded my fists against his bare chest. "What are you doing?"

He pulled his t-shirt off me and tossed it out onto the bathroom floor. "Keeping you from going back to sleep. We have a plane to catch."

After a bland continental breakfast in the hotel lobby, the three of us loaded our bags into the trunk of the rental car, and Warren headed in the direction of the airport. I looked in the back seat where Nathan was popping Skittles into his mouth.

"Isn't it a little early for that?" I asked.

He shook his head. "It's never too early for Skittles."

I laughed and rolled my eyes. "Do you think they'll be able to bust Abigail today?"

He nodded. "If they get the search warrant signed by a judge. They'll have to find a judge at home though since it's Sunday."

Warren shook his head. "That's exactly why I don't do law enforcement. Too many rules and way too much paperwork."

I relaxed in my seat as Warren pulled the car onto the freeway. The buildings of downtown looked small in the distance, and a light haze from the morning dew loomed over the city. I looked at the clock on the dashboard. It was eight-thirty, and our flight was at eleven. The thought of curling up in my quiet bed at home was intoxicating. I could almost feel the soft bamboo sheets and smell the lavender fabric softener in my pillowcase.

Nathan's voice snapped me out of my daze a few minutes later. "Dude, you missed your exit."

"Crap," Warren muttered. "I'll have to find another exit where I can turn around. I was off in la-la land."

I pulled my knees into my chest. "Me too," I said, still thinking of home. "I can't wait to get home to my bed, in my house. I think I might sleep all week long."

"Don't you have to go to work at some point?' Nathan asked.

My heart sank. "Oh, I hadn't even thought about that. I've almost forgotten I even have a job."

"When do you have to go back?" Warren asked.

"I guess tomorrow. I need to save my last couple of personal days to take you to Charlotte." I groaned. "I can just see the inbox on my office door overflowing into the hallway." I turned toward him. "Hey, speaking of jobs...did you tell Nathan to stay in Asheville and not take the job with the FBI?"

Warren glanced in the rearview mirror at Nathan. "Do you not have the ability to keep your mouth shut?"

I crossed my arms over my chest. "So, you did?"

He looked at me over his shoulder. "Not exactly. I just told him I would feel better if he stayed close by while I was gone."

"What's he going to do? Patrol my front porch like Scotland Yard?" I asked.

His eyes turned serious. "We haven't had a very good track record lately, and if we're making enemies somewhere in the spirit world, it would be a lot safer for someone who knows our secret to keep an eye on you."

I knew he was right, and it terrified me.

"It's fine, Sloan," Nathan said. "I like working for the county, and I have no desire whatsoever to go through another brutal training academy. I promise I'm not missing out on anything."

I looked back at him and scrunched my eyebrows together. "Asheville's not that exciting. You're going to get bored."

"Not true," he said. "I have you."

"Well, don't pin all your adventurous hopes on me. I'm taking the year off of supernatural B.S. while Warren's gone. I need a break." I flopped my head back against the headrest.

Warren got off the interstate and turned left, but he didn't get on the on-ramp in the opposite direction.

Nathan chuckled. "Warren, man, do you need me to drive? You're failing miserably at navigation this morning."

"Shut up," Warren said. "I think we can get there by going this way."

"You'd better be sure, or we aren't going to have time to get through security at the airport," Nathan said.

"Let me drive, Nate."

As we wound around the city seemingly further and further away from civilization, I was becoming very doubtful of my boyfriend's sense of direction. I looked at him out of the corner of my eye. "Maybe we should turn on the GPS."

"I know where I am," he assured me. "We're going the right way."

"Okie dokie." I turned my wide eyes toward Nathan, and he

covered his mouth to squelch a laugh.

Warren turned the car left down a small street lined with run-down buildings, and I waved my hand in front of his face. "Where are you going?" I asked.

Before he had time to answer, a bright flash, like an explosion of light with no sound, erupted around us. About fifteen feet ahead, a man was kneeling in the remnants of the spot where the light had dissipated. Warren slammed on his brakes so as not to run him over. I screamed as the car lurched forward, throwing the three of us toward the windshield. When the seatbelt slammed into my chest and my eyes refocused, Samael was standing at our front fender.

21.

"WHAT THE HELL was that?" Nathan shouted. He was rubbing his head where it had smashed into the back of Warren's seat.

I scrambled for the handle on the car door and pushed it open. "Samael!"

He met me in two long strides and grabbed me by the shoulders. "Sloan, you are in great danger." He gently shook me and pleaded with his captivating golden eyes. "You must leave. You must get out of here right now."

Warren and Nathan were out of the car. "What's going on?" Nathan asked, confused as he walked toward me. "And where the hell are we?"

Seemingly in a daze, Warren walked past the front of the car, then broke into a jog down the road away from us.

"Warren!" I yelled. "Where are you going?"

He didn't even flinch in my direction.

Samael shook me again. "It's no use. You must let him go and leave this place!"

I pushed Samael away from me. "I'm not going anywhere without him!" I took off in a sprint toward my boyfriend.

Warren rounded another corner, and when I caught up with him, he was stopped dead in his tracks.

Abigail—Kasyade—was standing in the middle of the street with her arms folded across her chest. Her long dark hair was blowing behind her, yet there was no breeze. Her face was set like stone, and her skin seemed to glow with some unnatural, radiated brilliance.

"Warren!" I shouted again, yanking on his arm with all the strength I could muster.

Samael caught up with me. "This was a trap to lure you here. The Siren has summoned him. He's under her control now."

"The hell he is," I argued. "Warren!"

He didn't respond.

A blue sedan was approaching in the distance behind Abigail. She didn't turn to look. Instead, she raised her hand and the car flipped backwards about twenty feet into the air before crashing down onto its roof.

I grasped Warren's arm and screamed his name again.

Nathan reached us as Samael tried to pull me away. "It is no use," Samael insisted as he closed his arms around me. "We must go!"

"*En magna, Samael,*" Abigail hissed.

My head snapped up at the sound of the bizarre language. It sounded like an odd mix of broken Latin and Klingon.

"*Retribues pro, Kasyade!*" Samael shouted over my head. "*Adduces enim super te formidabilis vindictae! Tuum erit dies!*"

I wrenched my body free and grabbed Warren by his head. I forced his face down to look at me and peered into his black eyes. His pupils were completely dilated and blank with incoherence. But there was something else. For the first time ever, I saw his mortal soul.

"Warren!" I shouted, shaking his skull. His glazed eyes stared right through me.

An unseen force knocked me sideways, and I landed hard on the concrete. Nathan rushed toward me, and my hip burned with a deep pain as he helped me to my feet.

"You believe you can defy my will, Praea?" Abigail roared, her voice echoing against the buildings with a hollow, inhuman pitch. "Did you not think I would know it was you? You betrayed me! Your very own mother!"

"You're not my mother!" I screamed.

Her hand waved through the air, and a ghostly slap across my face knocked me against Nathan's chest. He pushed me behind him with one hand and yanked his handgun from its holster with the other. He aimed and fired twice at Abigail, striking her in the chest. She faltered back a few steps, but straightened...and laughed. The two entry wounds were bloody and should have been fatal, but Abigail was far from neutralized. She raised her hand again and knocked the gun out of Nathan's hand.

She looked at Warren, and he began slowly walking toward her again. I scrambled to my feet. The pain in my hip seared through me, but I hobbled to him as quickly as I could.

Abigail turned toward me, but before she could act, Samael launched a fiery ball of light at her. The blow knocked her off her feet just as I reached Warren.

I grasped him by the face once more and forced him to meet my eyes. Without a thought in my brain other than the desperation of calling him back to me, I pressed both of my palms to his heart and screamed, "Warren!"

The familiar zing of electricity that regularly flowed between us was suddenly like the shock from a defibrillator. We both fell backward onto the street, and the skin was torn from my elbows by the asphalt.

Suddenly, Warren was on top of me. "Sloan!" Whatever control Abigail had on him was broken.

Samael grabbed Warren by the shirt and hoisted him into the air like my 220 pound boyfriend was nothing more than a flimsy rag doll. He placed Warren on his feet and grasped his shoulders, leaning so close they were nearly eye to eye. "You must sever the connection between her spirit and her body," he said. "I cannot kill her, but in spirit form, I can remove her from this place if you help me!"

I rolled onto my knees and tried to push myself up, but the pain was too great. Then Nathan's arm hooked around my waist and he pulled me up.

"Are you all right?" He was panting as he helped me stand.

Before I could answer, Nathan was ripped off his feet and pulled through the air. Abigail's palm was outstretched toward him, drawing him like a magnet. When his neck collided with her hand, she dangled him inches off the ground.

"Nathan!"

In horror, I watched as she lowered Nathan's face toward her own. Her fingers went white with tension as she closed them around his throat. Her mouth opened to a shockingly abnormal width that dislocated her jawbone. A screeching hiss and a high pitched sucking sound were released from deep inside her. Nathan's shoulders convulsed violently for a moment before going limp. She discarded him, slamming his body onto the nearby sidewalk.

I screamed again and pushed myself up off the road. Stumbling over my own feet, I took off in a clumsy, painful sprint toward him. Her hand flew up again, erecting an invisible wall in front of me. I slammed face-first into it and fell backward with a warm gush of blood flowing from my nose into my gaping mouth. I coughed and spewed a shower of blood into the air.

In my peripheral, I saw her move again, and then Warren and Samael were knocked backward out of my view.

Before I could turn and look for them, my body began to slide across the asphalt, the rocks ripping the back of my shirt open and tearing into my flesh. I slid to a stop at Abigail's feet, and her black shoe came down hard on my throat. "My daughter, Praea." The words dripped like poison from her mouth. Her eyes were a glowing golden color as she ground my skull against the rough pavement. "The events have already been set in motion, and there is no stopping it now. You'll see. This is only the beginning."

She leaned down, pressing her foot harder against my throat. Burning pain began to throb behind my eyeballs as my body starved for oxygen. "Whether you like it or not, this is your destiny. It is what you were born for, Praea."

I clawed at her shin, struggling to breathe. "My name is Sloan," I choked out.

She removed her foot, and then her hand sliced through the air above me. The intangible force hit me so hard that I rolled four times down the yellow center line of the street. I came to rest with my face in the gravel dust facing her. She slowly walked toward me, her feet seemingly not connected with the ground.

"You will greatly suffer, my daughter. I will destroy you and those whom you love. I will destroy your future and take what is rightfully mine!" Her hands shot forward, and my body lost its connection to gravity.

"Warren, do it now!" Samael screamed behind me.

As I levitated into the air, I caught a glimpse of Warren dropping down to one knee. Blood was running into my eyes, but I saw his hands shoot forward in my direction. A bright surge of electricity blasted through the air, rippling the space between us. The force spun me out of Kasyade's ethereal grip, and I slammed into the concrete again.

The distinctive clap of lightning exploded and was accompanied by the shrillest shriek I had ever heard. My head rattled with the splintering sound, and I covered my ringing ears. Kasyade's body crumpled to the street, then a cloud of energy rose and pulsed over her lifeless corpse. Suddenly, Samael vanished and a violent, hurricane-force wind rushed over me and collided with what I assumed was her spirit. With an audible *crack*, they disappeared like they had been sucked from this world into a black hole.

The street fell silent.

As I tried to push myself up off the ground, I felt Warren's large hands close around my middle. He pulled me to my feet and into his strong arms. My legs felt limp underneath me.

"Are you all right?" He was panting.

I winced as I tried to hold my weight. "I'm broken."

Out of the corner of my eye, I saw Nathan's contorted figure bent at an unnatural angle between the side of a building and the broken sidewalk which had cracked under the sheer force with which she had thrown him. "No!" I tried helplessly to work myself free from Warren's grasp, but he held me still until he turned and saw Nathan for himself.

A choking gasp caught in his throat. "Oh God, Nate." He wrapped his arm around my waist, and I winced as he carried me across the road.

When we reached Nathan's lifeless body, I sank to the ground beside him as Warren rolled him onto his back. His eyes were open and bloodshot and staring into nothingness.

Nathan McNamara was gone.

Though I knew I wasn't going to find one, I checked for a pulse in his neck.

"Sloan," Warren said.

Instinctively, I tilted Nathan's chin up and opened his mouth to begin CPR. I covered his mouth with my own and breathed into him.

When I straightened, Warren reached over and closed Nathan's eyes. He put his hand on my back. "It's no use."

I threw my fist at him. "You can help me or you can leave!" I shouted. "I'm not just going to give up on him!"

Patronizing me, Warren got on his knees beside Nathan's torso and pressed his large hands against Nathan's sternum. When I breathed into his cold mouth again, the audible grind from his broken rib cage as it expanded was almost enough to turn my stomach. Warren compressed Nathan's chest a few more times, and tears mixed with blood streamed down my face and dripped onto Nathan's lips. I breathed again and again.

Nathan's lower lip quivered ever so slightly, and I pulled away. "Check his pulse," I said.

"Sloan, it's no—"

"Check his pulse!"

Warren pressed his fingers against the side of Nathan's pale neck. "Nothing."

I bent and forced more air into his lungs. His chest rose and collapsed. My heart twisted as I hopelessly breathed into him again. When Nathan's chest fell a second time to its lifeless resting place, painful sobs erupted that I couldn't control. Warren reached to console me, but I pushed him away. I clambered to my knees and clasped my hands one on top of the other and placed them over Nathan's heart. With all my strength, I pushed.

A deep and hollow *boom* echoed around us. I toppled forward as the windows in the abandoned buildings around us exploded. Warren shielded me with his body from the falling glass where I lay with my head on Nathan's chest. Then I heard it.

Thump. Thump. Thump...

Warren and I slowly rose up. Warren must have sensed it as well because he moved around me and pressed his fingers to Nathan's jugular again. His eyes widened.

"Call an ambulance," I said, pushing him out of my way.

Warren moved a good distance away from us and pulled out his phone.

I cupped Nathan's face in my hands. "Nathan! Nathan, can you hear me?"

His eyes fluttered open ever so slightly. "Sloan." It was barely a whisper.

I cried and bent and kissed him on the mouth, not even pausing to think of the consequences that might follow. "Oh my God, Nathan!"

I sat up and looked at him again. Blood stained his mouth. I wasn't sure if it was his or my own.

"Sloan," he said again.

"Shh," I said. "Just breathe."

A bright flash of light lit up the street, and I looked back to see Samael standing over me. "Put your hands on him," he said with a voice so calm it was haunting. "Cast your life into him. You have the power now."

"I don't know how," I said.

"You don't have to know how. Your power is not limited by your ability," he said. "Put your hands on him."

Carefully, I placed my trembling hands on Nathan's chest and closed my eyes. Like something out of a bad, low-budget sci-fi movie, I concentrated on sending whatever energy I had into Nathan's broken body. Either to my surprise or to my horror, I wasn't really sure which, my hands warmed slowly against his chest. Heat surged through all of my fingers—even the ones I hadn't been able to feel in weeks. Underneath my palms, his bones were moving and grinding like rocks stuck in the chain of a bicycle.

Nathan cried out in pain.

"Don't stop," Samael said.

His joints popped and snapped. I felt his spine crack, but much more violently than the way mine did in the morning. Nathan was screaming and writhing in pain, but once again Samael instructed me to continue. Finally, the angel's hand came to rest on my shoulder, and I relaxed.

Nathan's breathing was even, and when I pulled away and looked in his face, his eyes were calm and no longer streaked with broken blood vessels. His lip quivered as he reached up and pulled my head down to his shoulder. We both cried.

For the second time, I had almost lost this man that I loved. I pressed my head to his chest just to hear his heartbeat. When his sobs subsided, I sat up to examine his face. He was in pain, but he was going to live. I picked up his hand and pressed my lips to his palm, leaving a bloody kiss behind.

Warren and Samael were talking quietly behind us. "How are we going to explain this to the first responders?" Warren asked.

I looked back, curious as to Samael's response.

"Easy," Samael said with a wink.

He turned and looked down the street we had come from, and a moment later, our rental car turned the corner and was rolling toward us. My mouth dropped open, as there was no one in the driver's seat.

"What the hell?" I mumbled.

When it neared us, Samael raised his hand, and our rental car floated off the ground. He waved his arm and sent the car careening into the front of the blue sedan Kasyade had flipped earlier.

Warren's mouth dropped open in amazement. "God, I want to learn how to do that." He nodded toward a man sitting on the curb whom I hadn't even noticed in the confusion. "What about him?"

Apparently, the driver of the blue sedan had crawled to the curb and had witnessed the whole crazy ordeal. He was visibly shaking, and blood streaked the side of his tanned face.

Samael outstretched his hand in the man's direction. The man slowly and gently slumped to the concrete. "When he wakes, he will have no memory of what happened," Samael said. "The accident report will show that the brakes on your rental car were defective."

Warren was shaking his head, staring at the mangled cars. "That's one hell of an impact for a backstreet accident."

Samael put his hand on Warren's shoulder. "Do not worry."

I pointed to Abigail's lifeless corpse sprawled out across the center of the road. "And her?"

"Her, I will make disappear." His steady voice sent chills through my body.

Samael walked over and knelt down next to the body that had once carried me and given me life. He gently placed his hand on the back of her skull, and his eyes seemed to roll back into his head. Her body began to disintegrate at his fingertips. In a matter of seconds, what remained of Kasyade's earthly form was reduced to a pile of dust. Samael leaned over it and blew with a force no human could muster, sending the particles sailing into the atmosphere.

Warren shook his head as Samael approached us. "You're good," he said in awe.

Nathan squeezed my hand, and I looked down at him. "You saved my life," he whispered.

Samael knelt down next to us. "She did more than that. She brought you back."

Nathan closed his eyes and shook his head. "I always knew you would get me killed."

I looked up at Samael. "How did I bring him back?"

His face was somber, but his eyes were glowing gold. His hand rested on my shoulder. "For a time, you will have powers greater than you've ever known."

"What about Abigail...uh, Kasyade?" I asked.

He sighed. "The Siren is not gone. She will procure another body, but it will take time for her to recover. She will come after you again, as will others."

An uneasy feeling was growing in the pit of my gut. "Samael, what did she mean that it was too late to stop it? What events have already been set into motion?"

Samael squinted his eyes against the sunlight as he seemed to search the horizon. "For that, I have no answer. I have many powers. Unfortunately, omniscience is not one of them."

Warren caught my eye. "What are you thinking?"

I didn't like what I was thinking. "I have a feeling we've only scratched the surface on what Kasyade was up to. It had to be about more than the money she was making."

Samael nodded. "The fallen are motivated by suffering, not monetary gain."

I gulped down his words with a hard swallow and shuddered. "How did you find us?" I asked. "How did you know she would lead us here?"

He took my hand. "The entire spirit world can see you now, Sloan. That is why you must be very careful. You've learned here today that not all spirits are friendly, and they are extremely powerful. Unfortunately, I am afraid this will not be the last attempt on your life."

Warren knelt down next to me and rested his hands on my shoulders. "What do we do to stop them?"

"You will have protection unseen," he said. "I do suggest that you not go looking for trouble. Trouble will find you easily enough on its own."

Sirens blared in the distance. Samael looked around. "I must go. Peace be with you," he said to us. "We will see each other again."

"Samael, wait!" I called.

He turned his golden eyes toward me. "Yes?"

"Kasyade is a demon, right?" I asked.

He nodded. "She is a fallen angel. That is correct."

"Then what does that make me? She said she created me on purpose." My frantic heartbeat was audible in my ears.

His smile was benevolent and kind. "We are all given the choice between the side of good and evil, Sloan. No one but you can decide."

I reached out and grabbed him by the hand. "Thank you."

He shook his head. "No. Thank *you*."

With another flash of light, Samael was gone.

22.

NATHAN WAS TAKEN by ambulance to St. Luke's Baptist Hospital. I rode with him, and I suspected I needed medical treatment of my own. On the ride there, I winced in pain as I felt the bone in my hip crack and snap into place.

Nathan's eyes were fearful. "Are you OK? What's happening?" He clasped his hand around mine.

I forced a nod as the ribs on my right side began to grind against each other. I squeezed his hand and cried till they popped back together. My nose, which the EMT had said was obviously broken, began burning and pouring blood once again. I dropped my face into my lap as it shifted into alignment. I cried out as my eyes flooded with tears.

The paramedic who was caring for Nathan put his hand on my back. "Ma'am, are you all right?"

I sat up, and blood poured down my face, splattering all over the floor of the ambulance. The paramedic's eyes widened with horror, and he quickly grabbed a towel and held it to my face. Bright dots speckled my vision as the pain slowly faded.

I couldn't even imagine what was happening to me other than somehow my body was rejuvenating itself. It hadn't done that when I was beaten by Billy Stewart. Perhaps Abigail had unintentionally unlocked some of my power. By the time we reached the hospital, I was able to climb out of the ambulance without any help.

Warren had ridden with a San Antonio police officer to the hospital, and he was waiting in the transport bay at the emergency room entrance when we arrived. I stopped and squeezed Nathan's fingers. "I'll be there in a minute."

He nodded. "I'll be OK."

As they wheeled Nathan inside, Warren walked over and tilted my chin up to examine my face. "You're a mess. We've got to get you cleaned up."

I could feel the blood crusting on my skin. "I look worse than I feel now."

"Thank God." He took my hand and led me inside.

A nurse stopped us. "Honey, let's get you to triage." The plump woman in scrubs took my arm.

I shook my head. "I'm OK. I just look like a mess. Can you point us to the bathrooms?"

Her eyes were wide. It was obvious she didn't believe me. "You're covered in blood."

"I know. We were in an accident, but most of this blood is my friend's," I said. "Can I get some towels, maybe?"

She nodded. "Absolutely." She walked around the nursing station and returned with a towel and two washcloths. "Come with me. A sink isn't going to be enough. You need a shower."

Her kindness almost moved me to tears as she led us down another hallway to a room with a private bath. She winked at me. "This will be our little secret. I'll try and find you something to wear."

I sighed and smiled. "Thank you."

Warren tugged me toward the bathroom. "Come on."

Once we were inside, I caught sight of myself in the mirror as Warren turned the water in the shower on. I looked like an extra from a *Night of the Living Dead* movie. My face was splattered and smeared with blood. It covered my mouth and was down my neck and the front of my shirt. Dark circles from my broken nose were already forming under my eyes. My t-shirt and my jeans were shredded like I had been through a wood-chipper. Tears streaked through the blood on my cheeks.

"I think you should let a doctor look at you." Warren pulled some matted hair away from my face. "Just to be on the safe side."

I shook my head. "No. I felt my bones come back together in the ambulance. It was excruciating." Holding up my hands, I flexed and straightened my fingers. "Even the nerve damage seems to be gone."

He stared at me for a moment. "What's happening to you?"

I turned to face him. "I don't know, Warren, but there's something else."

"What?" he asked, his eyes growing with alarm.

"I can see your soul."

His head jerked in surprise. "Really?"

I nodded. "Really."

He scratched his head. "Something must have happened with Abigail. Maybe she transferred some of her powers to you."

"A lot of things with Abigail, but I don't think that's it." I leaned against the sink. "The other day at her house, she told me that you and I were born with all of our angelic powers from our parents. We just aren't able to use them as well because we are human."

His head tilted. "Does that mean—"

"That I'm becoming less human?" I interrupted him. I held my hands up. "I have no idea what's happening."

He shook his head and laughed, though he clearly didn't think it was funny. "It's like the more we find out, the less we understand."

I sighed. "I know."

He reached over and untucked my shirt. "Let's get you cleaned up."

Gently, Warren eased the torn fabric over my head. My bones might not have been broken anymore, but that didn't mean they didn't hurt like hell.

I stepped into the shower and winced as the hot water ran over the open cuts in my skin. There was a light knock at the door, and the hinges creaked as Warren pulled it open.

"These might be a little big on her, but here are some extra scrubs I had in my locker. And here is some shampoo and a comb for her hair that I got from our supply closet," I heard the nurse say.

"You're a saint. Thank you so much," Warren replied.

"Are you sure she shouldn't get herself checked out?" the nurse asked. "She looks really banged up, and I'm afraid she could have some internal injuries."

"She says she's fine, but thank you again. I know she's anxious to get to our friend."

"I'll check back in a little while and see how she's doing," she said.

Warren handed me the shampoo, and it burned as I lathered it. I looked down and watched the suds swirling with blood down the drain. When I finished, I stepped out and let Warren wrap me in a towel. I put on the blue scrubs and shoved my clothes into the trashcan. They were irreparable. My torn scalp felt like it was ripping as I brushed the tangles out of my hair. I briefly considered using Warren's knife to cut my hair off, but I realized if I did, Adrianne would probably kill me when I got home.

Nathan was in radiology when I finished up in the bathroom. The nurse took us to the stall in the emergency room where they would bring him, and we waited in two chairs. I rested my head against Warren's shoulder and tried to release the stress that had built up throughout the day. It was hopeless. Even after fifteen minutes, my hands were still trembling.

An unfamiliar ringtone came from Warren's chest pocket. He pulled it out and looked at it. "This is Nathan's," he said. "It's a Texas number. Should we answer it?"

"Yeah, it's probably the FBI." I took the phone from him and hit the answer button as I put it to my ear. "Nathan McNamara's phone," I said.

"Hi, is this Sloan?" a woman asked.

"Yes, is this Agent Silvers?"

"It is," she said. "I wanted you to know that we've searched Abigail Smith's home and office and found very substantial evidence to support your statement. We didn't find Ms. Smith, however. It seems that either Rex Parker or Tito Juarez may have tipped her off. I thought you should be warned in case she suspects you might have spoken with us."

I actually laughed. "Thanks for the warning, Agent Silvers."

"Is something funny?" she asked.

"No, ma'am," I said. "I just really don't think this day could get any worse. We are at the hospital after a very serious accident."

"Oh, I'm sorry to hear that. Is there anything I can do for you?" she asked.

"Just find the girls Abigail has taken, and please get Larry Mendez off the streets."

"I'm doing everything I can on both fronts. Please let me know as soon as possible if you hear anything from Abigail," she said.

"I will." I kept my laughter to myself that time.

Warren looked at me. "Mendez is still out there?"

I stared at the phone in my hands. "Guess so."

He was quiet for a moment before turning toward me. "Will you be all right here by yourself for a while?"

I almost asked why, but the fiery look in his eye answered the question.

Nodding, I touched his cheek. "Go find him."

* * *

I was busy losing a game of Solitaire on Nathan's phone when two nurses pushed his rolling hospital bed into the room. He was sitting up at a slight incline, and he looked groggy. They had cleaned most of the blood off his face, and had changed him into a clean hospital gown. His arm was tethered to an IV pole.

I stood up, walked to his bedside, and took his hand. "Hey, how are you feeling?"

"Like I've been raised from the dead," he said with a hint of a painful smile.

I leaned over and pressed a kiss to his forehead.

"Where's Warren?"

"He went out to run some errands. What did the doctors say?"

He shook his head. "Not much. They took some x-rays and did a CT scan to check for broken bones and internal injuries. I wonder if they'll find anything."

"I wonder the same thing," I said.

Nathan's fingers squeezed mine. "What happened back there?"

Carefully, I eased down onto the edge of his bed. I looked around to see if there was anyone else within earshot of us. I lowered my voice. "The black guy, Samael, is another angel we had met before. Abigail can summon people like I can, except she's much better at it. She had summoned Warren to where she was waiting."

Nathan cracked a smile. "Did he tell you that to justify his awful driving?"

I laughed. At least he still had his sense of humor.

His smile quickly faded. "What happened while I was dead?"

My face twisted into a frown. "Well, Warren used his power to kill her body, and Samael did something—I don't know what—with her spirit."

"Warren used what power?"

I scrunched up my nose. "You don't want to know."

He pressed his eyes closed. "No, I probably don't. How did she kill me?"

I shrugged my shoulders. "I'm really not sure. I don't know if she choked you to death, sucked the life out of you, or if her slamming you into the brick and concrete was what did it."

He grimaced. "How did you bring me back?"

I dropped my head. "I have absolutely no idea." A nurse stopped in to check a machine he was attached to. When she was gone, I leaned closer to him. "Do you remember anything about it? Being dead, I mean."

He shook his head. "Nothing."

His answer was disappointing. I had hoped for a full report about what it was like on the other side.

Just then, a doctor appeared around the curtain. "Nathan McNamara?" He was holding a metal clipboard in his hand.

"Yes," Nathan answered.

I stood up and stepped over to my chair.

The doctor looked down at his sheet. "You're a lucky man, Nathan," he said. "Amazingly, you don't have any broken bones. Any new ones anyway. The CT scan showed quite a bit of scar tissue and inflammation around two different spots on your spine, a few places on your rib cage, and your right shoulder, but those appear to be previous injuries.

Nathan's mouth fell open. I'm sure his expression matched mine. Neither of us spoke.

The doctor looked down at him. "I would like to hold you here overnight, just to be on the safe side. And you're going to be very sore for a few days, I'm afraid."

"I can handle sore," Nathan replied.

The doctor smiled. "Once we get some paperwork done on our end down here, someone will come and move you to a room upstairs. I'm going to get you some pain medicine and have the nurse come and clean you up a bit more."

"Thank you, Doctor," Nathan said.

The doctor shook his head. "Don't thank me." He pointed up toward the ceiling with his index finger. "You need to be thanking someone a lot higher up."

Sometime later, they moved Nathan to a regular room. It had a chair that converted into a bed, and I was half-asleep on it when

Nathan turned the volume all the way up on the television. "Sloan, check it out!"

I pushed myself up. "What is it?"

He pointed to the television.

It was a news broadcast with a brunette anchor woman, and behind her was a picture of Larry Mendez. She spoke directly into the camera. "Panic broke out at a local Wal-Mart shopping center this evening in downtown San Antonio when there was what witnesses described as a loud explosion that left one man dead and many shoppers terrified. Alec Ortega is live on the scene. Alec, can you tell us what happened down there tonight?"

The screen switched to a scene in the parking lot with the Wal-Mart sign lit up in the background. "No one is really sure what happened tonight at this popular shopping center downtown. Numerous calls were made to police from customers who said an explosion happened inside the store." He held his hands out in confusion. "However, investigators have found no sign of explosives or any damage that could have been caused by one. What they did uncover was a man's body near the center of the store, but they say there is no sign of foul play. We spoke with Police Chief Albert Bechard and this is what he had to say."

The camera cut to an interview with a man in a police uniform. "At this time, we have found nothing that indicates there was any kind of explosion here at this store despite the testimony of countless shoppers and employees." The man looked genuinely puzzled. "We did recover a deceased person, but there is no sign the two events were related. The victim is forty-two-year-old Larry Mendez of Bexar County, and at this time, it appears as though he died of natural causes. We have found no evidence to suggest otherwise."

Nathan's jaw was dropped when he turned to look at me.

I pinched my lips together.

"Do you know something about this?" he asked.

My eyes widened, and I slowly shrugged my shoulders.

"Where is Warren?"

I shrugged again. "I don't know. I don't have a phone, remember?"

Just then, the door slowly opened and Warren's head peeked through the crack. "Is this the right room?"

"Yeah, come in," I said, sitting up on the edge of my makeshift bed.

He walked into the room. "Sorry, it took me forever to find out what room you guys were in. The nurse at the desk—" He stopped talking when he saw the horrified look on Nathan's face. "Uh, hey, Nate. How are you feeling?"

Nathan didn't answer.

I caught Warren's eyes and discreetly pointed toward the television.

"Larry Mendez is dead," Nathan said.

Warren blinked with surprise, but it wasn't very convincing. "Really?"

I almost laughed.

"How'd that happen?" Warren asked, walking over and sitting down next to me.

Nathan's expression was caught at the crossroads of confusion, anger, and fear. "I thought you might tell me. Where've you been?"

"Oh." Warren looked at me. "I've been out tying up some loose ends."

"Warren." Nathan's tone was scolding.

Warren smiled. "I almost forgot." He reached inside his jacket and pulled out a white plastic bag. "I got you a get well gift." He tossed the bag onto Nathan's lap.

Nathan unrolled it.

It was a pack of Skittles, inside a shopping bag...from Wal-Mart.

23.

NATHAN WAS DISCHARGED the next morning, and we were able to book a flight to Asheville that afternoon. When we got to North Carolina, I instructed Warren to drive us to my house. Nathan attempted a weak protest, but he was still in a lot of pain and didn't have his normal amount of arguing power.

He was still complaining as he leaned on me for support going up my front steps. "I'm fine, Sloan."

"That argument would be a lot more effective if you weren't using me as a crutch right now. You died two days ago. That's kind of a big deal. I don't want you staying in that apartment by yourself, so you're going to stay here with us. You can sleep in the armory."

He looked down at me. "The armory?"

"You'll see." I fumbled with my keys till I got the correct one in the front door.

I helped him up the stairs inside till we reached the guest room. "Holy mother," he said, looking around in astonishment at the arsenal.

I rolled my eyes and helped him over to the bed. "I know. I feel like I live at Fort Knox without the gold."

He winced in pain as he lay down on top of the comforter. I pulled his pain pills out of my coat pocket and put them on the nightstand. "You should take something and try to rest. We're going to run check on my dad, but we won't be gone for too long."

He nodded. "OK."

"I'll go get you some water." I scampered downstairs and retrieved a bottle of water from the refrigerator as Warren carried the load of suitcases in the front door. "Here, let me help." I took Nathan's backpack from him.

"Thanks," he said as he followed me up the steps.

I walked in the guest room and put the water on the nightstand and the pack beside the bed. "Call Warren's phone if you need anything. We'll bring you some dinner."

"Sounds good."

"Are you sure you'll be OK?" I asked.

He nodded. "Positive." As I turned to leave, he called out to me. "Sloan, wait."

I walked over to the side of his bed. "Yeah?"

He reached his hand toward me. "I never said thank you."

I laughed. "Nathan, I've almost gotten you killed once, and I actually got you killed a second time. You really don't need to thank me."

He nodded and pulled me down next to him. "Yeah, I do. You didn't give up. You saved my life."

Tears tickled the corners of my puffy eyes. There was so much I wanted to say to him, but I knew it wouldn't be fair to anyone. I leaned over and gently touched my lips to his forehead. I lingered there for a second to hopefully convey a message I could never say out loud.

"I love you," he whispered.

A tear slid down my cheek and dripped onto his. When I pulled away, his eyes were closed and he was smiling.

I stood up. "We'll be back in a little while."

When I walked out of the room, I pulled the door closed gently behind me. Warren was waiting with his hands in his pockets. If he had been watching from the doorway, he didn't say anything.

"You ready?" he asked.

I nodded. "Yep."

We drove to my dad's house, and he was sitting on the front porch when we pulled in the driveway. I jogged up the front path toward him and fell into his arms.

He sighed and kissed the side of my head. "Welcome home,

sweetheart."

"You have no idea how glad I am to be home," I told him as Warren caught up to us.

Dad put his hand under my chin and examined the bruising on my face. "What happened to you?"

I shook my head. "I'm fine. It looks worse than it is."

Warren smiled as he walked up onto the porch. "I promise I didn't do it."

He laughed and put his arm around my shoulders. "Come on. Let's go in. It's chilly out here." We turned and walked inside. "I expected a phone call when you met Sarah to tell me if she was actually your birth mom."

"Well, I broke my phone even worse when we were in Texas, and we had a lot going on. And yes, Sarah—her name is actually Kasyade—is the one who left me at the hospital."

We sat down on the sofa in the den. Take-out food containers littered the room. "What else did she have to say?" he asked. "Did she tell you who your father is?"

I shook my head. "No. She refused to tell me, actually."

He cocked his head to the side. "Really? Why?"

I blew out a sigh. "Oh, Dad, I don't even know where to start." I leaned forward on my elbows. "For starters, she's not a good angel. She almost killed us."

His eyes widened. "Really?"

"Yeah."

He looked confused. "She was so nice when I knew her."

"Warren and another angel we met ended up destroying her. At least for the time being," I said. "I know one thing. I'm not going to Texas again anytime soon."

He shook his head. "I would assume not. Is that how you got the bruises?" He pointed to my face.

"Yeah. It could have been a lot worse than it was," I said.

He rubbed my back. "I'm sorry your visit with her wasn't the reunion you had hoped for."

I smiled at him. "I got all I needed from her. I know a little bit more about where I came from and what I am."

He nodded. "That's good."

"Dad, we're going to stay at my house right now if that's OK. Warren leaves in a few days, and Nathan is staying with us because he caught the worst of the violence down in Texas. He really needs to be looked after for a while."

"Of course, sweetheart. I'm getting along pretty well here," he said. "I've cooked twice this weekend and haven't even had to call the fire department once."

I laughed. "That's awesome."

"Are you going back to work?" he asked.

"Yeah. I don't want to, but I need to go in tomorrow to do some catching up," I told him.

He nodded. "I think it would be good for you. I went to the office yesterday and saw some patients. Getting back into a routine will be good for us both."

My shoulders slumped as I looked from him to Warren. I wondered if anything about my life would ever be *routine* again.

* * *

When Warren and I left about an hour later, the sun was starting to set behind the mountains. Streaks of orange, pink, and purple swirled through the sky. A few bright stars twinkled against the dying light of the sun.

Warren wrapped his arms around me from behind. "You OK?"

I took a deep breath. "This is just the beginning, Warren. We haven't seen anything yet."

"Are you afraid?"

I nodded. "Did you hear Samael? He said the whole spirit world can sense me now. I can't hide from them." I shuddered in his arms. "They're coming after me to kill me."

He pressed a kiss to the bend of my neck. "Something tells me you're not that easy to kill."

"Is that supposed to make me feel better?"

He tightened his arms around me. "Think about it. If the evil spirits can see you, so can the good ones. You won't be alone, and don't forget what else Samael said. You'll have protection, even if you can't see it."

"I'm afraid."

"I know."

A faint ripple against the sky caught my attention. It was a very delicate shimmering wave against the colors of the horizon. I squinted and tried to focus on it, but couldn't make the figure any clearer. I pointed up to it. "Do you see that?"

His eyes followed my finger and carefully searched the sky. "See what?"

I knew exactly what it was and remembered Samael's words, *protection unseen.* For the first time, I knew I was seeing an angel. It seemed so obvious to me, splayed against the horizon, that I wasn't sure how I had missed seeing them before. I admired the silvery rippling figure again and felt a calm rush over me.

Finally, I smiled and hugged Warren's arms that were around my waist. "Nothing. Let's go. I want to stop by Adrianne's on the way home and heal her leg."

He smiled as he reached down and wrapped his hand around mine. "Do you think you can really do it?"

I nodded and glanced toward the sky. "I know I can."

24.

BY SOME MIRACLE, we made it three full days without any catastrophes, supernatural uprisings, or criminal disasters. But Thursday morning came, and it was more difficult to get out of bed than usual. I had been awake for a while, listening to the sound of the shower and then the hair dryer, but I had convinced myself that if I didn't get up, the day couldn't really begin. After a while, the door opened and Warren leaned in the bathroom doorway wearing only a pair of jeans. His black hair was hanging around his shoulders.

He smiled at me. "It's time. I need your help."

"No. Come back to bed."

"Sloan." His tone was even but cautionary.

Groaning, I pushed myself up off the bed. It was almost ten in the morning.

I walked into the bathroom, and Warren pulled out the vanity stool and sat down. He brushed his hair back and tied it with an elastic band. He looked at me in the mirror. "You ready?"

I ran my fingers through the end of his ponytail. "I can't do it," I whined.

He watched me in the mirror. "Am I going to have to do it myself?"

I sighed and shook my head. "No."

With trembling hands, I gripped his hair and took the pair of scissors he was holding over his shoulder. "It will grow back," he said as I stared at it. "Cut."

Cringing, I brought the scissors close to his head. The doorbell rang. I jumped when I heard it, slamming the scissors down on the counter.

"Damn it, woman," Warren grumbled as I ran out of the room.

When I reached the front door, I swung the door open to see Adrianne standing there holding an overnight bag and a cup of coffee. Her hair was cropped short in a pixie style, and she had on a pair of bright red, four-inch high heels that brought tears to my eyes. She stepped effortlessly over the threshold of my front door like she had never been injured at all.

"I'm so glad you're here. I need you." I was panting.

"Well, hold up because Nathan is coming in right after me." She nodded outside to where Nathan was climbing out of his truck.

"Nate, the door's open!" I called to him and grabbed Adrianne by the hand.

She looked down at me. "Maybe you should at least put on a bra before he gets in here, and have you even brushed your hair?"

"No. I just got out of bed." I dragged her up the stairs.

"What's so important?" she asked.

We walked into my bedroom. "Hair emergency."

Warren was still sitting in the vanity chair with his arms folded over his bare chest. She froze in the doorway and looked down at the scissors. "What's going on?"

"He wants me to cut it. I can't do it." I pushed her forward into the bathroom.

She stepped over behind him and put her hands on his shoulders. She leaned down close to his ear. "Trust me. You don't want her to do it. She cut her own bangs one time in junior high and wound up with a haircut like mine," she said, pointing to her own short hair. She leaned over him and picked up the scissors. "All of it?"

He nodded. "All of it."

I felt like I was going to throw up as the scissors sliced through his ponytail. I stumbled back a couple of steps into my room.

"Where is everyone?" I heard Nathan call downstairs.

"My room!" I shouted. "Come on up!"

Warren looked over at me. His hair fell just to his ears. "Please put on some damn clothes, Sloan."

"Whoops!" I yanked open a dresser drawer and grabbed the first thick material my fingers found. I slipped a black sweatshirt over my head.

Adrianne handed me the end of the ponytail. "Here you go."

My bottom lip popped out. "Will you guys laugh at me if I cry right now?"

"Yes," they said in unison.

Nathan walked into my room, holding a travel mug and a file folder. "What's going on?"

I nodded toward the bathroom where more black hair was falling to the floor.

He looked around the doorway. "Oh, that sucks," Nathan said. "Do you feel your superpowers fading right now?"

"I can still whip you in a fight if necessary," Warren said over his shoulder.

Nathan laughed. "Well, don't whip me till you've seen this." He handed Warren the paper. "It was in my email this morning."

"What is it?" I asked, stepping over next to Adrianne so I could peek over his shoulder.

Warren was shaking his head. "I don't believe it."

I read aloud the lines marked with a highlighter. "Department of Children and Family Services. Rachel A. Smith. 1992, 1997-2000."

Warren looked up at me. "In 1992, I was eight."

Both my hands shot up over my mouth. "Oh my god."

Adrianne looked at me with alarm. "What is it?"

No one answered her.

It wasn't by chance that Abigail was working there when Warren and Alice were placed in the home of a child molester. He crumpled the paper slowly in his fist.

Nathan crossed his arms. "If she was there, why didn't you feel it when she left?"

Warren shook his head. "I don't know, but right now I'm more concerned about what she was doing there in the first place."

I put my hand on his rigid shoulder and caught his eye in the reflection of the glass. "This isn't over."

The muscles working in his jaw. "No, it isn't."

After a long, awkward, and tense moment in the bathroom, Adrianne pointed to her watch and looked at us with wide and cautious eyes. "I hate to interrupt all the mysterious brooding in here, but we need to get a move on, Warren, if you want to keep to your schedule."

He cleared his throat and straightened in the chair. "You're right. Proceed."

Adrianne ran her fingers through what remained of his hair. "Do you want it all buzzed off, or do you want it within military regulations and as long as possible?"

"You can do that?" he asked, blinking with surprise.

She nodded. "Of course I can," she said. "Aren't you glad I came over? Please don't ever let Sloan near your head with a pair of scissors or clippers."

I swatted my hand at her, but she ducked out of the way. "Let me get rid of that," I said, taking the ball of paper from Warren. I bent to throw it in the wastebasket under the bathroom counter.

Nathan started laughing.

"What?" I asked, turning to look at him. Then I noticed Warren shaking his head with his eyes rolled up at the ceiling. My voice jumped up an octave. "What is it?"

Warren pointed toward the mirror. "Look at your back."

Craning my neck over my shoulder, I saw the reflection of the letters S.W.A.T. across my shoulders. I groaned. Nathan was doubled over, howling with laughter.

"What did I miss?" Adrianne asked.

My arms flopped to my sides in defeat. "It's Nathan's shirt," I said. "It's a long story."

She sighed and started cutting again. "I can only imagine."

Nathan dabbed at his eyes with his sleeve as his cackles subsided. "Not that I'm complaining about your outfit, Sloan, but why aren't you dressed?"

"She's not packed either," Warren said.

Nathan shook his head.

I pouted again. "It's too hard."

Adrianne jerked her thumb toward the bedroom. "Go get your shit together, right now."

Dropping my head, I shuffled to my bedroom, grabbing an overnight bag out of my closet as I went. I shoved some pajamas, clean underwear, and an outfit for the next day into the bag. My migraine medicine and my Xanax were on my nightstand. I dropped them in the top of the bag and zipped it shut. The sound of the clippers buzzing in the bathroom made me cringe.

When Adrianne was finished, my boyfriend looked like a giant GI Joe action figure. As he stood, she brushed the hair off his shoulders with a hand towel.

"You did a good job, Adrianne," he said, running his hand over the top. He turned around and looked at me. "Do you like it?"

I sighed. "You don't have the ability to look bad."

It wasn't the haircut I hated. It was the reason behind it. He leaned over and kissed me. "It will grow back, and then I'll never have to do this again," he said. "Are you about ready to go?"

I nodded, but dropped my shoulders in defeat.

After I had dressed, and Warren finished gathering everything he needed, the four of us walked out onto the front porch. I locked the front door behind us.

"What are we driving?" Adrianne asked.

"Not my truck," Nathan said. "Sloan's going to be puking all the way home with one of her migraines, and I just had the carpets cleaned from the last time."

I frowned. "Shut up."

"We're not taking the Challenger either." Warren looked down at me with eyes that dared me to argue.

"We'll take my car." I sighed and rolled my eyes. "You guys suck."

"Do you have your migraine medicine?" Warren asked, taking my keys from me.

I nodded. "In my bag."

Next door, a flag in the shape of a turkey fluttered on the breeze. Thanksgiving was around the corner, but I didn't have a thankful bone in my body. Warren was leaving, my mother was gone, demons wanted me dead...the list went on and on. As we walked to my car, I was already fighting back tears. It was going to be a rotten day.

Warren drove, and Nathan and Adrianne got in the back seat. I was glad they had both offered to make the trip to Charlotte with us. I knew that between Warren leaving and the migraine that would follow, I would be in no shape to drive myself home. Maybe the efforts of the two of them combined could keep me from completely going to pieces.

As we merged onto the interstate, Adrianne leaned between the front seats and looked at me. "So, have you heard any more from the FBI?"

I put my feet up on the dash and hugged my knees to my chest. "Yeah, they called yesterday to say that they've tracked down Abigail's establishments in Los Angeles, Chicago, and New York City. It's probably going to be one of the largest operations ever taken down before," I said.

Adrianne sighed and shook her head. "Wow. That's crazy."

Warren looked at her in the rearview mirror. "Did Sloan tell you how she was laundering the money?"

"Huh-uh." Adrianne shook her head. "How?"

"They think she was counting the payments as donations to Morning Star Ministries," Warren said.

Nathan sipped his coffee. "She was sending out end-of-the-year receipts and everything."

Adrianne's mouth fell open. "You've got to be kidding me."

I looked at her. "What's worse is the ministry reported over ten million dollars in income last year."

She covered her mouth with her hand. "That's sick. What's going to happen to those girls?"

I sighed. "I hope someone legitimate will actually try and help them recover."

Adrianne sat back in her seat. "It's hard to believe this stuff happens here in America."

Nathan was nodding. "They say sex trafficking generated more than nine billion dollars in the United States alone last year."

"God help us," she said. "Are they still looking for Abigail?"

"Of course. She's on the Most Wanted list now," Nathan said. "There's a reward for $500,000 from the FBI for information that will lead to her arrest."

She tapped her fingernail on my leather seat. "But they won't ever find her, will they? She won't return looking the same, right?"

"I highly doubt it," I said. "We watched her body turn to dust."

"But she will still come back?" she asked.

I nodded. "Samael said she would have to procure another body."

"Do you know how it's done?" Nathan asked.

"Demons possess people, right?" Adrianne said.

I shrugged. "I really have no idea, but I'm hoping it's a lengthy process."

Nathan leaned forward. "Hey, Warren, have you thought anymore about what you're going to do to Rex?" he asked. "You threatened him pretty good."

"Oh, I think about it every day," Warren said, looking at him in the mirror. "I'm going to let him sweat about it till I get home. Then I plan on paying him a little visit in prison."

"To do what?" Nathan asked.

Neither of us answered.

He held up his hand. "Let me guess. I don't want to know."

Warren looked at me and winked as he smiled. I reached over and meshed my fingers with his.

* * *

We pulled up to the front entrance of the Ramada Inn near the Military Entrance Processing Command Station in Charlotte. Warren put the car in park. "Nate, you wanna grab the bags while I go check in?"

"Sure," Nathan said, wrenching his door open.

Adrianne opened her door. "Come on. Let's go help Nate."

I was clutching my overnight bag when Warren came out and took it from my hands. He handed keys to both Nathan and Adrianne. "Thanks, guys," he said and dropped my bag back into the trunk.

Confused, I spun around toward him. "What are you doing?"

Adrianne nudged me with her arm. "Get in the car. We'll see you tomorrow."

I looked up at Warren. "What's going on?"

He smiled at me. "It's my last night with you, and as much as I like these two"—he nodded toward Adrianne and Nathan—"I'd really like to have you all to myself for a little while."

I felt my cheeks flush red. "All right."

I hugged Adrianne and Nathan goodbye, and Warren opened my car door for me. "Where are you taking me?" I asked.

He laughed as I got in. "You don't have to be in control of absolutely everything, Sloan. Stop asking so many questions."

When he got in and started the engine, I laughed. "Is this date going to end in chasing bad guys or fighting demons like all the other ones do?"

He chuckled and fastened his seatbelt. "God, I hope not."

Thirty minutes later, far outside the city limits, he turned onto a two-lane highway. We passed a billboard and two smaller signs on the road advertising the North Carolina State Gun Show. I turned in my seat and pointed at him. "If your idea of a romantic last night together has anything to do with a gun show, we might as well end this relationship right now."

He chuckled and reached for my hand. "I'm a little smarter than that." He nodded toward my window. "Look."

I followed the direction of his gaze and saw another sign that read *Willow Mountain Inn and Botanical Gardens.* My mind floated back to our date night in San Antonio when he so adamantly shot down my idea of visiting the gardens there.

I covered my mouth and laughed. Then I leaned over and kissed his cheek. "Well played, sir," I said. "Well played."

The inn was a beautifully restored Victorian, Queen Anne-style house, surrounded by lush greenery and flowers that were still blooming in the fall. The brochure in our room said it mostly functioned as an event place for weddings and parties, but there were six private villas which were rented out to overnight guests. Warren confessed he had help in planning the evening, but I already knew it the second we walked through the door. The place was Adrianne's style all the way.

We enjoyed a private dinner in the heated outdoor gazebo, shared a bottle of wine, and talked about anything and everything except for deployments or demons. For a moment, we were a completely normal couple.

He finished off what was left in my glass and offered me his hand. "Let's go for a walk."

A little dizzy from the wine and his intoxicating presence, I rested my cheek against his strong arm as we wandered along the stone pathways that wound around elaborate flowers and plants. We crossed over a quiet creek on a storybook stone bridge, and the faint scent of lemon balm and dill floated along the cool breeze.

I stopped walking and took a deep, refreshing breath. "Is this heaven?"

When I looked up at him, he was smiling. "If it isn't, I don't want to be there."

Turning to face him, I stretched up on my tiptoes and looped my arms around his neck. As we embraced, I closed my eyes to sear the moment into my memory.

After a minute, he reached up and took my wrists in his hands, pulling them gently down between us. "Do you remember when we were in San Antonio and I told you I wasn't going to propose to you?"

I laughed. "Yeah. I don't think I can forget about that conversation."

"Well..." He held up his hand. On the tip of his pinky finger was a large, circular diamond with a halo of smaller diamonds around it. It was glistening in the pink and orange glow of the last rays of sunlight.

My mouth fell open. "What is this?"

His eyes were wide, but his mouth was tipped up around the corners. "This still isn't a proposal," he cautioned.

"Then. What. Is. It?" I asked, carefully articulating my words.

He took a deep breath. "I know our life together is very complicated, and I'm sure it always will be. In fact, I'm pretty damn sure it's only going to get worse from this point on." He paused to laugh. "Angels and demons be damned because I don't want anything else in this world more than I want you and all the mess that comes with us being together."

I raised a skeptical eyebrow. "This sounds like a proposal."

He reached into his pocket and pulled out a ring box. He opened it, placed the ring in the cushioned velvet center, and snapped the box shut. I cocked my head to the side and glared at him as he tucked the box into the inside chest pocket of his jacket.

I put my hands on my hips. "Are you just trying to be an ass or what?"

He put his hands on the sides of my face. "No. I'm not trying to be an ass. I just want you to know how serious I am about us." He took a step closer to me. "I don't ever want to wonder if you might have any regrets."

I opened my mouth to spew my objection, as well as a few more obscenities, but he covered my lips with his finger.

"I know you love me, but you love him too." He bent slightly to look me directly in the eye. "While I'm gone, I want you to really consider it and decide, with absolute certainty, what you want for the rest of your life."

My brow crumpled. "Are you breaking up with me?"

He shook his head. "No, but I am giving you the next few months to really get honest with yourself and with me and Nathan." He put his hand over the pocket where he had stashed the box. "I want you to be sure because when I put this ring on your hand, it's going to be for forever."

I dropped my gaze to our feet, and a tear dripped from my eye and splashed onto the toe of his boot. Warren was right. I knew he was. Knowing it was the right thing to do didn't make it any easier though. I didn't deserve Warren. Hell, I didn't deserve either of them.

He tipped my chin up and brought his lips down to meet mine. "I love you," he said again when he pulled away.

"I love you, too."

* * *

Adrianne had a loaded smile splashed across her face the next morning when Warren and I met her and Nathan in the lobby of the Ramada Inn. "Well? Did you two have fun last night?"

I smiled and looped my arm through Warren's. "It was a beautifully spectacular evening."

She clapped her hands with glee. "Yeah? Did anything *exciting* happen?"

Heat rose in my cheeks. Lots of exciting things happened, but none of them would I share with Adrianne...at least not in Warren's presence—or Nathan's. I recognized her tone though, and I held up my bare left hand. "We're not engaged, if that's what you're wondering."

Nathan looked at Adrianne. "You owe me twenty bucks."

She rolled her eyes.

Warren laughed and looked down at his watch, then at me. "We've got to get going. Are you ready?"

I pouted. "No."

He sighed and tugged on my arm. "Come on."

Nathan drove my car down Whitehall Park Street till we reached a large four story white building. I was riding in the back seat, practically sitting in Warren's lap. When he parked in the lot near the front, we all got out. Warren pulled his duffel bag out of the trunk and dropped it on the curb.

Adrianne wrapped her arms around his neck. "Be safe. I'll pray for you," she said.

He smiled. "Thanks, Adrianne."

Next, he turned to Nathan. "Come home safe, brother," Nathan said.

Warren pulled him into a tight hug. It was odd seeing the two of them embrace. Odd, and perfect. "Take care of her for me," Warren said when he stepped away. "Keep your damn hands to yourself, but take care of her."

Nathan laughed. "I will."

Warren gave me a warning glare. "Don't let her run off and get herself into a shit-load of trouble while I'm gone."

I held up my hands. "I don't do that!"

"Right," the three of them said at the same time.

Nathan and Adrianne got into the car. Warren took a slow step toward me and reached for my hand. He rested his forehead against mine and closed his eyes. "In all seriousness, please be careful."

"I will be. I promise."

He tucked my hair behind my ears. "The gun you shot when we were in Texas is in your nightstand by the bed. It's loaded, just in case. Get Nathan to take you to the range again. You need to practice."

I groaned. "I don't wanna."

He put his arms around me and pulled me close. "I don't care."

Tears began to well up in my eyes. "Please come home to me."

He pressed his lips against my forehead. "Always."

Tilting my chin up with his finger, he kissed me long and slow. The magnetic energy surged through us, and I enjoyed its intoxicating tingle one last time. My knees felt weak when he finally pulled away. He lifted my left hand up and kissed the spot where I should have been wearing that sparkling diamond.

He cut his eyes at me. "Just out of curiosity, if I had asked, what would you have said?"

"You know what I would have said." I sniffed and rubbed my eyes, smearing mascara across my knuckles.

He cupped my face in his hands and wiped under my eyes with his thumbs. Staring into his eyes, I let the sensation of his kind soul burn itself into my memory. He kissed me one more time. "I love you," he said.

"I love you."

Stepping away, he picked up his black bag, slinging the strap over his shoulder. He headed toward the front door and paused at the entrance to look back and wave one last time. I still hated his short hair.

Then he was gone.

* * *

The car was silent till we got out of Charlotte's city limits. Adrianne reached back and touched my arm. Her makeup was smudged from crying as well. "Are you OK?" she asked.

My cheeks were still wet with silent tears. I nodded and squeezed her fingers. "Yeah. I'm OK."

"You wanna talk about what happened last night? I thought for sure you were going to show up engaged this morning." She pointed from Nathan to herself. "We placed bets on whether or not he was going to propose to you."

I folded my arms over my chest. "I want to know why Nathan was so sure he wouldn't."

Nathan kept his eyes on the road. "Because he told me."

My head snapped back in surprise. "He told you?"

"Yeah. He said he wanted to, but he needed to give you some time to make up your mind without him being in the picture."

Adrianne split a glance between both of us. "Make up your mind about what?"

Nathan and I both stared at her.

"Ohhhhh." She turned around and slouched down in her seat. "Well, this is awkward."

Nathan seemed as desperate to change the subject as I was. He looked over his shoulder at me. "How's your head? Is it starting to hurt yet?"

I looked up with surprise. "Not at all, actually."

He looked down at the odometer. "That's weird. I figured it would have started about ten miles ago."

A surprising thought exploded in my mind, and the puzzle pieces swirled and snapped together.

My new instant ability to heal.

Being able to see Warren's soul.

Detecting angels even though they weren't visible.

The reason why the spirit world was suddenly so interested in me.

The absence of my migraines...

Warren hadn't completely left me at all.

"Oh my God."

Adrianne turned around in her seat again at the sound of alarm in my voice. "What is it?" she asked.

I clamped my hand over my mouth to prevent myself from blurting it out.

I'm pregnant.

THE ANGEL OF DEATH

ELICIA HYDER

Book Three of
The Soul Summoner Series

For Rena.
Thanks for saving my life.
Literally.

1.

"YOU'RE GOING TO put that thing *where?*"

My eyes were double their normal size as I peered at Dr. Grayson Watts over the bridge the paper sheet formed between my knees. The long device in her hand looked more like a lightsaber than a medical instrument. My mouth was gaping so wide that I should have been at the dentist's office rather than the OB/GYN.

Dr. Watts cocked her head to the side and raised an eyebrow. "It's a transvaginal ultrasound, Sloan. It will be a little uncomfortable, but this is the only way we can get a clear picture of your uterus at this stage and determine how far along you are."

I winced. "It looks like you're going to battle the Empire."

She wasn't amused.

I sighed and flopped back on the exam table. "Go ahead."

"Relax your knees," she said.

I focused on the speckled ceiling tiles and gulped. "Oh, boy."

I sucked in a deep breath and whimpered as she impaled me like a jousting knight.

"Relax," she said again.

I considered kicking her in the face.

A moment later, she turned the screen on her computer toward me, and I rose up on my elbows again. "Here is your uterus." She was pointing to a cloud of white fuzz on the screen. "And this black blob is the gestational sac." She shifted her magic wand around some more. "And this little spot right here, that's your baby."

I squinted my eyes. A small, gray misshapen bean was inside the black blob.

My chest tightened, and I fell back onto my pillow again and took a few deep breaths.

"It looks like you're about eight weeks along," she said.

"Eight weeks?" I shook my head. "No. That can't be right. I know exactly when I got pregnant. October 19th."

I counted backward in my mind. So much had happened in the past few months it was hard to place the events and catastrophes in the order in which they occurred. It had been three weeks since my boyfriend, Warren Parish, was reactivated with the Marine Corps. The week before that, my biological mother—a demon, literally—tried to kill me. Two weeks before that, my adoptive mother died from brain cancer on October 19th. The tiny speck on the screen was the product of emotional, grief-stricken sex, when my boyfriend hadn't bothered to remove his boots or use any protection. I couldn't be eight weeks along.

"It's only been about six weeks," I told her.

She closed my legs when she removed the wand. "The weeks are calculated starting with the first day of your last period, so mid-October is right for the conception date."

"I knew it," I said. "Warren should be very glad the military has him because if he were still here, I might kill him."

Dr. Watts was trying hard to suppress a giggle. Her latex gloves snapped as she removed them. She pulled a sliding, paper wheel from her pocket and adjusted it with her thumbs. "This puts your due date as July 11th."

As she scribbled in her notes, I stared out the window. On one hand, July 11th felt like an eternity away. On the other, if I had learned anything in the previous four months, it was how much could radically change in such a short time period. Warren was lost to me in November, and there was no guarantee he would find me by July.

"Are you all right?"

I groaned and covered my face with my arms.

She rolled on her chair till she was by my head. "Sloan?"

I let out a deep sigh. "I'm all right. This wasn't exactly planned."

"I can tell." She helped me sit up. "Can I ask about the father?"

There was so much to say about my baby's father that I didn't even know where to begin. He was the son of an Angel of Death. He was a Recon Marine Sniper and then a mercenary. He had a body that could only be ranked on a scale of one to oh-my-god, and he made love like he should require a height restriction. Of course, none of this was the kind of information Dr. Watts was interested in.

"He's not here because he's off in Iraq or Israel or somewhere," I said.

"Military?" she asked.

I smoothed the paper sheet over my bare legs. "He's in the Marines, but I don't know where he is. He can't tell me anything."

She frowned. "I'm sorry to hear that. Does he know you're pregnant?"

"No one outside this room knows." That was true, unless you counted the supernatural world. "You won't tell my dad, will you?" My father and Dr. Watts worked in the same building.

She dumped her gloves in the trashcan. "I wouldn't dream of it. And legally, whatever you say in this room is protected under doctor-patient confidentiality."

"Really?"

"Absolutely."

I was skeptical. "What if I sound crazy? Could you tell someone then?"

"Not unless I thought you might harm someone else or yourself," she answered. "Do you need to talk about something?"

There were only a handful of people on the planet who knew I was part-angel, and none of them knew I was pregnant. So no one had heard the fears all my over-thinking had produced since those two pink lines popped up on the home pregnancy test. *Is it fair to bring a baby into the mess that has become my life? Will the baby be normal with parents like me and Warren? Can I even live through childbirth if the kid inherits Warren's big head and broad shoulders?*

I hesitated. "Did you notice anything abnormal about the baby?"

Her eyes widened with surprise, and she shook her head. "No. Nothing at all. Are you worried about something specific?"

I was worried about many specific things, none of which I could discuss with Dr. Watts. "My body has been through a lot lately, before I knew I was pregnant."

"Trauma?" she asked, pulling out my medical chart and a pen.

My fight with Kasyade was certainly traumatic. I had suffered a broken hip, a broken nose, several broken ribs, and was slammed into the concrete more times than I could count. Again, I couldn't tell the doctor about that either, since then I would have to explain how my body had healed itself on the way to the hospital.

"I've been through severe emotional trauma," I said, which wasn't at all a lie.

Her face twisted into a frown full of pity. "I heard about your mother passing recently. That must have been painful for you."

My mother had complained of a headache on Monday and was dead by Saturday. To describe the incident as 'painful' was almost insulting. I had successfully managed to not cry over it yet that day, and I wasn't about to start while I was naked from the waist down with my dad's colleague. So I bypassed the conversation altogether.

"I also have a panic disorder, and I take Xanax."

She grimaced. "You should avoid taking it, unless it's absolutely essential, especially for the first twelve weeks or so. It does carry a risk for your baby."

I cringed. "I've taken it a few times recently. Since my mom died, I've had nightmares that sometimes trigger panic attacks in the middle of the night."

She made some notes. "Pregnancy will probably increase your dreams."

I groaned. "That's just great." I thought for a second. "Also, I won't be able to do parts of my job without it."

She pulled her head back in surprise. "Your job induces anxiety? Aren't you the publicist for the county?"

"I am," I said. "I have to work at the sheriff's office some, and it's inside the jail. I always have attacks there."

"Fear of enclosed spaces?" she asked.

I laughed. "Sure. That's it." It wasn't, but it was a better reason than the truth.

"Maybe you should think about seeing a psychiatrist."

I laughed again but didn't comment. Any truthful explanation would only validate her suggestion. "What do I need to do as far as being pregnant? I'm a first-timer."

She scribbled something on a pad of paper. "Here is a prescription for generic prenatal vitamins, and I want to see you again in a month."

I nodded. "I'll make the appointment before I leave."

"Do you smoke?" she asked.

"Nope."

"Do you drink alcohol?"

"All the time."

She looked up with alarm. "How much do you drink?"

"I usually have a few beers a week," I said.

She tapped her pen on my chart. "Like, more than four in one sitting?"

"Never. I'd pass out around four."

She pointed the pen at me. "No alcohol."

"I figured."

"What about other meds?" she asked.

I shook my head. I had a prescription for migraines, but I wouldn't need it.

She looked over her notes. "So, no Xanax, and don't take any over the counter pain meds except Tylenol and only if it's absolutely necessary. Go easy on caffeine and stay away from raw and undercooked meat and seafood. Other than that, drink plenty of water and no heavy lifting. Have you had a flu shot this year?"

I shook my head.

"Get a flu shot," she said.

"OK."

She stood and pulled open the cabinet over the sink. She retrieved a thick paperback and handed it to me. "This book answers most questions I'm regularly asked, so I bought them for my patients. If you can't find an answer in there, call me."

I gripped the book, *What to Expect When You're Expecting*, with both hands. A lumpy looking woman with a suburban haircut, 1980's red trousers, and an orange smock was seated in a rocking chair on the cover. My face soured. "Do I have to dress this way?"

She laughed and patted my shoulder. "We're all done here. You can get dressed." She walked across the room but paused before she reached the door. "Sloan, please tell someone you trust that you're pregnant. You'll need support through this."

I took a deep breath. "I will."

"Oh, and happy Thanksgiving," she said.

A wave of nausea hit my stomach. "Happy Thanksgiving."

Before I left her office, I made an appointment for the next month.

On my way outside, I shoved the baby book in my purse and checked the screen of my brand new cell phone. It had been on silent since the nurse took me back to see the doctor. There were two missed calls and a text message from Warren.

Call me ASAP. Getting ready to board the C-130 and have to turn off my phone.

I hit the call button, and he picked up on the first ring. "Thank God, I was afraid you wouldn't call me back in time." He was out of breath. "Where have you been? I've been trying to reach you for about thirty minutes."

"I was in with my doctor," I told him as I sank back against the wall. A lump rose in my throat.

"The doctor? Is everything all right?" he asked.

"Yeah, everything is fine. I had a checkup." At least it wasn't a complete lie. "So, this is it?"

"This is it," he said. "We are flying out today. I may not be able to have contact for a while after this. I had to hear your voice one more time."

"Still no idea when you will be back?" I asked.

"Nope," he said. "Although, I think it will be shorter than we expected. Maybe three to six months."

I picked at my cuticle. "And you still can't tell me where you're going or what you're doing?"

"You know I can't, babe." There was a loud rumble in the background. "I've got to go. I'll be in touch as soon as I can," he said over the commotion.

God, I wanted to tell him about the baby. "Warren!"

"Yeah?"

I bit my lower lip and hesitated. "Uh…" *Say it.* "Be careful."

"I will if you will," he said, laughing. "I love you, Sloan."

"I love you too."

"I'll be back before you know it." He disconnected the call without saying goodbye.

My back was glued to the wall in the hallway. I couldn't move. I just stood and stared at the phone in my hand, thinking about what Dr. Watts had said before I left. *Tell someone you trust.* I stepped onto the elevator and pressed the button for floor three. If I trusted anyone in the world the most, it would be my dad.

Dad's office was almost empty when I opened the door to the

waiting room. There was only one elderly patient waiting to see him. Thankfully, Dad had been keeping his workload light since Mom wasn't there to help him. She had been his primary nurse since he opened the practice. When Mom was alive, I rarely visited during work hours, but since her funeral, I made it a point to drop in a few times a week to check on him.

The receptionist greeted me, far too bubbly before lunch. "Hey there, Sloan."

"Hey, Patty," I said. "Is my dad busy?"

She looked down at a piece of paper on her desk. "He's in an exam room with a patient, but you can wait in his office if you'd like."

I glanced around the small lobby. "I'll wait out here. Can you let him know?"

She stood from her desk. "Of course."

I took a seat next to an old man with sporadic white hairs encircling his mostly bald head. His skin sagged around his dark eyes and his jaw line. He turned a wide, toothy grin toward me. "Hello, Sloan," he said, his voice deep and raspy.

My eyes widened with surprise. "Hello."

He nodded. "You don't know me, but I've seen your picture on the desk in your dad's office. He's awful proud of you."

I felt my face flush. "Yeah, he is."

He offered me his hand. "My name's Otis Cash."

"Nice to meet you, Mr. Cash." Something about the old man caught my attention. I had gotten the same feeling from my mother before she died. Mr. Cash had cancer. "Do you come see my dad often?"

His head bobbed up and down. "Ever since they found the tumor in my lungs a couple of months ago," he said. "Your dad's been checking up on me every few weeks since I refused to see that cancer doctor they wanted me to go to." He laughed, wheezing heavily. "I told 'em, I don't need a cancer doctor. I'm eighty-nine years old. I've lived through World War II and Vietnam. My wife's been gone for twenty years, and my youngest granddaughter just had her first baby last year. I've lived too good of a life to go out sick with chemotherapy."

His chuckling turned into a fit of coughing. Sympathetically, I put my hand on his back. "Sounds like you've lived a pretty full life." I closed my eyes and focused on Mr. Cash's cancer.

"I have," he said. "It'd be swell to see it through Christmas one last time with my kids, but I'm ready to go on home when the good Lord wants me."

With my other hand, I patted his arm. "World War II and Vietnam, huh? That's pretty impressive."

"Yep." He paused to cough and catch his breath. "I was in one of the first groups that arrived at Hiroshima after they dropped the bomb on 'em. There was nothin'. I mean, no people, no military, no stray dogs even. It was all ash and black." He shook his head as my hand warmed on his back. "Then I was in Saigon for a year during Vietnam."

"That's incredible, Mr. Cash," I said.

He took a deep and easy breath and looked over at me. "You feelin' all right, young lady? You seem awfully warm to me."

I leaned into him. "I'm fine. Want to hear a secret?"

"Sure."

I lowered my voice and looked carefully around the room. "I'm pregnant."

He laughed. "No kidding? I'll bet your daddy's a happy man."

"He doesn't know yet," I said. "I think I might tell him today."

He pulled back and eyed me curiously. "I didn't know you were married."

I shook my head. "Oh, I'm not. So you'd better say a prayer for me before I go back there and break the news."

He pointed down at the carpet. "You're going to tell him right now?"

I sighed. "That's the plan."

He chuckled. "Well, that man is over the moon about you. I'm sure you'll be fine. Where's the baby's father?"

My hand cooled as the last ounces of my power left my fingers. I slowly removed it so Mr. Cash wouldn't notice.

I shrugged my shoulders. "He's a military man too. He's deployed right now."

"Really?" he asked. "What branch?"

"The Marines."

He laughed, this time with no rasp in his voice at all. "I was an Army man myself," he said. "But I won't hold it against 'ya that your man is a *jarhead*."

I clasped my hands together over my knee. "I try not to hold it against him myself."

The door into the waiting room swung open, and my dad stepped out with an elderly woman clutching his arm. "Now, don't you forget," she was saying, "to bake the casserole at 350 degrees for an hour."

"I won't forget," he replied.

Dad turned, his face brightening when he saw me. He looked down at the old woman. "Mrs. Hannigan, you be safe on your drive home now."

She patted his hand. "I will, Robert. I will."

The woman left the office, and Dad walked over to me and Mr. Cash. "Otis, I hope my daughter isn't causing you too much trouble out here," he said, reaching out to shake his hand.

I rolled my eyes.

Mr. Cash smiled. "She's just as wonderful as you say she is."

Blushing, I nudged him with my elbow. "You old charmer."

He laughed.

We both stood. Dad looked at me. "Mr. Cash is my last appointment before lunch. Do you have time to wait?"

I opened my mouth to answer, but Mr. Cash cut me off. "You know, Dr. Jordan, I'm havin' a pretty good day today. I think I'll reschedule my appointment and let you chat with this lovely girl." The old man winked at me.

Dad's mouth fell open a little. "Are you sure, Otis?"

"Yeah, I don't mind waiting," I told him.

Otis shook his head. "I'm sure. Maybe I'll go see my own daughter."

I smiled as he turned to leave. "Mr. Cash?"

He looked at me in question.

I hugged him. "Happy Thanksgiving, and if I don't bump into you again beforehand, have a Merry Christmas too. I hope you enjoy it with your family."

He cocked his chin to the side and beamed at me. "The good Lord willin'." Without another word, he turned and left the room.

Dad looked down at me and raised an eyebrow. "You healed him, didn't you?"

I pressed my lips together. "Maybe."

He sighed and shook his head. "People will start thinking I'm a miracle worker if all my patients keep ending up suddenly cured around here." He put his arm around my shoulders and steered me through the door toward his office.

"Is that such a bad thing?" I asked, looking up at him.

"Well, no, but it will raise questions. Mr. Otis has stage four terminal cancer," he said.

I grinned. "Not anymore."

He rifled through some files on his desk while I sat in the leather wingback chairs meant for patients and pharmaceutical reps. "How come you're not at work today?" he asked. "Are you already off for the holiday?"

I crossed my legs. "I had an appointment with Dr. Watt's downstairs."

He carried a folder to the filing cabinet in the corner. "A checkup?"

I scrunched up my nose. "Sort of. Dad, you need to sit down."

He turned and looked at me. "Is everything OK, sweetheart?"

A deep breath puffed out my cheeks. I slowly expelled it. "Well…"

His eyes widened, and he moved over in front of me, sitting down carefully on the edge of his desk. "What is it?"

"Warren just called," I said. "He left the States."

Relief washed over Dad's face, like he was sure I was about to tell him I was dying. "I hate that. He still doesn't know when he will be back?"

I shook my head. "Nope."

"Well, that's not exactly a surprise—"

I cut him off. "There's more, Dad."

His face fell again. "Oh no. I hate it when you say that."

I rubbed my fingers against my eyes. "Do you promise you won't freak out?"

He laughed. "Sloan, last month you told me your migraines were supernatural. Then you told me you were half-angel. After that, you informed me your birth mother was a demon, and she tried to kill you. Do you really think you could say anything to me at this point that would shock me?"

"I'm pregnant."

Dad slipped off the corner of his desk. He caught himself before hitting the floor. His mouth was gaping as he straightened. "What?"

I pulled the ultrasound picture from my purse and handed it to him. "I'm due July 11th."

His mouth was still hanging open as he looked at it.

"Dad?"

He glanced up. "Can I assume Warren is the father?"

I folded my arms across my chest and scowled. "Seriously?"

He held up his hands in defense. "It's a legitimate question that I'm sure Warren will probably ask as well."

This time, *my* mouth fell open. "He'd better not!"

"He's aware things aren't strictly business with you and Detective McNamara."

"That may be true, but Warren knows I'm not sleeping with Nathan. I'm surprised, and pretty disappointed, it even crossed your mind."

He sighed. "I'm sorry. I didn't mean it the way it sounded. Have you told him?"

I smirked. "Warren or Nathan McNamara?"

He frowned. "Sloan."

"I haven't told anybody, Dad. Not even Adrianne," I said, and it surprised even me. I'd been telling my best friend, Adrianne Marx, everything since I was thirteen.

"Why didn't you tell Warren?"

"Because I found out after he left. I figured it out when we dropped him off at the Marine station in Charlotte last month and I didn't get a migraine. It made everything make sense. My demon-mom trying to murder me, my sudden ability to heal, oh—and I saw Warren's soul for the first time ever."

"That's right. You could never see his soul," he said.

"But I can now. I can sense him like I can sense everyone else," I said.

He rubbed his palms over his face.

I leaned forward and rested my elbow on his desk. "Am I wrong for not telling Warren? It didn't seem right because he's already so worried about me, and I'm sure he's worried about the crap with me and Nathan…" I cast my gaze at the carpet. "He needs to focus on whatever dangerous stuff they have him doing. He doesn't need anything else to freak out about."

Dad sighed. "I don't know, Sloan. If it were me, I would want to know. Imagine what it will do to him when he shows up and you've got a belly out to here." He was holding his hand about a foot out from his stomach. "Or worse. What if you've got a baby in your arms when he comes home?"

I groaned. "You're probably right. Maybe I'll tell him if I get to talk to him again on the phone. I'm not writing it in a letter though."

He shook his head. "No, don't do that." He handed me the

ultrasound picture. "Does this mean you'll marry him?"

"We talked about it before he left, but he said I needed to take the time while he's gone to figure out what I want for the rest of my life," I said.

"Him or the detective?" Dad asked.

I nodded.

"Well?" he asked.

I turned my palms up. "Aside from the obvious fact that I'm in love with Warren, doesn't it kind of make up my mind if we're having a baby together?"

Dad was thoughtful for a moment. "Sloan, you can't put that kind of pressure on your child. You can't just marry him because of the baby. You still have to choose for yourself." He laughed a little. "I will say you won't come across another man like Warren. I wouldn't be so understanding if I were in his shoes."

Tears pooled in my eyes. "I can't help it. If I could turn off my feelings for Nathan, I would. I swear I would."

Dad got up and knelt down beside me. "Come here." He pulled me into his arms and let me cry on his shoulder.

"I don't know what to do. Why can't I just love them both?"

He pulled back to look at me. His eyes were serious. "You *can* love them both. But sometimes, the most loving thing we can do for someone is let them go."

I sniffed and wiped my nose on my sleeve. "I don't know how."

He tucked a loose strand of hair behind my ear. "You have to figure out how, sweetheart, because three-way relationships don't work. Pretty soon you won't have a choice, and you might lose them both." He handed me a tissue from the box on his desk. "May I ask you a question?"

I braced myself.

He studied my face. "What is it about Nathan?" He held up his hands. "Don't get me wrong, he's a good man. It's just you and Warren seem so perfect for each other. It surprises me you're still struggling with a decision."

I had asked myself the same question over and over since the fall. "You know, for years I pretended to be normal because I feared if people found out what I was really like, they'd be afraid or they'd hate me. For years no one knew except Adrianne, not even you and mom."

Dad squeezed my hand.

"Then Nathan showed up," I said, smiling. "The first day we met, he had me so flustered that I basically blurted it out." I took a deep breath. "And he did the opposite of reject me. He found out everything I wanted to keep hidden, and I think he liked me even more."

"And then Warren showed up," Dad said with a sad, soft expression.

"Yeah, and like you said, Warren's perfect. It's like he was made for me," I said. "Sometimes it feels like the universe shut everything down with me and Nathan and neither of us had a choice in it."

Dad grinned. "I wouldn't say it shut *everything* down. Otherwise you wouldn't still have to choose."

"Yeah."

He squeezed my shoulder. "Well, if your old man's opinion matters, I really like them both. I don't think you could find two better men to pick from."

I whined. "That is so not helpful."

"I know."

"You really won't tell me who you think I should be with?" I asked.

He shook his head. "Maybe someday but not today." He winked at me. "I don't want to give up any leverage I may have in case they start bribing me with gifts or money."

I wadded up the tissue and threw it at him.

2.

MY ABILITY TO summon people had drastically improved since I found out I was pregnant. So when my phone rang as I left Dad's office, it wasn't a surprise that Detective Nathan McNamara's face popped up on the screen.

I tapped the answer button and pressed the phone to my ear. "I was just talking about you," I said in lieu of a greeting.

He chuckled. "You know, it's not always you putting your voodoo on me. Sometimes I call or come by all on my own."

I squinted against the sunshine as I unlocked my car and got inside. "Whatever you say, Nathan. What's up?"

"Where are you?" he asked.

"I stopped in to visit my dad, but I'm heading back to work now." I started my engine and backed out of the parking space.

"Good. Come by my office on your way in."

I slammed on my brakes, bringing the car to a lurching halt. Nathan's office was located inside the jail, and I could no longer take my Xanax. "No."

"No?" he asked. "Trust me. You want to see this."

I groaned and put the car in drive.

"I'll see you in ten minutes," he said and disconnected the call.

Nathan knew how much being at the jail affected me, and he

wouldn't ask me to come if it wasn't important. So, on the drive there, I practiced deep breathing exercises and tried to think about anything but the panic attack I knew was on its way.

A few minutes later, I pulled into the jail parking lot and parked in the space beside Nathan's county-issued SUV. I took the steps to the front door two at a time and sucked in a deep breath before pulling the door open.

I breathed a small sigh of relief when I saw Virginia Claybrooks stuffed into the office chair behind the front desk. Her uniform was screaming at the seams, and her shoulder-length black wig was sitting a little too far back on her forehead. She was on the phone, and her bright red lips bent into a fake smile when she saw me.

She held up a long manicured fingernail, signaling for me to wait before continuing her animated verbal assault on whoever was on the other end of the line. "Honey, if you wanted to have Thanksgiving dinner with your baby boy, you shoulda raised him better so his ass didn't wind up in jail! I don't give a turkey's butt about whatchoo think is fair and not fair. Not fair is me having to sit my ass on this phone, listening to the whinin' and complainin' of you people when I oughtta be...Hello? Hello?"

She stared at the phone for a moment in disbelief. "That bitch done hung up on me!"

I tried to suppress my laughter, but I wasn't successful.

She rounded on me. "You think sumthins' funny?"

I covered my mouth with my hand and shook my head. "No, Ms. Claybrooks. I'm sorry."

"How 'you know my name?" she barked at me.

"Ms. Claybrooks, I've worked with the sheriff for years." I tapped my chest. "I'm Sloan Jordan."

She tossed her head from side to side. "I don't know no Sloan Jordan."

I sighed. "Can you please tell Detective McNamara I'm here?" I asked. "He's expecting me."

She looked me up and down so skeptically that I half-expected her to throw me out the front door. "Mmm-hmm," she said, pressing her lips together. She picked up the phone and pushed a few buttons. "McNamara!" She waited. "De-Tec-Tiv Mc-Na-Mara!" Her voice bounced off the concrete walls around us.

She slammed the phone down and looked at me. "He ain't

answerin'."

Her phone rang, and she picked it up. "Hello?" She rolled her eyes toward the ceiling and huffed. "They's six thousand offices up in this buildin'. How do you people expect me to remember 'em all. I got close enough for you to hear me so stop your bitchin'." She looked over at me. "You got a girl up here askin' for ya…Uh-huh, OK." She hung up the phone and forced a smile in my direction. "He'll be right with you."

Rather than sit, I paced the lobby. Evil reverberated off the walls like a heartbeat. The whole place pulsed with dark energy, and it tightened around my throat. I took a deep breath in and blew it out slowly. The mechanical doors slid open, and Nathan stuck his head out. "Sloan!"

I jumped, then scurried over.

Even my rising anxiety wasn't enough to completely suppress the butterflies that were disturbed every time I laid eyes on Nathan McNamara. He was in his standard outfit of khaki tactical cargos and an olive drab green fleece pullover. He wore his badge around his neck and a ball cap with an American flag patch on the front pulled low over his face.

Nathan was the guy mothers wanted their daughters to marry, and the one fathers warned them about, all wrapped up in one. He was the blond-haired boy next door with a baby-face smile and the ability to put a bullet between someone's eyes. He was also the kryptonite to my better judgement, and he had been nothing but trouble for me since the day we met.

"Hey stranger," he said. "Long time, no see."

That was a joke. Nathan had come by every night for the past three weeks. Warren had asked him to keep tabs on me since we found out I had a cosmic bounty on my head.

His eyes widened when I stepped through the door. "You OK?"

I pumped the collar of my blouse forcing cool air down the front. "You know I'm not. I hate this place."

He nudged me forward. "Come on. We won't be here long."

We walked past his office, and I jerked my thumb toward his door. "Where are we going?"

"Women's solitary," he answered.

I shuddered. "Isn't that where they keep the really bad people?"

"Sometimes."

"Nathan," I whined, dragging my feet.

He urged me on. "We'll be on the medical hall. I promise it'll be worth it."

My rising blood pressure stirred my doubt in him.

Once we were deep inside the jail, we went through one more heavy metal door that opened to a long hallway. Nathan escorted me by four locked rooms that reeked of evil before stopping in front of an empty cell. "What is this?" I asked.

He nodded toward the door. "Look through the window."

Curious, I peeked inside.

The stale white room was flooded with blinding light from the overhead halogens. There was a steel frame bed shoved against the wall, a metal toilet, and a matching small sink. "I don't get it," I said, looking back at him.

He looked in, then took a step back. "Under the bed."

I leaned toward the glass again. This time I saw long strands of red hair laying across the concrete floor, and the edge of a corpse peeked out from the shadows. I gasped. "Why is there a body in there?"

"Keep watching." He knocked his knuckles against the metal.

A hand shot out from under the bed in our direction. I jumped back. "What the hell?"

He put his hand on my shoulder and ushered me forward again. Covering my mouth with my hands, I watched an emaciated woman, paler than anyone I'd ever seen, drag herself out from under the bed. I scrambled to get away, but Nathan held me still.

He put his lips to my ear. "She can't get to you."

"She's not a *she*, Nathan." I gripped his sleeve as I looked at him. "She's not human."

He looked only mildly surprised. "They found her wandering around the Vance Memorial completely naked. She doesn't speak English, but she kept saying one thing very clearly."

"What was that?"

"Sloan Jordan."

My mouth fell open. "What?"

Then her soulless eyes settled on me. They were the color of flawless sapphires. "*Id vos, Sloan!*" The woman banged her fists against the glass, her nails caked with dirt, or blood, I wasn't sure which. I'd put my money on blood given the heavy white bandages on her forearms. "*Id vos! Id vos! Utavi! Ename utavi.*"

Had I not already been mid-panic attack, she would have triggered one. I stumbled back into Nathan.

"*Nankaj morteirakka!*" she screamed.

My heart was pounding. The air was as thick as soup. "Nathan, I can't stay in here."

He put his hand on the back of my neck. "Did you take your Xanax?"

I shook my head. "No. I forgot it," I lied.

The woman threw her body against the door. "*Ketka, Sloan! Ename utavi!*"

Nathan took hold of my arm, just as my legs wobbled. "Come on. Let's get you out of here." He hooked an arm around my waist.

She was still wailing in her cell. "Sloan! *Sloan!*"

My heart was pounding so loud I could swear it was echoing off of the walls. I feared my head might pop right off my shoulders. Nathan was carrying me more than I was actually walking. "Hold on," he said, pushing a door open.

When we got to the front of the building, we reached a door that could only be opened by Master Control. Nathan pressed the button and held it down. When no one answered, he groaned and pushed it again. Finally, Ms. Claybrooks came over the speaker. "Seriously!" she shouted. "They's only one of me up here, ya know!"

I bent at the waist and rested my hands on my knees for support as the floor spun in and out of focus.

"Ms. Claybrooks, it's Detective McNamara. I need you to open the door immediately." He was trying to sound calm but not doing a convincing job of it.

"Hold your horses! I'm just one woman," she said.

Finally, the door slid open, and I sprinted through it. I was panting when Nathan caught up with me at the front door. "Happy Thanksgivin', y'all," Ms. Claybrooks called as I bolted outside into the crisp, cold mountain air.

I sucked in an icy breath and blew it out toward the sky. "Oh my god."

He gripped the sides of my waist, and angled his head to look me in the eye. "Geez, Sloan. You about gave me a heart attack. Breathe."

I took a few deep breaths. "Please get me out of here."

He clicked the unlock button on his SUV. "Come on. I'll buy you lunch."

I didn't have time for lunch, but nothing in me wanted to argue. He opened the passenger side door, and I climbed in and rested my forehead against the dashboard. He got in and cranked the engine, peeling his tires as he exited the parking lot. When we were a safe distance away, my heart rate slowed to normal. I sat back in my seat and opened my eyes.

"I'm sorry. I had to leave," I said.

He shook his head. "It's not your fault. I didn't think it through before calling you."

I turned toward him. "What was that thing?"

He shrugged. "I was hoping you could tell me. Deputies brought her in this morning. They called me when she kept rattling on about you. No name, no ID. Nobody even knows what language she's speaking."

My stomach felt sick. "You've heard it before. I'm pretty sure that's my demon mom's language."

"You think so?"

I was still panting. "Yeah. And I don't understand much Latin, but I think whatever she was saying had something to do with someone dying." I tapped my chest. "Probably me."

He scowled. "Don't talk like that." He jerked his thumb back toward the building. "Do you think she's like you and Warren?"

I looked over at him. "Maybe. Or she could be like Abigail."

He drummed his fingers on the steering wheel. "Do you think there's a chance she could *be* Abigail?"

I cringed at the thought. I'd watched the body the world knew as Abigail Smith turn to dust, but the angel Samael had told us she would procure another body. I chewed on my fingernail. "Abigail doesn't strike me as the type to allow herself to be locked up."

He nodded. "I thought the same thing. That's the only reason I even considered letting you near her." He leaned toward his door and wedged his hand into his pocket. He produced his cell phone and handed it to me. "Look in my photo gallery."

After a moment of searching, I navigated my way to the pictures on his phone. I saw my own face before I saw anything else. There was a succession of photos of me making funny faces that I'd taken one night when Nathan left his phone lying on my sofa. It had been weeks before, and he hadn't deleted them.

"Check the folder called 'work' in the gallery list," he said, snapping me back to reality.

I tapped the work folder open, and immediately cringed at the sight of blood. "Eww."

"Look at the first few," he insisted. "That's what's under those bandages on that girl."

It took me a second to figure out I was looking at pictures of the red-head's forearms. Two different words were written on...no *carved into* her arms. The first one was a little hard to read. "Kot...*kotailis?*" I asked, looking over at him. "Is that what it says?"

He shrugged. "I'm not sure, but that's what it looks like."

"What does it mean?"

He shook his head. "I don't know that either. Could be something from a video game. Could be an online company in the UK. Could be crazy-person-speak for 'let's give McNamara a headache.' Beats me."

My bottom lip poked out as I looked at the second word. "Nathan, why does she have my name carved into her arm?"

He cringed and turned his palm up. "Sorry. I'm striking out with answers today." He held out his hand for his phone, and I gave it to him. "Is there any way I can get the info on her to Warren? I'd like him to see it."

I sighed and shook my head. "Nope. He called this morning. He's officially on his way to wherever they're sending him."

His face twisted into a frown. "That sucks. How are you doing with it?"

I shrugged my shoulders. "I hate it, but we knew it was coming sooner or later."

He pointed his finger down the road ahead. "Want to blow off work and go to the bar?"

"As tempting as that sounds, I can't" ...*because I'm pregnant,* I silently added. I rested my head back against the seat, and the cloth ceiling of Nathan's SUV caught my attention. It was covered with patches for his hat. "This is new," I said, giggling as I read some of them.

Finish your beer. There are sober kids in Africa.

My idea of 'help from above' is a sniper on the roof.

I'm here to kick ass and chew bubblegum and I'm all out of bubblegum.

He grinned. "It's become somewhat of an obsession. People at work are giving them to me now."

"It's definitely a conversation starter." After a moment, I rolled my head toward him. "What will the jail do with her?"

He turned his palm up on the steering wheel. "Probably release her to the mental hospital. She's not stable enough to be released into public, and they can't keep her locked up."

"What if she comes after me?" I asked.

He looked over his shoulder at me. "You know I won't let that happen. Besides, you won't be home this weekend to worry about her."

I straightened in my seat. "Oh, yeah! We're going to Raleigh. I've had so much on my mind, I almost forgot. When are we leaving?"

Nathan's family had been waiting for months to finally be able to lay his baby sister, Ashley, to rest. I'd promised to be moral support for the burial service.

He pulled into the parking lot of my favorite restaurant, Tupelo Honey. "Well, my mom invited you to come to our house for Thanksgiving tomorrow, but I told her you would probably want to spend the day with your dad. So we can leave on Friday if you want."

"Sure," I said. "What are you doing tomorrow?"

He shrugged. "Getting take out and watching football, I guess."

I rolled my eyes. "No, you're not. You'll come eat with us. Dad and I are cooking, so the food might suck, but it would be nice to have another body at the table."

He smiled as he put the car in park. "I'd love to. What can I bring?"

I laughed as we got out. "A backup plan."

* * *

My nerves were frayed for the rest of the day. Every time I blinked, I saw the red-haired woman's crazy blue eyes frantic with terror. Her screams were on replay in my brain like the theme song to my own personal horror movie.

When I pulled into my driveway and parked next to Warren's black Dodge Challenger, it was dark in Asheville. Mile markers could have ticked off the distance between my car and my front door and it wouldn't have seemed any further away. I was frozen in the driver's seat, unable to even will myself to turn off the engine. Gripping the steering wheel with both hands, I swallowed hard.

Nathan had offered to escort me home from work, but like the idiot I was, I insisted I was fine.

I wasn't fine.

I was very, very far from it.

Laying my face against the back of my hands on the steering wheel,

I focused on breathing.

A car horn blasted behind me.

My foot slipped off the brake and onto the gas pedal, sending the car barreling forward into the large rhododendron that crowned my driveway. I cursed.

Adrianne's red sports car pulled up behind me as I backed out of the bush. When I was completely on the gravel again, I put the car in park.

My best friend was laughing as I got out. "Are you drunk?"

I slammed my car door. "You scared the crap out of me!" I walked to the front of my car and shined the light from my cell phone onto the hood. "What are you doing here?" I began plucking leaves from the grill.

"Your dad dropped by my shop today and said I should check in on you. He was really worried, so I figured we'd need this." She held up a bottle of tequila. "Are you OK?"

I swiped my hand across the hood. Thankfully, I didn't feel any major scratches. "It's been a rough day."

She looped her arm through mine as we walked up the sidewalk. "I heard Warren left."

I frowned up at her. "That's only the beginning of it."

A faint ripple against the night sky caught my attention. It was an angel, or *angels,* I wasn't sure. I'd been seeing them regularly since we returned from Texas. Adrianne didn't notice.

"What else happened?" she asked, leading me up the front steps.

I unlocked the door and unwound my scarf as we walked inside. "Well, a crazy woman—who may or may not be a demon—was arrested downtown today. She was walking around naked with my name carved into the skin on her arm."

Her eyes widened as she shrugged out of her coat. "I heard about a naked woman downtown. I didn't hear anything about you though."

I followed her into the kitchen where she went straight to the cupboard containing my shot glasses.

"Nathan called me down to the jail to see her for myself. She started screaming in some crazy language, then I almost passed out from a panic attack." I plopped down in a chair at the table. "It was fun."

She filled two shot glasses full of golden liquor and pushed one in my direction. In one swift motion, she drained hers. "Who was the woman?" she asked.

I shrugged. "Nobody knows."

"What does she want with you?" she asked, refilling her glass.

"Don't know that either." I slouched in my seat. "Nathan almost had to carry me out of there, so I didn't have a chance to talk to her."

When she picked up her second shot, she noticed my first one was still sitting in front of me. She glanced up expectantly.

I looked at it, then back at her. "I can't drink it."

"Why not?" Before I had a chance to answer, her mouth fell open. She pointed at me. "Oh my god. You're pregnant!"

I slumped over the table. "And you accuse *me* of being psychic."

She gently shoved my shoulder. "Are you serious? When did you find out?"

"I figured it out when we dropped Warren off in Charlotte and I didn't get a migraine. Four positive pregnancy tests and then an ultrasound today confirmed it," I said.

She tossed her hands up. "You've known for a month and didn't tell me!"

I grimaced. "I didn't tell anyone till today."

"Have you told Warren?"

I shook my head.

"Nathan?"

"No. Just my dad. Nobody else knows," I said.

She rubbed her hands over her face. "Warren will be fine, but Nathan will freak out. You know that right?"

I felt a familiar hitch in my throat that always preceded tears. "Please don't make me cry again. I've cried all day." I blinked a few times to keep my tear ducts in line.

She pointed a perfectly manicured fingernail at me. "This is what you get for not figuring out your feelings before you hooked up with Warren."

I shook my head. "That's not helpful."

She drank her second shot. "Didn't mean for it to be." She screwed the cap back on the tequila. "Just stating the facts."

"Adrianne, how am I supposed to tell him?"

She sighed. "I don't know, but you need to tell him soon. The longer you wait, the worse it will be. And you've got to have some boundaries with him. You guys can't be together all the time like you are."

"I know." I slouched in my seat. "I'll tell him this weekend. We're visiting his parents' house in Raleigh for his sister's memorial service."

"Well, wait till after the funeral and then break it to him. Cut the poor guy some slack."

I nodded, still pouting. "You're right."

She drummed her nails on the table. "So, what does you and Warren having a baby together mean?"

"Samael, the angel that was with us in Texas, told me demons would try to kill me."

She rolled her eyes. "Not what I meant. I was wondering if you've decided to marry Warren, but I can see how that would take a back seat to being murdered."

I chuckled. Only Adrianne could make that statement funny.

"Why do they want to kill you?" she asked.

I shrugged my shoulders. "I'm not really sure, but I do know I've got a bunch of angel guardians floating around me all the time."

Her eyes searched the ceiling.

"You can't see them," I told her. "They don't come inside, anyway."

"That's creepy."

"Tell me about it." I put my hand on her arm. "Thanks for coming by tonight. I really didn't have it in me to be alone, and I know I can't keep relying on Nathan."

She patted my hand with her own. "Call me anytime, Sloan. I may be as much of a wimp as you, but at least we can puss out together." Getting up from the table, she offered me her hand. "Enough supernatural B.S. for tonight. We've got important things to discuss."

"Like what?" I asked as she pulled me to my feet.

She spun around and put her hands on her hips. "Like redecorating. Where the hell will you put a baby in this tiny dollhouse?"

Where the hell, indeed.

3.

THE REDECORATION PLANS began and ended with: Sloan needs to buy a bigger house. After that, I heard all about the new stylist her salon had hired and the rising rent crisis in downtown Asheville. Adrianne left when I could no longer hold my eyes open, despite my pleas for a slumber party. Once she was gone, I packed for my trip with Nathan, then stared at the ceiling fan for most of the night and seriously contemplated taking my Xanax against my doctor's advice. I should have had her define "absolutely essential" before I left her office. My fingernails were bloody by midnight.

After fading out of consciousness sometime around four in the morning, I awoke to the shrill ring of my cell phone. I picked it up and saw Nathan's picture on the screen. It was eight forty-five. I groaned and tapped the answer button. "What did I ever do to you?" I asked. "It's my day off."

"Good morning to you too, sunshine," he said.

"Screw you, Nathan."

He laughed. "I'm outside and it's snowing. Come let me in."

With a huff, I disconnected and dropped the phone on the mattress. I sat up, draped my blanket over my head, and wrapped it around my body instead of getting dressed. Barefoot, I trudged down the cold hardwood steps, through the living room, and to the door. I yanked it open.

His head snapped back with surprise. "Whoa. You look terrifying."

I rubbed my eyes. "I didn't get much sleep. Why are you here?"

Dusting the snow off his shoulders, he stepped inside and wiped his boots on the welcome mat. "It's Thanksgiving. You invited me."

I scowled as I closed the door behind him. "I invited you to eat with us later at my dad's. It's the butt crack of dawn."

He slipped off his camel colored jacket. "Thanksgiving is an all-day gig, Sloan. The parade starts at nine."

I tightened the blanket around me and cocked my head to the side. "The parade?"

"The Thanksgiving Day Parade."

I smiled. "I know what it is. You get up early to watch it?"

He held up his hands in confusion. "Doesn't everyone?"

I laughed and shook my head. "Not everyone over the age of seven."

"Shut up, Sloan."

The patch on the front of his hat said, *I'd be thankful if you'd shut the hell up.* Chuckling to myself, I rolled my eyes and turned toward the stairs. "I'm going to get dressed. You woke me up, so I expect coffee when I come back downstairs."

"What do I get in return?" he called after me.

I started up the steps. "You get to not die today."

Fifteen minutes and a hot shower later, I was much more alert when I went back down to the living room to find Nathan lounging on my white sofa. His socked feet rested on the coffee table, and his thighs cradled a bowl of dry cereal. The Thanksgiving Day Parade was live on my flat screen. It was kind of adorable.

He looked up at me. "You look less lethal now."

I was pulling my hair up into a ponytail. "I still might kill you."

"The coffee's fresh."

"Bless you," I whispered as I walked past him toward the kitchen.

On the third shelf of the cupboard above the coffee pot was one of Warren's man-sized travel mugs. I stretched on my tiptoes to retrieve it. One cup of coffee simply wouldn't be enough. As I filled the mug, Dr. Watts' voice came to mind. "Go easy on the caffeine," she'd said.

My shoulders slumped and I whimpered.

"Everything OK in there?" Nathan called.

"Yeah."

Damn it.

I put Warren's cup back and got my regular mug. I fought back bitterness as I poured it half-empty. I shut off the coffee maker and went back to the living room. "You ready to go?" I asked, taking a tiny sip of my drink.

Nathan looked over his shoulder. "Can we wait till a commercial?"

I giggled. "Sure." Stepping over his legs, I plopped down beside him. I eyed the bowl he was holding. "Where did you find Lucky Charms cereal?"

He offered me a rainbow marshmallow. "Brought it from home. I thought you'd have milk. I'm not sure why."

"Sorry," I said, taking the rainbow from his fingers.

He pointed at the screen. "You just missed the new Snoopy and Woodstock balloon."

I turned toward him. "It's like I've never met you before."

Laughing again, he funneled a handful of cereal into his mouth.

When the program went to a commercial break, Nathan picked up the remote and shut the television off. "Come on. Let's hurry and get to your dad's. I don't want to miss Joan Jett."

Before we left the house, I picked up the suitcase I'd packed and left in the foyer the night before.

He cocked an eyebrow as he eyed it in my hand and opened the front door. "You running away?" he asked, taking it from my hands.

We walked outside together, and I turned to lock the front door. "I'm crashing at Dad's tonight. You can pick me up there in the morning."

"Really? How come?" he asked.

I grimaced. "I'm kinda becoming a wuss at being alone. Nightmares and such."

A snowflake landed on my cheek. He brushed it away. "You don't have to be alone."

The nerve endings on my cheek tingled from his fingertip. "I know. Thanks."

He gestured toward the truck. "Ready?"

"Yeah." I paused before walking down the front steps and saluted the ripples in the sky. "Hold down the fort while I'm gone, boys."

Nathan looked around. "What the hell?"

I looked to the sky. "I'm talking to my guardian angels."

He laughed. "Are you cracking up on me?"

I pointed. "There's an angel right there, or maybe more than one. I'm not sure. They've been following me around since we got back from Texas."

He looked in the direction of my finger. "I don't see anything."

Rolling my eyes, I shook my head. "Mortal."

He sighed and offered me his arm as we headed out into the flurries. "You weird me out sometimes."

I gripped his sleeve as we carefully went down the stairs. "I know. I don't want things to get too boring."

My foot slipped on a patch of slush.

Nathan's bicep crushed my arm against his chest, while his other arm shot behind my back as my feet flew forward. Wide-eyed and panting, we both stared at each other a moment as I regained my footing.

He burst out laughing. "Boring? No one can ever accuse you of being boring!"

* * *

We took Nathan's pickup to my dad's house on the outskirts of downtown Asheville. The roads were wet and empty as we wound up the mountainside. It was that time of year when Mother Nature was stuck in limbo between the decay of fall and a glistening winter. The oaks and maples were bare, jutting out from the mountains like a dark skeleton of the forest. The thick branches of the hemlocks sagged with the weight of the almost-snow dropping from the gray sky in clumps. Soon, North Carolina would be a winter wonderland, but that day it was just soggy and cold.

Dad's stone chimney was pumping out smoke when we pulled in the driveway.

Nathan grabbed my arm when I reached for my door handle. "Get out over here on my side so we can avoid any holiday catastrophes, please."

I laughed and scooted across the bench seat toward him. He held me steady with both hands as I slid down from the cab.

When we walked in the front door of the house, a crash of metal clanged against the tile floor in the kitchen. "Dad?" I called out as I took off my winter coat.

"I'm all right!" he answered.

Nathan followed me to the kitchen where we found my father with a pile of pots and pans scattered around his feet. He shrugged his shoulders as he looked around at them. "I pulled out the bottom one, and they all fell," he explained.

We helped pick them up.

Once all the cookware was tucked back in the cabinet, Dad's eyes settled on Nathan. "Detective McNamara, I wasn't expecting to see you this morning."

Nathan stuffed his hands into his pockets. "Sloan invited me. I hope that's OK."

My father squeezed Nathan's arm. "Of course it is. You're always welcome here. I just assumed you would be with your family today."

Nathan shook his head. "Sloan and I are heading to Raleigh tomorrow to see them."

Dad's eyes widened, and he cast his gaze down at me. "Oh, really?"

"His sister's burial service is this weekend, so I'm going with him," I said.

"Oh." Dad's shoulders sagged. "Please send my condolences."

Nathan nodded. "I will, sir. Thank you."

Dad stepped over to the coffee pot. "Would you like some coffee, Detective?"

"Please, Dr. Jordan. Call me, Nathan," he said.

My dad smiled. "As long as you promise to call me Robert."

Nathan grinned as Dad handed him a cup. "Deal." Nathan motioned toward the den behind us. "Do you mind if I turn on the television?"

I giggled. "Nathan wants to watch the parade."

Dad held out his hands. "Be my guest."

I pulled out a barstool at the counter. "I want some coffee, Dad."

He shook his head. "Not in your condition, Sloan. It isn't healthy."

Nathan glanced back at me as he turned on the parade. "You can't have coffee now?"

Dad poured his own mug full and shook his head. "No. Caffeine isn't good for the ba—"

"My panic disorder!" I shouted to interrupt him with a loaded glare. "I'm not supposed to have caffeine due to my anxiety. Right, Dad?"

Dad looked at me, then at Nathan and back at me before a mental light bulb flickered on. "Oh, yes. Caffeine is no good for your anxiety, Sloan."

Nathan settled onto the barstool next to mine. "Oh man. That's bad news for everyone if Sloan can't have coffee in the morning. That was the only thing standing between all of us and a beheading before ten A.M."

I elbowed him in the ribs. "Shut up."

He grinned over the rim of his cup.

"So, Dad, what's on the menu for today?" I asked, leaning on my elbows.

He stepped across the kitchen. "Well, I went to the grocery store this morning and bought a turkey." He pulled the refrigerator door open and lifted out the plastic covered bird. He set it down with a heavy thud on the marble counter top.

My eyes doubled in size. "How big is that thing?"

He looked at the tag. "Twenty-two pounds. Do you think it's big enough?" He wasn't joking.

"It's only you, me, and Nathan eating, right?" I asked.

He nodded.

I exchanged a smile with Nathan and chuckled. "Surely, it's plenty." I got up and walked over to the turkey. "Now, does anyone know how to cook one of these things?"

No one answered.

I looked around at them. "Fantastic. Nathan, can you Google directions on your phone for how to cook a turkey?"

He whipped out his cell phone, and I carried the bird to the sink. "This thing is frozen solid," I said. "Can we cook frozen meat?"

My dad shrugged. "I don't see why not. It will thaw as it cooks, right?"

I shrugged. "I guess so."

"All these directions say to thaw the turkey first," Nathan said, glancing up from his phone. "Then you cook it on 325 degrees for 4 to 4 ½ hours."

Dad cocked his head to the side. "Well, if we start with it frozen, why don't we kick up the temperature a little to help it thaw and cook faster."

I studied the knobs on the oven. "That's a good plan. What should I set the oven on?"

"How about an even 400 degrees?" he suggested.

"Sounds good to me," I said, dialing it up to 400.

"I also got potatoes, green beans, and rolls from the bakery," Dad said.

I looked up at him. "What about dessert?"

He grimaced. "Oh, I forgot dessert."

Nathan jerked his thumb toward the front door. "I can run to the grocery store and pick up something. We passed an open grocery store on the drive here."

"OK, great." I looked around. "I need a knife."

Nathan stood. "Here you go." He produced a tactical knife from his pocket, opened it, and passed it to me.

I sliced open the plastic wrapping around the bird, and Dad handed me the biggest pan they owned. The bird clanged against the metal when I dropped it in the center.

"Let me lift that," Dad said, stepping in between me and the pan when I went to put it in the oven.

I opened the oven door, then set the timer for 4 ½ hours as Dad put the turkey inside. I washed off my hands and wiped them on my jeans. "All right, when should we cook everything else?"

Dad shrugged his shoulders. "I don't think the potatoes will take long, and the green beans are in a can."

I shook my head and laughed. "Somewhere, Mom is rolling her eyes and laughing at us right now."

Dad chuckled and put his arm around my shoulders. "I'm sure she is."

Nathan jingled his keys. "Sloan, do you want to go with me to the store?"

"If you don't mind, I'll hang out with Dad. I think you can manage dessert by yourself." I was still hugging my father around his middle.

He held up his cell phone. "Call me if I need to get anything else."

When he was gone, my Dad looked down at me and raised an eyebrow. "So you haven't told him about the baby?"

I walked to the den and plopped down on the sofa. "No."

He sighed and sat in his recliner. "You understand you won't be able to keep a secret like this for long, right?"

I kicked off my boots and curled my feet underneath me. "I know. I guess I was hoping I'd be able to tell Warren first."

"Do you think he'll call today since it's a holiday?" he asked.

"I doubt it."

"How would he feel about you spending the weekend with Nathan?"

I looked over my shoulder at him. "He wouldn't be surprised.

Warren's aware I was planning to attend the service. It's really not a big deal."

Genuine concern had contorted his face. "Can I be honest with you, Sloan?"

I hugged a couch pillow to my chest. "Of course you can."

His crumpled brow suggested he was struggling to choose his words. "You aren't doing anyone any favors by spending so much time with Nathan, especially time alone with him. Both of you may have the best of intentions at keeping the relationship appropriate, but I feel like you're playing with fire. I don't want to see you do anything you might regret once Warren gets home."

Dad was right and I knew it. "I appreciate the word of caution. I'll tell him about the baby after the funeral and work on figuring out how to put some space between us."

He cut his eyes over at me. "Please be very careful."

I nodded. "I will."

The familiar guitar riff of *I Love Rock and Roll* came over the television speakers. Joan Jett was performing Nathan's song, and he was going to miss it.

* * *

Almost two hours later, I was sound asleep on the couch when the doorbell rang. Dad slept in his recliner, snoring with his mouth hanging open.

I shuffled across the house in my socks and opened the door to find Nathan shivering in the cold, holding two grocery bags. His eyes were wide, his face pale, and he shook his head as he stepped inside. "You do not want to go to the grocery store on Thanksgiving."

I laughed and took the bags from him so he could take off his coat. I glanced at the clock on the wall. "You've been gone for hours. You were at the grocery store the whole time?"

"The whole time," he said. "That place is like the third ring of hell. People are freaking crazy. I considered getting my taser from the truck."

I peered into a bag. "Did you get dessert?"

He grimaced. "Sort of."

We walked to the kitchen, and I opened the bags. He'd bought a half-gallon of mint chocolate chip ice cream, Swiss Cake Rolls, and an economy-size bag of Skittles. I put my hand on my hip and glared at him. He held his hands up in defense. "There were no pies left! I even checked for frozen pies! Zero. So I improvised."

I rolled my eyes and put the ice cream in the freezer.

"Uh, Sloan," Nathan said behind me.

I turned to see smoke pouring from the oven. "Oh my god!" I screamed.

Dad sat up so fast that the foot rest slammed closed, jerking the seat back upright so violently he catapulted to his feet. He ran to the kitchen as I yanked the oven door open. Billows of black smoke rolled out into the room. Coughing, I waved my hand furiously in front of my face.

"Move!" Dad shouted.

The fire alarm wailed through the house.

Dad grabbed two pot holders and pulled the pan from the oven. The turkey was black, and one of its wings was on fire. Dad was chanting, "Oh no, oh no, oh no…"

Nathan doubled over laughing.

I smacked him on the back of the head. "Open the windows and shut off the alarm!"

Dad was horrified as I threw a wet dishcloth over the turkey to extinguish the flames. I wondered if he might burst into tears.

Instead he burst into hysterical laughter. "We are not responsible enough to do this!"

"I'm not going back to the grocery store!" Nathan shouted from where he fanned the smoke alarm with a newspaper.

I leaned against the counter and laughed. I pulled out my phone, took a picture of the charred bird, and sent it to Adrianne with the caption, *Happy Thanksgiving!*

Dad picked at the blackened skin. "Do you think we can save any of it?"

I grimaced. "I'm not eating that mess."

The bird was still smoking, so Dad carried the whole thing out to the back porch. Once the fire alarm stopped screaming through the house, Nathan came over and draped his arm around my shoulders. "Best Thanksgiving ever," he said, chuckling.

I elbowed him again.

Dad came back inside and closed the door. He turned and looked at us. "Well, what do we do now?"

Nathan shook his head. "Seriously. I'm not going back to the store."

I folded my arms across my chest. "Then we're having mashed

potatoes, green beans, rolls, ice cream, and Skittles for Thanksgiving."

Nathan beamed down at me. "And Swiss Cake Rolls."

Dad laughed. "Do you think anyone is delivering pizza today?"

I rolled my eyes and went back to the den. On the end table next to the sofa was a picture of Mom and Dad, smiling arm in arm. I picked it up and sighed as I ran my thumb over my mother's face. A haze of smoke still clouded the entire downstairs of the house. "I miss you, Mom."

An hour later, Dad was nervously watching the rolls brown through the window in the oven, Nathan was opening the can of green beans, and I was attempting to mash the potatoes with a fork when the doorbell rang.

I walked to the foyer and pulled the front door open. Adrianne and her parents were holding covered pans and casserole dishes.

"Happy Thanksgiving!" the trio sang in unison.

I laughed and stepped out of their way. "What are you doing here?"

Dad and Nathan joined us in the foyer.

Adrianne thrust a large pan covered in tin foil into my arms. "We brought Thanksgiving to you," she said as she unwound a fluffy white scarf from around her neck.

I felt tears prickle the corner of my eyes.

Gloria Marx, Adrianne's mom, gave me a giant bear hug and kissed my temple. "We can't let our favorite family eat burnt turkey on Thanksgiving," she said.

Adrianne wrapped her arms around me and looked down from where she towered over me at six feet some odd inches in her high heels. "I think we have a whole lot to be thankful for this year, don't you?"

I smiled. "Yes, I do."

4.

THE NEXT MORNING, Nathan sent a text message warning me at six a.m. that he was on his way to pick me up. I'd already been awake for an hour battling the first pangs of what I assumed was morning sickness. I was bloated, nauseated, and craving coffee, but I was dressed and ready to go when he rang Dad's doorbell fifteen minutes later.

Dad opened the door as I was coming down the stairs. "Good morning, Detective."

"Good morning, sir." The corners of Nathan's mouth twitched when he saw me. "Nice hair."

"Shut up," I said as I finished tying my unruly locks in a knot on the top of my head.

Dad closed the door. "Nathan, I must run. I have a patient I need to see at the hospital, but I'll be thinking of you and your family this weekend."

Nathan shook his hand. "Thank you, sir."

Dad pointed at both of us, but gave me a warning glance. "You two be careful."

I gave him a side hug. "We will, Dad."

He kissed the side of my head, then released me and headed toward the garage. "I'll see you at dinner on Monday, Sloan?"

"Yes. Love you, Dad."

He smiled back over his shoulder. "Love you too, sweetheart."

I did a double-take when I turned back to Nathan. He looked completely different. It was the first time I had ever seen him dressed like a normal guy. He was in blue jeans and a dark green plaid shirt over a white thermal. I blinked. "What are you wearing?"

He looked down at his outfit. "You don't like it?"

"It's weird. Aside from Mom's funeral, I've never seen you in anything but your GI Joe getup." I was still eyeing him suspiciously. "This is weird."

"You'll get used to it." He looked down at his watch. "How long till you're ready?"

My head flopped to one side. "I am ready."

His eyes went from my pink hoodie, down to my blue sweatpants, and then to my fuzzy brown boots. He sighed and shook his head. "It's a good thing you're hot."

I held my arms out. "What's wrong with my clothes? I thought I looked cute."

He chuckled. "Yeah, if we were popping popcorn to watch a movie in bed, but we're going to see my family."

I pulled down on the corner of my eye to show off my mascara. "I put on makeup."

"Those ugly boots cancel out the makeup."

"Hey!"

Laughing, he rolled his eyes and picked up the suitcase I'd put by the door. "Come on. I told my mom we'd be there by lunch."

It was a four hour drive to his parents' house outside of Raleigh in Durham, North Carolina. Half-way there it started snowing again, and by the time we pulled up in front of the blue, two-story farmhouse, there was over an inch on the ground. It was a grand, older home with white shutters, a wraparound porch, and a small barn in the back. Christmas garland twisted around the porch spindles, and two large wreaths with giant red bows hung over the front double doors.

I marveled at the house. "This is like something from a fifties Christmas movie. You grew up here?"

"Yep." He pointed up to the second floor. "I broke my arm in the second grade trying to jump off the porch roof and fly like Superman."

I motioned to a line of cars around the side of the house. "Who all is here?"

He turned off the engine. "Oh, my whole family is here, I'm sure."

I blinked with surprise. "Your *whole* family?" I asked. "How many are there?"

"Well, my parents are here. My sister, Karen—"

I cut him off. "You have another sister?"

He nodded. "I have two other sisters and a brother."

I cringed. "Are you joking?"

A thin smile spread across his face as he shook his head. "Is that a problem, Madam Sweatpants?"

"No," I lied, tugging on the strings of my hoodie. "You just never told me you have such a big family."

"I also have a bunch of nieces and nephews."

"And they'll all be here?" I asked.

"I'm pretty sure they all got here yesterday."

I looked back at the house. "None of them are serious criminals or anything, are they?"

He laughed. "What?"

I shrugged my shoulders. "Well, I have panic attacks around scary people, and I can't take my medicine."

"You can't take your medicine?" he asked surprised. "I thought you said you forgot to take it."

Dang it.

I scrambled for a recovery. "Well, the doctor took me off of it because of some of the side effects. You didn't answer my question."

He shook his head. "No criminals around here. I promise." He stretched his arm across the back of my seat. "Relax. You'll love them."

I took a deep breath. "All right. Let's do this."

When we got out of the truck, the front door swung open and a short, plump woman with straight white hair that curled under around her shoulders ran out onto the porch. She was wearing a white sweater with a red collar and a big sequined poinsettia on the front. She was clapping her hands and had a smile so wide I thought her face might crack in the cold. "Noot-Noot! You're here!" she cheered.

I spun around toward where he was pulling our bags from the back seat. "Noot-Noot?"

He pointed a warning finger at me. "Don't even start."

I laughed and followed him as he jogged up ahead of me to meet his mother halfway up the steps. She squealed softly as he put the suitcases down and hugged her tight. He turned toward me when I stepped up onto the bottom step. "Mom, this is—"

She came down the stairs to meet me. "This is Sloan. I know exactly who she is." She stretched out her arms and hugged me. "I'm Nathan's mom. You can call me Kathy."

I shivered. "It's nice to meet you, Kathy."

She curled her arm protectively around my shoulders. "Come on, honey. Let's get you in the house where it's warm."

The smell of cinnamon and apple pie made me close my eyes and inhale when we stepped through the front door. "Oh my goodness. This must be what Heaven smells like," I said, looking over at her.

She was smiling from ear to ear as she took our bags from Nathan. "Thank you. I hope you're hungry, Sloan. You got here just in time to eat!"

"I'm famished," I said as I unbuttoned my coat.

Tiny squeals and the sound of little rushing feet filled the hallway. "Unca Nate!" a munchkin voice squeaked.

Two children, a boy with long blond hair and a girl with brown curls, latched onto Nathan's legs. He laughed and picked up the little girl. "How are you, princess?" he asked.

She tossed her hair over her shoulder. "Gramma says I can't have cookies till after we eat."

He growled. "She's so mean."

His mom smacked him on the back of the head and he laughed.

The little girl rubbed her nose and pointed at me. "Who is this lady?"

He touched my shoulder. "This is my friend, Sloan. Sloan, this is Gretchen."

I shook her tiny hand. "Hi, Gretchen."

The boy tugged on my pant leg. "And I'm Carter!"

I laughed. "Nice to meet you, Carter."

Nathan put Gretchen down, and they took off running down the hallway again. Kathy headed up the stairs behind us. "I'll put these in your room, Nathan. You can go on into the kitchen."

"Thanks, Mom," he said.

I grabbed Nathan's arm as we walked down the hall. "Your room? Are we supposed to share a bedroom?"

"Calm down. I'll sleep on the couch, so you don't have to worry about me spoiling your virtue."

I rolled my eyes. "Does your mom think we're a couple?"

"Beats me," he said. "I haven't told her we are."

I cocked an eyebrow. "Have you told her we're *not?*"

He just winked at me.

We passed a formal dining room and a living room with a massive Christmas tree in it. There were no ornaments on the tree, but the smell of fresh pine was intoxicating. At the end of the hall, loud chatter was coming from behind a swinging, white door. He pushed it open, and stepped aside so I could enter. It was a large kitchen, but it was crowded with the McNamara clan all dressed in holiday sweaters.

And there I was, *Madam Sweatpants.*

No one seemed to notice, however. They all cheered when we walked inside and, instinctively, I clapped my hands over my ears. Nathan ceremoniously introduced me to everyone.

Nathan's sister Lara looked like she could be his twin. She and her husband, Joe, were Carter's parents. They lived about twenty minutes down the road.

His other sister, Karen, was married to Nick, and they lived in Columbia, South Carolina. Karen and Nick had four kids. The oldest two were out Black Friday shopping, but the younger two were ignoring us all in the adjoining den off the kitchen.

Nathan's brother, Chuck, was the oldest sibling and was the exact opposite of Nathan. He looked like a lumberjack with a thick brown beard, dressed in camouflage from head to toe. He was recently divorced and living in Tennessee. He was Gretchen's dad.

In five minutes, I was completely overwhelmed.

"Sloan," Nathan said, turning me around again. "This is my dad, James McNamara."

My head snapped back with surprise. James McNamara was a silver-haired, gray-eyed Paul Newman in a sweater vest. He was Nathan in thirty more years.

He shook my hand. "It's nice to finally meet you, Sloan. We hear about you quite a bit."

I blushed. "Really?"

"Absolutely. We owe you so much for helping us find Ashley after all these years of searching and wondering. You'll never know how grateful we are."

"I'm glad I could help, and I'm so sorry for your loss," I said.

He squeezed my hand again. "Well, we're happy you're here. I hope you'll make yourself at home."

"Thank you, Mr. McNamara," I said.

He shook his head. "Call me James."

"Ok."

Someone shoved a plate into my hands, and Nathan led me toward the counter piled with leftover Thanksgiving food. He leaned close to my ear. "See? You're the big hero here. They love you."

"They all seem really nice." There was a half-carved turkey at the end of the counter. Its skin was golden brown, not black. I pointed to it. "Maybe I can get your mom to teach me how to cook a turkey while I'm here."

He chuckled. "Still, best Thanksgiving *ever.*"

Nathan's mom had reserved us seats at what everyone referred to as the 'adult table' in the formal dining room. Everyone else scattered throughout the house. I sat between Nathan and his mother. She patted my hand. "Sloan, we are so excited you could join us," she said.

"And we are so glad you're not Shannon Green," Lara added with wide eyes and a chuckle.

I covered my mouth so I didn't laugh and spit food all over the table.

Nathan's cheeks turned bright red, and he dropped his eyes to his plate. "Don't start, Lara."

Lara looked at me. "Sloan, have you met Shannon?"

I laughed. "Oh yes. I grew up with her."

Lara rolled her eyes and groaned. "I am so sorry."

Nathan draped his arm across the back of my chair. "Don't feel too sorry. Sloan convinced their whole high school that Shannon had syphilis."

The table erupted in laughter.

Nathan's mom was hiding her red face behind her napkin. "Is that true?"

I held up my hands and gave a noncommittal smile. Nathan's ex-girlfriend, Shannon Green, had been my nemesis since we were teenagers. He had broken up with her about a month before, apparently pleasing more people than only me.

"That's terrible," Kathy said through her giggles.

Lara pointed her fork at both of us. "So what is this? Are you two finally a *thing?*"

"Lara!" Kathy snapped. "That's none of your business." Despite her words, her questioning eyes turned slowly toward us.

I glanced at Nathan for help.

"It's not like that," he said. "We're close friends. That's all."

I swallowed the bite of cornbread stuffing in my mouth. "I have a boyfriend. He's deployed with the Marines."

There was a collective, sorrowful moan around the table accompanied by condolences.

"How long will he be away?" Kathy asked.

I shrugged my shoulders. "He left a few days ago, and I have no idea when he'll be back."

"I was a Marine right out of college," James said. "I never saw any combat though."

"Dad's an engineer now," Nathan added.

"What kind of engineer?" I asked.

"Civil," James answered.

Kathy smiled. "James is working on the gridlock problem in Raleigh."

I nodded and looked at Nathan. "I remember you telling me you wanted to be an engineer before you went into law enforcement."

He tilted his glass of sweet tea toward his father. "Yeah. I think Dad's still a little bitter about it."

James shook his head. "No, son. We're all very proud of you."

"I know, Dad."

Lara mocked a cough behind her hand and said, "Golden boy."

Chuck did the same, but coughed out "mama's boy" instead.

Nathan wadded up a napkin and threw it at his brother. We all laughed. Kathy stood, waving her hands. "None of that! There will be no food fights in this house this year!"

That evening with the McNamaras was my first real experience with a big family. It was delightful. There was so much laughter and chatter, and it was nice to be a part of it. After dinner, we all gathered in the living room and helped his mom decorate the Christmas tree. The after-Thanksgiving tradition had been put on hold till Nathan and I arrived.

When all the ornaments were in place, James motioned to me from his spot by the tree. He held up the end of the Christmas lights' string. "Sloan, would you come and do the honors?"

Smiling, I pushed myself off the couch. "I'd love to!"

He handed me the plug, then rejoined his wife by the fireplace. I plugged in the tree and it lit up in a colorful glow. A melody of "ooo's" and "ahh's" echoed around the room. Nathan beamed at me as I settled back down next to him on the sofa.

Watching them all laugh and carry on as Kathy passed out hot cocoa to the kids, I felt a strong wave of guilt wash over me. Somewhere, Warren was off doing god-only-knows-what, and I was with another man, like part of his family. And I was enjoying it. A lot. My hands went to my stomach.

"You all right?" Nathan's voice was concerned.

I forced a nod. "Yeah. This is amazing."

He squeezed my hand, smiling as he looked down to where his fingers wrapped around mine. He took a deep breath and released it.

When it was time for bed, everyone became a little somber. The next day wouldn't have the same laughter and joy the evening had. It was hard for me to even imagine how devastated this sweet family must have been when their baby girl went missing ten years before.

Nathan followed me upstairs. "Did you enjoy yourself?" he asked.

I smiled back at him. "Yeah, I did. Your family is great."

"You were the star of the night." He put his hand on the small of my back to steer me down the hall when we reached the top. "Second door on the right."

It was obvious Nathan's bedroom hadn't changed much over the years. Sports trophies lined the walls, along with plaques and ribbons from different events. He had a queen sized bed with a navy blue comforter and a stuffed brown bear perched against the pillows. I pointed at it, looked back at him, and giggled. "Is that Noot-Noot's teddy bear?"

He grabbed my finger. "You leave my bear outta this."

Laughing, I pulled my hand away.

He picked up his suitcase and dropped it on the bed. He fished out a t-shirt and a pair of flannel pants. "That door is for the bathroom," he said, gesturing to the right side of the room. "It adjoins to Lara's room, so I suggest locking it from this side if you don't want Carter wandering in and out of here."

"Thanks for the tip."

He draped his clothes over his shoulder and walked toward the bathroom. "Are you sleeping in the same pajamas you've worn all day?"

I picked up his bear and threw it at him.

When he returned dressed and ready for bed, I was putting my black dress for the next day on a hanger.

"That's pretty," he said.

I smoothed out the front and hung it from the top lip of the closet door. "Thank you. I'm determined to make a better second impression on your family than I did the first."

"I'm only giving you a hard time," he said as he folded his clothes and zipped up his suitcase. "I couldn't care less what you wear, as long as you're here."

I smiled and pulled the comforter down on the bed. "Nevertheless, I plan on looking spectacular by breakfast."

He put his suitcase in the corner of the room, then walked past me to grab a pillow. He nodded toward the bed with a devious grin. "What Warren doesn't know won't hurt him."

I crossed my arms over my chest. "You want to take that chance with a guy who hunts people down for a living?"

He laughed and walked to the door. "I'll be on the couch downstairs if you need anything."

"Thanks, Nathan."

He paused in the doorway. "Goodnight, Sloan."

"Goodnight."

5.

"MIIISWOOOAN…"

"MIIIIIIIISSSSSWOOOOOAN…" THE voice came again, the second time a little more sing-song.

I rolled over in the dimly lit room and hugged my pillow. I had to be dreaming. Something was touching my face. My right eyelid was slowly pried open. Big blue eyes were inches from my nose.

I screamed.

Carter screamed.

I bolted upright in the bed.

With his tiny fists clenched at his sides, he screeched as loud as he could.

I stretched my arms toward him. "Carter! Carter! I'm sorry, bud! I'm sorry!"

He threw the door to my room open and screamed all the way down the hallway, then all the way down the stairs. I flopped back onto the bed and groaned. *I'm going to be a great parent.*

As if on cue, my stomach churned with nausea.

When I finally felt like I could stand without hurling all over the shag carpet, I walked to the window and peeked out through the blinds. A fresh blanket of snow covered the ground making the McNamara's front yard look like a scene from a Thomas Kinkade painting. I looked at the driveway and hoped I'd be able to walk in my heels.

My heels. Oh crap!

I ran across the bedroom and dropped to my knees beside my suitcase. Frantically, I tossed out every shred of fabric onto the floor. I'd forgotten to pack my shoes. I looked at my dress on the hanger, then down at my brown, sheepskin, fuzzy boots. Sitting back on my heels, I let out a frustrated huff toward the ceiling.

The morning got worse from there.

Half-way through my shower, just when I'd finished lathering up my hair, the water ran cold. Ice cold. Then my hair dryer shorted out with half my hair still soaking wet, and it took out all the lights in the bathroom. My teeth were still chattering by the time I trudged downstairs *not* polished and ready for the day like I'd wanted.

Kathy and Lara were in the kitchen when I walked in. "Good morning," Kathy said, her welcoming smile fading to wide-eyed concern when she looked me over. "Are you OK, dear?"

I slumped down onto a barstool next to Lara at the kitchen island. "I'm a train wreck. Please don't hate me."

She laughed and covered my hands with her own. "Nonsense. You look like you could use some coffee. May I pour you a cup?"

I sighed. "No, thank you. I'm trying to cut back on caffeine."

She looked around the kitchen. "How about orange juice or milk?"

The thought of milk made my stomach queasy again. "Juice would be great."

She stepped back toward the counter against the wall and pulled a glass from the cabinet overhead. "Lara, would you like some juice?"

Beside me, Lara slurped her coffee. "Mother, I haven't had juice not laced with some form of alcohol since elementary school."

I laughed, but Kathy sighed and shook her head.

When she handed me the orange juice, I smiled up at her. "Thank you."

Lara handed me a large wire basket lined with a red checkered cloth. "Mom made muffins," she said. "There are blueberry ones, and there may be chocolate chip ones if Carter and Gretchen didn't eat them all."

I plucked a blueberry muffin from the basket and put it down on a napkin Kathy handed me. "These smell amazing. You made these?"

"From scratch," Kathy replied.

The sugary topping crumbled between my fingers as I broke off a bite and popped it into my mouth. It melted on my tongue. "Mmm," I moaned. "This is delicious."

She was beaming. "Thank you."

I turned toward Lara. "I have to apologize. I may have scarred Carter for life this morning."

Her eyes widened. "All that yelling earlier. Was that to do with you?"

I grimaced. "We scared each other half to death."

Lara groaned. "He came into your room?"

I nodded. "And pried my eyeball open while I was sleeping."

She hid her flushing cheeks behind her hands. "Oh god, Sloan. I'm so sorry. That boy is impossible."

I laughed and squeezed her arm. "Don't worry about it. I doubt he'll do it again after the way I screamed out in terror."

"Other than the rude awakening, did you sleep well?" Kathy asked.

I sipped my juice. It was delicious. I needed to start buying it to keep at home. "I did, but my morning was a nightmare."

"Oh?" she asked.

"I forgot my shoes at home that go with my dress, and I may have blown a fuse in the bathroom upstairs when my hair dryer died."

"It happens all the time in this old house. James will set it right." Kathy's gaze rose to my crazy hair. "I have a hair dryer you can borrow."

Lara nodded. "And what size shoes do you wear?"

"Seven," I answered.

She sucked in a sharp breath through her teeth. "Well, none of us will be any help with that. We all have giant clown feet."

"Thanks anyway," I said. "You'll just understand now when I look like an Eskimo from the shins down later."

They both laughed.

"Have you seen Nathan this morning?" I asked.

Kathy pointed toward the back door. "He went out with his dad and brother early this morning to scout the woods for deer tracks."

Lara smiled over her mug. "That's what they call it, but they're really out there drinking Daddy's stash of whiskey and bitching about Chuck's ex-wife."

Kathy pulled out the stool on the other side of Lara and sat down with her coffee. "Mind your mouth, Lara Jane."

Lara chuckled.

I looked over at Kathy. "I'm sorry Nathan missed Thanksgiving with you all."

She waved her hand in my direction. "Don't apologize. I assumed he would be wherever you are."

That made me feel bad for a few different reasons. I scrunched up my nose. "I appreciated your invitation here, but I didn't want my dad to be alone."

Kathy put her cup down on the tiled countertop. "Nathan told us your mother passed away. I was sorry to hear it. She must have been young."

"She was fifty-one," I said. "It was a very aggressive brain tumor."

Kathy shook her head sadly. "I'm so sorry." She patted my hand. "I wish I could tell you that you'll get over it in time, but it never goes away. You learn to deal with it differently, and the day-to-day gets easier."

The way her eyes were fixed on the wood grain of the table, I knew her mind was on Ashley.

Thankfully, before we both burst into tears, Carter exploded into the room. He froze when he saw me, then quickly ducked between his mother and grandmother. He slowly peeked his head up, and I gave him a little wave, but he ducked down again.

Lara twisted around in her seat. "Carter, what have we told you about going into people's rooms when they are sleeping?"

I heard a faint "not to" come from the other side of her.

"You owe Ms. Sloan an apology," Lara said.

His eyes lifted just above Lara's knees. "Sowwy."

"It's all right," I told him. "I'm sorry if I scared you."

Without another word, he ran from the room again.

Lara sighed. "Kids."

"I've never really been around kids." I ran my finger along the rim of my glass. "I come from a really small family."

"Only child?" Kathy asked.

"Yes. I was adopted, and my parents never had any children of their own."

Lara laughed. "This circus must scare the bejeezus out of you."

I shook my head. "Not at all. It's been really nice. It's sort of like being in a Hallmark movie."

Lara put her hand on my forearm. "Don't be fooled. It's sometimes more like the Bundys than the Bradys around here."

The back door of the kitchen swung open and Nathan, his dad and brother, stepped inside. Kathy jumped up from the bar. "Take those nasty boots off on the porch! You're not tracking mud and snow in here!"

They all grumbled and walked backward outside again. A moment later, Nathan came in and pulled off the toboggan that covered his head. He smiled at me, then his eyes widened when they fell on my hair. "Morning."

I shook my head. "It's not my fault this time. I tried."

He pointed at my glass. "What is this?"

"Orange juice. It's amazing."

Nathan grinned. "Is vodka in it?"

Beside me, Lara laughed.

I stuck my tongue out at him. "How was the *hunt*?" I asked using air quotes around the word.

He winked. "It was cold." He pointed to the ceiling. "I'm going to hop into the shower. Do you need anything in the bathroom?"

"No, but I'm not sure the shower is a great idea." I cringed. "Something may be wrong with the water heater."

He looked confused for a second, then he laughed. "Oh! You got in late."

Lara patted my back. "The curse of big families."

"Did we run out of hot water on you?" his dad asked as he came in from the porch.

I was shocked. "I guess so."

Chuck was still dusting snow off his hat as he walked in. "Gotta get up early if you want a hot shower around here."

Kathy glanced at the clock. "It's probably had time to warm up now. Karen and Nick took the kids to see his parents earlier, so no one has been in the bathrooms."

Nathan squeezed my shoulder. "You OK?"

I smiled. "Yes."

"I'll be upstairs," he said and left the kitchen.

"Nathan!" his mother called out.

He stuck his blond head back through the door.

"You'll have to reset the breaker for the bathroom." She looked at her husband. "It blew again this morning while Sloan was getting ready."

"That explains a lot," Nathan teased.

She pointed at him. "You leave her alone."

He nodded. "Yes, ma'am." Then he was gone.

James poured a cup of coffee. "I'll fix it tomorrow."

Kathy rolled her eyes. "Tomorrow," she mimicked. "It's always tomorrow."

James kissed her on the cheek as he walked by to the den behind us. He turned on the television to the morning news. I hated the news. With all the evil in the world, it was like watching the inside of the jail through a thin piece of glass. I shuddered and turned away.

In my back pocket, my cell phone vibrated. I pulled it out and saw my dad's picture on the screen. "Hey, Dad," I answered.

"Hey, sweetheart. Are you with Nathan?" he asked.

"Sort of. He's upstairs. What's up?" I asked.

"The FBI was just here at my house. They were looking for you," he said.

My spine went rigid. "Are you kidding? Did they say why?"

"No, but it didn't seem like a social call," he said. "She left a card. Agent Sharvell Silvers."

My chest tightened. I swallowed the growing lump in my throat. "OK. Thanks for telling me, Dad."

"How are things there? Do you like Nathan's family?"

"Yeah. They're great. You'd like them too."

"I have no doubt," he said. "I'll let you go. Just thought you should be aware."

"Thanks. I love you."

"I love you. Bye."

Kathy put her hand on my arm. She must've noticed when my face fell. "Is everything all right?"

I forced a nod. "Yeah. Everything's fine." Slowly, I pushed my chair back and stood. "Excuse me," I said to the group before walking out the door. I took the steps two at a time till I reached Nathan's bedroom. The door was open, and I could hear the shower running in the bathroom.

I knocked on the bathroom door. "Nathan, get out of the shower!"

"What?" he shouted.

"Come out here! I need to talk to you!"

The water shut off, and I sat on the edge of the bed with my knees bouncing like they'd been electrified. The door opened and Nathan stepped out of the bathroom in a cloud of steam. He wore a pair of black dress pants and a belt. That was it.

"Sloan?"

I jerked my eyes up to meet his and immediately felt my cheeks heat up.

He was drying his head with a towel. "Are you blushing, Ms. Jordan?"

"No."

"Liar."

I held up my phone. "Put on a shirt. We need to talk."

A lone water droplet slid from his chest down the center line of his stomach. I thought about catching it with my finger, or my tongue.

Sweet Jesus.

"Sloan?" he asked again. This time he was laughing.

I shook my head in an attempt to clear it. "My dad called."

His brow scrunched together as he walked to his suitcase. "Congratulations. You got me out of the shower to tell me that?"

"The FBI showed up at my dad's house looking for me," I said, my voice elevating with every syllable. I watched him pluck a white t-shirt from his bag. "It was that agent from Texas."

He stopped with one arm in and one arm out of the shirt. "Silvers?"

I nodded. "Why would she come all the way to North Carolina looking for me?"

He didn't speak. Which was *never* a good sign with him.

"Nathan, I don't want to go to jail!"

His eyes snapped to mine. "You're not going to jail. They're probably following up with you because they're still looking for Abigail."

"That's not the reason. She wouldn't get on a plane for that." I pointed at him. "I'll bet anything she knows we were lying."

The corners of his mouth tipped up in a smile. "You're willing to bet *anything*?"

"Nathan! This is serious!"

He sat next to me. "Maybe, but don't jump to conclusions. It's a holiday. For all we know, she might have family in Asheville and she wanted to bring you a fruitcake."

"You're a terrible liar." I dropped my face into my hands. "Nathan, what will we do?"

He was quiet for a moment, and he put his hand on mine. "I'll find out what's going on as soon as we get home." He squeezed my fingers and let out a deep sigh. "But honestly, I don't have the headspace to worry about it today."

My shoulders slumped. I'd completely forgotten what the day would hold for him. My bottom lip poked out. "You're right. I'm sorry for being insensitive."

He released my hand, then stood. "Don't apologize."

"Are you wearing a suit today?" I asked.

"No. I've got a button up and a black sweater," he said.

I scrunched up my nose.

"What is it?" he asked.

"I forgot my shoes, so I'm wearing my pretty black dress with my ugly brown boots."

His shoulders shook with laughter. "Of course you are."

"What time are we leaving here?"

He looked at his watch. "Probably in about an hour. The service is at one."

* * *

The graveside service for Ashley was held at a small cemetery outside town. Nathan and I rode with his parents in the back of their SUV. In the snow, James had to use the four-wheel drive to make it up some steep hills. No one spoke in the car, allowing me plenty of time to consider the implications of the FBI's visit to find me.

When we arrived at the cemetery, about fifty people had gathered under a green tent surrounded by sprays of flowers. A shiny mahogany casket rested over a giant hole in the ground.

It reminded me of my mother.

The moment I stepped out onto the cemetery path, a strange sensation came over me. *Death.* Warren had once tried to verbalize his ability to detect the presence of the dead. He said it felt like a vacuum. It was an accurate description. Death pulled at my attention in every single direction.

I felt it because the baby felt it.

Nathan's hand on my back snapped me out of a daze. "I'm going to go talk to some people," he said.

My smile was gentle. "Do what you have to do. Don't worry about me."

He straightened the angel pin on the lapel of my coat. "Are you warm enough?"

I lowered my voice. "My boots may be hideous, but they're nice and toasty."

He laughed softly, but his eyes were sad.

I wandered the grounds as Nathan and his family mingled with people I didn't know and would probably never see again. It was eerie to be able to distinguish the empty grave plots from the occupied ones as I left my tracks in the untouched layer of snow. Unlike Warren, the awareness creeped me out, and I suddenly realized how far I'd strayed from the group. Turning on my heel, I double-timed my pace back to the tent.

Rows of chairs faced the casket, and I sat in the back and watched mourners come by and pay their respects. But something beyond the ornate box caught my attention.

Transparent against the scenery, three rippled figures hovered near the casket. Everyone but me was ignorant of their presence. Family members passed by and through them undeterred. It was chilling. Even more disturbing was, despite their lack of faces, I knew they were watching me.

They didn't strike me as sinister, but I got up and backed out of the tent nonetheless. Their gazes followed me, but they didn't leave their post. It was like they were guarding her, but I didn't know why.

As I watched them, my mind went to dark places. Had the angels been there in the woods where she was discarded and hidden for ten long years? Were they standing watch during her rape and torture? Did they really do nothing to intervene?

With everything I had experienced in the past few months, I could no longer believe the supernatural existed only in fairytales and Bible stories. God was real, and I knew it. But the more I found out, the more pissed off I became.

A tall, stout man who looked more like a politician than a minister, walked up in front of the chairs, clutching a brown Bible in his hands. "Everyone, I'd like to ask that the family please be seated. Friends and loved ones, please gather close for a word of prayer and a message of thankfulness for the life of sweet Ashley McNamara."

The crowd filed in, and I kept my distance near one of the back poles. Then Nathan waved to me from the front and motioned me forward. When I approached, I saw he'd saved a seat for me between him and his brother. I squeezed my way across the cramped second row and into the seat beside him.

The pastor opened with a prayer, then read a few letters written by various friends shortly after Ashley disappeared. Nathan's body tensed next to me, and when I looked at him, his face was frozen, staring ahead. I rested my head against his shoulder, and he wrapped his hand around mine.

I squeezed.

He squeezed back.

The pastor hugged his Bible to his chest. "Can I be honest?"

Everyone looked up at him.

He let out a heavy sigh and slowly shook his head. "For the life of me, I can't understand this tragedy." He took a step closer to Nathan's parents. "James, Kathy, I've looked at my little girls this week and wondered how a God who claims to love us like a father loves his children could let something so horrific happen. I'm sure you've wondered the same."

Kathy wiped tears away with a cloth handkerchief as they both nodded.

The pastor looked out over the crowd. "We've all asked this question, haven't we?"

A few people answered out loud in agreement while others bobbed their heads.

He shrugged his shoulders. "I honestly don't know why. No other memorial I have ever preached has stirred my doubt as this one has."

I withered with disappointment in my chair.

He held up his Bible. "But I know a few other things." He pointed to the casket. "I know Ashley's not here."

"That's true," I whispered to no one in particular.

The pastor tapped his chest. "This body—this temporal, decaying, grayer-every-day body—is just a container." He lifted the Bible again. "And if I believe what this book tells me, then I know to be absent from this body is to be present with the Lord! This life is only the beginning. Jesus told his disciples, *'Do not let your hearts be troubled. You believe in God. Believe also in me. My Father's house has many rooms. I am going to prepare a place for you. And if I go and prepare a place for you, I will come back and take you to be with me.'*" He looked around the group. "Ashley hasn't been missing all these years." He pointed up. "She's been at the Father's house."

Kathy dabbed at her eyes again, and her husband rubbed her back. Chuck reached up and squeezed her shoulder.

The preacher approached the family. "While I can't give you a reason why this happened, I can assure you this wasn't God's will. However, if we allow Him to be in this grief with us, He will use even this to do His good work. He promises us that. We won't see it for a while because right now our vision is obscured through the darkened glass of this world. But someday, when we stand face-to-face with Him in eternity, we will see clearly. We will see how even this evil, which was meant to destroy us, He used for good." He held his hands out. "Let us pray."

When he finished, a man with a guitar sang *Amazing Grace*, and Ashley's childhood friend read a poem. After a final prayer, each family member placed a single red rose on the lid of the casket. I held Nathan's hand during his turn.

When we were close to Ashley—close to the angels—I realized why they were there. Peace stirred in my soul, and they were the source. The angels weren't there for Ashley's bones. They stood guard for us.

We waited till the casket sank into the ground, then Kathy was ready to leave. The drive back to the house was even quieter than the drive to the cemetery had been. I stared out the window, watching small snowflakes drift to the ground, and thought about what the preacher had said again.

Typically, Bible verses frustrated me the same way poetry always had. All the words seemed to be a step beyond my comprehension level. Like there was a great message in there, but I was too dumb to get it.

The pastor that day, however, actually made sense. Maybe a positive ripple effect from all the crap we endure in this life *will* be unveiled in the next. It was a nice thought, whether or not it was true.

Nathan's hand touched my arm, drawing me back into the solemnity of the car. He didn't speak or look at me, but I understood his need for reassurance that the world was still real. I had felt the same when my mother died. Like a world without my mother in it, simply couldn't exist.

I wished my power to heal included the ability to mend broken hearts. Unfortunately, the divine didn't seem to work that way. The body I could touch; the soul I could only see.

The snow had stopped by the time we reached the McNamaras' home. Kathy's eyes were red and swollen, and she walked into the house and to her room without a word. James stopped with us at the stairwell and hugged his son. The other cars pulled into the driveway as I followed Nathan up the stairs.

When we reached his room, he walked over and picked up a framed picture. It was the first photo I had ever seen of Ashley. She wore a cheerleader's uniform next to Nathan in his football gear. His football number sparkled with glitter on her cheek. She had disappeared a week later.

For the first time all day, Nathan broke. He pinched the bridge of his nose while his shoulders shook with silent sobs. I put my arms around him from behind, and he laid the picture down and gripped the ledge of the dresser so tight his knuckles turned white.

When his breathing returned to normal, he turned around and pulled me into his arms. The subtle essence of fading cologne and testosterone made me light-headed.

He rested the side of his face against my hair. "Thank you so much for being here."

The soft fuzz of his sweater tickled my nose. "I wouldn't dream of being anywhere else. Can I do anything for you?"

He shook his head. "You're doing it."

We stood melted together for a long time, his fingers trailing up and down my spine, and his heartbeat quickening in my ear with each passing moment. Finally, he brought his hand under my chin and tilted my face up to look at him. He studied my mouth for a moment, then leaned in and kissed me.

The kiss was gentle at first, his mouth tenderly lingering on mine. Then his hand slid back into my hair, and he parted my lips with his tongue. Sidestepping toward the door, his free arm pushed it closed before he pinned my body against the wall. As the kiss deepened, his hands slid down my sides, and his fingers dug into my hips. The whole room seemed to spin.

I could empathize. A similar scene when my mother died spawned the predicament I was in. Frantically, I scrambled to muster the ability to stop him before things escalated any further.

I put my hands on his chest and pushed.

He stopped moving and pulled his lips away. He rested his forehead against mine, his eyes pressed close. "Please, Sloan," he whispered. "Please."

I gripped the collar of his shirt. "Nathan, I'm pregnant."

6.

NATHAN STUMBLED BACK like I had told him I was infected with the plague. I stayed glued to the wall. His face twisted with shock and confusion…and anger. "Pregnant?"

I nodded.

He raked his fingers through his hair and walked across the room. "You're pregnant?" he asked again.

I flinched at the tone of his voice. "About eight weeks."

He turned to look at me. His face was as pale as I had ever seen it—even when he was dead for a brief time. "Does Warren know?" he asked.

I shook my head.

He ran his hands over his face as he continued to pace. He was making me nervous, like he might spontaneously combust at any moment.

"Nathan, please say something."

"How long have you known?" he asked.

I took a small step away from the wall. "I realized it on our drive back from Charlotte when we dropped off Warren. It made sense when I didn't get a migraine that day. I found out from the doctor for sure a few days ago."

He stopped walking and tossed his hands in the air. "When were you planning to tell me?"

"I...I was trying to figure out how," I stammered.

He waved his hand toward me. "Well, I'm glad you figured it out before I tossed your dress onto my bedroom floor!"

I walked toward him. "Nathan, please—"

He held up his hand to stop me and shook his head. "No." He turned toward the door. "I can't do this anymore." He walked out of the bedroom and slammed the door behind him.

I started after him, but as soon as the door was open, I heard the front door downstairs slam. I sank back into the bedroom. Uncontrollable tears streamed down my cheeks, and I curled into a ball on the bed and cried.

At some point, I cried myself to sleep, and I awoke to the creak of the bedroom door. I opened my eyes and saw Nathan crossing through the room in the fading light of sunset. He stopped at the edge of the bed and looked down at me. I half-expected him to yell again.

Instead, he whispered, "Scoot over."

I slid over in the bed, and he stretched out next to me. He reached for my arm and pulled me close. I rested my head on his chest. "I'm sorry," he said, stroking my hair.

"I'm sorry too."

He tugged the blanket up around my shoulders. "This has to be over with me and you." His tone was low, serious, and unsteady. "I love you. I've loved you since that first day I walked into your office and you smacked your head on your desk." He sucked in a deep breath. "But this has to be over now."

I didn't speak.

"As much as I hate him sometimes, Warren's a good guy, and he really loves you. You're supposed to be with him," he said.

"Nathan, I—"

He cut me off. "Please, don't. Please, don't say it." His hand was still tangled in my hair. "I can handle being shot at and having my body broken in half by a demon, but I can't stand hearing you tell me you love me."

I closed my mouth.

He pressed a kiss to the top of my head, and silent tears dripped onto his sweater. My father's words floated to my mind. If I really loved him, I had to let him go.

I just wish I knew how.

* * *

After lunch the next day, we said our goodbyes to his family, promised his mother we would get our flu shots, and headed back to Asheville. We rode for a while in silence. Me staring out my window, and Nathan staring at the road ahead.

He finally looked over at me. "What are you going to do?"

"About the baby?"

The word made him flinch, but he nodded. "With you and Warren being whatever it is you are—"

"Seramorta."

"Right. Angel hybrids. What does that mean your kid will be?"

I sighed. "I don't know, but I'd guess it's why the supernatural world is so interested in me now. It's a big deal for an Angel of Life and an Angel of Death to even be together. I can only imagine the repercussions of us having a baby."

"Is that what you are? An Angel of Life?"

I shrugged my shoulders. "I guess so. That's what Kasyade told me before she went full demon on everyone."

He shook his head. "Life with you is starting to feel like a Hitchcock movie."

I leaned my head against the cold glass. "I can't argue."

"And you believe her?" he asked.

"Samael, the angel that helped us the day we fought her—"

"The day I died?" he asked.

My heart deflated. "Yes. The day you died. Samael said basically the same thing, and he's a good angel."

"Is it because you're pregnant that you could bring me back from the dead, and now can fully heal people?" he asked.

"Yeah. All the powers I had before are magnified like crazy. My summoning power works like a GPS now," I said. "I also seem to have developed Warren's ability to sense dead bodies. It was overwhelming at the cemetery yesterday."

"That must be weird," he said.

I nodded. "It was." Another thought occurred to me. "I wonder if I can kill people too."

Nathan looked at me with raised eyebrows. "So Warren can kill people?"

I grimaced. "I wasn't supposed to tell you that."

He sighed. "I already knew, but it's still alarming to hear it said out loud." He looked back out the windshield. "Is that what really happened to Billy Stewart and Larry Mendez?"

I didn't answer because I didn't have to.

After a minute, Nathan groaned.

"What?" I asked.

He rubbed his forehead. "I'm considering what Warren could do to me if he finds out what happened with us last night."

I laughed. "What did you think 'Angel of Death' meant?"

He shrugged and draped an arm over the steering wheel. "Honestly, I still have a little trouble believing all that."

Some days I still had trouble believing it myself.

When we reached my house, the sun was sinking behind the mountains. I was half-asleep with my head against the window listening to the moody drone of nineties grunge rock.

"This isn't good." Nathan switched off the radio.

Rubbing my eyes, I straightened in my seat. "Huh?"

"You've got company," he said.

A dark blue sedan was at the curb in front of my house.

"Oh god," I said. "It's the feds. I'm going to prison."

Nathan rolled his eyes and pulled to a stop behind the car. "Calm down and let me do the talking."

A man got out of the driver's seat, then the passenger side door popped open. FBI Agent Sharvell Silvers angled out of the car and tightened the belt on her wool coat as she marched to the curb.

I was sweating.

"Get out of the truck, Sloan," Nathan said.

I looked over and he was leaning against his door. I hadn't heard him move. Exhaling slowly, I opened my door and slid off my seat.

Even in the four inch black pumps she was wearing, Agent Silvers didn't quite reach my eye-level, but she made me feel about two inches tall. Technically, she was one of the good guys, but she could be one hell of a villain if she so desired. And I wasn't sure which side of the law she thought I was on in that moment.

Swallowing my fear with a heavy gulp, I extended a hand toward her. "Agent Silvers, it's nice to see you again."

"Good afternoon, Sloan." She looked at Nathan. "Hello, Detective."

Nathan stepped forward and shook her hand.

She looked toward the man with her. "This is Agent Clark"

Nathan shook his hand, then turned his attention back to her. "What brings you to Asheville?"

She looked me up and down. "I'd like to have a private word with Ms. Jordan, if you don't mind."

Nathan crossed his arms. "Absolutely not without a lawyer."

She shot him a daring look. "I could detain her and put her in jail on a temporary hold."

He smirked. "You have to have probable cause for that."

She held up a padded legal folder. "How about suspicion of conspiracy to commit sex trafficking, conspiracy to harbor aliens, and conspiracy to commit money laundering. I have a whole file full of probable cause." Sharvell looked at me. "Would you prefer a holding cell, Ms. Jordan, or shall we step inside?"

The spike in my blood pressure was enough to make my knees wobble. I shook my head furiously. "Of course we can go inside, Agent Silvers."

Without waiting for me to lead the way, the two agents turned toward the steps to my house. Nathan grabbed the tail of my shirt. "What are you doing?" he whispered.

"I can't go to jail, Nathan!"

He pointed at me. "You watch what you say in there, Sloan. They can hold anything against you."

We followed them, and I passed the agents on the porch. My hand was shaking so much I fumbled the keys, twice. Sharvell noticed. Once we were inside, I motioned toward the living room. "Please make yourselves comfortable. Can we get you some water? Or I can make coffee," I offered.

Agent Silvers shook her head and walked around my living room like a cat on the prowl. She stopped at the mantle and picked up a photo of my family. "Is this your mother?"

I looked at Nathan. He nodded.

"Yes, ma'am," I said.

She traced her finger over the edge of the frame. "I hear she passed away."

"In October," I answered, a familiar pain creeping through me.

Gently, she placed the frame back on the ledge. "How did she die?"

"Cut the interrogation tactics. Using her mom to rattle her is a low blow," Nathan interrupted.

Her gaze cut to him. "I simply wanted to offer my condolences."

"Bullshit," Nathan said.

Without further argument, she stalked to the sofa and sat down. The rest of us took that as our cue to find a seat. Nathan sat so protectively close to me, his hip touched mine.

Sharvell opened the business folder and balanced it on her thighs. "Sloan, I would like you to tell me again about your involvement with Abigail Smith."

I shook my head. "I'm not involved with Abigail and haven't seen her since Texas."

"What was your involvement with her prior to Texas?" she asked.

I turned my palms up in question. "We weren't involved. I only met her a couple of times."

She pointed at me. "You're lying."

My mouth fell open. "No, I'm not."

She pulled papers from the portfolio and handed them over the coffee table. "These were found inside her residence in San Antonio. Can you explain them?"

They were photographs. Of me.

One was a picture of me locking the front door of the apartment I lived in during my senior year of college. The second was me on the playground at school when we still lived in Florida. And the third was of me and Warren carrying boxes of his stuff into my house. A chill made me shudder. I felt naked. Exposed.

"I don't know what these are," I said.

Nathan was looking over my shoulder. "These are obviously surveillance photos taken without her knowledge."

I flipped back to the picture of me as a child. It was the same playground where I'd received the scar over my eye as a kid. Kasyade had been watching me the whole time. I thought of the teacher who had terrified me that same year and realized she'd been planted there on purpose. My chin quivered.

"Why would Abigail be watching you?" she asked.

I held up the photos. "I would love to know the same thing."

"Sloan, we recovered boxes and boxes of photographs like these, along with notes, newspaper clippings, medical records, school transcripts..." She tapped her finger on the folder. "For someone who claims to have only just met this woman, I find it odd she has a lifetime of information on you."

Nathan shook his head. "All this proves is Sloan has a stalker."

"And what does this prove?" She leaned forward, passing Nathan a manila folder from her portfolio.

Nathan opened it, and I leaned over his shoulder.

Uh oh.

"I believe that's an information packet about a woman you were investigating here in North Carolina, is it not?" she asked, her voice dripping with haughty derision. "You lied to me, Detective. You both lied."

The folder contained the original information he had gathered on Abigail when we still assumed her name was Rachel Smith and that she'd been murdered by our serial killer.

"My question is *why* would you lie?" she asked.

Nathan closed the folder. "I was out of my jurisdiction while investigating—"

"Now who's spouting off bullshit, Detective?" she snapped. She wagged her finger between the two of us. "I also know the two of you aren't a couple. Never have been."

I scowled at Nathan.

He ignored me and stood. "Well, unfortunately for you, Agent Silvers, our relationship status isn't governed by federal law. So unless you're going to charge us with a crime of which you have zero proof, our conversation here is over."

I was surprised Nathan didn't fall over dead under the heat of her glare.

Sharvell stood, as did the man with her. They walked toward the front door and we followed. She turned on her heel in the foyer and looked up at me. "I promise you, Ms. Jordan." Her eyes shrank into angry slits as she snatched the photos I was still holding. "I will find out what you're hiding from me. Make no mistake of it."

My skin prickled at her tone, and I shuddered as they walked out the door.

Nathan leaned toward my ear. "Stay inside. I'll get your bag from the car."

I couldn't have moved if I'd wanted to. And I didn't want to.

Nathan stood on the curb with his arms folded across his chest till the agents drove away and disappeared around the curve. Then he went to his truck and retrieved my bag. I was still frozen in front of the door when he came back in and closed it.

He waved a hand in front of my staring eyes. "Earth to Sloan. Are you OK?"

Snapping out of my daze, I nodded. "Yeah. At least she didn't arrest me." I turned toward him as he put my bag down by the stairs inside. "What did she mean by she could detain me on conspiracy of all that stuff? Is that true?"

He came back over and stood in front of me. "Technically, they can hold you without charging you, but they won't do that. Not if that's all the probable cause they have." His face wasn't convincing.

"That woman is going to bury me under the jail!"

He shook his head. "They have no evidence you're involved in this because no evidence exists." He bent to look me in the eye. "I won't let them bury you anywhere."

I wished his words were comforting.

"Just to be safe, we should look for a federal defense attorney," he suggested.

I smirked. "And tell them what?"

"It's still a good idea." He glanced at his watch, then around the room. "Are you staying in for tonight?"

"Yeah. I need to try to get some rest. *Try* being the keyword in that sentence."

He hesitated as he turned toward the front door. "I can sleep in the guest room if it will help you relax."

I squeezed his hand. "This has to end, remember?" I asked. "You moving in with me—no matter how noble the reason—isn't good for anyone. I can always go stay with Dad if I need to."

He looked down at the floor and sighed. "You're right."

"I'll call you if anything happens," I said.

He put his arms around me. "I hate this."

"I know."

From the door, I watched until he got into his truck and drove away, then I sucked in a deep breath and looked out over the horizon. The faint ripples were thicker and covered more of the sky. I wondered how many angels were out there, and if it was a good sign or a bad one that their numbers were multiplying. Slowly, I closed the door and walked back into my quiet house.

As I lay in bed, waiting for sleep to come, my brain replayed the events of the weekend. The FBI and the funeral were both overshadowed by the memory of Nathan's arms pinning me against his bedroom wall as we kissed. I still felt his fingertips on my hips and the weight of his body pressing against me. My stomach fluttered with the taste of desperation on his lips and the plea for escape dripping from his eyes. *Please*, he had whispered.

With so many emotions between us, that neither of us could reconcile, how would it ever be possible for me and Nathan to just be friends? Someone in our triangular affair was destined for heartbreak. I suspected it might be all three of us.

I didn't deserve the unnatural patience and understanding that Warren Parish afforded me. If he struggled between love for me and love for another woman, I would be devastated and possibly homicidal. I pictured his face and washed myself in the memory of the intoxicating buzz of energy I felt whenever we touched.

Into the darkness, I reached out with my gift to find his soul. He was there, but he was so far away. Lost in the delusions of a faceless embrace, I drifted off to sleep as tears dripped to my pillow and thunder rumbled in the distance.

* * *

The sound of my alarm clock came too early the next morning. Nothing in me wanted to get up and go into work. I briefly considered grabbing my phone and typing out a resignation email with my thumbs. *If I quit my job, I can go right back to sleep.*

I didn't. I got up instead and blindly crossed my bedroom to the master bath. When I flipped on the light, two bulbs blew out. There was barely enough light for me to see to brush my teeth, much less fix my hair and do my makeup. Just my luck.

I picked up my hairbrush and pulled it through the tangles in my long brown hair. My eyes were tired, and I blinked a few times to get them to focus. I put my brush down to wash my face, but my reflection in the mirror didn't change. I was still brushing my hair.

I wiped the sleep from my eyes and looked again. I stared back at me. "Sloan." The sound of my own voice, though it didn't come from my lips, was jolting as it echoed around the bathroom.

My reflection moved closer to the glass. "Sloan."

To my horror, blood spread over the midsection of Warren's gray t-shirt I wore. I looked down to see nothing amiss with the real me standing at the sink, and when I looked back again at the mirror, the eyes staring back at me were solid white and empty. I held up my shirt, showing a long bloody gash across my stomach. The inside was hollow. My baby was gone.

My scream echoed throughout the house.

I sat up in bed, sweat pouring down my face, when I looked at the clock on my nightstand. It was 2:13 in the morning. Instinctively, I grasped at my stomach. There was nothing wrong with me.

In the corner of my room, I saw something move.

A shadow, with the shape of a small person and bright, amber eyes, moved toward me. With my heart pounding so loud it reverberated around the room, I scrambled back as far in the bed as I could before the figure overtook me and slammed my body against the mattress.

I tried to scream, but no sound would come. I tried to fight, but the shadow had nothing to grab onto. Two chilly hands pushed through my chest and gripped my heart, squeezing and twisting. I fought to breathe, but the crushing weight on my chest wouldn't allow for any air. The veins in my eyes exploded as the life slipped from my body.

There was a flash of bright light, and then I was sitting up again. I looked at the clock. 2:13.

This time, I lunged for the lamp on my nightstand and jumped out of bed. There was nothing in my room. I was wearing Warren's shirt, and it wasn't covered in blood. I walked to the bathroom and turned on the lights. All the bulbs flickered on.

As I splashed cold water on my face, I avoided looking at my reflection—just in case.

"It's only a dream," I said, still panting. "It's only a dream."

There was no use in trying to go back to sleep because it wouldn't happen. I got up and walked downstairs to the dark living room. I grabbed the pregnancy book from the doctor and sat on the couch. An entire section dedicated to dreams and fantasies confirmed increased nightmares were normal during pregnancy. It made me feel slightly better. I pulled the fleece blanket off the back of the couch and curled up underneath it. The clock on the wall said 2:26.

The unmistakable sound of footsteps came from my front porch.

Slowly, I got up and moved against the wall. Whoever it was had seen my light come on. They knew I was home, and if they'd been watching my house for any period of time, they also knew I was alone. I should have let Nathan stay. My phone was upstairs.

My heart was racing so fast I was dizzy. Closing my eyes, I sent out my *evil radar*, as Nathan called it. There didn't seem to be anything sinister waiting for me, so I crept into the foyer and looked out the peep hole. On the other side of the door, the silhouette of a man flashed against the distant glow of the dim city lights.

I blinked and he was gone.

Gripping the sides of my head, I wondered if I was losing my mind. For a moment, I considered driving to Nathan's apartment, but I decided the idea was worse than staying home alone. I could have gone to my dad's, but if I woke him up that early, he'd never go back to sleep.

Wind howled in my chimney.

A branch cracked outside the window.

Screw this.

I ran upstairs, threw some clothes into a bag, then drove to the only place that made sense.

Adrianne's.

* * *

Adrianne was rubbing her eyes with her knuckles when she opened the front door. She leaned against the doorframe and surveyed my wild hair, disheveled pajamas, and the overnight bag in my hand. "This can't be good," she said through a yawn.

My teeth were chattering. "Can I come in?"

She stepped out of the way, and I rushed into her two-story loft apartment. She locked the deadbolt behind me. "What's up?"

I pulled the scarf from my neck. "There might be a demon at my house. Can I sleep here?"

"Did you bring the demon with you?" she asked.

I shrugged my shoulders. "I don't think so, but I can't be sure."

She shuffled toward her kitchen and flipped the light on. She pointed at the table. "Sit." Obediently, I sat down as she poured two glasses of water. She handed me one and sat across from me. "OK, what happened?"

Without pausing to breathe, I told her everything.

She was cradling her skull in her hands by the time I finished. "Are you sure you were still dreaming when that thing attacked you in your room?"

"I have no idea. I'm not completely convinced I'm fully awake right now."

She reached across the table and pinched my arm. Hard.

I yelped with pain. "Ow!"

She shook her head. "You're awake."

I scowled and rubbed the stinging spot on my arm.

"Did you call Nathan?"

I groaned. "No. He would have insisted on coming over to my house."

"Is that such a bad thing?" she asked.

I covered my face with my hands. "*Things* happened with us this weekend."

She rolled her eyes and sipped her water. "Oh, geez. What now?"

I blew out a long puff of air. "I told him about the baby, and it didn't go well."

"I thought you were going to wait to tell him," she said.

"Well, I was, but after the funeral, things got a little heated in his bedroom, and I sort of blurted it out."

Her jaw dropped. "You told him you were pregnant during sex?"

"No. Geez, get your mind out of the gutter, Adrianne."

She tossed her hands up. "How else am I supposed to take 'heated in his bedroom,' Sloan?"

I groaned. "I told him before things went that far. He freaked out."

"I told you he would."

I raked my fingers through my hair. "We're all right now, but he stormed out of the house. I was afraid he'd never speak to me again."

"*Pshhh*," she said. "He's too in love with you for that."

I ran both hands down my face, pulling my lips down into a frown. "I know, which is why I came here instead of going to him."

She pointed at me. "Smart girl. You need to tell him about this though. This is major."

"He'll be even more protective of me, and that's the opposite of what either of us need," I said.

"You need to work on having some boundaries with him, I agree. However, if you don't tell him, I will. I'm a hair expert, not a bodyguard," she said.

I nodded but said nothing.

A smile crept over her face. "So what happened in his bedroom?"

My mouth fell open. "We're not talking about that."

"Tongue or no tongue?" she pressed.

I got up and walked toward the bathroom.

She followed me. "Was there nakedness?"

"Adrianne!"

I tried to shut the bathroom door in her face, but she blocked it with her long arm. "Serious question though."

I put my hand on my hip.

"If you weren't pregnant, what would've happened?"

My shoulders dropped.

She pointed at me. "Bingo."

7.

ADRIANNE MADE UP the couch for me to sleep on, but sleep never came. My brain replayed the nightmares over and over again. Every time I closed my eyes, I saw the figure in the corner of my room. At six, I gave up and got ready for work.

Sleep wasn't so elusive once I got to my office. I woke up drooling on my desk, not once but three times during the day. By five o'clock, I was running on autopilot, but I'd promised my dad we'd have our regularly scheduled Monday night dinner, and I was desperate to talk to him more about the FBI.

When I walked out of the building, Nathan was walking up the steps. I narrowed my eyes. "Did Adrianne call you?"

He met me half-way. "She sent me a text message to come by today. I thought it was strange. What did you do?"

My brow wrinkled. "Why would you assume I did something?"

He crossed his arms over his chest and glared.

I rolled my eyes and walked down the stairs. Nathan fell in step beside me.

"Adrianne's worried because I had a pretty bad nightmare last night. I showed up at her house at three this morning." From the corner of my eye, I saw he was suppressing a smile. I pointed at him. "Don't you dare laugh at me. You don't know how bad it was."

"Tell me about it," he said.

"I dreamed someone cut the baby out of my stomach, then when I woke up screaming, something—or someone—was in my room, and it tried to crush me in my bed," I said as we crossed the lot.

He stopped walking. "Were you really awake?"

I shrugged my shoulders. "I don't know. After that, I got up and went downstairs, but I heard something or someone outside. I looked through the peep hole and maybe saw a man, but when I looked again, he was gone."

"Why didn't you call me?"

I kicked my toe against the gravel on the asphalt. "Because things are weird with us right now."

He rested his hands below the sides of his tactical belt.

"That's when I drove to Adrianne's. She thought I should tell you."

For a few moments, he stared down at the ground. Then he cut his eyes up at me. "I'm coming to your house tonight."

"I'll sleep on Adrianne's couch—"

He pointed at me. "No, you're not. What if that was a person standing on your porch or in your room? I'll sleep in the guest bed till we figure something else out."

"Nathan, I—"

He cut me off again. "Stop arguing. We've already seen what Kasyade is capable of, so we're not playing around with this shit anymore." He sighed. "I promised Warren, Sloan."

I put my hands on my hips. "He might feel differently given what's already happened."

He crossed his arms over his chest. "Do you not think he weighed that out before he asked me? He was worried enough to still take that chance, obviously with good reason."

I scowled but had no argument.

"When and where are you having dinner with your dad?"

"Red Stag in half an hour."

"Then I'll be at your place around eight." He turned on his heel and headed toward his tan SUV.

"Nathan, this is a bad idea," I called after him.

He stopped and looked back at me, laughing sarcastically. "When have we ever done anything that's been a good idea? I'll see you in a couple of hours."

Before I could protest further, he got into his car and slammed the door.

* * *

Thanks to Nathan's untimely visit, if I didn't hurry, I would be late for dinner with my dad.

There was a little-known shortcut through town involving a questionable road by the park and passing through two parking lots marked with No Entry signs. When I exited the first parking lot, I noticed a set of headlights in my rearview mirror.

When I entered the second parking lot, the lights were still behind me. I reached out with my gift, but my sixth sense was choppy and vague because I was distracted by driving.

I hoped Nathan was being overprotective and had decided to follow me. I dialed his number.

"McNamara," he answered.

"Hey, it's me." I turned left onto the main highway toward the Biltmore Estate. "Where are you?"

It was loud wherever he was. "Just walked into the jail to wrap things up."

"Someone might be following me," I said.

"Where are you?" he asked.

I checked my surroundings. "On highway twenty-five, near Biltmore. I'm almost at the Red Stag."

He was quiet for a second. "As soon as you get there, park in a well-lit area and get inside as fast as you can. I can't leave right now, but stay at the restaurant till I get there. I'll follow you home."

"OK."

"Sloan!"

"What?"

"Don't do anything stupid," he said.

I rolled my eyes and pulled into the parking lot of the Bohemian Hotel. "I won't."

"Stay on the phone with me till you get inside," he said.

When I put the car in park, I looked back over my shoulder. A car stopped on the curb of the street a block down from the hotel. "I can't be sure because it's dark and there are so many cars, but they might have parked near McDonald's."

"Can you tell what kind of car?" he asked.

"Of course not." I grabbed my purse and bolted from my car toward the entrance. When I slid to a stop in the lobby, I was breathless. "I'm inside."

"Stay there," he said. "I'll be there by the time you're done." He disconnected the line.

I loved the Red Stag Grill for its ambiance and perfect mix of gnarly mountain cuisine and trendy pretension. Only around Biltmore could venison and rainbow trout feel snobbish. The room flaunted rich shades of brown and red with a warm glow from honey-colored lamps illuminating its many guests. In the corner, an enormous Christmas tree, trimmed with holly berries and flameless lanterns, stood beneath the mounted head of a twelve-point buck. My father waved from a table between the bar and the silent baby grand piano.

A hardwood path wove in and out of crimson, candlelit tables across the room. When I reached my dad, he offered his cheek for a kiss. I obliged before pulling off my pea coat and sliding into my seat. "I'm sorry I'm late," I said, draping the cloth napkin over my lap. "It was a weird drive here."

"Weird drive?" he asked.

"Yeah. I think I was followed."

"Followed?" The alarm in his voice drove his pitch up an octave.

I nodded. "I called Nathan. He's meeting me here before we leave to make sure I get home OK."

Dad's shoulders relaxed. "That's good. I expected him to be with you."

"Not for dinner, but I'm sure you'll get to see him before the night's over." I opened the menu and looked over the choices. "I wonder what wild boar tastes like. What are you ordering, Dad?"

He pointed to his menu. "I believe I'll have the halibut."

I scanned the entry and frowned. "What on earth are duck fat baby potatoes?"

He chuckled and took a sip of his water. "They're tiny little potatoes. Very tasty. How's Nathan?"

"He's good." I looked over the top of my menu at Dad. "Do you think they yank the trout out of the river out back?"

Dad smiled. "I doubt that." He leaned toward me. "Why do I feel like you're avoiding Nathan as a topic of dinner conversation?"

I forced my lips into a smile. "I'm not," I lied. The truth was I knew I couldn't talk about my weekend with Nathan without blushing, and the last thing I wanted was for Dad to know Nathan was going home with me after dinner.

By the grace of God and all the good karma in the universe, our waiter appeared at the table with a basket of sliced multigrain baguettes. "Ma'am, would you be interested in a glass of wine?"

I blew out a sigh that puffed out my cheeks. "Oh, I'm interested, but no. Water will be fine."

"May I take your dinner order, then?" he asked.

I pointed across the table. "Start with him."

Dad ordered his fish, then both men stared expectantly at me.

I looked up at my dad, tapping my fingers against the sides of the menu. "Can I just have the chocolate lava cake?"

"No."

I frowned. "Then I guess I'll order the meatloaf." I closed my menu and handed it to the waiter.

Dad buttered a slice of bread. "How was the funeral?"

Heat rose in my cheeks. "It was very emotional." I picked up my water goblet and drained half of it.

Dad chuckled. "Are you OK?"

"Yup."

His brow rose in question. "Sloan?"

"Yeah?"

"You're as red as a beet," he said. "What happened?"

"Nothing."

He pointed his butter knife at me. "You're lying."

I scrunched up my nose. "That's twice in two days I've been called a liar."

He put the knife on the plate and lifted the bread. "Well, at least half the time it's been true. Who else called you a liar?"

"The FBI."

His hand froze midway to his mouth. "They found you, then?"

"Yeah. They were waiting at my house yesterday when we got back, and my guess would be they're following me now," I said.

He looked around the room. "What do they want with you?"

I turned my palms up. "I'm not really sure, except they believe I was lying in Texas about my relationship with Abigail."

"You *were* lying to them in Texas," he said, taking a bite of his bread.

"Was I supposed to tell them the truth?" I scoffed at the thought. "Do you want them to lock me up in the loony bin?"

Dad pressed his lips together in a tight grimace. "It'd be better than prison."

I groaned. "What did they say to you?"

The waiter returned with our salads. I smiled and thanked him.

Dad poured dressing over his wedge of iceberg lettuce. "Not much. They asked where they could find you. I said you were attending a funeral out of town with a friend. They inquired about Nathan. Apparently, they were under the impression the two of you were a couple. I set them straight."

"Ahh…that makes sense," I said.

"What makes sense?" he asked.

I skewered a grape tomato. "Nathan told them we were together. I was wondering how they found out we weren't."

Dad's eyebrow peaked. "Why would he do that?"

I rolled my eyes. "Because he's an idiot."

He folded his arms on the tabletop. "While we're on the subject…"

My fork clinked against the china when I dropped it onto the salad plate.

"Are you taking my advice and minding your boundaries with him?"

He wasn't going to let it go. I sat back hard in my seat and stared at him. "Dad, I've had two attempts made on my life in the past two months and have been promised that more will come. I've done my best to keep a safe distance from Nathan, but he's staying close to protect me like he promised Warren he would. Please stop insinuating I'm becoming the Harlot of West Asheville."

Dad couldn't suppress his laughter. "Are you a little defensive, my dear?"

"Yes."

"Pregnancy hormones will do that to you," he said.

I picked up my fork again and stabbed an innocent crouton. "So will meddlesome fathers."

He chuckled behind his napkin. "All right. No more questions about Nathan, I promise."

"Thank you."

His head fell to the side. "Is he following you home so he can stay with you?"

"Dad!"

* * *

Nathan arrived at dinner in time for dessert, and he pulled up a chair to our table set for two. He shook my father's hand. "Sorry to crash your date, Dr. Jordan."

Dad waved his napkin. "Nonsense. I'm glad you're here."

I handed Nathan the dessert menu. "Did you see anything strange outside?"

He shook his head. "No, but I'll keep an eye out on our drive to your house." He pointed to my plate. "What is that?"

"Chocolate lava cake. Do you want some?" I asked, offering him the bite on my fork.

He leaned over and opened his mouth. As the tines scraped across his teeth, I caught my dad rolling his eyes in my peripheral. I credited myself with paying attention to my father and not to Nathan's lips as he licked a drizzle of chocolate off them. Damn hormones.

The waiter stopped by and Nathan ordered a cup of coffee.

"No cake?" I asked, surprised.

He patted his flat stomach. "Trying to watch my figure."

I laughed. "Whatever, Captain Skittles."

He smiled at me, then rested his elbows on the table and lowered his voice. "What makes you think someone followed you here?"

I wiped crumbs off my mouth. "I took a few obscure back roads and headlights were behind me the whole way."

"Was the driver human?" he asked barely above a whisper.

"I'm not sure. They were far away and I was driving so I couldn't concentrate."

The waiter returned with Nathan's coffee, and he wrapped his hands around the steaming mug. "I'm sure it's the FBI. You've probably got eyes on you in this very room."

I carefully scanned the other tables. "Right now?"

He nodded and scooped a finger full of chocolate icing off my plate. "You need to be careful. They could tap your phone and bug your house too."

I pushed what was left on the plate toward him, and he grinned and picked up my fork.

"Can they do that?" Dad asked.

"They can if they get a warrant for it." He grimaced. "And I hate to say it, but if I were a judge, I'd issue one in this case."

I dropped my face into my hands.

Nathan squeezed my shoulder. "They still can't prove you're involved because you're not. I'll make some calls tomorrow and see what I can find out. Don't worry till there's a reason to."

I looked up at him. "Easy for you to say."

"If they're investigating you, they're investigating me too."

I scrunched up my nose. "I guess that seals the deal on no FBI job for you."

He finished what was left of my cake. "I'm sure it does."

I was yawning by the time we said our goodbyes to my dad in the hotel lobby. Dad hugged me and kissed the side of my head. "Are you all right to drive yourself home? It looks like it's flurrying outside."

I nodded against his shoulder. "Yeah. I'll be fine."

He shook hands with Nathan. "Thanks for looking out for her, son."

"It's my pleasure, sir."

Dad pointed a finger at me. "You be careful." His warning tone was loaded with double meaning.

Nathan walked with me to my car. "I'll be behind you the whole way," he said.

"Thank you."

Knowing the headlights behind me belonged to Nathan, I relaxed on the drive home. I called Adrianne and yelled at her, but I also thanked her for looking out for me by calling him. We chatted until I pulled into the driveway.

"Gotta go. We're home now," I said to her.

"OK," she said. "No staying up past eleven with him and always sleep in Warren's shirts."

I laughed. "Is that your recipe for chastity?"

"Yes. And don't let him wear cologne in the house. You're a sucker for that shit," she said.

She was right.

"Goodnight, Adrianne."

"Call me if you get weak."

Nathan was waiting by his car door behind me when I got out. "Sorry," I said, holding up my phone. "That was Adrianne."

"What did she have to say?" he asked.

I chuckled. "You don't want to know."

"Probably not." He froze when he noticed the crushed rhododendron in front of my driveway. "What happened to the bush?"

I squished my mouth to one side.

"Sloan?"

"I drove over it."

He cocked his head to the side. "Why?"

I looked down at my feet. "Adrianne scared me."

He pointed at me. "You scare me." We turned toward the sidewalk leading to the house. "Well, you don't have to worry about anything sinister that can be stopped by bullets. That's the upside of having the FBI on your tail."

"They're following me?"

He grimaced. "That would be my guess. Someone certainly is."

I dropped my arms and looked up at the sky. "Why?" I asked the angels, or God, or the universe. I scanned the dark street. "Where are they now?"

He jerked his head to the side. "They're in a truck a street over."

"Fantastic," I muttered as we walked up the steps to the porch.

As I unlocked the front door, he nudged my side. "Maybe you should give me Warren's key while he's gone."

Smirking, I pushed the door open. "Sometimes I worry you have a death wish."

"Been there, done that, Sloan."

I laughed as we walked inside.

8.

THE REST OF the week was remarkably uneventful considering an army of angels and the federal government followed me wherever I went, the world's hottest cop was sleeping in my guest room, and a person the size of a duck fat baby potato was growing inside me. On Friday afternoon, I was packing up my files and laptop when my boss walked into my office.

"Hey, Mary," I said.

Mary Travers was so small she could easily be mistaken for a child from behind if it weren't for her fondness of tweed and polyester skirt suits. She'd recently gotten a new hairstyle, an asymmetrical long pixie cut—a daring leap from her boring straight brown bob—and contact lenses to replace her thick black frames. In our office, it was the most peculiar metamorphosis since Kafka.

"I'm glad I caught you." She handed me a white envelope.

I blinked with surprise. "What's this?"

"Your valet vouchers for tomorrow night," she answered.

My brain raced. "Umm…"

"The office Christmas party at the Grove Park," she said, wide-eyed.

I laughed. "Oh my. With everything going on, I completely forgot about it."

"I hope everything's OK," she said.

I sank down into my office chair and motioned to the chairs across from my desk. "We need to talk."

Mary sat, worry lines creasing her brow.

I shifted uncomfortably on my chair. "I recently found out I'm pregnant."

She covered her mouth with her hand. "Really?"

"Really. I'm due in July."

She looked a little uneasy. "I hope congratulations are in order."

I smiled. "Yes. I'm happy about it." And it was true, despite my raging nerves and confused hormones.

Mary reached across the table and squeezed my hand. "Congratulations, Sloan."

"Thank you."

She tapped her fingertips together. "Have you considered how your job will fit into your new life as a mother?"

I shook my head. "I haven't even thought about it, but I'll let you know if I forsee any major changes."

"We'll do whatever we can to make your life easier so we can keep you here."

"I appreciate that," I said.

She glanced at the envelope. "Will you make it to the party tomorrow night?"

I stood and straightened my shirt. "If I can stay awake, I'll be there."

Laughing, she got up. "Wonderful. I'll see you then."

"Goodbye, Mary."

When she left, I crammed my laptop and files into my bag and locked up my office. It was freezing outside, and I saw my breath against the last rays of pink and orange sunshine. There were ripples watching me in the sky and a black truck watching me from the corner of the parking lot. I waved to both of them.

The truck followed me home.

Nathan, who had been camped out in my guest room all week, was idling at the curb when I pulled into my driveway. When I came around front, he was waiting by his SUV. He was carrying a pizza box from Asheville Pizza and Brewery.

I smiled. "I could get used to living with you."

He laughed. "Don't."

The patch on the front of his ball cap said, *The ATF should be a convenience store, not a government agency.*

I pointed at it. "You didn't work today?"

He took my bag from me as we walked up the stairs. "I went in for a few hours this morning, but I wasn't on the schedule. How was your day?"

"Exhausting." I looked over at him. "Do you have plans tomorrow night?"

"I'll have to check my social calendar." He shook his head as we went up the steps. "I've got this chick in my life who wears me the hell out—"

I playfully backhanded his arm. "Shut up."

"Why do you ask?"

"My office Christmas party is tomorrow night at The Grove Park Inn," I said. "I forgot about it."

He groaned.

"Have you ever been to the Grove Park Inn?" I asked as I put my key in the deadbolt.

He laughed. "I dated Shannon. What do you think?"

Rolling my eyes, I pushed my door open. "Have you ever been at Christmas time?"

"No."

"It will be nice," I said as we walked inside.

He locked the door behind us. "Does that mean I have to dress up?"

"Yes."

He groaned again. "How dressy are we talking about?"

I thought for a moment. "I'll probably wear a black dress and—"

He spun toward me. "The black dress you wore at the bar?"

I froze as I unbuttoned my coat. "What?"

"Short black dress, kinda shiny with a belt. You wore it to the bar the first night I met Adrianne," he said.

I closed my eyes and thought back to the first night I'd ever seen Nathan outside work. We were at a nightclub downtown. He'd shown up with Shannon. Ugh. I shook my head. "No. I hate that dress."

He pulled off his hat and hung it on a hook by the door. "I liked it, but it probably wouldn't fit you anymore."

I gasped. "Excuse me?"

He nudged my arm. "It's not bad. It's normal to have a baby bump."

"I don't have a baby bump."

He carried the pizza to the kitchen. "I've been looking at your body for six months. You have a bump."

I shrugged out of my coat. "I'm not sure what offends me more, your admission of checking me out all the time or you pointing out I'm gaining weight."

"If that offends you, then you'll really be pissed to know I've noticed your boobs getting bigger also," he said over his shoulder.

"Nathan!"

He was snickering as he pulled two plates out of the cupboard. "I thought you wanted bigger boobs."

Stalking into the kitchen, I punched him in the shoulder. "We're not talking about my boobs!"

"I meant it as a compliment." He laughed. "If you're putting on a few pounds, at least you're doing it in the right places."

"Please stop talking." I yanked open the refrigerator to retrieve two bottles of water.

Thirty minutes later, most of the pizza was gone. I ate half. I put my plate down on the coffee table and pointed a warning finger at Nathan. "Don't you dare say a word about how much I ate."

He laughed and swallowed his last bite. "I wouldn't dare."

I pulled the blanket off the back of the sofa before positioning the throw pillow against the arm of the sofa. I stretched out, tucking my cold feet behind Nathan's back.

He tapped my shin. "Hey, isn't that the guy you think they sent Warren after?"

On the television was a photograph of an Arabic man who Warren had shown me before he left. The terrorist, whose name I couldn't pronounce, had no soul which meant he was dead or he wasn't human. Since videos and stories kept flooding the news about him, I suspected it was the latter.

"And there's more breaking news out of Lebanon. Abdelkarim Abdulla Khalil Shallah, has released a new video on a known terrorist website claiming responsibility for the beheading of US Marine, Alexander Diaz..."

They showed a paused video image of another man in a black robe and face mask, standing next to a person who was on his knees in the dirt wearing multi-cam fatigues. A black pillowcase was over his head, and his hands were behind his back. I covered my mouth and gasped. "That's horrible."

The video played, and the pillowcase was ripped off the man's head. A tangle of long black hair fell around his shoulders, which the terrorist grabbed to pull him upright. Warren's eyes locked on mine, pleading in horror through the camera. Then a machete swung and blood splattered across the television screen.

I screamed.

"Sloan, wake up!" Nathan was shaking my arm.

When I opened my eyes, we were still on the couch, the news was still on, and a gray-haired man was showing a cold front moving into Western North Carolina. I rubbed my eyes and tried to catch my breath. "What happened?"

He helped me sit up. "You dozed off and then started screaming."

"There was a Marine on television," I said, pointing at the screen.

He nodded. "Yeah. Alexander Diaz died in Israel, but we saw that fifteen minutes ago."

I gripped my head. "Geez, I'm losing it."

"No, you're not. You're just exhausted. Go to bed," he said, pointing up the stairs.

Just then, a blast of thunder rattled the house. We both jumped.

Nathan got up and went to the back door. He pulled it open and a rush of wind blew inside, carrying a flurry of dead leaves into the room. My heart constricted—like it had the night the figure attacked me in my bed. I hugged my knees to my chest. "Nathan, close the door."

He looked over his shoulder at me. "What?"

Before I could answer, he was knocked backward off his feet. I leapt off the couch, stepping over him to shut the back door. I tumbled the deadbolt, then sank to the floor against it.

Nathan's eyes were double their normal size. "What the hell was that?"

I shook my head and crawled over beside him. "I don't know, but I've only ever felt like that in Texas and in my nightmares. Pinch me."

"Huh?"

I pinched his arm.

He yelped. "What was that for?"

"I guess I'm not asleep," I said.

He got up, jerking his sidearm from its holster. "How does you pinching me prove you're not asleep?" He walked over to the door and pulled back the curtains over the window. "There's movement out there. Lock the door behind me."

I scrambled to my feet and grabbed his arm. "Don't. Please don't leave me."

His mouth opened like he was about to argue, but he didn't. "I won't." He walked to the table and picked up his radio. "Dispatch this is 2201, off duty."

The radio beeped and a woman's voice came over the line. "Officer 2201, this is dispatch. Go ahead."

"Dispatch this is 2201. Current location is 7506 Bradley Avenue. Requests you dispatch the zone two unit to this area for patrol. Be on the lookout for suspicious activity or persons at current location. Unable to investigate at this time."

"Officer 2201, this is dispatch. 10-4. I'll have the zone two officer en route to your position."

He hooked the radio on his belt, then walked to the kitchen. I followed close on his heels as he peeked out the blinds behind the dinette. "No unusual cars on the street."

I was right over his shoulder. "Nathan, forget the cars. There's no wind, or storm!"

He didn't respond.

Pressing my eyes closed, I sent my evil radar out into the night, sincerely hoping to detect an armed robber or an axe murderer. They would be easier to deal with than what I feared was out there. There was no one. No humans, anyway.

Through clenched teeth, I let out a squeal. "Nathan, it's her. It's Kasyade. She's going to kill me."

He turned around and leveled his gaze at me. "You don't know that."

"Yes I do."

He shook his head. "It could have been a transformer blowing or kids setting off fireworks."

I pointed at his face. "Nathan, you know better."

He pushed my hand down. "Maybe it was Thor, God of Thunder."

I bit down on the insides of my lips to keep from laughing. Nothing about the situation warranted jokes, no matter how funny they were.

He winked at me. "Go to bed. I'll stand guard."

I smirked. "Right. Let me get right to that." I paced around the kitchen.

"Sloan, you'll trigger a panic attack if you don't calm down," he warned.

I was wringing my hands. "I'm trying."

He tucked his gun back into its holster and grabbed my hand. "Sit," he instructed, pulling a chair out at the dinette table for me. "Talk about something else."

"Like what?" I sat on my hands to keep from fidgeting.

"What will you name the baby?" he asked, opening a cabinet and retrieving a water glass.

I blinked with surprise. "I haven't really thought about it."

He filled the glass at the sink. "Don't all girls keep lists of what they want to name their babies? Or was that just Shannon?"

That time, I laughed. "It's not just Shannon, but it's never been me."

He handed me the glass and sat next to me. "Never?"

I shook my head. "No. I guess I always assumed kids wouldn't be in the cards."

His head snapped back with surprise. "That's crazy. Why would you think that?"

I shrugged and pulled the water close. "I've never been in a relationship long enough to imagine it going anywhere. I've always kind of been alone."

"Bullshit," he said, sitting back in his chair.

I sipped the water. "True story. The longest relationship I've ever been in was a few months, and it was long distance so it doesn't count."

"But everybody loves you, so why?" he asked.

A dog barked outside, and my eyes flashed back to the window.

Nathan snapped his fingers in front of my nose. "Focus on me. Why are you romantically defective?"

I took a deep, calming breath and thought for a second. "Adrianne once accused me of taking things too fast, not slowing down enough to get to know someone before deciding it won't work." I leaned on my elbow. "But it's the exact opposite. Immediately, I know people too well."

His brow lifted. "So that's why you jumped in so fast with Warren. He was mysterious."

I smiled. "The tall, dark, and smoking hot thing didn't hurt either."

He rolled his eyes. "Yeah, that too."

I drummed my nails on the sides of the glass. "It's different with him. I never worry that he's attracted to me because of my magnetic qualities." I added some finger flair to the last part of that statement for dramatic effect. "What most people feel for me isn't real."

He leaned toward me, cutting his eyes. "You still believe after everything we've been through that I care about you because of"—he waved his hand toward me—"whatever it is you are?"

"Nathan, Kasyade told me—"

"I don't care what she told you!" His voice was a little louder than he obviously intended. He dialed his decibels back down. "I'm not here because I'm some weak-willed mortal who can't resist the charms of the county publicist."

Whoa.

"Nathan, I didn't mean it like—"

He cut me off again, this time standing up so fast his chair legs squeaked across the tile floor. "How else could you mean that?" It was his turn to pace the kitchen. "Is that really the whole reason you and I aren't—"

The doorbell rang.

He muttered a few profanities before stomping across the room to the foyer.

How the hell we'd gone from a demon trying to blow my house down to the subatomic foundation of our relationship was beyond me. At least he kept my panic at bay. I was still scratching my head when a uniformed sheriff's deputy walked into my living room.

"Russ, this is Sloan. Sloan, Russ Hughes," Nathan said, not looking directly at me.

I waved to the deputy.

"Nate, I didn't see anything out of the ordinary, and we circled the area a few times," he said.

Nathan folded his arms over his chest. "Did anyone else report hearing some kind of explosion? Or have you gotten any calls about power outages from a transformer in the area?"

Russ shook his head. "Not that I'm aware of."

"How about a surveillance car? Usually a truck parked over on Hyde Lane. Did you see it?"

"I didn't see one," Russ answered. "Do you have a tail?"

"Maybe." Nathan offered him his hand, and Russ shook it. "Listen, thanks for coming out and checking."

"Not a problem. I'll be around tonight. I'll swing back by a few times and keep my eyes open."

"Thank you," Nathan said.

"Hey, did you hear the news about Gollum?" Russ asked.

Nathan looked at me, then back at Russ. "No. What news?"

"She busted out of the psych ward. They just called it in that she's gone missing," he said.

Nathan groaned. "I'd better keep my scanner on. Call me if you hear anything."

"10-4." Russ gave a slight nod in my direction. "Good evening, ma'am."

"Thanks, Russ," I said.

When he left, I looked at Nathan. "Who's Gollum?"

He swirled his finger around his ear. "Red-headed crazy chick."

I perked with alarm. "The demon lady who's looking for me?"

"That's the one."

I pointed to the door. "Perhaps that's what all the noise and wind was about."

Nathan shrugged but didn't look convinced. "Whatever it was, it's over now." He paused, but his mouth was still open and ready to speak. After a moment, he looked in my direction but not exactly at me. "I'm sorry for raising my voice."

"It's OK."

He finally made eye-contact. "No, it's not. Please forgive me."

"Forgiven."

He glanced toward the stairs. "You're exhausted. You may not sleep, but you still need to rest."

I walked toward the stairs but stopped in front of him. "I'm sorry too."

He cast his gaze at the ground, bobbing his head in acknowledgement. "It's over. Let's not bring it back up."

I nodded, but we both knew whatever *it* was, it certainly wasn't over. It was far, far from it.

9.

THE LAST TIME I'd had a social night out was the night before Warren's reactivation with the Marine Corps. He had almost proposed to me then, but he didn't because of Nathan McNamara.

Oh the irony, I thought as I stood in front of a full-length mirror in the ladies' room of The Grove Park Inn. I was polished and primped for a date at the most romantic hotel in all of Asheville...with the wrong man in my life.

"This is not a date," I corrected myself out loud. "This is *definitely* not a date."

A woman stepped out of a stall I didn't realize was occupied behind me. She had a teasing smile.

I shook my head. "It's really not."

The lady chuckled.

After tucking a loose curl back into the bird's nest Adrianne had sculpted on my head, I walked out of the bathroom, but Nathan wasn't where I'd left him by the piano. I walked around the Great Hall fireplace and all around the crowded bar, but I couldn't find him anywhere. I thought about calling him on the phone, but I remembered my cell was still plugged up at home on my nightstand.

I heard a familiar whistle somewhere in the distance behind me and turned to see him on the far side of the room, sitting in the back of a big red Santa sleigh.

I held out my arms as I walked over. "What are you doing?"

He stood, holding two full wine glasses. "All the other seats were taken," he said, stepping out of the sleigh. "What were you doing in there? You were gone for half an hour."

I rolled my eyes. "I was not."

He handed me a glass.

I frowned. "Umm?"

He smiled. "It's grape juice. It's *sparkling*," he added with a lisp.

I laughed and accepted it. "Thank you."

Halfway through the lobby, I heard my name over the commotion. It was a woman's voice. I turned and looked, as did Nathan. Finally, I spotted a waving arm in the crowd. "Sloan!" she called again.

My brain scrambled to place the older woman's familiar face.

A half a second later, three and a half feet of bounding energy burst through the crowd of legs in the room. Blond haired, blue and green eyed, Kayleigh Neeland sprinted toward me, her red patent Mary Janes click-clacking against the marble as she ran.

I knelt down in time to catch her in my arms. "Kayleigh!"

"Miss Sloan!" she cheered, throwing her tiny arms around my neck.

"How are you, sweet girl?" I asked.

She pulled back, pushing her curls out of her face. "We came to see the gingerbread houses. The one with the Barbie in the castle is my favorite."

"Really?" I asked, tugging on the hem of her sparkly red and green Christmas dress. "You're so pretty. Is this new?"

"Uh huh," she said, nodding.

Over our heads, Nathan greeted Kayleigh's grandparents.

Kayleigh pointed back behind her. "Did you see Santa?"

I shook my head. "No. I didn't know Santa was here. Did you sit on his lap and tell him what you want for Christmas?"

"Uh huh. I want the new Mary Ashley doll. The one that talks and goes to school. Not the Mary Ashley doll that cries and wears diapers," she said.

I laughed and bobbed my head like I knew what she was talking about. "How's kindergarten?"

She shrugged. "It's OK." Her head tilted to the side. "Miss Sloan, when's your baby coming?"

I blinked. "H…how did you know about that?"

She pushed her hair back again. "I saw your baby tummy."

Nathan nudged my leg with the toe of his dress shoe. "Told you."

I swatted his leg away, then turned back to her. "Well, my baby is coming this summer. Isn't that exciting?"

She bit her lower lip, swaying from side to side. "She's going to be pretty, just like you."

"Thank you," I said. "Oh, look what I still have." I held out the collar of my coat so she could see the angel pin she'd given me.

She touched it with her tiny finger.

"I wear it every day," I said.

"Nana says if I'm good we can have hot chocolate before we leave," she said.

I pinched her nose. "I'm sure it will be delicious."

She looked up at Nathan. "You're the police man."

He dropped to a knee beside me. "You remember me?"

"Uh huh." She rocked back and forth on her heels. "You found me that one bad day."

He sucked in a deep breath and smiled. "Yes, I did." He playfully touched the tip of her nose. "It was a bad day, but it was also one of the very best days."

She laughed. "Yeah."

I looked up at her grandmother. "It's so good to see you. How long are you in town?"

"Just tonight," she said. "We had a custody hearing yesterday, so we decided to make a weekend out of it. Few places are more beautiful than Asheville at Christmas."

"That's the truth," I agreed. "How did the hearing go?"

Kayleigh's grandfather nodded. "It went well. The judge granted us full custody."

"It was a bittersweet victory," Nana said. "But you can only imagine how happy we are."

I tucked a strand of Kayleigh's hair behind her ear. "Yes, I can." I opened my arms. "Can I have another hug?"

She lunged into me, squeezing my neck again.

"I hope you have a very Merry Christmas, Kayleigh," I said, kissing her on the side of the head.

"Merry Christmas, Miss Sloan."

Nathan gave Kayleigh a high-five, then helped me to my feet. I pulled one of my business cards out of my purse and handed it to her grandmother. "The next time you're in town, let me know so we can plan to meet. This has made my night."

The woman nodded. "I will."

"Merry Christmas," I said to them.

"Merry Christmas," they echoed back.

Nathan's hand at the small of my back turned me toward the hallway. I closed my eyes and let out a melodic sigh. "I love that kid so much."

He smiled when I looked at him. "I know you do. She's cute." He pointed toward the banquet room. "You ready to go in?"

I took a deep breath. "Yeah. Let's do this."

The annual Christmas party was the only social event my office ever had, and the county went all out for it. The room glistened with Christmas trees and twinkle lights, but the centerpiece of the decor was the view. Beyond the panoramic glass walls, the sun dipped behind mountains speckled with snow-covered pines, splashing the dark blue sky with violet and fuchsia swirls. I'm pretty sure if Heaven exists, then Asheville at Christmastime was modeled after it. It was so stunning that I almost didn't notice how every eye turned toward me and Nathan as we crossed the room.

"Why are people staring at us?" Nathan whispered behind me.

I shrugged.

Sheriff Davis, Nathan's boss, sauntered over in a black suit with a bright red Santa Claus tie. "McNamara!" He extended his hand as he approached. "Glad to see I'm not the only one representing our office tonight. You clean up pretty well."

He was right. Nathan's black pants and charcoal button up couldn't have fit any better if they were melted onto his body. He had a fresh shave and a haircut. And he smelled even better than he looked.

Nathan caught my eye and winked. "Thank you, sir, but no one is looking at me tonight."

This is not a date. This is not a date. This is not a date.

The sheriff turned toward me. "Sloan Jordan, you look like a million bucks." He gave me a side hug, jostling my shoulders with his large hand. "How 'ya feelin' these days, young lady?"

I nodded. "Pretty well, thank you. How's Mrs. Davis?"

He looked around the room. "She's good. Around here somewhere."

"If I don't have the chance, please wish her a Merry Christmas for me."

"Will do." He looked at Nathan. "You heard any more from the feds?"

Nathan crossed his arms over his chest. "No, sir. Though I believe they're still following Sloan."

I held my hands up. "Gentlemen, this is a party. Can we please not talk about things that might make me cry?"

Sheriff Davis laughed with a hearty chuckle. "I remember those tearful days when Rosie found out she was carrying our first. One time I told her we were out of egg salad; you'd think I told her our dog was dead."

I laughed, but I turned my wide eyes toward Nathan.

He shrugged.

The sheriff grabbed Nathan's shoulder and shook it. "On that note, I need to find my wife. You two have a fun night. You've earned it." He paused as he turned away. "Oh! And congratulations," he said with a wink.

As he walked away, I put my hands on my hips. "He knows I'm pregnant. Who did you tell?"

Nathan held up his hands. "I didn't say a word. Who did *you* tell?"

"Just my boss but only yesterday."

He helped me out of my coat. "Well, this is a pretty small town. News travels fast." He motioned toward an empty table near the exit. "Want to sit where we can make a quick getaway?"

Smiling, I nodded my head. "Please."

The room filled up over the next few minutes. I often forgot how many people worked for the county. Half of them I didn't recognize because they either worked in a completely different division or they were so dressed up I couldn't place them. Mary was one of those. I had to do a double-take when she appeared at our table dressed in a red gown that sparkled like a disco ball. She was even wearing makeup. "Hello, Mary. Don't you look beautiful!" I said, standing up to hug her.

"Thank you, dear. So do you!" When she stepped away from our embrace, she noticed Nathan. "Detective McNamara, I wasn't expecting you here tonight!"

He squeezed her hand. "I'm here against my will, I assure you."

I laughed. "Don't let him fool you. He's here for the open bar."

He grinned at her. "That too."

Mary blushed. He had that effect on people. "You two kids have a lovely evening. I'm going to go join my date."

I blinked with surprise. "Your date?"

She looked like she might squeal with excitement. "You're not the only one around here with a juicy love life these days."

My eyes widened. "Well, don't hold out on me! Who is it?"

"Calvin Jarvis."

The name sounded familiar. My brow crumpled.

Nathan laughed. "We were sworn in together."

I grabbed her hands. "Oh, I'm so happy for you!" Mary had called him a fox the first time we'd seen him—the day I met Nathan.

She was so excited, I was worried she might pass out. Glancing from me to Nathan and back again, she squeezed my fingers. "I guess both our wishes came true."

It wasn't till she was gone that I realized what she meant. I plopped down in my chair. "Everyone's staring at us because they all think we're having this baby together."

He popped the collar on his shirt. "What can I say? I'm a stud."

I laughed and swatted him with my cloth napkin.

* * *

After a delicious meal, dessert, and coffee—decaf, Nathan leaned into me. "You've yawned nine times in the past four minutes. You ready to head home?"

Home.

"Yes."

My eyes were watery with exhaustion while we waited for the valet to bring around his SUV. It was freezing outside and flurrying again, and all I wanted was to curl up in my warm bed. I was dozing in and out by the time we reached the bottom of the mountain. Soft Christmas music floated through the speakers.

Thoughts of what the next Christmas would be like danced around in my mind. I'd be a mother by then, and Warren would be home, hopefully. We'd have a tree; I'd never bothered to put one up before. And my dad would buy lots of expensive toys that were completely unsuitable for a baby. I smiled and leaned my head against the cold glass window as the car gently shifted around a curve.

"Whoa!" Nathan yelled.

I looked up in time to spot a skeleton shaped figure with stringy red hair standing in the dead center of the road. She was barefoot in a hospital gown. An IV dangled from her withered and scarred arm.

Nathan swerved to miss her, sending the SUV careening off the side of the road. We missed a telephone pole by inches and tore through a cluster of mountain laurel before going off an embankment.

The last thing I saw was the French Broad River in front of us before my face smacked the dashboard.

10.

NATHAN WAS SCREAMING somewhere off in the distance. I was bobbing up and down, floating on a faint stream of consciousness. Something was gurgling. My feet were cold. *I should have worn thicker stockings,* I thought.

When my eyes swirled into focus, Nathan was frantically jerking on my seatbelt. I blinked.

"Sloan!"

I blinked again. "Nathan?"

"Sloan, we've got to get out of here!"

I shook my head from side to side. It hurt like hell. I touched my fingers to a throbbing spot on my forehead, and when I pulled them back, blood dripped down my palm.

Water was everywhere.

Outside my window, water and ice sloshed up and down against the glass. I pressed my hand to it, trying to make sense of what was happening. Nathan's SUV was bobbing in the river. My feet were wet. One of his hat patches pinned to the ceiling above my head said, *All Work. No Pay.*

I chuckled. *It's sad all of Nathan's patches are going to drown in the river…*

"Sloan!"

I'm going to drown in the river.

Realization hit me like a freight train. Confusion gave way to panic. My fingers fought with Nathan's over the seat belt. He grabbed my hands. "Sloan," he said, trying to keep his voice calm. I focused on his gray eyes. "I need you to stay calm so we can get out of this. Unbuckle your seatbelt. I'll break the windshield."

I nodded my understanding.

Cold was spreading from my wet feet, up my legs, and deep into my bones. I shuddered as I fought with the seatbelt latch. It must have been damaged in the crash, but after a moment, I worked it free. Nathan turned around on his seat and yanked the headrest out of the seat. The water was sneaking up the glass on both sides of us, and we were moving downstream in the current.

I tried the button to roll down my window, but the electric opener was no longer functional. Perfect snowflakes were freezing on the windshield.

"Can you swim?"

My teeth chattered. "Yes."

"Take off your coat and your shoes. We'll have to get to the bank as quickly as possible before we freeze to death," he said.

The water was over two inches up my window. My hands were shaking but only partly from the cold. "We can't die in here!"

"Nobody is dying today," he said. "Take off your shoes."

I slipped off my heels and struggled out of my thick wool coat. I detached the silver angel pin and shoved it down into my bra.

Nathan slammed the posts of the headrest against the windshield. The glass cracked, but it didn't shatter. "It would be easier to bust out the side, but I'm afraid the car will sink before we can both get out. Problem is, the windshield's bulletproof," he said. "This could take a minute."

The water was at least four inches over the window, and it was up to my calves in the floorboard. Looking down at the water swirling around my feet, I noticed my hands—seemingly of their own accord —shielding my stomach. *My baby*. That was all the motivation I needed. I got up on my knees and pounded the windshield with the balls of my fist.

"Sloan, stop! You'll wear yourself out!"

"I'm not going to drown in your stupid car!" I screamed.

With all my desperation focused on getting out of the windshield, I slammed my fist into the glass again. This time, it splintered beneath my hands, and ice cold water gushed in. I sucked half of it down my lungs before realizing the barrier between me and the oxygen above was gone. My feet pushed against the sinking passenger's seat and kicked till my face pierced the surface.

I thrashed around in the freezing current until I saw Nathan pop up a few feet away. He gasped and began thrashing toward the river bank. The ice felt like needles in my skin as I forced my legs to kick for the shore after him. A small crowd of people had gathered on the snowy bank. Everyone was screaming. Flashlights were blinding me as they flailed in the dark sky.

I kicked and kicked, but I couldn't feel anything below the water anymore. As my arms reached for the riverbank, the burning sensation slowly faded. *A few more feet...*

The pain in my chest exploded as I went under the surface again. The beams of light from the shore grew more and more distant. I thought I was swimming, but there was enough light to see my arms floating motionless up toward the surface of the water. I could no longer close my eyelids.

Then a hand wrapped around my wrist, and a warm, familiar buzz of energy flowed into me. Only one other person had that touch. His energy ignited the life inside me. Warren's face was inches from mine under the water. *I'm dreaming again...*

We broke through into the icy night air.

For a split second, I saw his face.

Then the world went black.

* * *

"Get blankets!"

"Bring her here!"

"Get those wet clothes off!"

The world faded in and out for a few moments. Someone ripped off my dress, and another pair of hands wrapped a fleece blanket around my shoulders. I opened my eyes to look for Warren, but I couldn't find him. I was inside a minivan. Nathan was there, and I could hear his teeth chattering beside me.

I couldn't hold my head up on my own. I thought of my baby and slipped into oblivion once more.

Halogen lights blinded my eyes when I opened them again. The wheels of the bed underneath me squeaked as I rolled down the familiar hallway. Between Adrianne's accident, my near-death trauma with Billy Stewart, and Mom's death, the Mission Hospital emergency room was becoming like a second home.

A nurse with long dark hair bent over me when we stopped moving. Her name tag said, *Rena*. My jaw wouldn't stop trembling. "Wh... wh...where's N...N...Nath...than?"

Rena put her hand on my shoulder. "He came in right before you did. He's fine. Can you tell me your name and what happened?"

"M...my n...ame is S...S...Sloan J...Jor...Jordan. I w...was in a ca...car cr...rash. A w...woman w...was s...standing in th...the r... road," I replied.

She nodded. "Ms. Jordan, we've notified your father. He should be here soon. We need to check out your head, but your body temperature is coming back up."

"I'm pr...pr...egnant," I said.

Her eyes widened. "I'll let your doctor know."

"Is m...my b...boyfriend, here? W...W...Warren P...Parish?" I asked.

She looked around the room. "Just you and Detective McNamara were brought in."

When they wheeled me behind a curtain across from the nurses' station, they covered me from head to toe with warm blankets. I wiggled my legs and realized I wasn't wearing any pants. At least I'd worn pretty panties with my dress.

"Sloan, is th...th...at you?" I heard Nathan ask on the other side of the curtain divider. His voice was as shaky as my own.

"Y...yeah. Are y...you ok...k?" I asked.

"C...cold," he answered. "You?"

"A...l...live," I chattered.

Rena came back into my cubicle. She pulled the curtain back between me and Nathan enough so we could see each other. She winked at me. When I looked over, Nathan's face was blotchy and red. He was in a similar blanket cocoon.

Two deputies from the Sheriff's office walked in and went to talk to Nathan. My nurse returned and hooked me up to a warm IV bag. She paused after sticking the needle in my arm and cocked her head to the side.

My eyes widened at the look on her face. "Wh...what is it?"

Her brow scrunched together. "The gash on your forehead... It's closed now."

Because I was so cold, I hadn't felt it. "I'm a f...fast healer."

"That's impossible," she said.

I gave a sheepish shrug.

A doctor, a man I hadn't seen on any of my previous visits, walked in behind her. She motioned for him to come over. "Dr. Lambert, five minutes ago this mark on her forehead was a gaping wound. I've never seen anything like this before."

He pulled at the skin on my forehead with his thumbs. "Are you sure?" he asked.

"Positive," she replied.

He rubbed his chin. "That's strange." He looked at me expecting an answer.

"M...maybe I d...didn't hit my h...head as hard as w...we thought."

He scribbled something on my chart. "I'm still ordering a CT scan to make sure the bump on your head is OK. I've also paged the obstetrician on call to check on the baby."

Just then, I saw my dad walk up to the nurses' station behind them. "D...dad!"

He turned, and panic flashed across his face when he saw me. "Sloan, thank God you're OK." He walked over and kissed my forehead. "You're freezing."

"Your daughter is lucky," the doctor said. "The water temperature could have killed her."

"I know." Dad leaned down toward me. "How are you feeling?"

"C...cold," I answered.

He blew out a long sigh. "Are you hurt?"

I shook my head. "I d...don't think so. I'm gon...na need some dry c...clothes."

He squeezed my shoulder. "I'll take care of it once they confirm you're stable."

I nodded. "H...have you s...seen W...warren?"

His head snapped back with surprise. "Warren?"

"He p...pulled m...me out of the w...water," I stammered.

Dad looked around the room confused. "Honey, Warren isn't here."

I'm officially crazy.

* * *

Just as I suspected, the CT scan came back clear. If I had sustained any injuries to my skull, they would have healed before I reached the hospital. My teeth had stopped chattering, and I could once again feel my arms and legs.

Nathan was sitting in a chair, dressed in a dry outfit, and he stood when I was wheeled back into my curtained cubical. When they parked my bed, without a word he closed the space between us and bent over me. I wrapped my arms around him and squeezed the back of his neck. I cried into his shoulder.

"Shh…" he said. "It's over. You're safe." He eased down onto the bed beside me, and he brushed the tears off my cheeks with his thumb. His eyes were glassy. "I looked back and saw you go under." With each word, he struggled to not fall apart.

He pressed a long kiss to my forehead.

My father walked in behind him, followed by another doctor in a white coat. Dad motioned toward me. "Dr. Rhodes, this is my daughter, Sloan."

Nathan stepped back, drying his eyes on the back of his sleeve as he turned away.

The woman held up a fetal doppler. "Sloan, are you ready to check the baby's heart rate?"

I sniffed and sat up in the bed. "Absolutely."

Dad laid a black backpack on the chair beside the bed. "I got your clothes, sweetheart."

Nathan took a step back next to my dad.

A few moments later, a muffled *bump, bump, bump, bump, bump* echoed around the room. I covered my mouth with my hands. "I've never heard it before."

She smiled.

Dad walked over and put his hand on my shoulder.

Nathan was beaming in our direction.

"The heart rate's a little slow, but that's normal due to the drop in your body temperature," she explained. "I'll come back and check on you in a little bit."

"Thank you, Doctor."

When she was gone, I looked at Nathan. "Did they find the lunatic who was standing in the middle of the road?"

He shook his head. "No. The Sheriff's office is looking for her, but so far they haven't found anything."

"The FBI guys following us didn't see anything?" I asked.

He lowered his voice. "As far as I know, no one from the FBI was there."

Interesting.

In the cubical to my left, someone erupted into a violent coughing fit. Then a woman cried out in pain.

I pointed toward the bag on the chair Dad had brought from my house. "Hand me my clothes, please."

"You haven't been cleared for release yet," Dad said.

I shook my head. "I don't care. I can help her."

He hesitated. "This isn't a good idea."

"Dad, nothing I ever do is a good idea."

He tried not to, but he cracked a smile.

I held my hands up. "What will they do? Kick me out of the hospital? Hand me my clothes!"

Dad dropped the bag onto my bed and put his hands on his hips.

I unzipped it and pulled out a sweatshirt. It was a black hoodie with S.W.A.T. written across the back in bold white letters. I laughed. "Nathan, look," I said, holding it up for him to see.

He glanced over and chuckled. "That's hilarious."

"What's so funny?" Dad asked.

"It's Nathan's shirt," I said. "It's a long story."

Nathan had given me the shirt to wear the night we saved Kayleigh Neeland, and Warren hated I still had it. Thinking of Kayleigh reminded me that the angel pin she had given me must still be in my bra, wherever it ended up...or maybe it was at the bottom of the river.

I couldn't put the shirt on with the IV still in my arm. "Dad, can you take this thing out?"

He looked around for the nurse. "Sloan, I really don't feel right about this."

I cocked my head to the side. "Are you going to let me jerk this needle out of my arm and bleed all over the emergency room?"

He groaned and stepped over beside my bed. "You're so stubborn."

I winked at him. "I get it from you."

He rolled his eyes and removed the IV.

I slipped the sweatshirt over my head and caught Nathan grinning over at me. "It still looks good on you," he said.

I laughed. "Glad you think so."

Carefully, I wiggled into a pair of black yoga pants underneath my blankets. Almost all the feeling had returned to my extremities, so I was even able to tie on my sneakers without any help. I swung my legs off the bed and looked up at my dad. "Do you see anyone coming?"

He looked around the hall behind him. "Your nurse is two stalls down."

"Can you distract her?"

He frowned but nodded his head.

My legs wobbled a bit when I stood, so I gripped the bed for support.

"Where are you going?" Nathan whispered.

I didn't answer him. Instead, I quietly tiptoed over to the curtain, pulling it back slowly as to not make a sound.

In the cubicle next to me was Virginia Claybrooks, the guard from the jail. I gasped. "Oh, Ms. Claybrooks."

Perspiration was beaded on her forehead, and her cheeks were streaked with tears. A young man was holding her hand. She looked at me, full of fear. "How 'you know my name?"

I touched my fingers to my chest. "I'm Sloan Jordan from the county office. Don't you remember me?"

Her eyes narrowed. "You're the cute blond boy's girlfriend, aren't you?"

I laughed. "Detective McNamara and I are friends. Are you ill?"

She began coughing again. With each convulsion, she winced and more tears spilled out. "They say I got fluid in my lungs. Feels like I'm drowning from the inside out. I'm gonna die here."

I stepped to her bedside and took her hand. "You're not going to die, Ms. Claybrooks."

She moaned, triggering another coughing fit.

Gently, I sat on the edge of her bed and put my hand on her clammy forehead.

"Your hands are ice cold," she said, shivering.

"Well, speaking of drowning, I almost drowned in the river tonight," I said.

Her eyes widened. "What the heck were you doing in the river, child? Don't you know it's winter time?"

I laughed. "If I didn't know it before, I know it now." I put both my hands on either side of her face.

"What are you doin' to me?" she asked.

"Maybe my cold hands will help with that fever," I said, smiling gently. "Hey, that cute blond boy is here. Do you want to see him?"

She shook her head. "Don't nobody need to see me. They say this thing could be contagious. My son, David"—she gestured to the man beside her bed—"he's as stubborn as a bull, and he won't leave."

I laughed. "My dad just said the same thing about me." I glanced at her son. "Hi, David."

He waved. "Hi."

Ms. Claybrooks shuddered again and winced with pain. When she coughed again, it already sounded less congested. My hands warmed against her face as my whole body buzzed with energy.

"I feel all twisted up inside," she cried.

"Shh," I said. "It will be over soon."

"Cuz I'm gonna die," she whimpered.

"Virginia, look at me." Her swollen eyes focused on mine. I shook my head. "You're not going to die. Not today. And certainly not from a cough."

Her face relaxed, and she looked at me with fierce curiosity. "What are you?" she whispered.

I winked at her. "I'm a publicist."

* * *

Before the doctors caught on to the rounds I was making through the emergency room, I was able to heal Ms. Claybrooks from pneumonia, a single mom of three kids from a severe case of strep throat, and two old ladies who were dreadfully sick with the flu.

When the nurse brought my discharge papers, she was frowning. "Make sure you stop by and say hello when you're back in here with a productive cough and a fever in a couple of days."

I smiled and tucked the papers into my bag. "I'm sure I'll be OK. Thanks for taking such good care of us, Rena."

She pointed at me. "I don't want to see you again, Ms. Jordan." She turned toward Nathan who was standing next to my bed. "Or you, Detective."

"Yes, ma'am," Nathan said.

My dad looked down at me. "Are you ready to go?"

I nodded and he helped me to my feet. "Yeah. Can you drop us off at my house since neither of us have a car?"

"Of course. You about gave me a heart attack. I may never let you out of my sight again." He kept his hand on my back. "I'm so thankful you're both alive."

Nathan took my backpack and slung it over his shoulder. "We've all got Sloan to thank for that. She saved us by shattering the windshield." He looked over at me as we walked out to the lobby. "How did you do it?"

I thought about the way Kasyade had once thrown a car down a San Antonio street and how Samael was able to lock and unlock doors without touching them. "I think it must have been part of my power, but I have no idea how I did it."

"That's near death experience number three in the time I've known you, Sloan," Nathan said as he held the door open to the parking lot. It was still snowing, but it was wet and clumpy.

"I think I came a lot closer to death than you did this time," I said.

Dad looked at both of us. "It's not a competition, kids!"

I put my hood up over my head. "I never would have made it to the shore if…" I stopped before sounding completely nuts again.

"If what?" Nathan asked.

"I could have sworn Warren pulled me out of the water," I said, bringing our little group to a halt.

Nathan's brow crumpled. "Impossible. You had to be hallucinating."

"Nathan, I saw him. I felt him when he grabbed me. I didn't hallucinate that feeling."

"It's impossible," he said and started walking again.

I did a double-step to catch up with him. "Did you see who pulled me out?"

Nathan was quiet till we got to the car and Dad unlocked the doors. "I was in and out of it, and I remember seeing a man carrying you up the riverbank, but it wasn't Warren. It couldn't have been."

We all got into the car, and Dad started the engine. "It isn't uncommon to imagine things when you come so close to death, Sloan. I agree with Nathan."

I leaned my head back against the seat. "I know you're right, but I also know what I saw."

Dad sighed. "Well, I'm grateful to whoever pulled you out of the river."

"Me too," Nathan agreed.

We had an uneventful drive home, but when we turned on to my street, a black truck was parked in front of my house. Nathan pointed over my seat. "That's the truck that's been following you."

I strained my eyes in the dark. "That doesn't look like the FBI."

"No, it doesn't," Nathan agreed.

My father pulled to a stop behind the truck.

"Stay in the car," Nathan said as he wrenched his door open.

I smirked and pulled on my door handle. "You can't tell me to stay in the car at my own house."

Dad tossed his hands up. "What good is it to have the boy to protect you if you never listen to him?"

The street was dark, but in the moonlight, I saw a man standing on the front steps of my house. I couldn't sense his soul. I grabbed onto Nathan's hand and ducked behind him. "Not human," I whispered.

When we got closer, the man turned toward us, and light from the moon flashed across his face.

It was him.

11.

"WARREN?" NATHAN ASKED, cautiously moving forward.

I hesitantly side-stepped around him, but Nathan blocked me with his arm.

The man didn't move, making us come all the way to him at the foot of the stairs where he towered over us. I doubted it would be much different if we were on equal footing. Beneath him, I felt very small and was keenly aware Nathan had lost his sidearm in the river. We were completely unprotected.

The man was dressed in dark clothes and had short black hair. It wasn't Warren, but it could have been his clone. I gasped and covered my mouth with my hand. "Oh my god."

"Who are you?" Nathan demanded.

"My name is—"

"Azrael," I said, pushing Nathan's arm away from me and taking a step forward. "Your name is Azrael."

The man's black eyes widened with surprise. "Yes. My name is Azrael. How did you know?"

"Lucky guess," I said.

Nathan looked at me. "Who?"

"He's Warren's father." I studied Azrael. "It was you who saved me tonight. You were following me."

He nodded slowly.

"You've been following her?" Nathan asked, anger rising in his voice.

Azrael stepped down one step. "And where would she be if I hadn't been?" His voice was dark and dangerous, just like his son's.

"Are you here to kill me?" I asked, summoning courage I didn't know I had.

"If I were here to kill you, I would have let you drown," he answered. "You're in danger and, as I am Warren's father, I came to protect you...and your unborn daughter."

"How do you know about the baby? And what makes you so sure it's a girl?" Nathan asked.

He smiled, but it was more creepy than comforting. "Your child is well known in my world, Sloan."

My neighbor's porch light flickered on. My eyes darted down the street. "Can we go inside before someone calls the police?" I asked.

"I am the police," Nathan reminded me. "And no, we can't go inside." He stepped protectively in front of me again and looked up at the angel on my porch steps. "If you're here to protect her, then why all the secrecy? Who the hell do you think you are?"

Azrael took a step toward Nathan. "My name is Azrael, the Archangel of Death."

I swallowed and cowered behind Nathan's back.

Nathan smirked. "Sure you are."

I pressed my lips together and shrank back even more. I tugged on his arm and lowered my voice. "I don't think it's a good idea to get mouthy with him, Nate."

Azrael's face was inscrutable. "You don't have to believe me. It doesn't make it any less true. I am also her child's grandfather."

Nathan cast me a skeptical glare.

"Who, may I ask, are you?" Azrael said.

Nathan folded his arms over his chest. "I'm Detective Nathan McNamara. Sloan and I are close friends, and I promised the baby's father I would look out for her while he's gone."

"You know my son?" Azrael asked.

"How do we even know he's really your son?"

"Look at him," I said. "They couldn't look any more alike if you put Warren through a Xerox."

Nathan turned toward me and put his hands on his hips. "People think my dad looks like Paul Newman, but it doesn't mean they're related!"

"Your dad *does* look like Paul Newman!"

Nathan's head dropped to the side. "Focus please."

"Sorry."

"Even if he is Warren's dad, who's to say he's not a psychopath like your sadistic mother?" he asked.

I put my hands on his forearms and cut my eyes up at him. "Nathan, this is one of those leap of faith moments you'll have to take with me. I believe him, and I really want to hear what he has to say."

He ran a hand down his face in frustration. "You're impossible."

"I know."

I turned back in the direction of the car and waved for my dad to come, then Azrael stepped aside as I walked up the steps past him. When I reached the front door, I realized my keys were sitting at the bottom of the French Broad River. I patted my empty pockets. Azrael must have understood because he lifted his hand toward the door, and I heard the deadbolt slide open. My mouth fell open a little as I stared up at him.

He looked like he wanted to smile, but he didn't.

It was unnerving how much he looked like Warren. The jawline, the cheekbones, the tanned skin stretched smooth and taut over his face…it was all the same. What wasn't the same was the cavernous scar running from the inside of his eyebrow, across the bridge of his nose, and down the opposite cheek. I wondered what the other guy must have looked like.

Azrael followed me into the house with Nathan and my father quick on his heels. I flipped the light switch.

My father shrugged out of his wool coat. "Can someone please explain to me what is going on?"

I touched his elbow. "Dad, this is Azrael. He's Warren's father."

Dad blinked with bewilderment. "His father?"

"Angels don't age," I explained. "Azrael, this is my dad, Dr. Robert Jordan."

Dad extended his hand, but Azrael just looked down at it until my father awkwardly pulled it away. "Well, it's nice to meet you, I think, Azrael," Dad said, stumbling over each word.

"Come in and have a seat," I said, motioning toward the living room. "Make yourself comfortable."

Nathan and my father cornered me in the foyer.

"I don't like this, Sloan," Nathan said.

I rolled my eyes. "Surprise, surprise."

Dad pointed at him. "I agree with Nathan."

I looked at both of them and motioned toward the door. "Then you can both go home. You don't live here."

In unison they scowled at me.

I pushed through the middle of them, but Nathan's hand to my chest stopped me. He lowered his face to my ear. "You don't need to talk in here. I told you, the FBI's probably listening."

"It's OK," Azrael called out from across the room. "I swept the house for bugs before you got home."

We all turned toward him.

"How did he hear that?" Nathan asked quietly.

"I hear lots of things," Azrael replied without looking over.

He was settled in the corner of the loveseat, his black boot resting over his knee and his arm stretched across the seat back. He even occupied the sofa like Warren.

Cautiously, I walked over and sat in the middle of the couch across from him.

His dark eyes were taking a close inventory of me. "How did you know who I was?"

"Well, for starters, you look exactly like Warren," I said. "I thought you were him earlier tonight."

"How did you know my name?" he asked.

My knees were bouncing nervously. "Warren told me a story of when he was in Iraq a few years ago, and an old man freaked out when he saw him. He called Warren by your name, and it left such an impression on him that Warren had the name tattooed on his side. I'm assuming now, by looking at you, the old man had once seen you in person."

He nodded. "It's possible. I've spent time in Iraq. I think I was memorable for the few people I met there."

I didn't doubt him.

"You're in the military?" Nathan asked as he came across the room. He sat on my left side, and my father sat to my right.

Azrael shook his head. "Not exactly, but I have been present for most of the major world wars."

My father looked as though his brain was cramping. "I don't understand. How old are you?"

"Older than the ground you walk on."

That was sobering.

"How did you find me?" I asked.

"I've stayed close to Warren since he was born. Your union with him is quite notorious," he said.

I scrunched up my nose. "So I've been told."

Nathan straightened in his seat like he'd been electrocuted. "It was you!"

We all turned to stare at him.

He pointed at Azrael. "You were in Chicago when Warren was a kid!"

Azrael nodded.

My head swirled around with bewilderment. "How the heck did you put that together?"

"Remember when we found out your demon mom was in Chicago?" he asked.

I covered my gaping mouth with my fingers. "We wondered why Warren never got a migraine when she left." I looked at Azrael. "It's because you were there the whole time."

He nodded again.

I thought of Warren and his childhood foster-sister, Alice, being placed in a home with a child molester and stiffened. My hands clenched into tight fists. "You were there the whole time," I said again, my voice deepening with anger.

"Had I not been there," his tone was a warning, "Warren would not have been able to access his power and use it that first time."

My breath caught in my chest. "You're the reason he's so much better than me."

Azrael didn't respond.

Dad leaned toward me. "What are you two talking about?"

"Kasyade told me my exposure to Warren increased my ability to use my power. Warren's been around Azrael his whole life without knowing it. That's why he's so much better at using his gift than I am," I said.

"I don't think it hurts that Warren's more disciplined and focused than you are," Nathan added.

I pinched his side.

Azrael's foot dropped to the ground with a heavy thud. "You've met your mother, then?"

I smirked. "Oh yeah. We've met. She tried to kill me a few weeks ago."

Azrael's brow scrunched together. "I doubt that."

Nathan and I exchanged a puzzled glance. "Azrael, she tried to kill me." I pointed at Nathan. "And she succeeded at killing him."

"Him, I can believe she would kill. Not you. That would be counterproductive," he said.

"She beat Sloan within an inch of her life," Nathan argued.

Azrael leaned forward, resting his elbows on his knees. "Perhaps, but she would not kill Sloan." He tapped his fingertips together. "Not until my granddaughter is born, anyway."

No one spoke.

"She wants the baby?" my father asked. "Why?"

"Because Sloan is carrying the most powerful angel in all of history."

I couldn't help it. I burst out laughing. Beside me, Nathan was laughing too. Dad joined in as well, but his was more of a wide-eyed, nervous chuckle.

Azrael didn't move.

Or speak.

Or laugh.

Our cackles quickly faded with all the decrescendo of a cartoon balloon losing its helium.

I looked at Azrael. "You're serious?"

He turned his palms up. "Do I look like I make jokes?"

After a second, Nathan stood and wiped his hands on his pants. "That's my cue to get a beer. Dr. Jordan?"

"No, thank you," Dad said.

"Azrael?" Nathan offered.

Azrael shook his head. The way he was staring at me made me contemplate crawling behind the sofa. He pointed at my stomach. "I'm fairly certain this was planned before you were ever born."

Nathan returned from the kitchen, twisted the top off his beer bottle, then tossed it across the room into the fireplace. "I'm going to need some more information." He sat next to me again. "Why don't you start at the beginning?"

"Of time?" Azrael asked.

I snickered.

Nathan glared at him, but Azrael didn't seem to care...or notice.

He looked at me. "What do you know about my world?"

"Nothing good," Nathan muttered.

"Ignore him," I said. "We know Warren and I are Seramorta, part angel and part human."

Azrael nodded. "That's correct. But to understand what that means and why your child is so important, you must first understand what I am."

This was about to get interesting.

He held up seven fingers. "There are seven choirs of angels in Heaven. Messengers and the Ministry choir are the lowest ranked. Then there are Angels of Prophecy, Knowledge, and Protection. The Angels of Life—your mother—make up the second choir. First, are the Angels of Death." He tapped his chest. "That's what I am."

I wondered if I should get a pen and piece of paper. "Samael is an Angel of Death."

Azrael's brow rose. "That is correct. Samael is a guard of the spirit line. He decides who is permitted to cross, who must suffer the second death, and who must be turned over to The Destroyer."

I liked the sound of *none* of that. I gulped and kept my mouth shut, but Nathan didn't.

"The Destroyer?" he asked.

"The truly wicked souls are turned over to The Destroyer at their death." Azrael spread his hands out. "He is aptly named."

I closed my eyes. "My head hurts."

"Shall I continue?" Azrael asked.

I nodded.

"Each choir has an archangel like myself, and above the archangels was The Morning Star," he said.

I raised my hand. "Satan?"

He shrugged. "For simplicity's sake, sure."

"What makes him so special?" Nathan asked, sounding more annoyed than interested.

"The Morning Star was given both the gift of life and the gift of knowledge, making him more powerful than the rest of us."

Nathan seemed satisfied with the answer.

Azrael stretched his arm along the back of the sofa again. "Long after the angels were created, God created humans. Comparatively, humans were weak and inferior, but He favored them above all His other creations, even us. They were given a gift none of the rest of us had."

"What was that?" Dad asked.

"Free will," Azrael answered. "The angels were solely created to carry out the will of the Father. We have no right to choose which orders we will obey and which orders we will not. We rarely questioned it because we knew no different. Then humanity was born, and they were given the option to serve only themselves. And if that wasn't insulting enough, then God placed the angels in service to his new creation."

Nathan drummed his fingers on the arm of the couch. "You sound bitter about it."

Azrael gave a noncommittal shrug. "None of us were happy, but I'm certainly not bitter. The Morning Star, however, was furious. He argued that because the angels had been with God since the beginning, we should have dominion over humans. Not the other way around. When God refused the Morning Star rebelled and incited a war to take the throne. Of course, he and his followers were defeated and cast out of Heaven, exiled here."

I raised my hand again.

Nathan pushed it back down. "Knock it off. We're not in school. Just ask."

Azrael almost looked amused.

"Why would they be cast down here to Earth? Why not send them to Saturn or Pluto where they can't bother anybody?" I asked.

"Heaven is not up or down. Heaven is here"—he motioned around the room—"and Heaven is all throughout the universe, but it's across the spirit line."

I stopped myself before I raised my hand again. "Like a different dimension?"

"Sort of."

Nathan began humming the theme song to *The Twilight Zone*.

I rolled my eyes. "Azrael, please continue."

"The Morning Star vowed to torment man." He pointed at us. "Including all of you."

I held up my hands. "Why man? What did we do?"

"I can answer that one," my father said.

Nathan and I turned our curious eyes toward him.

"Because there's no greater pain than when your children are in danger," he said, looking right at me. "The worst punishment he can inflict on God is to attack his children."

Azrael nodded. "Exactly."

Nathan took a long drink of his beer. "But what does all that have to do with Sloan and this kid?"

"I'm getting there." Azrael leaned forward on his elbows and looked at me. "The Seramorta, like you and Warren, are children born to angels," he said. "There are few Seramorta in the world, and only twice before in the entire history of mankind, have two Seramorta borne children together. The child is born with both gifts and no human spirit at all."

My father's medical brain was trying to process the information, but it was clear from his face that it wasn't doing a good job of it. "So… like biology," he began, "the angel gene is the dominant gene, so that's what Warren and Sloan passed on to their child."

Azrael pointed at him. "Correct. That's a good analogy. It's like a loophole in the laws of the universe. Angels can't copulate with other angels to prevent this very thing from happening, but because Sloan and Warren are also human, they can have a child together."

Nathan looked over at me and pointed between us. "So let's say you and I had a baby. Would it get the angel gene?"

Azrael shook his head. "No. The angelic line would end, and the child would be a normal human. That's typically what happens. The odds of two Seramorta finding each other are minimal."

"You said this has happened twice before. What happened to those children?" Dad asked.

"Their bodies matured as a normal human would, but they never died. They were escorted across the spirit line by the Father himself, and their human bodies were frozen as they were."

My hands instinctively went to my stomach. "They never died?"

Azrael shook his head. "Metatron possesses both the gifts of life and ministry, and Sandolfin possesses the gifts of prophecy and knowledge."

Nathan rubbed his forehead. "So what's so special about Sloan and Warren?"

Azrael rose from his seat and slowly walked back and forth in front of the coffee table. He was wringing his hands as he paced. "Do you remember what I told you about the hierarchy? The Angels of Life and the Angels of Death are the most powerful choirs in Heaven."

I looked at Nathan. "I feel like I'm missing something."

He nodded in agreement.

Azrael stopped walking and knelt down in front of me. He gripped my hands. "Sloan, the birth of the child you carry will be the greatest event in angelic history. She will be known as the Vitamorte, born with the gift of free will as well as the power to control life and death. Your daughter will someday take the empty seat of The Morning Star." He leaned toward me. "The Vitamorte will be more powerful than Satan himself."

12.

MY MOUTH WAS gaping as his words sank in. Then I burst out laughing again, this time in his face. I doubled over, resting my forehead against Azrael's hands that still covered my own. "What the hell?" My voice was an octave higher than normal. I straightened and looked at him. "Do you hear yourself? Oh, geez. Maybe we're both delusional." I quickly sobered as a rational thought occurred to me. I grasped his massive forearms. "Maybe this is another one of my crazy dreams!"

Azrael sank back onto the floor and stared at me with a clear mix of confusion and frustration. "You're not dreaming."

I pushed myself up out of my seat and stepped over him. "Oh, Azrael. I'd better be dreaming, or this world is in trouble."

He got up and followed me to the kitchen. Since I couldn't drink alcohol, I reached into the freezer for a carton of ice cream. As I retrieved a spoon from the drawer, Azrael grabbed me by the arm and spun me around. His eyes were pleading. "Sloan, I know this is a lot to process, but you have to understand the seriousness of what I'm saying."

Dad and Nathan walked in behind him. My father looked like he had been punched in the stomach.

Nathan put his hand on my shoulder. "I don't think he's lying to you."

"Oh, don't tell me you're buying into this now too," I whined.

Nathan stepped closer in front of me as I shoveled a spoonful of mint chocolate chip into my mouth. "Think about all you can do now, Sloan."

Azrael nodded his head. "You possess and can use the power of the Vitamorte."

Everyone was quiet for a moment.

Dad pointed at me. "Then doesn't that make Sloan the most powerful angel in history?"

I sucked a chocolate chip down my windpipe and erupted into a fit of coughing. Nathan took the ice cream carton from me as Azrael thumped his large hand on my back. I leaned against the counter and gasped for air. Dad was ready to perform the Heimlich...or CPR.

When the coughing subsided, reality settled on me like the fallout from a nuclear warhead. My demon mother's final words echoed in my mind. *This is what you were born for.*

Huge tears spilled out onto my cheeks. My hands were trembling so much I dropped my spoon, and it clanged against the kitchen floor. I felt my knees give way underneath me, and I would have fallen if Azrael hadn't caught me.

The buzz of his energy was consuming, and immediately, my nerves settled. "Now you know why I've come," he said quietly in my ear. "And I will not leave you."

My father wedged himself between me and the angel who held me. Protectively, he curled his arm around my shoulders and guided me back to the sofa. Tears were still streaming down my face. As we sat down, I was shaking my head and quietly chanting, "I can't do this."

Nathan and Azrael followed us, and Nathan sat on the coffee table in front of me. He looked up at Azrael. "Why can't you find Kasyade and kill her?"

"Even I do not have the power to destroy another angel." Azrael reclaimed his spot on the loveseat. "And Kasyade is but a cog in a larger wheel. For thousands of years, Kasyade has kept close counsel with two other Angels of Life, Ysha and Phenex. I'm sure they're as much involved with this as she is."

"Involved how?" Dad asked.

Azrael laced his fingers together. "Have you seen the red-haired woman?"

"Yes!" Nathan answered.

Dad was shaking his head, but I straightened in my seat, anxious to hear Azrael's commentary.

Nathan was sitting on the edge of his seat. "Who is she? And what does she have to do with all this?"

Azrael pointed at me. "She's Sloan, or a different version of her, rather."

"Excuse me?" Nathan asked.

"As I said earlier," Azrael began, "I believe this child was planned before Sloan was ever born."

I didn't like where the conversation was headed.

"My son is unique," he said. "Never before has a Seramorta born of an Angel of Death ever existed."

"Warren's the only one?" I asked.

Azrael nodded. "The only one in history."

"So?" Nathan asked.

"When Warren was born, I believe Kasyade, Ysha, and Phenex saw it as their opportunity to create a weapon. The red-haired woman confirms to me they each created a daughter." He was watching me, like he was waiting for a light-bulb in my mind to flicker on. When it did, I suddenly felt nauseated.

"Kasyade said she created me for a purpose. She gave birth to me so I would someday breed this super angel." My voice sounded small and pathetic even to me.

"I believe so," Azrael said. "They planned for one of the daughters they created to have a child with my son."

Nathan scratched his head. "Why? So they can start another war?"

Azrael shook his head. "No. Their war with God is finished, but they're still subject to the law of Heaven. Think of this place as their prison. It's their goal to cut off the warden. The Vitamorte will have the power to destroy the spirit line, forever separating this world from my world, and they'll be free of the restrictions set forth to protect humanity."

"They'll rule the Earth," I added.

Azrael bowed his head slightly in confirmation. "And eventually wipe out the human race altogether."

Nathan bent forward, resting his elbows on his knees and pressing his palms against his eye sockets. He groaned. "I keep waiting for a movie director to walk in and yell 'Cut!' at any moment."

My stomach was churning. "I'm going to be sick." Covering my mouth with my hand, I ran up the stairs to the guest bathroom and barely made it to the toilet before losing the last remnants of my prime rib dinner.

Somehow I managed to flush before melting into a puddle of tears on the cold floor.

My father came in to find me sobbing in the fetal position. He sank down next to me and gathered me into his arms.

Nathan appeared in the doorway. "What can I do for you?" he asked.

I wiped my eyes. "I don't want any of this."

Dad squeezed the back of my neck gently.

Nathan knelt down beside my knees, a teasing smile on his lips. "Sloan, we all know, if I had any control over this situation whatsoever, *this*"—he gestured to my stomach—"would have never happened to begin with."

Through my tears, I chuckled.

"On a more practical level, what else do you need?" he asked.

"A toothbrush," I whimpered.

"That, we can manage." He glanced at his watch. "It's really late. Maybe you should brush your teeth and go on to bed. I think you've had enough excitement for tonight."

"Or a lifetime," Dad added.

"That's the truth," Nathan agreed.

The two of them hoisted me to my feet. Dad's arm around my waist steadied me as they escorted me to my bedroom. Nathan stopped at the door, and Dad helped me across the room. "What about Azrael?" I asked, sitting down on the edge of my bed.

Nathan waved his hand. "I'll grab blankets and a pillow for him or something, or who knows? Maybe he sleeps in a coffin in your backyard. Whatever. Don't worry about him."

Dad bent to look me in the eye. "Angel and demon nonsense aside, are you feeling all right? Your body went through quite an ordeal today."

"Yeah, I'm all right," I lied.

"I'm going to make a bed on the floor by the fire—"

I waved my hand to cut him off. "No, you're not. Go home and sleep in your bed. I'll be fine, Dad. Really. I won't sleep at all knowing you're on the floor."

It was clear from my father's pained expression he was torn. "Well, I'll call and check on you first thing tomorrow." He pressed a long, lingering kiss to my forehead. "I love you, Sloan."

I gripped his arm. "I love you too, Dad."

Dabbing his eyes with the cuff of his sleeve, he straightened and walked toward Nathan. They shook hands. "You'll stay with her?" Dad asked.

"I wouldn't dream of leaving," Nathan replied.

My father looked pleased. "Call me at any time if something happens."

"I will, sir."

When my dad was gone, Nathan pointed to the bathroom. "Do you need help getting ready for bed?"

I shook my head.

"OK. I'll deal with Azrael, then I'll come back and make sure you're squared away," he said.

"Thank you."

A little while later, when I finally climbed under my covers, it was Azrael who knocked on my door instead of Nathan. "May I come in?"

I didn't sit up, but I nodded.

Slowly, he crossed the room to my bedside and sat next to me. "I am truly sorry to be the bearer of such news, Sloan."

I didn't respond.

"But I am here, and I will not let anything harm you or the child," he said.

"The nightmares," I whispered. "They were real, weren't they?"

"In a sense," he said. "The veil between what is seen and what is unseen becomes thin when your mind isn't alert. The dreams were designed to torment you, to break you. If they can break you, they can control you."

"So last night, the thunder...that was you?"

He nodded.

"And the figure I saw in my room?"

"It was very real." He put his hand on my shoulder.

I blinked up at him. "And you got rid of it?"

"While I stand guard, no evil shall befall you. Now rest."

Azrael laid his massive hand on the top of my head, and the room swirled out of view.

* * *

In the morning, the aroma of sausage and fresh coffee roused me from the deepest slumber I had enjoyed since Warren left town, or maybe ever. Hysteria has some positive side effects, I guess, and having a father-in-law who can induce comas doesn't hurt either.

Part of me wanted to curl into my pillow and doze off again, but the other part—the rumbling in my stomach—urged me out from under the heavy warmth of my down comforter.

On the nightstand, the little light on my cell phone was blinking red. I picked up the phone and saw I had a voicemail from my boss, a missed call from Sheriff Davis, and a string of text messages and two missed calls from Adrianne.

Did you make it home OK?

You and Nathan are on the front page of the Citizen Times.

You really need to answer me.

Are you dead??

I dialed her number, and she answered on the first ring. "I was about to drive over to your house and kick your ass! Why haven't you answered the phone?" She was yelling into the receiver.

"I'm sorry," I said. "It was a really, really messed up night."

"I would say so! You almost drowned in the river, and I had to read about it in the newspaper!"

"I'm sorry," I said again. "I was going to call you, but things got weird."

"Weird?"

"Warren's dad was at my house when we got home last night," I said.

She was silent for a second. "Are you kidding me?"

"Nope." I rubbed my hand over my face. "He's been following me around in an attempt to protect me."

"Where is he now?"

"I'm guessing he's cooking breakfast downstairs."

"What the hell?"

"I told you things got weird."

"Does Nathan know?" she asked.

"Oh yes. And my dad," I said. "We all stayed up half the night talking about angels and demons and a cosmic war between Heaven and Earth. It was thrilling."

"Sounds like it," she said.

My stomach growled so loud I could hear it. "I need to go eat. Can I call you later?"

"You'd better," she said.

"I will."

I disconnected the call and trudged across the cool hardwood floor to my bathroom. I brushed my teeth and pulled my unruly hair into a knot on the top of my head before following my nose downstairs.

Azrael, who was dressed for the day in black cargo pants and a fitted white thermal shirt, was hunched over a frying pan which belonged to his son. "Good morning, Sloan," he said, recognizing my presence in the room though his back was turned.

Weird.

I pulled open a cupboard door and retrieved a glass. "Good morning. Did you go to the grocery store?"

"The contents of your refrigerator was quite abysmal." He flipped an egg over onto its yolk and turned to look at me as I ran tap water into my glass. "There's orange juice in the refrigerator."

My heart fluttered. "You bought juice?"

He pointed at the pink sticky note I'd put on the refrigerator door when Nathan and I returned from Raleigh. "The note said 'buy orange juice', so I did."

I dumped the water in the sink, then clapped my hands together with glee as I walked to the fridge. "Yay! Thank you."

"Did you rest well?"

"I slept like the dead." I poured my glass full and raised an eyebrow in his direction. "Which is ironic."

Either he didn't get the joke, or he didn't think I was funny. Instead, as if anticipating my next move, he handed me my bottle of prenatal vitamins. "Are you hungry?"

"Starving. Has Nathan come down?" I asked as I dropped a pill into my mouth.

"Yes," Nathan answered behind me.

When I turned around, he was rubbing sleep from his eyes. He was dressed in similar attire as me, sweatpants and a tank top.

"Good morning," I said.

He yawned. "No, it's not."

I poured him a cup of coffee, snuck a sip of it, then handed it to him. "You look like you need this."

He accepted the cup and carried it over to the table. "How are you feeling this morning?" he asked.

I pulled out a chair next to him and sat down. "I slept better than I have in weeks, so that definitely helps."

"You're not sore from the accident?" he asked.

I shook my head. "You?"

"Not even a little bit."

Azrael put plates piled with sausage, eggs, and biscuits from a can in front of both of us. Nathan looked up in amazement. "Breakfast prepared by the Angel of Death. Do you think his cooking will kill us?"

"I hope not." Smiling, I scooped up a forkful of eggs. "I'm kinda surprised these aren't deviled."

Nathan and I snickered quietly at the table. It felt good to laugh after the severity of the night before. Azrael carried a plate to the seat opposite mine and sat down. He wasn't amused.

Nathan sandwiched a piece of sausage between two halves of his biscuit. "What's on the agenda for today?"

I sighed. "I've got to figure out our living situation. I'm running out of space in this house."

Azrael nodded. "I need to gather my things from the hotel, and at some point, I'd like to find the woman who was in the road last night."

"I'd like that too," I said.

"Something tells me, she'll be back all on her own," Nathan said.

I looked at Azrael. "You said all three of them gave birth to daughters. Who is the third?"

He put his fork down. "When Warren was very young, Phenex arrived in Chicago. She was pregnant with a daughter. It was then I first suspected their plan because angels don't often decide to procreate."

"Why?" Nathan asked.

"Our gift is passed on to the child, creating a bond between us and our offspring that cannot be willingly severed," he explained. "As long as the child lives, the angel is confined to this earth. That's not an easy sacrifice to make for any angel, good or evil."

I was confused. "But I thought you said none of the angels who were cast out can cross the spirit line, regardless?"

He shook his head. "They can't cross back into Heaven; that is true. But they can move through time and space here unhindered as long as they aren't tied here. The bond with the child is a lot like gravity in a sense."

"What happened to Phenex?" I asked.

"I dispatched her from her human form," he said.

My eyes doubled in size. "You killed a pregnant woman?"

"No. I told you, I don't have the ability to destroy an angel." Azrael looked frustrated by that fact.

Truthfully, I was frustrated by it as well. If he couldn't destroy my demon mom, no one could. "That's why Samael couldn't kill Kasyade in Texas," I said. "He said she'll come back."

"That's correct," Azrael said. "It will take a full moon cycle, then Kasyade will be able to take human form again."

"How is that done?" Nathan asked.

Azrael held up two fingers. "Two different ways. We can either be born into a body or a body can be taken. I suspect it will be the latter because it doesn't take as long."

I shuddered. "So that exorcist stuff is real?"

"Quite real, but she won't be able to do it alone. She'll need an angel to help her. Therefore it is imperative we find Ysha and Phenex."

"How?" I asked.

Azrael smiled. "I have my resources."

"We are getting way off topic here. What about Phenex's baby? Did it die?" Nathan asked.

Azrael shook his head. "The child was full term, and she was born perfectly healthy and completely human."

I thought for a moment. "She wasn't part angel?"

"Only human," he said. "If the angelic spirit is severed while the child is in utero, no part of the spirit is passed on at birth."

Suddenly, I was no longer hungry. "What if something happens to me while I'm pregnant?"

Azrael hesitated.

"I want to know," I said despite every one of my feelings to the contrary.

He folded his arms on top of the table. "If something happens to you before the child can survive outside your womb, then you'll both pass into the spirit world."

He was quiet again.

Nathan and I exchanged a worried glance. "And if something happens once the child *can* survive?" Nathan asked.

Azrael took a deep breath. "If Sloan dies, then Kasyade will no longer be tied to this world. She'll be able to move across time and space freely, and she will get to the child before any of us can stop her."

Nathan said a bad word.

"Even you can't stop her?" I asked.

He shook his head. "Not if she's in spirit form and I am not. This is why Phenex is particularly dangerous. She has no bond here. She can come and go at will."

Resting my elbows on the table by my plate, I cradled my face in my hands and stared down at my eggs.

A surge of energy flowed into me when Azrael's hand stretched across the table to grasp my forearm. "Look at me," he said.

Numb and completely overwhelmed, I looked up at him.

"I won't let anything happen to you or the child. I am a formidable adversary, even as I am." He smiled and pointed at me. "And you are not easy to kill."

I wasn't so sure I believed the last part.

He nudged my plate toward me. "Eat. You need your strength."

Frowning, I dropped my head. "What strength?"

"Eat," he insisted.

Nathan offered me his coffee cup. "Here, have another sip. I know juice is your thing now, but this will make you feel better."

"Thank you."

As I drank it, he winked at me.

Azrael must have noticed the exchange. He split a glance between the two of us. "What is your relationship? I've been watching the two of you for weeks, and I rarely find one of you without the other."

Nathan blew out a sigh. "It's complicated."

Azrael sat back in his chair. "I was able to work that much out for myself."

"We're friends," Nathan said. "Warren asked me to take care of Sloan while he's gone."

"And does he know you're in love with her?" Azrael asked.

His blatant candor startled both of us.

Nathan tapped his fingers on the table. "I told him."

My head snapped up with surprise. "You did?"

"Yeah, I did."

"When?" I asked.

"When he moved in with you before we all went to Texas," he answered.

"Before Texas?" My voice rose. "That was months ago!"

Nathan shrugged. "He asked. I answered. It's not like it's some big secret. Everybody knows."

Azrael shook his head. "My son did not get his patience from me. I would have killed you."

I cringed. *Yikes.*

Nathan's head tilted. "I'm sure he's thought about it."

"Speaking of relationship drama," I said, looking at Azrael. "Who is Warren's mother?"

Azrael stared at me for a moment, then looked at his plate without answering. He devoured a piece of sausage like I hadn't even spoken.

"Kasyade all but admitted she raped the man who fathered me," I said, conjuring up a surprising amount of bravery. "Is that what happened with Warren?"

Anger flashed through Azrael's dark eyes, and I shrank back in my seat. Even from across the table, I could hear his teeth grinding. Warren did that too in the rare moments he was mad.

After a moment of steely silence, he spoke. His voice was tight and even. "I knew Warren's mother. I loved her very much."

My mouth fell open. Azrael didn't strike me as having the ability to love anyone. "You loved her?"

He slowly nodded his head. "She's the reason I tied myself here."

It was obvious Azrael didn't want to elaborate, but I didn't care. If he could inquire about my love life, then I entitled myself to knowing about his. "How did you meet her? What was she like?"

There was more teeth-grinding.

Nathan nudged my leg with his socked foot under the table. He was warning me with his eyes.

I didn't care. "Where is she?"

Azrael picked up his half-eaten breakfast and carried it to the sink.

"Where is she?" I asked again.

His head whipped toward me, his eyes fiery and his jaw set like stone.

We stared at each other. I could feel my blood pressure rising as we engaged in a silent battle of wills.

Finally, his shoulders dropped. "She's dead."

His words echoed around the room, and his anger melted into raw pain.

I'd won, but I was infinitely sorry I'd asked.

13.

AZRAEL WALKED OUT of the house and didn't return for an hour. When he came back, he carried in a large black duffle bag, a rolling suitcase, and a backpack. He deposited them in the foyer. I didn't remember an official agreement of him moving in, but I'd been so tired the night before, anything was possible. No matter, we all knew he wasn't going anywhere and as much as he made me nervous, I was glad.

None of us brought up Warren's mother again.

Despite the falling snow outside, Nathan had to go into work that afternoon. The city had extracted his SUV from the river early that morning, and he was called in to prepare a written report of the accident and list the contents of the vehicle that would have to be replaced. He also needed to go pick up a new cell phone since his sank to the bottom of the river with everything else. It was obvious when he left the house he was hesitant to leave me alone with Azrael, but I assured him I would be safe until he got back.

After we said our goodbyes at the door, I surveyed the stuff Azrael had brought in. With my hands on my hips, I sighed. "I need a bigger house." He walked up beside me, and I looked up at him. "I have no idea where you're going to sleep."

He shook his head. "I don't usually sleep."

I frowned. "That's creepy."

"My body doesn't require sleep in the same way yours does. I can sleep, but usually I prefer not to. The couch is fine," he said.

I groaned. "But what will we do with all your stuff?" I pointed toward the ceiling. "I'm going to see how much space is left in the guest room-slash-Nathan's room-slash-the armory upstairs."

When I got to the room, the sight was a little overwhelming. There was a dresser already filled with most of Warren's clothes sandwiched between the wall and two oversized, fireproof gun cases. Blocking the only window in the room, was a cabinet filled with ammunition. Nathan had two stacks of clothes on the floor beside the bed, along with two pairs of tactical boots and a spare belt. Surprisingly, the bed was made, but his toiletries bag and a laundry bag were deposited on top of the comforter. In the small closet were more of Warren's clothes and most of my summer wardrobe.

There was no place for Azrael's belongings, and even worse...no place for a baby.

"I need a bigger house," I said again.

"You seem stressed." Azrael's voice behind me almost caused me to pee my pants.

I gasped and spun around to see him leaning against the doorframe of the bedroom. "You scared the crap out of me."

He nodded. "I can tell. What are you doing?"

I scratched my head. "Trying to figure out our living situation. I really don't want the Angel of Death setting up residence in my living room."

"Why don't you ask Detective McNamara to return to his apartment? There is no need for him while I am here," he said.

In the closet, I gathered all my sundresses in my arms. "While I'm sure you see it that way, Nathan won't agree. He won't ever completely trust you. It's not in his nature, so I suggest you start getting used to it." As I walked past him, I motioned to the closet. "Can you grab all the men's clothes hanging up in there and put them on my bed?"

From his annoyed expression I could tell he thought the task was beneath him.

"And then can you grab all the shoes?" I added.

I heard him groan as I walked to my room.

After arranging all of mine and Warren's clothes in my closet, I returned to the guest room. Both of Warren's gun cases were standing open, and Azrael was holding a huge rifle. I froze in the doorway. "How did you get those open? I don't even know the combination."

He grinned over his shoulder at me. "Magic."

I shuddered.

The closet was empty except for the extra sheets for the guest bed. "I think there's room for your stuff in here now," I said.

He nodded. "I'll bring it up in a moment. You should get dressed."

"For what?"

"It's time to go to work," he said.

I looked at the clock on the nightstand. "It's time to go to dinner."

He looked down the barrel of the rifle as it was pointed at the floor. "You have training to do."

"Not today," I whined. "I want dinner and an early bedtime."

He snapped the barrel closed, and put the gun back in the case. "We won't do much today, but I want to get started. You exercising your gift will not only protect you, but it will protect others *from* you. Right now you're a liability."

I frowned. "You don't even know me."

"Maybe not, but I know what you can do. You need to master it." He looked at his watch. "You do this, and I'll treat you to dinner after. Deal?"

I sighed. "Deal. What should I wear?"

"Something warm."

I returned to my room and dressed in jeans and a turtleneck sweater. I pulled on my brown, fuzzy boots and picked up my cell phone off the bed. I tapped out a text message on my phone to Nathan. *Going out to practice my superpowers with Azrael and then to dinner. Be back later.*

As soon I pressed the send button, the phone buzzed in my hand. *Message Undeliverable.*

He obviously hadn't picked up his new phone yet.

When Azrael and I walked outside, he opened up the passenger side door of the truck parked on my curb. I narrowed my eyes and cocked my head to the side.

"What is it?" he asked.

I pointed to the bland black pickup. "I expected something cooler from you, Mr. Archangel. Like a Hummer…or the Batmobile."

He didn't laugh. "I'm sorry to disappoint. Get in."

Once we were inside, he put an address into a GPS device. I

couldn't help but snicker. He cut his eyes at me. "Is something funny?"

I folded my hands in my lap. "The Angel of Death needs Garmin?"

"Navigating was much easier and faster when I could cross in and out of this world," he said.

"Like teleporting or apparating?"

He put the truck into gear. "Something like that."

I looked out at the clumps of dirty white snow lining the streets. "That's so cool. Do you miss it?"

"Every single day," he said.

"What's so great about it?" I asked.

He rubbed his hand over his mouth. "Do you remember what it was like the first time you met my son?"

I laughed. "How could I forget? He showed up at my doorstep and scared the hell out of me."

He looked over his shoulder at me. "I'm talking about the first time he ever touched you."

The first time Warren's hand brushed mine, we were sitting on the curb in front of my house. It was like a bolt of electricity pulsing from his body through mine. The memory alone was enough to make me squirm in the passenger's seat of the truck.

The look on my face must have answered Azrael's question. He pointed at me. "That's what my world is like. It is euphoria all the time. You never get used to it. It never gets old. You can never have enough."

"It sounds like you're talking about heroin or something."

"Haven't you ever wondered why the world has so many addicts? So many lost souls seeking after the ultimate high?" he asked.

"Yeah."

He bowed his head slightly. "Now you know."

I laughed, but I didn't exactly think it was funny. "Are you saying drug abuse is linked to God?"

He gave a noncommittal shrug. "I'm saying everyone on this planet is born with the desire for that connection, that feeling. Some try to satisfy it with drugs, and others use sex, money, and even religion. But, ultimately, everyone's after the same thing."

"That's interesting," I said.

Azrael turned onto the interstate. The mountains were speckled with snow against the dreary gray sky. It was getting dark outside.

"Where are we going?"

A thin smile spread across his face. "You'll see."

His cool and disconnected tone unnerved me. "Maybe we should try this tomorrow," I said. "It will be dark soon."

"Don't worry. This won't take long," he said.

After ten minutes of driving, he got off the interstate onto a small access road near the Blue Ridge Parkway. My spine tingled as I realized I had been on the road before. Confirming my fear, Azrael turned onto an even more desolate logging road leading up the mountain. My eyes darted around the dim forest. "Why are you bringing me here?"

"You'll see."

I pulled out my phone and tapped a message out to Nathan. *Azrael is taking me to the woods where Billy Stewart tried to kill me. Not sure why.*

I hit send, but the phone buzzed and another *Message Undeliverable* alert popped up on my screen. I gulped, and my heart was racing. "I don't like this. Please turn around."

He kept driving.

My brain was scrambling for a way out, but I was trapped. I knew it, and Azrael knew it. My heart was thumping so hard I could feel it beating against my seat belt. I closed my eyes. "Nathan McNamara," I whispered.

When I looked at Azrael again, his creepy smile turned my stomach.

Finally, he stopped in the middle of the dirt road and slid the transmission into park. "Is this where it happened?" he asked.

"What are we doing here?" I asked, my voice cracking.

"Get out of the truck."

"Azrael, I—"

"Get out of the truck!" he roared.

He wrenched his door open, and I sat frozen in my seat as he got out and slammed his door. I hit the lock button. He looked back at me and grinned, then he held up his hand. The lock clicked and my door flung itself open.

"Damn it," I muttered.

Before I got out, I closed my eyes once more and pictured Nathan's face in my mind. "Nathan, I need you here."

Carefully, I slid out of the cab and tightened the belt of my coat. Snow was sporadically spitting through the high beams from the headlights as I walked in front of the truck. I stood there hugging my arms and shivering, partly from the cold and partly out of sheer terror of what was coming next. Once again, I had walked blindly into the open trap of a demon.

"Are you afraid?" Azrael asked as he took a few slow steps toward me.

There was no point in lying. "Yes."

"Did you summon the detective here?" he asked.

I nodded.

"Good."

He turned away and navigated down the embankment on the side of the road. He motioned his fingers toward me, beckoning me to follow. When I didn't move, a magnetic force pulled my body in his direction, forcing my feet to keep up. I followed Azrael into a small clearing in the woods. Not a hundred feet from where we stood was the spot where serial killer, Billy Stewart, had buried Leslie Bryson and had dug my grave right next to her.

Icy tears slipped down my face.

Azrael turned toward me. "Close your eyes."

I knew if I didn't close them, he would close them for me, so I pressed my eyes shut.

A moment later, I heard twigs cracking under his weight next to me. "Your life is in my hands, Sloan. The life of your child is putty at my fingertips. I can destroy you and your baby, and no one will be able to get to you fast enough." His warm breath singed the exposed skin of my neck. "I want you to burn this feeling into your memory," he hissed.

My shoulders trembled with silent sobs.

"Oh, don't cry," he taunted. "Each tear is your strength dripping off your cheeks. Your tears make you weak."

"Please," I begged.

"Remember this feeling, Sloan. Let it seep into your bones. Let it flow through your veins," he said. "Open your eyes."

When I opened my eyes, Azrael was standing inches in front of me. His hands were outstretched and between them was a razor-sharp, white, pulsing light. It danced violently in the space between his palms. "Hold out your hands," he ordered.

Trembling, I stretched out my freezing hands.

He carefully extended his arms till his hands reached mine. Then, as if passing me a basketball or a loaf of bread, he placed the light in my hands. My eyes widened so far I feared they might freeze that way.

The light sizzled like *Pop Rocks* in my hands. It tingled and burned and felt icy hot as it pulsed from one palm to the other. My terror was replaced with fascination as the bolt surged between my fingertips.

Then the light fizzled out.

Azrael's eyes met mine. "You forgot your fear."

My mouth was still hanging open. "What?"

"The fear. That radical feeling of desperation," he said. "That's the key to unlocking your power over death."

I put my hand on my hip. "So you aren't planning to kill me?"

He grinned and shook his head. "Not today." He took a step forward and looked down at me. "I needed to make you fear me and fear for your life and for your daughter. I'm sorry it had to be this way."

I shoved him backward. "That's a jerk move, Azrael!"

He smiled. "It wouldn't work any other way. I could explain it all day long, but you wouldn't understand unless you felt it," he said. "Let's just say this training exercise was done in a secured environment." He gestured toward the truck. "It's freezing. Let's get out of here."

Azrael walked back to the truck, but I stood motionless in the clearing, frozen to the ground, my mind working overtime to process all that had occurred in the five minutes we had been there.

"Are you coming?" Azrael called from the driver side door.

I thrust my hands into my coat pockets and trudged back up the hill to the road. I got in the passenger's side and slammed the door behind me. "You're such an asshole!"

"Yes," he said as he looked over his shoulder to complete a three-point turn. "Call your detective friend and tell him to meet us for dinner. Does the baby like Mexican food?"

I felt like kicking and screaming. "Azrael! I thought you were going to kill me!"

"I know. That is what I intended you to think. Better me than someone who actually wanted you dead, don't you agree? Now you know how to access your power without me needing to write a textbook about it." He pointed at my phone. "Call your friend."

I sighed. "I can't. His phone isn't working."

Azrael scowled over at me. "You don't need a phone."

Using my gift, I called out to Nathan and after a few moments of silence, my phone rang and his face came up on my screen. "Hello?" I answered.

"Hey. I just got my new phone. Where are you?" he asked.

"Driving. Where are you?"

"Well, I got turned around on the interstate and accidentally wound up in the forest," he said.

I sighed. "It's because I summoned you. I'm fine now, though. Want to meet us for dinner?"

He paused for a moment. "Uh, sure," he said. "Where are you going?"

"Azrael wants Mexican food. How about Papa's and Beer over near your apartment?" I asked.

"I'll see you there in ten minutes," he said and disconnected the call.

Azrael glanced across the cab at me. "Like I said earlier, now that I'm here, there really isn't any need for the detective to stand guard over you all the time."

I smirked. "Try telling him that."

"It really isn't safe for you to be so close to anyone," he said. "Angels can use other humans to get close to you, even against their will."

I shuddered at his implication and hugged my arms. "Nathan won't leave me, so you're wasting your breath."

"Are you in love with him?" Azrael asked as he drove.

I rolled my eyes. "You dragged me up into the woods like Ted Bundy, and now you want to discuss my love life?"

He reached across the cab and squeezed my shoulder. "I said I was sorry. You learned though, didn't you? Now you will know exactly what I'm talking about when I tell you to focus on your fear."

"Why does it have to be fear?" I asked. "Why can't it be love? Or happiness?"

"Because fear is more powerful than even love," he said. "Fear forces you to reach into places within you to summon courage and power you never thought you had." He cast me a serious look. "Fear is also ultimate respect. And if you are about to end the life of another being—you had better be fearful and certain of that choice."

His words gave me chills. "I really don't want this, Azrael."

He shook his head. "You don't have a choice."

* * *

I decided to extend the dinner invitation to Adrianne also, to smooth things over after not calling her about the accident. She said she'd be right behind us.

Nathan was seated at a table when Azrael and I walked into the restaurant. He stood when he saw us. I huffed as I slid into the booth, and he sat next to me. "What have the two of you been up to?" he asked.

I glared across the table at Azrael. "Well, he tried to kill me."

Azrael grinned. "I did not."

I turned toward Nathan. "He took me up to Billy Stewart's spot in the woods and made me believe he was about to murder me!"

Nathan's eyes darkened, and he looked at Azrael. "You did what?"

"Tell him what else happened," Azrael said to me.

I sighed. "He handed me this lightning ball thing, and I held it till I got distracted and it burned out."

"What?" Nathan asked.

Azrael seemed proud. "I taught her how to harness the power of death on that mountain."

Nathan sighed and looked down at the menu. "Geez, I hope it's happy hour. I have a feeling I'm going to need a drink."

"But the light went out," I said to Azrael. "What good does that do me?"

Azrael looked around the restaurant toward the bar. He held up one finger. "Give me a second."

When he was gone, Nathan tugged on my arm. "You're all right?" he asked.

"I'm fine. I thought I was going to die though."

His eyes followed Azrael. "I'm still not sure about him."

I put my hand on his forearm. "He is unorthodox, but he could've hurt me and he didn't. How was your day? Did you get the stuff with your car straightened out?"

His face fell. "The car was destroyed. Most everything was gone. Almost all my weapons were swept downstream."

I leveled my gaze at him. "Better the weapons than you and me."

"Absolutely."

Azrael walked back to the table. He had a cigarette lighter in each hand. "Are you ready for a cosmic physics lesson?" he asked.

I put my hands in my lap. "Dazzle me."

"OK, this is what happened up on the mountain today." He held up a pink lighter. He pressed the button down. "You can't see it, but you know gas is leaking out of this thing, right?"

Nathan and I both nodded.

Azrael held up the other lighter and struck it with his thumb. A small flame danced at the end. "For lack of a better word, I ignited my power like this little flame. And then"—he held the flame over the other lighter and it ignited also—"I passed off that power to you."

He let his lighter go out and held out the one representing me.

"Your power burned until you forgot how afraid you were," he said. Then he let the flame go out.

"But I can get the flame back?" I asked.

"When the gas is flowing, all you need is a spark." He ignited the lighter again.

"How?" I asked.

He put the lighters on the table and held up his hands in front of him. "You focus the energy to that spot," he said, nodding his head to the space between his hands. "And if you choose to use it on a human, you will separate their spirit from their body."

"And kill them?" Nathan asked.

Azrael glanced at him. "The human spirit is what animates the body, is it not?"

My cheeks puffed out as I blew out a deep sigh. "I'm not mature enough for this kind of responsibility."

Azrael stood back up. "I must return these lighters to their owners."

When Azrael got up, Nathan draped his arm across the back of the seat and leaned into me. "I still think he's nuts."

I agreed. "He is. He's right though. I know exactly what he's talking about."

"You actually held that light?" he asked.

I put my hands up in front of me. "Just like this."

He tugged his ball cap down lower over his eyes. "Remind me not to get on your bad side."

I nudged him in the ribs with my elbow.

After we'd gotten our drinks and ordered our food, I chewed on the end of my straw, replaying everything he'd taught me. I looked at Azrael. "So does my power only work on humans?"

He shook his head. "No. It would work on me if you chose to use it."

I pointed at him. "I'll remember that."

It was the first time I'd ever heard him laugh.

Nathan tapped my arm. "Your girl's here."

I looked up to see Adrianne walking through the door. Even in yoga pants, she looked classier than me. I waved and called out her name. "Let me out so I can say hello."

"Hey, sorry I'm late," Adrianne said as she approached. "I wouldn't have been if I hadn't been an afterthought." She was glaring at me as Nathan and I slid out of the booth.

I gave her a hug. "You weren't an afterthought. It was a last-minute decision."

Azrael moved over to make room for her on his side of the table.

Adrianne did a double-take when she saw him. "Is this...?"

I pointed at him. "This is Azrael. Warren's dad. Az, this is my best friend, Adrianne Marx."

He slightly bowed his head. "Hello."

She looked him over again, absolutely mesmerized. "Ho...ly...crap. The genes run strong in this family, don't they?"

"They certainly do," I agreed as we all sat down. Nathan took the inside so I could sit across from Adrianne.

She picked up a menu and held it up in front of her face. She mouthed the words 'Oh my god' and dropped her mouth open dramatically.

I rolled my eyes.

"Is he single?" she whispered.

"I don't know, but he has supernatural hearing," I said.

She dropped her menu and looked over at him. He was smiling. Her face turned four different shades of crimson.

Nathan looked at him. "Are you single?"

Azrael's eyes slowly slid toward him. "I hope you're not asking for yourself."

I giggled. "Listen to that. He makes jokes."

Azrael raised an eyebrow. "Who said I was joking?"

Nathan sighed and picked up his drink.

"I am single," he finally said.

Adrianne leaned toward him and stuck her hand out. "It's nice to meet you, Azrael."

"Oh, no! Absolutely none of that," I said.

"None of what?" Adrianne whined, batting her eyelashes at me.

"I know that look," I said. "And I'm putting my foot down now."

She winked at Azrael. "She never lets me have any fun."

He leaned on his elbow a little too close to her. "Somehow I doubt that does much to deter you."

"Mmm, an angel and a mind reader," she said.

I held my hands up. "That's it!" I got up and pulled on her sleeve. "You can sit by Nathan."

She laughed and stood, but she grabbed my hand and cut her eyes at me with a grin. "Can I flirt with him instead?"

"I learned how to kill people today," I warned.

Laughing, she pressed a kiss to my forehead, certainly leaving a bright red lip print behind.

14.

THAT WEEK, REFUSING to leave my side, Azrael began accompanying me to work every day. While I fielded holiday news requests and worked on my end of the year expense reports, the Angel of Death sat opposite my desk and played Angry Birds on his cell phone.

Each evening we practiced my superpowers. Most of that time was spent teaching me to conjure up my own deadly light ball and project it onto nearby trees and bushes. Note: no natural vegetation was harmed in the practicing of this skill. Despite popular belief in the mountains of North Carolina, trees don't have souls.

I still hadn't heard a word from Warren.

Friday afternoon, I had a scheduled day off for my follow-up doctor's appointment from the accident. Nathan left for work, and I slept in. When I came downstairs around eleven, I found Azrael standing in the middle of my kitchen.

"Let's go out. The baby is craving cheese grits for breakfast," I said as I walked to the refrigerator.

He rolled his eyes. "It's not breakfast anymore, and the baby will have to settle for a sandwich and potato chips. I've got something special planned for today."

He successfully piqued my interest. "What are we doing?"

"Playing with fruit," he answered.

There was a bag of navel oranges on the kitchen counter. My brow scrunched together. "Is this a joke?"

"I never joke," he said as he ripped the bag open.

That was the truth. One thing had become obvious about my mysterious faux-father-in-law: the Almighty didn't instill a sense of humor within His angels. I hopped up on the counter and peeled an orange. Azrael yanked it from my fingers.

"Hey!" I objected.

"This fruit is not for eating," he said.

A thin smile spread across my face. "Is that what God told Adam in the Garden of Eden?"

He pointed a warning finger at me. "You tap dance on blasphemy, you know."

I pretended to zip my lips sealed.

Azrael carried an orange across the kitchen and placed it in the center of the dinette table by the window. He turned to look at me. "I'm going to teach you how to move the orange."

I cocked an eyebrow. "Move it?"

"Without touching it," he added. "Stand up."

Obediently, I jumped down from the counter. With a smile plastered across my face, I walked to the center of the kitchen. I spread my feet apart, bent my knees, and rubbed my palms together furiously. "Let's do this."

Azrael folded his arms across his muscular chest. "I need you to be serious."

I pressed my lips together and straightened my posture. "I'm sorry. I'll be serious."

"Close your eyes," he said. When my eyes were sealed, he continued. "For the next several moments, I want you to forget we are standing in your kitchen. I want you to forget we are even connected to this world you live in."

I wanted to ask if he would be burning incense, but I kept my mouth shut.

"Where you exist, Sloan, is inside this shell called the body." I felt his fingertips tap lightly against my forehead. "The part of you that makes decisions, that loves, that hurts, that fears—that is who you really are. Your body actually limits you. Let's do an exercise," he said. "Where's the most beautiful place on Earth?"

I smiled. "Bora Bora."

"Have you been there?" he asked.

Sadly, I poked out my bottom lip and shook my head.

"That's even better. Can you see it right now?"

I smiled again. "Yeah."

"What's it look like?" he asked.

"I see a turquoise lagoon with thatch-roof bungalows built over the sparkling water. Behind it are green mountains against a bright blue sky," I said.

"Is it warm?"

"Yes, but there's a cool ocean breeze that smells like coconut and limes."

He chuckled. "Now open your eyes."

My eyes popped open, expecting to see that we'd been teleported across the globe to tropical Tahiti. Nope. We were still in the middle of my kitchen. The only thing I could smell was lemon scented bleach from the sink. I shook my head and pointed at him. "That's a dirty trick, Azrael."

He waved his hand down my face. "Close your eyes again."

With a huff, I obeyed.

"Everything in this house, in this city, in this country is standing between you and Bora Bora, correct?" He tapped my forehead again. "You're already back there in your mind, aren't you?"

I was. I was currently peering through the glass bottom floor of my bungalow watching a school of blue and purple fish swim under me.

His large hand gripped my skull. "This is the most powerful tool you possess, and everything outside of it is simply matter that can be moved and bent to your will."

"Is this like, 'Do not try to bend the spoon, Neo'?," I asked with a grin.

"What?" he asked.

My eyes opened again. "The Matrix? Keanu Reeves?"

Azrael was glaring with disapproval.

"Sorry," I whispered, closing my eyes.

"The art of what you know as telekinesis is really a simple process. Your body is a store of potential energy, and if you consider your potential energy as an accessible entity, you can learn to harness it and project it as kinetic energy onto an external object."

I groaned. "I should have paid more attention in high school physics."

"Please stop talking," he said.

I nodded.

"I want you to try to see that energy inside you, the same way you created your vision of Bora Bora."

My eyes opened again. "Are you serious?"

He was standing only inches in front of me. His expression was a mix of frustration and annoyance. "Yes. Do you want to learn this or not?"

"I'd rather learn how to teleport."

"Someday I'll teach you."

He had my attention. "Really?" I asked.

"Yes, but not today. Focus."

I closed my eyes again and huffed.

Two of his fingers touched my forehead. "You were given creativity for a reason. Use it to create your energy into a viable resource. See it in your mind."

I took a few slow and deep breaths to rid my mind of how ridiculous this all was to me. On the next inhale, I held the breath. It was surprisingly easy to dream up a glowing haze of energy. I imagined it to be like the first orb of light Azrael had passed to me when we were on the mountain road. It sparkled and sizzled and danced around in my mind like static electricity in the clouds on a dry summer night.

He removed his fingers and walked in slow circles around me. "Hold on to that image and then imagine forcing that energy into the space between you and the orange I placed on the table. Use your hands to direct the energy toward the orange, but do not open your eyes."

I raised my hands and imagined sending the ball of sparkling light across the room and into the orange. I slowly exhaled.

A deafening crack exploded behind me and reverberated around the room nearly sending me flying out of my skin. I clapped my hands over my splintered ear drums and opened my eyes in time to see the glass shattering as the orange crashed through the kitchen window. I spun around on Azrael who was holding a small handgun pointed toward the ceiling. He was smiling.

"Jesus, Mary, and Joseph! What did you do?" I screamed.

He tucked the gun into his waistband and grabbed my shoulders.

He was laughing with pride. "No! It is what *you* did!" He turned me back toward the window.

"Did you shoot the orange?" I shouted.

"No! I fired a blank!" He pointed toward the window. "You did that! You broke the window!"

My jaw dropped as another piece from the pane of broken glass crashed to the tile floor. I whirled back around and punched him as hard as I could square in the nose. His head snapped back and blood poured down into his mouth, but he was still laughing.

"I absolutely hate you!" I roared. "You are an evil man!"

He pulled his shirt up to catch some of the blood. Even though I really wanted to hit him again, I retrieved a towel from under the sink and handed it to him so he wouldn't track blood all over my house. He pressed it to his nose. With bloody fingers, he pointed to the window again. "You did it, Sloan!"

"Why did you fire a gun in my kitchen?"

He examined the amount of blood on the towel. "Adrenaline makes it easier."

My ears were still ringing, and I pressed my palms against them. "I think you ruptured my eardrums!"

"It's a tiny gun. You'll be fine," he said. "I think you broke my nose."

"I hope I did! You're lucky it wasn't your neck!"

He pulled the bloody towel away and pointed to his crooked nose. "Can you fix this so the bleeding will stop?"

"Fix it yourself," I grumbled.

He shook his head. "I can't. It won't kill me, but I do not heal as you do."

I crossed my arms over my chest. "Well, if it won't kill you, I should let you suffer."

"I'll go sit on your sofa," he warned.

I narrowed my eyes. "You're such a jerk."

"I know."

For the sake of my white upholstery, I placed my hand over Azrael's face. For a moment, I considered cutting off his oxygen supply but healed his nose instead. He winced as the cartilage and bone popped back into place and fused back together. "There," I said when the process was finished. "I hope it hurt like hell."

"It did. I'm going to go wash the blood off upstairs."

I pointed to the window. "I hope God gave you some carpentry skills because I expect you to fix this!"

"Don't worry, I will."

* * *

I still hadn't completely regained my hearing by the time we reached my doctor's office downtown. While we waited in the lobby, Azrael thumbed through a pregnancy magazine.

I looked over at him. "Can I ask you a question?"

He put the magazine down. "Of course."

"I'm sorry for the way I brought this up before, but will you tell me more about Warren's mother?" I asked.

His hands and the magazine dropped into his lap. He looked at the floor.

I leaned into him. "I understand if you don't want to talk about it."

He sighed. "I don't like to talk about Nadine."

"That's a pretty name," I said.

"She was a beautiful person." He looked over at me. "What would you like to know?"

"Where did you meet?"

He closed the magazine and put it on the table. "Nadine was a field nurse in Vietnam during the war." Leaning sideways in his chair, he pulled his wallet from the back pocket of his jeans. He opened it, took out a small picture, and handed it to me.

It looked like a copy of a Polaroid yellowed with age. The woman in the photo was standing next to a window in a short white tank top dress with a wide patterned sash around her waist. Her long, straight dark hair fell around her shoulders, the front pulled to the side and fastened with a barrette. She was laughing.

"Warren has her smile," I said.

He tucked the photo back into his wallet. "I stayed close to her for several months, and after the fall of Saigon, I returned with her to Chicago."

"Did she love you?"

He chuckled. "She didn't like me at first. I terrified her."

"Warren terrifies people when I'm not around him," I said.

He shrugged his shoulders. "Humans naturally fear death. But Nadine was different. She could *see* me."

I turned toward him. "What do you mean?"

"There are a few humans born with the ability to see us. They get glimpses of the spirit world. It's called the gift of discernment," he said. "Nadine was one of those few."

I was skeptical. "I can't even see other angels. Kasyade said it was my humanity that prevented me from seeing."

"That's true. Your human spirit doesn't have the gift."

Looking down at the photo, I studied Nadine's exotically beautiful face again. "What was she like?"

Had I blinked, I might have missed the split second Azrael's dark eyes glazed with the unmistakable swell of sweet remembrance. "She was feisty."

Not exactly the answer I expected.

"She knew her own mind, didn't back down to anyone. And she was tough. She never once flinched during that war, and it was brutal." A hint of a smile tugged at the corners of his mouth. "Maybe she flinched once." His expression was fascinating as he traced the line of the scar down his face. "She was with me when I got this."

I'd always been curious about that scar but too afraid to ask. "Oh, I have to hear that story."

"We slipped away from the hospital one night to an abandoned hut in a village the Viet Cong had lost to the army. On our way through the village, I ran up ahead and ripped down the Vietnam flag left behind." He looked away, but I swear I saw a tinge of pink rise in his cheeks.

"And?"

"The flag was rigged with a grenade."

My hands flew to cover my mouth.

He laughed. "Blew half my damn head off."

"Are you serious?"

He nodded, still shaking with chuckles. "Yeah. It took a while to come back from that one." He looked over at me. "Needless to say, my seductive plans for that night were thwarted by my own stupidity."

"Did she freak out?"

"Of course she did, but by then she knew I'd come back." Azrael's laughter subsided. "She never let me forget it though."

I gave the photo back to him. "What happened to her?"

"She died when Warren was born." He shifted uncomfortably in his seat and cast his eyes down at the floor. "There were complications during his delivery that were compounded by Warren and I being what we are. The doctors couldn't stop the bleeding, and her heart gave out."

My heart ached. "I'm sorry."

He forced a smile.

"Warren refuses to go around sick people with me because he says his presence makes them worse," I said.

He nodded. "That's true."

We were both quiet for a while. I touched my stomach. "Azrael, when this baby is born, will I die?"

He gently took my hand. "No. Warren's birth was complicated, and his mother was not an Angel of Life, as you are. I'm sure you'll be fine."

I sighed with relief and relaxed in my chair.

A nurse walked into the waiting room. "Sloan Jordan?"

We both stood.

She looked up at Azrael. "Is this the baby's father?"

"No, this is the baby's..." I caught myself before I said *grandfather*.

Azrael stretched out his hand. "I'm the father's brother."

She smiled, obviously confused. "Oh, OK." She looked at me. "Well, this appointment won't be as invasive as the last. Dr. Watts is going to do a different type of ultrasound if you would like for the baby's uncle to come with you."

I looked at Azrael. "Want to come see your *niece?*"

A genuine smile came over his face. "I would love to."

"Follow me," she said.

We walked back to an exam room. The nurse opened the door, and we followed her inside. She motioned to the weight scale by the window. "I need to get your weight and your vitals," she said.

I kicked off my tennis shoes and stepped onto the scale. I had gained two pounds since my last appointment. She took my blood pressure and temperature and then pointed to the exam table. "Go ahead and have a seat. Dr. Watts will be in shortly."

When she left the room, I looked over at Azrael who was studying a three-dimensional model of a pregnant woman. It was cut in half to show her insides. He touched it, and the fake baby toppled out of the model's uterus and bounced across the floor.

I laughed.

Dr. Watts came in, hugging her clipboard. "Hello again, Sloan."

I smiled. "Hello."

She stuck out her hand toward Azrael, and he actually shook it. "I hear you're the baby's uncle. Welcome."

"Thank you," he replied.

She put the clipboard down by the sink and sat on a chair with wheels. "How are you feeling these days, Sloan?"

"Tired and I cry *all the time*. Is that normal?" I asked.

She chuckled. "Yes. It's perfectly normal and it may get worse." She patted the pillow behind me. "Sloan, you can go ahead and lie back. No need for a gown this time. Just pull your shirt up," she said.

Obediently, I lay back on the table and tugged my sweatshirt up to my ribs.

She rolled the ultrasound machine over beside the table. "Normally, I don't do ultrasounds this early, but with your accident a few weeks ago, I would rather play it safe."

"I understand," I said.

"I read the report. That must have been quite the ordeal," she said as she turned the machine on.

I nodded. "It was terrifying."

"I'm glad you were able to get out of the car."

"Me too."

"Me three," Azrael added.

Dr. Watts squeezed warm blue jelly out of a bottle onto my stomach. Then she rolled a wand around in the jelly, pressing it into my abdomen. After a moment, we all heard a fast *bump, bump, bump.*

"Is that the baby's heartbeat?" I asked.

She smiled and nodded her head. "Yes, and it's very strong." She put her finger on the screen. "See the little blinking light? That's the heart."

Azrael leaned close to the screen and sucked in a deep breath. "That's the baby?" he asked.

"That's him," she said.

"Or her," he corrected.

She laughed. "Yes. She looks wonderful, Sloan."

I sat up on my elbows for a better view. The little bean actually looked like a baby this time. It had tiny arms and legs and a giant head in comparison to the body. My eyes prickled with tears.

Azrael was completely mesmerized by the screen. "It's really real," he said.

"It's quite a miracle, isn't it?" Dr. Watts asked.

He looked back at me. "You have no idea what a miracle it is."

Dr. Watts printed out a photo for me to take home, and I tucked it into my purse. Before I left, she asked me a ton of questions about my health. Have I had any abnormal bleeding? Have I had problems with my anxiety? Have I had any more migraines? I assured her all was well, and we were free to leave.

On our way back to the car, Azrael looked over at me. "What do you think about the migraines?"

I groaned. "They're terrible. That's actually how I knew I was pregnant. I didn't have a migraine when we dropped Warren off at the military station."

He nodded. "Even though I've never been pregnant, that makes sense. When I left Warren at the church in Chicago, I was sick for a week."

"I believe it," I said. "Warren figured out our migraines usually start around the thirty mile mark of us being separated. Is that how it works?"

He shook his head. "Not exactly. Your power is limited by distance, but it's not an exact science. The closer two angels are in proximity, the worse the separation."

"Is that why Warren never had migraines before me?" I asked. "Because you kept your distance?"

"Correct. His side effects would have been mild."

For a moment, my mind replayed the horrific headaches I'd experience. "I guess that makes sense. My first migraine happened immediately after Warren left, certainly not after thirty miles."

"And Warren's likely happened later," he said. "Warren's body was more adjusted to the physiological response than yours was."

I stopped walking.

He turned toward me. "What is it?"

"When I figured out Kasyade was my mother, I called her, and she was out of town. When I talked to her in Texas, she said she had a headache when she got back. She was with another angel while she was traveling."

He raised an eyebrow. "Did she say where she went?"

I shook my head. "No, but I'll bet we can find out." I tugged on his arm. "Come on. We need to find Nathan."

* * *

When we got back to my house, Azrael yanked my keys out of my hand when I tried to use them at the front door. "You don't need them anymore."

"My bladder says otherwise," I answered.

He dangled them in the air, just out of my reach. "I guess you have some good motivation then."

"Some days I think you're a demon."

He winked. "Some days I would agree." He pointed to the lock. "Focus like you did this morning."

For five full minutes, I focused on the damn deadbolt. And for five minutes, nothing happened. "You're not projecting your energy into the lock," he said. "See it in your mind. Slide the bolt open."

My knees were pinched together, and I was bouncing. "I see it in my mind, and I'm sliding the stupid bolt open. It's not working."

Suddenly, the door swung open. But it wasn't my supernatural doing. It was Nathan. "The door's unlocked," he said.

I spun with a glare toward Azrael. "How can I unlock an unlocked door, you stupid angel?"

He laughed, holding his hands up in the surrender position. "Maybe you should've tried the handle first."

With a huff of frustration, I thrust my purse in to Nathan's arms and ran past him into the house. I took the steps two at a time upstairs to the closest bathroom. When I was finished, I trudged back to the living room. Nathan was sitting on the sofa watching the news. He looked up at me. "Still haven't mastered your superpowers, huh?"

"Maybe I have. I guess we'll never know," I said, sitting down next to him on the arm of the couch.

He gestured toward the door. "I can lock you outside if you like."

I rolled my eyes.

He handed me my purse. "How was the doctor's appointment?"

"Oh!" I found the photo Dr. Watts had given me and thrust it in front of his face. "Look!"

He smiled. "That's awesome. She looks just like you." He turned in his seat to look at me. "Did you know the kitchen window is busted?"

I pointed at Azrael as he walked in with water from the kitchen. "He did it."

He pointed back at me. "You did it."

"Only because you fired a gun next to my head!"

Nathan jerked his head toward Azrael. "You fired a gun in the house?"

Azrael shrugged his shoulders. "They were blanks."

"Still!" Nathan shouted. "What the hell were you doing?"

I crossed my legs and let them dangle off the arm of the sofa. "Azrael was teaching me how to move things with my mind."

Nathan was almost too angry to laugh. Almost. "What?"

Azrael put his hand on my shoulder. "She did it too. That's how the window was broken."

Nathan narrowed his eyes. "Is that why I found an orange on the sidewalk?"

I patted him on the back. "Good work, Detective."

He sighed and shook his head.

I grabbed his shoulder. "Speaking of detective work, guess what I figured out?"

He looked up at me. "What?"

"I'll bet Kasyade visited Ysha or Phenex, or maybe both, right before the second trip we made to Texas. If we can get ahold of her travel records, then we can possibly find them," I said.

"What makes you think that?" he asked.

"Because she had a migraine when she got back which means she was with another angel," I said.

He laughed. "I want to be on the line when you explain this theory to the FBI."

"It's possible to find out though, right?" I asked.

"Yeah, it's possible."

"And if we find the other two sisters, then we find Kasyade and end this thing," I said.

"There is a lot of *ifs* in that assumption," Nathan said. "*If* we find them and *if* she's with them and *if* they don't kill us all before we can do anything about it." He looked back at Azrael. "I'm not even so sure it's such a good idea to go looking for them if we have no way of killing them. What's the point?"

Azrael opened his mouth to answer, but the doorbell rang.

Nathan looked at me. "You expecting company?"

I shook my head and moved to get up.

The doorbell rang again.

Azrael held up a hand and signaled for me to stop.

It rang a third time.

Then a fourth.

And a fifth.

I sent out my evil radar.

Nothing human was pressing the doorbell as it chimed over and over and over again...

15.

NATHAN STAYED IN front of me as a shield as we turned and watched Azrael walk to the door. His heavy footfalls on the hardwood creating an eerie sound against the incessant chimes. Without looking through the peephole, he opened the door.

And through it fell the red-haired woman, tattered and bloody.

I gripped Nathan's arm as I peered over his shoulder.

Azrael caught her as she collapsed over the threshold, and I relaxed when I realized she was unconscious.

"Where can I put her?" he asked, lifting her limp body into the air.

"On the couch," I said.

She wore a pair of thin sweatpants and a men's v-neck white t-shirt. That was it. It was freezing outside. Blood was crusted on most of her skin, except for the places it was still sticky on arms and feet. Azrael hesitated before laying her down on my white furniture.

"It's only a couch," I told him. "Put her down."

Her body was emaciated, like something off the cover of a National Geographic story on third world poverty. Her skin was so thin it was translucent, showcasing thin blue veins and tendons everywhere clean enough to be visible. Her sunken eyes were open but fixed on the ceiling, staring into nothingness, or maybe not staring at all.

Nathan felt for a pulse. "She's alive." He stretched out one of her arms along the sofa. My name was still freshly carved into her flesh. I shuddered.

Her pale lips were cracked and raw. She looked like a corpse—and felt like one too.

I looked at Azrael. "This is Ysha's daughter? What happened to her?"

He took a step back. "My guess is she was raised by Ysha."

"I thought that wasn't allowed or something," Nathan said.

"It's not." I looked at Azrael. "This is why, isn't it?"

He nodded. "That is correct. Imagine a lifetime of constant electroshock. It breaks the mind which all of us still have. This, or some version of this, is always the result."

"Can I heal her?" I asked.

He looked at me with sadness in his eyes. "She's like you. She already has your healing power."

My shoulders sagged. Had different choices been made for me, I could have ended up on someone's couch, clinging to life or standing half-naked in the middle of the road in the dead of winter.

Nathan stretched out her other arm. "Azrael, what does this mean? *Kotailis.*"

"The kotailis is the time the earth is most inclined toward the sun. Light is greater than darkness on that day," he explained.

I frowned. "Are you speaking literally or figuratively?"

He pointed out the window. "Right now it is dark. In the morning, it will be light."

I relaxed again.

"In America we call it the first day of summer," Nathan said.

"What does that have to do with anything?" I asked.

Azrael simply turned his palms up in question.

"What do we do with her?" I asked.

Nathan pulled out his cell phone. "I'll have a car come pick her up and take her to the station."

I grabbed the phone out of his hand. "No! You can't do that."

His eyes widened. "Why not?"

Gripping the phone with both hands, I shook my head. "Because if she's like me...Nathan, you can't lock her up in jail. I would rather you shoot me between the eyes. Nobody deserves that."

He put his hands on his hips. "Well, what else can we do?"

I gave him his phone back. "We'll have to keep her here."

Nathan swore. "Are you kidding me?"

Azrael folded his arms over his massive chest. "This woman is completely unpredictable, Sloan. We don't know why she's here or what she wants with you."

"Look at her," I said. "I could kill her with a fly swatter."

Nathan paced the room. "She's been court ordered to be in that facility. They'll keep looking for her."

I pulled the blanket off the back of the couch and gently draped it over her. "I'm not sending her away so she can wind up in jail again. Besides, I want to talk to her and find out why she's here and why the heck my name is engraved on her skin."

"She doesn't speak English, remember?" Nathan asked.

"Yeah." I pointed at Azrael. "But I'll bet he can translate."

From the expression on Nathan's face, it was clear he was surprised he hadn't thought of that. He looked at Azrael. "What language do you speak?"

"*En makkai est molingui ine tempronera.* It is called *Katavukai.*"

Suddenly, the woman on the couch convulsed like she'd been electrocuted. She jumped upright and scrambled into the corner of the couch, facing away from us. I ducked behind Azrael.

Nathan crossed his arms. "Looks like you said the magic words, Az."

The woman's head turned slightly, just enough for one glassy eye to peek back over her shoulder. Then she jumped over the arm of the couch, sending the side table lamp crashing to the floor as she scurried toward the corner. She was terrified, shielding her face with her arms, crouched like a wild animal against the wall.

"Azrael, say something to her," I said, grabbing his sleeve and pushing him forward.

"*Nankal taracebit amaityano.*" He cautiously moved toward her with his hands raised. "*Amaityano. Nakal uteves auxil.*"

She was peeping through the crack made by her arms. I'd never seen anyone look so afraid...except Kayleigh Neeland after she'd been kidnapped, beaten, and left to die in a dark attic. My eyes teared up imagining what this poor creature had endured.

Azrael's voice was barely above a whisper. "*Nakal uteves auxil.*"

She slowly unveiled her face.

"*Quid peyar?*" Azrael asked.

"Taiya." If mice could speak, that's what she'd sound like.

Azrael looked over at us. "Her name is Taiya."

"Ty-ah," Nathan said slowly.

The woman stretched out her arm and burst into tears. She pointed to my name.

Taking that as my cue, I slowly walked over to her and knelt down. She grabbed my hand, still sobbing. Puzzled, I looked at Azrael. "Ask her how I can help her."

"Taiya, auxi uta Sloan," he said.

"Nadas auxi," she replied.

"She cannot help me," he translated.

"Nadas auxi," she said again. *"Praea morteirakka."*

I gulped. "She just said I'm going to die."

Azrael's face snapped toward me.

Nathan walked over. "How do you know that?"

"*Praea* is the name Kasyade gave me, and I know enough Latin to know *morte*-anything is probably bad news." I looked at Azrael. "Am I right?"

He nodded.

The woman babbled to Azrael, her words coming out so fast Azrael squinted like it was difficult to keep up. I heard a few words I recognized. *Kasyade* was one of them. *Ysha* was another. My name was said a lot.

"What's she saying?" Nathan asked.

Azrael held up his hand to silence him. He said something to the woman instead that sounded like a question.

Then the woman looked at me. *"Morteira kotailis."*

* * *

By some miracle, I made it out the back door and over the porch railing before dispelling the contents of my stomach onto the frozen ground. It wasn't exactly new information. I'd known for a while I was a target. But now I knew the demons had a timetable; they were planning to kill me on the first day of summer.

A hand rested on my back. "You know I've seen you puke more times than I've seen all my other friends and family puke combined." Nathan's tone was light. I knew it was to calm my nerves. It didn't help. "It was very considerate of them," he continued, "to give you the date of your demise."

I spat on the ground. "Indeed. It was very thoughtful."

He tugged on the hem of my shirt. "Come here."

I turned and stepped into his arms.

"This doesn't change anything," he said quietly. "We still won't let anything happen to you, and actually knowing this will help us do that."

That did help me feel a little better.

He pulled back. "Let's go in before we freeze to death and the demons aren't a problem anymore."

Back inside, Azrael had coaxed Taiya into the kitchen. She was drinking a glass of water, and he appeared to be making her something to eat. As we passed my couch where she'd been lying, I sighed. The white fabric was defiled with blood and grime.

Nathan guided me to the loveseat. "Sit. I'll get you some water."

In the kitchen, I watched Azrael put a plate down in front of Taiya before walking over and sitting on the arm of the couch across from me.

"What else did she tell you?" Nathan asked as he returned with a bottle of water. Without sitting down, he handed it to me.

Azrael hesitated, looking down at me.

"It's OK," I said, unscrewing the cap. "I want to know."

He drew in a deep breath. "As I assumed, she was raised by Ysha, but she was left in the house in Chicago about two months ago. She was taken into custody with the other girls."

In the kitchen, I watched Taiya nibbling on a Pop-Tart. "Why can't I see her soul?"

"Excuse me?" Azrael asked.

I looked at him. "I couldn't see Warren's soul till I was pregnant. I still can't see hers though."

"Taiya's human spirit is very weak," he said. "It's part of the consequence of her upbringing."

A question was bothering me; I was almost afraid to ask it.

Azrael must have noticed. "What's the matter?"

I put my hand on my stomach. "Will I have to give her up?" I asked. "So she doesn't turn out like Taiya?"

He shook his head, offering me a gentle smile. "Your humanity tempers the effect you'll have on her, so you'll be fine to raise her as your own."

"How did she get here?" Nathan asked.

Azrael shrugged. "She escaped the facility where they took all the girls, but she doesn't know how she got here."

I looked again at the woman hunched over the dinette table. I would have been surprised if she could find her way across town, let alone the country.

"She's kinda got a Houdini thing going on. How does she keep escaping these places?" Nathan asked.

Azrael's brow rose. "Don't underestimate her. She's been around angels her whole life. She's more powerful than you think."

Nathan looked over at her. "Is she dangerous?"

Azrael took a deep breath. "I do not yet know."

After I made up a bed for Taiya on the couch, Nathan followed me upstairs. He stopped in the doorway to my bedroom, and I turned back toward him after switching on my bedside lamp. "You never come in here anymore," I observed out loud.

He braced his arms against the doorframe and tapped his fingers against the wood. "It doesn't feel right now," he said.

I smiled. "You're such a good guy."

He laughed. "I promise, I'm really not."

I took a few steps toward him. "Crazy day, huh?"

"I expect no less." He jerked his thumb over his shoulder toward the hall downstairs. "You OK? That was a lot."

I nodded. "I will be. You're right. What she said doesn't change anything. I know I'm safe." *For now*, I added silently.

His face was serious. "You are safe."

I nodded again.

"I'll be in my room if you need me," he said.

"Goodnight," I replied.

When he backed out into the hallway, I gently closed the door. Then I turned the knob lock before shutting off the light.

* * *

It was still dark in my room when I opened my eyes. The clock on the nightstand said it was just after three. Sleeping through the night was becoming rarer as bathroom trips became more and more frequent. I had assumed bladder control would be one of the final hurrahs of pregnancy. I was wrong.

I also didn't have to pee.

There was a strange noise so soft it was curious rather than terrifying as most noises are in the middle of the night. Maybe a slip of paper had fallen into the air vent. Or maybe a leaf was trapped in the windowsill outside. No. It was more subtle than that, and it was closer than the window. It was a tearing sound.

My heart quickened in my chest, and I sat up in the middle of the bed. Straining my eyes in the dim light of the moon, I searched.

Between my nightstand and the wall, a pair of wild eyes blinked in the corner.

I screamed and scrambled across the bed in the opposite direction, thankfully toward the door. But my legs were tangled in the sheet, and I tumbled off the side of the bed onto the hardwood floor. I half-crawled, half-ran to the door and twisted the handle but it wouldn't budge.

Screaming for help, I yanked as hard as I could, rattling the door against the casing.

There was commotion on the other side. Someone had heard me. Perhaps all of Bradley Avenue.

"Sloan?" It was Nathan's voice.

"Nathan!"

"Sloan, open the door!"

"I can't! It won't open!"

Whatever was in my room, was standing right behind me. I had to get out.

There was a click, and the door swung toward me.

Then I was through it and into Azrael's arms on the other side.

Nathan was cursing behind him. "What the...?"

I didn't want to look, but I did.

Taiya was standing a few feet behind me in the long white night gown I'd given her to wear. Her empty eyes were glassy and slightly crossed. At her sides, her bony hands were covered in tangles of her long orange hair. I buried my face in Azrael's chest again.

He spoke to her in their language.

"Taiya," he said louder. "Taiya! *Auyuketkai!*"

Azrael pushed me behind him.

Nathan grabbed the sides of my face. "Did she hurt you?"

I was still shaking so much I could hardly move my head from side to side.

He pulled me backwards across the hall into his room and closed the door behind us. "What happened?" he asked, looking me over for injuries. "Your knee." He nudged me toward the bed where I sat down and he knelt beside me.

My knee was flushed bright red and split open straight down the middle. Blood was trickling out. "I...I f...fell off the b...bed."

He stood. "I have a first aid kit out in my trunk—"

"No!" I grasped the tail of his white t-shirt.

"Shh." He sat and pulled me into his arms. "It's over."

I sobbed against his shoulder until the door creaked open. It was Azrael.

"Are you OK?" he asked, stepping into the room. He was fully dressed, of course.

I straightened and swiped my fingers under my eyes. "She was in my room! She was ripping her hair out, watching me sleep!"

"What was she doing in there?" Nathan asked, tightening his arm protectively around my shoulders.

Azrael crossed his arms. "Something like sleepwalking. I don't believe she was conscious."

"Where is she now?" Nathan asked.

"Back asleep on the couch," Azrael answered.

I raked both hands back through my hair, still heaving for oxygen. "I can't do this!"

Nathan shook his head. "I'm calling dispatch to have her taken in."

Azrael held up his hand. "Let's wait. I'll sit and watch her till morning and we can—"

"You were supposed to be watching her tonight!" Nathan shouted, cutting him off.

"She went to the bathroom," Azrael said.

"She moved through a locked door!" I cried.

Azrael dropped his gaze to me. "It's not that hard to do."

"Thanks, that makes me feel a lot better!"

The angel wasn't moved by my hysteria. "Let's wait until morning to decide her fate. If she was going to harm you, she would have."

I buried my face in my hands. "Just go watch her and make sure she doesn't budge off that sofa."

Without a word, he walked out of the room.

When he was gone, Nathan turned to me. "Forget about what he said. What do you want me to do? I can get her out of here tonight."

Pressing my eyes closed, I sucked in a deep breath. "Right now, help me clean up my leg."

When I looked at him again, he was nodding. "Can I get a

washcloth from the bathroom?"

"I'll come with you."

He helped me to my feet. There was no pain in my leg. I looked down to see the blood had stopped oozing and was starting to crust, and while the wound hadn't closed, it did already look like a fresh scar.

Nathan's eyes widened. "You're getting better at this."

I groaned as we went to the bathroom. "Great. Maybe my head will reattach itself when she severs it in my sleep."

16.

THE NEXT DAY, I didn't send Taiya to jail. When I left my bedroom, I stepped on a plate with a peeled brownish banana, a handful of crackers, and a bite-size Milky Way. Beside the plate was a pink sticky note from the pad I kept in the kitchen. I picked it up and read, *I sory. Taiya.* The handwriting reminded me of Kayleigh. I'd have to be a demon for that not to melt the ice around my heart. Pun intended.

Azrael made waffles.

"What will we do with her long term?" Nathan asked, pointing at Taiya. She was next to me, swiping up syrup with her finger. "Is she going to live here too?"

I leaned my elbow on the table and rested my chin in my hand. "I guess she can stay on the couch."

Nathan looked around the room. "This place is getting crowded."

I rolled my eyes. "It's been crowded since Warren moved in."

Behind his hand, Nathan snickered.

"Shut up, Nathan," I said.

"You said it, not me," he defended.

Azrael cleared his throat. "Nathan, you don't have to stay. I'm fully capable of taking care of things here on my own."

Nathan's fork clanged against his plate when he dropped it. "Like you took care of things last night?"

"Boys," I said with a warning tone. "I am in no mood to referee this morning. Last night sucked, but it's over. Let it go." I looked at Nathan. "Do you have to work today?"

He shook his head. "I'm off all weekend."

"Can you take me shopping?" I asked. "I want to get her some clothes that fit. Mine swallow her up."

His entire countenance fell. I might as well have asked him to take me to the third ring of hell. "Why can't Azrael take you?"

I pointed at Taiya. "Would you rather stay here with her?"

He huffed. "No."

"It's settled then," I said.

"What will happen when we both go back to work?" he asked. "Azrael won't stay here with her, and he can't bring her to your office."

"Well, if we can figure out Monday, I'll talk to my boss about working from home this week." I wiped my mouth with a napkin and dropped it on my empty plate. "I'll blame it on pregnancy stuff."

"How are you feeling these days?" Nathan asked.

"I'm finally over the caffeine headaches," I said. "I still feel kind of queasy on and off through the day, but other than that, I'm OK." That wasn't the complete truth, but I didn't feel like talking to Nathan and Warren's dad about my overactive bladder and painful boobs.

"Ding, dong," Taiya said, reminding us all of her presence at the table.

We all looked at her, just as the doorbell rang.

I looked at Nathan as he got up. "That's freaking creepy," I whispered.

He answered the door.

"Morning, Nate!" Adrianne was entirely too chipper for so early in the morning. She rushed in, unwrapping her bright red scarf as she came. "It is freezing out there!" She slid to a stop in the middle of the kitchen and froze at the sight of our new houseguest. "Uhh…"

I looked up at her. "Adrianne, this is—"

She held up her hand. "I know who this is. She tried to kill you. Why is she…" Her head angled sideways. "Why is she drinking maple syrup out of the bottle?"

I turned to look as Azrael snatched the bottle from Taiya's hands. "*Nil,*" he said, wagging his finger in her face.

Taiya dropped her hands in her lap. Pouting was clear in any language.

I jerked my thumb toward her as I turned back to my best friend. "This is Taiya. She's a long story. What are you doing here? Aren't you working today?"

Nathan pulled out his chair for her. "Have a seat, Adrianne. You want some coffee?"

She held up the travel mug she'd carried in. "I'm all set. Thanks." She flashed a flirty smile at Azrael. "Morning, Az."

I groaned.

Laughing, she plopped down into the chair and crossed her long legs. "I took today off because I have done zero Christmas shopping."

"Crap," I said. "Me either."

She slapped my leg. "Good. I came to make you go with me."

"We were literally just talking about shopping when you walked in," I said. "I need to go get our new friend some clothes."

Nathan was at the refrigerator, but he spun around with a bright smile. "Hey! We can give Adrianne some money and we can stay here."

I rolled my eyes. "Nice try. We're going."

His shoulders slumped again.

"Great." She gripped my arm. "We can buy maternity clothes!"

Behind me, Nathan mumbled, "Kill me now."

"I *so* do not need maternity clothes yet," I argued.

"You'll need them soon enough." She pointed back toward the stairs. "Go get dressed. The mall will be nuts today. We'll probably be there all day as it is."

Nathan cursed under his breath.

* * *

Nuts didn't begin to describe the state of the Asheville Mall. We parked in the last space of the highest deck of the parking garage and entered into the overwhelming lingerie section of a department store. We were greeted by women dressed as elves handing out coupons as *Hark the Herald Angels Sing* blared over the store's sound system.

Nathan put his hands on his hips and looked at me, shaking his head. "The things I do for you."

I pinched his nose. "Santa's going to bring you an extra big present this year."

"Speaking of Christmas," Adrianne said as we wound our way through the crowded department store. "My boss won a private dinner party at the Deerpark restaurant at Biltmore next weekend. She's out of town and offered me the tickets. You guys want to go?"

"I don't know." I looked back over my shoulder. Nathan's eyes darted in every direction, and his hand was poised to grab the handgun I knew was tucked under his jacket. I giggled. "Nathan, did you hear Adrianne?"

He looked at me. "Huh?"

"Do we have plans next weekend?"

He dodged left out of the way of a woman with two armloads of shopping bags. "I don't think so."

Adrianne looped her arm through mine. "It would be so much fun. We can get all dressed up and wine and dine like royalty. What do you think?"

The corners of my mouth dipped into a frown. "Can't have wine."

"Well, you can have chocolate cake for two."

My mouth watered at the mention of chocolate.

"Did I hear something about getting dressed up?" Nathan asked, doing a double-step to catch up with Adrianne's long stride. "If so, I'd like to vote no."

She looked at him over her shoulder. "You don't get a vote, McNamara."

He grumbled something too low for me to hear.

"What do you say?" She bumped me with her hip. "I bought a new dress for that hot father-in-law of yours."

"Good luck getting him into it," I said.

She rolled her eyes. "You know what I mean."

I sighed, exasperated. "You have the worst taste in men."

Her bottom lip poked out. "I thought you liked him. How could he be bad for me?"

"For starters, he's not human." I held up two fingers. "Secondly: He's. Not. Human."

"Warren's not human," she said.

I tugged her on toward the junior's department. "Yes, he is."

"I agree with Adrianne," Nathan interjected behind us.

"Your opinion doesn't count," I called over my shoulder.

She leaned against me. "But he's beautiful, smart, and kind...and he can cook."

I stopped walking and looked up at her. "He's the Angel of Death, Adrianne. The Grim Reaper. Death personified!"

Nathan laughed. "You have to admit, he's still a step up from that Mark guy she dated."

I jabbed my finger down my throat and faked a vomiting noise.

"Look! Baby clothes!" Adrianne squealed. She dropped my arm and quickened her pace toward a rack covered with Christmas dresses for babies...or dolls, I wasn't sure which. She held up a red sequined, velvet Santa dress with cuffed, fuzzy white sleeves and a big white bow around the middle.

I put my hands over my stomach. "I think it's a little big for her."

Nathan snickered beside me.

Adrianne held the dress against her chest. "Little Adrianne can wear it next Christmas."

"Little Adrianne?" Nathan asked.

She nodded. "Of course."

"And if it's a boy, same name spelled with an I-A-N. *Adrian*," she said.

"Azrael says it's a girl," I told her.

She dangled the dress on the tip of her finger. "Then it's perfect! I'm buying it."

Nathan looked at me. "I feel bad for this kid already."

I chuckled.

"Nathan! Sloan!" a familiar female voice called out behind us.

Nathan's head fell back, and he pressed his eyes closed in agony. "Dear God, why?"

We both slowly turned around.

Shannon Green's hips were swinging from side to side so dramatically she cleared a path all the way to us. As usual, she was overdressed in a long wool winter green coat...or maybe it was a dress, with her blond curls dangling beneath a leopard print beret. She wore more makeup than I'd worn all year collectively, and I could smell her pungent perfume from fifteen feet away. "Fancy meeting the two of you here." She tossed her hair back over her shoulder as she stopped in front of Nathan.

He forced a smile. "Hello, Shannon."

She blinked her heavy eyelashes at him. "I'm a little surprised to see you here, Nathan." She glanced at me. "Or, maybe I'm not."

"How have you been, Shannon? I haven't seen you at all since we got back from Texas," I said.

She shrugged. "Why would you?" Her eyes ran the length of my body like she had X-Ray vision and she was giving me a body scan. "I hear you're pregnant."

"That's right," I said.

She looked at Nathan. "Dare I ask?"

Nathan rolled his eyes. "I'm not the father, Shannon."

"Where's Warren?" she asked me.

"He was deployed," I answered.

She waved her finger between me and Nathan. "I'll bet he loves this arrangement. I've heard you're living together. Is it true?"

Nathan crossed his arms. "I'm not sure how that's any of your business."

She jabbed her fingernail into the center of his chest. "Because everyone is talking about it. You and I just broke up!"

Adrianne raised an eyebrow. "It's been like two months."

She cut an evil glare at Adrianne. "Was I talking to you?"

Adrianne took a step toward her. "Oh, you don't *want* to talk to me!"

My eyes widened. "It's like we've time-warped back to 1997." I stepped between Adrianne and Shannon. "It's Christmas. Let's all be nice."

Tears were brimming in the corners of Shannon's eyes. "I really hate you, Sloan."

Ouch.

She spun on her heel and stalked away, the heels of her knee-high boots tapping out a sharp staccato against the tiles. I jogged to catch up with her. "Shannon, wait."

"What?" she snapped, spinning to face me. She tried to catch a rogue tear on her sleeve before I saw it.

"For what it's worth, I'm really sorry about you and Nathan," I said. "And I hope someday you'll be able to forgive me for whatever part I may have played in it. I never meant any harm."

She sniffed.

I smiled and touched her arm. "Have a Merry Christmas, Shannon."

As I turned to leave, she called out after me. "Sloan."

I looked back at her.

She didn't say anything. She just stared at me for a second, then walked away. We might never be actual friends, but I didn't hate Shannon anymore. And as hard is it was for me to admit, in more ways than one, she was a better person than I'd ever be.

*** * ***

It took begging and extortion, but Adrianne finally agreed to hang out with Taiya for the day on Monday while Azrael went with me to work. Mary agreed for me to work from home for the rest of the week, and the following week was Christmas. Hopefully by the New Year, we'd have a permanent solution to our babysitting problem with Taiya.

When we got home that evening, my kitchen looked like a crime scene, the weapon of choice—hairdresser's scissors. Bright orange locks lay all around the dinette table, and Adrianne stood in front of Taiya with her head cocked to the side and her scissors raised at the ready.

It was like a sacrificial offering to the gods of cosmetology.

Taiya looked stoned.

"Did you drug her to get her to sit still?" I asked, walking up next to Adrianne.

Adrianne shook her head. "I gave her wine and melatonin." She snapped her fingers. "Works like a charm."

Taiya's hair was cut in an angled bob just above her shoulders. It had been blown dry with mousse, flat-ironed, teased, and hosed down with enough hairspray to freeze time. I looked up at my friend. "Give her some big earrings and a guitar, and she could be the lost ginger from Jem and the Holograms."

Adrianne's face scrunched up. "I know. I'm not sure it works for her."

"Taiya?" Azrael asked.

She blinked up at him and smiled.

He rolled his eyes.

Behind us, the front door opened and Nathan walked in. His eyes widened as he looked around the kitchen. "What happened in here?"

"Adrianne has been playing a game called *Give the Angel a Makeover*," I answered.

"Cool." He looked over at me. "Are you next?"

I rolled my eyes. "Funny."

He nudged my arm. "I need to talk to you, and you'll want to sit down." His tone was unnerving.

"OK. What's going on?"

Azrael and I followed him to the living room, where we sat on my sofa that was covered with a bed sheet. He opened a file folder he was carrying and handed me a piece of paper. "I got ahold of Kasyade's travel record for around the time right before you went back to Texas."

"Great!" I scanned the paper. "Where was she?"

"Here."

I looked up at Nathan. "What?"

He leaned toward me and pointed to a line item on the page. "Look. She was in Asheville the day she confirmed she was your mother on the phone."

The paper clearly said she flew into Asheville on Wednesday that week and flew back to San Antonio on Friday. "How can that be possible? What was she doing here?"

He shrugged. "The bigger question is—"

"Who was she with, and what was she doing while she was here?" Azrael interrupted.

Nathan tapped his finger on the paper. "I'm sure the FBI is asking the same questions."

I looked at Azrael. "Do you think Ysha or Phenex is here?"

He stared out the window. "The presence of the angelic has been so concentrated since your child's conception that it's hard to say. I believe so, and I know they have both been here before, but as good as I am at tracking, they are equally good at evading."

"Can you dig around some more?" Nathan asked.

Azrael was thoughtful. "I've already got some contacts working on it, but I'll go out tonight and see if I can find anything close by."

I stood. "Well, let's get a move on because I promised Adrianne dinner at Chestnut tonight."

Azrael nodded. "OK. We'll rendezvous here later then. I'm not sure how long I'll be—"

I held up my hand to silence him. "No. You'll have to go after dinner." I rolled my eyes toward Adrianne who was grinning mischievously at me from the kitchen. Then I looked back up at him. "Dinner with you was the deal."

17.

"ADRIANNE HAS BALLS," Nathan said as we sat in the living room eating Chinese takeout in our pajamas.

I popped a forkful of sesame chicken into my mouth. "That she does," I replied around the bite.

Azrael had been grinning—quite a feat for him—when he left the house with Adrianne for dinner. She was a crafty one. Not only did she force me to relinquish my stance on her chastity where he was concerned, she cornered him into the date whether he wanted it or not. They'd been gone for a while and I hadn't heard a word from either of them, except for a photograph Adrianne had taken with her phone at the bar. Both of them were smiling, a feat for Azrael.

Nathan crossed his socked feet at the ankles on top of my coffee table. "Do you think he's interested in her like that?"

"How am I supposed to know?" I asked. "He's about as readable as braille on sandpaper."

"True."

He chewed in silence for a moment. "Do you trust him?" he finally asked.

I looked over at him. "With Adrianne or in general?"

"In general."

"That's an odd question."

He jammed his fork into the container of fried rice and put the container on the floor. "I feel like he's hiding something from us. I mean, we still don't know anything about him. I thought about trying to pull his travel records today and realized we don't even know his last name."

"Does he have a last name?" I asked.

His expression was smug. "Do you see my point?"

"I don't think I *don't* trust him," I said.

He chuckled. "That's a solid position. You either trust him or you don't."

"I trust him," I said, trying to sound more confident. "It's hard when things fell apart so quickly with Abigail."

"I know what you mean."

"What will you do about it?" I asked.

"Dig. I nosed around in his stuff a little when he first showed up, but didn't find anything. I might try to lift some prints or find out who that truck was rented to," he answered.

"It's a rental?"

He nodded.

"Why don't we ask him?"

He picked up the remote control. "Because everyone lies. It's better to find out via other methods."

I smiled. "Do you lie?"

"Never," he said with a wink. "Were you lying to Shannon yesterday when you told her you were sorry?"

It was a valid question, and I thoughtfully considered it for a moment. "Actually, no. That was the truth. I am sorry for whatever role I played in her getting her heart broken. As much as I don't like her, I wouldn't wish that on her."

He raised a skeptical eyebrow.

I laughed. "OK, maybe I would have wished it on her in high school but not now. We're not the same people we used to be."

"Just for the record, you weren't the reason I broke it off with her," he said.

"I know."

He nudged my ribs with his elbow. "I will admit I wanted you to be the reason."

I knew that too.

"Can I tell you something that's been bothering me for a while now?" he asked quietly.

I put the rest of my food on the table. "Of course you can."

He turned slightly toward me. "The night we got into the fight about you saying I was only attracted to you because of your power, I've thought about it every day since. Honestly, I've hoped it was true."

His words stung, but I understood what he meant.

"But it's not true," he said. "It can't be."

His tone wasn't wistful or amorous. Nathan was in detective-mode and stating facts.

"Why?" I asked, genuinely curious.

He draped his arm across the back of the couch. "Remember what Azrael said. Your power is limited. Maybe the thirty-mile theory was off base, but at some physical distance your power loses effect." He lowered his voice. "How many times in the past few months have I been gone to Raleigh or Greensboro or Winston-Salem? For god's sake, when you were in Texas, I dropped fifteen hundred dollars on a plane ticket to come see you."

"But the investigation—"

He cut me off. "Screw the investigation, Sloan. I came because you were there. I came because there is no force in this world—or the next —strong enough to change how I feel about you."

Sometime during his explanation, his tone had changed. So had the distance between his face and mine. I sucked in a deep breath and laughed to cover my nerves or keep from bursting into tears. I scooted back several inches on the sofa.

He obviously realized the conversation took a turn he didn't intend, and he held his hands up. "I'm sorry. I didn't mean to—"

Shaking my head, I stood. "No, don't be sorry." I wiped my sweaty palms on my pants and looked at the clock. "Wow, it's gotten late." It was four minutes after eleven.

"Yeah, we should probably get to bed. I've got work in the morning."

"So do I," I said.

He motioned toward the coffee table. "I'll clean up our mess. You go on up."

I forced a smile. "Thank you."

My tears stayed corralled till I reached my room, but when the door was secured behind me, I fell spectacularly apart. Nathan was right, and I'd known it all along, but that only made everything infinitely harder. I collapsed onto my unmade bed and sobbed into the pillow.

There was a soft knock on my door. As Nathan opened it, I quickly dried my eyes on the sheet. "Can I come in?"

I sniffed and wiped my eyes with the edge of the sheet.

He walked slowly across the room. "I heard you crying." He sank down on the side of the bed. "Are you OK?"

I nodded.

He winked and pointed at me. "See, I told you everyone lies."

Through my tears, I genuinely smiled.

Nathan pulled the comforter up over me. When he started to get up, I grabbed his hand. "Will you stay with me till I fall asleep?" Even to me, I sounded pathetic.

He hesitated for a second. "Sure."

Sliding down in bed beside me, he pulled the covers up over us. Against both our better judgements, he pulled me close and I rested my head on his shoulder. My soft sobs subsided as I paced my breathing against the warmth of his neck. Still, tears slid down onto his t-shirt. "I'm sorry for all this. I'm so sorry I hurt you."

He pulled my hand up and rested it over his heart.

"I love you, Nathan."

His breath caught in his chest.

When he remembered to inhale again, his hand traced the shape of my arm all the way up until his fingers raked through my hair. He paused for a moment while he certainly contemplated the consequences of his next move. My fingers curled into the center of his chest, and that was all the encouragement he needed. He rolled toward me, and in the darkness, his lips found mine.

For so long I had dreamed about feeling the warmth of his body on top of mine, and the reality of it was so much sweeter than the fantasy. My fingers gripped the hem of his t-shirt, and I tugged it up until he grabbed the back of it and pulled it off in one fluid motion. He tossed the shirt on the floor before covering my body again. My fingernails traced the gentle waves of the muscles in his back as his tongue explored my mouth, and his hands explored my body. I pushed with my hips and rolled him onto his back, sitting up in the moonlight and dropping my knees on either side of his hips.

His stomach flexed as he curled up to grasp my tank top and pull it over my head. He smoothed my hair back into place as his mouth covered mine once again. His hand trembled as it touched my breast for the first time. The sensation of his cool fingers against my warm skin triggered a desperate whimper I barely recognized as my own.

Breathless, he pulled away and graced the bottom of my throat with his lips. "If you're going to say no, please say it fast."

In response, I tightened my thighs against his and pulled his head back by his hair to kiss him as I scraped my nails down his spine.

He rolled again, discarding his shorts in the process, until he rested on me so my heart beat against his. He braced my arms against the pillows over my head and breathed into my neck. "Do you really love me?"

"Yes."

"Say it again," he whispered.

"I love you, Nathan."

His hands slid carefully down the length of my arms to my collar bone as he pressed his hips into mine. "Do you love me enough to die for me?"

My eyes fluttered open. "What?"

His fingers closed around my throat. The streaks of light from the window danced across his perfect face, and when his eyes met mine, they were a sea of black.

I grasped at his hands, trying to pry his fingers away, but his grasp was too tight. He pressed in as he constricted my throat against the pillows. I clawed at his chest, drawing blood with my fingernails, but he wouldn't stop. The blood vessels in my face throbbed, some bursting and splintering my skin in agony.

I heard Azrael's voice in the back of my mind. *Hold on to your fear.*

I drew my hands together, and a flash of light appeared between my fingertips. As I drowned in the void of oxygen, I prayed to not have to kill my best friend. Then, as the life drained out of me, I pressed the light into Nathan's chest. Sparks exploded around the room and screams echoed through the night.

"Sloan!"

Taiya was shaking me, and Nathan was shouting. I blinked. Panic was etched on both their faces.

"Sloan, are you awake?" Nathan asked.

My eyes focused on him, and I recoiled from his touch. "What happened?"

"You were screaming," he said. "In your sleep. We both ran in here.

Taiya unlocked the door."

I was panting so hard I felt light-headed. I looked down for my shirt; I was still wearing it. Then I dropped my face into my palms and cried.

"Are you OK?" Nathan asked as the bed dipped under his weight.

My eyes pouring tears, I glanced up at the clock. It was 3:04 AM. My hands were still shaking.

"Where's Azrael?" I asked.

Nathan shook his head. "I don't think he's back yet."

"Call him," I cried.

"OK."

When he moved off the bed, Taiya took his spot. She placed her hands against my face, and immediately peace washed over me. My breathing slowed to almost normal.

"They come," she said. "They come in sleep."

"You can speak English?" My voice was quaked.

She smiled gently. "Little."

Nathan returned with his phone in his hand. "He's on his way back now," he said. "What can I do?"

I shook my head. "Nothing. I want to go downstairs. I can't stay in here."

He offered me his hand, but I refused it.

"I'm OK," I insisted, standing up.

"Look at me," he said, putting a hand under my chin. He turned my face toward him. "Your neck."

I touched my fingers to my throat and felt pain.

"It's really red. Looks like bruising," he said, alarm rising in his voice.

Nathan faltered back a step, quickly withdrawing his hands from me. Terror flashed in his eyes.

A chill rippled through me. "What is it?"

He slowly pulled up the front of his shirt. First, I saw his chiseled abs. Then I saw the long, bloody scratches down his chest.

18.

"TELL ME *EXACTLY* what happened." Azrael sat on the coffee table to face me without even removing his coat. "Start at the beginning."

Nathan was pacing in front of the fireplace. Taiya had fallen back to sleep with her head in my lap since I was sitting on her bed, the sofa. "I don't know what the beginning was. None of it felt like a dream," I admitted. "I don't even remember going to bed."

"You fell asleep on the couch," Nathan said. "I carried you to your room, then I went to bed."

"We ate Chinese food?" I asked.

He nodded. "We had it delivered."

"Where was Taiya?" Azrael asked.

Nathan pointed to a spot on the floor, but Azrael held up his hand to silence him. "I only want Sloan to answer."

I closed my eyes and tried to remember. "She wasn't there," I said, looking at him.

He touched my knee. "Of course she wasn't because you can only see her physical form."

Holy crap. He's right.

"What else happened?" he asked.

"Nathan and I were talking about a fight we had a few weeks ago. I

- 647 -

had told him his feelings for me existed because of my power, and he got upset. Last night he said he'd figured out that wasn't true because of what you'd told us about my power being limited by distance."

Azrael shook his head. "Nathan wasn't there when I told you your power was limited. That happened when we left your doctor's office."

"Oh, that's true," I said. I rubbed my hands over my face. "I can't tell what's real and what's not anymore."

He leaned toward me. "Sloan, it's all real. Do you not realize that?"

My chin quivered.

"What else happened?"

I swallowed hard. "Um...I went to my room and cried. Nathan heard me and came in to comfort me. We started to...um..."

Nathan turned his back to us, his hands folded on top off his head. "Did you have sex?" he asked.

"No," I answered. "Before that happened, he tried to kill me."

Azrael tilted my chin up. "He choked you?"

I nodded.

"I swear, I was asleep in my room the whole time. I woke up to her screaming and ran across the hall," Nathan said. "The door was even locked. Taiya had to open it."

Azrael silenced him with his hand again. "Sloan, how did you stop it?"

I covered my face as the tears spilled out. "I used my power. There was a huge explosion, and I killed him."

Azrael's mouth fell open a fraction of an inch.

Nathan walked around to face him and pulled up his shirt, displaying the marks on his torso. "Azrael, what does this mean?"

The Angel of Death straightened and looked at him. "It means, Detective McNamara, you are *very* lucky to be alive."

* * *

I'm pretty sure Azrael used his magic to put me back to sleep for several hours, and when I woke up again, it was daylight and Nathan was gone. Azrael and Taiya were talking quietly at the table in the kitchen when I came downstairs. "Good morning," I said to both of them.

"Good afternoon," Azrael corrected me. "Do you feel better?"

"No."

"How is your throat?"

"It's better," I said. "Did Nathan go to work?"

"Several hours ago." He pushed the chair out across from him with his foot. "Sit down. We have things to discuss."

"Azrael, I'm too tired for deep conversation this morning."

"I don't care."

After retrieving a water from the refrigerator, I sat in the chair. He reached around to my prenatals on the counter behind him. He slid the bottle toward me. I dropped one in my mouth, washed it down with a gulp of water, and slid the bottle back to him. "All right, what do you want to discuss?"

"You're not safe like this," he said with zero emotion.

I tapped my finger on the table. "I'm fine as long as you're here and you weren't here last night. Where were you, anyway?"

He leaned his elbows on the table. "You know where I was. I was looking for Ysha and Phenex."

"Were you?" I asked. "Or were you fooling around with my best friend?"

His face slipped into a scowl. "I was *exactly* where I said I was. My involvement with Adrianne was *your* doing. Don't forget that."

I rubbed my hands over my face. "I'm sorry. I'm tired and completely freaked out today."

"Which is why we must change our situation here. You're not safe. Humans are too vulnerable," he said. "And that puts you and my granddaughter in danger."

"I'm not leaving Nathan," I said.

He folded his arms over his chest. "How long do you think you can keep this up with him, Sloan? Will you be able to leave Nathan when Warren comes home? How about when your child is born? Where will you draw the line?"

"It's not that easy," I said.

"Let me make it easy." He slammed his index finger onto the table. "This child holds the fate of humanity, and compared to that, your *feelings* are worthless. This is your destiny."

I smirked. "You sound like my demon mother right now."

"Perhaps I do, but that doesn't make me wrong," he said. "And if you're so in love with him, do you not even care you could've taken his life last night?"

"Of course I care!" I screamed. "I've already lost him once. I don't want it to happen again."

Azrael leaned back. "Lost him when?"

"Kasyade killed him in Texas," I said. "I brought him back."

He sat back in his chair, dropping his hands into his lap. "That explains a lot."

I pushed back from the table in frustration. "Well, explain it to me."

"You cannot kill what you've already saved and vice versa," he said. "If you used your power to heal him—"

"I used my power to bring him back from the dead," I said.

"If you used your power *at all*, you can't harm him."

I stood. "Great. It's settled then." I put a hand on the table and leaned over it. "He's staying."

"No, I'm not." Nathan's voice came from behind me, but I hadn't even heard him come in.

I spun around toward him.

He looked around me to Azrael. "Can I talk to Sloan alone?"

Azrael said something to Taiya in Katavukai, then I heard their chairs move. A second later they both walked past me toward the door. "We'll be outside," Azrael said.

When they were gone, Nathan gestured toward the loveseat. "Can we sit?"

I followed him across the room and sat down beside him. "Nathan, I don't know—"

"Let me talk first," he said, interrupting me.

I bit down on the insides of my lips and relaxed back in my seat.

He gathered my hands in his and looked down at them for a long while before he finally spoke. "I need you to allow me to take a step back from this."

"Did Azrael put you up to this?" I asked.

He shook his head. "Azrael has nothing to do with it. This isn't about what physical danger you or I might be in. This is about me not being able to stop my mind from replaying being in your bed last night."

I was surprised. "You remember it?"

"It's jumbled and doesn't make much sense, but yeah." He let out a deep sigh. "It doesn't matter if I was in control of myself or not; what matters is I don't want to be in control anymore. I want all of you, and it's too damn hard being this close and not being able to have you."

He gripped my hands tighter, still not meeting my eyes. "I've been an asshole, and I've passed the responsibility of what happens with us completely to you. I've stayed right here because I told myself I was doing it to protect you and that I was doing it because Warren asked me to. And while those things are true, they're also bullshit. I did it for me because I can't stand being away from you."

We were both quiet as I let his words sink in. He was doing it. He was really saying goodbye.

"I do love you, Nathan." My voice was barely a whisper.

When he finally looked up, his gray eyes were glassy. "I know you do, and somewhere in another lifetime, I'm sure we have an awesome life together." He tucked a loose strand of hair behind my ear. "It's just not in this one."

"Where will you go?" I asked softly.

He shrugged. "I don't know. Maybe back to Raleigh."

I looked down and tears splashed in speckled shapes onto my pants.

Nathan put his hand under my chin and lifted my face to meet my eyes. "I need you to be OK though, and I need you to be happy."

"How can I be happy?"

His smile was gentle. "It'll come. Warren will be home soon, your daughter will be born, and you'll have a good life with them."

"What about you?"

He winked at me. "I've always got bad guys, booze, and college basketball."

I laughed and wiped my eyes.

"Look at me, Sloan," he said.

Nathan studied my face carefully for a moment, like he knew it was the last time he'd see it. Then without hesitation or apology, he slid his hands up my jaw and pulled my lips to meet his.

The kiss was long and slow. Deep and memorable...because that's exactly what we both knew it would become.

A very distant memory.

19.

NATHAN TOOK ALL his stuff back to his apartment without even a final goodbye before he left. No matter how many times Azrael said the words '*he did the right thing,*' nothing made Nathan's departure any easier. By lunchtime the next day, I still hadn't gotten out of bed.

"Knock, knock," Adrianne said, announcing her presence as she pushed open my door.

I looked around the pillow I was hugging. "Hey."

"Hey," she said.

"What are you doing here?"

"I'm on my lunch break. Your dad called me. He's really worried about you," she said, sitting down next to me.

"I'm fine," I mumbled.

She frowned. "I'm looking at your hair. You are *not* fine."

"You're right," I said, rolling over to look at her. "I'm not. I'm a horrible person, destined for hell or equally bad things."

"I can't argue with you there," she said, grinning at me.

I threw the pillow at her.

"Get in the shower, you nasty skank," she said. "And get your ass out of bed. Geez, this isn't a moody teen melodrama. You need real food and real human interaction…or at least non-human interaction. Just get up."

I snuggled further under my blankets. "I'm so tired."

With an exasperated huff, Adrianne yanked back my comforter. "Get up!" She stood and pointed at me. "Don't make me push a pregnant lady on the floor."

Obediently, I sat up in the bed.

She aimed her finger at the master bath. "Shower. *Now.*"

Twenty minutes later, I came downstairs, showered and dressed for the first time since we'd all gone Christmas shopping. Adrianne was sitting next to Azrael on the couch, a little closer to him than I was comfortable with. Taiya was sitting on the floor with a coloring book. She clapped when she saw me.

Adrianne and Azrael looked up.

"Back from the dead," Adrianne announced.

Azrael looked at her. "You're a miracle worker."

"Stop being dramatic," I said. "It's only been a day."

Adrianne put her hand on Azrael's arm. "You have no idea the miracles I can work."

I wanted to throw up. "Move over," I said, pushing them apart and dropping down in the seat between them.

"Are you hungry?" Azrael motioned to the box of pizza on the coffee table. "It's extra meat and extra cheese."

"Azrael, you eat like you're preparing for a reality show intervention someday, but you never work out. How is it you're built like a tank?" I asked.

Adrianne made a soft purring noise beside me.

I rolled my eyes.

"The cells in this body are programmed to work at maximum efficiency all the time," he said. "Outside factors have no influence on them."

"I hate you," I said, leaning toward the pizza box.

He grabbed my arm and pulled me back. "No. I'm sorry. You have to work for your dinner."

I was confused. "What?"

"If you want pizza, you can't use your hands."

"Are you serious?" I asked.

He let go of my arm. "You can use your hands to eat it, but not to get it."

"Azrael," I whined.

"Close your eyes," he instructed.

With a huff, I pressed my eyes closed.

"Think about what you want to happen. Visualize it. Use the space around you to move the pizza onto the plate and not your lap," he said.

Adrianne burst out in nervous laughter beside me. "What kind of voodoo shit is this?"

I cracked up, and my eyes popped open.

She leaned over, dropped a slice of pizza onto a plate and handed it to me. "Problem solved," she said.

Frustrated, Azrael sighed and shook his head.

"I have to get back to work before you two circus monkeys get any weirder." Adrianne stood, then leaned down to look at me. "Will you be OK?"

"I'm fine. Thanks for dragging me out of bed."

She pointed at me. "No more sulking."

"Yes, ma'am."

"I love you, freak."

"I love you too."

She tousled Taiya's hair. "Goodbye, beautiful."

Taiya waved at her, smiling from ear to ear.

Azrael walked her to the door.

"So...will I see you on Friday?" she asked, running a finger under the collar of the jacket he was wearing.

I groaned.

"I'll let you know," he said, opening the front door.

She held her pinky and her thumb in the shape of a phone up to the side of her face. "Call me."

When she was gone, he brought me a bottle of water from the kitchen before reclaiming his spot on the sofa. "Here," he said.

"Thanks." I pointed the bottle at him. "What's happening on Friday?"

He cleared his throat. "She said we're all going to some fancy dinner thing."

I groaned. "I forgot about that. We're having dinner at the Deerpark restaurant."

"I don't know what that is," he said.

"It's probably the most romantic restaurant in all of North Carolina." I sighed. "Just the perfect place for me to have my debut starring role as a third wheel." I pointed at Taiya. "What about her?"

"She'll have to go with us, I guess," he answered.

"Is that a good idea? Taking her out in public?" I asked.

He shrugged. "Taiya's not exactly a wanted criminal. Besides, I doubt anyone would even recognize her now."

That was the truth. Between her haircut, her new clothes, and the five pounds she'd packed on in the week she'd been at my house, Taiya looked like a completely different person.

"Adrianne really worked some magic on her, didn't she?" he asked.

The melodic notes of his tone caught my attention. I looked over at him. "What's going on with you and my best friend?"

He shook his head. "Nothing."

"Liar."

"She's nice," he said. "And she's tall. I like that."

I took a long drink of water. "She's off limits."

He turned toward me. "How come?"

"Because you're a dead guy!"

His brow crumpled. "I am most certainly *not* a dead guy."

"You're not a human," I said.

"That's correct." He winked at me. "I'm better."

I picked up my slice of pizza again. "You can't give her a future, and she deserves one. I don't want her to wind up with a broken heart."

"I have no intention of breaking anything," he said, putting his feet up on the coffee table.

"You'd better not. I'm just getting used to having you around, so I'd hate to have to use my light ball on you."

He watched me retrieve a second slice of pizza from the box. The thick mozzarella drew out into a long greasy string for as high up as I could reach. I had to use my other fingers to break it.

"Do you ever plan on practicing your skills, Sloan?" he asked with a hint of exasperation.

"Of course," I said.

He crossed his arms. "When?"

I lowered the stringy cheese into my mouth and winked at him. "It's my New Year's resolution. I promise."

* * *

On Friday afternoon, Adrianne came to my house to get ready for the party. She claimed it was so we could all ride together, but I really knew it was so she could make sure I looked presentable next to her in public. "You should wear the black Ivis Mishi dress I got you," she said as she pinned a hot roller into my hair.

I made a sour face. "The monstrosity that looks like a jeweled garbage sack?"

She made a sharp screeching sound that echoed around the bathroom. "You take that back!"

"I wish you'd taken that dress back," I teased.

She yanked on my hair.

"Ow!"

"You're such a brat," she said, rolling her eyes at me in the mirror.

I slathered on a layer of sheer lip-gloss. "I know."

"You look so hot in that dress," she whined.

My heart sank. Nathan had said the same thing not too long ago. In the five months we'd known each other, hardly a day had passed that I hadn't heard his voice until that week. He'd been gone four whole days.

"Earth to Sloan," Adrianne said.

My eyes snapped up. "Sorry."

"What's the matter?"

I scrunched up my nose. "Thinking about Nathan."

"Have you talked to him at all?" she asked.

I shook my head. "Not even a text message."

She twisted another long strand of my hair around a hot roller. "Was it really that bad? You never told me exactly what happened."

I sighed. "Yeah, it was *that* bad. The night you were out with Azrael, I had another one of those crazy weird nightmares. Only this time, Nathan was a part of it. It was pretty, um…" My cheeks flushed red.

"Explicit?" she asked.

"Very. But then he tried to kill me in the dream and I almost killed him."

She looked confused. "But it was a dream."

"Well, somehow I woke up with bruises around my throat, and he had bloody scratches down his chest. God only knows what really happened."

"That's terrifying."

"Yeah."

She hosed down the set curlers with hairspray. "So that's why he left?"

"That and he said he's tired of being so close and not being able to have me," I said.

Her bottom lip poked out. "Ohh…that's so sad."

"I know." I slumped in my chair. "And he kissed me."

"Shut up. Really?"

I nodded.

"Like a real kiss?" she asked.

"Closed eyes and everything."

She gasped. "Not closed eyes."

"And face-holding," I added.

She put her hands on my shoulders. "You poor thing."

"And now he's gone," I said. "We weren't even a couple, and it's still the worst breakup I've ever been through."

She grimaced. "Will you tell Warren? He's going to know something major is wrong if he comes home and Nathan is gone."

"I don't want to lie to him," I answered.

Adrianne shook her head. "No. You can't do that. Maybe he won't ask."

I laughed. "Right. Because Warren is about as oblivious as a hawk at dinnertime."

"Sorry."

I waved her off. "Let's talk about something else before I start crying and ruin my makeup."

"Right! There will be absolutely no sad tears tonight. This will be a glorious evening!" She spun around toward my closet. "Now, what are you going to wear?"

* * *

"I look like a California Raisin," I grumbled, tugging at the hem of my skirt as I followed Adrianne and Azrael—who were locked at the elbows—up the stone steps to the glass front doors of the Deerpark Restaurant.

Adrianne flashed a painted smile back at me. "You look gorgeous."

"I look *alone*," I corrected her.

Azrael, who was wearing a black suit against his will at Adrianne's insistence, glanced over his shoulder. "Not true. You've got Taiya."

Taiya.

I stopped walking and looked around for her. It was the second time we'd lost her that evening, and we'd only left the house a half hour before. The first time, she'd disappeared through my neighbor's backyard to the street behind my house. Azrael had brought her back. This time, she was wandering down the cobblestone handicap ramp. I shouted her name, but she was looking everywhere but at me.

"*Eshta!*" Azrael called out.

Taiya spun toward us, causing the short skirt of her dark blue velvet dress to swirl around her thighs. Adrianne had found the frock in the children's department at the mall, and it almost fit perfectly, except for the sleeves which were barely long enough to cover her scars. The square heels of her strap-on dress shoes clopped against the path as she ran over.

I took her hand. "Stay with us." I pulled a pen out of my purse, yanked up Taiya's sleeve and on the outside of her pale forearm I wrote my phone number and *If found, please call Sloan Jordan.*

She ignored me and smacked her lips together like she had been doing ever since Adrianne put pink lipstick on her at the house.

"Azrael, tell her to quit doing that. She looks like a guppy," Adrianne said.

"Oh, leave her alone." Azrael reached for the door handle and held it open for all of us.

I imagine there are few places in the world as grand and spectacular as the Biltmore Estate. The 250 room home, nestled against the backdrop of the Blue Ridge Mountains, was nothing shy of a fairytale castle. Even in my current, irrevocable state of melancholy, it was hard to be blasé about the Biltmore at Christmas.

Inside the spacious restaurant lobby, we were greeted by ten-foot, flawless Frasier firs sparkling with white twinkle lights and silver jingle bells. Fresh pine garland and poinsettias of every size garnished every stationary furnishing in the room. Soft Christmas music drifted from the instruments of a string quartet somewhere nearby.

Dinner at the Deerpark was like dining inside a Hallmark snow globe.

I missed Warren.

And Nathan.

The hostess led us through a maze of banquet tables and buffet stations. Taiya swiped a handful of cheese cubes from an artisan platter as we passed by. Our round table, draped with a pristine white tablecloth and set for a party of six, was tucked into the corner beside the windows that overlooked the center outdoor courtyard hidden at the heart of the restaurant. Adrianne and I had attended our high school prom out in that magical space beneath the stars. I smiled as I pulled out the chair closest to the window.

Adrianne grabbed my hand. "Let me sit there. You know I hate having my back to the action."

Rolling my eyes, I stepped back beside Taiya while Adrianne eased into the seat right next to Azrael.

Deep inside my belly, a distinct flutter tickled my bladder.

My hands covered my stomach. "Whoa."

Azrael looked up with alarm. "What's the matter?"

I giggled. "I think I felt the baby move."

Adrianne clasped her hands together. "Really?"

"I think so." I froze, waiting to feel it again.

Everyone was watching me. Well, everyone except Taiya. She had walked around to the window and was pressing her cheek against the glass.

Azrael snapped his fingers in her direction. "*Eshta. Por dova.*" He pointed to her chair, and obediently she pulled it out and sat down.

Giving up on feeling the flutter a second time, I sank down beside her. "That was weird."

"What did it feel like?" Adrianne asked.

I bit my lower lip. "Kind of like I had to go to the bathroom."

Adrianne's face soured. "That's gross. Isn't it kind of early to be feeling her kick? When my boss was pregnant, she felt her son the first time at the salon and she was further along."

Azrael shook his head. "You can't expect this to be a normal pregnancy. It's not a normal child."

Even if it was true, I didn't like him calling my baby abnormal.

A waitress took our drink orders and invited us all to help ourselves to the buffet tables. Normally, I didn't like buffets. It reminded me of cattle being herded to a trough, but for the Biltmore, I'd make an exception. And since my dad wasn't there to argue, I started at the dessert table.

It was clear from Azrael's scowl that he didn't approve of my chocolate raspberry cheesecake and triple chocolate mousse. "The baby needs calcium," I said, putting my plate down on the table.

Perhaps she heard me using her as my gluttony defense because she moved again.

I smoothed the soft fabric over my midsection. "I feel her again!"

When I glanced toward Adrianne, movement behind her in the courtyard caught my attention. A tall, broad figure was poised in the moonlight, and when he looked up, his black eyes locked on mine.

It was Warren.

20.

GASPING, I COVERED my mouth. "Oh my god."

Everyone in earshot turned to look outside.

Warren stuffed his hands into his pockets, smiling from ear to ear.

In my haste toward the door, I knocked over two chairs and caused an older gentleman to dump his untouched slice of cheesecake onto the floor. I didn't even stop to apologize. My feet didn't stop till I was through the door, across the courtyard, and on top of him. "Warren!" Under the canopy of stars in the cloudless sky above, every nerve ending in my body came alive when his strong arms closed around me. He lifted my feet from the ground and stumbled backward from the force of my impact.

I buried my face in the bend of his neck and cried. "I can't believe you're here!"

He set me down on my heels and pulled back enough to see my face. "Surprise!" Tears sparkled at the corners of his eyes as he cupped my face in his strong hands and pressed his lips to mine. The baby tumbled in my stomach as his energy surged with mine. When he finally broke the kiss, he rested his forehead against mine, sliding his hands down my bare arms till his fingers tangled with mine.

"Are you real?" I asked quietly.

He chuckled. "Of course I'm real. What kind of question is that?"

"A valid one," I said, rubbing my nose against his. "Weirder things have happened lately." I opened my eyes and looked into his. "What are you doing here?"

"We got back yesterday," he said. "I have until Monday to spend at home before I have to go back and process out."

"How did you know…" I blinked up at him. "Adrianne organized this, didn't she?"

He grinned. "Yeah. I called her last week. I wasn't exactly sure this would work out, so I didn't want to get your hopes up."

His black hair was growing back out, and he was as formal as Warren ever got: nice dark jeans that clung to all the right muscle groups, a fitted, black button-up shirt covered by a steel-gray jacket. The jacket looked amazing, but I knew it hadn't been a fashion choice; Warren likely hid an arsenal beneath it. I slipped my finger between two buttons on his chest. "Is this new?"

"I literally bought it"—he glanced down at the tactical watch tucked under his sleeve—"forty-seven minutes ago. Adrianne told me to dress up."

"You look amazing."

"*You* look amazing," he said. "And you look cold. Let's go inside."

I grabbed his hand to stop him. "Wait. Before we go in, I need to tell you something." Over dinner was not how I wanted to tell him about the baby and waiting till after wouldn't be an option given my new affinity for chocolate as an appetizer.

Concern flashed in his eyes. "What's going on?"

Standing in front of him, I sucked in a deep breath and held it.

"Sloan?"

Say it.

"Warren, I'm pregnant."

His face froze.

"Warren?"

Nothing.

I stepped to the side, but his eyes stayed fixed on the spot I'd vacated. I waved my hand in front of his face. "Warren?"

He blinked twice, his mouth gaping. "You're pregnant?"

I nodded.

"Pregnant?"

I nodded again. "I didn't want to tell you inside with everyone."

His gaze fell to our feet. "Are you sure?"

"She's due in July."

"She?" His voice broke.

I shrugged. "Your father says it's a girl."

His eyes doubled in size and he angled his ear toward me. "My *father?*"

Crap.

I covered my mouth with my hands. "Oh, geez. Warren, we have so much we have to talk about."

He looked around the courtyard. "I think I need to sit down."

Behind us was a waist-high wall built in a semicircle. I tugged him toward it. "Here."

Carefully, he sat down on top of the bricks, and I stood wringing my cold hands in front of him. "I'm sorry this is a lot of overwhelming information to dump on you."

He held up his index finger. "One thing at a time. Are you really pregnant?"

"Yes. I'm sorry I didn't tell you sooner. I didn't figure it out till you were gone." I put my hands over my stomach. "Please don't be mad."

In an instant, he was on his feet in front me. He gripped my hands in his and held them against his chest. "Sloan, I could never be mad about that." He blinked back tears. "I'm going to be a dad."

"Yeah." I laughed and burst out crying at the same time.

Warren pulled me into his arms and kissed me, his tears mixing with mine. He was breathless when he pulled away. "This is the absolute best news I could come home to. I love you so much."

I gathered the fabric of his jacket in my hands. "I love you too."

His large hand rested against my stomach, and the baby fluttered again.

I laughed. "I think she's kicking."

His eyes whipped up to meet mine. "Really? I can't feel anything."

"I think it's too soon. I never felt her before tonight."

"Are you feeling OK? Have you been sick?" he asked.

I sighed. "Honestly, with all the drama, there's not been much time for normal pregnancy stuff. But I'm healthy, and so is she, I think."

"She," he whispered.

Gripping his forearm with one hand, I pointed back to the restaurant with the other. Our party was watching us intently on the other side of the glass. "The guy next to Adrianne is Azrael."

Warren's shoulders dropped and his jaw slowly opened.

"He's your father," I said.

All the blood drained from Warren's handsome face. He ran his fingers over his head, raking his hair back till it stood on end and then fell in different directions.

"He showed up a few weeks ago and has been taking care of me," I said.

"How did he find you?" he asked, still staring at Azrael.

I tightened my grip on his arm. "He says he's been watching you your entire life. He came straight here when he found out about the baby."

Warren looked up at the sky and blew out a long sigh. "This is a lot to take in. A baby and a father in five minutes."

"I'm sorry." I tugged on his sleeve. "Let's go meet him."

His Adam's apple bobbed with a hard swallow. He nodded. "OK."

I'd never thought it was possible for Warren Parish to look nervous. I was wrong. Before we walked through the door, he pulled me to stop. "Do you trust him?" he asked. "We've not had such good luck with biological parents."

"Well, he could have killed me plenty of times since he got here and he didn't." I shrugged. "He's a bit unconventional, but he's not like Kasyade."

Warren relaxed. "Thank God." He gazed through the window again. "Did he tell you anything about *my* mother?"

I laced my fingers between his and hesitated.

He looked down at me. "She's dead, isn't she?"

I nodded and squinted up at him. "How did you know?"

His eyes darted from mine. "Do you remember that I can see the number of people a person has killed?"

My shoulders sagged with the weight of the statement I knew he was about to make next. "Yes."

"Every time I look in the mirror, I see one death I can't account for." He looked at the ground. "I've always wondered if somehow I killed her."

I squeezed his hand. "There were complications when you were born. She loved you too much to be separated from you."

His jaw was set, and he nodded stiffly, still not meeting my eyes.

I stretched up on my tip-toes and kissed his cool cheek. "Come on. Let's go in." I pushed the door open, and he followed me inside.

Azrael stood as we approached the table and when they were face to face, Azrael extended his hand. "Hello, Warren."

When their hands touched, Warren straightened with a jolt.

Azrael's lips spread into a thin smile. "It's nice to finally meet you, son."

Warren cleared his throat. "Uh…it's nice to meet you too." His tone wasn't convincing. The pleasantry sounded like it needed a question mark at the end. Warren was studying his father's face like he was preparing for a quiz, and Azrael was having one of those rare moments where he genuinely looked happy.

Realizing the two men were both too stunned or awkward to speak, Adrianne broke the silence by getting up and pushing her way in between them. She threw her arms around Warren's neck. "Welcome home, Warren!"

He pulled back and smiled at her. "Thank you, Adrianne." He reached back for my hand. "And thank you for being my co-conspirator in all this."

"I'm just glad it all worked out so you could come. Sorry I couldn't warn you about everything else." She gestured between me and Azrael.

"I'm a little impressed you kept your mouth shut," I said.

She put a hand on her hip. "You didn't make it easy with all your moping around lately."

My eyes flashed at her, and I bit down on the insides of my mouth. The last thing I wanted to discuss right then was my McNamara-induced funk.

Adrianne took the hint. "She's been absolutely miserable without you, Warren."

He pulled me under his arm and kissed the side of my forehead. "I know the feeling."

I noticed the empty chair next to mine. "Where's Taiya?"

"Who?" Warren asked.

My gaze followed the direction of Azrael's finger across the room.

She was making her way across the dining room with a salad plate piled high with deviled eggs. I couldn't help but smile.

Taiya froze when she looked up and saw Warren. Her cheeks flushed red and her hands went limp, spilling the eggs from her plate and sending them bouncing across the tiles. She dropped to her knees, crouching behind the tablecloth of an empty table near us.

"Taiya?" I called out.

She gathered up a few scattered eggs and peeked between the tables at us.

"*Por ata dova, Taiya,*" Azrael called out. "*Misha forste Warren.*"

The surrounding patrons were mortified. Either by Azrael's strange language or probably by the grown woman crawling under the tables of the four-star establishment.

"*Por ata dova,*" Azrael said again.

"What's going on?" Warren whispered in my ear.

I pointed to Taiya. "She's a little skittish."

"Who is she?" Warren asked.

I sighed. "She's a long story. Her name is Taiya. She's Seramorta like us."

His head snapped back. "Really?"

"Yeah. She showed up in town around Thanksgiving," I said, purposefully omitting a lot of details. "She's the daughter of one of Kasyade's cohorts named Ysha. She's with us now. I think."

"Kasyade has cohorts?" The alarm in his voice was obvious.

"Two of them, unfortunately." I looked up at him. "We have a lot to talk about."

"I'll say."

"Be right back." I walked down the aisle, picking up stray eggs as I passed them. When I reached the last table before the salad buffet station, I lifted the skirt of the tablecloth and peeked under it. "Taiya."

She was hiding her red face behind her hands.

"What are you doing under here?" I asked.

She shook her head wildly.

I reached under for her arm. "Come on. Come meet Warren."

"*Keshtaka mi noviombre uta.*"

I had no idea what she was saying. "Come on," I said again. "You'll love him."

"Love him," she softly echoed.

"That's right." My fingers found her wrist. Gently, I pulled her out from under the table.

As she stood upright, she swiped an egg off the floor and stuffed it into her mouth before I could stop her. I almost puked on my shoes. I steered her by the shoulders back to our table, apologizing to each table on the way for the scene we'd created.

Taiya pushed back against me when we got closer to Warren.

I looked over his shoulder. "Taiya, this is Warren."

"Hello," he said, offering her his hand.

She tugged the collar of her shirt up over her face and squealed.

Adrianne giggled. "Look at her. She's totally crushing on him."

"Of course she is," I said. "He's beautiful."

Warren rolled his eyes.

Azrael pointed at Warren. "She's probably been told her whole life that she'll be with him, remember?"

"What?" Warren asked.

My heart sank. "Oh, that's sad." I looked at Warren. "You'll have to let her down easy."

Warren tossed his hands into the air. "What the hell are you guys talking about?"

Adrianne walked around the table and took Taiya's hand. "I'm going to go fix her a plate while you start explaining to your poor boyfriend what all is going on." She looked over at Warren. "I hope you brought something to take notes with."

Azrael and I took turns filling Warren in on the details about Taiya, Ysha, and Phenex. I told him about the FBI investigating me and about Azrael pulling me out of the river. Azrael spoke about the angel world and about teaching me to use my powers. We talked about the baby and the demon's plan to kill me in the summer. By the time I finished my chocolate mousse, Warren's head was resting in his hands with his elbows propped up on the table.

I squeezed his knee under the table. "I'm sure this overload isn't what you had planned for tonight."

He looked up and chuckled. "I really expect no less from you, my dear." He crossed his arms on the tabletop. "I do have another question though."

"What?" I asked.

"Where's Nate?"

My mouth snapped shut. Adrianne stopped chewing. Azrael's face was set like stone. Taiya was swirling ketchup into her mashed potatoes.

Warren glanced around the table. "OK, this can't be good. Where is he?"

There was another beat of awkward silence.

"Ice fishing!" Adrianne blurted out.

We all looked at her.

"He went on an ice fishing trip to..." She looked at Azrael for help.

"Alaska?" Azrael said.

Adrianne nodded. "Yes. Alaska."

Now it was my turn to want to crawl under the table.

Warren raised a skeptical eyebrow. "Alaska?"

"He won a trip on the radio," Adrianne added.

Oh, geez. It wasn't any wonder that we never got away with breaking curfew in high school.

It was obvious that Warren was debating calling us all out at the table or trusting that our lie was with good reason. He pointed across the room. "I'm going to go get some more prime rib. Anybody need anything?"

I slouched in my chair. "No, thank you."

He was still eyeing me curiously as he got up from the table.

When he was out of earshot, I glared at Adrianne. "Ice fishing? Really?"

She held up her hands. "It's the first thing that popped into my head."

Groaning, I buried my face in my hands.

Adrianne smacked me across the top of my head. "Don't you dare spoil his first night back with your guilty conscience."

Knowing the Angel of Death would have a strong opinion, I turned my gaze to him.

Azrael shook his head. "She's right. He's been through enough tonight. Wait till tomorrow, but you'd better tell him soon. This kind of news only festers with time."

When Warren returned with his second plate of beef and mashed potatoes, I was anxious to avoid revisiting the subject of Nathan's phony fishing trip. "Can you tell us now where you've been?"

Warren scanned the room, then lowered his voice. "We were right about them sending me after the terrorist in Lebanon." He looked over at me. "But we were wrong about him being a demon. He was dead."

"Really?" I asked.

Warren nodded. "And he'd been dead for quite a while when I found him. They believe he was killed by a US drone months ago."

Adrianne seemed confused. "Why would they send you across the world for a dead guy?"

Warren sliced into his meat. "They weren't a hundred percent sure they'd killed him since his terrorist organization keeps releasing propaganda with his name and picture on it. Now that the US has his body, the organization loses a lot of their power."

I drummed my nails on the tabletop. "It seems strange they would send you of all people in the military."

Warren shrugged. "I found all those bodies Billy Stewart hid in the mountains. I guess they figured I knew what I was doing."

"Will they discharge you now?" Azrael asked.

Warren nodded. "This week I'll process out. They said we'll be back home by Christmas Eve."

"And be done for good?" I asked, perking up in my seat.

He reached over and squeezed my hand. "And be done for good."

* * *

When dinner was finished, the five of us walked out to the parking lot. Warren tried to put his arm around me as we ducked into the cold, but Taiya wedged herself between us and held onto my arm. When he tried to talk to her, she giggled and slipped around my back to my other side. It was adorable, and a little sad.

"Did you drive here?" I asked as we neared Adrianne's car.

He pointed to a gray sedan parked at the end of the row. "I rented a car this morning."

I split a glance between Adrianne and Azrael. "I want to ride with Warren, so we'll see you at the house."

Warren's hand tightened around mine. "No you won't."

I looked up at him. "I won't?"

He laughed. "If you don't mind, I'd like to have you all to myself for tonight. I've made other plans. *Private* plans."

My heart quickened at the thought.

Azrael shook his head. "That's not possible."

Warren's brow lifted, and he was trying and almost succeeding at suppressing the smirk on his face. "No offense, *Dad*, but I didn't ask you."

I bit down on the insides of my lips.

Adrianne's eyes widened.

Azrael took a step toward his son. It was creepy how much they looked alike. "Warren, things are not the same as you left them. Sloan is in danger and she needs—"

Warren held up his hand. "I'll be the judge of what she needs. Tonight, she's spending with me, so you might as well save your breath."

The two stared at each other with so much intensity I worried one or both of their heads might start smoking at any second.

Warren finally pointed at Adrianne. "She knows where to find us if there's an emergency, and we won't be too far from home."

The muscles around Azrael's eyes softened just enough to make it clear he knew he'd lost the argument. He looked at me. "Keep your phone on. If the weather changes or if you dream, call me at once."

Warren pulled me close. "I don't intend on letting her sleep."

There was a small squeak in the back of my throat, and I hid my face behind my hands.

"I mean it," Azrael snapped.

Still cringing with embarrassment, I nodded. "I promise."

Warren wrapped his hand around mine and pulled me in the direction of his car before anyone could say anything else.

"You two have fun!" Adrianne called after us.

I waved back over my shoulder.

When we got to the car, Warren opened my door. "Is he always like that?"

"Hard-headed and argumentative?" I laughed as I got into the car. "You haven't seen anything yet."

* * *

Warren had booked a king sized room at the Inn on Biltmore Estate, just up the road from the Deerpark. It had only been open a couple of years, and I'd never been inside it. Like every other property on the lavish estate, the Inn was fit for American royalty with a grand mix of gothic elegance and contemporary comfort. To be honest, I felt a little out of place as we walked up to the registration counter to check in.

"You're fidgeting," Warren said, leaning against the marble counter.

I hadn't realized I was. Perhaps it was the ritzy hotel. Or maybe it was my nerves about the whole thing with Nathan. Hell, maybe it was the ungodly amount of sugar I'd consumed at dinner.

He ran his fingers down my arm. "Would you be more comfortable at home? I should've asked that earlier."

I snuggled under his arm. "No way. This is wonderful. Thank you for planning something so special."

He looked down at me, his face a mix of concern and hesitation. "I feel like we need to talk about stuff."

"I won't lie and say we don't, but I'd rather save it for later. It's nothing that can't wait till tomorrow."

He was obviously skeptical. "Are you sure?"

I smiled. "I promise."

Our room was on the third floor. It had an oversized mahogany bed with a pristine white comforter and fluffy white pillows. There were two leather wingback chairs with footstools facing the private terrace which I was sure had a glorious view of the mountains in the daylight.

Behind me, Warren wrapped his arms around my waist. "I missed you, Sloan."

I covered his arms with my own. "I missed you too, so very much."

He pressed warm kisses to the side of my neck sending tingles rippling down my spine as his fingers worked loose the buttons on the front of my winter coat. Slowly, he peeled it back off my shoulders before draping it over the back of one of the chairs. His hands slid across the smooth fabric covering my stomach.

"I still can't believe you're pregnant," he said quietly in my ear.

I turned around in his arms and locked my fingers behind his neck. "Are you ready to be a dad?"

"Nope." He laughed and pulled me closer. "But I'll figure it out."

"I'm sure you will," I said.

He dipped his head and pressed his lips to mine. The room seemed to spin around us as I melted into his strong arms. I had almost forgotten how it felt to be wrapped up with him—like the earth could implode, and it wouldn't even matter. His hands slid down the curves of my back till they settled behind my thighs. He lifted me up until my legs draped across his hips, and my curls spilled down over his shoulders. I cradled his head in my arms as he kissed me. Carefully, he slid one arm behind my back and used the other to brace himself against the bed as he lowered me down onto it.

As he knelt between my legs, he shrugged out of his jacket and tossed it on the chair with mine. He unclasped his double holster, slipped it off his shoulders, and lowered his two guns carefully to the ground. He unbuttoned his shirt and peeled it back off his shoulders. Then with one hand, he reached back between his shoulder blades, grasped his white t-shirt, and tugged it off over his head. Over his chest was a tribal dragon's talon tattooed across his shoulder and down the center of his torso. On his waist, just above the normal resting place for his sidearm, was the name Azrael. I dragged my nails down his stomach till they found the clasp for his black belt. He slid out of his slacks as he bent down over me.

He undressed me slowly, taking extra care to trace every inch of the new landscape of my figure. "You've never been more beautiful," he whispered as he trailed kisses down the center of my tender, swollen breasts to my stomach and then back up again.

Warren was hesitant, nervous even, to cover my body with the full force of his weight, but I pushed his support arm up toward my head forcing him to settle slowly on top of me. He hooked his hand behind my knee and drew my leg up toward his hip. After that, everything swirled out of focus.

* * *

True to his word, Warren didn't let me sleep. Not much anyway. We'd dozed on and off between sweaty bouts of lovemaking. It was the best non-sleep I'd ever had, and that was saying something. My lips were raw and my legs felt like Jell-O by sunrise.

When we pulled up in front of my house, Adrianne's red sports car was still parked at the curb. I frowned. "That's not good."

Warren slid the transmission to park. "She stayed the night?"

"Looks like it," I grumbled.

He looked over at me. "I gather from your tone this isn't exactly great news."

I glared at him.

"You can't protect her from everything," he said.

"I can't protect her from *anything*, Warren. She never listens to me."

He pointed toward the house. "Do you think she needs protecting from him?"

I groaned. "I think best-case scenario is that she'll wind up hurt when he can't give her what she wants."

We walked inside to find Taiya watching cartoons on the couch and no one else around. Upstairs I heard the sound of the shower in the guest bathroom. "Good morning, Taiya," I said as I dropped my purse on the floor with a heavy thud and kicked off my high heels.

Her face broke out in a wide smile when her eyes settled on Warren. He waved, and she ducked her head into her pillow.

"She lives here now too?" he asked, following me to the kitchen to get my prenatal vitamins.

I nodded. "Yeah. It's been a little less crowded since Nathan moved out, but it's still—"

He cut me off. "Nathan was living here?"

My back was to him at the refrigerator so he couldn't see me cringe.

I grabbed the orange juice and carried it to the counter. "I was attacked while I was home alone one night. After that, Nathan moved into the guest room."

Warren pulled out the chair at the dinette table and sat down. "Are you ready to tell me where he really is and not that bullshit story about ice fishing?"

My bottom lip poked out. "No."

He crossed his arms. "Babe, I promise you don't want to leave this one to my imagination."

Sadly, I feared his imagination couldn't be much worse than the truth. But the last thing I wanted was to tell him the truth and then send him away for a few days to stew on it. So, instead, I shook the carton of Tropicana in his direction. "Do you want some orange juice?"

"No, Sloan. I don't want any juice," he said, his voice dark and bordering on anger.

Buying myself a few more seconds of pre-fight peace and happiness, I dropped the vitamin into my mouth and drained the entire glass of juice. When I finished, I washed the glass by hand in the sink, dried it slowly, then tucked it away in the cabinet. When I turned around to look at him, Warren's jaw was twitching. That was never a good sign.

I leaned back against the counter for support. "You asked Nathan to take care of me while you were gone, remember?"

His eyes tightened, and he drew in a deep breath. "Yes."

I looked down at the tiles. "Well, things with us—"

Just then, Adrianne jogged down the stairs wearing a pair of my sweatpants—that only reached half-way down her calves—and one of Azrael's shirts. I was almost too relieved by her interruption to still be mad at her. She froze when she saw us in the kitchen.

I put my hands on my hips. "What are you doing here?"

A sly grin was on her face. "Good morning to you too, sunshine."

I rolled my eyes as she entered the kitchen. "I don't even want to know."

"You probably don't." She winked at me as she grabbed a banana out of the fruit basket. "How was the hotel last night?"

"Really nice," I said. "Have you been there?"

She nodded. "I've done hair for a few bridal parties there."

Warren cleared his throat. "Not to be rude or anything, but Sloan and I are kind of in the middle of something."

Adrianne cringed. "That doesn't sound good."

I jerked my thumb toward the stairs and looked at Warren. "Come on. Let's go talk upstairs in our room."

He got up and walked toward me. Over his shoulder, I saw Adrianne mouth the words *good luck*.

I practiced deep breathing as we crossed the living room.

"Ding dong," Taiya said from the floor.

My eyes widened, and I looked at the door just as the bell rang.

"Did she do that?" Warren asked, confused.

My heart pounded in my chest. I knew somehow I'd slipped up and summoned Nathan McNamara, possibly to his death. Warren must have realized the same thing because we both bolted toward the door at the same time. My hand reached the knob first.

"Sloan, wait!" I heard Azrael shout upstairs.

But it was too late.

I pulled the door open.

It was Agent Silvers…and a team of other officers.

"Sloan Jordan, you're under arrest."

21.

"PLEASE STATE YOUR last name."

My wrists ached from where they'd just removed the handcuffs. I rubbed the red marks left behind. "Jordan."

Agent Silvers looked up from the paper. "And your first name?"

I looked at her in disbelief. "You know my name."

"This is procedural, Ms. Jordan. Please answer the question."

"My first name is Sloan."

"Middle name?"

"Bridgett."

"Can you spell that please?"

"B-R-I-D-G-E-T-T."

"Date of birth?"

"January 24th, 1986."

We went through a list of *procedural* information before Agent Silvers let me go to the bathroom and get some water. I'd cried the entire drive in the back of the unmarked car, until I realized they weren't taking me to jail as I'd assumed. I had driven past the stone and glass building on Patton Avenue a thousand times but had never been inside. Little did I know the FBI field office was housed there.

When we came back into the interrogation room, someone else, a man who looked like he might play golf with my dad, stared at me from across the table. Agent Silvers excused herself and left, closing the door behind her.

The man extended his hand to me. "Hi, Ms. Jordan, I'm Special Agent Elijah Voss. It's nice to meet you. I'm sorry it had to be under these circumstances."

My smile was awkward.

"Ms. Jordan, as you know, we've been investigating Abigail Smith for the past several weeks, and in the course of our investigation, we have discovered substantial evidence that brings us back to you. Now, I'm pretty new on this case, so I'm hoping you can explain to me how an upstanding county employee such as yourself has gotten mixed up in a federal investigation." He smiled. "You have certain rights I'm obligated to advise you of before I talk to you. You have the right to remain silent. Anything you say can and will be used against you in a court of law. You have the right to talk to an attorney before answering any questioning or making any statements now or in the future. If you can't afford an attorney, one will be appointed for you before any questioning if you wish. Do you understand?"

I nodded.

"You can decide at any time to exercise these rights and not answer any questions or make any statements." He folded his hands on top of his notepad and file folder. "Now, knowing and understanding your rights as I have explained them to you, are you willing to answer my questions without an attorney present?"

This is the part where you're supposed to say no.

But I didn't. "Yes."

My curiosity about what evidence they'd come up with outweighed my good sense in the matter.

"How do you know Abigail?"

"I really don't know her well. I met her a couple of times in Texas," I said.

"What took you to Texas?" he asked.

This was one of those questions, I knew I shouldn't answer since we'd already lied about it the first time we met with Agent Silvers. "I'd rather speak to my attorney about that."

He made some notes. "Very well. Will you tell me how you came across the information that led to human trafficking charges being brought against Ms. Smith?"

"She invited me to her home, and while I was there, I was snooping in her office. I found bond paperwork on an individual I knew had been arrested for trafficking," I said. All of that was completely true.

Thin lines of confusion rippled his brow. "Why were you snooping in her office?"

I shrugged my shoulders and kept my mouth shut. The truth was a voice in my head told me to go in there, but that wasn't the sort of thing you tell a detective...or anyone.

"What happened after you found the paperwork?" he asked.

"I heard Abigail on the phone in the other room, and then I left her home," I said.

He tapped his pen against the pad. "What was she saying on the phone?"

"It's in the notes from my previous statement," I said.

"I'd rather you tell me."

I stared back at him. "I'd rather you look them up."

"Are you refusing to answer the question?" he asked.

"Yes."

He looked annoyed, but he didn't say anything. "Are you aware surveillance photos and other information spanning most of your life were found at the residence of Abigail Smith?"

I nodded. "Agent Silvers showed me some of the photos."

"Any guess as to why she would have such information on you?"

I shook my head. "I wish I knew."

While that was true, I also had a very good idea why she would have kept close tabs on me over the years. She'd had a plan my entire life that brought me to where I was presently—pregnant with Warren's kid.

"Where were you on the morning of October 31ˢᵗ?" he asked.

"Halloween," I clarified.

"Yes. Halloween."

That was the day I called Abigail and asked if she was my biological mother. That week, Warren had stayed with my dad while I dipped in and out of my office trying to catch up from being gone and trying to prevent falling even further behind.

"I went into work that morning." I thought for a moment. "I remember sending out something to our newsletter subscribers about trick-or-treating safety."

He made some notes. "What else did you do that day?"

"I left work early—"

"At what time?"

I thought back. "It's hard to remember exactly, but it was probably around four or so. I remember skipping lunch so I could leave early."

"And where did you go?" he asked.

"Back to my father's house. My boyfriend and I stayed with him all week because my mother had just died," I said.

"I'm sorry to hear that. Your boyfriend...Detective Nathan McNamara?"

I rolled my eyes. "No. My boyfriend's name is Warren Parish. I have had a close relationship with Detective McNamara, but I was with Warren on Halloween. We had dinner at the Sunny Point Cafe, then went back to my father's house in time for trick-or-treaters to show up. Oh yeah, and we stopped to buy candy for them on the way home."

"Anything else happen that day?" he asked.

I swallowed. "I spoke to Abigail on the phone. She asked me to come back to Texas for a meeting."

"Did she call you or did you call her?"

This was a test to see if I'd tell the truth. I was sure he'd already seen my phone records.

"I called her."

He blinked with fake surprise. "You called her? Why?"

I shook my head. "I'll only answer that question with my attorney."

For a moment, we stared at each other in a battle of wills. I won, and he looked at his pad of paper again. "Did you visit anywhere else on the day of October 31st?"

"No."

He nodded and made some notes.

"Sloan, where do you bank?"

That was an odd question. "Western Carolina Credit Union, why?"

He glanced up at me. "Do you utilize any other financial service institutions?"

I thought for a second. "I have a deferred compensation retirement plan through my work, plus a Roth IRA through Smithson Investors Services."

"No others?"

I smirked. "Are you planning on freezing my assets or something?"

He just stared at me.

I sank in my chair. "No other institutions. I want to contact an attorney. I won't answer any more questions."

"We haven't even discussed the—"

I cut him off. "I don't care. I'm exercising my rights. I want an attorney."

He closed his notebook. "Very well."

Never in my life had I needed an attorney for anything other than closing on my new house. I knew a few from my dealings with work, but those were generally prosecutors or sleaze bags covered in the media. But my dad knew lots of people, so I called him. When he answered the collect call, he sounded panicked. "Are you OK?" he asked before even saying hello.

"I'm OK. I'm in an interrogation room downtown," I said. "I need you to call Nathan, and I need you to find a federal criminal attorney."

"We've already made some calls. I came to your house as soon as Warren called me. Azrael and Nathan are both here with us as well," he said.

Relief washed over me. "Thank you."

There was some commotion on his end of the line. "Nathan says they'll take you to appear before the federal magistrate and they'll set bail. We'll get you out then."

"OK. Please find someone quickly."

"We will, sweetheart. Be brave."

I heard Nathan in the background. "Keep your mouth shut, Sloan."

"Tell him I will," I said. "I love you, Dad."

"I love you, Sloan. We'll figure this out."

"I know." I almost believed it too.

When I hung up the phone, Agent Silvers returned to the room. "Were you able to contact an attorney?" she asked.

"My father's handling it," I answered. "When will I see the magistrate?"

A thin smile spread across her painted lips as she looked down at her watch. "In a few days once you're back in Texas."

My heartbeat quickened. "Texas?"

"Correct. Your transport has already been arranged."

My lower lip quivered. "What will happen to me until then?"

She walked toward the door, then paused and looked back over her shoulder. "I think you're familiar with the Buncombe County Jail."

* * *

By the time we reached the Buncombe County Jail well after midnight, I was in the fetal position in the back of the car. Rather than parking in the front lot and going through the main doors, we were admitted through a high gate covered in barbed wire to a back covered entrance I'd never seen before. The car door opened, and one of the male federal officers pulled me out by my handcuffs. My legs faltered and before I could get my feet underneath me, my knees buckled and slammed into the concrete.

"I'll take it from here!" an angry voice shouted.

A man hooked his arms under mine and hoisted me to my feet. I recognized his face but didn't know his name. His eyes were full of confusion and pity. "Are you OK?" he asked quietly in my ear.

All I could do was shake my head.

"I've got you," he said, wrapping an arm around my waist to help me walk. "Baynard, get me a wheelchair!"

They helped me sit down and wheeled me inside.

Movement in the far corner of the room caught my attention. "Sloan!"

My blurry eyes focused on Nathan just as two deputies caught him by the chest to prevent him from reaching me.

"Get him out of here!" a gruff voice I didn't recognize barked from a nearby hallway.

"We're working on getting you out of here!" Nathan shouted before he was forced through a door and out of my view.

The deputy who had brought me in wheeled my chair up to a tall counter and handcuffed my arm to it.

Behind us, there were murmurings from the federal agents warning the deputies about procedures and preferential treatment. The woman behind the counter looked terrified to talk to me. I didn't know her, but it was obvious she knew me. And judging from the whispers and wide eyes around the room, she wasn't the only one.

She slid a sheet of paper and a pen toward me. The top of the page read *Female Inmate Intake Form*. I shuddered. "Please fill this out," she said.

There was an entire section about pregnancy. I snorted at the line, *Is your pregnancy high risk?*

When I was finished, she placed a clear plastic box in front of me. "Ms. Jordan, I need you to place all your personal belongings inside this container for inventory."

They hadn't even allowed me to change out of my dress before taking me into custody, so I took off all my jewelry and put it in the box.

"I'll need your shoes as well," she added.

I slipped off my heels and dropped them into the box. The deputy who had gotten the wheelchair brought a pair of rubber, slide-on flip-flops. He knelt down and slipped them onto my bare feet. He stood and un-cuffed me from the counter, then helped me to my feet.

"We need to get your photos," he explained. "Can you walk?"

I nodded but leaned heavily on his arm for support.

He backed me up against a wall marked with measurements for height and took a step back. Another woman tapped a webcam positioned on top of a computer. "Please look here, Ms. Jordan," she said.

When my mugshots were finished, they took me to a computer that electronically scanned my fingerprints. "Your dad treated my grandmother last year," the deputy at the computer said.

I tried to smile.

After he clicked a few more buttons, he motioned toward a woman standing behind me. "Deputy Knox will take you back to shower and change," he said.

I shook my head. "I don't need a shower."

He grimaced. "It's policy. You don't have a choice."

Deputy Knox took my arm. "This way, Sloan."

Her tone caught my attention, and I looked at her. Her name when I'd known her had been Kellie Bryant. "Kellie?" I asked.

She cast her gaze at the floor.

Ten years before, Kellie had been on the high school cheerleading squad with me and Adrianne. We had shared a lab table in Advanced Placement Chemistry and had ridden the same school bus before her family moved to Arden. Now she was escorting me across the booking room toward a curtained hallway wearing rubber gloves. That could only mean one thing.

"Do you want me to get someone else?" she asked, still refusing to meet my eyes.

My chin was quivering. "No. Thank you, though."

Once we were behind the curtain, she stood behind me and held my arms out to the side. She proceeded to thoroughly canvas my body, from my ears to my ankles. "Turn around, please," she said.

I turned to face her, and she lifted my arms up again. Then she completely patted down my front, swiping under my boobs and between my legs. I refused to cry, but I'd never been so mortified and shamed in all my life. That is, until she instructed me to disrobe, squat...and cough.

"I'm so sorry," she whispered.

I stood back up, covering myself as much as I could with my arms.

She motioned to a concrete shower with no curtain and a chipped floor behind her. "Step into the shower and use the lice shampoo. Everyone has to do it. It will sit on your hair for three minutes, and then you can wash it out. There's regular shampoo in there you can use after."

I nodded my understanding.

"Your dress and undergarments will be inventoried with the rest of your things," she said. "You'll get them back when you leave."

I thought about telling her she could just trash the dress, but in that moment, I wanted nothing more than that expensive ugly garbage bag.

My teeth chattered as I soaked my head under the ice-cold water. Then, naked and shivering, I leaned against the concrete wall while the lice shampoo burned into my scalp. I slid down the concrete blocks and wrapped my arms around my legs, my tears mixing with the suds as I cried into my knees.

When I was finished, Kellie waited for me with a white cotton sports bra and panties, a white thermal undershirt, a pair of drawstring orange pants and matching top, thick white socks, and black slide flip-flops. As I pulled up the orange pants, I noticed the elastic strain as it went up over my belly.

How lovely.

My first memory of my baby bump would be forever tainted with the scent of lice killer and the cold steel of handcuffs.

22.

WHEN I WAS a child, maybe four or five, I had a horrific nightmare after attending an Easter egg hunt at my Aunt Joan's church. Twenty years later, graphic details of that dream were crystal clear in my memory.

I was dragged to the basement of the building by a scaly creature with a forked tongue and razor-sharp claws. It had glowing amber eyes and smelled of sulfur, rotten eggs. The thing slithered through a door, slamming me against the doorframe as we moved.

I knew there were hundreds of people on the floor above the basement, but something invisible, with the weight of a thousand bricks, was crushing my windpipe. I couldn't scream.

With a violent fling, I was slammed against the cold, wet tiles of a bathroom. They were tiny tiles, maybe an inch in size, and they were green, a fluorescent lime that gave the room a sinister glow. Something sticky was splattered on the tiles; I assumed it was blood, but it had the consistency of tar and the tackiness of superglue. In my discarded heap, I was paralyzed, unable to move. Or run. Or fight.

The creature opened a long box—a vertical, wide coffin, maybe—that was nailed to the wall in front of me. Inside it, were my parents, seemingly made of stone with their eyes fixed but full of terror. Hot tears stung my cheeks, but I couldn't cry because I couldn't breathe.

Helpless and screaming on the inside, I watched the creature use its claw to dissect the body of my mother first. Her dripping bowels splashed into a puddle of blood on the floor. I could feel her pain. Every bit of it, but there was nothing I could do to save her—or save myself.

That panic. That nightmare. That feeling—magnified tenfold—was what the inside of my cell at the Buncombe County Jail felt like. All night long. It was an all-consuming nightmare from which I could not escape.

Because of the baby and my hysteria, I wasn't put into the general population. I was put in a cell on the medical floor, as far away from the other inmates as possible, but that was little consolation. Under my metal bed, I curled into a ball with the itchy down pillow clamped down tight over my head. My face was slick against the polished concrete floor, resting in a pool of tears, snot, and saliva.

For hours and hours, I couldn't stop the shaking.

At some point, I heard my name. "Sloan? Sloan, can you hear me?"

Prying open one of my eyes, I saw the face of Virginia Claybrooks peeking under my bed. Her hand closed around my wrist, yanking me along the smooth floor out into the halogen light of my cell. She plopped down on her backside and pulled my head into her lap. Stroking my hair, she quietly sang a song I'd never heard.

"When peace, like a river, attendeth my way, when sorrows like sea billows roll; whatever my lot, Thou hast taught me to say, it is well, it is well with my soul..."

I tried to focus on her words, but the melody was like a baby's mobile lullaby chiming in a horror house.

"The sheriff is coming," someone said.

Virginia flinched.

Heavy footfalls echoed down the hall, then a gruff male voice was in the room. "Virginia, you aren't authorized to be in here."

"I know that, Sheriff, but you can't blame me," Virginia said. "So fire me if you want. I ain't sorry."

He grunted his disapproval. "Go on now," he said. "Get out of here before I have to put you in handcuffs."

Squeezing her shin as much as I could, I moved off her lap back to the cold tiles.

The sheriff dropped to a knee beside me. "Sloan, are you all right?"

I wanted to scream at him, *Do I look all right?* But I couldn't, and I wouldn't.

"Do you have meds you need to be taking?" he asked.

It was a fair question because I was acting like a lunatic. I was sure my doctor would have deemed this a "Xanax-essential" situation, but I shook my head.

"They tell me you're not eating or drinking any fluids. That's not healthy for you or the baby. You know that," he said.

Honestly, I hadn't even noticed.

"McNamara's been here all night, of course, but you know I can't let him back here to see you," he said. "Your lawyer just got here, so you'll see him in a little while."

I pulled my knees up to my chest. "Thank you," I whispered.

He squeezed my hand where it lay on the floor. "I hate this, Sloan. I wish you the best of luck."

Before he left, he took the blanket off my bed and draped it over me.

A little while later, I heard footsteps again. "Jordan," a man said.

I forced myself to look up.

The deputy didn't look old enough to be a deputy. "Ms. Jordan, I need to cuff you to take you down to see your attorney. Can you come put your hands through this slot in the door?"

It took a few tries and several deep breathing exercises to get me off the floor. When I finally made it to the door, I stuck my hands through it and let him put handcuffs back on my bruised wrists.

The kid held onto my arm as we shuffled down the hallway. He smelled of Axe Body Spray and had teenage boy acne and a taser. I felt very safe.

We turned a corner and stopped in front of a bright white room. Inside, a man with strawberry blond hair and pale skin was looking through a file folder on the table in front of him. Alarm bells went off in my head. *Not human. Not human. Not human.*

Then the man looked up and ice ran through my veins when I locked on his eyes. They were striking blue, the same color as Taiya's.

Ysha.

The boy-deputy urged me forward, but I dug the heels of my flip-flops against the concrete floor. "Ms. Jordan, I need you to move your feet," he said, looking at me like I was crazy. Maybe I was.

The angel stood when we entered. He was dressed in a tailored, navy suit and tie. A briefcase was laying on the table with pens and a legal pad. He certainly looked the part of a lawyer.

"Let me get those," the deputy said, snapping me out of a fearful daze. He turned me toward him and removed the handcuffs.

"Are you leaving me in here?" I whispered.

He nodded. "Attorney-client privilege. Your meeting will be videotaped, but there will be no audio recording."

I rubbed my aching wrists as he backed out the room, closing the door behind him. A clock on the wall said it was almost four. I'd already spent all night and all day in jail.

"Good evening, Sloan." The angel's voice was deep and melodic, and even though I was terrified of him, his simple presence calmed my nerves.

Slowly, I turned to face him, and he extended his hand. I didn't accept it; I took a step back.

He squeezed a fist and dropped it to his side. "My name is Abner Tuinstra. Azrael sent me today when you were arrested."

"You're lying," I said, stepping back into the corner.

He studied me for a moment, then his face split into a creepy smile. "What makes you say that?"

"I know who you are," I said.

He unbuttoned his jacket and sat down. "And who is it that you think I am?"

"You're Ysha, aren't you?" I asked.

He smiled again. "How did you know?"

Azrael could have mentioned Ysha was a man, not a woman as I'd assumed. Maybe gender was an extraneous detail in the supernatural world.

"I know your daughter, Taiya."

His head bowed slightly. "Ahh, yes. My little half-wit puppet. How is she?"

I could have clawed his perfect eyeballs out. "You destroyed her."

"Oh, nonsense," he said. "I made her better."

"Better?"

He sighed and folded his hands together on the tabletop. "Humans are so much more efficient after they've been broken down and rebuilt. Empires have been conquered on the backs of broken humans. Ask that military boyfriend of yours."

"But there's no sense in what you did to her."

"I don't do anything without reason, Sloan. You have no idea what I have planned for my daughter."

"You're sick," I said.

"I've been called worse." He motioned to the chair across from him. "Please have a seat, Sloan." His eyes snapped up. "Or should I call you Praea?"

My jaw clenched. "My name is Sloan."

"Your mother would argue," he replied. "But it doesn't matter. Please sit."

I shook my head. "No."

He glared at me. "You're of no use to me dead, my dear. I won't hurt you." He pulled a file folder from his briefcase. "I do, however, have a copy of your arrest paperwork. I'm sure you're curious to see it."

He was right.

"How do you have it?" I asked.

The angel turned his palms up. "I'm an attorney."

"A real attorney?"

"Of course." He touched the ID wallet hanging around his neck. "Would you like to see my Bar Association credentials?"

I sucked in a deep breath.

He offered me the folder. "Take this then."

Ysha must have realized that, even for the paperwork, I wouldn't budge from my spot in the corner. He opened the folder and took out the papers. "Shall I read it?" When I didn't respond, he nodded. "It's quite a list: conspiracy to commit sex trafficking, conspiracy to harbor aliens, money laundering, forgery, obstruction, perjury…"

My mouth fell open. "But that's not true! How can they arrest me for something there's no proof of? You and I both know I had nothing to do with that."

"Do we?" The pleasure on his face was grotesque.

"What?" I asked.

He flipped to another sheet of paper. "According to this affidavit, there is video surveillance footage of you entering the Asheville Savings and Trust on Merrimon Avenue at 10:19 AM on Thursday, October 31st in the company of Abigail Smith."

"What the hell?" I shouted.

"Apparently, you opened a safe deposit box." Abner rifled through some paperwork, then slid a sheet of paper toward me. "Is this your signature?"

It was.

"I never visited any bank or opened any safe deposit box!"

He read over another sheet of paper. "Inside the box, they found a forged passport with your photograph, a new Texas driver's license, a new social security card"—he looked up at me—"and a hundred thousand dollars in cash."

I gripped the side of my face. "What is happening?"

And then it hit me.

I heard Abigail's voice in my head when she was talking to me about how she raped my biological father. *"When I summon someone for a purpose, they often don't remember it."*

I slid down the wall till my knees touched my chin.

Abner stood and walked around the table, sitting on the corner of it. "This is quite the predicament you're in, isn't it?"

Refusing to cry, I glared up at him. "So this is your master plan? Plant evidence to have me locked up while I'm pregnant?"

He shook his head. "No. It had been our hope you would come willingly, but I must say, this is one hell of a backup plan." He chuckled as he swung his leg back and forth. "With this evidence, you'll certainly be denied bail once you get to Texas, and when the case goes to trial, it will be a slam-dunk for the prosecution. Then we wait till that precious little asset growing in your womb doesn't need you anymore, and you'll officially be"—he held up his hands—"case closed."

I wanted to throw up. "Did you just come here to torture me?"

He glanced up at the halogen lights, then back down at me on the floor. "Yes."

Slowly, I rose to my feet. "I don't have to listen to this." I banged my fist against the door. The deputy opened it. "Please take me back to my cell," I said holding my wrists toward him.

He looked surprised.

I glanced over my shoulder at the demon. "And please tell Sheriff Davis not to allow Mr. Tuinstra in here again to see me."

The lawyer stood, shaking his head as he closed his briefcase. He walked past us as the deputy put me in handcuffs. He winked at my jailer. "Some prisoners don't know when they've been beaten, do they, son?"

The kid seemed too confused to answer.

Abner walked down the hall. "I'll see you soon, Sloan."

"Go to hell, Ysha."

He cackled till he was out of sight.

* * *

I spent the next twenty minutes vomiting bile into my metal commode.

My assumption about Abigail being with another angel during her travels had been correct, except instead of Ysha or Phenex...it was me. And with no way to argue otherwise, I would spend the rest of my life in prison. Not the county jail. Federal prison.

That is if I survived giving birth which was more doubtful than ever.

For hours, I prayed for sleep to come. It never did. Each time I closed my eyes, the room would spin and the nausea would return. Somewhere a woman was screaming, and I couldn't tell if it was inside the jail or only inside my head. Sweat soaked through my clothes and bed sheets.

Sometime, when all was quiet, I heard the bolt of the cell door slide open. I prayed whoever it was would kill me and end my misery.

Instead, I felt a hand on my back. Tingling warmth spread through me and immediately my nerves began to settle. I inhaled the deepest breath I'd taken in hours and blew it out slowly.

When I looked up, a pair of sapphire eyes sparkled down at me in the faint glow of the security lights.

It was Taiya.

I pushed myself up to face her. She was wearing the same jail issued uniform that I was. "What are you doing here?"

She smiled and pushed my matted hair out of my face. "Help."

I grabbed the crazy waif and hugged her. "Thank you."

When I pulled back, she stood and pointed to the open cell door. "Go."

Shaking my head, I gulped. "Taiya, we can't go!"

Her eyes widened, and she raised her hands in question. "Stay?" she asked, genuinely puzzled.

Wait. Who am I talking to? "Let's get out of here, Houdini."

Taiya was truly a master at getting out of places. She knew when to hide, when to duck security cameras, and most importantly...how to open locked doors without a key. She took me down a couple of hallways I'd never visited and out a side emergency door. She was even able to silence the alarm.

We were in the yard but still behind a locked security fence when I felt the presence of two humans coming toward us. Back inside was the only way to go, and that wasn't an option. She looked at me with wide eyes. "Run."

Grabbing my hand, she bolted in the direction I'd felt the people coming. I had no choice but to follow. We turned a corner and passed two unsuspecting guards who were sharing a cigarette as they patrolled the grounds. Immediately, they were shouting and running after us, but Taiya didn't slow or stop. She ran directly toward the huge gate meant for vehicles.

She threw her hands toward it and slowly it slid open. She jerked my arm forward, pulling me in front of her. "Run!" she screamed again.

I raced through the gate but looked back in time to see Taiya tackle the two guards, clotheslining them with her outstretched arms.

I'd been in the parking lot of the jail a million times but never at night and never running like a madwoman on foot. As fast as my feet would carry me, I ran toward the street. Suddenly, headlights flickered on behind me accompanied by the loud roar of a souped-up engine.

My jail-issued flip-flops pounded the asphalt as the car raced up next to me. It was Warren's black Dodge Challenger.

The driver's side window slid down. "Good evening, ma'am, would you like a ride?"

It was Nathan.

23.

NEVER IN MY life was I a rule breaker. I'd never so much as gotten a detention in school or even let a library book go overdue. But getting in the passenger side of that getaway car was the easiest choice I ever made. Once my seatbelt was fastened, Nathan stepped on the gas, slamming my head back against the leather headrest. "Hang on!"

The car's tires screamed around the right turn onto College Street, then laid rubber tracks down as we cut a left onto Charlotte. A half a second later, we were barreling down Interstate 240, and I turned to look behind us. No one was following. The city planners certainly hadn't put a lot of forethought into the road system when they built the jail.

Nathan was furiously shifting gears and checking the rearview mirror. He relaxed a tad when he merged onto Interstate 40 East, and still no one was behind us. He grasped my hand. "Are you OK?"

"Oh my god! You broke me out of jail!" I leaned over the middle console and wrapped my arms around his neck. "Oh my god! Thank you, thank you, thank you!"

"Technically, Taiya broke you out," he said.

I covered my mouth with my hands. "Oh no. They got her."

He glanced over at me. "Something tells me, she won't be there for long."

I planted a loud, wet kiss on his cheek. "You're my hero."

He shook his head and checked the rearview mirror again. "Don't call me that till we get out of this mess," he said.

I gasped. "They're gonna know it was you. Nathan, you're going to lose your job."

He laughed. "Sloan, if they catch us, I won't have to worry about a job because I'll be in jail."

"Where's Warren?" I asked.

Nathan checked the rearview. "We'll see him shortly." He jerked his thumb back over his shoulder. "In the back is a bag with some clothes in it and your purse."

I found the backpack in the back floorboard, and I pulled out my purse that was laying on top in the main compartment. I dug around inside it for my phone.

"Where's my cell?" I asked.

"At home. Those things can be tracked." He looked over at me. "My sweatshirt is in that bag. You're going to need it."

I pulled out the black S.W.A.T. team hoodie that was inside. In any other situation, I would've at least laughed, but about that time, blue lights flashed inside our car. I squealed with panic as I yanked the sweatshirt over my head.

Nathan pressed the gas again. "You buckled?"

I clicked the belt back into place. "Yes."

"Good."

The engine roared as we sped down the interstate, weaving around the few cars we passed. There were more flashing lights behind us, but they were pretty far off in the distance, and they kept disappearing around the hills and curves through the mountains. Nathan took the exit to Black Mountain. It was a death trap of dangerous roads, but I kept my mouth shut till he dipped off the shoulder of the road and began driving through a field.

"Have you lost your mind?" I shouted, gripping the handle above my door.

"Obviously so," he answered.

Just then, up ahead of us, lights descended from above. I bent and looked up to see a helicopter lowering toward the tall grass. "Where the hell did you get a helicopter?"

"Long story. When we stop, get ready to run," he said. "And bring the bag because that may be the only change of clothes you get for a while."

He slammed down hard on the brakes when we were closer, throwing me toward the dashboard. I cursed and caught myself with my arms.

"Go! Go! Go!" he was screaming.

Hugging the backpack to my chest, I pushed my door open and was knocked backward by the force of the wind from the propellers. Nathan grabbed my hand as we ran toward the chopper. The machine was as black as the night around us, except for the lights and the shiny gold letters down the tail: *Claymore.*

Claymore Worldwide Security had employed Warren as a mercenary till he quit and moved in with me.

A man dressed all in black tactical clothes with an assault rifle slung across his chest, jumped down to the ground. Before I even saw his painted black face, I knew it was Warren. He grabbed my face and studied me for a second, relief evident in his eyes. Then he thrust me up into the open door on the side of the helicopter.

Nathan, who had already gotten in, pulled me up beside him. Warren climbed in behind me as Nathan pushed me into the very back seat. Warren closed the door, just as headlights and flashing blue lights lit up the field.

"Put these on!" Nathan shouted over the noise, handing me a headset.

Obediently, I slipped it over my head as he dropped into the seat next to me. Just then, the helicopter rocked slightly, then lifted into the air.

In the seats in front of us, Warren buckled himself in then watched carefully out the window as we rose into the air. In the cockpit, the pilot and co-pilot were dressed in full tactical gear. When the pilot turned toward the side window, I was surprised to see she was a woman.

When we were well into the air, Warren turned in his seat to look at me. He pulled the microphone on his headset up to his mouth. "Are you all right?"

I nodded. "I am now. You called Claymore?"

Warren exchanged a curious glance with Nathan, then he looked back at me and shook his head. "Azrael did."

My head tilted to the side. "Azrael has connections at Claymore?"

"Sloan, Azrael *is* Claymore," Warren said.

My mouth fell open. "What?"

Nathan leaned his shoulder against mine. "I was right about him hiding something from us. The name on his driver's license is Damon Claymore."

My brain was suffering from information whiplash. I gripped the sides of my skull. "You're joking."

Nathan shook his head. "Nope."

I pointed at my boyfriend. "You didn't know?"

He shook his head. "I've heard the name for years, but never met the man."

I looked around the helicopter. "Well, where is he now?"

Warren shrugged. "We have no idea."

Nathan looked at me. "He took off last night when I got the call from Sheriff Davis saying you'd been visited by a lawyer named Tuinstra," he said. "What the heck was that about? Your dad said he sent a lawyer, a woman—"

I held up a hand to save his breath. "Tuinstra was Ysha," I said. "Taiya's father."

Nathan's head snapped back. "No shit? I assumed Ysha was a chick like Abigail."

"Nope," I told them. "He's a lawyer, and he showed up to see me at the jail tonight."

Nathan sat back in his seat, bewildered. "Az must've known, but he didn't tell us."

"He just left and told us to carry out the plan without him," Warren said. "What did the lawyer want?"

"To gloat, I think," I answered. "The only good thing about his visit is I now know why I was arrested."

Warren nodded. "We found out too."

"About the video?"

"Yeah," Nathan said. "Care to explain?"

I shrugged my shoulders. "I wish I could. All I know is Abigail once told me she has the ability to make people do things without them remembering it. That was her argument for not telling me who my father was."

Warren let out a deep sigh. "If I didn't know you so well, I'd never believe a word of this."

"I fear a jury will feel the same way," Nathan said.

Refusing to break down in tears yet again that day, I looked out the side of the helicopter and watched the red and blue flashing lights getting smaller and smaller in the distance. The pilot said something to Warren about positioning and rally points and he leaned toward the cockpit to talk to them.

Nathan nudged me with his arm. "I told you I wouldn't let them have you. Sorry it took me so damn long to keep my word."

"I still can't believe you did it," I said. "I was honestly beginning to wonder if I would ever see you again."

He rolled his eyes. "Well, next time just summon me. Or hell, call me on the phone. Don't go and get yourself arrested by the FBI in hopes that I'll stage a rescue. Geez."

I laughed for the first time in days. "I missed you. I've been a wreck since you left."

He patted his flat stomach. "I was so upset I couldn't even eat Skittles."

The tension eased in my neck and shoulders. I looked out over the dark mountains, barely lit by moonlight. "Where are we going?"

Nathan shook his head. "I actually have no idea."

* * *

Sometime during the flight, I'd fallen asleep with my head against the vibrating wall of the helicopter. I woke up to Warren squeezing my shoulder. He turned the nob on my headphones as my eyes fluttered open. "We're landing," he said.

It was still dark out. I looked at his watch. I'd been asleep for over an hour which was pretty impressive considering helicopters are probably ranked among the worst places to take a nap.

The pilot looked back over her shoulder. "A car is waiting on the ground to take you to your next destination."

"You're not coming with us?" I asked.

The co-pilot shook his head. "No, ma'am. We have orders to return to headquarters."

"We appreciate the safe ride," Warren said to them.

They both nodded. "Our pleasure," the man replied.

When the chopper was safely on the ground, Warren, Nathan, and I unbuckled our harnesses and thanked the pilots one more time. Another soldier in full uniform with green night vision glasses on, approached the side to help us out.

Warren grabbed him by the arm. "Enzo?"

The man smiled and nodded his head. He motioned back toward

the black SUV that was waiting across the field. We all slowly jogged across the grass and out of the screaming wind from the propeller blades.

"Good to see you again, Parish," the soldier said to Warren.

The two shook hands. Warren pointed to me and Nathan. "This is Detective McNamara and my girlfriend, Sloan." Warren looked at us. "Enzo and I did field training together when I first went to work at Claymore."

Enzo's face was curious. "So I guess the secret is out now?"

Warren crossed his arms. "About our boss being my dad? Yeah, you can say that. You knew?"

Enzo nodded. "I've worked for Azrael almost since the beginning."

"Of time?" Nathan asked.

I snickered.

Enzo apparently didn't get the joke. "For a little over ten years, ma'am."

Nathan was still chuckling.

"What's the plan, Enzo?" Warren asked.

"I'll be taking you to the compound," he said.

"Is it close?" I asked.

He nodded, opening up the back door of a black SUV. "Thirty miles or so."

I grimaced. "Can we stop and use the bathroom?"

"I'm sorry, ma'am. My orders are to not stop till we reach the compound," he said.

We were in the middle of nowhere. Nathan jerked his thumb toward the tree line. "You can go squat in the woods."

"Ew. No," I answered.

"Thirty miles," Warren said. "Could be an hour before we get there."

My mouth dropped open. "I *cannot* pee outside."

Nathan smirked. "Of course you can. It's not that hard."

"Maybe not for you," I said.

"Come on. You're a mountain girl. It's in your blood," he said.

"That's"—I wanted to say 'sexist', but that wasn't the right term —"*regionalistic!* Stop assuming things about me because I live in Asheville. I don't know how to shoot and I can't pee in the woods!"

Nathan doubled over laughing. Warren and Enzo laughed too.

"Besides, I'm from Florida, remember?" I asked with my hands on my hips.

"So you're gonna hold it?" Warren asked.

"Yes." I turned toward the SUV. "No. Damn it!"

"Would you like a flashlight?" Enzo asked.

My bottom lip poked out. "Please."

Enzo reached into the front of the SUV and came out with a flashlight as long as my arm. "Here you are, ma'am."

"Come on," Warren said, offering me his hand.

"Dude, be sure to check for bears," Nathan said.

I glared back at him. "I hate you."

He just grinned.

"Don't worry ma'am," Enzo called after us. "We haven't seen any bears around here in almost two years!"

Warren and I walked through the tall, dead grass. "If that kid calls me 'ma'am' one more time, I'll beat him with his giant flashlight."

Warren grinned down at me. "Aw, did prison make you tough?"

I stuck my tongue out at him.

When we reached the tree line, he scoured the area with the flashlight. "The area is clear, just don't fall down the hill," he said.

"Did you check for snakes?" I asked as he handed me the flashlight and walked past me toward the car.

"It's December, babe," he said.

"That doesn't answer my question, Warren!"

"Yes, it does. Hurry up. It's cold!"

I shined the flashlight over the area and decided to go far enough downhill so my butt would be hidden if anyone tried to peek. I laid the flashlight in the grass and pushed down my prison pants. Squatting with my backside against the hill, so I wouldn't roll backward, I waited. And waited. And waited.

"Sloan!" Nathan yelled. "You're gonna get frostbite on your ass if you don't hurry!"

I ignored him, but my butt *was* numb, hanging out in the cold. Finally relief came, soaking my white socks as it ran down the hill. I screamed.

I heard feet pounding in my direction. "No! No! Stop! I'm fine!" I yelled before they reached me.

"What's going on?" Warren asked.

"Are you all right, ma'am?" Enzo called.

"Ugh." I yanked up my pants. "I'm fine."

"What happened?" I could almost hear Nathan trying not to smile.

I pulled off my wet socks, exposing my toes to the icy air. "I hate my life."

Thankfully, by some miracle, my pants were completely dry. I prayed for forgiveness for littering and left my socks in the grass before trudging back to my waiting companions. "We can go now," I said, walking past them.

"You OK?" Warren's tone was more curious than concerned.

"Yes. Let's just go." I opened the back door and climbed inside.

Warren followed me. Enzo got behind the wheel and Nathan got in the passenger's seat in front of me.

Before he closed the door, Warren dropped my backpack on the floorboard and his eyes fell on my bare feet. "Sloan, where are your socks?"

I balanced my elbow on the armrest and rested my chin into my hand. "I don't want to talk about it."

Chuckling, he closed his door and the interior light flickered out.

* * *

We drove for a while on small, narrow roads that aggravated a case of car sickness I didn't know I had. Maybe it was yet another pregnancy side-effect. We passed a feed store and The Honey Pot Cafe, and then there was nothing but trees for miles and miles. At some point, I began whistling the theme song to *Deliverance*, and Nathan told me to knock it off.

A road sign caught my attention. "Did that sign say 'Calfkiller Highway'?"

"It's named after Calfkiller River," Enzo answered.

I sucked in a deep breath and blew it out slowly. "Oh, boy."

"Where are we?" Nathan asked.

"Halifax County, sir. Between Raleigh and the coast, about ninety miles away from headquarters."

Warren stretched his arm across the back of my seat. "Claymore uses this place for escape and evasion training."

"You've been here before?" I asked.

He nodded.

"And sometimes we get to deer hunt," Enzo added.

After what felt like an eternity, he turned left onto a dirt road that was blocked by a metal chain strung between two wooden posts. "Sit tight," Enzo told us as he got out of the car. In front of the headlights, he used a key to open a single padlock.

"Very secure. That will keep demons and the FBI out for sure," I said, looking at Warren with wide eyes.

He grinned.

The truck bounced over a washed out dirt road for another mile before lights speckled the darkness. He rolled to a stop in front of a handful of pull-behind campers that looked like set props from a National Lampoon movie. They were arranged in a semicircle with a fire pit in the middle.

I looked around. "This is it?"

"Yes, ma'am," Enzo answered. "You'll want to watch your step getting out."

When my feet hit the ground, they sank down into a deep hole filled with squishy, cold mud. I groaned and pulled my feet up. The mud sucked off one of my flip flops. "Nathan, help," I whined.

He shook his head. "I'm not touching those shoes."

I whimpered.

Enzo grabbed my arm and helped me onto solid ground. "Thank you, Enzo."

He tipped the bill of his camouflage hat. "My pleasure, ma'am."

"Sloan," I corrected him as Warren walked up beside me. "Just call me Sloan."

"Yes, ma'am."

I rolled my eyes.

"Detective McNamara," Enzo said. He held up a set of keys then tossed them to Nathan. "You and I can bunk together in the gold Jayco."

Nathan nodded and started off across the yard.

"Come on," Enzo said to us. "I'll show you two to your home away from home."

Three wobbly and rusted steps led the three of us inside the largest soup can I had ever seen. The carpet had been stripped out, leaving only the sub flooring. There was half of a kitchen, a coffee pot, no television, two twin bunk beds in the corner, and lawn chairs instead of furniture. I put my hands on my hips. "I feel like Mother Mary in the stable in Bethlehem."

Warren laughed.

Enzo knelt down and turned on an electric heater that was on the floor. "I don't recommend running this all night for safety reasons, but you shouldn't need it once you go to bed. There are sub-zero sleeping bags in the closet with hand warmers you can toss in the bottom."

"Is there food?" I asked, moving closer to the heater.

He stood and pointed to the cabinets. "MREs and bottled waters. There's also a small amount of hot water if you want to take a shower, but I suggest you make it fast."

"Do you know when we might see Azrael?" Warren asked.

Enzo shook his head. "No, sir. He didn't give us an ETA." He held up a finger. "But he did have me pack a rifle case for you. It's in the back of the car."

Warren nodded. "I'll come grab it." He kissed my forehead. "I'll be right back."

As the two of them left the camper, they passed Nathan at the bottom of the steps. He held up the backpack he'd brought for me. "I forgot to give Sloan her bag."

Warren tipped his head up in approval, then followed Enzo into the darkness.

Nathan came inside and looked around. He pointed to the lawn chairs. "At least you have furniture. We've got hard-side coolers to sit on in our camper."

"It's better than a jail cell," I said. "I wouldn't have made it through another night in there. Thank you."

His eyes fell to my feet. "I tried so hard to get you out of there, Sloan."

I bent to look him in the eye. "You did get me out."

He shook his head. "Not fast enough. I know firsthand what that place does to you."

"It's over now."

Nathan opened his mouth to speak, but he didn't. Instead, he handed me the backpack. "There's a toothbrush in there. I know you can't stand not being able to brush your teeth."

He remembered my freaking toothbrush.

The simple thoughtfulness was enough to bring me to tears again.

I wanted to hug him, but I couldn't. Swallowing back every emotion inside me, I pulled the backpack into my arms instead of the man holding it. "Thank you, Nathan," I whispered.

Neither of us spoke for several moments, then finally, he put his hand under my chin and tugged at my lower lip with this thumb. His eyes were fixed on my mouth. "I need you to do something for me," he said quietly.

I blinked up at him.

His lips spread into a thin smile as he met my eyes and lowered his voice to a whisper. "Please go wash your feet."

I laughed and wiped my eyes on the back of my sleeve…his sleeve. "Shut up, Nathan."

He smiled. "I've actually missed hearing you say that." He stared at me for a second, then he turned toward the door. "Goodnight, Sloan."

He opened the door, just as Warren stepped up on the first step outside.

Nathan stood back out of his way to let him in. Warren came inside and put the big, black rifle case down on the counter.

Nathan nodded toward the door. "I'll see you guys in the morning if none of us freeze to death."

"Hey," Warren called out as Nathan stepped toward the door. He reached out his hand to him. "Thank you, Nate. I couldn't have done this without you."

Nathan nodded and gripped Warren's hand. He smiled over at me. "Of course."

When he was gone, Warren came to face me. His eyes were bloodshot with heavy, dark bags under them. "Come here," he said, pulling me into his arms.

All at once, I fell apart. My knees went weak as I cried, but Warren held me tight against him. He stroked my hair as he eased me over to the bed.

I was a mess for a lot of reasons. Adrenaline was leaving my bloodstream, and a slight case of shock was settling in. I hadn't really slept in…I literally couldn't remember when. On top of it all, I was pregnant—enough said.

But I was mostly a mess because I was tired of being dishonest. Dishonest with Nathan, dishonest with Warren, and dishonest with myself.

Tears streamed down my cheeks as I looked at my baby's father. "I need to talk to you."

He brushed my tears away with his thumbs and studied my face carefully. "Not tonight." There was a perceptive resolve in the way he studied my face. "It's nothing that can't wait till tomorrow."

24.

THE SOUND OF a car's engine woke me from a deep sleep the next morning. I sat up and looked around the dingy camper. Warren was gone, and I was alone. I shimmied out of the cozy sleeping bag and into the brisk mountain air. Male voices were outside. One of them was Azrael. I hurried to the bathroom to brush my teeth, then slipped on the sneakers Nathan had packed for me. My flip-flops were in the trashcan.

A fist pounded against the front door. "Anybody hungry in there?" Azrael called out.

I ran across the camper and threw the door open, only touching the top step before jumping into his unsuspecting arms. He laughed as he set me on the ground. He pulled back and tucked my tangled hair behind my ears. "You gave us quite a scare, young lady."

I hugged him around the neck again. "You saved me."

He shook his head. "My son and McNamara saved you. And Taiya. I only provided the ride." He squeezed my shoulders. "And the FBI won't find you till we're ready for them to."

"How can you be sure?" I asked.

He winked a black eye at me. "You don't walk the Earth for thousands of years without picking up a few tricks along the way."

I laughed and looked around for Warren. I spotted Nathan instead sitting at a picnic table with a plate of eggs and bacon and a large blue thermos. "Where's Warren?" I asked.

Azrael pointed to the trees in the distance. "He's out with some of my guys securing the perimeter. Did you sleep well?"

I smiled. "Your son is home. Of course I did."

Several men in multi-cam were carrying boxes, bags, and military-grade weapons from two more SUVs, one of which was pulling a large white trailer.

I put my hands on my hips. "I still can't believe you own Claymore."

Azrael shrugged. "We all have our secrets." He gestured toward the table. "Let's get you some breakfast, and then I'll answer all the questions you want. I'm sure you have lots of them."

"You bet I do," I said with a warning tone.

"Good morning," Nathan said as we approached.

I smiled and sat beside him. "Morning."

"Morning," he said, handing me a plate from a box on the ground near his feet.

Azrael sat across the table from us.

"Who made breakfast?" I asked, lifting the lid off of a cast-iron skillet.

Nathan glanced toward one of the other campers. "Enzo."

"God bless him," I said as I piled eggs onto my plate.

"I trust you were in good hands last night," Azrael said.

I nodded. "Your team was great."

"They really were," Nathan agreed.

Behind us, the loud rumble of a motor fired up. I turned in time to see one of the soldiers driving one of the biggest, camouflaged ATV's I'd ever seen. I counted four, maybe six, seats. Another ATV followed behind that one. I chuckled. "I didn't know they made ATV buses."

"We call them HOKs," Azrael said. "High-occupancy karts."

I used a piece of bacon as a pointing device, motioning all around the camp. "I don't understand though. How is it you came to own one of the biggest private military companies in the world?"

He sprinkled a ton of salt onto his food, far more than any human heart should have to suffer. "I started it when Warren joined the Marine Corps. I had to find some way to keep up with him. Turned out to be a profitable idea."

"But how did he not know his own boss?" I asked.

"Claymore has thirty thousand employees and contractors spread over four continents. I'm everyone's boss and no one's." He pointed to the guys who were still carrying stuff in and out of the campers. "These guys are part of a core group I work with directly, but they're an exclusive bunch. Most people who work for my company never see my face."

I thought back over everything Warren had told me about the company he had worked for in various capacities since his release from active duty with the Marines. I found it hard to believe that after three years there would be so much disconnect between him and the company's owner. Then it occurred to me the disconnect was certainly intentional. Azrael would have made sure to stay off Warren's radar, all while calling the shots like an intergalactic puppeteer.

My mouth dropped open. "Just after we met, Claymore offered him a lucrative transfer to the West Coast." My fork clanged against the plate when I dropped it. "That was you!"

Nathan scooted closer to me on the bench.

Azrael stared at me without speaking.

Bits of information were snapping together in my mind like loose pieces of a jigsaw puzzle. "*You* offered him the job in Oregon, didn't you?"

He nodded slowly.

I gasped and covered my mouth. "You tried to split us up!"

Nathan scooted even closer to me. "He did split you up," he mumbled.

"Wait." I looked at Nathan. "What do you mean?"

Nathan pressed his lips together, refusing to answer.

I shot my gaze back at Azrael, who was holding up his hands in defense. "Sloan, you must understand how detrimental this child has the potential to be for all of us."

"What did you do?" I demanded.

He hesitated.

I threw a slice of bacon at him. "Azrael!"

"The US government has contracted my company for years to handle situations all around the globe, so I have plenty of friends at the Pentagon—"

I jumped up from the table. Nathan's hands grabbed me to hold me back.

"You had him recalled to the Marines!" I yelled.

Azrael stood and stepped away from the table—away from me. "I may have suggested he would be able to deal with their terrorist problem in Palestine. I knew Warren would be able to find the body of Shallah."

I lunged at him over the table, but Nathan stood and held me tight. "I'm going to kill you!" I screamed.

" she'd take this news well," Nathan said sarcastically over my shoulder.

A couple of Azrael's soldiers had cautiously started in our direction. Azrael held up a hand to stop them.

"Nathan, let me go," I ordered.

He didn't. "Sloan, you're going to hurt yourself. Consider the possible outcomes of this. He's the Angel of Death."

"Yeah? Well, so am I!"

"Dude, she has a point," Nathan told him.

Azrael still kept his distance. "Hate me if you will, but I would do it again if it might save us from this fate. Surely, you must be feeling the same way."

I pointed an angry finger at him. "I would never wish Warren away from me."

"Perhaps not, but your world and mine are now at stake," he said.

Taking a deep breath, I tried to relax but it was hard. I wanted to claw his angel eyeballs out.

Nathan shook my shoulders. "Come on," he said. "Let's sit back down like civilized people and talk this out."

I huffed, but I sat down.

Cautiously, Azrael returned to his seat as well. "I'm sorry I deceived you, Sloan."

Refusing to look at him or accept his apology, I stabbed at my eggs with the fork.

Nathan squeezed my shoulder. "It's water under the bridge now. We've got bigger things to worry about."

Azrael wiped his mouth on a napkin and leaned his elbows on the table. "Sloan, are you aware of who you met during your time in jail?"

"Ysha. How did you know who the lawyer was?" I asked.

He smiled. "The name, Abner. It literally means *the father of life and light*."

"Seriously?" I asked.

"Seriously."

"Was it Abner you went after?" Nathan asked.

Azrael drummed his fingers on the tabletop. "Not exactly."

"Then what were you doing while I was rotting in prison?" I asked.

Azrael frowned. "You're so dramatic."

Nathan's eyebrow peaked. "Still a valid question."

"I was preparing," Azrael said, "to lead Ysha here."

My head snapped back with shock. "You were doing what?"

His smile was wild and mildly frightening. "It's the perfect plan, really. Here we have the upper hand. There are no witnesses, no risk for human casualties, and we'll be ready."

I laughed toward the sky. "You're insane! What if Ysha shows up with all his friends?" I asked.

He rubbed his palms together. "I'm counting on it."

"Even if those friends include Phenex and Kasyade?" I pointed between me and Nathan. "We took on just one of that trio by ourselves not too long ago. It didn't go well."

He jabbed his thumb into the center of his chest. "You underestimate me, my dear. And you certainly underestimate yourself."

I cackled in mockery. "I think I've done an excellent job at proving exactly what my estimation is lately. I've spent the past twenty-four hours barely containing my bladder because I was locked inside a building with petty thieves and wife beaters!"

He stood and leaned on his arms toward me. "You chose those bars, Sloan Jordan. You weren't locked inside anywhere." His words stung almost as much as the look in his eyes.

Nathan held his hand up. "Whoa, whoa, whoa. That's over the line, Az."

Azrael smacked Nathan's hand away. "I wasn't talking to you, McNamara."

What the...

I jumped out of my seat and walked around the table till I was in the angel's face. "I don't know where you get off, but while you were out playing *Marco Polo* with the *father of life and light*"—I used air quotes for dramatic effect—"*McNamara* was busy protecting the life of your precious granddaughter!"

"She's not his responsibility!" he roared, taking a step toward me. "You failed her, and you failed yourself!"

My hands were shaking I was so angry. I turned to stalk back to the camper.

"That's right. Run away, Sloan," he taunted after me. "You were right when you said you weren't capable of saving anyone. You aren't capable of—"

I whirled around to lunge in his direction, but he was knocked sideways and backward off his feet by an invisible force radiating from my fingertips. The Archangel of Death crash-landed into the center of the picnic table sending the skillet, eggs, and bacon flying in every direction.

I froze, my hands in mid-air.

Nathan's mouth was gaping.

Azrael started laughing and clapping his hands wildly in the air.

"Holy shit," Nathan muttered.

The angel sat up. He was still clapping. "Congratulations."

I dropped my hands. "What is wrong with you?" I shrieked.

He pushed himself up, walked over, and put his hands on my shoulders. "You must stop doubting yourself, Sloan. You are more powerful than you know."

"You are a madman!" My fists were balled at my sides.

He leaned toward me, smiling. "You will be ready," he said. "I promise."

I shook my head. "You have egg in your hair. I can't even take you seriously right now."

Nathan was still mesmerized at the table. His eyes fixed on me, he pointed at Azrael. "I can't believe you did that."

"I can't either," I said, reclaiming my seat beside him.

Azrael shook the scrambled eggs out of his black hair. "It really isn't complicated." He looked at me and pointed to his head. "Did I get all of it?"

I nodded. "Egg free."

"Not complicated?" Nathan asked. "How do you figure?"

He sat across from us and motioned between himself and Nathan. "What's between us right now?" he asked.

"Uh, the table," Nathan answered.

Azrael put his hands on the table. "Correct. What else?"

Nathan looked curiously around. "I dunno. About three feet of space."

Azrael didn't laugh. "Yes, and that space is made of millions of particles." He counted on his fingers. "Oxygen, nitrogen—"

I raised my hand. "Carbon dioxide."

Azrael nodded. "Yeah. Methane and argon. What else?"

Nathan and I looked at each other, confused.

"What about dust?" Azrael asked.

"Pollen?" Nathan asked.

I looked at him. "Not at this time of year."

He chuckled.

"Close your eyes," Azrael said. "Breathe in."

We obeyed.

"What do you smell?"

"Pine," I answered.

At the same time Nathan said, "Smoke."

"All those things are particles that make up what you perceive as the empty three feet of space between us," Azrael said.

Nathan raised an eyebrow. "OK."

"If I were to stand and push this table, you'd feel it, right?" Azrael asked him.

Nathan cringed. "Probably more than I'd want to. Please don't throw the table at me."

Azrael smiled. "What if I push the air? Would you feel that?"

Nathan smirked. "Sure. If *you* did it."

Azrael looked surprised. "Really? Then what's the purpose of fanning your face when it's hot outside? Your hand creates force against the air, causing those particles to move."

I held my hands up. "Hey, that's true."

Nathan looked impressed.

"What Sloan did to me is no different, except she—instead of the hand—is the force against the air."

A wide grin spread across my face. "That's badass."

Nathan laughed, but he nodded in agreement. "That's definitely badass."

I leaned my elbow on the table. "So why did you say all those mean things?"

"A few reasons," he said. "Adrenaline makes it easier, as I told you the day I shot the gun in your kitchen."

I scowled at him.

"And you were visualizing exactly what you wanted to do to me if you could get your hands on me fast enough, correct?"

"I wanted to backhand you across the face," I admitted.

He pointed at me. "And by taunting you, I made you specifically think about accessing your power the way I showed you."

I nodded, impressed with his teaching skills. "That's all correct."

Nathan winked at me. "I feel safer already."

"Ha." I smirked and rolled my eyes. "It's all well and good that I can throw one angel across a table, sure. But we'll need a lot stronger supernatural power than just me."

Azrael got up from the table. "Speaking of strong supernatural powers, I need to find my son. I suggest the two of you get some rest."

When he was gone, Nathan looked over at me. "What do you think he meant by leading the demons here? How will he do that?"

I thought about it. "Well, Samael said the whole spirit world can see me now. He made it sound like this baby is some kind of supernatural homing beacon."

He picked up his coffee cup. "I don't think so. If it were that easy, Azrael wouldn't have had people out looking."

I shrugged. "I don't know."

Nathan pointed toward the woods in the distance. "You haven't told Warren yet, have you?"

"No."

"Are you going to?" he asked, not meeting my eyes.

I shoved my hands into the front pocket of Nathan's sweatshirt I was still wearing. "Of course. I don't want to lie to him."

He shook his head. "I don't either, but who's going to do it?"

"Want to flip for it?" I asked, smiling as I nudged him with my elbow.

He laughed out loud. "Hell no. I already died once because of you. It's your turn."

* * *

While Nathan took a nap, I sat at the table and practiced picking up and putting down the iron skillet without touching it. After an hour, I was able to lift it into the air, move it all the way to the steps of the camper, and bring it back to the table without so much as a wobble.

"Very good, my little protégé," Azrael said from behind me.

Startled, I dropped the pan, and it crashed onto the metal camper steps.

"Geez, you scared me!" I spun around to see him clapping.

"My apologies," he said.

The camper door flew open, and a red-eyed, squinting Nathan stumbled outside. "What's going on?"

"Sloan's throwing pots and pans," Azrael said.

"Nathan, look!" I held my hand up, and the pan flew into it with so much force it stung my palm.

He nodded. "Nice. I'm going back to bed."

"Hold up," Azrael called out. "We have a camp-wide meeting in five."

Nathan groaned and disappeared back into the camper.

"Mortals need their sleep," I said, cutting my eyes up at Azrael.

Azrael's finger pointed up at the sky. "No time for sleep. Do you hear that?"

The sky was gray with clouds, and there was a low rumble in the distance. "A storm's coming?"

He walked past the table toward the campfire. "You could say that."

I got up and followed him. "What's going on?"

"That isn't thunder." He put more logs into the fire pit. "That's the sound of company arriving early."

I listened again. "Are you sure?"

"One of these days you're going to trust me." He clenched a fist, and when he opened it, a crackling flame danced in his hand. He knelt down and lit a small pile of kindling on fire.

"Whoa," I whispered.

He dusted his hands off as he stood.

"Where's Warren?" I asked.

His head tilted toward the field beyond the campers. I looked out to see three of Azrael's soldiers and Warren carrying shovels and duffel bags toward us. Nathan appeared at my side, yawning and rubbing his eyes. "What's going on?" he asked.

I turned my palms up. "I don't know. Azrael says the thunder isn't really thunder."

Nathan sighed and rolled his eyes. "Of course it's not." He looked at Azrael. "What now?"

"Nate, I need you to grab chairs out of the blue camper, and Sloan, bring the picnic table over here by the fire so no one freezes to death," Azrael said.

"Are you joking?" I asked.

He shook his head. "It's twenty-four degrees out here."

I put my hands on my hips "Not what I meant."

"I know what you meant. Bring it over here."

"Az, that thing's made out of concrete," I said.

He shrugged. "And?"

Nathan looked at me and laughed as he folded his arms over his chest. "I want to see this."

Blowing out a sigh that puffed out my cheeks, I turned toward the table and raised my hands. My fingers strained and trembled as I tried to move the table. It wouldn't budge.

"Close your eyes," Azrael said behind me.

My index finger whirled in his direction. "I swear to God I'll kill you if you fire a gun near my head."

The Angel of Death chuckled. "Close your eyes."

I closed my eyes and relaxed my shoulders.

"Now lift it," he said.

I could feel the weight of the table as it lifted off the ground.

"Good," Azrael said. "Now open your eyes so you don't clunk anyone over the head with that thing."

When I looked again, the table was floating inches off the ground. I pulled it toward me…and it came. Nathan was slowly clapping beside me as I turned, moving the table around us toward the fire. Gently, I set it down on the grass.

"When the hell did you learn how to do that?" Warren asked, walking up on the other side of the fire pit with his mouth gaping in awe.

I smiled as I sat down at the newly positioned table. "Lots has changed since you've been gone, Mr. Parish."

He straddled the bench next to me and leaned in for a kiss. "I like it."

Azrael gripped Enzo's shoulder when he approached. "Get the map for me."

Enzo nodded and carried his load toward his camper.

Nathan unfolded a few metal chairs around the table, then sat on the other side of Warren. The other soldiers unloaded their equipment before joining us.

I leaned toward Warren and lowered my voice. "I feel like there were more army dudes this morning."

"There are more of them," Azrael answered. "And they're not *army dudes.*"

I forgot he could hear everything.

"Some of his guys are already in position around the perimeter," Warren said, swinging his leg over the bench and leaning his elbows on the table.

Enzo walked over and spread a large topographical map on the table, then went and stood beside his boss.

Azrael used his finger to draw an imaginary circle around the map. "This is where we are. Approximately four hundred untouched acres with one road in and one road out. I've got five armed guys watching the perimeter, and we've got cameras posted here, here, here, and here." His finger moved to four different spots around the circle, then he looked out over the mountains on the horizon. "They're coming in from the east."

"How do you know that?" Nathan asked.

"The thunder," Enzo answered. "It's in the east."

Nathan's brow crumpled in confusion. "What?"

"When spirits cross into this world, it creates an effect similar to the sonic boom of an object breaking the sound barrier." Enzo's answer was so nonchalant he might as well have been explaining the process of making our morning scrambled eggs. "To us, it sounds like thunder."

Warren's head fell to the side, baffled. "How the hell do you know that?"

Enzo seemed equally puzzled. "You don't?"

Azrael held up a hand to silence them. "I'm sorry. I believe proper introductions are in order." He pointed around our group. "This is Enzo, Special Operations Director of SF-12."

I turned my ear toward him and raised an eyebrow. "SF-12?"

Enzo turned toward me. "SF-12 is a covert division of Claymore, kept completely off the corporate books and out of the main organizational structure."

"Like *Ocean's Eleven*?" I asked with a grin.

"Twelve, Sloan," Nathan corrected me.

I giggled but forced a straight face. "It has a nice ring to it, *Azrael's Twelve*."

Azrael wasn't amused, as usual. "SF-12 works directly with me. Most of them, like Enzo, have been with me almost since the company's inception."

"They know what you are?" Nathan asked.

"Yes," Azrael said.

Enzo looked at me. "And we know what you are."

My heart stopped when I met his gaze. Enzo knew what I was

because he could see me. He could *really* see me. And he had one blue eye...and one green.

25.

HAD I NOT been sitting, I would've fallen down. I gripped the side of the table and stared at the concrete while my mind raced in a thousand different directions. Only one other person I'd ever met had eyes like Enzo's, and she'd been the first person ever to call me an angel.

Kayleigh.

"What is it?" Warren asked, concerned.

I looked at Azrael. "Enzo is like Warren's mother."

Azrael nodded.

"It's the eyes?" I asked him.

"It's the eyes," he said.

Warren rubbed his forehead, squinting in confusion. "My mother?"

I gripped Warren's arm. "Enzo can see angels. So could your mother. It's called a discerning power."

Nathan glanced around. "Will someone please explain what they're talking about?"

I beckoned Enzo to come closer, then I pointed to Nathan. "Nathan, look at him."

Nathan and Enzo stared at each other. "His eyes are blue and green," Nathan said. "That means he can see angels?"

"Yes. And who else has eyes like that?" I asked.

His mouth fell open a bit. "Kayleigh Neeland."

"Who?" Azrael asked.

I raked my fingernails back through my hair. "When Nathan and I first met, I helped him rescue a little girl named Kayleigh. She's five. She told me I was an angel." I chuckled in awe. "I thought she was being metaphorical."

Azrael smiled. Even he looked impressed.

"So all of *Azrael's Twelve* can see angels?" Nathan asked.

Azrael rolled his eyes. "SF-12," he corrected. "And no. Several of them can." He pointed around the circle. "Enzo and Kane can."

Kane pulled off his hat and glasses. His eyes were blue and green as well.

"Cooper and Lex cannot, but they've seen enough to know what we're up against," Azrael said, gesturing toward the two men. "A couple of the guys in the field can see as well."

"And NAG, sir," Enzo said.

Azrael nodded. "Oh yes. NAG, your pilot last night. She can see you as well."

I blinked. "Her name is NAG?"

Enzo chuckled. "I believe her real name is Mandi. NAG is her call sign. It means *Not A Guy.*"

The rest of us laughed.

Warren rubbed his palms together. "I'm feeling much better about our odds now." He looked up at Azrael. "Finish explaining the plan."

Azrael smiled and leaned back over the map. "By my estimation, Ysha and his crew will arrive on foot maybe this time tomorrow."

I raised my hand. "His crew?"

"I hope Phenex and Kasyade will be with him, but I'm sure he'll bring others as well."

"Other demons or humans?" Nathan asked.

"Both," Azrael answered.

Enzo crossed his arms. "We've had no sign of Phenex, sir."

"We might still get lucky," Azrael said.

"And by our last count, Ysha travels with two humans, one with sight, and two AOPs, Mihan and The Destroyer," Enzo said.

Warren looked up. "AOPs?"

"Protection, warrior angels," Azrael said.

I looked at Azrael with alarm. "You've mentioned The Destroyer before. You said Samael decides who can cross the spirit line, who must suffer the second death, and who must be turned over to The Destroyer. Are we talking about the same person?"

"The Destroyer is not a person," Enzo said.

I rolled my eyes. "Is it the same *Destroyer?*"

Azrael nodded. "That is correct."

My stomach churned. I held up five fingers. "That's five potential angels, one of which is like the worst tormentor on the planet, and they're all showing up here tomorrow. And we've only got you on our side?"

"And you and Warren."

I groaned. "Oh my god, whatever."

"And Reuel," Enzo added.

Azrael pointed toward the woods. "Reuel, our own AOP, is on the perimeter. Abaddon, The Destroyer, will be his responsibility. Ysha will flank us. He won't come by the road, and we've got every measure possible to slow him down out there," Azrael said.

"Like what?" I asked.

"Snipers, for starters," Azrael answered, looking at Warren.

Nathan turned his palms up in question. "What good will guns do us? When we were in Texas, I emptied a clip into Sloan's demon mom, and I might as well have been pelting her with Cheerios. The bullet holes closed right up."

Enzo spoke first. "The whole group isn't immortal. We can certainly pick off the humans and have less bullets flying through the air."

I nodded. "And Kasyade was different. Not all of them will heal the way she does." I pointed at Az. "I broke his nose in my kitchen, and then I had to fix it."

"Correct," Azrael said. "Ysha is the only one with the power to heal as Kasyade does. Mihan and Abaddon can be injured."

Kane and Enzo exchanged a glance. "If you can hit them," Kane said.

Warren looked at the two men. "Where's the list of stuff we still need?"

Enzo pulled a small pad from the chest pocket on his camouflage jacket. "Got it."

"Pick up as many packs of tent stakes you can buy. The sharpened metal kind." Warren held his hands about a foot apart. "Maybe twelve to eighteen inches or so."

I looked up at him. "Stakes? They're demons, not vampires."

Warren smiled. "I'm aware. We'll dig a trench, and when the demons step into it, their legs will be impaled on the stakes. It might buy us some time."

"You scare me sometimes," I said.

He nodded. "Good."

"So how do we kill them?" Nathan asked.

There was silence all around the group. Finally, Azrael shook his head. "We don't." Then he turned toward me. "Sloan does."

My head snapped toward him. "Excuse me?"

He leaned against the table. "I told you. The Vitamorte has the power to control life and death." He lowered his voice. "That power is not limited to human life."

My mouth was gaping. "Are you saying I have the power to destroy angels?"

He just stared at me.

I balanced my elbows on the table and dropped my face into my hands.

His hand rested on my shoulder. "You're the only one, Sloan."

Azrael had once told me that my fizzling light ball would work on him if I chose to use it, but I didn't realize it would do more than just separate him from his human form. If he'd kept that information from me to prevent more tears and vomiting, he'd been smart. My stomach felt queasy and my hands trembled.

His hand tightened around the back of my neck. "Look at me."

I looked up into his stern face.

"Remember, you were created for this. Even your enemies know how strong you are. They wouldn't try so hard to break you if they weren't afraid of what you can do." He bent so we were eye to eye. "You're even more powerful than me. Don't you forget it."

I sincerely wished that made me feel better. It didn't.

He lifted my chin. "Faith without doubt isn't faith at all. Just because you don't believe it right now doesn't make it any less true."

And as if adding a cosmic exclamation point at the end of his sentence, another loud boom of thunder shook the mountains in the east.

* * *

Before Enzo and Kane left to make a run to the store back near the exit we'd taken off the interstate, I added a few more things to their list including clothes, socks, underwear, and a hair dryer. While they were gone, I retreated to the camper to take a nap, but sleep was elusive. Every time I closed my eyes, all I saw was Ysha's hateful, jeering eyes.

The door creaked open. "You awake?" Warren asked softly.

"Yeah," I replied.

He walked inside, ducking through the doorway. "Did you sleep at all?"

I laughed sarcastically in response.

The dusty old mattress dipped under his weight as he sat down beside me.

"Where have you been?" I asked, rolling onto my back to look at him.

"Digging trenches." He slid his hand over my stomach. "Are you feeling OK?"

I smiled. "I'm good, just tired."

"Can we have that talk now?"

Reluctantly, I held up my hand. "Yeah. Help me up."

Warren pulled me up, and I slid out of the warm sleeping bag. I groaned, slumping forward and balancing my elbows on my knees. "You know how much I love you, right?" I asked.

There was a deep rumble in his throat. "I don't like how this is starting out."

I turned toward him, studied his worried face for a moment, then drew in a deep, brave breath. "Back around Thanksgiving, you know I went to Raleigh for Nathan's sister's burial service, right?"

He nodded.

"Things were really emotional, as you can imagine." My hands started to sweat. "I hadn't told Nathan about the baby—or anyone besides my dad and my doctor, for that matter. Well, after the funeral, he was really upset, and he kissed me, but I stopped it before things went too far and told him I was pregnant."

Warren's Adam's apple bobbed with a strained swallow. He was clenching his jaw. "He kissed you?"

"Yes, but then he told me the whole 'Nathan and Sloan drama' had to end and he needed to put some distance between us," I said.

He relaxed a little. "OK."

I scrunched up my nose. "Well, that didn't exactly happen."

His eyes darkened.

"I started having all these crazy nightmares, like demons trying to choke me in my sleep and stuff."

"You told me about that."

"He kind of moved into the guest bedroom after that." I quickly held up my hands. "But absolutely nothing happened."

The muscle in his jaw was working again. "OK."

"Like a week later was the car wreck and from that night on, Azrael lived with us. Then Taiya moved in."

"Did Nathan leave when Azrael showed up?" he asked.

My head fell to the side. "You know Nathan better than that. He doesn't completely trust Az."

Warren crossed his arms. "That's not why he stayed, and you know it."

My shoulders dropped. "I know, but that's beside the point."

"What is the point?"

"As long as Azrael was with us, I didn't have any of the crazy dreams, but one night he went out looking for Ysha and Phenex, and I had another nightmare." I hesitated, then cut my eyes up at him. "I won't lie to you, all right?"

He held his breath. "All right."

"I dreamed I was crying and Nathan came into my room to console me." I took a deep breath. "Things got really physical, but then he started choking me to death, and I started clawing at him to get him to stop. When he wouldn't, I used my power to kill him."

He cocked an eyebrow. "So, you dream cheated on me?"

I rubbed my palms on my jeans. "Well, I woke up screaming with Nathan and Taiya both shaking me. He had been asleep in the guest room the whole time." I touched my neck. "But I had bruises on my throat, and he had really bad claw marks down his chest." For the safety of everyone, I left out the part about my lips being bruised from Nathan's kisses.

He was staring at me, his expression caught somewhere between hostile and confused.

I held my hands out. "I really don't know what happened that night, Warren. But the next day, Nathan moved out because he didn't want to take any more chances."

He frowned. "He moved out because he's in love with you and couldn't take it anymore."

"Well…"

He rubbed his palm down his face. "That's it?"

I bit down on the insides of my lips till I tasted blood.

He groaned and cursed under his breath. "What else?"

"When he told me he was leaving…" I sucked in a deep breath and closed my eyes. "We kissed. I was fully awake and knew exactly what I was doing, and I kissed him."

Warren's head dropped. He didn't look up at me. "You kissed him?"

"Yes."

He was silent for a long time, staring at his boots. Finally, he cut his eyes up at me. "I want the truth, Sloan. No lies to protect me. No lies to protect him."

Hesitantly, I nodded.

He stared at me. "Are you in love with him?"

My heart was pounding so hard I felt dizzy. "Yes."

He cringed and pinched the bridge of his nose. "Are you still in love with me?"

I gripped his arm. "Yes."

He pushed himself up and walked over to the counter where his guns were spread out and ready to be used. He gripped the tabletop and hung his head. His knuckles went white, and the sound of splintering wood crackled around the camper.

I struggled to my feet and cautiously walked over to him. Tears were building in my eyes as I reached to touch his arm. He flinched away from me. "Please talk to me," I begged.

He released the counter and folded his hands over the top of his head.

I placed my hands on his sides. "I *choose* you. I *choose* us."

He blew out a deep breath slowly and turned around. He stared down at me, his black eyes smoldering like hot coals. I had never felt so small standing in front of him.

Just then, a fist pounded against the door. "Hey, guys! Enzo and Kane are back from the store and they brought food!" Nathan shouted.

Warren's eyes widened and shot toward the door. He turned, and before I could grab him, he was across the room and exploding through the door. All I could do was scream.

"Nathan, run!"

* * *

Sheer panic flashed across Nathan's face before Warren rained down on top of him, tackling him onto the ground. I ran to the door in time to see Warren's fist come up and slam onto Nathan's face. My feet couldn't get down the steps fast enough, and before I jumped onto Warren's back, he got at least three solid punches into Nathan's skull.

"Warren, stop!" I shrieked as I pulled on his shoulders with all the strength I had.

My hands slipped, and I stumbled backward till I landed on my butt in the grass behind them. I pushed myself up on my elbows to see Warren's fist drop to his side. He rolled off Nathan onto the ground and sat there, fuming. Nathan was too stunned to move, or maybe he was unconscious, I wasn't sure.

Laughter was coming from the campfire. I looked over to see it was Azrael, standing and holding Enzo back to prevent him from intervening.

Covered in dirt and grass stains, I pushed myself up and crawled over to Nathan. He was panting with wide eyes and sweat rolling off his forehead. The side of his jaw was bent at an awkward angle and starting to swell. His cheek bone was bright red, and blood poured from his nose.

Warren sat motionless except for massaging his knuckles.

"I think your jaw is broken," I said. "Maybe your cheek bone too."

"He's lucky it wasn't his neck," Warren grumbled.

I leaned over top of Nathan and pressed my hands to both sides of his lower jaw till I felt the bones grind and snap back into place. He winced with pain and swore as tears leaked from the corners of his eyes. When it was over, he opened his mouth and moved his jaw around but didn't dare speak. I gave him a hand and helped him up till he was sitting.

Warren pulled his knees up and draped his arms over them, staring out into the field beyond the campers.

Nathan rubbed his swollen jaw. "I guess you told him what happened."

I bit my lower lip.

"Warren, I'm really sorry—" he began.

Warren snapped. "Shut the hell up, Nathan." He pushed himself off the ground and walked back inside the camper, slamming the door behind him with so much force a side window fell open.

Nathan sighed. "Well, at least he didn't kill me."

I shook my head. "I wouldn't be too relieved just yet. He's got a lot of guns and ammo in there."

A shadow fell over us. It was Az, offering a hand to pull Nathan up. "Can't say you didn't deserve that one." He pulled Nathan to his feet.

"I know," Nathan said.

I stood and slapped Azrael's chest. "You could have stopped that."

He rested his arm across my shoulders, turning me back toward the fire. "My dear, had I stopped it, Warren would have come up with nineteen ways to kill Nathan before sundown. And we don't have time for that."

"I should go talk to him," I said.

Azrael held me still. "No. You need to let him cool down. Then you can talk." He pointed toward a chair. "Sit."

Rather than taking the empty seat beside me, Nathan sat on the opposite side of the fire. Enzo handed him an ice pack from the cooler, and he pressed it against the side of his face.

"Here," Azrael said, handing me a plate of gas station fried chicken.

"Thank you, but I'm really not hungry."

He sat down next to me. "Your daughter is hungry."

"Do you have a course on guilt trips in the spirit world?" I asked, accepting the paper plate.

He just smiled. "I need to talk to you about something, and I want it to stay between us."

That didn't sound good. I frowned. "Why do I have a feeling this is very bad news?"

"It isn't news at all." He rested his arm along the back of my chair and leaned into me. "What was the FBI agent's name who arrested you?"

I pulled the skin off the chicken leg on my plate. "Sharvell Silvers."

"I want you to summon her here," he said.

"You want me to do what?" The question definitely went well beyond the volume of 'just us' dialogue. Everyone looked our way.

He rolled his eyes. "Keep your voice down."

When the rest of the group returned to their own conversations, he continued. "Sloan, the government will never believe you're completely ignorant to everything Kasyade's been up to. Every shred of evidence they find against her will always point back to you because you're central to her plot. Don't you realize that by now?"

I stared into the fire, knowing he was right. I'd known it since the first night Nathan and I sat across from Agent Silvers in Texas.

"If you bring her here, she'll see for herself what you could never explain." He pressed his finger into my shoulder. "She'll see what no jury will ever believe."

I dropped my chicken leg. "And what will stop her from hauling me back to jail when she gets here?"

He motioned around the campfire. "No one here will allow her to haul you anywhere. Besides, she'll be completely unprepared to encounter you. She won't know where she's going, remember?"

"This is a bad idea."

He bent forward to look me in the eye. "Sloan, trust me."

Across the campfire, Nathan was watching me, obviously curious as to what we were so deep in discussion about.

"Why don't you want anyone to know?" I asked.

Azrael's gaze shifted to Nathan, but he kept his voice low. "You know as well as I do that my son and Nathan will do everything they can to keep you from going back to jail." His eyes snapped to mine. "But nothing they can do will actually work aside from keeping you hidden for as long as possible. Is that what you want? To sleep in that camper or something similar for the rest of your life, always on the run and always looking over your shoulder? To ruin Nathan's career and make them both accomplices to crimes you can't prove you're innocent of?"

Looking down at my chicken, I felt sick. A bloody vein ran through the dark hunk of meat bared by the missing skin. I added it to my newly written mental list of food aversions in my first trimester, right behind deviled eggs—thank you, Taiya.

"You need to decide this for you, Sloan." He stood, but he paused before walking away and looked down at me. "Let me know what choice you make."

Unable to eat, I put my plate on the ground and tugged my sleeves over my cold, bare hands. I stared at my feet as my mind played out all the possible scenarios that could unfold if I did as Azrael suggested. Maybe it would clear my name if Silvers were allowed to peek behind the curtain to the supernatural world. Or maybe instead of prison, she'd have me committed. Given my recent string of luck, Silvers would probably wind up dead and I'd be able to add homicide to my long list of federal charges.

But I had more than just me to consider. Rusty and dilapidated campers I could live with; ruining Nathan's life and Warren's, I could not.

I closed my eyes and reached into the universe with my gift. In the darkness, I found Agent Silvers' spirit and before I could convince myself otherwise, I pulled her to me.

"What are you so lost in thought about?"

Nathan's voice snapped my attention back to reality. He sat down in the seat Az had vacated. His face was still swollen, and the redness was deepening to purple.

I looked away. "So much has happened in the past few days, I might never find my mental way back here again."

"I can sympathize with that." He nodded toward Azrael. "What did he say to you?"

I shook my head. "Nothing important."

"Liar."

I didn't even bother to argue.

Dark blue blood had begun to pool under his left eye, and the skin was split just above his cheekbone. "How's your face?" I asked.

He pulled back the slide on one of the Glocks. "It's throbbing, but it isn't broken anymore. Thank you."

"Do you want me to fix that gash under your eye?" I asked.

He shook his head and laughed. "Nah, it's all right. It will probably make Warren feel better to look at it."

I nudged him with my shoulder. "I guess I have to forgive you for leaving me, huh?"

He pointed to his face. "Yes. You have to give me a pass for all transgressions past, present, and future because I haven't taken a beating like that in my life."

I poked out my bottom lip. "I'm sorry."

He shook his head. "Don't be. It's my fault. I would have kicked my ass too."

Behind us, the door to my camper flew open and Warren stomped down the metal stairs. Nathan was out of his seat and five feet away before Warren looked in our direction. He stopped near the pile of shopping bags Enzo and Kane had brought back. After rummaging through them and repacking some of the contents, he slung a bag over one shoulder, his rifle over the other, and picked up two cans of gasoline. He walked by me without so much as a glance in my direction.

"Where are you going?" Nathan called out.

"To the woods to think about killing you," Warren replied, storming off toward the field.

Nathan put his hands on his hips, hung his head, and groaned. "Well, that's great."

I pointed at Warren. "Seriously, where's he going with the gas?"

He nodded toward the trees. "Probably to mix napalm and fantasize about burning me up with it."

"Warren's making napalm? That's frightening."

He nodded. "You've got a Recon Marine for a boyfriend, Sloan. Napalm is pretty low on the frightening scale of what he's capable of."

"How long do you think he'll be pissed off?" I asked, leaning on my elbow.

Nathan looked up as Warren cut through a pile of brush. "If I were him, forever."

* * *

The sun was low in the sky by the time Warren returned from the woods. He glanced at me by the fire as he walked wordlessly to our camper. I took that as my invitation to follow him.

Inside, I sat down on the bed as he silently unloaded his gear by the sinister red-orange glow of the space heater. "Are you going to talk to me?" I asked.

There was no answer.

Instead of joining me on the bed, he sat in one of the rickety lawn chairs. Its hinges creaked under his weight. He didn't even look at me.

After what felt like eternity, his deep voice echoed off the metal walls. "Is it over now with you and him?"

I got up and crept over beside him. "It will never happen again. I promise."

His eyes reflected the burning coils of the heater when he turned his head to look at me. "You didn't answer my question. Is it over?"

"I think so." It was the most truthful answer I could give. "I want it to be."

He looked out the window.

Dropping my head, I took a step backward. But he grabbed my hand, pulling me down till I straddled his lap. Studying my face, his hands gripped my hips, then he stood and carried me to the counter. With his arms braced beside my thighs, he dropped his face and cut his black eyes up at me. "It's him or me. I love you and I will always take care of our daughter, but I will not share you. Ever. Do you understand?"

I nodded. "I swear, I'm yours. Please forgive me."

"Not today."

I gulped. At least I couldn't fault his honesty.

Warren straightened, his eyes still smoldering as they searched me. His fingers found the hem of Nathan's sweatshirt I was still wearing, and silently, he yanked it up and over my head. "I never want to see you in this again." He threw the shirt toward the door.

I nodded, hugging myself to shield my bare skin from the chill of the room.

He peeled my arms from around my body, and his warm hands slid up my sides, slipping underneath the white cotton of my prison-issued sports bra. Sexy.

As he dropped it on the floor with one hand, the other raked through my hair till he could pull my mouth down onto his. The kiss was fierce, hot, and angry. His teeth scraped across my lower lip as he worked the button on my jeans. When he got them down to my ankles, he freed one leg from the denim and didn't bother with the other before he buried himself inside me.

And in that moment, we both knew it.

I'd made my choice.

I was irrevocably his.

26.

MY STOMACH RUMBLED so loud Warren raised up on his elbow and looked down at me. I laughed and covered my face with my hands. "I haven't consumed enough calories today to do what we just did."

Smiling for the first time since that morning, he settled back down on the pillow beside me, resting his hand on my stomach where we lay, our naked and sweaty limbs tangled under the mound of thick sleeping bags. "We should fight more often," he growled in my ear. "That was amazing."

I snuggled against him. "I think I blacked out a couple of times."

He laughed and tightened his arm around me. "Is that a good thing or a bad thing?"

"Definitely a good thing." My stomach growled again. "I smell burgers."

He pushed himself up. "Let's go grab something to eat before it's all gone."

As he stood, he pulled his cargos up over his bare, perfect butt. I smiled, enjoying the view. I reached for his hand and tugged him back toward the bed. He sat down beside me and pushed my hair out of my face. "Are we OK?" I asked.

"We will be," he said. "But I meant what I said. My patience has run out and I'm not doing this wishy-washy bullshit anymore." He tugged the blanket up around my shoulders. "Do you swear you told me everything? No more secrets."

"I swear," I said.

He was quiet for a moment, and then he leaned down pressed a kiss to my forehead. "I forgive you. Let's try to forget about it."

As if on cue, we heard Azrael's voice outside. "Nate, are those burgers about ready?"

I grimaced and traced my finger along the thick black line of the tattoo down the center of Warren's chest. "Will you forgive Nathan?"

He shook his head. "Probably not, but we do need him to help fight a war."

I caught his eye. "And it sounds like he has dinner."

Warren smiled again. "I am pretty hungry." He grabbed my hand and pulled me up. "Get dressed. Enzo bought you some clothes earlier."

He crossed the dark room and flipped on the light switch. By the door were a few shopping bags. He tossed me one that was tied shut. Inside was a black thermal shirt, some black jogging pants, a fleece pullover, and three plastic packages of women's underwear. I looked up at him. "Eighteen pairs of underwear? How long will we be here?"

He shrugged. "I have no idea."

There was a pack of granny panties, a pack of bikini briefs, and a pack of animal print thongs. I held up the last one over my head. "Seriously?"

He stopped tying his boots and pointed at me. "Speaking for all men everywhere, cut them some slack. We don't have any business shopping for women's underwear if it's not split crotch and covered in lace." He stood and zipped up his coat. "I'll see you out there."

* * *

The campfire cast an ominous glow over our group as we ate charred burgers and canned baked beans. No one said it out loud, but despite Azrael's confidence, we all knew it could be the last peaceful dinner we ever ate. And 'peaceful' was a generous description of the meal. The tension between Warren and Nathan was almost palpable across the campfire.

Breaking the silence, Azrael cleared his throat and poked the embers with a long stick. "Tomorrow, we're moving away from the campsite," he announced. "This area is too wide open with too little cover."

"Where will we go?" I asked between bites of my hamburger.

"There's a mountain spring that serves as the headwaters of Calfkiller Creek about a half a mile, directly north of here. It will give us a high vantage point because everything below and around the spring is an open meadow."

"Plenty of spots to pick people off from above," Kane added.

Warren looked at me. "And there's a cave back in the rocks where the spring is."

My eyes widened. "I hope you're not insinuating the cave is for me."

He shrugged. "Just in case."

I shook my head. "I'd rather be out fighting demons than be stuffed into a dirty cave with spiders and snakes and god-only-knows-what-else."

Nathan sighed. "You're so weird. Do you even hear yourself?"

I nodded. "Ysha, I can see coming. A brown recluse can slip into my shoe and inject me with skin-rotting poison while I shop for shoes on my cell phone. Those things are no joke."

The guys around the fire were softly chuckling.

Azrael held up his hand to silence us all. "Quiet."

I didn't hear anything.

Azrael tossed his paper plate into the fire and slowly rose from his seat, his ear angled up toward the sky.

"What is it?" I asked.

"Silence!" Azrael demanded, walking closer to me.

I bit down on the inside of my lips.

"Surround positions!" Azrael called out.

What the hell...

The unmistakable sound of gravel grinding under tires came from the road. I watched the soldiers scatter from the campfire and put on gear waiting at the ready nearby. They moved like pieces of a well-oiled machine. I, on the other hand, ran in circles like a squirrel stuck in rush hour traffic.

I grabbed Azrael's arm. "I forgot to tell you!"

"You summoned her?" he asked.

I nodded.

He patted my back. "Good girl. You stay behind Warren, no matter what." Before I could say anything, he turned away, slipping an earpiece into his ear. He pulled on a pair of black gloves that had been tucked into his pocket and handed Warren the assault rifle that had been sitting next to his camping chair.

Warren slipped the gun's strap over his head. "Sloan, what's going on?"

"I need to tell you something."

He looked down at me. "What now?"

I covered my mouth with my hands. "I summoned the FBI here."

His head snapped back. "You did *what?*"

I ducked behind his back as headlights flashed through the sky. "It was Azrael's idea. He told me to summon Silvers here to let her see what's going on. He said it's the only way to prove my innocence."

He raised the rifle to his shoulder. "Why the hell didn't you tell me?"

"Azrael told me not to." I gripped his sides. "And, honestly, I kind of forgot about it with...you know, everything else."

The black sedan rolled to a stop behind one of Azrael's SUVs.

Nathan appeared at Warren's side. "Human or supe?" he asked, looking at Warren.

"Human," Warren answered. "Sloan summoned the feds here."

Nathan's angry gaze shot to me. "Excuse me?"

Before I could explain, we heard more than one car door open.

"I guess she brought friends," Warren said.

I balled my fists at my sides in frustration. "I don't know why I listen to that guy!"

Suddenly, the faces of Agent Silvers and Agent Voss were lit up by the flashlights mounted on the assault rifles pointed at them by Azrael's men.

"Who's the guy?" Warren asked me over his shoulder.

"He's the agent who questioned me at the federal building," I answered.

Sharvell Silvers looked surprised but not the least bit intimidated. "My name is Agent Silvers, and I work for the Federal Bureau of Investigation. I must advise you of—"

Azrael took a few steps forward and held up a hand to silence her. "Lady, I don't care who you are or who you work for. You're in my world now." He pointed to her chest. There were two bright red dots from laser sights gleaming in the center of her breast bone.

Even from our distance, I could see her gulp.

"I don't want to kill you." Azrael spread out his hands as he walked to face her. "But I will."

His malevolent threat was enough to make me shudder.

Sharvell shifted on her feet.

Azrael crossed his arms and cocked his head to the side. "Stand down, Agent. You and I both know the government doesn't pay you enough to put your family through a funeral at Christmas." He put his hand over the top of her pistol.

She hesitated for a second, then released it into his grasp.

Agent Voss lowered his gun as well, and Cooper came out of the darkness and immediately disarmed him.

Satisfied, Azrael took a step back. He raised a finger in the air and swirled it around. "Check that car, boys," he said into his microphone.

Enzo and Lex walked to the sedan, keeping their aim on the driver who was still seated behind the wheel with his hands raised in the air.

Azrael reached into the pocket on the front of his vest and tossed a handful of zip-ties to Warren. "Staff Sergeant, you and Nate make our guests comfortable."

That's when Sharvell saw Nathan and her expression morphed from anger to confusion. "Detective McNamara?"

He groaned as he walked up and grabbed her hands. "Yeah."

"Is Sloan here as well?" she asked as he tied her wrists together with the plastic strip.

I walked straight up to her, much braver with her in restraints. "Nice to see you again, Sharvell."

Her mouth was hanging open.

I shook my head. "Don't try to make sense of what's happening to you right now. I do promise I won't let them hurt you."

Nathan and Warren walked the two agents over to the campfire and pushed them down carefully onto the ground. Enzo brought over the driver, Agent Clark if I remembered correctly, and put him down beside them as well.

Nathan dusted his hands off and looked at the agents. "It's nothing personal guys."

"Your career is finished, Detective," Sharvell spat at him.

"Yeah, I figured. But I have a feeling you'll see why."

Her brow rose, and she glared at me before mumbling something to her partner.

Azrael walked up beside me. "You made the right choice, Sloan."

Warren spun around toward him. "What were you thinking,

Azrael?"

Azrael held his hands up in defense. "This is the only way the three of you get to go home again."

"Home again?" Sharvell asked from the ground. "You're harboring a fugitive from federal custody. No one here is going home."

Azrael smiled. "Those are mighty words from where you sit in the dirt." He looked around at us and his men. "Nothing changes tomorrow." He gestured toward the agents. "They'll be coming with us."

There was a collective gasp around the circle, along with lots of wide eyes and dropped jaws.

Warren crossed his arms over his chest. "You can't be serious. You're going to let them see everything?"

Azrael put his hand on Warren's shoulder. "Son, sometimes it's in everyone's best interest to not keep things hidden. This will certainly be what's best for you."

"Will you leave them tied up?" Nathan asked. "They'll get killed out there!"

Azrael nodded. "It's possible."

The agents squirmed uncomfortably, but none of them spoke.

Nathan scowled. "They may be sorely misguided in their attempts to uphold justice, but they're still the good guys."

Azrael grinned at me. "Maybe I'll stick them in Sloan's hideout cave."

I held up my hands. "As long as you don't expect me to go in there too."

"I demand to know what's going on here!" Sharvell shouted.

Azrael walked over and knelt down in front of her, leaning forward on his knee for support and intimidation. It worked because Sharvell shrank back. "Tomorrow will be a war unlike anything you've ever seen. You can decide which side of that war you want to be on. I trust you'll recognize where you went wrong in this whole mix up."

"There is no mix up," she argued. "We have Sloan on videotape working with Abigail Smith."

"Perhaps," he said. "But tomorrow you'll see that not everything you believe to be true actually is."

"Who are you?" she barked viciously at him.

Slowly, he rose till he towered over them again. "My name is Azrael. And I'm the Angel of Death."

* * *

The next morning, I was awake before the sun which by itself was a miracle. Warren was still sleeping, also a miracle. Maybe it would be a good day for miraculous things to happen. God knows, we needed all the help we could get.

It was so cold I could see my breath, but I was snug under the weight of several sleeping bags and the heavy arm of the man of my dreams and beyond. His breath was warm against the back of my neck where he was curled protectively around me from behind. Our legs were tangled under the blanket.

Outside, hushed voices carried over the sound of something sizzling in a pan over the open fire. It smelled like sausage.

Warren stirred slightly, then I felt his lips grace the back of my shoulder. "Good morning," he whispered in the early morning light.

I snuggled closer into him. "Good morning."

His arm tightened around me. "I need about four more hours of shut-eye."

"I didn't sleep well either," I said, lacing my fingers between his under the blanket. He slid our locked hands down to my stomach, and the baby's tiny body fluttered. I glanced back at him over my shoulder. "I think she can sense you. She's moving again."

He flattened his palm against my stomach. "I still can't believe you're pregnant."

"Some days, neither can I." I rolled over till we were almost nose-to-nose and I curled my arms up under the pillow. I studied his handsome face to burn all his features into my memory.

"What are you thinking about?" he whispered.

"If something happens today—"

He shook his head to cut me off. "Don't talk like that. We're going to win, you'll see."

"You don't know that, Warren." I hugged the pillow a little tighter. "If something happens to me, I want you to know how much I love you."

The corner of his mouth tipped up into a smile. "You showed me pretty well last night, a few times."

I didn't laugh. "I'm serious."

He pushed my hair behind my ear. "I love you too, Sloan. This will all be behind us soon. We'll go home and have a beautiful little girl, and we are going to be happy. You'll see."

I smiled and wanted to believe him, but it was hard considering that the hounds of hell were coming with the day.

"I hope she has your eyes," he said.

I grinned. "I hope she has your hair."

He laughed and rolled over on top of me.

* * *

When Warren and I walked out of the camper later that morning, Nathan was sitting at the table alone, buttering a piece of toast. He was wearing multi-cam like the rest of Azrael's soldiers, and his face was flushed with bright shades of blue and purple. His eyes widened with worry as we approached and sat down. Cautiously, and silently, he slid a couple of empty plates toward us.

Warren poured two cups of coffee from the aluminum pot on the table and handed one to me.

"She can't have that—" Nathan began, then quickly snapped his mouth closed.

Warren glowered across the table.

Not another word was spoken as we ate, and Nathan chewed his food slowly as though it may be the last meal he would ever taste. Warren punished his eggs with his fork, clanging the tines so hard against the plate that the birds in the nearby tree line scattered each time he went for a bite. I nibbled a piece of sausage, praying for something to break the awkward tension.

That something turned out to be one of the HOKs appearing in the field from the tree line. Driving it was Azrael, and in the passenger seat was another man—no, *angel*—that I didn't know. They rolled to a stop about twenty feet away. "Good morning, all," Azrael said when he was close enough.

I smiled up at him. "Good morning."

Azrael leaned against the table. "Have we all kissed and made up?" His smile was taunting.

Warren nor Nathan even looked up.

Azrael laughed. "Well, if you'd all take a break from your brooding this morning, I'd like you to meet a friend of mine." He turned toward the man with him. "This is Reuel. We spoke of him yesterday."

Reuel was twice Azrael's size, a remarkable achievement by anyone's standard. He reminded me of a life-size action figure—or a professional wrestling entertainer, like John Cena without a soul. Reuel was terrifying.

Azrael spoke to him in Katavukai and told him all our names.

Unsure of angelic introduction protocol, given Azrael's aversion to hand-shaking, I waved awkwardly from my seat. "Nice to meet you, Reuel."

Azrael shook his head. "Reuel, doesn't speak English. He understands it perfectly well, but he never speaks it."

Weird.

I motioned toward the food. "Are you hungry?"

"We already ate," he answered. "I came to make sure everyone is up and moving. It will be a busy day."

"Where did you stash the FBI?" Warren asked.

Azrael pointed to his camper behind us. "I hope they enjoyed their accommodations." He turned in the direction he had pointed and began to walk. "Let's go find out."

A few minutes later, Azrael, Reuel, Kane, and Enzo escorted the FBI team out to the campfire. They looked awful, sleepless and afraid, and they were all still bound at the wrists. I knew what that felt like. "Are the wrist ties really necessary?" I asked.

"Yes," everyone else answered at the same time.

"They don't have weapons and they can't go anywhere," I reasoned.

"Not happening, Sloan," Azrael said. "Let it go."

I got up from the table. "Have you at least given them water or food?"

"No," Agent Clark answered.

I put my hands on my hips and looked at Az in disbelief. "Seriously? They're not our prisoners. Bring me some bottles of water."

Azrael looked annoyed, but then he smiled. "OK, but you have to get it yourself."

With a huff, I turned toward the cooler and took a step.

"No!" he shouted.

I looked back at him.

"You can't use your hands."

"Fine," I said, pushing up my sleeves.

Everyone was watching me. I took a deep breath and focused on the blue and white cooler sitting outside of Azrael's camper.

This will be tricky. I need to open the cooler, then somehow count out three bottles of water. Hmm. A smile spread across my face. *Or...*

Much easier than I expected, I lifted the entire cooler off the ground. Just like an invisible person was carrying it, it traveled across the lot, past me, and directly at Azrael's face. I dropped it with a thud right at his toes, making him jump out of the way.

The entire campsite exploded into cheers.

Warren's mouth was gaping at the table, and he was clapping his hands.

Nathan cupped his hands around his mouth and yelled, "Woohoo!"

Laughing, Azrael bent, pulled out three waters and carried them over to me. "Nicely done, Ms. Jordan. Nicely done."

"Thank you," I said, bowing before my teacher.

We unscrewed the caps and passed the waters out to the dumbfounded FBI agents. I saved Sharvell for last. "Here," I said, handing it to her.

"Thank you."

When she reached up and grabbed it, I held on. "I'm not who you think I am."

She stared at me, indignant but maybe mildly impressed.

Warren was still grinning from ear to ear when I walked back around to my place at the table and sat down. "When in the hell did you learn how to do that?"

"Baby, lots has changed since you've been gone," I said, smiling.

He leaned over and gave me a quick peck on the lips. "That's clear." He pushed his plate away and looked up at his father. "I'm assuming you've got an armory around here somewhere. I'm a little low on ammo."

Kane chuckled. "Yeah, we have an armory."

Nathan turned toward Azrael. "Speaking of weapons, I can't tell demons apart. I won't know who I can kill and who I can't."

Enzo looked at him. "Shoot all of them in the head, and if they get back up, blow out their kneecaps."

Nathan nodded. "I can do that."

I glanced sideways at our FBI friends. A couple of them were whispering with each other, but Sharvell's hateful gaze was fixed on me. I smiled and gave her a tiny wave with my finger.

Warren pointed at me. "What about Sloan? What's her role in all this?"

Azrael looked at me. "Sloan will be on the ground with me tonight."

Warren's eyes widened. "In the middle of everything?"

"Correct."

"Absolutely not," Warren said.

Azrael turned his palms up. "Warren, you don't have a choice. We're the offensive team here. I brought them out here so Sloan can kill them."

"So *Sloan* can kill them?" Warren asked, pointing at me in case anyone was confused by who Sloan was, apparently.

"She's the only one who can," Azrael said.

Warren's tone was laden with sarcasm. "Her little mind movement trick is really *neat* and all, but do you really think I'm going to allow the mother of my child to be—"

As if of their own accord, my hands began flailing wildly in the air. "*Allow* me?"

Out of the corner of my eye, I saw Nathan's hand clamp over his mouth. Muffled chuckles were coming from Azrael and his crew.

Warren shifted in my direction, glaring as he waited for my outburst.

I lifted my eyebrows and blinked. "Allow me?" I asked again.

Nathan's head was hung, and his shoulders were shaking with silent giggles.

Warren crossed his thick arms. "You can't expect me to be all right with the thought of my pregnant girlfriend battling a bunch of demons out in the middle the woods."

I scowled. "I don't expect you to be *happy* about it, but just because I'm pregnant doesn't mean you get to make decisions for me."

Azrael walked around the table and leaned between us. "OK, kids. Calm down." He draped his arm around Warren's shoulders. "I understand your hesitation about this. I really do. But she's more capable of ending this, once and for all, than any of us. I'll keep her safe, but I need her with me."

Warren looked at him. "Then you'll have me with you too."

Azrael tapped his finger on the table. "You're the best long-range shooter we've got. You can protect her better from somewhere else."

"He's right, Warren," Nathan said. "You're far better than anyone I've ever seen with a rifle."

It was obvious Warren didn't completely trust his father, which was understandable given how much of a whack-job my demon mother turned out to be and given Azrael's track record for keeping his own counsel. After a long moment of obvious internal debate, he looked at

Nathan with a pained expression.

Nathan must have understood because he nodded. "I won't leave her."

Azrael glanced around our group. "It's settled then?"

Warren gave a thumbs-up, but he didn't look happy about it.

"She'll be safe in my charge," Azrael said.

I raised my hands again. "I don't take orders from you either, Oh-Archangel-of-Death."

Warren looked at Azrael. "She's always this difficult, so get used to it."

Azrael slapped him on the back. "Tell me something I don't know."

"I'll tell you something you don't know." Enzo's voice caught us all by surprise as he pushed his way into the center of our group with his finger pushed against the speaker in his ear. "We've got heavy movement coming in the back east quadrant."

Azrael shoved his earpiece into his ear, and after a second looked around at all of us. "Our guests are early."

27.

"ALL RIGHT, BOYS. Let's go to work!" Azrael announced. "Enzo and Kane, you've got the HOKs. I want you to take Sloan, Warren, Nate, and our FBI friends to the clearing. Haul as much shit as you can. Reuel and I will take care of the rest."

"Roger that," Enzo said.

Azrael looked at Lex. "Lex, hook Warren up with the ghillie suit you found last night."

"Sweet," Warren said, getting up and then following Lex across the camp.

Azrael pointed at Nathan. "You've got my M-4, right?"

Nathan nodded. "Do you need it back?"

Azrael shook his head. "Nope. Keep it. You got mags?"

"Yes, sir."

I held up both my hands. "What do you want me to do?"

Azrael smiled. "Don't get killed."

"Not encouraging," I said, shaking my head furiously.

"Just kidding." He held up his hand. "Enzo! You've got two minutes to fit Sloan with some body armor!"

"Roger that, sir!"

Azrael pointed at me, then pointed at Enzo, whose head was sticking out of Azrael's camper. I jumped up from the table and scurried across the grounds. Enzo offered me a hand and pulled me up into the RV so sharply that I missed the top step.

The inside of Azrael's camper was worse than ours. His bunks didn't even have a mattress. It smelled like mold and there were rat droppings on the floor. "Ew," I said, looking around.

With a loaded smile, Enzo reached into the closet. I heard a switch followed by the unmistakable sound of hydraulics. The bottom bunk slowly lifted a few inches into the air, and Enzo swung it sideways on a hinge back against the wall. My bottom jaw dropped. "What the hell?"

There was a staircase underneath and halogen lights flickered on.

Enzo started down the stairs. "We're down to seventy-eight seconds, ma'am. Please hurry."

I followed him down into the underground bunker. "Shut up!" My voice echoed off the walls.

There were rows of barracks-style bunk beds, lockers along the walls, a large lunchroom table with bench seats, and even a door marked as a bathroom. At the far end, Enzo unlocked a large steel cage. "We're down to a minute, Ms. Jordan."

I shook my head to clear it. "Sorry." I scurried into the cage where he helped me put on the smallest vest they had. The bulky, camouflage Kevlar hung off my chest, even after he'd tightened it to the end of the Velcro strap. "I feel like a turtle," I told him, unable to lay my arms down flat against my sides.

"I'm sorry we don't have anything that fits better. I don't think we've ever even had a woman here before besides NAG and she took all her gear with her," he said.

I shook my head. "It's OK. I'm more pissed off I've been sleeping in that tin stable out there while you guys have been living it up down here in the Taj Mahal of hidey-holes ."

"The boss doesn't let us open it if he's not here. And last night, you and Staff Sergeant Parish crashed out early before we had a chance to move your stuff."

"I think Az just wanted me to suffer," I said.

"I doubt that, ma'am," he replied. "I'll see you on the HOK."

Just then, Cooper and Warren jogged down the stairs. Warren's reaction had to have been similar to my own, but he got over it a lot quicker than I did. "Don't you look hot?" he asked, grabbing me by the collar of my vest and kissing me before brushing past me into the cage.

"Have you ever seen anything like this place?" I asked.

He nodded as Cooper handed him a box full of ammunition. "Yes."

I rolled my eyes. "Of course you have. I need to grab a few things from the camper. I'll see you up top."

Warren didn't reply. He was distracted by all the big guns.

Less than ten minutes later, I was in the back seat of Enzo's HOK with Warren. Agent Silvers was stuffed into the passenger's seat up front, and Nathan was riding with Agent Voss in the very back. All our laps were loaded down with everything from grenades to gauze. My vest rode up over my chin the second I sat down, making it hard for me to talk as the group discussed the danger zone we were entering.

I had nothing helpful to add, anyway. Regardless of what everyone thought they knew, no one really had any idea what was coming our way. And we had no idea if we would win—or even survive. The battle in Texas with Kasyade hadn't gone well, and this one promised to make that look like a cat fight. I pressed my eyes closed and talked to the only person who could hear me behind my oversized armor.

Dear God, we need help.

* * *

It was a quick ride to the mountain spring in the middle of the plot of land. Enzo parked the HOK in the middle of the worn grassy path. "We'll unload here, then I'm stashing this thing in the woods."

We all got out, and I took in our surroundings. Up ahead was a rocky and shallow creek. The path opened up to an unleveled clearing with tall grass and thick leaves left to decay during the winter. Beyond the grass, a large rock jutted out from the earth forming a long crack in the mountainside, and toward the top, a small stream of water trickled out onto the rocks below. Near the bottom, a larger swell of the waterfall splashed into a rocky pool. And between the two spouts was an open, jagged space in the rock formation.

I pointed to it. "If that's the cave, which I'm sure it is, I'm putting everyone on notice, there's no way in hell I'm going in there."

"What are you mortals waiting for?" Azrael shouted down from the top of the rock.

I looked at Warren. "I thought he was behind us?"

"So did I," he said.

Warren draped the M-4's strap around his neck and reached for my hand. "Let's go."

It was at least thirty yards straight up the side of that *hill*. Warren looked back over his shoulder. "Hey, Nate. What does this remind you of?"

Behind us, Nathan began mimicking my voice. "I'm tired. My legs hurt. This is too steep. I want to go to the car."

If I had something I could throw at him, I would have.

Warren was chuckling. A good sign, considering he'd almost killed Nathan hours before.

Azrael was waving us forward when we reached the top of the falls. "Bring it in," he said. "We've got lots to cover in a short timeframe."

We all gathered around him, including the FBI.

"We already have eyes on at least six targets, three humans and three angels, including Abaddon. Reuel is en route to the border, to Abaddon's last known position. Do *not* engage with him. He's known as The Destroyer for a reason."

I shuddered. That didn't sound good.

"Any questions?" he asked.

"What about us?" Agent Voss asked, holding up his hands that were still bound at the wrists.

"Kane and Enzo will escort you to the cave." He lowered his glasses and glared at him. "I suggest you stay in it." Azrael looked around our group and used both hands to motion all the way around us. "These woods are rigged to kill people. If you don't want to die a painful and fiery death, don't cross the tree line."

As soon as the words left his mouth, a deafening blast shattered the silence of the woods. A black billow of smoke rose above the trees against the gray winter sky. A blood-curdling scream echoed through the forest, accompanied by the sound of startled woodland creatures scuttling through the fallen leaves. The screams sickened me as much as they brought me hope. Then, as if silenced by a cosmic mute button, the shrieks abruptly ceased, and the land was silent again. A chill ran down my spine, and I shuddered under Warren's arm.

"One down." Azrael's voice was even and sinister. "Get to your positions."

Warren grasped my arm and turned me around to face him. "Are you armed?"

I shook my head. "I should keep my hands free. Besides, there's no point. You know I can't shoot."

He pulled me close and pressed his lips to mine. "I love you, Sloan."

"I love you too."

He tucked my hair behind my ear. "Stay with Nate and don't do anything stupid."

I kissed him again.

"Ready?" Nathan asked, stepping to my side.

Warren grabbed him by the front of his vest. "Don't you leave her."

"You know I won't." Nathan stepped back and offered Warren his hand.

Warren looked at it before accepting. "Thank you," he said.

Nathan nodded. "Stay safe."

They stared at each other a moment, some sort of unsaid sentiment passing between them.

"Warren, get in position," Azrael ordered.

Warren turned to look at him. He pointed his finger at his father's face. "You'd better not let anything happen to her."

"You have my word, son," Azrael replied.

After a bit of heated staring, Warren nodded. He looked at me one last time before turning and jogging toward the trees.

"We've got to go," Azrael said, taking me by the arm.

Going down the mountain wasn't much easier than going up. Azrael had to hold me vertical to keep me from sliding down on my backside. I watched the three agents duck into the cave, then Enzo and Kane scaled off the falls to meet us at the bottom.

Back to back, Azrael, Nathan, and I formed a triangle, looking out toward the trees. Enzo and Kane were in opposite corners of the clearing.

For what felt like hours, but could have only been minutes, my eyes scanned the layers of the knotty pine trunks in front of me. I could only see about fifty feet beyond the tree line before the brush became too dense and the shade of the trees became too dark. There was no movement except for the pine needles that were rustled by the breeze.

The loud crack of a rifle rang out over our heads, followed by angry men shouting in a language I was becoming more and more familiar with—Katavukai. I shifted my weight from foot to foot and ground the toes of my boots into the earth. There was a second blast from a rifle, and after a moment, another one. More shots crackled through the woods, overlapping each other as the assailants in the woods returned fire. Then, *pop pop pop...pop pop pop...pop pop pop...pop pop pop!*

"They already switched from long range to assault rifles," Nathan said. "That's not a good sign."

There was commotion behind me, and Nathan opened fire. I spun around in time to see a man—a wicked human—dressed in all black, go down sideways in a trench. His light eyes bulged as he cried out in pain. The life extinguished in his expression as he fell backward into the leaves.

There was another explosion from a mine closest to Enzo's post, followed by more shots from the assault rifle and gunfire on the ground. My heart was pounding so loud it seemed to harmonize with the sound of the gunshots. Azrael sent a fireball into the woods, sending everything in its path up in flames.

Another demon—a woman with short brown hair—came through the trees where the first man had fallen. She extended her arms and two trees uprooted themselves. She flung them in our direction. Azrael caught them in midair, but gunfire on my other side caught my attention.

I turned in time to see Enzo fly backward off his feet amid a shower of bullets.

Before Azrael or Nathan could stop me, I sprinted toward him, my helmet clanging against my skull as I ran.

When I dropped onto the ground at his side, blood was gurgling out of his mouth as he struggled to breathe. A crimson stain spread from under his left arm where a bullet had caught him between the plates of his body armor.

"Stay with me, Enzo," I shouted, shoving my hand into the bloody cavern on his side.

As my healing power swelled at my fingertips, two more men, one human with a huge gun and one demon with empty hands, ran through the tree line toward me. I collapsed over Enzo's chest, and a sharp crack sailed through the air. A bullet caught the human directly in his right eye socket, exploding his skull in a shower of blood and bone as it knocked his body sideways onto the ground.

The demon kept charging like an angry bull until another bullet caught him in the knee. He faltered but kept coming.

Just before he collided with me on the ground, a brilliant white light exploded in every direction. The demon flew backward, feet over his head, taking out two small pines as he skidded into the woods.

When the light dissolved around us, a figure cloaked in what appeared to be fabric made of the night sky turned to face me. "You called for help?" Samael asked, his golden eyes dancing like flames.

"Sloan!" Azrael shouted.

I looked to see him pinning the brunette demon against the ground. Enzo gasped for air underneath me. "Can you breathe?" I asked.

He nodded. "Yes. Go."

I leapt from the grass, and Samael followed me to Azrael. Nathan was firing into his side of the woods. "Is that Phenex?" I asked as we ran up on them.

Azrael shook his. "No, but kill her anyway. She tried to club me over the head with an oak tree."

The woman's throat was caught under Azrael's hand, but she was cackling anyway. "This bitch can't kill me," she croaked out.

I opened my fingers and a bright light burst to life in my palm. "Wanna bet?" I slammed the light down right into the dead center of her chest.

The light splintered through her body quickly before it detonated with the force of a nuclear warhead. Azrael, Samael, and myself were all blown back by the explosion. The ground shook like an earthquake and shattered the rocks around the waterfall. Dazed and deaf, I sat up and looked around. The blast had leveled everyone on the field. And the spot where the brunette had been was black and covered in something that looked like shiny salt.

Azrael and Samael looked as shocked as I felt as they struggled to their feet.

An arm scooped me up around the waist and hauled me up. I turned to see Nathan, blinking like he was dizzy.

"Are you OK?" his lips asked. My hearing was slowly returning, but he sounded hollow and muffled.

I nodded. "Are you?"

He gripped the side of his head. "I think so."

An electric charge surged through me as a hand closed around my arm. It was Azrael, and he spun me around toward the woods. "He is here," he said, his voice so calm it made me shiver.

In front of us, there was an explosion of a different kind. Shards of broken earth shot up and speckled the sky as the sound of splintering wood and crashing trees reverberated through the forest. I needed no explanation. Like Azrael said, they called him The Destroyer for a reason. And he was coming.

I inhaled and stretched my fingers as trees toppled like bowling pins in front of us. A land mine detonated under the force of a fallen tree, erupting the timber into a blaze. Fiery napalm showered down onto Abaddon, clinging to his clothes and skin as it burned. Still, in the firelight, I saw him walking toward us with so much power the woodland floor vibrated with each step. The flames cast wicked shadows of his figure dancing among the trees.

Abaddon's hands shot forward, sending me sailing backward into Nathan. I toppled him over, landing hard on the solid earth. Pain radiated through my bones. I rolled onto my side in time to see Abaddon cross over the dismembered tree line into the clearing. All I could think of was The Incredible Hulk, except Abaddon wasn't green...he was black, charred by the napalm which still burned in some places on his massive frame.

A gun shot cracked through the sky and knocked him sideways, but he regained his footing quickly and charged me. I threw my hands toward him, sending up an invisible wall that knocked him completely off his feet.

I seized the moment and leapt to my feet as Azrael lifted Abaddon's stunned body into the air. He slammed him into a nearby tree, causing the demon to bounce like a giant pinball back to the ground. Without pausing to recover, Abaddon waved his arm toward the blaze behind him, sending a wave of fire over his head and through the clearing straight at us.

I shielded my face in time, but my hands were burned and the smell of burning hair turned my stomach. Samael's arms reached toward the stars, and a shower from a cloudless sky rained down and extinguished the flames.

Abaddon was on his feet and barreling toward us. More bullets sailed through the air in bursts from Nathan's assault rifle, but the demon wasn't deterred. Azrael sprinted toward him, then dove at his legs. The two collided and tumbled together into the woods, sending dirt, leaves, and brush flying like shrapnel.

Out of the corner of my eye, Kane was tackled to the ground by the demon Samael had knocked into the woods moments earlier. He outweighed Kane by at least a hundred pounds. With fists flying faster than I could see, the demon pounded Kane's face. My hands rose in their direction, the sizzling charge of light dancing at my fingertips, and I hurled the death blow into the demon's torso when he rose up to slam Kane again.

Another blast like before knocked everyone back again, and Kane's broken body was showered with electrified, glowing ash.

I scrambled toward him as Nathan and a bloody Enzo aimed and fired their weapons into the woods. Kane was wiping blood from his eyes with the back of his sleeve. "I'm OK," he said. "Thank you."

He may not have been dying, but he was far from OK. Had I not known who he was, I wouldn't have recognized him. I gently touched the sides of his face.

"The rocks," he choked out.

My head whipped toward the waterfall. Another demon was standing on the rocks, dangling Cooper over the side by his vest. When the inhuman man caught my eye, he laughed.

Then he dropped the soldier.

I screamed, throwing my hands in her direction. Cooper froze in the air, inches above the jagged rocks in the bottom pool. I exhaled so heavily, I almost collapsed. On the far side of the field, Samael seemed to vaporize into a cloud, then the cloud sailed through the air and collided with the demon on the rocks. The two of them disappeared into thin air with a crack.

"Sloan, look out!" Nathan shrieked.

Before I could react, my body sailed into the air, the force of gravity against the power holding me, nearly ripped my body in two. I cried out in pain as I hung suspended fifteen feet off the ground, my arms plastered against my sides, immovable. All I could think of was my baby.

There was a loud explosion from one of the mines in the distance followed by a fireball that rose through the trees. Azrael was nowhere to be seen.

Beneath me was Ysha.

"You don't want me to drop her," he said, daring Nathan and Enzo with his wild eyes. His hand that was stretched toward me, bent my body to an excruciating degree.

My piercing scream echoed around the woods.

They cautiously lowered their weapons.

"Come out! Come out!" Ysha called. "Warren, I know you're up there! Drag your friends out here too!"

A moment later, at the top of the waterfall, Warren in a ghillie suit walked out to the edge with his rifle raised over his head. Lex walked up beside him.

"Drop your guns!" Ysha told them.

Warren and Lex slowly slid their rifles off the edge of the rock they were standing on and they clattered down the side of the mountain.

There was another loud crash of trees somewhere in the distance.

With a satisfied nod, Ysha lowered me a few feet, then he let me fall. I crashed to the ground, my leg crumpling at an awkward angle underneath me. I screamed again. The blistering pain rendering me helpless. I looked down to see bloody bone poking through my pants.

Nathan lunged for me, but Ysha flung his hand toward him, knocking him off his feet.

Ysha grasped hold of my hair, tearing strands from my scalp as he ripped me off the ground. Somehow, through my hysterics, I managed to conjure up a flicker of my killing power, but before I could touch him with it, Ysha slammed me into the ground again.

He jerked my head up to look at him. "Did Azrael tell you what happens if you kill me?"

I could hardly see him through my blinding tears, but I could feel his hot and sticky breath on my face.

"If you kill me, Taiya dies instantly," he hissed. "I suggest you come quietly."

Without another word, I was dragged by my hair across the terrain. Jagged rocks from the creek bed ripped through my clothes and into my flesh. The lower half of my leg slapped against every surface it hit like dead fish. The icy water burned instead of numbed my skin as Ysha jerked my body through the stream. With one hand I fought against him while the other covered my belly. His merciless stride didn't slow as he ascended the mossy rocks. Where he was taking me, I wasn't sure, but my skull clanged against every rock he climbed.

Halfway up a huge boulder, the blast from a gun sounded over our heads. Ysha's grip went slack as he fell backward, taking me with him. Over his shoulder in the middle of our free fall, I caught a glimpse of smoke rising from the barrel of Warren's discarded rifle and, through the haze, I saw Sharvell Silvers holding it.

28.

WE CRASHED INTO the shallow pool, Ysha's full weight on top of me. My tailbone snapped and the back of my skull smacked against the rocks. Somehow I didn't die.

Ysha thrashed until he got his hands on me. My face broke the surface at the same instant his hands closed around my throat. Before he submerged my head again, I saw that half his skull had been blown away by the gun shot.

It didn't stop him from drowning me.

I had no other choice.

My baby and I would die if I didn't act.

This was my only chance.

My power surged into him and detonated.

The blast knocked me unconscious.

Nathan's face was the first thing I saw when I opened my eyes and inhaled for the first time since I'd gone under the water. He was hauling me out of the icy pool by the front of my body armor. We fell in a heap with my broken body landing across his lap. Inside my chest, bones were broken. I coughed and a shower of blood splattered back down onto my face.

"Can you breathe?" he asked.

Sort of. I nodded.

"The baby…are you cramping at all?"

I shook my head, gingerly touching my fingers to my stomach. "I think she's fine."

Sharvell sloshed her way through the water toward us. "What can I do?" she asked, dropping to her knees beside me.

"Someone has to put my leg back together and hold it," I said through my sobs.

She looked at me like I was crazy.

"Please," I begged.

Warren jumped down from one of the rocks. "Move," he said to her.

Sharvell crawled back out of his way as Warren pulled a knife from his vest. He knelt down next to my leg and cut my pant leg off.

"Don't look," he said.

I was struggling to breathe. "Warren, you have to put the bone back in. It can't heal like that."

"We need to get you to the hospital and let them—"

"Do it!" I shouted.

Warren unvelcroed his vest and dropped it on the ground. He peeled off his camouflage shirt and tossed it to Sharvell. "Here. Cut this up. I need something to bind her leg." Warren looked at Nathan. "You'll have to hold her still."

Nathan pulled me back against his chest, wrapping his arms around me as tight as he could.

My blood-curdling scream pierced my own eardrums as Warren grabbed the dangling piece of my lower limb. When he shoved it back in place, the world went black again.

* * *

"What happened?" I asked when I woke up. My leg still hurt like hell, but the worst of it was over. The bone under the bandages felt wrong, but solid. My chin was quivering from shock and the freezing air against my wet clothes.

Warren was holding me on the ground. "You're like the bionic woman. I don't know how the hell you survived that."

"I told you. Things have changed." I looked around. Nathan, Cooper, and Lex were gathering up the weapons. Enzo and Kane were carrying another soldier out of the woods. And the FBI agents were sitting on the ground a few feet away from us. "Where's Azrael?"

He shook his head. "I'm not sure. Shit got crazy between him and the big guy. The woods went silent not long after you killed the ginger."

The ginger.

"Taiya," I said, slumping in his arms.

"What?"

I looked up at him with tears in my eyes. "Ysha said if I killed him, Taiya would die."

He didn't say anything. He just kissed the top of my head.

Something heavy was coming through the woods to our right. When we looked, Reuel stumbled into the clearing. The trunk of a tree, at least four feet long and six inches in diameter was running through his chest between his right shoulder and his breast bone.

When he saw us, his shoulders wilted with relief.

Warren gently slid me off his lap and got up. He jogged over and caught Reuel under his left arm before the big guy stumbled. I gasped and struggled to my feet.

My left leg was significantly shorter than it had been before the break. The bone had healed at a horrible angle, but it was a small issue compared to the man standing before me who was impaled by a poplar.

"I guess this explains where you were when shit got ugly," Warren said as helped Reuel kneel down.

Reuel grunted.

He looked up at me, his eyes pleading.

I grimaced. "I'll heal you, but we've got to get that thing out first."

He nodded.

"Dude," Nathan said as he and Enzo walked over.

"I'll hold his chest, if you want to push," Enzo offered, looking at Warren.

"You sound experienced in this," I said.

Enzo smiled. "It's happened to Azrael more than once."

Warren blew out a heavy sigh, shaking his head. "Let's get this over with."

Enzo braced Reuel from the front while Warren pushed the log forward. Nathan ended up having to help him. It was the nastiest thing I'd ever seen which was saying quite a lot. It took forever to heal. Everyone else began packing up the HOKs while I closed the gaping hole in Reuel's chest.

"You owe me big time for this," I said.

He chuckled, though it was obviously painful.

"I wonder what would happen if I didn't heal it."

Reuel's head jerked up and he looked around.

"What is it?"

"Shh."

The look on his face was worrisome.

He grabbed my arm, his eyes wide with alarm.

The second I looked up, the sound of rapid-fire gunshots ricocheted off the falls again. Most everyone dove to the ground, except Enzo, who face-planted in the grass. Reuel pulled me behind him and Warren and Nathan ducked behind one of the HOKs. Agent Silvers showered the area in bullets with an M-4, shooting Agent Voss in the head and blowing out the kneecap of one of Azrael's soldiers I didn't know.

Then she stopped, but she didn't lower the weapon.

"Silvers, what are you doing?" Agent Clark shouted.

She didn't respond. Her eyes were glazed over and not really staring anywhere in particular. I'd seen the same look on Warren's face when Kasyade was controlling him in San Antonio.

Suddenly, the HOK flipped forward, landing upside down a few feet from me and Reuel, leaving Nathan and Warren exposed and vulnerable. Silvers turned the gun toward them.

Lex raised his sidearm in her direction, but before he could fire, he was knocked sideways off his feet by an invisible blow. My eyes frantically scanned the area, looking for the demon responsible. Then I saw her. A young Hispanic girl, maybe thirteen, standing at the edge of the woods.

Reuel saw her too. "Phenex."

I expected someone older.

"Kill them," she said, her calm voice eerily amplified for all of us to hear.

She aimed the rifle at Nathan.

I screamed.

Silvers fired.

And Warren jumped in front of the bullets.

* * *

Azrael had once told me that adrenalin makes everything easier, which explained why I broke from Reuel's powerful grasp like his fingers were coated with butter. Power exploded from my fingertips like a nuclear explosion blasting the Hispanic girl off her feet. Before she hit the ground, Samael appeared out of nowhere, grabbing her and vanishing into the air.

Another agent fired a round from a handgun into Silvers from behind. She toppled forward, losing her grip on the rifle. Lex jumped on her, and someone else grabbed the gun.

Warren landed on top of Nathan.

Blood was everywhere.

I ran across the field, falling twice before I reached Warren. The front of his shirt was riddled with bullet holes and soaked with blood. His dark eyes were vacant and staring into the sky.

Nathan was checking for a pulse.

A pulse I knew he wouldn't find.

"Get out of my way!" I yelled at him, fanning out my fingers, igniting my fingers with every ounce of power I had. As I reached toward his lifeless body, Samael descended on top of me, yanking me away and holding me back.

"Sloan, you must not!" Samael's lips pressed against my ear.

With all my strength, I kicked, elbowed, and punched him. "Let me go!"

He held me firm, covering my arms with his own to keep me from using my power on him. "Listen to me!" His voice was unyielding. "If you succeed in summoning him back to this body, his being will be splintered between this world and the next." He shook me. "He will likely die a painful death, regardless. And if he lives...it's not a fate that should be sentenced on anyone."

I crumpled in his arms, but continued to writhe against him. "I have to bring him back!" I screamed through my tears.

Samael tightened his grasp. "You must not. You must love him enough to let him go."

His words jarred me. My father had said those words before.

29.

SAMAEL HELD ME as I cried. When he finally released his grasp, I sank to my knees next to Warren and touched his blood-speckled face. Tears streamed from my eyes and mixed with the blood on his cheeks. I cradled his head in my arms, and our daughter kicked in my womb as I bent and kissed his frozen mouth.

Someone else was sobbing behind me. I glanced back to see Nathan seated in the grass, his eyes buried in his palm as tears dripped off his chin. Samael put a hand on his shoulder, but Nathan flinched away from his touch. He pushed himself off the ground and walked away from us all.

A few feet away, Warren's armored vest lay draped over the rucksack he'd carried in.

As I withered into hysterics again, the air came alive, buzzing with energy all around me. I looked at Samael, just as his face snapped up. Across the clearing, Reuel stood to his feet, angling his ear toward the sky.

Impulsively, Samael grabbed me again, hooking his arms under mine and pulling me swiftly backward. Warren's upper body slumped onto the grass as I was dragged from under him.

A gentle vibration grew beneath us, spreading and building until all the terrain rumbled violently. The rocks along the waterfall split open and tumbled into the waters below. Nathan and the few soldiers who had been standing fell to the their knees.

"What's happening?" I shouted over the thunderous quake.

A violent wind rushed over us, and the air around Warren's body visibly fractured in a thousand different directions. The space suddenly erupted into the most brilliant light I had ever witnessed. It was both blinding and inviting—the whitest white, icy and warm at the same time.

Samael's arm shielded our eyes against it as splintered through the sky.

There was another flash and as the light dissolved around us, the storm faded. Then standing before us was Azrael…and Warren.

His strong chest heaved with heavy breaths.

My heart stopped.

I'd slammed my skull pretty hard during my fall with Ysha, certainly bruising my brain. Maybe this was a hallucination. Maybe I was dreaming again. Maybe I had actually died and this was some vision of the afterlife. But the pressure from Samael's grip on my arm when we stood, convinced me it was reality.

"What. The. Hell?" Nathan's words were slow and over-enunciated as he walked up beside us.

Warren took a step forward. "Sloan." It was his voice, strong and even.

My feet were rooted to the forest floor.

He closed the space between us, and then his arms were around me. I couldn't move, and I stood there like a mannequin, petrified in place as he lifted me from the ground. His body was no longer rigid with death, his warmth seeped into my skin, and his energy surged through my nerve endings, stronger than it ever had before. I remembered to breathe as he settled me on my feet again. Our daughter fluttered in my belly.

Everyone else withdrew a few steps in horror.

"Sloan," Warren said again.

I pressed my eyes closed, and then reopened them. "You're alive?" I stammered.

He nodded. "I'm alive."

I shook my head. "No. This isn't possible. You were dead."

"I'm not dead anymore."

Carefully, I searched his face. There was no trace of blood on his skin or on his clothes. His eyes were sparkling in the mid-day sun that was peeking through the dissipating gray clouds, but something about him was alarmingly different.

I couldn't see his soul.

Recoiling from his touch, I grasped the sides of my head, fearing my skull might explode. "No, this isn't you. You're different."

Azrael appeared at his side. He was smiling. "You're right. He is better. Much better. He no longer has the weaknesses of humanity."

My head snapped back. "No longer human?" I started laughing. Hysterical, maniacal laughter. I spun on my heel and walked away from them, still shaking my head and holding my head together with my hands. Nathan, with his mouth hanging open, grabbed me by the arm to stop me. I looked into his eyes and pointed back over my shoulder. "You're seeing this shit too, right?"

He nodded but didn't, or couldn't, speak.

Warren spoke behind me. "Sloan, look at me."

I turned back around.

Slowly, he approached with his hands up in surrender. "Everything we've been told is true. Our little girl is very special. Now I have the power to protect her, and you." He took my hands and pulled them against his chest. I could feel his heart beating. "Please trust me."

For a long time, I stared at him. I touched his cheek, and his eyes closed as my fingertips graced his warm skin. When he reopened his eyes, peace washed over me. Tears slipped down my face. "You were dead."

He swiped his thumbs under my eyes. "And now you'll never worry about that again." He leaned in and kissed me, his power making me dizzy.

When he released me, Nathan was waiting with his hand outstretched. Again, Warren looked at it for a moment. Then, instead of shaking it, he stepped forward and embraced him. Neither of them spoke, but neither of them had to.

Azrael's hand came to rest on my shoulder. He looked down at me. "I assumed you would have known I'd have the power to bring him back."

"Seriously?" I asked, crossing my arms.

"You have the ability to control the human spirit; I command the Angels of Death. I thought this would be a natural conclusion given our circumstances."

I shook my head. "Not really. An explanation would be helpful."

"I'll explain everything soon," he said.

My eyes narrowed at him. "Where were you?"

"Trying unsuccessfully to subdue The Destroyer," he said.

"Where is he now?"

Azrael shrugged. "I couldn't stay with him and go after my son."

A thought occurred to me. "Can I recall Warren's human side now, so he'd be the same as he was before?"

Azrael sighed and shook his head. "Warren's human spirit is gone forever."

"But Samael said he can't survive if—"

Azrael cut me off. "As a human, he could not easily survive without the power his body has become dependent on over the years." He touched my forehead. "Remember those migraines?"

"It would kill him," I said quietly.

"Most likely."

"What about Taiya?" I asked. "Could she still be alive?"

He hung his head. "It's doubtful."

Tears pooled in my eyes. "I killed her."

He gripped my shoulders. "You can't think that way. It was not your choice." He pulled me against his chest as I began to cry. Of all the things Azrael was capable of, I was surprised tenderness was one of them. He dipped his head and spoke quietly just to me. "And you know it is not an empty platitude when I tell you if she is gone, she's in a better place."

His words made me feel better, but only slightly.

Just then, sirens howled in the distance.

"Someone must have heard all the explosions," Nathan said. "We're about to have some confused and angry deputies on our hands."

My eyes widened at the mention of law enforcement. The rest of our group was still scattered around the field. I took a step in their direction, but Azrael put a hand on my chest to stop me. "Agent Voss is dead."

I looked at him.

He pointed to the field where Agent Clark was performing triage on Agent Silvers. "This is your opportunity to do more than just bring someone back."

I rubbed my palms together. "It's time to clear my name."

* * *

The Halifax County Sheriff's Department was thoroughly perplexed when they descended on Calfkiller Creek and found the FBI and Claymore Worldwide cleaning up from a "training exercise." I don't know what the agents told them, and I didn't care. All that mattered was I wasn't going back to jail...not yet, anyway.

Just as I had no memory of being with Kasyade at the bank in Asheville, Sharvell Silvers had no memory of trying to kill us all with the M-4. Before she'd fallen under Phenex's control, she and the other agents had been able to sever their restraints on the jagged rocks inside the cave. They had freed themselves at just about the time that Ysha was dragging me up the rocks. Silvers had found Warren's rifle and shot Ysha in the face blowing us both off the rocks into the stream below.

Before the cops showed up, I healed her shoulder and, in front of all of them, brought Agent Voss back to life. He was in severe pain and completely freaked out, but he was alive.

Warren slipped an arm around my shoulders. "Are you all right?"

I leaned my head against his chest. "This was a terrifying day."

"I agree."

I looked up at him. "Kasyade wasn't here, Warren. That means this still isn't over."

"I know," he said. "But we'll be ready for her next time."

"Sloan?" Agent Silver asked behind us.

We turned to see her walking over from where the agents were loading up the helicopter. She had a thick file folder in her hand. She offered it to me when she was close enough.

"What is this?" I asked.

She crossed her arms. "It's a copy of all the information I have on Abigail Smith."

I raised it in my hand. "You realize it's kind of worthless, right?"

"You might be surprised," she said. "I'm fairly certain the young girl who..."

Warren's head tilted. "Who took control of your mind and forced you to go full-blown Scarface on all of us?"

Her gaze fell to the ground. "Yes. I'm sure she's in this information."

"Interesting," I said. "Thank you."

After a moment, she glanced back up at me. "You were right."

"About what?" I asked.

"You're not who I thought you were," she said.

I rocked back and forth on my heels. "I hope that means you won't send me to prison."

She shook her head. "No, I won't. I'll make sure the charges are dropped and the evidence against you is destroyed."

I pointed across the camp to where Nathan was eating Skittles by the fire. "And what about Detective McNamara?"

She shrugged. "Maybe he was with his family for the holiday."

I smiled. "Thank you."

"No. Thank you." She tapped the top of the file folder. "Let me know if you need any help. Just please find Abigail and the others." She cut her eyes up at me. "And when you do, make sure you kill them."

"I will."

30.

ALL I WANTED to do was go home and crawl into my bed, but a lot of business still had to be handled. A larger Claymore helicopter picked us up and flew us to Azrael's headquarters in New Hope. Over dinner in his conference room, Azrael explained how he'd been fighting Abaddon when he felt Warren die. For the first time in three decades, the Archangel of Death was released from his confinement to this world, and he crossed the spirit line to find his son. He said in order to bring Warren back, Warren had to choose for his human spirit to be completely destroyed.

"You *chose* to come back?" I asked, putting my fork down.

He nodded. "Of course I did. I couldn't leave you here alone."

"I don't understand." I looked at Azrael. "How does that work?"

Azrael pushed his plate back and crossed his arms on the tabletop. "Human spirits are not able to come back into this world once they cross the spirit line."

"Then how did Sloan bring me back?" Nathan asked before Azrael could continue.

"She brought you back before you crossed over," he explained. "Because Warren is my son, he basically went straight to the front of the line and passed through before anything could stop him. Even if Warren hadn't crossed the spirit line, Sloan would only have been able to recall his human spirit to his body, splintering him between both worlds. It would likely kill him, and if it didn't we'd all be sorry he lived."

That was what Samael had tried to explain to me on the battlefield.

"So what did you do to bring him back like this?" Nathan asked.

"As the archangel, I have the power to inflict the second death. I cannot destroy another angel, but I can completely obliterate a human soul." Azrael seemed sickeningly pleased. "Without the hindrance of his humanity, Warren stepped fully into his power and is now able to pass freely between this world and my own."

"Even with the baby? Isn't he *bound* here, or whatever?" I asked, pointing to my own stomach.

Azrael shook his head. "I told you, your child is different."

Nathan seemed confused. "But he was dead for maybe five minutes. How did you pull all that off?"

Warren looked at him. "Time does absolutely not work the same way on the other side. I felt like I was gone for hours."

"Correct," Azrael agreed.

"What was it like?" I asked Warren.

He leaned back in his chair and thought for a moment. "It really wasn't that different than here. More peaceful maybe and definitely more beautiful. There was so much sunlight." His voice had a note of wonder to it. "A lot happened that I can't explain. Something really weird happened with my body."

"Yeah," Nathan said with a chuckle. "It was blown full of bullet holes."

Warren shook his head. "No, after." He looked to Azrael for an explanation.

"Your physical body evolved," Azrael said. "Bullets will no longer be a problem."

I raised my hand into the air. "But at what price?"

Azrael was obviously surprised by my question. "At the price of weakness," he answered.

I was skeptical. "You keep saying that, but there must be something that makes us favored above the angels, right?" No one said anything. "Warren lost whatever that is. It's got to be a pretty big deal."

A muscle was working in Azrael's jaw. "This was the only way."

"And I appreciate that," I said. "I'm just not naive enough anymore to believe that such a miracle won't come with some consequences."

Nathan knocked his knuckles against the table, then lifted his beer into the air. "Well, let's not worry about it tonight. This day has sucked enough." He looked at Warren. "For whatever reason, I'm glad you're still here."

All our eyes widened with surprise.

Grinning, Warren raised his glass. "Thanks, Nate. Even though we all know it's a load of bullshit."

Everyone burst out laughing.

* * *

Some things with Warren were definitely improved. I found that out the nice way when we went to bed in a private housing unit after dinner. Like Azrael, he didn't really need to rest anymore. That had all kinds of benefits for both of us.

The next morning was Christmas, but it certainly didn't feel like it. Azrael gave us an SUV to drive to Camp Lejeune so Warren could collect his things from the barracks and deal with his command. Azrael stayed behind to take care of some business, but he promised to see us before the new year.

Nathan and I spent an hour at a sports bar on base while we waited for Warren to return.

"Did you call your dad?" Nathan asked, pointing to an old pay phone.

I nodded. "I called him from Claymore when we got there, and I called him this morning to wish him a Merry Christmas. Did you call your family?"

He nodded. "Mom said to give you a hug and she invited you to come celebrate the new year with us."

I smiled. "I love your family."

"They love you too," he replied.

"Have you checked in at work yet?" I asked.

Nathan sipped his beer. "Yeah, I called the sheriff last night. He asked if I was having a good vacation."

"That was it?"

"That was it. He played completely ignorant of everything else."

"Thank God. Did he say anything about Taiya?" I asked.

His face fell as he shook his head. "She escaped from the jail shortly after you did, but they haven't seen her since. I will find her, I promise." He tapped his fingers on the outside of his glass. "What did Azrael say about her?"

I sighed. "He said it's true. She probably would have died when I killed Ysha."

He frowned. "That sucks. I was starting to like her."

I slouched in my seat. "I know."

"Things will be very different when we get home," he said.

I stared at the table. "About that..."

Nathan took a deep breath. "You're going to marry him, aren't you?"

"Yes."

He forced a smile. "Congratulations."

"Will you forgive me?" I asked.

He reached over and squeezed my forearm. "There's nothing to forgive. It's how it should be."

"Will you come to the wedding?"

"I wouldn't miss it for anything."

Just then, the front door chimed when Warren walked inside. He was smiling, but it quickly faded as he approached the table. "It looks like someone died. Everything OK?"

I nodded. "Yeah. How'd it go?"

He handed me a white envelope and put a plastic bag down on the table as he slid into the booth beside me.

"What's this?" I asked, sliding the papers out.

"My discharge paperwork."

I looked briefly at the papers and then back at him. "Does this mean you're completely done?"

He nodded. "Completely finished."

I sighed with relief.

"You're officially out of the Marines?" Nathan asked.

"I'm out of the Marines," Warren said.

Nathan cracked a smile over the rim of his glass. "That's convenient now that you're in the Lord's Army."

Warren narrowed his eyes and Nathan's beer sloshed out across the front of his shirt.

"Damn it, Warren!" Nathan cursed, slamming the beer down on the table and grabbing a fistful of napkins.

I laughed and Warren winked at me.

Leaning back in my seat, I folded my hands over my stomach. "I see you're not having any issues using your powers. It took me forever to learn how to do that."

He grinned and stretched out his fingers. "I've gotten a bit better."

Warren's veiled modesty wasn't fooling anyone. While we waited for him to return, Nathan and I had discussed at length what had happened in the woods. Without a mortal soul, there would be nothing to dilute Warren's power. The thought was creepy but comforting when I considered Kasyade and Phenex were still out there somewhere.

I nodded toward the bag. "Did you buy me a present?"

His head snapped up. "Oh, I almost forgot." He handed the bag to Nathan. "It's actually for you. I found it at the MPX on base. Merry Christmas."

Nathan's eyes widened with curiosity as he accepted it. He reached into the bag and pulled out a small rectangle. His brow crumpled, and he scowled at Warren. "Really?"

Warren dropped his forehead onto the table and laughed harder than I had ever seen him laugh before. I held out my hand. "What is it?"

Nathan huffed and handed it to me. "It's a patch for my hat."

I turned the brown patch over in my hand. The front of it read, *REGULAR GUY.*

I covered my mouth with my hand and tried to suppress my chuckles. I wasn't sure what was funnier: the patch or Warren so tickled over it.

Nathan smacked Warren across the back of his head. "Asshole."

When Warren sat up, there were tears in his eyes from laughing. He held up his hands in defense. "Man, I'm only trying to help. Sloan told me you lost all your patches in the accident."

Nathan held up his middle finger and drained the last of his beer.

Warren regained his composure and pulled the car keys from his pocket. "I don't know about you guys, but I'm beyond ready to go home."

Home. From his lips, the word had a nice new ring to it.

* * *

We said goodbye to Nathan in our driveway when we got home. He promised to work on getting Warren's car out of impound and then bid us farewell with a cheesy, "I'll see you next year."

Even though we knew we'd see him again in the next couple of days, there was an odd finality to our waving goodbye from the front porch. Judging from Warren's heavy sigh, he felt it too.

A glint in the sky caught my attention. I looked up to see the angels standing guard. I pointed. "Can you see them now?"

Warren followed the direction of my finger. Then he looked at me. "There are more than just those, babe. Angels are everywhere."

I looped my arms around his neck. "I only need one."

He smiled. "Speaking of that." He reached into his jacket and pulled out a ring box. "Are you ready to wear this thing now?"

"You still want me to?" I asked, heat rising in my cheeks.

He flipped the box open. "Sloan, I never stopped."

My hand trembled as he slid the diamond on my finger. "Will you marry me?" he asked.

Happy tears almost froze to my face. "Absolutely." I stretched up on my tip-toes and kissed him. "I love you, Warren."

He cradled my face in his strong hands. "I love you too."

I squealed with glee as I held my hand up to watch the ring twinkle in the last rays from the pink sunset. "I want to go call Adrianne."

He laughed and picked up our bags off the porch. "I expect no less, but you'd better hurry. We need to get to your dad's."

Without touching the front door, I unlocked it and we walked inside. Someone had left my phone plugged in and laying on the coffee table. I skipped across the room and picked it up.

On the screen I had eleven missed calls and more text messages than I could scroll through. But one of them caught my attention; it was a picture message time-stamped that morning.

I clicked it open.

The picture showed Taiya tied to a chair. Her blue eyes were open, but they were dangerously weak. Someone held out her arm toward the camera.

If found, please call Sloan Jordan.

THANK YOU FOR READING!

★ ★ ★ ★ ★

Please consider leaving a review on Amazon! Reviews help indie authors like me find new readers and get advertising. If you enjoyed this book, please tell your friends!

The fourth novel in
The Soul Summoner Series
is in stores now!

Want more of your favorite detective?

There's a FREE Book from Elicia Hyder waiting for you at
www.thesoulsummoner.com/detective

THE DETECTIVE
A Nathan McNamara Story

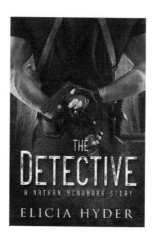

66771443R10424

Made in the USA
Columbia, SC
19 July 2019